A JACK STERN ADVENTURE

Resurrection in Mauritius

M J JURAND

Copyright © 2021 M J Jurand

ISBN: 978-1-922565-18-1
Published by Vivid Publishing
A division of Fontaine Publishing Group
P.O. Box 948, Fremantle
Western Australia 6959
www.vividpublishing.com.au

 A catalogue record for this
book is available from the
National Library of Australia

CONTENTS

1

CLUB IT

Once Jack Stern had attended to the formalities of meeting the parents and gaining their acceptance he literally spirited Yvette away to Club Med Mauritius. The popular resort is located on the northwest side of the island close to la pointe aux canonniers.

No long air flights to endure, no boring transit times to fill, no obnoxious immigration officials to pander to, simply say the word hold your beloved and you are there.

Yvette had become quite used to this form of travel and began to exhibit the same capabilities in her own right.

They 'landed' at the front entrance to the resort with nothing more than passports, credit cards and cash, perfectly equipped for such excursions, as Jack would always say.

He did not foretell of their destination wishing it to be a surprise. Jack had selected Mauritius out of respect for the French, a catholic saint and his love of warm tropical climates. He also wanted Yvette to see how the various peoples of the island had adapted the French culture to their own needs.

The island was lush with greenery. It was the wet season. The natural vegetation and sugar cane were doing extremely well in the rich volcanic soils fed with just the right amount of sun, wind and water.

It was going to be Jack Stern's immense pleasure to show the enchanting Yvette Bell around the island once she had settled into the Club's unique philosophy of fun.

Brendan and the girls were already there, having arrived three days earlier. The group's presence had already set tongues wagging and stories of their probable relationships circulated amongst the guests and staff of the complex.

No one agreed with the official story namely that Father Brendan O'Reilly was the girls' carer. "What utter nonsense these are eight highly charged sexual women!!! Who is he trying to fool? Surely he provides them with all sorts of erotic favours"!!!

"But then, on the other hand he is extremely handsome! Perhaps, he is an up and coming film star and this is his bevy of beauties '? Were just some of the thoughts that abounded? No matter which it was Brendan and the girls had all of the resorts ladies intrigued to the point that they each desired to know him intimately, much to the annoyance of their respective boyfriends and husbands.

Jack Stern and Yvette Bell held hands as they slowly walked along the cobbled road that meandered through the resorts chipping and putting greens. The large stylish building that lay ahead of them housed reception, the main dining room, the bar and entertainment arena. Outside and adjoining it was the main outdoor swimming pool from which they could hear the lively commotion of the day's pre-lunch water activities.

Brendan and the girls were a team taking on the villages GO's (gentil organisateur – kind organizer) as their opponents. Dozens of oogling women lined the pool's perimeter and admired Brendan's innocent charms and frolics which all of them mentally translated into erotic delights. No matter what he did someone in the crowd attached a sexual innuendo to it.

The girls were well aware of this and collectively formed a buffer that protected him from it. The GO's were no match for Brendan's team. Normally they would toy with the GM's (gentil membre- kind members) allowing them some sense of victory, today it was different. No matter how hard they tried they could not defeat the weakest member of Brendan's team at water polo, twenty-five meter sprint races, surfboard balancing or pond hopping.

Jack sensed what Brendan had been up to.

"Cheeky boy" he thought as he smiled in his direction. Yvette stood close by Jack's side and tuned into his thoughts.

"Using your supernatural abilities to their utmost advantage" she thought as she also smiled.

Brendan was oblivious to the golden pair's presence. He remained focused on his girls and their individual involvement in the ongoing war that had reached fever pitch with the GO's going all out to win at least one battle.

As Jack watched he realised that Brendan was not using his powers for his own personal gain. It was for the elation and benefit of the girls. His motives it was quite clear were to cement that "winner" feeling into each of his charges. The GO's were understandably frustrated. Over the past three days no matter which contest they had participated in whether it was golf, archery, water polo, tennis, water skiing, volleyball or sailing, Brendan and the girls had always emerged as the victors.

On each occasion the GO's were tantalizingly close to winning only to be dashed at the last moment. Now they faced overwhelming defeat at the hands of amateurs. Duty called on them to remain gentile, ego shouted at them to "kill crush and destroy" all rather difficult considering the circumstances of having to play water polo by wearing a life jacket as a "nappy" nine on nine; nine male GO's, all young, muscular, athletic, experts in their fields against one lonely male and eight voluptuous women. Score 20 goals to nil!

Brendan cleverly played midfield, if there is such a place. Elegantly poised he deflected any attempt at goals by the opposition. Brendan moved effortlessly as dolphins do, the waters offered no resistance to his fluid movements which was also true for each one of his girls. It was sheer delight for any observer to watch their poetic display of skill and power. The GO's could bear it no longer. They attacked as one and roughly pushed the girls away in a final desperate attempt to score that one goal. Brendan smiled sympathetically at their futile collective effort. Equipped with a deep knowledge of the waters he summoned the cystalline's to support and uplift each one of his charges. The girls became immovable. They "stood" in the swimming pool like pillars of stone and effortlessly halted the GO's advance. The whistle blew game over, the crowd cheered, the GO's swore in French and Philippe the club's director happily congratulated all involved.

"Another victory for our new playboy and his bevy of beauties, oui; Gentleman you may need to ask him what his secrets are, oui" Philippe suggested to the men in the audience as he winked and seductively played with his long cylindrical cordless microphone.

The GO's forced an inaudible miserable reply, saluted Brendan and made their way to the main eating area dragging their towels behind them.

"At least the food might make them feel better" Jack optimistically remarked as he gazed upon their forlorn sight.

"Umm, I'm famished" Yvette whispered

"Of course you are, how inattentive of me! Why don't you go and join Brendan and the girls whilst I check in. Find a nice table for us."

"I shall" Yvette obediently replied and then she made her way through the crowd.

Jack wasn't entirely truthful all that he needed to do was collect the key and give instructions as to how many bouquets of flowers he wanted delivered to the chalet which was located in the newer part of the village overlooking the picturesque bay.

'That didn't take you long" Yvette remarked when Jack suddenly appeared by her side.

"I'm rather efficient when it comes to matters of the heart" he chivalrously replied.

"Good to see you again Mr Stern" Brendan cheerfully said as he extended his hand.

"And you Father O'Reilly" an exchange of words which caused quite astir in some of the onlookers who were constantly tuned into the groups conversations. Jack sensed this and without batting an eyelid said tongue in cheek "He's starting a new order of nuns to meet the demands of the ever changing new world"

"Don't take any notice of him, he's just joking" Brendan countered as he ushered his group towards the open restaurant the main doors of which were flanked by the resorts highly trained chefs who welcomed the GM's as they arrived. Yvette's angelic beauty immediately captivated them and they responded by bowing at the waist in complete admiration.

Although Yvette had heard about the legendary Club Med buffets it took her a little while to truly appreciate the extent and variety of goods presented. The dishes were neatly laid out and stacked on the tables that skirted the perimeter of the obliquely L-shaped room. In the middle stood two separate islands, one being a large open rectangle that served as a chef's station at which hot food was continuously prepared according to customer demand. The arrangement and distribution of breakfast, lunch and dinner was done in such a fashion as to guarantee flow and minimize congestion. The eating areas were entirely open allowing fresh sea breezes to change the air and cool the patrons. The abundance of ceiling fans was activated on still and excessively humid days.

Humans were not the only guests. All manner of birds and squirrels frequented the place without causing the slightest flutter amongst the staff who welcomed their presence.

"The menu changes every day" Felicity said as she took the large dinner plates and handed them out.

'Where do I begin"? Yvette shyly asked

"At the beginning darling, at the beginning" Jack warmly said as he guided and pointed the young damsel towards the entrée section.

"I'm only a small eater"

"Then take only small portions"

"Even so I shall get fat in no time." Yvette protested

"I'm certain that won't happen here. The Club's activities will burn off any extra calories and more" Jack confidently stated.

"Do you really think so"?

"He's telling the truth. After three days of being here and eating three large meals each day I've actually lost weight'!! Brendan gladly exclaimed as he stood before Yvette with a plate piled high with delicious treats.

"Very well then, perhaps, I should indulge." She giggled. In parrot like fashion Jack Stern mirrored Yvette's selection and followed her to the round table where some of the girls were already seated. Jack positioned himself next to Brendan and arranged his place. After he had taken and swallowed a mouthful of fluffy omelette he looked around and asked.

"Have any of you ladies started to explore the island"?

"Not as yet. We've all had too much fun at the Club. Perhaps in a day or two" was one response followed by "I don't know if I want to. The Club and the nearby private operators offer enough for me. Why it was only yesterday that I experienced the most exhilarating water skiing in a rubber donut"!!!

"Oh my God, that was fun! Best ride I've ever had"! Another agreed suggestively. Quite amused by their spontaneously childish responses Jack looked at them and for the first time started to see each one individually. Felicity and Naomi had been the only two that he had sufficiently interacted with before. Brandy, Candy, Samantha, Brittany, Jamie and Holly were superficial strangers; his only knowledge of them was through eye contact and the depths of their soul that he had encountered. Yvette he realised had a better working knowledge of them and Brendan it appeared even more so. The past three days it appeared to Jack had sufficiently relaxed Brendan to the point that he was becoming quite familiar and at ease with his ladies. Up until then he had his hands full contending with the aftermath following their first adventure namely the Archbishop and his church politics. His Grace was totally displeased with Jack's interfering nature made worse by the Archbishop's conclusion that Brendan needed a much deserved holiday. Jack wondered how long it would be before the Church's espionage team tracked them down to Mauritius. It didn't matter. He would elude them again until the circumstances were right for Brendan's return. Meanwhile perhaps the observations of all those at the Club were correct; Brendan and the girls were intimate with each other. This was one question that he was eager to have answered. Jack shifted his gaze to where Yvette was seated.

"Oh you're such a lovely creature! Just what I was looking for! Would you like some more? Yes? Don't worry I'll give you some as well. Don't be jealous." She said as she gently played with the birds of paradise that sat on her head and shoulders.

"What did you say......never......I'll have to investigate that. Are you sure? Very well I promise to do something about it." She then remarked as a waiter walked past and thought her to be quite mad. Sensing his disapproval Yvette asked.

"Would you like to hear"?

"Er" was his uncertain response.

"Here take my hand and you too Felicity" Yvette gently invited as she extended her delicate, soft hands. The waiter did not know what to do until he saw Felicity accept the invitation and then he hesitantly decided to play along. All of a sudden his head became filled with numerous voices chattering about all manner of things. The waiter disconnected immediately and the voices in his head stopped. He looked at his hand in blank amazement and then reluctantly reconnected again when his courage allowed. The voices returned louder and clearer. He disconnected once again and ran away shaking his head and muttering incoherently about witches and demons. Felicity on the other hand remained coolly composed, maintained her grip and delighted in hearing the conversation.

"Go on say something." Yvette urged. Sensing her power Felicity obeyed.

"So what is it like being a bird" she innocently asked. The chattering stopped and the birds looked at each other not knowing how to answer. Then one of them bravely answered.

"Kind ladies, we have nothing to compare it with as we have always been in this life form."

"What can you tell us"? Felicity persisted

"Even though humans attempt to fly in all sorts of crude machines you will never be able to immerse yourselves in the wonders of the air as we can do" the bird merrily chirped

"Tell us more"

"The air is a wonderful mother. She nurtures us, teaches us, takes us to places all over the world and shows us things that only we can understand"

"Why is that? Surely our sciences are sufficiently advanced to explain everything to us" Yvette seriously questioned.

"Not at all, you humans are limited by your perception which is a product of your senses. You are not birds. It is only our species that truly understands the essence of air."

Yvette wrongfully thought that this philosophical aspect might be a little deep for Felicity and she changed the subject by asking.

"What can you tell me about Mauritius"?

"Nothing that you cannot find out for yourselves except for one thing that you need to know considering your nature."

"And that is"?

"In the region of the coloured sands stands a building that needs your attention" and with that directive the bird flew away merrily chirping with the others that had decided to take flight as well. The waiter who had been earlier spooked returned with several of the restaurants staff.

"Touch her hand and you will see, I mean hear, what I told you is true" he confidently and somewhat nervously said as he pointed to

Yvette. Those whom he had brought along tentatively smiled at his urgings and one by one in turn briefly held Yvette's soft hands.

Silence! Not a thing! No whispers! No murmurings, nothing!

"You've been at the rum again! We warned you what would happen! You stupid stubborn man! Apologies mademoiselle he is a little loco, ever since he came to the island he's been drinking and dunking in the rum like it's the local water" one of the waiter's colleagues apologised.

"Why is that"? Felicity sympathetically asked

"His friend will tell you, he shares a room with him, wait on." One of the other dark strangers replied as he went in search.

Yvette continued to eat and waited patiently as she reflected on what the birds had conveyed to her. The dark stranger returned in a matter of moments with one of the chef's who was on duty at the cooking station. The chef was not at all happy about being forcibly taken away from his creative crepe making but mellowed in an instant when he set eyes upon Yvette.

"Tell her Simon" instructed the one who fetched him. The chef instantly obliged.

"It is true mademoiselle my friend Jacque is a little crazy. He keeps having bad nightmares every night. He drinks to forget but I sometimes think it makes it worse. He drinks to forget what happened to him and his family members in the Sudan.

"Explain"

"Oh you know the same ongoing stories of civil wars, fighting, territorial politics, terrorist activities, human atrocities, etcetera, etcetera" The chef slowly and painfully detailed in his rich French-Mauritian accent.

"That is sad, very sad. I wish I could somehow help him" Yvette genuinely answered.

"Perhaps you will mademoiselle; beauty like yours is exceptionally rare. It is very………how do you say……..pacifying….oui?

"If you say so" Yvette sweetly answered as she lowered her head.

9

"Jacque needs help. He turned to religion but the local Catholic priest was of no help. He is rather hopeless himself, little wonder hardly any people go to him. Jacque tried the other religions here without success. I suppose his only salvation is still the local rum. Thank you for listening mademoiselle, enjoy your lunch, hope to talk to you again sometime au revoir"

"Au revoir Monsieur" Yvette genuinely replied. Simon the chef smiled passionately bowed and left with the rest of the staff. Jacque continued to shake his head in disbelief as he repeatedly looked at the palm of his hand and put it to his ear hoping to hear something.

"Charming fellow and a gentleman to boot, only a few minutes here and already the men are falling at your feet. I fear the competition may become too great for me"! Jack jokingly teased. Yvette remained silent and reflected for a moment before answering.

"More like being given an assignment" She replied.

"Then your holiday will be full of surprises"!

"Did you know about this" Yvette curiously asked.

"Not at all, I'm as much a tourist as you are"

"We shall see" She replied as she took a mouthful of Creole style noodles that the Club's chef had so expertly prepared from the local produce.

"These are the best noodles I have ever tried"! Yvette exclaimed

"Better than......"? Felicity inquired ambiguously.

"The one's I always used to buy at the local noodle shop back home. Except it didn't matter what dish I bought they would always taste the same"!!

"Never wiped his wok, makes one wonder what his sexual etiquette was like"! Jack said in complete deadpan fashion, which caused his entire group to spontaneously explode into roars of side-splitting laughter.

"Oh my God" gasped Felicity as three nuns resplendent in their white habits floated past.

"Sister Ambrosia"? She questioned with an air of expectant

hesitancy "Am I right, it is you"? She continued to inquire half expecting to be let down by the thought that her eyes had deceived her. The trio of nuns slowed to a halt, turned and looked in Felicity's direction.

"Order of the Servants of Mary at your service" Brendan proudly said as he stood up and extended his hand in good faith.

"You know your orders well Sir"! Sister Ambrosia answered in a no nonsense fashion.

"I should do as I am your male counterpart"

"A priest, a very relaxed priest it would seem, Father" Ambrosia dryly assumed.

"On holidays"

"From which parish"?

"Nothing specific actually you could call me more of a roaming missionary at the call of his Archbishop's whims and fancy's"

"I see! How is it that you are in the company of.........Felicity isn't it"?

Ambrosia sternly asked as she looked inquiringly at the young lady.

"Yes Mother Superior"

"No longer my child, that was a long time ago, something I'd rather forget" Sister Ambrosia bitterly replied.

"Please don't you were so wonderful at your job"

"Others didn't think so. I still bear the mental and physical scars of their disapproval"!

"Father Brendan can fix that for you" Felicity knowingly gushed.

"New breed of priest, are you Father"?

"Still finding myself"

"Aren't we all" Ambrosia fiercely concluded.

"Tell me Mother Superior how did you come to be here"? Felicity curiously asked grateful that fate had given her the opportunity of crossing paths with the nun once again.

"Before I explain tell me child, have you mended your ways"? Felicity nodded in the affirmative.

"Why is it that you are in the company of Father Brendan here"? She asked as she looked directly at him with an intense inquisitive glare"One wonders, Father, what sort of priest you are? Perhaps you're dabbling with the pleasures of the flesh? After all Felicity was the favourite of the men. I'm sure she could teach you a thing or two; in fact I'm sure you all can"! Ambrosia sarcastically said as she looked at each one of his ladies in turn until she set eyes upon Yvette who innocently returned her stare.

"I'm afraid you have it quite wrong Sister"! Yvette politely corrected the belligerent nun. "Father Brendan rescued these fine ladies from their sexual slavery and is in the process of helping them find new lives. I can tell from your mannerisms that humanity has dealt you many blows and hardened your otherwise loving nature" Sister Ambrosia reacted visibly to Yvette's intuitive finding and knew it to be accurate. The image of her true self flashed before her and caused tears to flood her eyes.

"I think your soul wants back in" Yvette softly whispered as she appeared by her side. "Come sit with us" she then warmly beckoned. The trio of nuns agreed and seated themselves between Brendan and Jack Stern, being in the company of ex-prostitutes caused Sister Ambrosia to painfully relive past episodes at the nursing home that she was once in charge of, Brendan sensed her anguish especially when she periodically phased out of the groups polite conversation.

"It was never like that you know and if you're not careful it will happen"

He cautioned the nun startling her in the process.

"What? How do you mean"? She said as she regained her bearings.

"The Past"

"What of it"

"It doesn't exist" and with that Father Brendan O'Reilly described his understanding of the mystery of time and its involvement with life. "Far better for you to create than to dwell upon something that brings discord after all you are a Servite" was his conclusive statement.

Ambrosia determined that Father Brendan was no ordinary priest and before she could ask any further questions of him Yvette interrupted their brief intimacy.

"I'm sure Felicity still expects to learn what brought you here"

"My apologies, after my "accident" I wandered the world searching for an acceptable reason as to why I was not protected by our heavenly Father. I found none. After three years of doing menial work I grew tired and decided to return to my original vocation. The previous religious Order to which I belonged no longer satisfied me and after a little research I decided to give the Servites a go. It was then that I saw the purpose behind the "accident" it was two fold, to change Orders and to journey to Mauritius. The Servites are champions of the arts. After joining an opening presented itself for missionary work on the island I immediately volunteered the rest is as many say history" Ambrosia said with warm admiration for the given opportunity and then went on to say.

"Although the island is relatively affluent many poor exist. My fellow sisters and I realised the people had more to offer than merely growing sugar, pineapples, or making rum and Ralph Lauren. They had an inherent culture that needed artistic expression. We experimented with all forms and found that the people were best suited to weaving cloth of original designs and texture. With the help of overseas funds we managed to set up a cottage industry, which presently employs some seventy individuals and provides them with sufficient income to support their respective families. All of their produce is sold at Port Louis. We use hawkers to sell to tourists at all of the resorts and high-class hotels.

"You're doing well" Brendan commented which lay halfway between a question and a conclusion.

"Beyond our expectations"

"I gather you're not talking from a monetary sense" Yvette put forward.

"Correct! My belief, faith and confidence have partially returned and restored themselves in my makeup to some extent. In the process of changing my devotion to the Virgin Mary I dared to ask Her son as the highly venerated Infant of Prague for help. In essence I was putting Him and His associated folklore story to the test. Surprisingly it worked all of a sudden prosperity was ours. I constantly pinch myself and pray that all of this is not a dream and that we can continue to grow and rescue those who wish to extract themselves from the tin shanties that dot the landscape"

"I'm more than certain that your combined beliefs of hope and faith will carry it on." Brendan enthusiastically said in a supportive fashion.

"Tell us more" Felicity urged the nun as she thirsted for more knowledge.

"Having come from an affluent western society I have come to the realization that mass production has many pitfalls. In my experience the local weaver with the aid of his primitive machine gives a material that is full of warmth, the human touch and emotion. Something that no highly advanced inanimate object can duplicate. Theirs is sterile. It is far better to have an original than a lifeless print that will fade into obscurity with time" Ambrosia philosophically expressed as she reflected on the quality of her weavers efforts.

"An artist who wishes to alter the fabric of human society with the instrument of social change" Jack powerfully interpreted.

"And in the process plants the seeds of love and understanding changing the landscape forever" Brendan added.

"Yuuummm.....yuuummm...yum,yum,..Yuuummm.... yuuummm......yum,yum" The tall black groom sang in tune to Mendelssohn's bridal march as he escorted his black "bride" around the tables.

"Bon appetite, bon appetite" 'She' he attempted to sing in a high soprano voice to the same melody. The pair looked ridiculous, but this is what it was meant to be.

"Congratulations on your marriage. You make a very handsome

gay couple"! Jack joked as he stood up to greet them. "May I kiss the bride"? He then asked.

"Sir, make no mistake I am a respectable woman now"! 'She" he answered.

"My apologies Madame your beauty is overwhelming, outstanding! I have never seen such a mop of hair on a woman before"! Jack said alluding to the 'brides' carefully coiffured, white cotton strands.

"You like"?

"But of course; however a little too light in colour too much of a contrast with your shinny skin, apart from that you look positively stunning"!

"Thank you Monsieur"

"Where are you going on your honeymoon"?

"To the beach shack, would you like to come and see'?

"A little adventurous for me, I am still a shy boy"! Jack excused himself.

"I do not believe that! Come it will be fun! Just the three of us"! The 'bride' said in a very low seductive voice.

"Later perhaps"

"Promise" Before Jack Stern could reply a blood-curdling scream shocked the ears of the GM's. Another tall black man heavily bandaged in mummy fashion and wearing a straight jacket burst into the room, he appeared to be running away from a doctor who was carrying an excessively large syringe.

"Please save me! Anyone please save me! This madman wants me to marry his daughter and become insane! Heeeelp, someone heeellllllp!!! He screamed as he ran about hiding behind pillars, people; chairs and under tables.

"Don't worry, it won't hurt a little"! The 'doctor' said as he unexpectedly pushed the syringes' plunger and randomly squirted many onlookers.

"Come on you little miserable cretin, come here! Stop making a fool of me. You know insane people end up in the mental institution of marriage! Come marry my daughter she will cure you of your sanity"!

"I don't want to! She's ugly"!

"No she's not"!

"Yes she is! She's got bandy legs, no boobies, false teeth, warts on her fingers and toes"!

"There's no need to whisper"! The 'doctor' shouted.

"Why not"?

"Because she's deaf as well"! The 'doctor' said pointing to his ears.

"Heelllp, heelllp, someone heelllp"! The hapless 'patient' screamed as he ran towards Jack and the 'bride' and 'groom'. He screeched to a stop, dropped his jaw, opened mouthed he stuttered, splattered, shook, rattled his body, rolled his head and screamed "Aaaaaahh-hh.............h" uncontrollably and then fled the building with the 'doctor' in hot pursuit.

"It's quite a circus in here! Tell me where's your certificate of insanity" Jack asked the 'newly weds'.

"Come to the shack and we will show you"! The 'bride' whispered in his ear as 'she' winked and wiggled 'her' way out of the dining room with the groom or should one say the broom in toe.

"Is it always like this"?

"Never a dull moment, but be careful"!

"Why Brendan"

"Because those two people teach how to water ski"

"Meaning"

"They might drag you off somewhere and have their ways with you"!

"You've been there'?

"Boys stop it"! Sister Ambrosia commanded like an overbearing primary schoolteacher. "Now sit down this minute and behave yourselves'!

"Yes Sister" They replied in unison.

Yvette found this entire comedic distraction very entertaining and made nothing of the insults levied at the holy sacrament of marriage even though she was above all a very seriously minded person.

"Tell me Sister Ambrosia do you know of a broken down Catholic Church in the region of the coloured sands. She asked in the hope that the Nun was a local expert.

"If you mean Chamarel, no I don't. Why do you ask"?

"Something I need to know in order to work out a puzzle that I was recently handed."

"There are many puzzles in life, my child, that's what makes it so wonderful"

"I'm glad you see it that way as well. Perhaps you could provide us with the whereabouts of the island's catholic church."

"Better still, I shall take you there this Sunday for morning Mass."

"That would be wonderful"! Yvette said with the utmost glee. Sister Ambrosia smiled and said nothing more.

2

VARIATIONS OF LOVE

Jack Stern and Father Brendan O'Reilly whilst in the company of their beautifully desirable women remained true to their word. No Hanky Panky even though it was difficult for both.

Brendan felt very comfortable with his collection of ladies and so it was that at long last he began to question the Church's authority that prevented priests from marrying and having a family. Two events magnified this thought, the pool of priests that he personally knew, those he had heard of who had made the bold decision to leave the priesthood and pursued the loves of their life and the vivid description that an elderly Sister of Mary once gave him about children.

"Gifts from God trailing clouds of glory behind them"!

"If the Catholic Church revised its position perhaps the scandal of paedophilia might even disappear" He postulated to himself. In his circumstances however, if he was to marry one of those in his present care the enormity of the public scandal were it to become common knowledge might destroy the sanctity of the very Church that he was attempting to restore. Brendan O'Reilly needed guidance.

Jack Stern on the other hand had no difficulties all of his previous love interests were almost perfect in every detail. He never intentionally misled or mistreated any girl and certainly did not place any sexual demands upon them. If lovemaking occurred it did so at the instigation of the woman. Jack Stern was always the gentleman, perhaps too much.

Invariably it was the women who broke off the relationship for numerous unfounded reasons. He reflected on his past encounters and trusted Yvette unlike the rest would not let him down. This was the fragile side of him.

It was early morning around 6am. Jack Stern had decided to take a solitary walk along the beach and allow the pristine seawater to wash away some of his anxieties. In the distance he could see storm clouds gathering heralding a tumultuous deluge scheduled for about 2pm in the afternoon.

He walked slowly and observed the endless unabated ripples that he caused on the surface of the water. Further along his watery mosaic met with interference and he looked up to see Brendan O'Reilly walking towards him.

"Good morning my friend, I see you also have troubles to resolve"!

"Very perceptive of you as always" Brendan replied

"So tell me what bothers you"

"The priesthood no longer satisfies me"!

"That is not unusual, it's made worse by your present evolving state which demands continual expression"

"What are you saying"?

"You have a number of options available to you. Stay in the priesthood and do everything you can to improve the status of your Church or take a chance and go outside of Her and see if you achieve greater things. Here take a store, cast it across the waters and observe what happens." Jack put forward.

Brendan selected one from the waterline and threw it in. Before it had time to hit the surface a mushroom shaped column of water ascended towards it, enveloped it and dragged it into the depths of the ocean without making the slightest sound. Brendan stood aghast.

"That rock was you, my son, consider the symbolism. Try a smaller flatter rock and see what you can do."

Brendan acted on Jack's instruction and found a suitable specimen. He played with in his hand and when he thought that the conditions were optimum sent it scurrying across the surface of the waters. The stone skipped and danced merrily unrestrained until it disappeared from view.

"I think I know what to do, but it creates another problem which I think may involve you as well." Jack remained silent and continued to look into the clear shallow water and observe the baitfish that darted to and fro.

"It involves virginity. Surely it must have crossed your mind especially in your blossoming relationship with Yvette."

"How do you mean"? Jack replied un-phased.

"Well I've deduced that you are a man of the world and as such has had many conquests"!

"Poor choice of words" Jack bluntly remarked unemotionally.

"Well what I am struggling to say is…how do you view your loss of virginity with Yvette's…err………..wholesomeness"?

"Who says I'm not a virgin"? Jack boldly replied completely unabashed and stumped Brendan in the process.

"I, like the girls that are presently in your charge are all virgins"

"Impossible"!! Brendan loudly protested.

"Not at all, my fellow student, remember what you have learnt the universale law that pervades all things seen and unseen is change."

"What of it"? Brendan shot back.

'Everybody, everything is in a constant state of virginity because everything, everybody constantly changes and as a result is constantly new. Everything that you do is for the first time because every time you do it all of the parameters surrounding it have changed."

"But what about the experience of it before"? Brendan swiftly retorted.

"Then unlike you I am a sexually experienced virgin"!!!

"You have no difficulty with Yvette's concerns about your past"?

"Not at all" Jack coolly replied

"Let me get this right! What you are saying is that I should think of all of the girls in my charge as being virgins"?

"Experienced ones, rather novel approach, don't you think, except it might play havoc with your concept of the Virgin Mary"! Jack stated joker faced. Brendan didn't know whether Jack was toying with him or not. However judging by the deep philosophical look that he had upon his face Brendan quickly gathered that he wasn't.

"Well, well look who we have here. If it isn't yesterday's bride and groom au naturale" Jack said as the two GO's approached them.

"Bonjour gentleman, you are both up bright and early. Most people sleep in." One of them gaily said as a mater of fact.

"My friend and I are taking advantage of Nature's early morning serenity to dwell on matters of theology." Jack sharply replied.

"Oh yes sounds quite impressive"

"Look it's rather rude of me, we haven't been properly introduced. I'm Jack Stern and this is Brendan O'Reilly and you are..........let me see the tattoo on your arm has RR love's MM with an arrow through the heart. How touching! Which are you? Jack asked disguising his mockery.

"Ravishing Roberto"! The tall Afro-Mauritian proudly proclaimed.

"So this must be.........."?

"Mischievous Moreno" Roberto once again proudly proclaimed.

"He looks the part. Quite a performance the two of you put on yesterday. I bet you get up to all sorts of mischief"! Jack cheekily inferred

"Oh Monsieur you don't the half of it. Would you like to enjoy some of the early morning kind that we get up to"?

"Pardon" Jack answered raising an eyebrow.

"You look the adventurous type. Come with us to the jetty over there and we will take you water skiing before breakfast"

"Just what I was hoping for' Jack replied consciously aware that he was playing into their hands.

"That includes you Mister Brendan, we can tow two at once" Roberto said as he licked his lips.

"Very well, but I need a life jacket" Brendan hesitantly replied.

"No problem, come follow us" Mischievous Moreno gaily beckoned as he took his lovers hand and swiftly jogged ahead.

"What are we letting ourselves in for"? Brendan sighed.

"It could be pay back time or you're simply too irresistible for them"!

"Wrong sex"!

"Not to them you're not" Jack remarked as he and Brendan caught up and climbed the stairs that lead up to the jetty's platform at the end of which stood an enclosure .As they walked cautiously towards it a voice rang out.

"Here we are, you handsome gentlemen! You've found us! Well come on let's play"

Brendan gingerly approached not knowing what to expect whereas Jack remained cool with all of his senses on full alert.

"Hello I'm over here, Roberto's in the boat, hotting it up"! Mischievous Moreno sang out.

Brendan and jack crept around the corner and found the enclosure empty much to Brendan's relief. Moreno was on the landing below preparing the towropes for the skis.

"Nothing to worry about all will be fine" Jack whispered from the side of his mouth into Brendan's ear as they descended the stairs together.

"Which one's mine"? Jack asked macho style.

"You take the left, you devil and you Monsieur the right"

Brendan and Jack followed orders, sat at the edge of the platform after removing their footwear and carefully slipped on their skis.

"You've both skied before"

"Veterans" Jack replied as though he was a toughened ex commando.

"I thought so! Are you ready"?

"Just about" Brendan replied as he preoccupied himself with the towrope's handle, but before he or Jack could adjust themselves, before he could request a lifejacket Moreno gunned the boats powerful engine and accelerated the craft at high speed out to sea.

"I think its pay back time" Brendan squeaked as the rope lines snapped tight and whipped them away.

"I disagree, he's testing our virility'! Jack shouted back seemingly in charge of his situation. Moreno glanced back, grinned and gave the thumbs up sign. Jack and Brendan struggled to keep balance. Both looked like drunks staggering about on ice-covered streets in winter. They continued their foolhardy display as Moreno weaved the boat in and around moored vessels in an attempt to plaster the skiers into oblivion.Every swerve was dangerously close; every sharp turn caused Brendan and Jack's muscles to strain with agonizing pain, every attempt close to shore also failed to dislodge the intrepid duo.

"I'll see how good you veterans are"! Moreno cursed as he pointed the powerful speedboat towards a treacherous expanse of exposed razor sharp rocks and coral. Jack and Brendan both straightened up and Jack shouted at the top of his voice with all of his might.

"Great stunt work! Give us more"!

"Coming up" Moreno yelled maliciously.

"I don't like the tone of his voice"! Brendan loudly said as he manoeuvred himself closer to Jack.

"I thought as much! It all seems too easy now doesn't it? I wonder what he has up his sleeve" Jack replied as he cast his analytical eye upon the sea ahead. "Very clever Moreno very clever indeed! Gay sadist! Jack muttered as he alerted Brendan to the rapidly approaching danger that lay just seconds away.

"He can't possibly be serious, he'll smash his boat"! Was Brendan's mental reaction as he stared in complete disbelief as Moreno flicked a switch and several small hydrofoils shot down from underneath the craft and lifted it sufficiently high to pass over all of the exposed volcanic rock, in a matter of moments Brendan and Jack would be put to the ultimate test of avoiding injury and death.

"Time for an uplifting experience"! Jack commanded as he sharpened his reflexes in anticipation of the daunting challenge. Brendan's mind had already raced ahead of them and prepared the stage for their salvation.

In a blink of an eye the surrounding waters without any warning became furiously agitated, boiled over into a synchronized flurry of activity as hundreds upon hundreds of flying fish burst forth and lifted Jack and Brendan into the heavens as far as the towropes would allow. The fish remained in tight formation. With wings outstretched, they coasted and glided upon the firm bed of supportive air like an engineless plane made out of hundreds of interlocking pieces. Moreno's eyes were glazed over with murderous intent as he sped the boat over the long curved reef. Half way through he looked back and saw nothing. He laughed with victorious satisfaction and turned the boat back to shore.

"That will teach you"!

"Hello we're up here! Were you looking for us'? Jack cheerfully called out with a wave of his hand.

"Huh!! Impossible'!!! Moreno cursed in French as he viewed Jack and Brendan floating high in the sky like two people enjoying a para-gliding joy ride.

"Damn You"!!! He grunted as he reached into a forward storage hold and pulled out a powerful revolver.

'He's becoming annoyed! I think He's going to do a spot of duck shooting! I don't fancy having my feathers blown off! Let's put a stop to this once and for all"! Jack said with a mixture of flippancy and seriousness. The fish as if on command, one by one broke formation and dive bombed Moreno until Brendan and Jack were safely back on water.Brendan then with a wave of his hand tilted his and Jack's skis back. Using his intimate knowledge of water he caused the sea to freeze over in front of them to a distance of six meters.

"Hold on tight" He then commanded

"Won't the rope break"? Jack's immediately replied quite concerned.

"Not at all, trust me" Brendan confidently replied as they both watched their respective towropes tense as the impact of the exponential weight gain exerted itself on the rear of the speedboat. It caused the watercraft to lift up and fly over them describing an arc of 180 degrees before it came hurtling down with an almighty explosive bang behind them.

"How did you do that"? Jack asked feigning surprise at Brendan's effort.

"Something I've learnt with time"

"Impressive, Master very impressive, now what"?

"Let's walk back" Which they both did on the sheets of ice that spread endlessly before them until they reached shore.

"Thank you" Brendan said in appreciation to the waters once they landed on the pebble and seashell studded shoreline. Some of the genuine GO's who were in charge of water sports were on the jetty preparing for the day's activities by bringing out life jackets, towels, sunscreens, and water skis from their secure storage areas.

"Bonjour" They happily greeted as they observed Brendan from the jetty.

"Bonjour" Brendan cheerfully returned the early morning salutation. "How long have Roberto and Moreno worked here." He then asked.

"Who"?

"Roberto and Moreno"

"No one of that name works here Monsieur" They replied as they shook their heads vigorously.

"But we saw them yesterday during lunch performing a bride and groom comedy skit in the main restaurant"

"As we did, nobody seems to know where they came from. Strange things happen here"!

"So it seems." Brendan replied somewhat satisfied with their explanation.

"Coming for a ski'?

"No thank you, we've had enough today"

"If you change your mind we are more than willing to teach you. Perhaps you could teach us how to catch the ladies."

"I'll keep that in mind" Brendan politely answered as a curtain of concern descended upon him.

"Jack, do you think Roberto and Moreno were assassins'?

"Don't know. Perhaps it's all very innocent, after all no one besides us should know that we're here, unless they have connections everywhere?"

"Who"?

"Badcock and his cronies of course I believe he still wants the girls back"! Jack correctly assumed.

"But we're in Mauritius" Brendan naively said.

"And prostitution is a global business probably run by a handful of well heeled families who have contacts everywhere; one handsome gentleman in the company of eight beautiful women; travelling together, a little obvious, easily identifiable time to watch your back."

Brendan stopped and looked very apprehensive as he dwelled on Jack's accurate words.

"Come on don't worry about it, let's have breakfast, I've been thinking about it ever since I smelt the aroma of freshly baked croissants and sweet breads floating on the fresh outdoor air." Jack suggested making light of the situation. Back at the chalet Yvette oblivious to Jack's absence was enjoying herself on the field of dreams whilst her body slept soundly. The beautiful maiden was in the company of highly evolved souls who continued to educate her in the unforseen mysteries of the ever-evolving universe her lesson was rudely interrupted by the persistent ring tone of Jack Stern's mobile phone, which demanded to be heard. Yvette threw back the thin cotton sheet that covered her naked body and walked boldly through the connecting door of the adjoining apartment to where the impatient electronic device jumped up and down on the hand crafted coffee table.

"Hello, err, good morning. Jack Sterns phone may I help you"? She softly greeted.

"That doesn't sound like a man's voice, where's Mr Stern'? The caller gruffly demanded to know.

"My apologies Sir, I honestly don't know. He doesn't appear to be in his apartment."

"Very well take down this number and have him me back call as soon as he returns. It's important, very important, and very urgent! Do you understand'?

"Yes sir, I do and I shall" Yvette sweetly obliged somewhat intimidated by the caller and his aggressive attitude. "Whom shall I say called" she asked slightly afraid.

"The Archbishop of course"!

"I shall tell him your Grace, God bless and goodbye" Yvette stuttered

"Oh yes, goodbye and all that"! His Grace roughly said as he abruptly clicked off.

Then another click sounded, this time closer as Jack unlocked the door to his chalet. Startled and naked Yvette knew she didn't have enough time to escape back to her bedroom so she quickly leapt into Jack's bed, covered herself up and pretended to be asleep. Jack entered moments later and was surprised to find her lying there.

'Good morning mademoiselle, what are you doing in my bed" He asked as though he was Papa bear asking Goldilocks.

"Pardon, what do mean your bed"? She answered coquettishly.

"It is my room unless you have decided to change accommodation or your mind." Jack suggested raising half a smile.

"I'm not that sort of girl"!

"Not for now you're not"

27

"What are you suggesting"?

"That we all change"

"Speaking about change, the Archbishop rang"

"What here" Jack asked rather perplexed

"Yes he did."

"On the Club's phone"

"No, your mobile" Yvette replied as she adjusted the pillow behind her head.

"That's impossible" Jack said a little angry.

"I assure you it's not, he was very coarse not at all what I expected from a man in his position" Yvette confessed quite disappointed.

"First Brendan now me" Jack mumbled.

"What are you talking about"?

"Nothing much" Jack replied as he approached the bed and sat down next to Yvette. "You are extremely beautiful has anyone told you that'?

"Many people, it has become second nature to me"

"Yes but how have they told you? Was it in simple terms, physical terms or in poetic ways with complete appreciation of that which you possess?

"I've forgotten"

"Perhaps you would allow me to express my thoughts"?

"Very Well"

"When I first met you I didn't take much notice until I saw you scrubbing the floors. Only then did I realize the innocence that you held, one that is shared by all things true to the earth, wind, water and fire." Yvette took Jack's hand and kissed it tenderly allowed it to caress her virginal breast and he responded by lowering himself down from the waist and then gently imparted a kiss on her neck, cheek and lips.

Yvette's breast felt wonderful, it was both full of motherly warmth and youthful excitement at the same time.

"Perhaps you could lie next to me and we could embrace for a moment or to" She softly purred as she felt the stirrings of her sexuality.

"Perhaps" He agreed as he wrapped his arms around her and felt their hearts fuse and beat together in three quarter time.

3

SERMON OF THE SOCKS

Sister Ambrosia was true to her word. On Sunday morning at 9am she collected Yvette and all those who wished to attend mass. The only time available was 10am as the congregation was invariably small and continued to decline with time.

The church if it could be called that was in a sad state of disrepair. It resembled many of the half built homes that were scattered throughout the island. The only features that suggested that it was a church were the awfully large wooden crosses that adorned each and every exterior wall. An inspired graffiti artist probably the only one that existed on the island painted one of the crosses bright Mexican red and encircled it giving the impression that the building was either a Red Cross or blood transfusion centre. Yvette was very distressed by its overall image.

"Oh my God what happened here'?

"Lack of interest my Child" Ambrosia sadly explained as she drove her transit van into the parking lot" As you can plainly see Father does his best to keep the gardens neat and tidy, and the interior and

30

exterior of the church clean, apart from that, he is restricted through lack of local funds."

"He needs help"

"In more ways than one" Ambrosia hinted as she led them towards the building after securing her vehicle. The main doors to the church were marginally open and rusted in place allowing only the less obese person to slip through. Ambrosia and her party had no difficulty in gaining entry.

The interior was as Ambrosia suggested however what struck Yvette were the statues and wall plaques all of which had been fashioned out of sugar cane. A local artist had found a way of fusing the dried cane together and then sculpturing an abstract form that looked rather jagged in appearance.

The effect was overwhelmingly eerie as it gave the impression that even the saints had bits and pieces missing from their personal make-ups which made them seem imperfect. Everything about the church was holey. Pieces were missing from the furniture, floor, walls, windows, ceiling and altar; it resembled a war zone. Jack Stern wondered if the building had been used as a guerrilla training ground. Yvette on the other hand thought it to be the result of random acts of vandalism. Both would have their suspicions answered during the homily.

A handful of worshippers were already seated in and around the central aisle, they whispered in low voices as they fervently recited the rosary which brought a glimmer of hope to Yvette's heart.

"Come child better take our seats, mass is about to start"

"Yes Sister" She obediently replied as she selected a suitable pew with an uninterrupted view. Brendan and Jack sat behind and remained silent as they had from the very beginning of the journey. A small bell chimed as if on queue to herald Fr Bruno Bogliani. He made his way towards the altar from the back of the church. The white tattered vestments that he wore enlarged his demure figure and the 10cm Cuban heels elevated his stature further.

"Cute" thought Jack.

"Sad" thought Brendan

"I hope you've improved." Ambrosia secretly wished.

Father Bruno went through the customary motions before addressing the small congregation.

"Good morning; sniff…..sniff….snort, nah"!

"Good morning Father."

'Today…..nah….I will after the introductory prayer and reading dwell on the subject of charity……..nah…….snort." Bogliani explained after he wiped his nose on his freshly laundered alb.

"Well chosen topic, considering the amount of poverty that exists here"! Jack thought.

"So let us begin. Nah…..will the assigned readers come forward……nah…so we may proceed….nah…sniff, snort…sniff. Very good…nah…. snort." Fr Bruno beckoned with a show of his hands as he took his seat near the pulpit. Yvette sat in total disbelief at Bogliani's bizarre mannerisms whilst the girls tried as best as they could to contain their laughter without success, a little snigger managed to escape now and then.

"Sssush" Give him a chance." Yvette pleaded. Jack winked at Brendan who like Yvette sat in a state of suspended disbelief.

"Is this man a real catholic priest assigned here or is he a refugee escaping from the Catholic Church? Where do these priests come from"? He mentally anguished.

"Thank you fellow….nah…readers…sniff….sniff….if you could return to your seats…..nah. In the name of the Father, Son nah and Holy Spirit nah. Today I shall talk about charity and what it means to me…nah sniff snort cough. The sort of charity I want to talk about is nah, not like the one, nah, that we practice…sniff snort cough. I want to talk about the divine type. Very often we as nah…..true Christians…sniff…help someone as best we can…nah sniff snort cough in all different ways…sniff. Giving a plate of food, giving a gift for a celebration….nah….giving of our time to visit…Nah!….giving an ear to listen…..no matter what it is….nah…..it is always limited and likened to a pair of socks. Supposing you saw a derelict walking on the street nah….looking very cold and hungry….nah…you noticed that his shoes had holes in them….nah sniff snort cough….and…. he wore no socks! He like his feet was feeling very miserable….nah sniff snort cough……you have no spare money on you….nah..nah.. so you decide to take off your socks and give them to him……nah sniff snort cough. He is thankful…nah..nah…but those socks will soon have holes in them because he has no soles on his shoes…. nah…..and he is once again back to being cold! Nah!!! Our Father in heaven does not give us socks as gifts….nah…instead he provides us with talents that last a lifetime….nah…nah…sniff….providing we do not use them as socks in which case they will get holes in them and become useless!!! Nah..nah…sniff snort cough.

We could wear the socks on our hands…nah…and use them as gloves…nah…but they are not intended for that…nah…we could try and wear them on our heads…nah…. and tear them in the process or we could even putt them on our……..nah, sniff snort cough. It doesn't matter! What we must always remain mindful of…..nah…. is….. what sort of socks our father gave us. We give woollen…nah… cotton or blended socks in sorts of colours…nah…shapes and sizes.

We can even give socks that look like mini-gloves…nah …in all sorts of thicknesses…but our socks remain good only for a short time…nah! If we store them away…nah…we might forget about them and the moths and silverfish will have their ways with them… nah…feasting in delight…nah! Our socks are useless….nah…but… nah…but…nah….the socks our Heavenly Father gives us…last us a lifetime….nah sniff snort cough. These socks we should never ever give away…nah…or store away….instead….nah…we should always use them without getting holes in them….nah! So think of charity as being a pair of socks…nah…keep them together….nah…never lose one…nah…..always make sure you keep them clean, wash on a gentle cycle, never spin dry or tumble dry in a hot drier…nah sniff snort cough. Lovely warm, fluffy, knitted socks....what more could any one wish for in life? God our Heavenly Father...nah...knows our needs well...nah...God bless you all! Now let us continue with the mass" Bruno said as he descended from the pulpit and strutted towards the rear of the altar.

The congregation with the exception of Yvette and the others bobbed their heads up and down in total agreement and appreciation of Fr Bogliani's deep and meaningful homily, for them the prayer the Our Father did not include "gives us this day our daily bread" instead it was "give us this day our pair of socks"!

No matter what topic of discussion it was, socks and only socks held and embraced the truth about all things in their divinely knitted way; this is how Fr Bruno Bogliani saw all of creation as being.

Yvette accepted Bogliani's idiosyncrasies and respected the fact that he was an ordained priest once consecration was over she obediently went up and received the holy Eucharist from his hands. Shortly afterwards when the sorry collection plate went around begging for funds it received a sock with a difference, courtesy of Mr Jack Stern, the clothing item was filled with all good things that heaven had wished for Bruno Bogliani to possess at long last.

"That was certainly Mass with a difference"! Brendan commented as they made their way out of the church.

"That's an understatement, my friend! Do you think we should help him"? Jack asked as he breathed out and waited his turn to squeeze through the main doors.

"Nah, I think he's too far gone! Makes one wonder what sort of life he's had to make him that way'? Brendan glibly said

"Foot fetish, failed podiatrist"?

"Stop it! That's far too obvious, but then again, perhaps, you could be right! Where to now? Back to the village for lunch or shall we rough it at one of those roadside café's?

"I'm not particularly hungry as yet" Jack courteously replied as he caught up to Yvette and overheard her, say.

"Can we go to the coloured sands region of Chamarel? Will you take us there Sister"?

"But of course my child, it's about forty minutes drive from here. You will enjoy the countryside. We need to go the back way through the mountains if we take the coastal road it will take us approximately three times longer and by then all that you will be thinking about is food. We can stop off at a charming restaurant situated on one of the mountain slopes overlooking the plains and ocean."

"That would be very nice, but after seeing that poverty stricken priest I feel rather guilty at the thought of it." Yvette replied sympathetically.

"I think we all understand, onwards then, but should you change your mind there are plenty of cheap places along the way that we can stop at."

The route that Sister Ambrosia took meandered through varied villages and small towns. It was full of surprises. The island was a true melting pot of different cultures; each bravely attempted to stamp its influence upon the general population. As they ascended into the mountain region of Vacoas the atmosphere changed from semi-tropical to alpine. The air became crisp and cool loosing much of its humid weariness. The scenery around the water reservoir was spectacular that suggested the Black Forest of Germany with tall majestic pines inhabiting the region.

They journeyed past the Hindu Temple and glimpsed the sacred monkeys arrogantly walking about and eating the locals' offerings to the gods whilst tourists busily photographed everything in sight including the large monkey like statues.

"Not as clean as Bogliani's." Yvette's observed not meaning to be disrespectful.

"They have different priorities" Ambrosia diplomatically replied as she tooted the transit van's twin air horns. "It's all-downhill from now.........geographically speaking" She then added as she concentrated on her driving.

"That was close"! Jack remarked as Ambrosia swerved to avoid a Japanese pedestrian, she picked up on his innuendo and said no more.

"Horns and brakes all the way" He further flippantly remarked as they sped along the curving road and picked up speed.

Sister Ambrosia was a capable driver, alert and considerate, she kept the van on track, around tight hairpin corners, narrow roads and crowded intersections. Everything flowed smoothly until without warning they left the main road and careered onto a loose gravel track.

"Is this the right way"?

"It is my child we are on the 'road' to the coloured sands. Don't despair I've taken a short cut" Ambrosia assured them as she firmly controlled the van's desire to drift wildly on the loose gravel stones.

"In the region of the coloured sands there stands a building that needs your attention." Yvette mumbled to herself.

"What did you say"? Ambrosia asked as she briefly took her eyes of the road and looked at Yvette who sat in the passenger seat next to her. She repeated the statement only louder.

"Hum, it could mean any number of things, just look around and see what you can see."

"Only a bird can see unlike you humans."

"You're behaving very strangely." Ambrosia replied

"Is there a road that goes around the sands"?

"No; one road in and the same out, no circular route."

"How big is the region"?

"Not large, region could mean anything, it's not specific enough, it might even mean nearby." Ambrosia suggested as she concentrated on her driving.

"I wonder if I…we need to go up to higher ground" Yvette guessed.

"Then you will need to walk" Ambrosia dryly replied matter of fact.

Disappointed with Ambrosia's reply Yvette mentally drifted back to the National park near the Chateau Alpine a place she frequented when she wanted to interact with the rare Rose that grew there. She remembered how she had taught Brendan to 'see' by using a purple cloth and she concluded that the purple of Easter was not about covering up but more about seeing the unseen. Easter was not only about rebirth it was more importantly about discovering the normally unseen.

Yvette wondered if the Holy Catholic Church had recognised the hidden symbolism and the true message of it all. Purple, violet, and crimson were the colours that her mind flicked through as it searched through all of their available hues as she remained silent and appeared to blankly look out of the window. The road became bitumen once again Ambrosia relaxed and drove through the farmland taking the appropriate turns to reach the coloured sands.

"Stop the van, please"! Yvette unexpectedly shouted. Ambrosia slammed on the brakes and looked around quite confused. There were no people, animals nor cars that posed a danger.

"What did you see"? She demanded to know obviously quite annoyed.

"Back there, it's back there"! Yvette excitedly babbled as she leapt out of the van and hurtled down the road leaving everyone quite dazed.

"What's out there"? Jack shouted after her.

"The purple violets" He heard her reply in the distance as he observed Yvette run into a farmer's field.

"What is she doing"? He said shaking his head.

"I think I know" Brendan confidently replied as he slid open the van's side door, jumped down and followed her path until he stood by her side.

"It's right here just as the bird said it would be"! Yvette exuberantly said as she pointed to a spot in the ground. Brendan strained his eyes but couldn't see anything significant.

"Wait, let me try something." He apologetically said as he produced a piece of purple cloth that Yvette had given him some time ago.

"You remembered"! She exclaimed visibly touched by his remembrance.

"How could I ever forget? You taught me to see. I've been trying to do it ever since that moment by myself, but I'm not that good at it yet. I need a little help now and then." He bashfully replied as he intoned several mystical words that would allow him to accelerate the process of 'seeing'.By the time the others had joined them he was in a state of readiness.

"It's absolutely breathtaking; I've never seen anything like this before. There are thousands of them.......the question is why? He exclaimed.

'Why.......is the question" Jack brashly interrupted as he accentuated the word 'why'.

"You must be hungry Mr Stern"! Yvette coldly rebuked Jack as she glared at him for disrupting such an important find. "Don't fret we'll feed you soon"! She then snapped. Jack immediately retreated and bit his tongue until further notice.

"Can I see"? Felicity respectfully asked.

"Of course, my friend, here take my hand" Yvette answered as she extended her delicate hand. The stupendous vision of massed purple violets rapidly unfolded and hit Felicity with force.

"Wow, this is incredible, I've never seen anything like this. What does it mean"?

"These purple wonders are protecting the last remaining fragment of the Church and I think they want us to help in some way" Yvette carefully explained.

"Where is the Fragment"? Felicity asked as she tried to determine its exact location.

"Some where in the middle, look for the ice blue coloured stone" Yvette replied as she lead Felicity and Brendan to where it lay.

Brendan lowered himself to one knee as an act of genuflection and gingerly touched the stone.

"It's colder than ice and that doesn't make sense! In this tropical climate it should be warm"! His description encouraged Yvette to touch the stone as well.

"I can feel a very feeble heart beat, it's hardly alive. It needs love and attention" She intuitively reasoned.

"It appears to be very dense" Brendan deduced as he continued to examine the stone.

"As would be expected"

"Meaning"

"It has all of the materials necessary to rebuild itself" Yvette suggested confident of her answer.

"Perhaps I can do the reverse of what Jack did with his Ferrari when we rescued the girls from Badcock" Brendan bravely put forward as he started to visualise his next move. Yvette gave her nod of approval and removed her hands from the fragment. Brendan intoned Omra seven times and soon found himself within the Church's interior. It was deathly cold almost minus 273 degrees absolute where it is argued that all matter ceases to exist. The red tabernacle light barely flickered.

"Who is the keeper of this building" Brendan shouted. His voice reverberated around the walls, the ubiquitous coldness changed its pitch and it came back, reached for his ears and attempted to fill his head with premature senility.

"I am too young for this nonsense! Show yourself"! He commanded. An image of frozen dehydrated decay formed before him. Brendan remained calm unafraid. He loved his church and would do anything to save it. His image in contrast to that of Decay burnt with youthful desire. The two opposites stood before each other.

"Where have you been"? Decay impatiently asked.

"Finding myself"! Brendan answered without any degree of shame.

"I've missed you. I'm almost dead from neglect. It's not fair. If it weren't for the violet's I wouldn't know if I could survive any longer"! Decay stuttered as it choked on its own words.

Brendan sensed its desperation and without any hesitation embraced the hideous looking being.He felt the rejuvenating energy of love flow out of him, the more Brendan thought about his beloved Church and how much it meant to him, the more the love flowed out of him until he heard.

"You can stop now"

"Pardon" He replied as he slowly opened his eyes apprehensively.

"I said you can stop now." Yvette softly repeated herself. Brendan blinked repeatedly, rubbed his eyes and looked around at his new surroundings. Decay had transformed itself into a magnificent place of worship complete with miraculous features as intended by its unearthly builders.

"The Church of the Coloured Sands with its natural source of healing waters" Felicity coined the description as she moved about its interior with arms stretched out wide until she reached the ornate baptismal font. Her movements caught Brendan's eye and he focused his attention on where she was standing. He watched as the water continuously bubbled up from the centre of the font cascade over its perimeter's edges and drain away into the stone floor beneath it without leaving one drop behind. He walked over, hesitated briefly before he scooped up a handful of the water in his cupped hands and drank it. Satisfied with its purity and effect he signalled for the others to do the same.

"Drink my friends it will cure you of your hunger and thirst"

Jack was the first to try. He found it to be true after a moment of self-analysis. Each of the ladies followed in turn, all with the exception of three obtained a measure of varied relief

"It is not for everyone" Jack remarked to himself as he closely observed each individual's outcome. Ambrosia was the greatest affected, she remained deeply silent as she came to grips with all of her past grievances and the demons that they had created. She watched them dissipate before her eyes and became at peace with herself.

"We must tell Bogliani about this place" Jack wryly said.

'What, so he can sabotage and destroy it'!!! Yvette snapped back clearly annoyed by Jack Stern's inappropriate and flippant remark.

"What do you propose my angel"?

"Brendan takes charge, it was meant for him"?

"And how did you come to this conclusion? A little birdie tell you"? Jack teased completely unafraid of the consequences.

"Perhaps" Yvette replied visibly wounded by Jack's stabbing comment.

"Very well, how about you organize and I advertise"? Jack challenged the fair maiden as he threw down the imaginary gauntlet.

4

MIRACLES IN MAURITIUS

When Jack Stern had something of importance to attend to, he did not have any time for distractions and unfortunately Yvette irrespective of how much she meant to him became one.

During the following week Jack devoted himself entirely to making the Island's people aware of the existence of the Church of the Coloured Sands and that Mass would be celebrated on Sundays at 8am, 10am and 12 O'clock noon. Everyone was welcomed no exclusions.

Jack when left to his own devices without any interference executed any task brilliantly. His methods stimulated, teased, provoked and 'begged'. Within days of his propaganda hitting the streets people started appearing outside the church in numbers just to have a look. To each the Church outwardly appeared different possessing a colour that attracted and held its observer. Inside it was the same. Strangely not one individual related to another person what they had seen.

The Church demanded universale acceptance, it wanted, never, ever, to revert back to its former state of decay.

As Jack worked diligently to ensure that the first Sunday would be an overwhelming success he reflected on previous days' incidences and he realised that he was once again all alone. Yvette spent most of her time with Brendan.

The idea, that, he like each one of us goes through life alone disturbed him. Jack realised that even though we may share some part of our life with some one or others, these were nothing more than fleeting encounters that were superficial in nature. No one really knew him or would know him in the true sense of the word. All that they might offer was some degree of comfort, direction or accomplishment. Granted he and Yvette had spent time together during the morning and evening meals even though it was in the company of others it did nevertheless allow them to progress in learning about each other and themselves. Recent events had however cooled their relationship and Yvette appeared to have become more attracted to Brendan.

"Perhaps it only appears so; perhaps she is spending all of her time with him because she wants the Church to look perfect on its opening day. God knows why? It's perfect as it is. Doesn't she realise that this is one extraordinary building"? Jack thought to himself and for the first time in his earthly existence he felt the pangs of jealousy.

Jack Stern's main adversary for Yvette Bell's affections would always be the Church and all that was contained within it. He postulated to himself that Yvette was experimenting with him, as he was the first true gentleman that she has ever encountered. If this were true then he should stop worrying immediately and with those thoughts in mind jealously swiftly vaporised never to be seen again.

Sunday was not far away. Jack intuitively knew that the day would be a huge success, for besides his marketing efforts, the Church of the Coloured Sands worked independently as well. Brendan might have caused Decay through his immense love of the Catholic Church to revert back to its former glory but Jack possessed a deeper knowledge of its workings and could hear its whispers spreading throughout the Island and infiltrating the minds of its inhabitants causing them to discuss matters of philosophical religion without the customary associated violence.

The Church of the Coloured Sands would in time become the grain that fed the souls of all those who thirsted for true knowledge.

"I'm a little nervous this morning."

"And why is that my precious little butterfly"? Jack warmly asked as he stretched his arms out wide in the hope that Yvette would take advantage of the opening and give him a good morning hug.

"For Brendan's sake"! She replied ignoring the invitation. "To day's the day"!

"I'm certain he will cope, after all he's more grown up now"

"What do you mean by that"!

"Nothing much" Jack innocently replied as he felt Yvette's defences rising to the occasion.

"I don't think I'll have breakfast this morning"!

"Why, too far to travel"? Jacks callous remark caused Yvette to sulk." Come here what's bothering you"? He tenderly asked realising the mistake he had made.

"You don't seem to have any time for me anymore. This week I felt so alone that I buried myself in the work that I'm used to. It's almost as if you don't want to know me anymore"! Yvette confessed as tears filled her eyes.

"Is that what you thought my precious pussycat? It's not the case at all. I decided to work especially hard so that the excitement I saw on your face when you first discovered the Church in the field of purple violets would never fade"!

"The greatest I've ever experienced is when I first met you"! Yvette emotionally replied as she approached Jack and lowered her head on his shoulder after lovingly embracing him.

"You must have picked up on my thoughts. I've been thinking about you all week fearing the worst."

"Which was"?

"Brendan and the Catholic Church are more important."

"Than you, I hardly think so! Let's make a promise "! Yvette said, as she looked deep into Jack's blue eyes.

"Which is"?

"To understand each other better no matter what happens; promise"?

"Promise" Jack truthfully answered as he reflected on the error of his ways and cursed himself for being such a fool.

"I've come to appreciate that you can be likened to an extremely fragile piece of fine porcelain, extremely beautiful, precious and delicate. Therefore it is my duty to treat you with the utmost care and respect."

"Don't say anymore. All that you have to do is love me. I ask for nothing more." Yvette softly replied.

"Will you teach me how to"? Jack answered as he kissed her hands one by one before he kissed her tenderly on both cheeks.

"I will."

"I need to understand what love is from a woman's perspective."

"It is not difficult."

"I'm certain it's not." Jack was pleased to say as he then realised that Yvette came into his life for the purpose of completing his education. They kissed and kissed some more, exchanged sweet meaningful nothings and then when the time was right held hands and transported themselves to the newly discovered Church of the coloured Sands.

Brendan O'Reilly, Sister Ambrosia and the girls were already present applying the finishing touches. Not one of them had dared out of sheer nervous excitement to peer outside and see what awaited them. Jack and Yvette appeared on the main altar as the perfect couple.

"Well, what's happening"? Jack asked as he peered at the nervous group which stood halfway down the main aisle.

"We're too scared to look" Candy stuttered

"Then let me take charge." Jack boldly offered.

"No need for that Mr Brash Stern. None of us here is incapable thank you very much"! Bellowed Sister Ambrosia as she sharply clicked her heels together turned on the spot and marched towards the main front doors.

"Insolent fool"! She audibly mumbled as she approached the heavy solid timber doors. Ambrosia was about to reach out and grab one of the door handles when they automatically swung open and caught her off guard causing her to lose her balance.

"Did you do that"?

"No my darling I am not that way inclined" Jack honestly replied as he witnessed the potentially humorous mishap. Ambrosia quickly regained her stance, brushed away the annoyance of the incident and made it a point to greet every person as they filtered into the church.

As the pews filled one by one, the internal atmosphere changed from dark to light.

"I know many 'hands make light work' but this is ridiculous"! Yvette said as she watched the increase in numbers cause the walls to exude a warm golden glow that transformed all into warm living wonders of life.

"They never looked so good" was Jack's sublime observation as he noticed the upper walls change into various forms of coloured quartz that created symbolic images of light, love and eternity. "I think we had better take our leave" He then hinted as he took Yvette's hand and headed towards the sacristy. Once inside he was greeted with Brendan's query.

"Is it my imagination or is the church growing"?

"Nothing's impossible my boy"!

"Then it's true we are dealing with a living entity"!

"How could you possibly think otherwise after all that you've been through"? Jack asked making reference to all they had experienced together at Newburn.

"What shall I call it"?

"Who"?

"The keeper of the building" Brendan vaguely answered.

"I don't know, invent a name or two, or better still, ask it! Perhaps it's something catchy like universe all, or even cat-holic, intoxicating don't you think? Probably not a good time to think about it; time for Mass, Brendan, ladies you all know what to do, let's get on with it"!

Jack hurried them along as he glanced at his watch, which was rapidly approaching 8am. They looked at each other shyly and then sprung into action.

Felicity took hold of the large gold processional crucifix, Brandy picked up the leather bound red copy of the bible, Candy made sure that the thurible had sufficient charcoal in it, Jamie carried the incense and Samantha held the silver bucket of Holy Water in which the Aspergillum was immersed. They exited the sacristy through a side door, made their way down a secret corridor and emerged in the main foyer.

Felicity was at the front of the line, she proudly held the gold crucifix up high; those without anything to carry were next, then Jamie, Candy, Samantha, Brandy and Brendan at the rear. Instead of audibly making the sign of the cross Brendan broke into song and sung one of his favourite melodies 'Ave Maria No Morro" in English, unbehnownst to him everyone else heard it in their preferred language. The lyrics were as follows:

Ave Maria
In our moment together we two lovers go out walking
Walking to the shrine on top of the hill
Everything we do we do together no matter whether they're the small things or the big things so we will share saying a prayer
Give me your hand dear now as we stand dear pray that our love will last forever may we never wonder or wish for anything more
The joy of living is in the giving so we give our love Ave Maria

The joy of living is in the giving so we give our love Ave Maria
Ave Maria Ave Maria
Love hath to last forever never to banish not ever
Ave Maria, Ave Maria

The words profoundly meaningful extended themselves into embracing all forms of love especially those that related to humans and divinity. The walls of the building selectively took hold of various individual human voices and transformed them into instruments of music that culminated in a grand symphony of sound adding to the overall effect. As the final Ave Maria faded out the processional column floated down the central aisle ascended the raised altar and everyone assumed his or her position.

"Good morning ladies, children, gentleman, it is very good to see all of you here today. It is truly a miracle that this magnificent church stands here and that you have come to share in its experience. If it were not for the efforts of a very special young lady who has the gift of 'seeing', none of this would have occurred." Brendan thankfully said as he made eye contact with as many of the congregation as he could. Yvette meanwhile secretly prayed that he would not identify her.

"However we will not pay her homage instead it is our intention to teach each one of you that you also possess special powers and that this was the driving force behind Jesus from the very beginning of his ministry. The beautiful young lady that I spoke of taught me how to see just as the Virgin Mary taught her son. Many eminent biblical scholars largely overlook this little known fact. It is continually supported by the apparitions of the Virgin Mary in her quest to educate us for there exists a well of souls here on earth that requires nurturing in order to prepare its offspring for the spiritual world. Life my friends is a gift which coincidentally has a mind if its own."

"Well done my boy, you have truly become a free thinking individual" Jack mentally applauded the young priest as he sat back to hear the rest of Brendan's opening address.

"Life experiments with life meaning that it experiments with itself to see how it can adapt and master its physical environment. Each one is a unique experiment in life. This building is known as the Church of the Coloured Sands. It is no accident that it came to be here, nor is it a mistake that it is called by that name. The coloured sands of Chamarel are a beautiful example of what life is trying to achieve here on earth. The sands represent all of the different races of people and clearly demonstrate that they can live in perfect harmony. The sands show how individual races are best suited to different localities and in doing so confirm that life in experimenting with itself it did so with many parameters in mind and it waited patiently to see the effect that they would have upon intelligence and adaptability. We are not all created equal, being a unique experiment we have each developed different abilities, however, we do have equal rights and that is what is important. The one thing that welds us together and makes it work is love that is the reason why you came here today. This church will not let you down, ask, knock, seek, it will be given to you, but first you must love each other without reservation for without love you cannot achieve anything.

The great wonders of the world, the great individual achievements were all done through the process of love. In the corner over there stands a baptismal font with a difference. It has its own natural water supply something that I have never come across before. This freely flowing water, unlike that of many commercial bottled varieties, actually possesses genuine curative powers that tailor themselves to the individual's personal needs. Today once Communion or Mass has concluded I invite each and every one of you to partake of your own personal miracle from the font."

Father Brendan O'Reilly's introductory greeting was adapted by the building's walls to suit each listener's yearnings irrespective of their age, colour or sex, something that Jack Stern, Yvette Bell and Brendan picked up on, apolitical, at its best.

Brendan's suggestion that human souls originated on earth

49

perplexed Jack Stern he accordingly dwelt on the matter. "Could it be true that they have their origins here and they require physical experience as a means for their advancement or is it a two way street whereby highly advanced souls return to show the road ahead"?

The Mass proceeded smoothly; the homily was brief, very brief, with Brendan saying. "Thank you for attending, enjoy and truly love one another Amen"

The distribution of Communion, the highlight of any Mass, was exceptional. The Church of the Coloured Sands did not want to disappoint. Each communion wafer tasted different to every partaker, more along the lines of a forgotten memory that dealt with his or her first love. The wine was sweet, an endless supply of it, handed out by eight celestial virgins. Brendan administered the sacrament with tireless devotion until he was confronted with the satanic eyes of the heavily disguised Harshman. Father Brendan O'Reilly placed the host on the man's outstretched hands.

"Body of Christ" He fearlessly said.

"Amen Mr Stern! We meet again except this time I am better equipped'!

"God bless you my son. Drink the Baptismal water it will cure you of your ailment"!

"You will need more than that to protect you"! The Harshman barked as he turned and swept his way out of the church. Unperturbed Brendan continued to distribute Holy Communion. Jack and Yvette meanwhile both of whom stood nearby viewed the incident out of the corner of their eye and then looked at each other to gauge each other's reaction. Yvette looked rather worried and gave the impression that she feared they would soon be attacked. Jack on the other hand smiled and winked as a way of saying "don't worry I'm here.' Yvette accepted his vote of confidence and continued to give out Communion.

The Church's interior was a hive of activity, people going to Communion, people partaking of the font's Holy Waters, people respecting each other, people behaving in an orderly manner, people accepting, welcoming, sitting and reflecting, praying and simply being.

Brendan had found his ministry in life, it wasn't on his native soil but that's how it normally goes. The Church of the Coloured Sands was his, he could feel it from the moment he had embraced Decay. It used his love to physically demonstrate his devotion to his beloved Church. This Church was Brendan O'"Reilly; it was an extension of him and it caused all things to happen that he had so long wished for. Without him the Church would not exist, without him the miracles would not happen, without him it would surely die at worse or at the best it would hibernate until another Brendan O'Reilly discovered and reactivated it. Brendan and its keeper needed to reach an understanding as to what would happen when he was away; miracles had to continue in abstentia.

The entire Mass and its content was a timeless affair at the end of which Brendan and his helpers came away fresh and ready to go again. Brendan did not ask for any donations during Mass. The people touched by his warmth and unselfish sincerity contributed as they left. A group of children brought offerings of Mauritian currency and others, and left them at the footsteps of the main altar, three bags full. They made no impact upon Brendan, he simply thanked and blessed the children, turned to Sister Ambrosia who stood behind him at the time, and said. "For your mission"

"That's very kind of you father, but you will need it for the upkeep of your Church"

"It can look after itself, all it needs is me"! Ambrosia looked at him sideways with a degree of impertinent disbelief and thanked him for his generosity.

The 10am and 12 O'clock noon Mass's produced similar results even though the mix of people was different. After they had tidied everything away Brendan and his group assembled outside amongst the purple violets.

"Excuse me Father, its 2 o'clock in the afternoon. I've had no morning tea, no lunch and I'm rather tired. What are you going to do about it the Club's restaurants are closed"?

"Have you stopped complaining, you sound like a whinging, whining, spoilt brat, Mr Stern"! Sister Ambrosia sharply said as she wished she could clip him around the ear.

"Not really, I'm on a roll here'!

"So I gathered"!

"Come on lets join hands"! Jack playfully said as he jumped about

"And play ring a ring a rosy, I suppose"! Ambrosia angrily replied, as her opinion of Jack Stern worsened. This was a man she definitely disliked and it was visibly evident.

"Come on Sister do as you're told otherwise you'll miss out on the fun and games" Jack continued to tease.

"Complete nut case"! She thought as she took her place in the circle.

'Right all close your eyes, ready" Ambrosia like the rest of her sisters thought that Brendan O'Reilly was about to say a number of thanksgiving prayers but instead in a flash of white terror she found herself being transported beyond the speed of light to a restaurant situated on a mountain slope that overlooked the sea and plains on the eastern side of the Island.

"Did you enjoy that"? Jack jovially asked as he suppressed his laughter.

Ambrosia touched herself all over and the Sister next to her, she stumbled about and tried to orientate herself with some difficulty.

"Madame has been at the altar wine oui"? The waiter joked as he approached the group and smiled at Ambrosia's apparent drunken stupor.

"Actually no, first time as the flying nun"! Jack flippantly remarked.

"You joke Signor"!

"Only if it keeps you happy, now, let me see we will probably need………"

"A long intimate table; we can accommodate you Signor, please, give us a few moments, come, enjoy the scenery from the balcony." The Laughing Cuckoo Restaurant's waiter instructed as he rubbed his hands in anticipation of a big lunch bill and many hot tips.

"Follow that man! Ladies, Sisters, Yvette my darling"! Jack light heartedly directed with a wave of his hand

Yvette and Felicity took Ambrosia's arms and led her in; she remained quite dazed and un-accepting of the 'miracle' that she had just experienced, Jack waited patiently until Abrosia had steadied herself against the veranda's solid railing and then he asked.

'Recovered yet"? Neither Felicity nor Yvette sided with Ambrosia for they understood Jack Stern's flippant ways. Ambrosia looked down on the vast green plains below gathered her thoughts and half answered.

"Beautiful isn't it"?

"What's that? The landscape you mean"?

"No, the idea, that someone has answered my prayers" Ambrosia reluctantly replied.

"And they were"?

'One day I would meet an Angel"

"I'm no angel"!

"I know that, you fool! How is it that a simpleton like you has been given immense powers"? Ambrosia bitterly asked.

"Because I'm simple, just like, the Little Flower Saint Theresa of Lisieux."

"Don't blaspheme"!!!

"I never do! I'm always serious and mischievous at the same time"!

"I sensed that"!!

"You're wondering what else I can do. Is that right"? Jack probed.

"Perhaps"

"If I did, do you think it would prove anything'? Jack once again probed.

"Only that you know how, nothing more, it does not prove that you're good"!

"Precisely, there's no point to it then"! Jack said in complete agreement

"No, there isn't"!

"Changed you mind about me"?

"No! Never will"!

"What will it take"? Jack asked in a charming fashion.

"More than your supernatural abilities"!

"Would you like to learn"? Jack offered once again in a charming fashion.

"Not really! I prefer the human ways"!

"I see" Jack replied sadly.

"I'll let the good Lord do all of those things"!

"Don't you think he would like us to have a little power" Jacked quizzed.

"For what purpose"? Ambrosia asked acidly

"To help with creation"

"Are you suggesting He's incompetent"?

"Misunderstood is a more realistic viewpoint" Jack bravely put forward.

"What are you driving at"?

"He needs our help! So why not learn what you are capable of doing'?

"No thank you"! Ambrosia emphatically stated.

"Who's being simple now"?

"No need for personal attacks"!

"Very well"

At that moment Jack Stern's ultra sophisticated hand crafted mobile phone rattled away angrily indicative of his callers aggressive nature. Jack retrieved it from his trouser pocket and viewed the screen, not recognising the number he activated the retrieve button.

"I hope that's you and not your personal assistant" The Archbishop coarsely said in a loud threatening voice.

"It's your lucky day! Finally managed to find my telephone number hey"!

"That's quite enough of your insolence Mr Stern! God only knows why I'm even talking to you"!

"Because I'm the best"!!!!

The Archbishop made no comment, Jack allowed his Grace a few moments silence and then he asked.

"Well what fine mess have you got yourself into this time"?

His Grace did not answer.

"Still with the brothers in black, don't tell me you haven't as yet divorced yourself from the Mafia"? Jack persisted.

"Let us say that we are fine tuning our organisation" His grace replied rather aloofly.

"I see! So where dose the trouble lie this time"? Jack asked even though he already knew as the Archbishop had broached the subject some time ago.

"With Australia"!

"What are you doing in Australia"? Jack asked feigning surprise.

"We had the misfortune of investing considerable monies in a natural therapies company"

"We..........meaning"

"Well, I actually" The archbishop arrogantly replied as he attempted to cover up his embarrassment

"And the money"

"Was a collaborative effort".

"In other words, not yours"! Jack Stern accurately surmised.

"One could deduce that if one examined the books very carefully." His Grace awkwardly replied.

"What about the company"?

"It was doing brilliantly well until the Australian Health Authorities got stuck into it and shut it down'! His Grace replied quite bitter with the entire affair and its mismanagement.

"Explain"

"The company is known as Napp Pharmaceuticals. It was the countries largest manufacturer of natural therapies. Its phenomenal growth was due to a number of factors. The quality of its goods, it researched and developed original products which were outstanding in their applications and it also contract manufactured for just about anyone."

"Let me guess, they grew too big for someone's liking" Jack correctly deduced.

"Precisely, it seems that the natural way is frowned upon, not by consumers, but by the medico-pharmaceutical organisations."

"Which suggests to me that Napp Pharmaceuticals was having an adverse effect on the profitability of the previously mentioned" Jack heartily concluded, he then asked." Tell me what happened"

"We believe that Napp was caught napping! From the evidence available to us it is our conclusion that Napp was sabotaged by members of the established rival industry with the assistance of corrupt government officials"!

"What are you saying"? Jack asked starting to take an intense interest in the subject matter.

"The collapse of Napp was entirely orchestrated with government approval"!

"Surely you jest"? Jack said with a degree of disbelief so as to taunt his Grace into telling the truth.

"Not at all, the health department seized on one batch of an innocuous product, I think it was a natural laxative, saying that it was contaminated with something that made consumers ill"!

"What proof did they have"? Jack asked raising one eyebrow.

"Nothing's been put forward as yet"!

"I see, I thought it would have been more prudent on their part to simply suspend one product" Jack intelligently determined.

"Not so, the officials went completely berserk! They raided all of Napp's manufacturing plants and claimed afterwards that they had discovered unhygienic premises, evidence of cross contamination, inaccuracies in weights and measures; you name it they found it"! His Grace expressed in a manner that demanded revenge.

"Sounds serious"!

"It is, the company has had its licence to manufacture terminated"! His Grace said with gritted teeth.

"Bit harsh"!

"That's an understatement"!

"Legal proceedings underway" Jack asked sizing up the situation.

"Not by the company or the government. I Believe negotiations are being conducted behind closed doors. I am also led to believe there is more to the story than meets the eye'!

"Tell me more"

"After the raids one of the manufacturing plants mysteriously caught fire."

"What else"?

"Rumour has it that the company had discovered an earth shattering breakthrough in the treatment of Alzheimer's disease"!

"I thought everyone knew how to treat that"!

"Very well you upstart, tell me"! His Grace growled.

"Simply eat Garlic. The ancients knew that garlic soaked in lemon juice produced a substance that kept you mentally alert"! Jack wisely said as he demonstrated his diverse wisdom.

"Your knowledge impresses me Mr Stern. Napp Pharmaceuticals had devised a specialised light activated alcoholic extraction of pre-treated garlic. The resultant elixir literally reversed the disease and rebuilt brains"!

"Well if that is the case then some one wanted the formula" Was Jacks understanding.

"Sadly they did not find it. We have it in a safe hiding place."

"How great is your involvement with Napp"?

"We've more than share holders" His grace answered almost choking on his words.

"Meaning"

"I trust this telephone line is secure"?

"Absolutely' Jack confirmed well aware of what lengths his techno-friend Stanley had gone to in order to keep his mobile phone untouchable. Although the line was the location wasn't, not far away, from where the Archbishop was talking, two unauthorized Australian Federal agents were listening in, using highly sensitive laser devices.

"How's it going"? One of the agents asked the other.

"Not good, getting a lot of distortion, this tape will need heavy editing, if we're going to use it." He answered frowning.

"Well then your Grace can you enlarge upon your relationship with Napp"?

"Mr Stern as you know for the Church to be known as Catholic it has had to embrace all peoples irrespective of their theological inclinations and beliefs."

"Yes."

"As you also know there are many Orders within the Church."

"Yes."

"There is also a sea of changing opinion."

"Yes."

"For some time many have been displeased with the traditional medicine, saying it is a gross departure from that which is divinely provided and therefore we should be actively involved in returning our flock to God's ways in terms of their health management. We could not do it directly from the pulpit, which is political suicide; therefore we decided to involve ourselves indirectly."

"With Napp Pharmaceuticals, good company, poor choice of geographical location"! Jack with total disregard for political correctness completed the Archbishop's sentence.

"So it would seem." His grace reluctantly admitted.

"Well it was nice chatting to you." Jack replied playing hard to get.

"Wait, wait a moment."

"What for"? Jack asked as he felt the Archbishop's embarrassment.

"I need to........."

"Yes.........." Jack answered sensing his Grace was choking.

"Ask for your assistance."

"There now, that wasn't difficult was it and you even said it nicely."

"Look Mr Stern, it's not my idea." His Grace rudely barked back.

"Really, care to tell me who the other players are"?

"I can't! Bear with me please" His Grace tactfully, replied,

"Very well" Jack answered well aware of his Grace's delicate circumstances

"We need the services of a good negotiator. The people who are presently looking after our interests in Australia are not doing a very good job."

"Sounds like you need a little leverage"!

"As much as we can possibly get"! His Grace stoically agreed.

"Sounds like fun, count me in. I can't promise to be there immediately, give me a week or two."

"Yes I understand you are in the company of the highly desirable Yvette Bell, bring her along with you if you wish. I shall advise our people to suspend any further negotiations on some pretext until you arrive." His Grace thoughtfully suggested.

"It will be my pleasure, your Grace; by the way wouldn't it be funny if other religions thought about going natural as well." Jack said making reference to the treatment of disease.

"The world is a funny place Mr Stern anything can happen"!

5

ISOLATED ORIGINS

Maxwell Dhaarling sat in the relative safety of his Baby Store Warehouse executive room and quietly listened to the Sudanese radio programme that was located at 96.66FM on his radio dial. As he did so he slowly consumed the lunch that his wife Merry had so lovingly prepared and he reminisced on the good times that he had had back home when he was younger.

Every working day Maxwell would time his midday meal to coincide with this cultural event, because, irrespective of how well Australia had treated him as a refugee, Sudan would always remain home. He needed to constantly remind himself of that fact for he was not a true refugee in the proper sense of the word.

Mr Maxwell Dhaarling and his family were what one might describe as 'assisted' meaning that the Australian officials who attended to his paperwork were extremely well paid for their efforts both abroad and at home.

Initially the Dhaarlings were meant to settle in Melbourne but after a short stay they journeyed to Perth, the most isolated city in the world so the locals say where the multi-racial mix and weather suited them better.

Maxwell throughout always dreamed of returning to a safe part of the Sudan, to live in peace forever, for the time being it was his duty to gather information for those to whom he was indebted. He often wondered how long it would be, for he had spent twelve years in Western Australia and not a word from the faceless people who had arranged his passage. Maxwell was growing impatient and if anything did not happen soon, the encouraging radio reports about life in the Sudan would cause him to move back once his daughter Precious had finished her university studies, which was only two years away.

There were many like Maxwell Dhaarling scattered throughout the whole world but mainly in nations, which were involved in the numerous wars that ravaged Sudan. Only the Sudanese knew of this. The official story that was printed in newspapers and magazines outside of the country painted a different picture.

One of internal social, political and economic turmoil, but in reality the Sudan was used by many developing countries as a play-ground in which to experiment with their latest weaponry and revised espionages skills.

In essence it was a training ground and often disputes between waring nations were settled there without the need to engage in damaging attacks on each others sovereign soils.

The Communist nations tried to put an end to the needless blood shed but failed, the West's vast propaganda machine was far too powerful. The only good thing to emerge was the formation of a secret organisation headed by an individual known by the improbable name of Max Climax.

Step by step just as religions do he welded Sudan's people together he gave them strength, faith and an ideology to live for. No longer were his people fighting amongst each other, the skirmishes and battles were now against those who sought to fragment Sudan, even though outwardly they were reported as being something else. The war would be won when Max Climax could inflict pain in those nations who experimented in the Sudan.

Maxwell Dhaarling was one of his many operatives who shared a common history of family desecration; loss of farming land, poverty, lack of eduction and constant fear. It was only when they encountered Max Climax's philosophy that they had any flicker of hope enter their miserable lives. Food, shelter, teachings were suddenly abundant; all they needed to do in order to partake of these treasures was pledge allegiance.

They were not required to under take any military training or kill anyone directly; the means of defeating the enemy was by a process of mental chess where the opponents unwittingly destroyed themselves.

The religion that they were required to follow was Islamic in principle based on Max Climax's belief that he possessed the only true version of the Koran and its proper interpretation which came about as a result of the epileptic seizures that he regularly experienced. Mr Climax did not see these as a medical affliction but rather as an act of God whereby his brain he believed underwent specific neurological alterations in order for him to be able to see the truths of the universe. Furthermore it was also his belief that these occurred at the most opportune moments in his life.

Max Dhaarling like the others received regular correspondence from the Master in the form of teachings that contained hidden mystical messages in a variety of ways. He and the others were required to go in search of these and this meant frequenting the public libraries and Internet cafes.

Merry Dharrling was especially pleased with her husband's effort to continually educate himself as she was an accomplished high school teacher who taught at a prestigious all girls college in the disciplines of chemistry and physics. At the same time both she and her husband were ecstatic with their daughter Precious and her study of Pharmacy even though they were initially sad when she did not qualify for Medicine, which was her first choice after sitting the public tertiary entrance examinations, however if she continued to excel as a student there was a strong likelihood that she could enter the school as a master's postgraduate student. Precious understood that this was her father's dream, it became her obligation to fulfil it as it had been deeply ingrained into her by the numerous stories that he told her when she was a small child, of how the white men came and healed the chronically sick members of his family with their miraculous medicine, being the only child made it worse.

Maxwell Dhaarling was a very clever retailer who jumped aboard the franchise wagon and quickly established a profitable chain of well-placed Baby Stores through the state. These rivalled the department, discount and variety stores on all fronts, price, quality and range. Maxwell's success came about by his uncanny ability to read the needs of all peoples and parents. Every day he made careful notes as to the idiosyncrasies of the Australian people's behaviour. Maxwell Dhaarling was the backroom boy who orchestrated the entire operation; his silent backer was none other than Max Climax who funded the entire set up and that was all, for he was not interested in monetary gain.

At the end of the Sudanese radio programme instead of the customary talk of forthcoming events "your stars for today" suddenly and unexpectedly came on.

"Virgo; Pisces, Cancer, Capricorn, news from afar, stop procrastinating it's time to strike"!

The phone as if on cue sprang to life startling Max in the process. He let it ring four times before lifting the receiver.

"Hello Baby Store, Max Dhaarling speaking."

"Mr Dhaarling."

"Yes."

"My name is Expedita Shocker I am a friend of Master Franck."

"Oh yes." Dhaarling cautiously replied as he started to feel rather uneasy for he had not heard from the Master in over eight years.

"We need to meet, know of any intimate Café's"?

"Quite a few" He honestly replied.

"Very good, I prefer the ones without the Net."

"I see, I suggest we meet at the..............."

The Duckstormer in the Swan Valley at 3pm on the dot"! Expedita suddenly and unexpectedly completed his sentence.

Maxwell Dhaarling stunned at the aggressive nature of his caller tried to remain calm as he sat in his expensive executive chair. He struggled momentarily to assess his situation; before he could say or do anything else Expedita Shocker terminated the conversation by saying. "See you there goodbye"!

Luckily for Max the afternoon was free of appointments. The work he had set himself could be rescheduled to the next day depending on what his caller's future demands were likely to be. The Baby Store was situated in the suburb of Malaga, a semi industrial area located northeast of Perth. It would be a short twenty-minute drive from there to the arranged meeting place. Twelve years of waiting were over, just like a dormant seed, the weather had changed and he was called to life.

The Duckstormer was located on the West Swan Road in Henley Brook, a combined restaurant and microbrewery in the German-Austrian style, light, bright and very friendly. Max parked his run of the mill Holden sedan in one of the customer parking bays available and made his way to the main entrance. The entire place bristled with activity as the tourists who had been brought in by various excursion companies were finishing the delights of their late lunch. An impeccably dressed Mr Maxwell Dhaarling looked around to see if he could match his mental impression of Expedita with someone in the crowd before him and as he did so he was oblivious to the attractive waitress who approached him.

"Mr Dhaarling." The young lady addressed him.

"Mr Dhaarling." She repeated after waiting a while.

"Eh? My apologies" He replied as he bowed from the waist and wondered how she knew his name.

"Your lady friend rang and instructed us to inform you that you must now make your way to the Paris Beat in Haynes Ave Kalamunda."

"Thank you, pity I couldn't stay" He apologised.

"Perhaps next time Mr Dhaarling."

"I'll bring my family." Max replied with half a smile and half the truth.

"Do that, auf weidersein." The attractive young waitress responded unconvinced as she turned on the spot and went about her duties.

Mr Maxwell Dhaarling looked quite perplexed as he walked towards his vehicle. Expedita Shocker he assumed had given such an accurate description of him that he was easily identifiable by the Duckstormers' staff. Had he or she met before? Was she working from a photograph or was another involved? Why the change in location? Were they presently being watched? Was Mr Climax's organisation under international surveillance? Had anyone of his followers' dobbed him in? Max didn't think that any of these applied, his analytical mind was simply doing its job. Max Dhaarling relaxed, the furrows on his forehead disappeared, his focus now shifted to working out the most direct route to his new destination as he thought; "In this part of the world all they do is endless disruptive road works"!

It was a bit of a jigsaw initially and then a straight run into the picturesque hills. The road spiralled up and levelled out at the Kalamunda townsite, which was not very large. Its name was aboriginal in origin and meant "Men of the trees." Max Dhaarling found the restaurant easily and parked outside of it in the main street. An abstract twenty foot replica of the Eiffel Tower stood in its courtyard surrounding by a mass of tables and chairs complete with red, white and blue umbrellas.

The Paris Beat was a converted retail store tastefully decorated throughout. It had a fine reputation for exquisite pastries and genuine French cuisine as all of its chefs were French, many came over during their holidays to experience the Australian way of life and as a consequence the food menu continued to vary much to the patrons delight.

Max Dhaarling entered the restaurant and stopped in front of the glass cabinet that displayed the pastry chef's daily masterpieces, art forms in themselves it was almost a shame to consume them.

"There you are Mr Dhaarling, the baguettes and cakes you ordered and of course the coffees that will be $26.90 thank you."

Max opened his wallet and gingerly obeyed. He handed over the payment and accepted the plastic bag of goodies.

"Your lady friend is in the park down the street. Thank you very much." The cheerful shop assistant said as she pointed in the direction that he should take and then she added with a wink of the eye." Please come again."

"Yes, I will, er thank you." Max vaguely answered. He exited the restaurant and stood on the footpath next to his car. Max then glanced up and down the street and caught a glimpse of greenery that suggested the park that the assistant had directed him to. He briskly walked towards it. The park was deserted.

"This is ridiculous"! He thought to himself and sat himself down on one of the available benches that overlooked numerous rose bushes in bloom.

The sun was warm, the breeze cool and the foods odour tantalising. Max took one of the baguettes out of the bag and un-wrapped it. Smoked salmon on lettuce, garnished with fresh cucumber, Brie cheese, capers and a hint of mustard made with freshly baked bread. If anything Mr Dhaarling's appetite had been stimulated by all of this cloak and dagger stuff. He was halfway through eating when a young fully attired nun silently came from behind and sat next to him. Startled, Max apologised and made room for the nun, to which she answered.

"That's quite alright my son; do you have a spare baguette for me"?

"Yes I do, how did you know"? Max reacted quite surprised.

"Your bag looks rather full and you appear to be a charitable person who comes well prepared."

"Thank you I guess. May I offer you coffee"?

"Most kind of you and it's still warm"! The nun said as she accepted the freshly brewed beverage.

66

"I wasn't aware that nuns existed in Kalamunda." Max said truthfully.

"Yes there is the order of St Joseph of the Apparition, the house is located on the main road leading into the town, but I am not from there, I am out of town on missionary work.

"What do you mean by that"?

"I am from overseas."

Maxwell Dhaarling put down his baguette and picked up his container of coffee. He turned to face the nun and looked carefully at her facial features.

"I'm sorry I didn't catch your name." He politely stated.

"Sister Eanswida, I was named after the saint of the same name who had a reputation for being quite expeditious. My vocation in life is reformation as directed by the Mother Superior of our Order."

"Which I believe is unknown and nameless." Max interrupted.

"Correct."

Maxwell Dhaarling confirmed to himself that his initial impression that the nun is his company was Expedita Shocker in disguise was correct. He also correctly determined that he was meant to continue this line of deceptive conversation so as not to alert anyone at all. Obviously the topic to discuss further was reformation.

"What does your Order expect of you? Is it personal reformation or does it have an outward expression"? He genuinely asked.

"We are outgoing in our activities. Our vision is one of localised global change for the benefit of all races.' Eanswida ambiguously answered.

"That sounds confusing to me how can you have a localised global event"? Max asked fishing for a proper answer.

"By that I meant that the globe becomes influenced all over by a solitary event that spreads by the mechanism of disease"! Max Dhaarling understood what she meant by that expression and he then asked.

"So you are travelling the world looking for a suitable origin"?

"Precisely"!

"Enjoying you baguette"?

"Immensely quite delicious thank you" She sweetly answered.

"I also have pastries"! He said as he opened the bag and took out a white cardboard box that contained four in total.

"Do you have anything else to offer"?

"Perhaps" He smiled "Here take my business card, call me anytime. I'll even give you my private home number and email address." He then offered.

"That wouldn't be necessary! I'm quite computer illiterate! I'll probably give you a call at work. Do you think that you could come up with some suggestions that could help in the reformation of the Australian people'?

"I'll try."

"Good. How long have you lived here"?

"About twelve years. What made you think I wasn't born here"?

"I can tell." The nun confidently replied.

"Do you always approach strangers so openly'?

"But of course"! She replied with a tilt of her head. My habit is persuasive and remember the words "knock and the door will be opened, seek and you will find, ask and it will be answered"

"I've heard them before"? Max Dhaarling guessed rather than confirmed.

"From Mother Francesca"

"Whom did you say"? Max asked

"Mother Francesca, she's our Mother Superior." Her statement made Max realise even more that he was indeed dealing with Expedita Shocker a charming sweet nun.

"Curious that she should refer to Franck Max Climax in the feminine gender; most appropriate, considering how well he looks after the hapless men, women and children in Sudan. A perfect blend of male and female emotions, no wonder many refer to him as being a God. Never seen; always providing." Were the thoughts that flooded

Max Dhaarling's mind as he responded "She sound's very intelligent and I must try it" Max said making reference to the words of wisdom.

"Do it, you'll be surprised what you'll discover"! Expedita nodded vigorously.

"You say that with such confidence" Max remarked.

"It's the driving force behind every achievement no matter how it is interpreted."

"Well said"! Max congratulated her as he examined her physical form. Tall, about five feet eight inches, svelte figure, C cup breasts, firm, with a hint of softness, long athletic legs, vivid green cat like eyes, wide full mouth complete with succulent lips, high cheek bones, peaches and cream complexion, probably a mixture of European races with a trace of something exotic like Sudanese.

"Yes Mr Dhaarling it is a pity that I am a nun otherwise we could take advantage of your physical attraction." She purred.

Startled by the accuracy of her comment Max cleared then lump of embarrassment from his throat.

"Was it that obvious"? He ashamedly asked.

"You could say that" Expedita smiled and exposed her pearl white teeth.

"I apologize"

"Accepted but not necessary, it's quite flattering, I use it to my advantage."

"Use what"?

"My good looks; a beautiful young nun always gets bigger donations"!

Max didn't know how to interpret that, Expedita continued. "Men deep in their hearts search for the perfect virgin. A nun like me is a fine example" She smiled again, this time cheekily.

"You're quite mischievous, does Mother Superior approve of your behaviour"?

"She doesn't know she's too busy with reformation. A subject we should talk more about." She suggested.

"Not now, it's far too beautiful out here, I don't want to spoil the moment." Max explained as he bit into his orange glazed almond croissant.

"Reformation doesn't have to be violent or upsetting"!

"I'll keep that in mind." Maxwell Dhaarling replied as he reached out and touched Expedita's hand.

6

MEDICAL MADNESS

As Maxwell Dhaarling ate his evening meal in the company of his daughter and wife he remained surprisingly quiet when questioned he answered that it was due to an exhausting day at the office. They accepted his feeble explanation but the truth of the matter was that Max could not get over the effect that Expedita had upon him.

His was in love a result of instant attraction and immediate infatuation. Given his marital history it was inevitable that such an event should occur.

Max married at the tender age of seventeen more out of comfort and self-preservation than love at all. Merry his wife came from a noble family, highly educated she was four years his senior, but looked younger. Intelligent, resourceful, hardworking, determined and domineering, it did not take her very long once in Australia to become a highly qualified high school teacher.

Max's success was more through the insistence of his wife than through his own devices. In some ways she was the brains of the business and definitely the seat of practical intelligence within the family. Max was an obedient student in all respects; he performed well and was suitably rewarded in the bedroom, although sexually satisfying, it lacked that emotional quality of love. Expedita seemed to possess that elusive essence in abundance and as consequence Max thought of nothing else but her.

When the dinner plates had been cleared away and the freshly brewed coffee served Precious looked sadly at her parents. Unable to contain her emotions her tears freely cascaded down her cheeks.

"What's the matter child"? Her mother kindly asked.

"I'm sorry, I'm really sorry"! Precious stuttered as she sobbed uncontrollably. Max and merry looked at each other blankly.

"I've…..I've……failed……."

"Your exams" Merry sternly asked, fearing the worst as a strict mother and teacher would do.

"No"!

"Give her a chance"! Max demanded knowing full well that he would have to bear the consequences of his abrupt action. Merry silently glared at him in response.

"When you're ready my child" He softly said to his distraught daughter who by then had started to rebuild her courage.

"Father, I am about to fail both you and mother."

"How will you do that"? Max asked somewhat disbelieving.

"By leaving the School of Pharmacy I've had enough. It's not meant for me. It's all so wrong"!

"What's made you think such thoughts"? Max asked now quite perplexed.

"Because she's fallen in with the wrong crowd I've seen it time and time again as an undergraduate and now as a teacher! Peer pressure, drug takers, alternative thinkers, ga……..! Max put up his hand in an effort to stop his wife's over reactive ranting. Merry was not impressed by what she perceived to be insulting behaviour. She snapped to attention and marched out of the dining room.

"I wish she wouldn't do that"! Precious remarked obviously disappointed with her mother's haughty attitude.

"Too highly strung, an over achiever, she'll simmer down once she retreats into her academic world."

"I'd like to believe that"!

"So would I." Max genuinely replied with a downward smile as he stood up and extended his hand for Precious to accept. "Come let's go to our hiding spot, we can talk in private up there." A smile broke through Precious' facial gloom and she happily joined her father arm in arm.

Their secret hiding place was in the vast expanse of the upstairs attic. Max had over the years cleverly arranged all that needed storing into a well constructed 'cubby house' big enough for two and with a view to the outside world. Often the two of them would escape there especially when Merry was in one of her moods made worse by extra workloads and the pressure of marking examination papers.

"I see you've been busy in here" Max made the observation as he sat down and crossed his legs.

"I have." Precious replied as she shifted piles of papers out of the way.

"Okay where do we begin"? Max gently asked as he shifted his gaze out of the window. Precious gathered her thoughts and arranged them so they would not only make sense but a convincing argument as well.

"I have been very happy studying pharmacy, it is a fascinating discipline especially the art of compounding, however ever since I started working in the commercial world my eyes have suddenly been exposed to the corruption and immoral practices that exist in western society's medico-pharmaceutical empire."

"Strong words, I hope you have concrete evidence to back up your allegations."

"It is based on personal observation and the advice given to me by one of the partners who owns the pharmacy at which I am doing my practical work." Max sat motionless and watched the motion of the stars. He occasionally looked at Precious; this was his way of listening without making the speaker nervous.

"I've never talked much about my work environment because mother is so preoccupied with herself and we always seem to do nothing else but become immersed in her troubled world. Instead of boring you with a long-winded description of what has happened I think it best to tell you what I've seen. The University assigned me to the Sensible Pharmacy group for a two-week period. On completion the owners offered me permanent part-time work. The business is very diverse largely as a result of the principal and original owner Mr Ramon Abdullah. He is not a very good looking man, he is of Indian ancestry and fancies himself as being a ladies man .He has this enormous protruding lower lip, a sign that he wants to suck out everything that he touches to his advantage. He has over the years built up a business that is completely money orientated with no consideration for the customers or their welfare at all."

Max hoped that this wasn't her entire argument; surely changing workplaces would alter her perception.

He services Nursing Homes, the aboriginal community, manufactures and sells illegal steroids to the body builders and even exports drugs overseas once again illegally. The size of the operation got out of hand when he purchased two other pharmacies. Not wishing to have any part of his business unprofitable, he falsified trading figures and took on a part owner, Mr Raymond Gossling. He is the complete opposite to Abdullah, a real gentleman, very well versed in the natural therapies of disease and illness. Abdullah saw him as a perfect candidate for partnership, not only for the money but also as a means of expansion into the alternative therapy market. It wasn't long before the two were at each other's throats. This came about as a result of information that disgruntled staff members freely volunteered to Mr Gossling on leaving their employment. Mr Gossling couldn't do anything about the situation, as he was more than certain that great harm would come to him by way of Abdullah's shady friends. In any event being part owner meant he had full knowledge and gave full approval to all of Abdullah's illegal practices. Ignorance is no defence."

"This is all very good Precious all you have to do is leave their employment and find work in an ethical environment to your liking. I am certain all is not that bad." was Max's fatherly advice.

"I understand what you are saying, Father, however my reasons for leaving are not based upon the corruption that I've seen but rather the medical madness"!

"What madness are you referring to my sweetheart"?

"It is a disease that pervades the entire Australian mentality at all levels from the simplest to the academic highnesses." Max sensed that Precious was about to run a comical routine.

"Nursing homes do not like dispensing an inmate's prescription medication from the original pack so they want us to prepare a blister pack. In essence what they are saying is:

"I'm not allowed to be giving you the medication from this box because I am incompetent; but it's alright for me to be giving it to you from that box. But I can only be giving the medication out from the box if the medication is packed in the correct coloured folder otherwise I cannot be giving you the medication that the doctor ordered"!

So what happens? The medication gets packed by us and delivered in the wrong coloured folder. The staff refuse to administer it, no matter how sick the patient is. They don't get their medication until it is put into the correct coloured folder. Then the patient is admitted to hospital and guess what happens next?

"We cannot be giving you your medication from these blister packs, it is against hospital policy, please be suppling us with the original containers"!!!! This is nothing more than petty minded strangling bureaucracy and what makes it worse is that the drugs may not even work"!!!!!

"Is this what the University teaches you"? Max Dhaarling asked in an effort to learn where exactly Precious had obtained her invaluable insight.

"Of course not, others have shown me the path of truth"! Precious replied indignantly.

"Crackpots, I surmise………."

"Not at all, the path is like a jigsaw puzzle, you find bits and pieces all over the place, for me it came from, Mr Gossling, little understood television documentaries, cutting edge magazines that mainstream media label as absurd and through my own reasoning once I had digested and assimilated what I had seen, heard and read"!

"What are you inferring"?

"That I am about to make one totally unsubstantiated sweeping statement"!

"Go on"

"Not one of the pharmaceutical drugs on the market is either fully proven or understood, what makes it worse is that it requires at least twenty years of intensive unbiased research to establish the efficacy and safety of what the poor public is taking.

The vast majority of these are in phase four which means that they are allowed to be marketed pending further research, which is not conducted by independent researchers. Instead the companies themselves fund it. Who then under these circumstances will publish an adverse finding after they have been invited to partake in the project? Nobody! If they do, they will soon find themselves discredited, ostracized, marginalised and probably unemployed"!

"My precious, precious child you sound more like an angry student who wants to change the world rather than one who studies to better themselves"

"You are quite correct father. The latter is for those who are prepared to satisfy the system, the former is for those who think for themselves. I am not prepared to become a sheep! I want the best for people and I want to leave pharmacy"! Precious resolutely stated as she held her head high.

"I do not think that this is a very good idea. You are so close to finishing. Is it not better to understand your enemy so as to destroy it"? Precious pondered on the intelligent suggestion and sought its merits. Her father meanwhile continued.

"Finish your present degree, it will, irrespective of what you want to do later open doors for you. A degree is a degree"! This further deepened her analysis of the subject.

"If what you have said is correct, tell me, what have you found to be a better alternative in curing the sick"? Max then further challenged her.

"That is just the problem! The medicines that are being marketed do nothing more than suppress symptoms. They give no relief at all, in fact they keep the patient sicker for longer and if taken to excess cause more disease to emerge. Not one of the drugs that I've seen address's the cause of the disease."

"Surely you're wrong my child. What about antibiotics, anti-epileptics, anti-diabetic, anti-depressants, heart medications, answer me"! Max taunted as he assumed the role of the devil's advocate.

"Precious took a deep breath and summoned all of her scant pharmacological knowledge.

"Pain relievers mask pain! Pain is the first step in the healing process. When taken too long analgesics cause disease to manifest itself by two processes. Firstly the disease that caused the pain proceeds further and secondly the suppression of the pain causes a frustration to occur within the body that precipitates other problems notably digestive and liver.

Antibiotics are no longer as effective as they are synthesized. Being unnatural they are not in the way they were meant to be and as a consequence the microbes that they target become elusive.

Antidepressants cause psychoses and neuroses, as no one truly understands the Neuro-biochemistry of the brain. It is far too complex and has an enormous amount of divergence. This is also true of the anti-epileptics.

Anti-diabetic drugs exhaust the body's ways of dealing with food distribution via the cardiovascular system and therefore these people will become insulin dependent, the heart system………"

"Enough said my child and might I say with impeccable

authority"! Max interrupted.

"I haven't finished! Although what I have just described seems primitive and without qualification the evidence is available in the recognised medical and scientific journals, pharmacopoeias', drug indexes and textbooks as well as the cutting edge magazines that I previously mentioned in which the articles are usually written by people in the know.

It needs a sharp mind to access the information, comprehend it and in so doing form the inescapable conclusion that the vast majority of drugs manufactured are highly addictive. Once the patient takes these, they are 'hooked' within a week It is very, very sad to realise that we live in a drug ridden and addicted society both legally and illegally"!

"Surely you exaggerate"?

"No not at all. The statistics shout for themselves. In this country on average the federal government pays out for about two hundred million prescriptions each year under its National Health Act. This number does not include non-claimable, private or workers compensation items. The illegal drug trade is enormous. I learnt this first hand from the methadone patients who dose at the pharmacy. It seems bizarre but sadly it's true and it has caused to me think differently. Whenever I see a person driving an expensive car, wearing high-class clothes and dazzling diamond jewellery, I wonder to myself 'what racket are you in'." Precious paused to catch her breath which gave Max an opportunity to say something?

"It seems to me that if you decided to become involved in alternative treatments you would face an uphill battle."

"Firstly they are the true medicine; secondly it depends where you find yourself in the ever changing world. Last year people in the USA went to and spent more on natural therapies than at the doctors."

"The outcome"

"Witch hunts against the true medicine practitioners. Vitamins and herbals considered as drugs, if it weren't for prominent actors and lobby groups standing up for consumer rights the pharmaceutical companies would have won. We have this problem right here, with the example of what happened to Napp Pharmaceuticals, with the exception that the people here do not fight for their rights they allow themselves to be walked on."

"I see...."

"I don't know why people worry about terrorist bombers; the biggest terrorist is the government itself"!

"Now Precious it is a better place to live in than Sudan. Safe, more opportunities...."

"And more corruption father"! Max Dhaarling could feel his daughter's pain brought about by her perceptive and intuitive reasoning.

"Are you suggesting that we return"?

"When the time is right, I would like to." Precious truthfully answered.

"Is the time ever right"? Max philosophically asked in response

"For me, it would mean becoming extremely well versed in all forms of natural medicine, proper nutrition and being able to harness the power of family love. Something that is lacking in this fragmented society where the government deliberately sets out to destroy families"!

Max Dhaarling mentally agreed. Was this the target of Expedita's reformation? It would mean changing the world's western nations political system which would not happen by the process she mentioned; it had to be something else. "I form the impression that you think that the pharmaceutical industry has far reaching influence"?

"Correct"!

"Surely it is subjected to the same strict regulatory controls as the others"? Max suggested.

"It is not a level playing field. The big well-established multi-national companies are hardly ever prosecuted. The health department only picks on the smaller companies with limited resources to justify their existence and make themselves look good."

"What would happen if one of these big companies made a mistake"?

"They would simply issue a recall, nothing more."

"I see." was Max's reply as he looked at the night sky's available stars.

"It's still difficult for me to accept your argument which has done nothing more than criticize the industry; that in itself does not make the other the better alternative by default alone you must argue the benefits of natural therapies"!! Max then countered.

"I suppose in order to argue the case for natural we need to understand what natural is with respect to its application to illness and why the sickness occurred. There is such a fine line between illness and disease. I am beginning to understand why people become sick and I think it has to do with emotional discord, karma and personal beliefs. What prevents disease is a loving stable home environment that includes all family members; proper foods, music, herbs and flowers are other sources of this stability. Each food has something to offer us in terms of keeping us healthy, preventing and even treating disease. Mr Gossling alerted me to this fact. He has spent many years and a great deal of money collecting books on the subject. The majority of these have been written by eminent medical anthropologists who have studied the cultural use of food over thousands of years. Mr Gossling often passionately informed customers of his discoveries, some embraced them others simply nodded their heads and continued their miserable lives without making the effort to correct their errors. For example, Mr Gossling promotes the use of blueberries, stinging nettle tea, neem leaves in the dietary resolution of diabetes, celery seed and bee pollen in honey for arthritis, mistletoe cold infusion for hypertension or hypotension, strawberries for viral infections, pumpkin seeds for prostatic problems, tomato juice for liver regeneration, onions, garlic, olive oil to correct high blood cholesterol levels........." Precious confidently rattled off before being cut short by her father.

"I see you have begun to understand the mysteries of life."

"And more father." Precious proudly replied.

"Very well tell me."

"We are without doubt electro- magnetic life forms in principle, vibratory in nature, so that each one of us is tuned to a certain specific frequency. The world that we live in is certainly very beautiful and free. Those who created it did so in an integrated fashion, so that no matter where man found himself, help was always available for him to cure his ills, the plants of this world are light transformers." Precious paused to allow her father to consider her postulations.

"I've never heard that before." Max replied not wishing to seem totally ignorant.

"It's not a new concept, merely put into different words."

"Explain." Max asked eager to learn more.

"Plants transform light into physical entities."

"But I thought and understood that they used the energy of the light" Max recalled.

"Yes but think about it in a different way. The energy is converted into physical forms and finds its expression by having its entire frequency range stored in infinitesimal amounts by specific molecules. The information contained in light's entire frequency spectrum is too great for any one molecule to store so it is distributed to thousands if not millions of different unique molecules.

We as humans select foods, herbs, fragrances and whatever else we need to accumulate the spectrum that is best suited to our individual needs and in so doing we maintain our health and vitality. The pharmaceutical drugs contain no such life force and rob us of that which we store."

"Can we heal with light"? Max questioned as he thought that this was a natural extrapolation of her hypothesis.

"I am certain we can, but it must be from the sun and not generated by man made means."

"Why do you say that"?

"Because all light is not the same, that generated by our sun is the best"!

"Does that apply to music as well"?

"Music is food for the soul."

"Does it matter what sort."

"Not really as long it provides the listener with a sense of happiness and does not lead them into discord that is why I prefer classical music."

"It seems to me that you have done your homework well" Max said in a congratulatory fashion.

'Thank you father" Precious replied with a degree of modesty.

"Where has this discussion taken us? Will you finish pharmacy"? Max asked directly without reservation.

"I promise, I will." She reluctantly answered.

"Good, now tell me more about Mr Gossling he sounds like an interesting chap."

Precious accepted the invitation and proceeded to tell her father about Mr Gossling's view of the not so caring medico-pharmaceutical industry. She told of its never-ending changing face, of how the doctors were puppets and how the industry created the fashionable nature of disease.

Max became engrossed in her vivid descriptions; he likened it to the baby industry, in that similarities existed in the area of what was trendy. Diseases came and went, fashions came and went. Mr Dhaarling realised that it was based and driven by greed, western culture needed to learn from others before it destroyed itself and those it had infiltrated.

7

SAVE THE CHILDREN

A week had gone by Max Dhaarling dreamed about Expedita Shocker everywhere he went, everyday, every night, she was the perfect woman that he had secretly lusted after all of his life.

Merry was content now that Precious was back on track committed to finishing her degree. Perhaps she had been wrong about her husband; perhaps he was a real man after all and not a man's man like others had suggested. The events of the past week had changed Merry's attitude and behaviour towards Max, almost as if she sensed that another woman vied for his affections. Merry became more attentive and playful in a physical and vocal fashion, which was filled with sexual innuendo, and provocative advances. Not wishing to disappoint his wife or alert her to the fact that he had fallen in love with another woman, Max played out his part to perfection.

"Yes you are perfect in every way, Expedita, my darling, how I yearn to taste your forbidden lips." was the thought that constantly filled Max's mind as he walked about the lower floor of the Baby Store and yet he was able to project a professional image of himself. Max Dhaaring was examining a row of girls mid-range tracksuits, for price, quality, correct labelling etc when one of his shop assistants with a cordless phone in hand came running over.

"Mr Dhaarling, phone for you." The middle-aged shop assistant gushed.

"Who is it"?

"I didn't catch the lady's name, I think she said she was a sister of your's." Somewhat confused Max accepted the hand piece and walked to a quiet corner.

"Hello......... Max Dhaarling here, how may I help you"?

"Good morning kind sir I am Sister Thomisina from the Carmelite Monastery in Nedlands."

"Are you looking for donations"? Max wondered.

"Not at all my son, your organization has been very generous in the past. I rang because we would like to invite you to afternoon tea tomorrow afternoon." The nun sweetly said in an angelic tone of voice.

"That's awfully good of you Sister, I'm rather busy these days and don't have much time to socialize, perhaps, you could mention me in your prayers."

"We already do that on a regular basis Mr Dhaarling. I cannot emphasize how important it is to have your company. We have a number of Sisters visiting us from overseas not only from our Order but others as well. They are from your part of the world and would like to meet a successful business man as yourself."

Max's heart quickened, was Expedita one of them?

"In that case Sister I shall be more than glad to attend"!

"Will three thirty be a satisfactory time for you"?

"Most certainly"!

"Very well then, our monastery is situated in Adelma Rd Nedlands. Come into the chapel first, one of our Sisters will greet you and lead the way."

"I look forward to our meeting." Max replied as he tried to hide the excitement in his voice.

"God bless you, goodbye."

"Goodbye Sister Thomisina." Max signed off. "Contact at last"!!!! He excitedly thought as he felt his heart race and body temperature rise.

The day could not go quickly enough it was a prolonged agony for Max to endure before 2pm the following day when he set off to attend afternoon tea. Everything went painfully slow until he reached the Monastery's outer walls and then it accelerated as he leapt out of his parked vehicle. Max's nostrils flared, his olfactory receptors strained to catch a whiff of Expedita's seductive personal fragrance. He spun his body 360 degrees around with every sixth step until he entered the chapel. There in the entry hall his nose was hit with a confusing mixture of smells. Max's brain frantically analysed each one until all had been accounted for. "Nothing, she's not here"!

"You can't always rely on your memory, Mr Dhaarling"! A voice softly said behind him.

It was her! No mistaking it! The pain of true love tore at Max's heart. He was too frightened to turn around in case he made a complete and utter fool of himself! Feeling helpless Max stood still and cleared the lovesick lump from his throat. Expedita stood behind him.

"Good afternoon Mr Dhaarling, nice to meet you. My Name is Sister Thomisina, I called you yesterday."

"You did"? Max nervously answered.

"Yes I did." Expedita confirmed.

"But... but... "?

"You couldn't recognise my voice is that it? That's understandable; telephone voices are often different to those in the open. Is you car outside"? Expedita sweetly and seductively asked.

"Yes it is." He replied as he adjusted his embarrassment.

"Excellent, I suggest we have afternoon tea after we say a decat of the Rosary before the Blessed Sacrament." Expedita purred as she walked with a swish of her hips towards a side altar and humbly knelt before it. Max respected Expedita's wishes and solemnly knelt next to her as she passionately recited the ten Hail Mary's. When she had finished she made the sign of the cross, stood up, adjusted her habit and said.

"Take me to Fremantle and drive slowly"!

Max weak at the knees, obeyed like a love struck puppy dog. Expedita was in control; her motives were quite plainly evident. She used the car as a mobile conversation chamber. In the midst of heavy traffic it would be difficult to record any discussion between them. Mother superior had trained her well.

"Well Mr Dhaarling, give me your impressions about Australia. First tell me what you dislike about the country."

Max remembered the comment that Precious made about the strangling bureaucracy and used this as the platform for his observations.

He then went onto deduce how it had affected the nations peoples at large and how it had driven them into the various levels of escapism that had reached epidemic proportions thus catapulting Australia internationally into one of the highest achievers in each of those activities. Alcohol, drugs, debt, marital break-ups, gambling, the list seemed endless.

"This is indeed a troubled nation"! Expedita remarked after listening to the statistics. Then she asked. "Where does one begin to undo the mess? There is much in need of reformation"

"Otherwise it is a good country in which to live, an abundance of most things, freedom in the restricted sense and opportunities providing you do not become too successful, in which case the automatically fine tuned "tall poppy reduction " system will seek you out and cut you down to size"! Max glumly ended

"Sounds blood thirsty"! Expedita exclaimed

"Tears that are invisibly shed" Max glibly replied as he turned his vehicle right from Stirling highway onto the old Fremantle traffic bridge road and remained silent thereafter as he drove down Queen Victoria St, Adelaide St onto South St, then past Notre Dame University before finding a parking place in Marine Terrace quite close to the Esplanade Hotel.

"Lovely part of the world" Expedita remarked as she observed the small park in front of her. "The pine trees and seagulls don't have a care in the world."

"I suppose not" Max replied as he thought her comment to be most odd.

"Shall we" He then advanced.

"Thank you sir, I would like that."

"Then Sister let us enjoy the Esplanade's sumptuous interior"!

"Very well" Expedita eagerly replied as the two of them set off and walked closely together. Max felt quite awkward like a puppy dog on a leash learning what he could and could not do.

A young down and out couple pushing a pram with an eight-month-old baby in it chanced to come by. Two nine-year-old twin boys noisily rushed past upsetting the baby and visibly ruffled the parents. The women lashed out verbally at her husband and said. "Didn't you remember to give them their Ritalin and dexie's"?

"I'm sure I did darling." The husband answered uncertain as to whether he had or hadn't.

"Damn it, love, they're not working again"! His wife said as she accepted his lame answer." Guess I'll just have to increase their dosage once again"! The husband forced a half-hearted smile and nodded his head slightly. Their passing conversation caught Expedita's ear, she turned towards Max Dhaarling and asked. "What is it that she spoke about"?

"A pharmaceutical disgrace, something my daughter spoke about a week ago. It is a subject very dear to my heart." Max whispered.

"Tell me more" Expedita begged as she tagged at his shirtsleeve.

"Chemical straightjackets"!

"Really.......that's a shame."

"Beyond your expectations, I'll tell you all about it over coffee." Max replied hoping that it would be a drawn out affair. Unfortunately for him it did not eventuate. Expedita took control from the first spoken word and was more concerned about the décor and how well he was doing in Australia than anything else. She treated him as a stranger whom she had met for the first time, after twenty minutes she indicated it was time to go and without further warning suggested they walk to the beach and make their way onto the South Mole.

Max remained tight lipped during the stroll to the Mole's rocky escarpment, which Expedita had no difficulty in climbing. Once on Fleet St they headed towards the lighthouse, it was then that she started her inquisition in earnest. Expedita very cleverly asked general questions about the size of the pharmaceutical industry and how dependent Australians were upon their products. Max unknowingly gave all the right answers that she was looking for but was unable to answer those of a technical nature. When Expedita heard how large the illegal pharmaceutical industry was, namely that run by criminals intent on amassing a highly dependent human database, she was visibly traumatised. This worsened when they discussed the ADD (Attention Deficit Disorder) pandemic that gripped the nation's young children.

"Do you think Society is a living entity"? Expedita asked as she stopped and stared at an old Greek fisherman who stood on a flat rock near the water's edge and slowly reeled in his line.

"It would have to be, after all each one of us contributes to it." Max agreed after a moment of reflection.

"What then guarantees its survival, its lifeline, its blood"? She asked this time a little more intensely.

"A beating heart"

"Young or old"

"Depends on the mix of its age" Max replied making reference to Society's mean statistical age.

"Very well, let me rephrase the question." She thoughtfully replied as the Greek fisherman shouted.

"Bless these waters for me Sister so that I may catch plenty of fish and feed my family"!

"For your cats and dogs, old man"! Expedita cuttingly shouted back.

"No, my grandchildren, my daughter is a single mother, she struggles everyday to survive."

"In this land of plenty, I think not"! Expedita retorted stone-faced.

"It is true, the social security system keeps her just above poverty" The Greek bitterly expressed as he recalled his daughter's struggle.

Expedita said nothing; she looked at Max Dhaarling for guidance. He remained blank. She looked back at the elderly Greek and sighed.

"How often do you come here"?

"Everyday" He replied as he rebaited his hooks.

"Doesn't you wife become lonely"?

"She passed away seven years ago." He said with a lump in his throat.

"I'm sorry." Expedita regretfully said.

"Yes, she died from a broken heart." The Greek man said in such way that suggested he also would have liked to have passed over. Expedita did not pursue the topic instead she let the old Greek speak uninterrupted.

"When my daughter's marriage failed, mixed marriages don't work very well. She warned my daughter not to marry that stupid Aussie, mom had a bad feeling, but what can you do, young love is stubborn. Now my daughter struggles, that Aussie bastard pays no up keep, all he was good for was shooting off a few rounds making my daughter pregnant and shooting through. I help as best as I can, the children need me"! He slowly and graphically described in his simple English. Expedita allowed the wave of emotion to subside before adding to the conversation.

"So you have become their father."

"Boys need a stable man in their lives. I don't want them taking any medicines to control their, how do you call it, frustr…a….tions"?

"All they need is love. Is that right old man"?

The Greek fisherman nodded and cast his baited line into a clear patch of deep water near a weed bank.

"Your prayers have been answered my son." Expedita positively said in a low voice. The words reached his ears just as his rod violently dipped under the strain of a big strike, the Greek took position as the line ripped off his reel and sped into the waters.

Max and Expedita watched as the seasoned fisherman wrestled with a giant of the deep. After twenty minutes of playing cat and mouse a flash of silver appeared near the surface of the water and with the sound of something croaking.

"Madonna"! He screamed as the shape of a thirty pound Mulloway began to make its appearance. "Come quick, help me"! He screamed with overwhelming excitement.

Max rushed over and carefully descended the slippery rocks until he stood on the same flat rock as the Greek and carefully followed his instruction to hold the rod and line tight while the Greek with gaff in hand made for the fish. One quick jag and it was all over. The old Greek lifted the watery beast ashore with all of his might and wrapped it securely with a large wet Hessian bag. He beamed from ear to ear and praised the nun's blessing.

"There's more there if you want it." She calmly said as she pointed to the waters.

The Greek needed no further encouragement. He furiously rebaited and recast his line once he was convinced that his catch would not 'flap off'.

"Shall I stay and help you." Max inquired like a young schoolboy who had just discovered the magic of fishing.

"He can manage by himself. Come we have to head home." Expedita commanded as her black and white habit fluttered in the fresh southwesterly sea breeze. Max scampered up the rocks and caught up with her.

"You haven't answered my question." Expedita coolly stated as she lead the way.

"I was distracted; in any case you haven't re-phrased it." Max replied as he tried to assert himself.

"Correct, let me see." She said as she joined her hands together as if in solemn prayer." Any living body can only survive if it is capable of......?

She then 'begged'.

"ER...er..."? Max Dhaarling mentally struggled to find the correct answer which would make him look good.

"Starts with the letter ...R"

"Reproduction" He randomly guessed.

"Sort of, think of the body itself, not of its desire to replicate and include its generations."

"Regeneration" Max quizzically replied.

"Correct! At what level"?

"From...er.... the.... er.... basic"?

"Correct, once again which confirms that for society as a living body to exist and remain healthy, it must have... "?

"Healthy children for they are the stem cells of our nations civilization"! Max quickly caught on.

"Excellent.... Mr Dhaarling! Now follow me"! Expedita commanded as she veered left and climbed onto the South Moles northern aspect, a large ocean going container ship guided by two pilot tug boats slowly drifted by. Expedita analysed it for its applicable symbolism.

"Do you think that we have the right to incarcerate children like the goods that are in those steel boxes and ship them out and leave them stranded in an unemotional chemically laced Sargasso Sea"?

"Not at all"

"Then why is it happening again"? She angrily asked.

What do you mean"?

"Children have become enslaved once again. Previously it was centuries ago when they were forced to work as young as eight years of age in mines and factories. Now they have become enslaved once again for the same purpose, the generation of monies by unscrupulous men, you would have thought that they had learnt their lesson previously"? Expedita sighed before continuing. "Man's ascension into the higher realms of morality does not appear to have prevented the emergence of those types. So Maxwell Dhaarling where lies the answer"?

"By the inductive reasoning that such things are restricted to those who have repeated the life cycle many times."

"Very well said Mr Dhaarling, your café excursions have served you well"!

Max could not help himself from pouncing on the word 'serve' he wished that he could service Expedita physically then and there. His manhood swollen with thirst needed immediate quenching.

'Somehow we must save the children. The Greek was correct all they need is love. These chemicals that are forced upon them or that they seek are no substitute, love is not a cerebral experience it lies in the depths of the soul. Perhaps that is our project Mr Dhaarling to make this society abandon its chemical pleasures and teach it to love properly."

"What do you suggest Sister Thomisina that we poison all of the wine, beer and spirits and attack every gambling venue"?

"Far too primitive Mr Dhaarling, our quest will be to save the children irrespective of their age. After all Maxwell everyone is a child. Let's put the morality of this nation to the test"! Expedita strongly challenged.

Max contrasted the murky waters of the harbours inlet to that of the crystal clear waters of the southern side of the Mole and wondered which represented the nation's morality. Deep down he secretly knew which one it was likely to be, however that information would never be publicly known for decades.

8

SQUIRREL KEEPER

Franck Max Climax was a man of a thousand faces. This is not to be confused by saying that he was a master of disguise for that is to suggest that he physically changed his appearance by the use of theatrical makeup and costumes. Mr Climax had elevated himself to a very high level of mystical and supernatural ability through his 'epileptic' experiences and through his intense reading of the only genuine copy of the original Koran. Every time a person would meet Mr Climax it would be for the first time, for Mr Climax was never remembered, he was an unrecognisable face in the immense crowd of humanity. To meet Mr Climax was a unique experience each and every time, only his name was remembered largely by its sexual-religious connotation.

Mr Climax had developed this non-recognition character unknowingly; its existence dawned on him later in his life. Not wishing to rely on it solely, he used the concept of many actors on many stages and delighted in dressing up to satisfy the occasion.

Wearing a dark blue double-breasted jacket complete with Holland and Sherry buttons, medium grey flannel tailored pleat-less trousers, crisp white Ermenegildo Zegna pure cotton shirt and

Wimbledon silk tie, he walked awkwardly in his black Italian shoes towards the English Nationals Immigration checkpoint at London's Heathrow International airport.

Forward step, forward step, wobble to the side, step back, forward step, forward step, wobble to the side, step back, was his gait, somewhat similar to a neurologically dysfunctional hospital patient. Common onlookers pitied his state, medical people tried to analyse his disease.

"Good afternoon, Lord Tingle! A pleasure to see you back home"! The British official greeted.

"Thank you my friend."

"Exhausting time as usual"?

"Always is, diplomacy is very draining you know"!

"Yes, my father told me, when he worked for the Indian government." The official agreed as he added "Did you achieve much"?

"Managed to rout several rotten scoundrels, made me feel rather good"!

"Excellent, so will you be taking a little vacation at home then"?

"Not at all, need the free time to do more research." Max Climax, alias Lord Tingle explained in a rather posh accent.

"Hope you find what you are looking for, go through Lord Tingle, everything is in order." The Indian born British official said as he handed back Max Climax's 'official' passport.

"Thank you my good man, regards to the wife and children, a little gift for them." Max warmly replied as he produced a large box of fine chocolates. The Anglo-Indian British official beamed with gratitude and said no more.

Max Climax alias Lord Tingle lived in the well to do suburb of Kensington in London, in a stately three storey semi-detached house a few doors from the Kensington Thistle Hotel. His choice of location was for one purpose only, to be as close as possible to the Kensington-Hyde Park gardens and his beloved furry friends.

Max Climax would often spend all day in the company of the

park's squirrels. They unlike humans had no difficulty in recognising him. Tourists delighted in watching the squirrels rest on Max's hand, allowing him to stroke, caress and feed them exclusively, much to the envy of the children who frequented the park. When Max saw and felt their despair he would use his intimate rapport with the animals and instruct them to attend to the peoples needs.

Squirrels offered joy, delight; therapy and more, they provided an immense wealth of insight into the mechanisms of the world. Max was their student; it was his desire to adapt some elements of their society to the human variant.

No matter which season it was, Max was always there; no matter how long he had been away for they remember Max would never take one away with him, instead he believed in leaving them in their natural homely environment.Whenever people took photographs of Max and the squirrels at play the result was always the same, a faceless man with animals.

Today once Max had returned to his Kensington apartment he would relax briefly, change into comfortable clothes, attend to sending out the latest mystical instructions via the Internet and then when the hour was right, Max once he had eluded the buildings' security would emerge as a dirty homeless beggar, dressed in the most vile smelling old and tattered clothes. For the next week Franck Max Climax would live on the comfortable streets of London without any fear of becoming hungry, cold or violated. He would associate himself with the honest people who had shunned society for all of its values and worth in preference for the beauty of their own inner worlds. Max Climax had a special spot in his heart for these and he cared for them with his band of mobile beggars and thieves.

You would need to have a very keen eye to spot the mobile beggar for it related not to methods of transport but rather to the possession of a mobile phone, something that you would hardly expect a penniless person to have, unless of course they were a thief. This was not the case at all. These mobile beggars were an elite group of information gatherers who doubled as mobile thieves, namely taxi drivers. Once they had completed their shifts on the roads, they would roam the streets begging and transmit their acquired information to the central data room in cyberspace, access of which was restricted to Max Climax only.

As taxi drivers they had a strict code of behaviour to adhere to. Their main targets of overcharging by dubious acceptable means were wealthy people only. The average struggling person was never taken advantage of, if the taxi drivers did, severe consequences would head their way.

Those that befriended him knew Max as 'Robbie'; not one of them knew that he was the Master, for he genuinely appeared to be a homeless man.

Thus Max was in the middle between his well to do band of men and the destitute people that he cared for.

The caring came from in the form of companionship, protection and the provision of just enough material goods to keep them sufficiently happy, simple pleasures that were profoundly rewarding.

On this night Max had decided to roam the streets of London's theatre district, with head down and stooped over, Max waited patiently at the cross walk opposite the Queens gate of Kensington gardens on Kensington road. The traffic was fierce even at this late hour and took precedence over pedestrians crossing the road. Finally the crosswalk signal to safely cross over came on; Max shuffled across and had almost reached the other side of the road when a black car came from nowhere. It completely ignored the red stoplight and flew at him. To the observer Max was surely dead.

There was the inevitable screech of tyres as they desperately tried to hold onto the road as the vehicles brakes' applied all of their force, then there was the almighty "bang" as bodies of different makeup collided together followed by the sweet sound of broken glass dancing erratically across the roads hard surface.

The hot headed Asian driver got out of his car and examined the damage to his heavily modified vehicle and totally disregarded the crumpled heap that lay nearby.

'Yuck-A-Moto"!! He grunted disgustingly as he turned intent on violently kicking the man who was down. He let loose one almighty left kick that hit its target, there was no groan, there was no 'ouch' in response, instead the victim's clothes flew up into the air and scattered themselves across the footpath. The Asian male punk stood dumbfounded, he looked around, there was nothing to see, he looked back, again there was nothing and then he looked at his precious status symbol and cursed "Yuck-A-Moto" once again.

Fear then took hold, what had he hit, where was it, how would he explain the damage to the insurance company? Before he had time to answer these questions the rear end of his car swung around and hit him. The force of the impact propelled him upwards and forwards against the gardens wrought iron gates, he hit hard and lapsed into unconsciousness.

"Instant Karmic Response"! Max Climax whispered as he picked up his coat and walked away through the open gates past the public toilets and onto the scenic walkway where his furry friends lived.

"Good night" He softly said as he scattered popcorn delights across the flowerbeds. The night was cold, the wind more than brisk, a hint of rain threatened otherwise it was perfect to be out of doors.

Franck Max Climax went back onto the main road and walked along the footpath until he was opposite the Royal Albert Concert Hall. He stopped to watch the happy patrons exit after having seen and heard a world famous orchestra perform a variety of music. Franck listened intently to their varied chatter and formed the opinion that good music was better than any medicine. A smile formed across his face and then he looked down to see the pages of a dismembered daily newspaper circulate around his feet. Max picked up several pages and made it seem as though he was about to stuff them down his clothes as extra padding to keep him warm during the freezing night. It was an act of distraction, for Franck kept himself warm by his thoughts and underneath all of that the ultra thin polar fleece complete with Gortex lining. The story's headline on page twelve caught his eye:

"12 million people in UK suffer with chronic arthritis"

Franck Max Climax locked that statistic away for future reference. It was 11.15pm he suddenly realised that he had not eaten since noon that day.

There would be several charitable soup kitchens along the way that would offer him sustenance otherwise he could examine the refuge bins and the rear of several prestigious restaurants as he had done in the past. If his luck held, a chef or his assistant might recognise his plight and offer him a rejected cordon bleu meal on the house. Hot or cold it didn't matter to him. Franck found the French to be very charitable in this respect, which was in keeping with their absence from any covert activities in Sudan.

Max Climax alias 'Robbie" the tramp made his was to Piccadilly until he reached the Circus by the same name, from there he meandered his way around the streets which allowed him to pass theatres such as; The Prince of Wales, The Criterion, The Cambridge, The Strand and the Mermaid as he seemingly wearily trudged his way towards the Royal Opera House. There he would find his evening meal and comedy in the form of an advertisement promoting the latest classic Italian Opera. The music would be good the plot ridiculous.

Parked in a disabled bay was an Artic white converted Mr Whippy ice cream van, complete with an illuminated neon crucifix on its roof.

No'Greensleeves' music played instead an eerie beckoning silence prevailed. The majority of the homeless in the district had already been fed, the Sisters on duty patiently waited for the stragglers to arrive before they set off home.

Franck Max Climax slowly approached the van that was manned by an elderly nun in her seventies and her assistant who appeared to be no more than twenty-five years of age. Both were dressed in the Sisters of Mercy winter habits. As Franck's outline appeared in the van's light the young nun stood up and greeted him.

"Good evening Sir, looking for something to eat"?

"Yes I am." Franck feebly answered.

"What takes your fancy? You may choose from the board. I am more than certain everything is in stock." She confidently and cheerfully said as she pointed to the blackboard, that leant against the van.

"Um, pea and ham soup, hot chocolate sounds good."

"Been quite a demand for both tonight, must be the change coming on, won't be a moment." The young nun answered making reference to the weather.

"Thank you." Franck mumbled as he rested against the van. Meanwhile the old nun busily microwaved the pre-measured and sealed containers of food.

"Haven't seen you before Sir" The young nun said making conversation.

"I've been away on diplomatic matters"

"So have I"!

"Really, where"?

"Australia and you"

"Switzerland, New York and Paris"

"Marvellous, absolutely marvellous"!

"There you are old man"! The elderly nun rudely interrupted as she handed across the containers of hot soup and cocoa.

"Thank you." And without saying anymore he turned and began to leave.

"Wait a minute! You'll need some paper napkins, take these." The young nun kindly offered. Franck Max Climax gratefully accepted the gift and disappeared into the shadows.

"Really Sister Eanswida I hope you didn't believe him, silly old git"!

"Not at all, just humouring him"

"Nice touch offering him the napkins, practical, very practical, however next time give him the scented wipes, much more sanitary you know"!

"Yes Sister I know, perhaps we could go home now"?

"A good idea, my Rheumatisms' playing up"

"So I'll drive'?

"I'm not a cripple, thank you very much"! The old nun replied quite indignant.

The hot pea and ham soup warmed Franck's insides and made him feel quite alive, the chocolate would further enhance that feeling; desert would be in the contents of the paper napkins once he had activated his phone and so in a dark and remote ally Franck retrieved his mobile phone from his waist band wallet and switched it on. He punched in SUDAN which caused the screen to change colour, he punched HOLD which caused it to stay on for a full ten minutes and then by this specific light he made visible the cryptic information that Expedita Shocker had written in their otherwise invisible ink.

Satisfied with its content Franck used the phones camera to commit the information into his ultra secret cyber space storage facility; then he destroyed the napkins and disappeared into the night.

9
RATHAUS

I f it wasn't one thing, then it was another that caused Jack Stern momentarily to lose interest in the ravishingly beautiful Yvette Bell. Previously it was the challenge to fill the Church of the Coloured Sands with worshippers now it was the Archbishop's demanding invitation to rescue the Catholic Church's investment in Napp Pharmaceuticals.

Jack loved love there was no doubt about it especially when it came to women, but he also loved the war-like conflicts of commerce. It he had to choose between the two the latter would always be his preference.

Jack Stern was an extremely highly evolved soul far more advanced than Fr Brendan O'Reilly, a soul who achieved results by the subtlety of his actions. Jack already knew of the Napp fiasco even before his Grace called for 'assistance' because there was another more powerful individual to whom Jack was answerable.

Within hours of their conversation Jack Stern set about collecting all manner of sensitive information on the sinister TAG team that he would ultimately wrestle with. He enlisted Stanley's exceptional computer skills on the physical level and Grandpa's spiritual abilities on the cyber space plane. Their combined talents would be unstoppable.

The human pentagon that Jack Stern would ultimately do battle with comprised the following individuals. Jacque Uzzi (surveillance), Ivy Humblebug (investigative officer), Rip Knoche (general product approvals), Arthur Grimrod (scheduled medicament approvals) and Annette Manoff (head of department), these wielded the ultimate power that sculptured the Australian medical landscape.

Jack had seven days in which to assemble his armoury; as the data came through it took him to various trading banks located around the world.

It was in Bremen Germany that he took special notice of the Town Hall's 'Rathaus' plaque as he emerged from the city's Deutche National Bank branch.

"Seat of governmental, bureaucratic power, house of rats is more appropriate"! He thought to himself as he flicked through the documents that he had just collected. Jack Stern stood in the middle of the town square and admired the old buildings. To his right he spied a bronze statue of four animals piled up upon each other. A donkey formed the base, upon him stood a dog, upon the dog stood a cat and upon the cat at the top was a rooster. A three-metre structure dedicated to the fairy tale. 'The Town Musicians of Bremen' recorded by the Brothers Grimm. Enthralled by its hidden message Jack filed away the important documents into his jackets inside breast pocket and walked across to eavesdrop on the tourist guides explanation of the folklore story. Thoroughly enchanted by it he decided to purchase a copy from the local government information and souvenir store, after which he delighted on the local delicacy, Bratwurst in a long bread roll covered with lashings of mustard.

With a little piece of heaven in hand Jack drifted though the main shopping mall and made for the café situated near the ornamental windmill which displayed the greatest array of flavoured ice creams that a connoisseur could wish for.

"Street eating at its best"! He thought to himself.

Completely satisfied after devouring a mountain of ice cream Jack meandered about the windmill's gardens and admired the flowers in bloom, the ornate pattern in which they were planted and the white swans that slowly drifted by on the stream that flowed through that little piece of European paradise. He sat down on a wooden bench that was covered in a blanket of pink flowers deposited from the branches of the adjoining tree above; he thought of Yvette and briefly saw her face before him. This time her look of love appeared somewhat distant, Jack pouted his lips, forced a downward smile, nodded and unwrapped his German copy of The Town Musicians of Bremen.

The similarities between his forthcoming encounter with the TAG administration and the folklore story were strikingly abundant. There was no doubt in Jack's mind that TAG's big five were the thieves; he on the other hand represented all of the animals rolled into one. Jack would need to kick like the donkey, bite like the dog, scratch like the cat and shout like the rooster in order to steal the robbers' treasures. Very carefully over the next few days he built up an accurate psychological profile of each individual and assigned the correct animal that would dispatch him or her. His dedication would cause him to alienate himself from all external influences in the process and that unfortunately included Yvette.

Programmed and loaded Jack Stern by the speed of thought and through the process of Spiritus Ruah arrived in Canberra.

He did not like the city, its location or its vibrations. Sterile, aloof, detached, it harboured mindless individuals whose purpose in like was to scale the ladders of success and achieve the epitome of incompetence whilst deluding themselves in the process. It was not a place for the individually minded and for that very reason Jack Stern decided that his stay would be as brief as possible.

No hotel reservations, no accommodation of any sort, simply land, find a public change room and transform yourself into a variant of Mr George Striker, namely Geoffrey Striker IPM emissary. This disguise was identical to that which he used when he and Brendan had infiltrated Newburn's Feelgood Pharmacy some time ago. Then he was a Federal Health investigator now he was a high ranked representative of International Pharmaceutical Management an expert on global regulatory matters.

All of Jack's requirements were carried with him in ultra compact form, almost microscopic, all space eliminated, they neatly condensed into balls of infinite resource, which instantly responded to his mental commands.

His meeting was scheduled for 10.30am on the understanding that the department had set aside the entire day in order to resolve all of the issues at hand.

Jack sat on one of the public benches at the edge of Lake Burley Griffin and watched the fountains of water stretch into the sky.

"Complete waste of money" He thought to himself as he prepared himself mentally for the conflict ahead." One against five, quite good odds" he reassured himself.

The entire perimeter of the lake was empty, not a soul in sight, obviously the wrong time of the year for tourists and foreign diplomatic missions. All of the car park and taxi stands were empty. Jack enjoyed the brief solitude and selectively listened to the fountains' waters as they screamed during their descent from the top of the water column into the lake below.

"Perhaps it's not such a waste after all; fun for nature, there's a nice change"

It was time to go; the main street was the place to obtain transport. Within seconds Jack stood next to a yellow taxi.

"Are you free"?

"Yeah, mate, come-on-in"!

"Thank you." He replied and as he was about to open the rear door the taxi driver roughly said "No mate, come and sit next to me, better view up front, ya know"!

"Thank you very much" Jack replied after he had clambered into the front seat, gently closed the door and connected his safety belt.

"Where to mate"?

"Department of Therapeutics and General Medicines please"

"Ah the ballistic centre, have you there in a jiffy"! The taxi driver loudly said as he pulled his car out of its parking bay and without looking sped down the road.

"What did you call it"?

"The ballistic centre mate, they're all crazy in there, don't say I didn't warn ya"! Jack's curiosity aroused itself but he remained silent.

"Look mate, it's like this. The building looks like a frigging military installation. If you don't play their game they bloody well bomb the hell out of you"! The taxi driver gruffly said.

"I suppose you've had first hand experience "?

"Bloody oath, I do mate! My missus was very, very sick, could hardly walk! Some sort of mystery virus! It hit her years ago! Doctor's didn't know anything! One theory after another that's all we got! And the medications I reckon made her worse! Bloody quacks"!

"What precisely did she have wrong with her"?

"Multiple this and that, first it was sclerosis, then arthritis, then auto disease. I don't know mate, all I know is that she got fancy medical names attached to her with no frigging help at all! Until she came across this weird naturopath! She set her straight. No worries! But then that f.... ing Tag team got stuck into the company that produced my wife's pills"!!!

"Were they natural"? Jack asked.

"Of course they were mate, bloody good shit they were, got my missus back into shagging"!

"So what are you saying"?

"If it's any good and natural those bastards will tag it illegal and shut it down"!! Jack sensed the bitter anger and sexual frustration in the man's voice.

"Can any thing be done about this"?

"Nah mate, the pharmaceutical industry is too strong if you know what I mean"!

"You believe they're behind this"?

"Course mate they don't sell anything that's good, they're in it to control the market and make squillions"!

"I see. You're not Australian is that right"?

"Yeah mate, parents were from eastern Europe came out after World War II had a bloody frigging hard life out here, outcasts they were, never fitted in, always looked down upon. They raised me to be strong"!

"How"?

"Street smart, keep my ears to the ground, know how to make a quick quid, if you know what I mean"!

"I do."

"Good mate, good"!

"And your wife"

"She's eastern European descent as well, same upbringing as mine, we think alike."

"Is she well now"?

"Very mate, did it the hard way, taught herself when the pills were taken away, healed herself with herbs and meditation, she's the picture of health, not like that bloody horrible building over there"! Jack looked across to where the taxi driver was pointing and understood the meaning of the man's apt description.

The structure attempted to look like a disguised military site. Excessively tall cylindrical stainless steel chimneys that resembled intercontinental ballistic missiles flanked every wall, the building was isolated and heavily secured. It was full of paranoid people

"They are so worried in there that security started eight miles from here"!

"Pardon"! Jack replied quite astonished.

"Every f.... ing lamp post we passed had cameras and all sorts of spy gear screwed into them"!

"Do you think they take medications"?

"They would need to mate, they are a bunch of loonies; they speak some sort of foreign language! When my missus couldn't get any more of her pills, I wanted to kill every one of them! Only my good missus stopped me, bless her heart! She said she would find a way, she was right, God bless her"!

"I'm sure he has." Jack assured the driver as he went on to say, "Do you think any one will"?

"What's that mate"?

"Shoot some of them"? Jack asked as he tried to feel his way into the building.

"Nah, too many gays in this country"!

"Really"

"Yeah mate, we've got the biggest gay Mardi Gras in the frigging world Huge it is, attracts people from all countries. Bloody disgrace"!

"Is that why Australians don't fight for their rights"?

'Probably mate. Probably"! The taxi driver glumly replied as he manoeuvred his car towards the first checkpoint.

"You got your ID and all that"? He then asked Jack

"Do I need to"?

"Sure do mate checkpoint numero uno"! Jack looked somewhat astonished and unprepared as the taxi came to a halt just in front of the checkpoints manned booth. Before he knew it six armed guards swooped down on the vehicle and went over it with highly sophisticated electronic equipment. They looked for anything that could remotely or potentially be used as a weapon. Jack was forcibly ousted from the taxi and bodily searched. Not a word was said by anyone. Jack continued to observe and compare the behaviour of the individuals to that of oaf at Longevity Plus.

"More mindless wonders"! He concluded as they dissipated as

quickly as they had appeared. The taxi driver signalled to get in, Jack nodded and together they drove slowly towards the next checkpoint.

"What's this, a car wash I suppose"? Jack asked making reference to the up and coming bizarre structure.

"Nah mate, it's a Be-do, you know what the Frenchies use"!

"A bidet" Jack correctly said making reference to the basin in which one can wash one's genital area.

"No mate, look at the sign, Biological Decontamination Unit"! The taxi driver struggled to say as the small print on the sign came into view.

"And after that" Jack frowned

"We get X-rayed"!!

"I've had enough of this madness"! Jack Stern mentally said to himself. In a matter of seconds just before the taxi entered the sterilising complex Jack Stern was gone. He left behind two hundred dollars for the driver's trouble and invaluable information.

Jack materialised in the public male toilet on the third floor, thus avoiding the stupidity as he saw it of having to negotiate the main entrance, the ground floors security booth and the Head of Departments nauseating secretary. He adorned himself with the proper departmental ID appropriate to his visitor status and with complete unquestioned authority made for the conference room and made himself very comfortable.

The room was bare, windowless almost like a Russian KGB interrogation room, not welcoming at all. The colour scheme in contrast to the rest of the building threatened to incarcerate anyone who dared to oppose the Tag teams thinking and commands. Complete abeyance was their objective.

Jack entered into pray as he waited for the big five to assemble outside the conference room. One by one they appeared and stood at the closed door.

"Has or does anyone know if that Mr Striker has arrived"? Annette Manoff asked of the group. "No, very well then, Ivy, check with the secretary to see if he's in the building, will you darling"?

"Yes Ann" A meek voice responded.

"Lady gays" Jack mumbled to himself as he opened the door.

"That won't be necessary! I'm already here, come in won't you; make yourselves comfortable, no need for introductions I feel as though I know you intimately well. Oh yes, as you can see by my identity tag I am Mr G Striker from IPM, that's right IPM, you may have heard of them, if you haven't here's a business card for each one of you to help get better acquainted! Never know when you might need their services, do you now? Jack grinned. He then waved to the secretary and said. "Thank you we're all here now" The secretary stared blankly unaware of anything that had been said and nodded in response.

"She's probably had one of her late nights"! Ivy suggested.

"You're very boisterous Mr Striker. American, are you"? Annette Manoff coldly said as she took an instant dislike to the man.

"I do live there, however my origins are elsewhere."

"Really"!

"However that does not matter unless of course you wished to have dinner with me tonight. Me, you and Ivy, we could make quite a threesome, if you know what I mean"? Annette Manoff continued to look at Jack coldly but he knew that he had struck a cord in her sexual preferences.

"That depends how well this morning's meeting goes Mr Striker"!

"In which case we could all be bitterly disappointed"

"Enough of the pleasantries, can we get on with this"? Jacque Uzzi sharply interrupted.

"Of course, but what's the rush we have all day"! Jack countered as he made eye contact with Uzzi.

"That's not the case Mr Striker"! Arthur Grimrod firmly said as he lent support to Uzzi.

"Explain"?

"We have re-evaluated the situation with respect to Napp Pharmaceuticals and have decided to implement the following plan.

If you or the Company's directors do not agree to it we will instigate immediate legal proceedings and seek the harshest penalties possible under the current legislation, which is presently under review. By the time the case is listed for trial the penalties will be harsher and made retrospective"!!

"As is the immoral practice in your land"! Jack bit back as he accepted the documents that Uzzi violently thrust at him.

"Um, give me a minute to digest these will you"? Jack calmly said as a true professional used to overbearing bureaucrats. He walked back into the conference room and sat down in his chair. The others remained standing and crowded around him in an intimidating manner, only Ivy Humblebug appeared to be different. Jack sensed that she was the newest member of the team and had not as yet been initiated into their sordid ways.

Jack pretended to be uneasy and buried his head in his hands as he read the first page of the disassembling document. In true theatrical fashion he allowed grief and despair to form on his face as he slowly flicked through the pages analysing their content as he went. Jack took his time for one purpose only, to allow the bureaucratic 'killers' to falsely think that they held the upper hand. All that remained was for him or the chief executive officers of Napp Pharmaceuticals to accept the conditions offered and allow the vultures in.

Jacks normally generous lips became tight, now he had a slit for a mouth. He continually sighed and forced perspiration to bead on his brow. When the time was right he put the document face down, stared into space and said.

"Weed, pathetic miserable weed"!

Annette Manoff took exception to his comment she raised her voice and roughly barked.

"Are you being personal Mr Striker? Because if you are, you can leave right now"! Jack stood up to face his adversary.

"Not at all, I was merely making reference to Marijuana and how it makes life difficult for you"!

"You're being absurd"!

"Not really, all I wanted to know is what your department is going to do about it"?

"Mr Striker, stop this nonsense! You know very well that this is not our jurisdiction"!

"But it is"! Jack commented innocently.

"How"? Annette Manoff almost shouted visibly angered by his insolent absurdity.

"Just think about it. It's legal to own the substance in moderate amounts."

"For personal use only"!!! Manoff retorted.

"Agreed, however Marijuana affects the physiological processes, has medicinal properties, and therefore any person who grows it, dries it, cuts it, packs it is guilty of manufacturing a therapeutic substance. Hence it should be registered with you"!! Jack correctly argued as he made a mockery of the law and its administration.

"Only if they supply other people" Ivy Humblebug said coming to Manoff's defence without realising the error of her rash statement.

"How naïve are you? Of course they do! You society is drug ridden! It is your duty to fulfil your administrative obligations, do us all a favour and register Marijuana and alcohol, as being therapeutic substances. There are no exemptions to the rule." Jack brilliantly argued.

"Mr Striker you're changing the subject! Let's get back to Napp"!

Annette Manoff roughly commanded. With complete disregard for her authority, Jack insolently replied.

"I'm afraid, there will be no agreement, and yes, you were correct, when I spoke of weed, I was referring to you. The only exception is Mrs Humblebug who has not as yet been indoctrinated into your aberrant ways, primarily because she has only been here for, what has it been, three months"?

"Correct" She meekly replied.

"Then you my young sweet lady are in for a series of shocks"!

"Knocke, call security immediately"! Manoff commanded as she exercised her departmental authority.

"Yes M'me." He obediently replied as he rushed for the door. Knocke attempted to turn the handle. It refused to co-operate. A futile desperation filled his body.

"What's the matter Rip? Get on with it"!

"I can't the door refuses to budge"! He stuttered in a high-pitched voice as he looked back and blushed with embarrassment at his failure.

"Force it! Oh bother, get out of my way, you imbecile, let a woman do the job"! Manoff violently screamed as she shoved Knocke off his feet.

Jack's deep blue eyes danced and sparkled with amusement as he watched their bureaucratic bumbling rise to the occasion.

"Damn it! Somebody press the panic button"!

"Yes sir, straight away, sir"! Arthur Grimrod immediately responded by pushing the secret device that was situated under the conference table. Nothing! Deathly silence!

"Do it"!! Manoff screamed

""I have"! Grimrod shouted back somewhat panic stricken as he repeatedly pressed the button like a monkey that had learnt a conditioned response.

"Do it again"!!!

"I am! I am"! Grimrod angrily snapped.

"Uzzi to the camera! Write a sign! 'Help get us out quick' do it man"!!

"It won't do you any good. In any case what are all of you so sacred about? There's only one of me, unless of course you are pathologically afraid of being unmasked"! Jack piercingly said with arms and legs crossed over.

'We have nothing to hide Mr Striker"!!! Manoff defiantly said as she attempted to fake her innocence.

"Why all of the commotions paranoid are you"?

"Not at all"!! Both Grimrod and Manoff aggressively replied.

"I'm not convinced, judging by all of the security precautions you have gone to, commencing some eight miles from here, I would say otherwise."

"I repeat, Mr Striker, we, have, nothing to hide"!!!! Manoff slowly said as she walked up to Jack Stern and stared menacingly at him.

"I'm glad you clarified the situation." Jack calmly replied as he magically produced fifty concisely typed pages dealing with the official corruption that each member of the TAG team with the exception of Miss Ivy Humblebug had been involved in.

"Its authenticated, detailed and my negotiating device! The question is to whom shall we make the information available"? Jack gestured towards his listeners.

"If I give it to you Ivy and you decide to do something with it, your life will probably be in danger if not shortened. If you choose to do nothing, your acquired knowledge I am certain will have you allocated to another government department, your colleagues will make certain of that. No point going to the federal police, they're in on it. No point going to the political opposition parties, they wrote the legislation, which leaves us with two avenues, the Senate and the media. Which one do you suggest I try Annette"?

"Neither, Geoffrey"! Annette Manoff sarcastically said. "Do you for one moment think that anyone will believe you? One corrupt government official perhaps, an entire department, I think not! Your discovery is useless to you and anyone else who might want to use it"!

"Then Ms Manoff, we should obviously focus our attention on one person, how about you, hey"? After all you appear to have reaped the most out of everyone here. It is only your signature that appears on all of the important documents, you alone had the final say"!

Ruffled but aloof, Manoff said nothing; she remained arrogantly motionless as she calculated her position. The others looked on in desperation and then at each other quizzically.

"Oh I understand you wish to see how explicit the information is;

that right? Let me help you! Here you are"! Jack flippantly said as he handed out a duplicate copy to each member that highlighted his or her personal level of involvement in the official corruption.

Perspiration beaded on Manoffs forehead, her skin started to pale, her breathing accelerated as did her heart rate, quite audibly but only to Jack, who sensed her imminent downfall. Ivy Humblebug frowned with gross disappointment as she flicked through the pages of her copy that embraced every member of the TAG team.

"United we stand……divided…we…fall"! Was Manoff's strained statement just before she fainted and fell to the floor narrowly missing the edge of the conference table Jack made certain she landed softly. He looked unashamedly at her and sat down. The Tag team's eyes were upon him and condemned Jack for his ruthless actions, only Ivy Humblebug went to Manoff's assistance and administered first aid as best as she could, the remainder continued to stupidly seek outside help.

Jack remained seated, secretly smiled and said nothing. He closed his eyes, lowered his head so as to feign guilt and went in pursuit of Annette Manoff's soul.

In that place where the subconscious goes to find solutions Jack Stern found her there and started the process of proper negotiation. What you are about to read is not what was said for the language of the soul and brain are not of the physical world.

"It will do you no good to hide; for this place does cater for sinister motives."

What are you saying"?

"That you are immersed in morality or Vestibulum Moralis as it is known to the ancients. You stand at its threshold with no invitation to enter"!

Manoff's soul looked at Jack Stern's image, which was made up of an infinite mass of brilliant white dots. Sensing her confusion he explained as he pointed to each one of them.

"These come from Vestibulum Moralis courtyard's endless supply;

they are naturally attracted to me, as they sense my noble intentions. Each represents the correct solution to a problem. But enough of that let's look at you, for this place is the place to bear one's inner soul, the soul within the soul."

The dots disappeared and nothing was present not even darkness. Shocked at the nothingness, Manoff emitted a cry of terrifying anguish. She desperately tried to run here and there but the nothingness prevented her and then a dim light appeared and spread before her. It was her inner soul.

The complete ongoing history of her physical life, a myriad of differently coloured dots all interconnected. Manoff screamed again as she felt the pain of her spiritual autopsy.

"No anaesthetics here I'm afraid. This is the inevitable pain of your physical reality. No one escapes this."

Manoff's subconscious grappled with the abstract picture.

"As you see it is beyond your life's history. Everything that you did and its consequent impact on others; is recorded without exception. Nothing terribly dramatic until you entered TAG and became seduced by its multi- national opportunities; through them, by them, with them, you influenced the writing of the federal health legislation and were instrumental in deriving from them huge amounts of money for political election purposes. The companies were always seen as apolitical, it did not matter where the money was channelled as long as all of their hidden agenda's were achieved. You have frustrated the lives of millions of people one way or another and in so doing have created unnecessary discord and hardship. You alone have stifled the true ways of medicine and have subjected the nation's people to an endless supply of poisons that do nothing but create even more disease"!

"Stop it! I say, away with you, how dare you, enter my dream! Be gone with you"!!!!

Jack remained silent and commanded her inner soul to fold onto itself. Nothingness returned, Manoff screamed relentlessly, Vestibulum Moralis moved further away, Manoff's physical greed had destroyed her true subconscious nature, it felt powerless, lost, bewildered and down trodden at the realization that it had been robbed of coupling with Vestibulum Moralis.

"Why is she screaming? What have you done to her Ivy"? Jacque Uzzi shouted, as he demanded to know more.

"Nothing at all"!

"Liar"! Arthur Grimrod then accused the distressed Ivy who was doing everything in her power to make Manoff comfortable.

"You know she's got a bad back! Get out of the way! Let me deal with this"! Grimrod said in a raised voice as he pushed the hapless woman aside.

"Very well" Ivy meekly replied as she fled to a neutral corner of the room.

"United we stand, divided we fall, do you remember those words." Jack teased.

"I think you better leave Mr Striker." Grimroad roughly said.

"Not until we reach an agreement." Jack bluntly replied.

"Not possible under the circumstances"!

"And why not"? Jack asked pretending to be ignorant.

"Because you trouble making fool the Head of the Department is out to it." Arthur Grimrod blurted out visibly frustrated with the situation of being trapped in the conference room with no visible means of exit.

"I don't think so, she's merely playing Possum, isn't that right Annette"?

Jack without any hesitation replied as he levitated her into the upright position, opened her eyes and proceeded to handle her as a ventriloquist's dummy from a distance.

"Yes, he's quite right, I was playing possum all the time, it was my only line of defence, now if you will all excuse us, I will deal with this matter privately." Jack made her say as part of the illusion.

"What about the blackmail evidence"?

"Blackmail evidence? What are you taking about Mr Knocke or

may I call you Rip"? Jack smartly jeered.

"The stuff you produced"! Knocke thrust his empty hand at Jack.

"All I see is an open hand, did you drop something"?

"What, uh, impossible"! The TAG team muttered to itself as it searched in vain for the other copies. Only Jack Stern knew the whereabouts of the true copy and that was in Ivy Humblebugs bedside drawer.

"Now do as you were told, back to your places like good little school children, off you go now, Annette and I have important matters to discuss." Jack then advised them as Manoff ushered them away and locked the door behind them leaving each one to deal with their recollection of the same surreal experience.

Jack positioned Manoff in a chair with her back to the outside corridor and waited patiently for her to return from the realm of nothingness as he set about resolving the Archbishops dilemma.

He rewrote the TAG's document dealing with NAPP's dissection and made it look as though no major procedural or manufacturing errors had been found. All that Napp needed to do was to tighten up on their documentation, nothing else matters to bureaucrats.

This tactic allowed him to carefully word a media release that would ensure the saving of face for TAG; after all it was the custom of the nation's governing bodies never to admit their mistakes, even though members of the media delighted in making a mockery of the entire system.

Jack made certain that all of what he had constructed was permanently locked and cross referenced in all of the TAG's computer system and then in true theatrical fashion he prepared with the equipment available to him, a video interview with Annette Manoff as the puppet. Once he had cleverly tweaked it as being an official copy, he dispatched it directly to the department's public relations officer, who once he was satisfied with its authenticity and the attached paperwork, shipped it out together with the written statement to the appropriate radio and television networks and print media.

When all was said and done and Jack Stern was happy with his achievement, he returned to nothingness and helped Annette Manoff home. As soon as she stirred back into the reality of the physical world Jack Stern departed unnoticed.

10
THE SPIRITS HAVE SPOKEN

It took Jack Stern twenty-four minutes and forty- six seconds to despatch the unscrupulous TAG team after two weeks of intense statistical preparation. He could have done it differently, more easily in fact, however he preferred to do it the hard way and come into the confrontation cold rather than use his developed supernatural powers. Jack felt that this approach honed one's combat skills and it was this attitude that he employed when assessing his present or future staff.

Jack Stern had no time for those who passed examinations by reviewing past papers, he preferred the individual who made the effort to learn off all of the taught material. These he perceived were better self-educated than those who were lucky enough to have guessed what sort of exam questions might be asked and consequently scored an artificially high mark.

Jack Stern had the ability to remote view but kept it to himself. The last thing he wanted to happen was to be abducted by the US military for espionage purposes. Although the official story stated that this avenue of spying had been thwarted by the instillation of so-phisticated electromagnetic shielding devices at extremely sensitive sites of varying natures and it was therefore disposed of, the opposite was true.

Jack would use this ability to keep an 'eye' on the TAG team in the aftermath of his visit thereby safeguarding NAPP Pharmaceuticals and its innovative discoveries.

It was at the insistence of his beloved ghostly Grandpa that Jack multiply this gift. He would often retire to the mountain hide away where the Genius Loci presently existed and under Grandpa's super-vision view a wall that held sixteen identical television screens in a four by four matrix.

It had taken several years for Jack whilst in his teens to master watching all screens simultaneously and report in detail on each and every individual programme that had been broadcast at the same time over a forty-five minute period on one of the sets. Jack was con-tinuously thankful for Grandpa's intuition and his decision to stay behind after his physical demise instead of moving on.

Jack loved his Grandpa intensely and delighted in being his student even though his was rapidly reversing the tables and becoming the teacher's teacher. This had come about by his desire to see and hear first hand what the master Jesus had taught. Jack had progressed to the stage of being able to remote view up to six different locations anywhere on earth at any given time. During his learning he realised that his gift could be used to view events retrospectively, this is not to say that he could go back in time, which is not true.

Jack deduced correctly that time is layered upon itself, so that one steps across and accesses what one wishes. His profound insight enabled him to view Christ's life on earth from his birth to earthly departure and this recorded history was vastly different to that of the biblical version. This information was constantly and repeatedly channelled into Jack's memory so as to ensure he did not miss one aspect of the Christ's behaviour. The only thing he could not do was to invade the mind of Jesus as this was outside the jurisdiction of remote viewing.

All of that which Jack learnt he kept secret until he was satisfied through personal trial and error that he could teach the principle he had learnt. During the time that he was away from Mauritius much had happened at the Church of the Coloured Sands. Brendan's intense love for his Catholic Church coupled with Yvette's unwavering devotion to the Blessed Virgin Mary caused Decay to blossom in an intelligent way. This constant interplay between the beings of the spiritual world and those of the physical is available to everyone.

Franck Max Climax was one of those who embraced this concept. As Robbie the Vagabond he first encountered the spirits during the celebration of the Day of the Dead – Dia de los Muertos – at one of London's many cemeteries. This Mexican festival believed that the souls of the dead return each year to visit their living relatives, to eat, drink and be merry, just like they did when they were living. Robbie however soon discovered that this return was not restricted to calendar determined events, it was an ongoing process governed by true democratic rules.

It was 2am in the morning Max was doing his weekly round ensuring that all whom he cared for were safe and well. He shuffled along one of the main shopping streets, taking note of everything that he heard and saw. He halted in front of a home theatre entertainment specialty store and listened to a repeat of the previous day's current affair programme by placing his fingertips on the storefront glass window.

The presenter told of consumer groups' dissatisfaction with adverse drug effects and the steps they were taking to remedy the situation, which included class actions against the powerful pharmaceutical companies. The topics of discussion dealt with issues besides the cox-2 inhibitors scandal and clearly demonstrated that the companies were guilty of severely comprising the health status of individuals exposed to their products. The question of indirect manslaughter for profit was raised, this presented both a moral and legal nightmare, to Franck Max Climax there was no debate to be had, in his mind they were guilty of misrepresentation, lies and deceit that ultimately led to the death of the individual.

As he watched he noticed the reflection of a luminous body on the glass window. Franck turned around to locate its source and saw it floating as it were along the footpath on the opposite side of the street. He walked across the road with authority and stopped alongside the apparition. Max looked at the tragic figure and sensed its hopeless despair and without saying a word spoke to it through the language of the soul.

"You don't know that you're dead." was his introduction to conversation.

"I do, but I don't, I suppose, but I suppose not, I don't want to accept the fact for which I was unprepared, it happened without warning."

"Before your time as well"

"Yes, of course, what happens now"? The ghost asked with tears in its eyes.

"Time to go home"

"But this is home."

"Only for a brief moment or two" Max truthfully replied. The ghost appeared very confused at the philosophical suggestion and its light began to dim.

"How long have you walked the streets"?

"I can't answer that question, I've lost all concept of time."

"What was your earthly name and where did you live"?

The ghost thought for a while and continued to hopelessly look around as it avoided eye contact with Franck, who remained calm.

"It doesn't seem important now, there's.... a.... group of us. We're all the same. I come out at night to find the way, away, so far none of us have been successful...."

"Because you lacked faith" Franck concluded on the lost soul's behalf. The ghost's life force dimmed a little more. Franck then commanded.

"Take me to your group, perhaps I can help."

A smile of hope spread across the ghost's face and he appeared brighter as the excitement of being shown home captured its heart.

"Do you really mean it"?

"Yes I do."

"You're not lying"?

I have no reason to." Franck replied genuinely as a police car stopped near him. A middle-aged voice from the front passenger seat roughly barked.

"Move along, don't want your types hanging around here"!!

Franck lowered his head submissively and mumbled. "Yes officer." He then walked away in the direction of the lost soul.

"Schizophrenic vagabond"! The police officer grumbled as he wound up his window to shut out the night's cold air.

"The city's becoming full of them." His partner for the night remarked.

"And the nut houses are full"!!

"The system can't accommodate all of them. Careful you could end up like them." The partner warned.

"Not a chance"! The middle aged policeman seriously replied as he observed Franck alias Robbie the vagabond in the patrol car's side vision mirror. Within minutes Franck was gone, engulfed by the early morning mists that heralded sunrise in the making.

Franck Max climax found himself in the grounds of a rich oil sheik's mansion located in the posh suburb of Greenpark, halfway between Mayfair and Piccadilly Circus. The group of lost souls were assembled around the family's private mausoleum. A collection of sexless spirits, they exhibited all forms and degrees of negative emotion. As Franck Max climax approached them he said "Good attempt, but they've long gone, you wont find the door here, it's only a hotel for the dead, come follow me, are there any others"?

There was no response, Franck walked out of the estate without even a whisper from the sophisticated surveillance equipment by virtue of his non recognition ability, thirty minutes on they reached the ornate gilded gates of one of London's many cemeteries, known as the boneyard it was located between Eutace and Camdentown train stations. The early morning mist had thickened and flowed over the graves and in between the expensive upright statues of angels, saints and sinners. Franck approached one with his entourage of souls in tow. The statue's static life form stretched into the sky, it was carved out of the finest white marble into the shape of a non-denominational angel with metallic sword in hand.

"Janitor janitor ad vivus aqua resare" Franck repeatedly pleaded.

Static became fluid and from the exact anatomical position belonging to the fallopian tubes, two hands emerged with fingers that moved rhythmically to capture the essence of life as they would in the living body. They beckoned, they called, the souls stood still uncertain of what they should do, each assumed that they would encounter that brilliant tunnel of light that many who had experienced near death had spoken of.

Franck Max Climax nodded his head to indicate that all was well and that this was in fact the route to the womb of spiritual development. Reluctantly one by one slowly passed him by and left behind a token of their life experiences and the cause of their physical death.

As each approached the angel's sword came down, touched them on the shoulder and reduced them to the spiritual seed that they were intended to become. Their journey would take them to a place where the Father waited intent on fertilising their ultimate destiny determined by their life's achievements.

Franck Max Climax played with the disc's of life knowing full well that he had only twenty-four hours in which to view their contents, after which time they would disperse and feed the plants who thirsted for their knowledge.

Morning had broken, the mist clung desperately onto the cold stone that filled the cemetery, knowing full well that its life was short lived until the next given opportunity. The cold, dense early morning air magnified the stirrings of the humans and their machines; it carried not only their sounds but their smells as well. These stimulated, seduced and teased Franck's olfactory senses, his mouth lusted for an opulent breakfast, but alas, it was not to be, there was much to be discovered. This day's offerings would present him the tasks that he would have to undertake to completion if he wanted to stay in his maker's favour.

Food would come at the right time and place when his body felt hungry, for now it was content with the euphoria it received for helping the lost souls find their way home. Tears of joy cascaded down Franck's cheeks as he played with the soul's tokens, each resembled an ancient coin complete with the owner's unique profile. He withdrew one by one from his left hand trouser pocket, studied each carefully and allowed his fingers to explore the throat region of each profile, the information contained within rapidly ascended the neural pathways of his radial and ulnar nerves and his third eye projected the images onto his cerebral screen.

Franck Max Climax out of respect for their intimacy sought only the information that dealt with extreme sufferings. Mesmerized by the workings of his inner world mechanisms, Max walked straight into the path of an intensely bizarre individual.

"Nice coins you have there, old man. Care to swap them for the experience of your lifetime"? The prematurely wrinkled twenty-four year old male propositioned as he spread his legs apart, adjusted his skirt and fiddled with his ponytail. Franck gripped the precious coins tightly in his hand as he gazed at the heavily made up face of the aged transvestite.

"What would an old man wish or desire for besides youth"? He asked.

"Can't give you that, old man, can't cut away the years like a plastic surgeon's knife, but I can do better! I can promise you the trip of a lifetime! Where you'll experience everything you wished for and couldn't get, know what I mean eh"?

"Afraid not sonny, let me be, I've heard it before"!

"Ah yes, but have you ever encountered these"? The gaily-dressed transvestite asked as he produced two different plastic covered balls, one from the left the other from the right buccal region between the teeth and inside of his cheeks.

"This one's brown sugar and this one's a little bit of icy crack"!

"What would I be wanting with these? Especially when they come from your unhygienic orifice! Look at you! You don't know whether you're a man or a woman. No guessing where your mouth's been, your cheeks are swollen, you've probably got a case of mumps or some other horrible disease"!

The transvestite took grave offence to Franck Max Climax's comments and lashed back by angrily saying.

"I'm a respectable business man! People know me as 'Louis Armstrong'"!

"Really........... blowing your trumpet again"?

"No! Cause me mouth's me warehouse"!!! The dealer attempted to shout as he struggled orally to retain his expensive cargo. It was then that Franck realised how tall his aggressor was and how rapidly his karma was ascending towards explosive heights.

"You better remain tight-lipped otherwise you'll spill the beans"! Franck cautioned as he pointed to the plastic covered drugs of addiction. "Let me guess, brown sugar is Turkish heroin and icy crack is not to be confused with what plumbers experience during winter"!

The colourful transvestite spat out the contents of his mouth into his hands and pocketed the slimy plastics covered balls of addiction. He wiped away the saliva from the corners of his mouth with his left hand as his right felt for the knife that was concealed in his back trouser pocket.

Franck looked him in the eye and froze like a statute not out of fear but rather out of desire to know his enemy well. He had voluntarily entered into a Petite Mal state of epilepsy, which allowed him to prod and probe his potential assailant at the soul level.

Mister Armstrong was used to getting his own way after all he was the King of the Card Boys and had built a nicely sized territory in which he promoted the ladies of the night and their wares, by leaving their calling cards firmly attached to the inside walls of public telephone boxes.

"Look here old man I've taken a fancy to them coins so hand them over"! He violently demanded as he thrust the sharp point of his seven inch flick knife at Max's throat.

"I said, hand them over"!!!

"It might be safer for you to attend to your calling cards." Max replied showing no fear as he slowly chanted "Janitor; Janitor; prae-sidium" several times. Outraged by Max Climax's apparent senile stupidity 'Armstrong' lashed out with his knife. Two flashes of light simultaneously occurred. In his mind there should have been the sounds of screams, the splatter of blood and the thud of a body falling, instead nothing. 'Armstrong' stood perplexed, Franck Max Climax was intact, 'Armstrong' felt for his knife, but his hand was bare, then his victim spoke.

"I think you had better turn around."

Frightened by the event he obediently obeyed and was awe struck by the presence of a two and half metre white marble angel that stood behind him. The statue had come to life and held 'Armstrong's' flick knife in its free hand fearing that his time was over, 'Armstrong' fled into a nearby red telephone box. As he made haste the angel threw his own knife after him, it followed in close proximity until it pierced the telephone box's closing door and nailed it shut against its doorframe. Franck Max Climax approached the box and peered inside. 'Armstrong' shook uncontrollably as he voided his urinary bladder.

"I think you're in need of emergency assistance." He said in a deadpan fashion as he observed the deeply troubled drug dealer. The angel who stood nearby overheard Max's comment and acted on his behalf without penetrating the telephone box, it punched in triple zero and gave the operator the exact location of the emergency, all by the power of telekinesis, which further worsened 'Armstrong's' already fragile state and caused him to truly believe that he was hallucinating. Max continued to loiter around as a curious simpleton would do until the police officers who had ordered him to 'move along' the previous night arrived.

"M..maan , mmaan in there look no good." Franck stuttered with a mouth full of saliva, as he pointed to the figure shivering in a corner of the telephone box.

"Move along sonny, there's nothing for you here." The policeman ordered as he took stock of the situation." Wait a minute, don't I know you"? He then asked

"I, I..d.don't… t…think so." Franck once again stuttered after which he smiled in an innocent way that people with Down's syndrome do. His realistic play acting filled the policeman with sympathy.

"Where's home"? The policeman asked.

Franck smiled once again, looked left, right and left again, shifted his weight from one foot to the other and then quite innocently answered "Over there"! as he pointed to the graveyard.

"Are you sure"?

"Yes, me mom's over there."

The policeman on hearing these words momentarily choked and was about to reply when his partner summonsed him.

"Harry, come over here quick! Look what we have here! Our local Big Mouth, except this time he's all out of wind"!

"He's got balls in his pockets" Max giggled. Harry quickly grasped the significance of his statement and said nothing so as not to alert 'Armstrong' into swallowing the evidence.

"I'm sure he has, now run along sonny, nothing here for you today."

"Okay officer, I go now, I think me mommy's calling me." Franck replied in a childish voice as he moved away from the chaotic scene. Armstrong continued to shake out of morbid fear at the image of the large angel even when the other rescue teams arrived.

"Take me away, take me away"!!! He incessantly pleaded as his rescuers broke open the door.

As they were about to yank him out of the red telephone box, the prostitute's calling cards magically flew from the interior walls and attacked every part of 'Armstrong's' anatomy, causing him hundreds of very painful paper cuts and shredding his clothes completely.

"Instant Karmic response" Max whispered happily to himself as he turned and sauntered down the street seemingly without a care in the world as he went in search of his next adventure.

It wasn't long before he was back on a busy street, as he walked he looked at everybody and everything that he passed by. The majority of people acknowledged him in one way or another, a minority deliberately looked the other way, those who accepted his presence returned his smile and some who had breakfast on the run offered some of their sustenance.

Max accepted a few morsels here and there and without exception blessed each one for their kindness.

He continued with this behaviour until he reached his final destination; which was on the street outside of London's Natural History Museum. There he retrieved his necessary equipment from its secret hiding spot in the Museums gardens and set up his shoe-polishing stand after he made subtle changes to his appearance.

Franck Max Climax waited patiently to clean the shoes of those who were 'superior' to him, including the occasional corporate giants. The morning passed without incident, his regulars of the day came and went nothing untoward until the flashy Indian arrived.

Swarup Phiandi was the closest you could ever find to that of a coloured aristocrat in the House of Lords, not that he was a proper Lord mind you, but rather, as a consequence of his brilliant success, he came to behave like one. Aloof, detached and arrogant are but some of the many applicable descriptions that could be appropriate if it were not for the fact that he was extremely ruthless and cold blooded in his approach to accumulate immeasurable wealth at the expense of the common man.

Dressed in the finest hand made clothes, which just about included everything that he wore including his underpants, Swarup or 'swamp' as many of his colleagues called him behind his back because they perceived everything that he did to be somewhat murky, alighted out of the rear of his Bentley Mulsanne turbo that his Nigerian chauffeur conveniently parked in the handicapped zone.

Mr Phiandi's Indian parents originated from the border region adjacent to Pakistan. Sick of all of the turmoil, unrest and unnecessary killings that surrounded them, Mr Phiandi senior took himself and his wife to Hong Kong in search of a better life. Sadly the situation there was no better.

Mr Phiandi could only obtain work as a security guard, which was in keeping with the Chinese attitude towards all Indians as being low class disposable citizens. Mr Phiandi senior could only tolerate six months of such abhorrent treatment and once again he sought refuge in another foreign land. This time it was Kenya.

In that country the Indian immigrants were paler in skin colour than many of the indigenous Kenyans and they quickly used this to their advantage by establishing profitable business ventures through the dubious art of exploiting the labour market. It must be said in defence that Mr Phiandi senior was a little more charitable than his fellow Indian and as a result built a fine rock solid coffee empire. His growers, the native Kenyans were relatively happy with their meagre payments. When the time was right Mr Phiandi senior secretly purchased a stately mansion in England.

There his wife and offspring would live and be raised in the English traditions. His one and only son Swarup once he had reached his sixteenth birthday would be expected to return to Kenya each and every summer holidays and help manage his father's coffee business which enabled Swarup to become extremely street smart and manipulative.

Swarup had neither care nor intention of involving himself in the same line of activity as his father; he sought other areas of opportunity.

"Well my shoe cleaning cretin, get on with it"! He growled at Franck, as he sat down and placed his fine black leather zip up boots on the polishing board.

"Yes Master." Franck humbly replied as he attended to the command.

"At least you know your place in the world"! Swarup summed up as he gazed down at Franck who busied himself with the cleaning cloth.

"Still living on the streets, you Africans never do amount to anything, do you'?

"I'm not."

"You're not a failure"? Swarup jeered

"African"

"What then"?

"Sudanese" Franck proudly replied.

"See that man over there"? Swarup asked as he pointed to his chauffeur.

"Yes"

"He's Nigerian and doing better than you"! Swarup was about to render more verbal abuse when his mobile phone rang. "Phiandi.... Yes, how the devil are you? All things going well, what's that you say? Really, excellent, tell me more, that's absolutely marvellous"!

Franck Max Climax shook off any desire to punish his client with Instant Karmic Response instead he listened intently to Swarup Phiandi's extraordinary conversation.

His caller was the Chief Executive Officer of a major international food additive company, whilst Phiandi himself was second in charge of a large pharmaceutical conglomerate with his eye on the top job. Carried away by his passionate greed Phiandi was unaware of Franck alias 'Robbie' 'listening in' and was ridiculously oblivious to the fact that during the intense twenty minutes that he was on the mobile telephone he had each shoe cleaned and polished six times. Swarup always used shoe cleaning to disguise his criminal activities for two reasons, one to ensure privacy out in the open and second to symbolically wash away the dirt before it had a chance to accumulate.

With phone in hand Phiandi stood up and threw a fifty pence coin onto the ground before him as crumbs from the corporate table. Franck scooped it up eagerly as a beggar would do and thanked his client profusely.

"Peasant"! Uttered Swarup as he made for the rear door of his limousine held open by the ever-smiling Nigerian who gloated in his own success.

Franck Max Climax glared at the duo as they drove away and he tried desperately not to allow harmful anger to creep into his persona. The gentle happy face of Vivienne the shop assistant from the French patisserie that was located several doors down from Harrod's department store broke the mood.

"Good morning Robbie, here you are, lunch for today, I'm sorry it's a left over from yesterday. As you know Gustav will not let me give you a fresh baguette, at least I snuck out some fresh pastries for you"!

"Oh thank you, let me clean your shoes"!

"You always say that" Vivienne reminded him before she invited him to eat. "Come let's have lunch." Franck Max Climax alias "Robbie' the shoe cleaner needed no further encouragement, he quickly closed up his stand and hung a 'back in 10 minutes' sign on it.

Together they found a nice quiet bench on the northern side of the museum that was bathed in the warm daylight. It was one of their favourite spots. Their relationship had started out of Vivienne's charitable concern for 'Robbie' when she spied him searching the rubbish bins at the rear of the restaurant that she worked at some fifteen months prior. Unaware that he was looking for something else she offered him sustenance for the day in the form of yesterday's bake and seconds.

"Vivienne"

"Yes Robbie"

"Do you think the patisserie's food is addictive"?

"How do you mean"?

"Do people come back again and again, in search of their fix"?

"Not really, we do have our regular's who come I suppose out of habit, otherwise we have a different mix of customers every day."

"Does any one come in everyday and eat the same food"?

"Not at all, why do you ask"?

"Intrigued I suppose as to why people become addicted to fast foods and junk foods."

"Advertising, image, laziness, I suspect" Vivienne surmised

"Do you think it could be more"?

"Perhaps the taste, but if it was, why aren't they addicted to our food, I ask you. Ours is more delicious, nutritious and made from the finest fresh produce."

Franck agreed and reflected on what he had learnt from over-hearing Swarup Phiandi's telephone conversation, as he cast small pieces of bread to the hungry pigeons that busily cooed at his feet.

"You're a very generous man Robbie."

"Just looking after God's creatures"

"I've never asked this question before forgive me, if it is too personal. Do you have any family"?

"I walk alone." Franck Max Climax unemotionally answered.

Vivienne forced a downward smile and regretfully replied. "That's sad."

"Only if you want it to be I have a great many friends and I get the chance to meet nice people like you"! He said in a complimentary fashion.

Vivienne blushed and although she was clearly attracted to him said nothing more. Her lunch hour went all too quickly and without further comment she rushed back to the shop to help with the hungry crowds.

Franck was in no mood to clean any more shoes, if any cleaning was to be done, now was the time to cleanse on a massive scale and rid the hapless population of the parasites that fed on them in the name of Medicine. Today he had learnt by chance some would say and others would argue that it was predestined that the likes of Swarup Phiandi crossed his path to teach him that conglomerates deliberately inflicted disease upon the public in a number of unsuspecting ways.

Phiandi's company was involved in the manufacture of long acting pharmacologically active food additives that enhanced flavour and smell to the extent that consumers became unknowingly addicted to them. Swarup employed cutting edge nano-particle technology that bypassed the regulator's authority.

The additives went into places within the human body and acted in ways unheard of before, they caused a wide range of side effects that included: metabolic alterations, cardiovascular effects, neurological disorders and behavioural changes. No one recognised the fast foods or snack foods as being the culprits and merely put down their health problems as being a result of the stresses of modern day life.

The other avenue that Phiandi introduced disease was via immunization and its specific target was the nervous system. He knew that vaccines were largely ineffective and that almost 50% of children were not resistant to the disease for which they had been immunized; he also was keenly aware that vaccine adjuvants such as aluminium and mercury were neurotoxic.

Phiandi made certain that his company used a highly developed unique version of these two substances, which appeared innocent enough in seemingly producing an enhanced immunological reaction, but in reality they produced a delayed toxic effect some twenty years later once the recipient entered adulthood. Needless to say Phiandi's group of companies had available the appropriate treatments for the flotilla of artificial diseases that had been launched by the same corporations, a money- makers dream.

"Robbie me old chum, you're going in the wrong direction"! A boisterous middle-aged red headed man shouted as he grabbed hold of Franck's coat tails.

"I didn't know I was."

"Oh yes you do! Don't you remember? You promised to come with me this afternoon and visit Al."

"Who"?

"Al alias Keith Wholagan the man who keeps us well. The man with the cat! Remember"?

"Vaguely"

"Don't give me that, the other day you said you weren't feeling well. So me mate I've come up with the solution for you. Come on then, hurry along, and don't dilly-dally." The jovial Mr Percival Phillips said with much gusto as he led the way.

They the odd looking couple walked and walked here and there almost in circles it seemed at one stage until they reached a rather dubious looking flea market whose stalls were run buy all sorts of 'legal' refugee's, selling all manner of ethnic goods. Not exactly the place one would expect to find a healer.

"Brilliant location, hey what old chap"?

"If you say so"

"Of course I do! Breathe in; fill your nostrils with the smells! Riveting, absolutely riveting, if I do say so myself"! Franck nodded somewhat in agreement.

"Oh I see you're confused, is that it? Well then let me explain, our man Al makes herbal concoctions, somewhat smelly some of them, so what better place to do it then amongst other outrageous smells. What do you think, eh, absolutely brilliant? If it ain't stinky or horrible to taste then it ain't any good for you, health wise that is"!

Franck nodded once again somewhat in agreement.

"Careful where you step now, if you please" Percival commanded as he pushed his way through the tightly crowded passageways of the dilapidated complex.

Franck could feel himself peered at, analysed by a thousand dark eyes in a thousand dark places as he closely followed his guide. Countless hands touched his garments as he passed by dark skinned people from the African states offering their wares. Sadly he declined each one and he wished he could help them all. When he looked back, they were gone replaced by someone new. Each time he did this it was the same, a constant shifting landscape of faces not unlike that of the seashore.

Franck questioned what he had seen, was it real or was it a hallucination induced by the intoxicating odours of the place.

Incense sticks burnt everywhere, offerings to the Gods pleas for help, prosperity, shelter, food and protection. There was only one who could help them and he was now amongst them. The atmosphere's oppressive nature was too much for him, fresh air was all that Franck wished for.

"Enjoying yourself old chum" A blank stare was all that Franck could muster in response.

"Not much further now; get ready"!

"For what"? Franck thought.

"I hear you, London's private jungle." Percival mysteriously replied.

"Not in this climate"! Franck muttered to himself.

"You'll be surprised"! Percival sang as he made his way through a stall selling thousands of hanging silk scarfs and disappeared from view.

"This is ridiculous"! Franck said quite impatiently.

"Follow your nose"! A distant voice called, its location disguised and distorted by the swaying fluttering scarfs.

Ten paces on, the scarfs became wispy vines with mistletoe attached. The breath of fresh air that Franck Max Climax had so longingly wished for was not forthcoming, instead it was replaced by the odour of seasonings; rosemary, sage and thyme. Several of the vines came alive and hundreds of exotic butterflies filled the air.

"Come on you're almost there"! He could hear Mr Phillips call as he stepped into the interior of a huge disused factory that resembled ancient ruins hundreds of years old. The entire building was covered by a giant olive green glass dome that managed to keep the interior's temperature and humidity constant at 79.5 degrees and 85% water content irrespective of the outside weather.

"Do you like it? A forgotten remnant of the great exhibition, don't mind the people they're waiting their turn with Haws, that's the cat and please no corny CAT scan jokes please and no snide remarks about promiscuity or prostitutes just because his name makes him sound like an animal gigolo."

Percival Phillips gushed as he approached Franck who was mesmerized by the contrast between the enormity and intimacy of his surroundings.

A long circular line of patients stretched out before him, each patiently waited for Haws to place his feline paws upon them and diagnose the origin of their complaint. Keith Wholagan would be close by and after asking a series of questions would write down the necessary herbal prescription and pass it on to one of his assistants who would dispense it then and there. The process did not take long and was invariably very accurate.

"I think we've come at a bad time." Franck suggested.

'Not at all, appearances can be very deceiving. Al has in fact finished up, all these people before you have already been treated; they're staying to play with the cat. Come on let's take you into Al's laboratory if we can call it that and have a cup of herbal tea." Percival said as he made the appropriate gestures to Keith with respect to his intentions.Franck was amazed at the lush tropical greenery that abounded everywhere and he wondered how it all came about and managed to live.

"To answer your quizzical look; on the sewer system" Franck stared at Percival blankly who flashed a cheeky smile and then explained.

"Al's fed all of the plants an energy boasting herbal that stimulated their root systems into finding nutrients, a major sewer pipe runs underneath us, the plants easily found the cracks and crevices in the walls and are happily feeding in the richness below.

"What was this place"?

"A slaughter house, ironic isn't it? Once used to kill animals and now used to heal them. Come on let's go to the root of all evil." Mr Phillips said with intrigue as he spun around on the heel of his shoe and snapped his fingers indicating that Franck should follow him at once. Percival took Franck through an open archway that lead onto a downward spiral of wooden stairs. As they descended deeper into the ground the walls of the stairwell lost their smooth texture and became increasingly burdened with tortuous root systems until they disappeared altogether and were replaced by a three dimensional mosaic. Everything was green until Percival opened a well-hidden door and a flash of white light burst upon them. Franck was temporarily blinded, lost his footing and stumbled forward. Two welcoming arms caught and prevented his fall.

"Thank you Percival, I wasn't expecting to fall." Franck gratefully expressed as he clutched onto his rescuer.

"A pleasure, however Mr Phillips is already inside the lab."

"How did you come down so quickly, you were just upstairs a minute ago, I didn't see you leave"! Franck exclaimed quite astonished at the identity of his rescuer.

"Because I haven't that's my twin brother. I'm Kevin, we're identical twins, he'll be down directly, come in, make yourself at home. Percival tells me you're in need of some attention."

"It's nothing serious."

"We'll be the judges of that." Kevin answered as he ushered Franck into the pristine herbal laboratory where hundreds of labelled two litre amber glass bottles sat. Behind each was either a framed lithograph of an ancient seeker of truth or a quotation originated by them. The list of names was not restricted to medicine and covered all fields of human endeavour. Each contributed a little more to the understanding of life.

Franck was duly overpowered by the attentive devotion put into setting up this facility and then he realised that each bottle contained a herbal concoction that coincided exactly with the sage that it was assigned to represent.

Exasperating wouldn't you say"?

"Indeed I would, indeed I would; it must have taken you years of painstaking effort to create all of this. Is that right Kevin"? Franck quietly asked.

"He's over there by the doorway, I'm Keith I've just come down and I've brought my wife Judy with me."

Franck looked closely at Keith and then at Kevin. A number of things immediately struck him; the smooth flawless skin that each had, a living testimony to their herbal belief, their height, their apparent youth and the fact that they appeared to be married to identical twins who shared the same countenance.

"A pleasure to meet you sirs"

"Likewise, may I introduce you to my wife Judy and over there is her identical twin sister June who is and you guessed it, married to my identical twin brother Kevin."

"Extraordinary, quite extraordinary do you ever become confused, as to which one is your wife"?

"Never because there are dissimilarities between the two that only I and Kevin know about, you're very privileged to be here, Percival doesn't normally bring people down here, it's only reserved for those seeking wisdom."

"You haven't had many visitors then"?

"Only a few, can't take any chances otherwise we'll be persecuted and prosecuted before we know it. That's just the way this world is and always has been."

These words explained the introductory upstairs events that Franck had experienced prior to entering the factory and the lengths that Keith and Kevin had gone to in order to safeguard their operation and their own safety.

"Come with us, to the preparation room."

Franck reluctantly followed not wishing to be treated at all; however he realised that this was an important occasion, a lesson to be learnt. Haws the cat was already waiting, purring with content as he sat at the end of a large dispensing bench.

"Oh don't tell me he's been at it again"! Kevin said quite annoyed at the state of the cat.

"Haws, what have you been up to"? Judy sweetly asked, as she approached the cat that looked the other way out of shame.

"Occupational hazard, it's to be expected, especially when one experiments trying to perfect exquisite liqueurs. Haws you're forgiven, but not you June, please be more careful next time and don't leave any samples lying around, last thing we need is an alcoholic cat."

"Yes Keith." June answered visibly embarrassed by her carelessness.

"Do you use a lot of alcohol"? Franck asked out of curiosity but not wishing to inflame the situation. His comment caused the foursome to burst into raptures of laughter.

"Colossal amounts, thousands of bottles." Judy answered as she pretended to swagger about like a drunk and then she pointed to a circular stainless steel grating in the floor. "Come, look and see." She cordially invited; Franck accepted the invitation knelt down and peered through its square holes.

"Oh my…. only when the best will do" He remarked as he surveyed the bottles' labels. "Swedish, Danish, Finnish and a few Polish producers, you have expensive tastes"!

"We would prefer to call them high standards. We only use grain based vodka's from cold climates as these provide us with excellent character filled alcohols for our needs." Keith explained.

"It must cost you a fortune"!

"Not really, when each patient comes in they bring a 750ml or 1 litre bottle with them, at no cost to us. We then offset the cost of their herbal tinctures so it balances out quite nicely and everyone remains quite happy with the arrangement. We discard the empty bottles into that chute over there and the bottles simply roll away never to be seen again."

"Where do they go"? Franck asked taken by its mystery.

"We don't know, you're lucky to have seen anything at all, one day they're here, the next they're gone without even a whisper or the faintest clinker."

"And the herbs"

This time Kevin answered "A similar process, but a little more complicated because we follow the ways of Nicholas Culpepper who had a profound understanding of astrology and its influence on plants. We harvest according to his methods and employ two types of individuals for our purposes, growers and gatherers. Those who grow do so according to the astrological requirements of the herb, they are sowed at the correct time, grown in the correct time and conditions and harvested at the correct time. Result the very best medicinal herbs that one can obtain. There are herbs however that we cannot cultivate, these prefer to grow wild in their own ways, the best we can do is pick them at the right time and that is the role of our gatherers who have such knowledge. All of the herbs are then cut and dried according to the correct individual method and sent to us via numerous and varied routes so as not to attract any undue attention."

"Does it mean that you have hundreds of different herbs coming in"? Franck asked out a desire to understand the extent of herbalist's operation.

"We only rely upon a short list, the very best; the most effective that is found in this great nation of ours. It is our belief that no matter where mankind finds himself, there are botanical cures available to him in that location, for ailments in the location. Here in England we have fine-tuned our approach in accordance with the philosophy of

the Abbe Knepp who wisely said 'there is a plant for every illness'"
Before Kevin could continue Keith interrupted by saying.

"Thanks to June's and Judy's efforts in acquiring ancient texts
and articles in obscure journals, we have come to support the idea
through trial and error that a belief held by the German neurologist
Dr Waaper- Jauregg is true."

"Which was"?

"Two thirds of mentally ill patients would not need to go to a
psychiatric institution if they had healthy kidneys. Depressions,
delusions, fits of rage are due to kidney disorders. Treat them with
Bedstraw, Golden Rod and Yellow Dead Nettle, sit them in a Horsetail
sitz bath and watch the illness disappear." Keith confidently stated as
he saw that Judy wanted to add her learned observations.

"There are three requirements for Health. Firstly complete
nutrition as required by that race of people, secondly adequate san-
itation and thirdly always be happy irrespective of your situation,
laugh a lot, because it regenerates the body through the release of
many different hormones and that's why we push baby poo."

"Huh"? Franck exclaimed dumbfounded.

"There in the jars behind you." She pointed and Franck turned
to view the dozens of 8 ounce square plastic jars, which contained a
yellow-brown substance not unlike the consistency of baby poo.

"What is it"? He asked disbelieving her apt description.

"Baby poo, like I said." June once again reiterated and remained
silent until she saw that he was reluctant to accept the description so
she ceased her teasing and said.

"Baby poo is our nickname for the bee-pollen- honey mixture that
we make. The bee pollen comes from New Zealand it is the best we
can find, it varies in nutritional content depending upon the season
but it never fails to rejuvenate the person when taken internally. Here
have a read of this." She instructed as she handed him a compiled
readout on the miraculous natural substance.

"As you can see it doesn't take much to keep the human body

healthy, it is in fact one of the most resilient pieces of biological machinery ever conceived, remember what you have seen and keep up the good work in the Sudan." She politely explained as she kept pace with his reading speed.

Franck was completely taken aback by her profound statement; he was meant to be totally anonymous. How did she know, who had informed her?

"No one; you're not the only one who can see"! June dramatically said in a fashion designed to shock Mr Franck Max Climax and before he could utter anything in reply she added. "Oh my god, the bottles have disappeared, here take a look"!!

Completely bamboozled by his bizarre experience Franck was left floundering and he meekly obeyed. He stepped onto the grating and looked down which was to become his last memory of the laboratory. In less than a heart beat he plunged into total darkness and rapidly slid down a slippery carpet of moss and landed softly on the right bank of an underground river. Judy was already present on the opposite side.

"I can see that you're wondering what will happen next. Fear not; follow the river it will lead you to safety, but not before you build up a sweat for you see the river flows down into the bowels of the earth where all that it carries is purified by the intense heat to be returned pristine into the open world by the streams and fissures that empty into it. Remember there is no truth in the saying 'a black cat crossing your path causes you bad luck'" With that Judy disappeared from view.

For once in his adult life Franck Max Climax was not in control. He had found himself in a situation where his powers had failed him, all that he could do was to rely upon his basic instincts and find a way out. He nervously walked along the edge of the narrow riverbank in the direction of current flow and constantly monitored the ambient temperature as he kept a sharp eye out for any stray cats.

The river mischievously threaded its way erratically through the earth's soil and as it did so its current flow grew steadily faster, with it the temperature of its surroundings started to become uncomfortable hot. It was not dark as one might expect for the walls abounded in glow-worms that emitted a pleasant phosphorescent light.

As he proceeded further the air became thick with a fine mist which damped to some extent the thunderous sounds of falling and swirling waters that assaulted Franck Max Climax's ears and threatened to deafen him permanently; the river had reached its end point and its contents cascaded downward into a whirlpool that spiralled into the depths of the earth never to be seen again. Franck was at a dead end; there was nowhere left for him to go. Had Judy lied to him? Was he also meant to disappear without a trace? Was Percival a foreign agent intent on eliminating him? Franck decided to turn back, Judy's directions were entirely wrong! With each step that he took the glow-worms went out like candles in the wind. Franck tried desperately to induce a voluntary 'fit' but it would not work, the intense heat prevented it from happening.

Franck Max Climax found himself in total darkness, the rods and cones of his eyes failed to detect any photon of light for there was none, completely blind Franck was aware that if he lost his footing and fell into the river he would be swept away into the whirlpool and surely dragged to his death. He inched along and used the wall that the river had gouged out of the earth over hundreds of years as a guide; caution was not a good strategy, the intense heat was merciless, Franck in spite of the high humidity perspired profusely, the prolonged exposure had taken its toll, severe dehydration had set in, Franck grew steadily weaker and confused until his body could not compensate any further and blackness filled his mind.

11
RECESSIVE ADDICTION

Drip…drip…thump…thump…restriction Drip…drip…thump …thump…restriction; that's all that Franck Max Climax could feel and hear in his head; the unbearable heat had gone, freshness had entered his body, he lay quite still and enjoyed the revival. He slowly crept back into consciousness and realised that the epicentre of his recovery was in the flexure of his left forearm. Franck opened his eyes and visually explored his surroundings; he was back in the comfort of his own bed with an intravenous drip of some sorts attached to his left arm.

The chiming of the grandfather clock downstairs signalled it was 12 O'clock midnight, the bedroom was dark, the air still, nothing moved. Franck Max Climax no longer felt safe, someone had infiltrated his inner sanctum, someone knew where he lived, he was no longer anonymous, he was now completely naked, an easy target. The question was twofold how did it happen and who was responsible?

What errors in judgement had he made? Who recognised him and why would they want to do this to him? Franck looked at the intravenous plastic tube and wondered what was being deposited into the vein. Was it good or was it evil? Was it safe for him to leave it in?

He could not take a chance. In an act of complete and utter panic filled desperation he ripped out the intravenous needle and stemmed the subsequent bleeding by applying direct pressure with a folded facial tissue that he had taken from a packet located on top of his bedside table. He sat up and contemplated his situation. The sound of the front door clicking shut sent a fearful shock wave through his entire body. Franck strained his ears to pick up the minutes' movement. Nothing, not a sound; he looked about the room.

The mixture of subdued light and shadows that entered the room through his bedroom window cast eerie figures in his troubled mind; not since his youth had he experienced such trauma. His autonomic nervous systems were on red alert, ready to fight or take flight; fright was already well and truly entrenched.

Without any warning the shadowy figures on the walls that resembled abstract pine trees leapt before him and a wind blew through them with such ferocity that it pushed him back into his bed. As the wind screamed through the pine needles each cut, whipped and whizzed the air until they became transformed into the individual pages of the entire Koran, these deposited themselves upon him and all was still once again. Shocked at the sacrilege Franck furiously grabbed at the pile of pages and tried to rearrange them into their original order and hoped that this was not his precious original copy.

"If you are looking for the secret of life in these you won't find it! Neither will you find the words of the creator written in the works of man"! Franck stopped what he was doing and searched for the source of the words.

Once again without any warning the unexpected occurred. Haws the cat leapt out of nowhere and landed at the bottom of Franck's bed. The cat's huge yellow sapphire eyes stared at Franck with a burning intensity that he had never seen before in any living creature.

"It is I who has come alone to instruct you"!

Franck could not answer, he was held rigidly in place by his fearful emotions and the questions they poised. "If the cat had done all of this what else is he capable of? This is no ordinary feline."

Aware of Franck's frightful state Haws the cat moved up the bed every so slowly and hissed loudly as he approached Franck's chest. He then plonked himself down heavily on Franck's abdomen and with total disregard for his safety, began to preen himself.

Franck Max Climax could not breathe his heart pounded away, his blood gasses were seriously inverted and consciousness began to ebb away until Haws reversed the situation by massaging his kidney region. Peace once again re-entered Franck's body and with it a healthy level of homeostasis.

"Who are you? Are you some sort of demon"? Franck mustered up the courage to ask.

"Other cats think so, because…. I…. am…. Possessed"!!!!

"By what"? Franck nervously asked as he could feel his urinary bladder ready to void itself.

"By a reincarnated being, who hides within me"!

Franck's fears worsened, as did his confusion.

"It's true what he says." Another voice suddenly confirmed, as a wispy luminous body slowly emerged from the cats left ear. Within moments the image of a young maiden with flaxen hair appeared and sat itself down on the edge of Franck's bed. She smiled and knew that her time in the outer world was brief as she was unsuited to it and therefore it would cause her great harm.

"My name is Lumina; I come from a planet far away from here, in human terms, yet so near in ours. I chose the body of a cat to reside in, rather than that of a human, as it would be more acceptable once people recognised my talents. I can heal directly but that is not my purpose. Mine is to educate in the ways of plants and return your ravaged world to one of natural beauty. If I had come in the form of a human your kind would have killed me. I leave you with one request, help me to achieve my goal, study the discs, for they will show you the way." She hurriedly but precisely and clearly said just before her time expired. Lumina's spirit re-entered the body of Haws the cat and as she did so the jumbled up pages of the Koran re-assembled and fused themselves correctly into the holy book.

12.29 am Franck had only a number of hours left before the discs would disintegrate. He leapt out of the bed and frantically searched for his clothes. They were nowhere to be found. He searched every inch of his apartment except for the obvious, which was the wardrobe. There hanging in his suit closet was the uniform of 'Robbie' the vagabond, all pristine and clean. Haws lead him to the living treasures and once Franck retrieved them, haws the cat disappeared never to be seen again.

With discs in hand and completely naked, Franck retreated to his operations room and downloaded the precious information. One would have expected that it would have been a simple matter. Find the end point of the individual's life and read the cause of death or transition as some would like to call it.

Unfortunately it did not work that way, for death was compartmentalised and included every living soul that the person had come into contact with. It was in fact the Internet of Death.

Franck Max Climax had twenty nine discs to read, he had thought that it would be twenty nine deaths instead it ran into the hundreds of thousands through the process of each individual's all seeing third eye or subconscious as it should be properly known.

Franck was both surprised and appalled at the extent of drug addiction; both legal and illegal; 81.67% was the statistic; which embraced the subliminal forms of a paracetamol a day keeps the doctor away right through to the myriad of consuming numerous unnecessary medications to threat health risk factors that were sensationalised into pseudo disease; medications for fashionable disease and hardcore narcotic addictions, all without any realisation of what harm the synthesized agents were doing to the human body.

His disgust deepened as he read about the chemical straight jackets that people with supposedly behavioural disorders were put into from as young as three years of age, never to escape the clutches of the medico-pharmaceutical drug lords or should I say warlords. The more he read the colder the room became until ice formed all around him. Yet Franck although naked was not, the heat of his emotions kept him warm.

The target of his aspirations was becoming increasing clear, the arrow that finally scored the bullseye came in the form of one of the last remaining life discs; which belonged to one Damien Brace-girdle a geneticist who had worked for Jeansdesign Incorporated, a misnomer, for it was in fact a highly sophisticated research facility with grandiose ideas for the future of mankind.

This fine upstanding elderly gentleman was a product of World War 2. His German father Hans was an officer in the elite SS who defected and fled to hide in a remote village in Norway in 1941. There he fell in love with a pretty Norwegian girl Damien was the result of their intense love for each other. Once the war was over and things settled down, Hans, his wife Agnetha and baby Klaus migrated to England to help rebuild the nation.

The falsified identity papers that they used were extremely good, perfect in other words and by some people's standards, even Hans's qualifications passed the most rigorous scrutiny. It was there that Klaus became Damien Bracegirdle, Hans adopted Alfred and Agnetha was renamed Hyacinth. It was no coincidence that the family managed to inhabit the Bracegirdle's old family home as they were just one of the targets that the SS eliminated in an early attempt to undermine the social infrastructure of Great Britain through the process of look-a-like substitution.

Damien was an only child raised in a strict environment of morality and learning. His mother did her best to fit into the English class system but the strain of it was far too much and she left when Damien was eighteen years of age to live in her beloved Norway. This left a deep impact upon the young boy and caused him to shy away from the opposite sex and devote himself entirely to study at which he did exceedingly well. Gifted with a precise German mind, it enabled him to gain a rare insight into whatever interested him and which eluded others. It was no accident that he chose genetics, as this was already underway as one of the previously unknown secret avenues available to ensure the propagation of the Aryan race, one of Adolf Hitler's many dreams, something that Damien's father also held deep in his heart. Damien did not pursue this aspect, his ambition was to understand, discover, describe and teach the world about the genetic basis of disease. He wanted to know what activated destructive genes.

Damien was quickly scooped up within days of passing his doctorate of philosophy with honours and employed strangely enough in exactly the field that he wanted to investigate. Unknown to him Jeansdesign whilst outwardly British was in fact funded by the American Military. They had spent an enormous amount of money in successfully mapping out the human genome, what was left was to identify the role of each gene or gene sequence for one end only, the creation of biological weapons. None of what they were doing was ever leaked to the researchers; they always remained in the dark oblivious of the outcome of their meticulous work.

To Damien the human genome was like the night sky, with some genes sparkling brighter than the rest, whilst others clustered together in an effort to produce the same light intensity. Once at Jeansdesign Damien was assigned to research a specific cluster, which it was suggested was responsible for Multiple Sclerosis, an emerging disease in western society.

All of the genes within the cluster were recessive in nature, which meant you needed to inherit two sets, one from each parent to enable the disease to manifest itself given the right circumstances. The hypothesis that Jeansdesign expected Damien Bracegirdle to solve was whether it was possible for a recessive gene to become dominant and in so doing would in effect arrest the disease at any given point in time. Jeansdesign sought to answer the following questions. Was it possible for a gene to change character, can it be recessive one minute and dominant the next and if so, is it permanent or transient and more importantly can it be made to be permanent?

Damien leapt at the opportunity. To him the analogy was the hair on one's head, for any individual fibre can either grow as a vellus (baby) or terminal (solid thick shaft) fibre depending upon its state of mind, bald people invariably had all of their terminal hair replaced by vellus. To be able to permanently change the nature of the gene expression had far reaching ramifications because it suggested that once he had determined the method, anyone could by switching the character of the genes stop autoimmune diseases; cancer otherwise known as the Spanish dancer and the like dead in their tracks.

In order to achieve this breakthrough technology, which belonged to the realm of the gods, money was no object and equipment was not a problem. Whatever he wanted he could have, providing he without fail constantly and obediently presented the data he had accumulated.

Over the years everything was going extremely well until one day per chance Damien received a cryptic email in error from the head of one of the largest American Pharmaceutical companies asking for information relating to project Recessive Addiction.

Initially Damien had no idea what it was about until his sharp German mind swung into action and deciphered the hidden messages. Realising that it was not safe to investigate the matter from his laboratory or office computer he carefully copied all of the information he required onto a USB stick and conducted his detective work from various Internet Café's.

Damien did not bother turning up for work on the pretext that he had 'burned ' himself out and as a consequence was quite 'sick'.

Damien Bracegirdle was no computer hacker nor was he a simpleton. He found that the Internet bore a remarkable similarity to the way that genetic material behaved and once he had assigned different identities to what he was doing, he was able to easily navigate his way around and access all of the information he wanted.

To those who think that emails once destroyed are destroyed Damien found this concept quite wrong. The Internet like genetic material never relinquishes its information, it keeps it forever. Therefore all messages written decades ago can be accessed albeit slowly.

Six days and six nights of relentless computer work took its toll upon Damien, before he called in sick as an excuse to hideaway, now he was truly unwell from exhaustion and the prospect that all of his life's work was in vain, an absolute waste, soul destroying stuff.

If anything the experience had provided Damien with invaluable information that he could use at a later date once he had extracted himself from Jeansdesign employment and found a new more ethical job. Damien Bracegirdle was a pawn like many other gifted academics that were used for commercial gain and rewarded with a middleclass lifestyle.

On the seventh day of his quest the pack of 'sniffer dogs' that he had sent out into cyberspace six days earlier returned with their 'sticks' of information all neatly laid down. The gene cluster that Damien had been working on for so long had nothing to do with multiple sclerosis at all, its main activity was associated with human social behaviour in particular chemical addiction, exhibited in individuals who had inherited the necessary recessive genes responsible for the addiction from both parents. Environmental factors it was postulated activated the genes causing the individual to seek out chemicals that would pacify an outraged cerebrum or some part thereof. It had also been determined that certain chemical moieties which possessed a certain spatial configuration turned one or more of the genes 'on' in much the same way as a lock and key arrangement in people who were otherwise detached or disinterested in any from of substance or drug addiction.

Somewhat unscrupulous individuals who managed to keep secret their activities from their peers and had sold this information to highly receptive drug company executives.

So that as time went by it became common knowledge by various novel means of skulduggery with the result that any new form of a so called anti-depressant therapy became extremely addictive rendering the patient a lifelong consumer. Not content with that the companies wanted a bigger market and were more than keen to discover how to render the resistant portion of the population accessible to their wishes. This meant that if they could convert the individuals that were blessed with a dominant- dominant or dominant-recessive gene combination into a completely irreversible recessive-recessive situation, they could substantially increase their sales of drugs once the individuals had succumbed to the barrage of environmental insults.

All of this sickened Damien to such a degree that he vomited over the keyboard of the computer at which he sat. It was not only a response to the horridness of what he had just read but also that his own work may have contributed to the manipulation of millions of people and that he indirectly caused harm rather than good. Even though he was naïve of the fact Damien's upbringing did not and would not excuse him of his involvement.

Damien Bracegirdle wanted to bring the monster down. But how, what was its Achilles' heel? What could he really do in the scheme of things? He clutched his stomach as he threw tissues over his vomit and hastily gathered the outcome of his work.

Outside of the Internet café an unruly demonstration was in progress. A large number of dissident Saudi Arabians were shouting and waving crudely written placards about some new dispute in the Middle East. The owner of the café looked rather nervous, Damien thought it had something to do with his gastric upheaval and was about to apologize when a Molotov cocktail came hurtling through the front window, it crashed into the left bank of computer terminals and everything exploded into flames, it was no ordinary gasoline mixture, it had been expertly made from ethanol, naphthalene and detergent. The safest way for Damien to escape the heat was through the front door as the all-engulfing fire was behind him and rapidly spreading down the shop towards the rear of the building. He ran with all of his might not caring who he bowled over or what he might hit survival was utmost in his mind. Once outside he stopped and confronted the hostile gathering. The Arabs were not interested in him; it was the anti-Palestinian who ran the café that they wanted.

Realising that he was an innocent victim of the attack Damien cautiously made his way through the heated crowd, the sound of approaching police and fire brigade sirens filled the air; onlookers and inhabitants from the surrounding area came to look at the fire, which greedily devoured the building.

The pains in his stomach intensified and he gripped his abdomen even more. Then another pain struck, unexpectedly this time sharp and to the point, a warmth covered his left kidney area and spread down his left leg until it oozed onto the pavement and painted it bright red. Damien Bracegirdle had been stabbed, precisely and with murderous intent, there was no salvation, no one to save him, the bleeding could not be stopped, there was no body or anything to stem the flow, he felt cold, bitterly cold, winter had set in and he fell dead.

The official story was one of mistaken identity in which Mr Damien Bracegirdle respected research scientist was killed in an unfortunate incident. He was simply in the wrong place at the wrong time.

Franck Max Climax thought he could feel the razor sharpness of the knife that terminated Bracegirdle's life but in fact it was his own. The ice that had started to form in the room had grown so rapidly that it now hung from the ceiling as long thin sabres and pierced his skin. Franck dared not straighten his posture for it would have meant certain trauma instead he remained motionless and examined one last life disc before the time to do so ran out.

Dean Trodden, the man of three's, three times a drug addict, three times rehabilitated and three times he returned to his former addiction. One would have thought that with such a history he would have been successful in kicking the habit but it was not to be for the foundation of his failure was his circle of friends, one that he could never break away from. All that they could do was talk incessantly about endless highs and how they could obtain money to ensure continuity. Their sole purpose in life was to explore the ever-increasing expansion of consciousness as created and driven by narcotic ingestion, an obsession that robbed them of genuine realities and caused them to live in a world of absurd distortions. Franck did not wish to view these but the swords of ice forcibly prompted him so that he could experience the horrors that certain humans inflicted upon their fellow man.

All of the images were out of this world and out of mind; haphazard, horrendous and horrid; sickening, sordid and satanic, how Franck wished for something divine.

During his last weeks in jail Dean supposedly found salvation in the copy of the Bible that his mother sent him. Many before him had turned to religion in an effort to kick their dirty habits; Dean obtained some measure of solace but not enough as the constant talk of Heroin in the cells amongst the inmates fuelled and fired his desire to dance with the white powder once again. Five years of separation from the outside world was sufficient time for all those that he had previously known as sources of the enigmatic substance to move on, change identities, locations and ways of making black money. Now everything was new, the old ways of obtaining supply was still there and available to those who remembered how to access them.

The Oxford Arms pub was one of those reliable places to find dealers, it was located as one might expect on Oxford St London. The wisest time to go there was late Friday night when the popular drinking venue was full to the brim with people from all walks of life, desirable and undesirable, which was reflected by the language that bounced off the pubs walls.

Dean edged his way into the crowded building and tried to make eye contact with as many people as he could. Most avoided him, one or two gave him a moment or two otherwise all were immersed in their little worlds of joyous expectations, especially when it related to the physical coupling of the sexes later that night. Realising that he was wasting his time Dean Trodden decided to approach one of the rougher looking barmen.

"Excuse me" He shouted above the din.

"I'm having trouble locating Harry." Dean then said lowering his voice as he bent forwards towards the bartender.

"We have lots of Harries in here mate, could you be a little more specific"?

"Brown, Harry Brown, you know, the Brownies, they're very uplifting sort of people, if you know what I mean"!

"Not here mate; moved on, your best bet is Cambridge Circus, opposite the miserable ones"! Was the cryptic clue that the bartender gave as he attended to making his next order and then he asked. "What might be your pleasure tonight"?

"Something strong and exotic, been an extra long time between drinks, almost forgotten what's it's all about"!

"One remembrance coming up Governor"!

The bartender was true to his word, with a dazzling display of juggling ability and alcoholic knowledge; he created a multi-layered tropical paradise in a tall glass complete with exotic fruits and the customary cocktail umbrella. Dean took the liquid work of art after paying for it and settled into an empty seat in the upstairs gallery that overlooked the seething pandemonium below. Every sip of the complex alcoholic beverage took him to a different equatorial location, Jamaican rum completed the journey, he drained the last drop from the glass and enjoyed the Dutch courage and spiritual optimism that it filled him with, full of it, he departed the pub and made his way up Oxford St. Once past Tottenham Rd he turned into Charing Cross Rd, then into Litchfield St and finally into Shelton St where the Cambridge theatre stood, as he walked he kept his head down and constantly prayed that he would find a seller.

"Please God, let me find one; I'm Desperate"!

"Please God let me find one; I need it"!

"Please God answer my prayer"! He repeatedly pleaded, from the darkness a voice rang out.

"I believe you are looking for me"! A tall well-built black stranger dressed completely in black said with a Jamaican accent.

"Not that I'm aware of." Dean replied fearing that this ominous looking man was intent on robbing him.

"My name's Harry Brown. I belong to a family of high flyers. Care to get on board, my good man, got lots of tickets to sell, any destination, any way you want to go, now what might be your pleasure Governor"?

Dean thought a while, it made sense; the bartender was a drug pimp. Dean Trodden quickly made the connection; the tropical drink was made with fine Jamaican rum, an omen of what was to come. This man was Jamaican. A runner or text message had been sent ahead, that fully described Dean and his desires; this was no co-incidence not wishing to draw attention to themselves the seller suggested.

"Let's walk, Governor and let me describe what Jamaican delights I have to offer you"! Dean agreed and stepped in time with the stranger. He looked ahead and saw a huge billboard with a French flag held up by downtrodden civilians upon it.

"The miserable ones"! He whispered to himself.

"Don't sell anything like that my friend. I'll tell you what; I think that the Jamaican cocktail will suit you the best. Smooth and warm to start with, followed by a sudden jolt and you're away like one of those tunnel of terror thrill rides you get in space mountains, except no terror, just pure pleasure. Much, much better, than your standard Brown Sugar, what about it"?

"Sounds good, really good"! Dean answered convinced that his prayers had been heard.

"Well then Governor how many of those 'G's' do you want"?

"Pardon"! Dean replied unfamiliar with the Jamaican's terminology.

"'G's" of force, like gravity man, except its pure gravity"!

"As many as you can spare"! Dean bravely said as he threw all sense of caution to the wind.

"You look like a man who can take seven big one's Governor"! The Jamaican pronounced as he produced a 9cm long white package.

"That'll be one hundred quid, Governor"!

'What's this"? Dean nervously asked as he handled the bag and tried to discern its contents.

"Jamaican Special, premixed syringe, no messing about, all done expertly for you, just mainline and you're away, modern technology at its best"!

Dean happily parted with his money and accepted his fate.

"Thank you Sir, a pleasure doing pleasure with you. Hope to see you soon. Remember; see the bartender for the next location"! And with that the Jamaican disappeared into the eerie shadows of the night.

Dean Trodden's excitement was unbearable, he wanted to inject then and there, the years of craving heightened by listening to talk of hits and experience was making him uncontrollable. He started to shake, desperation seized him and carried him to a quiet ally way where he ripped open the package and gasped at the sophisticated device. The syringe was pristine, obviously assembled in a sterile environment, it contained two chambers, the first was filled with a clear fluid, obviously the pre-warmer but in fact it was a solution of Epsom salts or magnesium sulphate being its chemical name, the second chamber contained the heroin. As one depressed the plunger, the first chamber delivered its contents and when the user was ready and had experienced sufficient foreplay, the diaphragm separating the two chambers, ruptured and made available the heroin dose.

Dean Trodden took off his overcoat and rolled up the sleeve of his left arm and searched for an available vein. The years of drug abuse had collapsed the majority of them, which worsened his desperation; again he turned to his 'God'.

"Help me, help me, I need it now, don't deny me"!!! He pleaded as he flexed and extended his forearm muscles and repeatedly opened and closed his fist. Blood flooded into his arteries and veins in response and soon a site reluctantly presented itself for injection. Dean inserted the needle, by itself it felt so good, he moaned with a mixture of relief and sexual excitement as the needle sat in his vein and stimulated its vascular wall, next he depressed the plunger and a warmth filled his entire body, a strange warmth, an unusual warmth caused by bursting red blood cells and the start of the inflammatory response, then when all was said and done, he partook of the ecstasy that he waited for almost an eternity, then he was no more.

"Stupid, stupid Christians, what a stupid religion, what a stupid accumulation of believers"!!! Franck Max Climax profoundly said as he watched the death of Dean Trodden and with that death the discs of life exploded, the ice in the room vaporised, the cold sabres of death disappeared and all was normal again, apart from the markings that sabres had left behind on Franck's back. The swords of ice had cut deeply into his skin and the resulting lesions healed as reactive keloid tissue leaving behind a date written in Latin and Roman numerals.

12

LOVE RE-IGNITED

Jack Stern returned to Club Med Mauritius and did not find his group of friends there.

"I am sorry Monsieur, your close acquaintances moved out over a week ago." The obliging GO stated in broken English as he openly displayed his dismay at their departure.

"They were a joy to behold; they brought so much fun and laughter into the complex, such good people"!

"Has the account been taken care of"?

"One moment Monsieur, I shall check. Yes everything is in order."

"May I have a copy please?" Jack politely requested. "Purely for accounting purposes" He then added.

"There you are Monsieur, I hope you enjoyed your stay, except, correct me if I am wrong, you were only here for a day or two and always in the company of the exquisite Yvette"!

"Yes, my life is not my own"!

"You are…. excuse me…. my English is not that good, you are a …er..a..pee shooter."

"Pardon"

"I get that wrong…. I…. er…perhaps you are a…a..sharp shooter"?

"The correct description is trouble shooter and you were right the second time, I usually hit the target. Thank you for your assistance good-day." Jack warmly replied and set off towards the Club's main entrance.

"One week away and already they've disappeared. Anyone would think that the Club is not good enough for them"! He thought to himself as he walked briskly through the main gates and turned right towards the three-way traffic intersection. Satisfied that no one had taken any notice of him Jack wandered off the main road into the scrub, intoned Spiritus Ruah and by the speed of thought materialised in the grounds of the newly erected Church of the Coloured Sands. Four new buildings adorned the site, a presbytery, a large parish hall and a modest primary school. Behind the presbytery stood what appeared to be a convent. There was a constant flow of worshippers in and out of the church. It all made sense.

'Well!!! What are you going to do about me"? The angry dishevelled man roared as he shook his fist behind Jack's back. Thinking that he was deranged and talking to some fictitious person Jack ignored him and his aggressive behaviour and made a move to find his friends.

"Don't walk away when I'm talking to you! You…. you…. double-crossing heathen"!!!

Jack Stern had no idea what this madman was on about until he turned to face Father Bruno Bogliani dressed in the most appalling tattered clothes and looking quite gaunt.

"Since you opened this monstrosity no one comes to me anymore. My life is ruined! Why did you come here? Why couldn't you have stayed away? I was comfortable, I did God's work; I did it humbly with reverence"!

"A little too humbly"! Jack interrupted, his words further infuriated Bogliani.

"Swine! Blackguard! Thief! You're already cursed by the religions on the Island. They want you out, we damn the day you arrived"!!!!

"And I, Sir, bless the day I set my eyes upon you" These ambiguous words sufficiently calmed Bogliani and allowed Jack the chance to further his pacification.

"You are in need of help. Life is not about socks or keeping your tootsies warm. It is about self- discovery, for this very reason, the monstrosity as you call it came into being.

It is not here to rob any religion of its members; it is here to fill in the gaps. It was discovered by one of the beautiful young maidens who has the gift of sight and it was brought to life by the intense love for his Catholic Church by one Father Brendan O'Reilly." Jack firmly and unequivocally said as he stared Bogliani in the eye.

"He is Catholic"? Bogliani nervously answered.

"But of course."

"What is he doing here"? Bogliani asked as he scratched the crown of his balding head.

"He's on sabbatical leave looking after eight previously destitute young ladies. It must have taken you a long time to muster up the courage to face your fears and the unknown to come here." Jack correctly deduced as he maintained his stare.

"How did you know"?

"Because your entire life revolves about socks. You have never elevated yourself from the ground level; you have never attempted to take the view from the mountaintops. Your life Father Bogliani was not meant to be lived in dust alone"!

Bogliani glanced at his dirty feet, which were housed in a pair of extremely worn out sandals held together by dust alone. He then compared them with Jack's pristine appearance, swallowed hard and wiped his feet against his grimy cassock. Very little dirt fell away.

"It will take more than that to clean yourself up"! Jack declared. "Why not come inside and wash away all of your fears, anxieties and misgivings; not forgetting your socks and discover what wondrous things Brendan's love has achieved."

Bogliani looked reluctantly away and then with a slimy grin he slyly asked the following question that fished for more information.

"Why doesn't my Archbishop know about this"?

"Because we haven't told him or anyone else for that matter; it's early days, news will spread, controversy will follow, political warfare will result and revolution will create a new world of understanding. Our church and mankind might even benefit from it if they're clever enough. The question is, do you want to be part of it or do you want to continue living your life in the dirt with your pair of socks"?

"Is the Church of the Coloured Sands a new order"? Bogliani slyly asked.

"If you want it to be"!

"Can I see"? Bogliani asked somewhat resentful of Jack Stern's attitude.

"Let's go together, it's a great adventure, much to discover"! Jack confidently replied as he ushered Bruno Bogliani along.

Max Dhaarling was constantly pining for the infatuation of his life, Expedita Shocker; it forced him to think and dream of her twenty-four hours a day without rest. He was truly lovesick and his physical disposition showed it. His wife however did not become suspicious, Merry Dhaarling was self immersed and cared only for herself; she fleetingly acknowledged his haggard appearance and put it down to work pressures. One last time, that's all he needed, one last time to hear her unforgettable voice or gaze upon her extraordinary countenance, that wish was answered in a telephone call.

"Good afternoon, Max Dhaarling here."

"A pleasure to hear you voice" The caller softly whispered. "Do you have the time to talk"?

"Yes, how may I help you"? He replied nervously after clearing the lump from his throat.

"Mother Superior is most curious to discover what would make tablets and capsules fail to work. Do you think you could find out for us, because one of our Sisters is not responding to her medication, we are very distressed and fear for her good health"?

"Yes Sister I shall do my utmost." Max assured Expedita as he felt himself coming on heat.

"By Tomorrow please, there is some urgency"!

"Yes by tomorrow." Max replied as he felt his embarrassment strain against his trousers zipper.

"Thank you and God bless." Before Max Dhaarling could say anything more Expedita clicked off. He cursed himself for being impolite and not having the ability to extend the telephone conversation further.

It would become an agonising twenty-four hours for him and once it was over, he knew that he would hear her voice for the last time and it would signal the end of his responsibilities to the Master; for the Master would not continue to use him. Any operative of which there were thousands would only be used once so as not to expose them to any sort of danger.

Precious Dhaarling responded to her father's request for help, in their secret attic hideaway in a most comfortable fashion, having been expertly taught by highly experienced University lecturers, she left no stone unturned, Max made detailed notes in anticipation of being thoroughly quizzed by Expedita and in the hope that she would thank him in person one day before he died.

"Bonny Davison is her name, Pharmaceutics is her game, in fact she plays it here and abroad, she's so good at her sport that she umpires for the T.A.G."

Max Dhaarling looked rather perplexed and his daughter sensed it. Precious giggled at his ignorance and admired the genius of her own flippancy.

"Oh don't look so lost, I'm just toying with you"!

"Okay" Max hesitantly replied.

"Well if you must know, it's Ms Davison, cos she never married, you know one of those types academic types who married her vocation."

"Wish your mom had done that"!

"Hey, that's not nice; then I wouldn't be here"!

"Oh I don't know some how you would have managed to find your way into my heart probably through a different mother, sorry"! Max apologized.

"That's better. Well, she knows everything." Precious replied as she made reference to Ms Davison.

"Just like your mom"!

"Dad stop it; you're here to learn now stay silent and make notes"!

"Yes darling."

"Okay let's start again. I was taught by the big government advisor and I must tell you, she was around before the legislation which was written to ensure medical quality and that should give you some idea about her age, lots of medicines and I mean lots of medicines were found to be ineffective before the legislation came to be."

"How"?

"Tablets passed through the gut intact, same for capsules, liquids didn't deliver, injections caused blood clotting problems, people really suffered badly."

"But only those who were dependent upon them by virtue of their subjective beliefs" Max philosophised.

"Yeah…whatever"!!

"Why didn't they work"?

"Well it's rather simple, it's all a matter of attention to detail, once you have the proper physiological understanding, that is." Max was none the wiser and it clearly showed on his face.

"Everything that enters the stomach has to be able to be digested or go ka-boom"!!

"Ka-boom"

"Yes Ka-boom, meaning it has to break up prior to digestion and absorption." Precious kept it simple so that her dad could understand.

"Before they understood, manufacturers pounded out the tablets like little fruit stones. These went straight through the gut with no benefit to the patient apart from heavier stools. Then someone realised that Ka-boom was necessary otherwise the toilets would get clogged up and consequently a disintegrant was added."

"You mean an explosive to clear the blocked toilets"?

"Not quite, they added starch to the formulation which when exposed to water swelled up and broke the tablet or capsule apart into smaller pieces. Everyone was happy, the manufacturer, the patient and the plumber."

"And the TAG people"

"Don't be silly they're never happy! They introduced tests"!

"What sort of tests"?

"To make certain that the tablet or capsule disintegrated within a certain minimal time in a test tube. This was meant to approximate stomach conditions. If it took too long, it meant there was a strong likelihood that it would pass through the gut intact no effect once again......... understand"?

"Yes I do any other variants"?

"Many which include complicated digestive functions, interactions with the active ingredients, with foods or other medications, acidity of the stomach, transit time of the bowel, the way the active medicament binds to the tablets' or capsules' other ingredients, a whole host of factors, the health of the patient etcetera, etcetera, etcetera" Precious expertly detailed.

"I think I get the picture." Max said as he made finishing touches to his notes.

"Good, I'm glad you understand, is there anything else I can explain to you"?

"One more thing"

"Yes"

"I've noticed that you have been very happy recently, you haven't by any chance met someone"? Max asked as a caring parent.

"Perhaps" Precious answered without giving anything away.

"I'm glad." Max Dhaarling shakily replied as he gazed into the heavens and watched clouds streak across the face of the full moon, the shadows that they cast accurately represented his emotional misery.

The sung words:

"Though the Moon is shining brightly, even brighter is your smile" caught Jack Stern's ear and tugged at his heartstrings. What a fool he had been not to have given Yvette the courtesy of a telephone call now and then; still that was the way he had always been, duty first, personal pleasures second and money as far removed as possible. Bogliani had sufficiently distracted Jack from instantly realising that something special was happening at the complex. People were not leaving as he had initially thought; they were entering the parish hall instead and attending a celebration of sorts.

The words of the song continued to demand his attention and they forcibly drew him out of the church into the hall's large lobby. Jack followed the trail of the music and entered the main auditorium, which turned out to be a richly decorated ballroom complete with ornate teak parquetry floor, soft neutral sound absorbing curtains, an abundance of very comfortable tables and chairs, a fully equipped kitchen and a stage upon which a full sixteen piece orchestra could be assembled. On this occasion a sophisticated audiovisual hi- fidelity electronic system provided the entertainment. The song 'Ciribiribin' recorded by a famous Belgium male tenor textured the air with love and emotion. In the middle of the floor entwined in each arms were Yvette and Brendan dancing as one. They had much in common, both were virgins, both had an intense love for the Church and both were devoted to the Blessed Virgin Mary. Not wishing to be seen Jack assumed invisibility and watched unnoticed from a quiet corner of the ballroom.

"Alone once again, it doesn't matter" Jack said to himself as he observed Yvette and Brendan dancing the dance of romance. "Look at them the beautiful couple, they don't know it yet, no one has told them; they don't even realise that they are meant to be together forever." He thought just before he intoned Spiritus Ruah and by the speed of thought returned to the welcoming arms of his ghostly grandfather at the Genius Loci.

"With hearts so free we'll dance this melody ciribiribin, ciribiribin"

"With one romance these beating hearts will sing and dance this melody loving hearts in ecstasy"

Brendan sang along with the tenor as he glided around the floor with Yvette and when the music had finished, he let go of her, bowed at the waist, kissed her hand and thanked her for the pleasure of the dance before proceeding to partner with one of the other girls. Candy eagerly pounced on the opportunity and quickly filled the void in his open arms.

"Not only are you handsome but you can dance and sing extremely well"! She congratulated him as she pressed her warm body against his.

'Do you think so"? Brendan shyly asked somewhat caught off guard.

"Oh yes"! She enthusiastically replied in a seductive voice as she took his hand, placed her arm upon his shoulder and assumed dancing position in readiness for the next waltz. This parish get together as it was advertised had been done on the spur of the moment at Candy's insistence who thought it a good idea to weld the community at large using the universal languages of music and dance. The Chosen theme was love, only waltzes and rumbas were allowed, each in their own way represented love, one was hot and spicy whilst the other flowed forever.

What Jack Stern saw between Yvette and Brendan was a chance singular event, a glimpse of a potential future, they did not dance the night together to the exclusion of others, on the contrary each had a multiple of partners with whom they shared their joyous experience of dancing. Jack should really have waited, but being a true gentleman he was not one to sway the hearts or minds of others. It was Jack's belief that love occurred through recognition of itself in others; infatuation was a clever magician who caused its illusion.

Jack Stern sat in a comfortable chair on the top level of the Genius Loci's complex and out of respect for the couple that would eventually see the love in each other; remote viewed random events at the Federal House of Representatives in Canberra Australia.

"Harvey."

"Yes Cyril."

"What time did you say we were meeting with Annette Manoff"?

"3pm sharp"!

"I can see that you're quite mad"!

"You had better believe it especially after that stupid publicity stunt of hers over the Napp affair"! Harvey Jarwood one of Australia's longest standing Prime Minister snapped back as he walked briskly towards his office door.

Cyril Pinewood his deputy deeply admired Harvey for his manliness after all Cyril was gay, a closet homosexual who married for political purposes, behaved very professionally as a heterosexual but secretly was in love with the tall white-headed P.M. What Cyril did not know was that the P.M. was also that way sexually inclined and moulded his life and public appearances to suit his political ambitions. Harvey Jarwood also harboured intense feelings for Cyril and possessed hours of video footage of Cyril doing private things. The P.M. had instructed numerous government agencies to keep tabs on Cyril on the pretext that he had received very reliable and accurate information that the Deputy P.M. had behaved in an irregular fashion whilst deputising for the P.M. during an international Heads of State summit. All of this was fictitious; Harvey Jarwood was a voyeur who had future intentions of marrying Cyril once they had both quit politics.

"Three O'clock on the dot"!

"I can read Cyril, I can read"! Jarwood madly retorted as he looked at his Rolex wristwatch and simultaneously opened the door to find Annette Manoff seated in one of the visitors chairs.

"Who let you in"? Jarwood angrily barked.

"I did"

"I have a mind to call security and have you arrested"!

"On what pretext"?

"Spying"!!

"Oh don't be stupid Harvey we're all in it together"! Manoff fired back with gusto.

"Well then, how about I arrest you for undermining the integrity of the T.A.G. department"?

"How"?

"By performing that ridiculous press release what were you thinking about? You almost destroyed our source of election funds! I just spent days and sleepless nights pacifying the lot! Wake up woman we live in a freely elected dictatorship set up by the funds of big business! No one has any say any more! We're all puppets of the monetary monster! I want you to destroy Napp, do you hear"?

"Yes sir" Manoff feebly replied as she waited for the ringing in her ears to subside.

"Good, how you do it, is your concern, perhaps you could initially try frustrating them out of existence." Jarwood suggested calming down a little.

Manoff thought a while and then answered.

"That could work; I remember a decade ago a similar incident occurred. One of the 'big' companies had a problem with locally manufactured indomethacin; we stopped its production but allowed its import. We then tested every carton at the company's expense that company no longer exists." Manoff replied with a satanic tinge in her voice that complimented the victorious gleam in her eye.

"Then do the same here"!!

"Yes Sir, will that be all Sir"?

"Yes it Will"! Jarwood abruptly commanded as he dismissed her with a wave of his hand. Manoff took her leave and mentally scribbled down her strategy for bringing down Napp Pharmaceuticals once and for all by using every power available to her whether it was state or federal.

"Well that was short, sharp and to the point"! Cyril Pinewood bravely commented.

"It had to be! I am not going to waste or sacrifice thirty years of my life even though it was with the help of the opposition, moulding this country to the point where the control of its population through legislation and both houses of parliament is jeopardised by some incompetent fool"!

"Well said Sir"!

"Thank you"! Jarwood arrogantly answered as he stared into space and reflected on all those he had eliminated over the years.

Disgusted with their double crossing brat like behaviour Jack Stern switched his remote viewing onto Annette Manoff and watched as she set about organising T.A.G officers to take up permanent residence at Napp Pharmaceuticals. Their prime objective it was revealed was to unreasonably delay the release of all products whether they were listed or not, thus frustrating the public at large and adversely affecting the companies cash flow.

"Some people just don't learn"! He correctly thought to himself as he felt the brewing of a huge political Tsunami that was about to engulf Australia.

13

OPTION 1 JUST PASSING THROUGH

In the cellar beneath the cellar of the Ricci mansion the Small Dark Figure had assembled an emergency meeting of all the important members of the Organisation; present were, Louis Badcock, the Ricci twins, the Harshman, members of the PhD clan, their henchmen and a charismatic stranger known only to the Small Dark Figure by the name of Dennis Sauvage.

It had been six months since the disastrous episodes occurred at The Infirmary, Longevity Plus and the Feelgood Pharmacy in Newburn, everything had since been rebuilt; Louis Badcock and the Small Dark Figure had settled their differences with the latter assuming control of all operations.

"I don't know why you called this meeting! Everything as far as I am concerned is proceeding extremely well. I've rebuilt The Infirmary much to the disgust of that obnoxious puritanical Fire Chief and his Town Hall cronies, restocked it with lusty high performing ladies and re-established Longevity Plus's reputation."

"And the big picture Louis"? The Small Dark Figure asked.

"I will open similar complexes around the country."

"Too messy too many people too much opportunity for it to go wrong once again! It must have cost us a fortune to quieten our official friends! How much did it cost us Louis"?

Badcock began to squirm, this was not the time to divulge official figures, instead he side stepped the question and answered as a clever politician.

"Something that will not take long to recoup based upon past and current trends."

"You're speculating, the truth of the matter is, our official friends have yet to decide whether or not to follow through with the prosecutions. No amount of money is going to stop that! They value their freedom more than the petty fortunes you throw at them"!

"Every man has his price"! Badcock firmly retorted.

"And freedom is priceless"!

"At least I've found where that Brendan O'Reilly and Jack Stern character are, their strength's and how I can get my girls back"!

"Causing trouble again? Forget the revenge; it won't do you any good"!

'Rubbish, absolute rubbish"! Badcock reddened with rage.

"Oh yes, tell me what you've done Louis and don't miss anything out"!

"I sent the Harshman to Mauritius and had him observe them at Club Med and other places. I hired two gay assassins to take them out but they failed. The Harsh man saw it all and can report if you wish."

"Well Louis it seems that we have more in common than I thought after all"!

"What do you mean"? Badcock asked looking quite perplexed.

"Our fondness of gay's"!

"I am not that way inclined thank you very much"! Badcock answered indignantly as his face reddened even further.

"Very well, tell me Harshman what have you to report"?

"Thanks to Louis and his contacts I have been able to discover some of the secrets imbedded in the pins that the D-man left behind after his demise." The Small Dark Figure's ears pricked up at this revelation and it began to tingle with anticipatory excitement.

'Tell me more"! It hungrily asked.

"I, given time, will become as powerful as he and even more so if Louis's weird friends' predictions are correct"!

"With such supernatural information we could build an army of supermen, our organisation will become invincible"! The Small Dark Figure wildly postulated as it counted the chickens before they hatched.

"I'm afraid not." The Harshman reluctantly advised.

"What do you mean, not"?

"Louis was quite intuitive on the day and had the foresight to drain as much of the D-man's remaining blood as he could with the help of his friends. I carry some of that blood within me." The Harshman proudly stated.

"You're genetically modified"!

"Increasingly so"! The Harshman replied with heightened pride.

"When will you realise the full extent of your powers"?

"No one does"!

"I would like to be the next"!

"Again I'm afraid not"! The Harshman stated matter of fact.

"I don't like, not! Explain"! The Small Dark Figure angrily commanded.

"One needs to be of a certain twisted mentality that is genetically predetermined."

"Don't I look twisted enough"? The Small Dark Figure asked making reference to its physical and behavioural aspects.

"Perhaps, but if it is environmentally caused then you are not a suitable candidate. Louis's weird friends will need to do tests to determine your eligibility."

"Very well, later perhaps, we have more important matters to discuss." The Small Dark Figure said changing the topic of conversation.

"That would be nice"! Louis Badcock sarcastically agreed and impatiently waited for the next instalment of nonsense to begin as he saw it.

"In order to take the heat off us by our wavering official friends, we have to give them something else to preoccupy their time with, so they lose interest in our pending prosecutions to the point that they will abandon them all together."

"What do you propose"? The Harshman and Badcock asked simultaneously.

"We all know that there is an enormous untapped market available to us, one that is presently supplied by the legal entities, the legal drug dealers."

"Yes, which one might that be"? Badcock asked as he looked around the room and analysed the stone faces of the PhD clan and the smiling face of Dennis Sauvage who was nodding his head in agreement.

"All those individuals who are addicted to anti-depressants and anxiolytics"

"Oh yeah, sounds a bit far fetched to me." Badcock jeered.

'Only because Louis you don't see the big picture"! The Small Dark Figure reiterated. Badcock sat silent as did some of the others and waited for the nonsense as he saw it to pass. The Small Dark Figure flipped open its powerful Hitachi lap top computer and pressed the necessary buttons to activate its infrared function, then the power point presentation began.

On the far white wall via the ceilings digital projector a series of slides flashed that presented accurate statistical data on the different classes of drugs, their effectiveness, addictiveness, unit sales, dollar value in the USA as a whole and state by state.

"This is the market, Ladies and Gentlemen that we need to attack and satisfy."

"And how do you propose we do that"? Badcock asked seemingly disinterested as he sat with crossed arms.

"My gay fried Dennis Sauvage will explain, Ladies and Gentlemen, may I introduce you to Doctor Dennis Sauvage PhD.

"Not another one"! Badcock sighed.

"Be nice Louis for once in your life, be nice! Dennis holds a double doctorate in biochemistry and microbiology"!

"At what University or research facility does he work"? Badcock asked openly growing impatient.

"None"

"Oh wonderful, great, that's all we need an out of work academic" Next you'll be telling us is that his degree's have been purchased on line from some fictitious Internet University called Montana's Camp Queer"! Badcock babbled intent on disgracing the Small Dark Figures endeavours at which Dr Dennis Sauvage stood up, stretched to his full one metre and ninety-three centimetre height and then walked over to Badcock's side of the table and towered over him.

"I'm not out of work! My degree's come from Stanford and Mr Badcock unlike you I have no problem loving males. Give us a Kiss"! Dr Dennis Sauvage quietly stated as he told hold of Badcock's hand and gave it a warm and friendly squeeze.

The Harshman didn't know whether to come to Louis aid or remain seated. Badcock swallowed hard and then uttered in a squeaky voice.

"How can this lovely man help us"?

"Thank you Louis I thought you might come back to your senses, there's nothing like a little sexual persuasion to help the day, is there now"?

"No…?

The Small Dark Figure smiled and proceeded with the next series of slides.

"Here we have Dr Sauvage's life work in a nut shell. As you can see Dr Sauvage postulated that virus's and bacteria invade us for one purpose only, to steal some proportion of our genetic material necessary for their own evolution. This theory was met with scorn made worse by the entrenched anti-gay attitude of university staff. Dennis has found it impossible to find an academic position and therefore has remained with his first love namely theatrical ice-skating. He travels the world with an international ice show while he continues to privately research his theories.

"How can this big bug man help us"? Louis asked as he tried to extract his hand from Dennis's vice like grip.

"Dennis understands bacteria and viruses extremely well almost to the point that he can easily communicate with them albeit via bio-chemical means."

"That's not possible." Badcock argued without any scientific foundation at all.

"Oh Louis, how ignorant you are, you obviously haven't heard of mRna."

"What of it? Sounds more like a rap artist"!

"It stands for messenger ribonucleic acid. Dennis knows how to programme it and in the process talk to the microbes." The Small Dark Figure confidently said.

"Will you tell him to let go"! Badcock pleaded as he desperately tried to free himself.

"Please release him Dennis."

"But he's so cute and what a surname! Bad cock! Does it live up to its reputation"? Dennis Sauvage cheekily asked as he finally released his grip.

Louis blushed at the suggestion and remained tight lipped.

"Enough of the innuendos please sit down Dennis, thank you. The next slide says it all'! The Small Dark Figure exclaimed as the all-important data danced before them.

"As you can plainly see, Dennis has explained DNA which as you know is the genetic foundation of our bodies in a rather controversial manner. To him it represents a biological micro-processor and you can't get more micro than that"! The Small Dark Figure paused mid sentence expecting a wave of laughter at its feeble attempt at humour, there was no response apart from Badcock who simply raised his eyebrows and rolled his eyes out of disgust, disappointed it continued.

"It stores, retrieves, sends out information, receives feed-back and acts accordingly, all via messenger RNA. DNA constantly changes with respect to environmental conditions and adapts the individual depending upon its accumulated knowledge; otherwise it postulates a solution if it is at all capable and that capability is dependent upon the individual's evolutionary status."

"Next you'll be telling us that bugs are intelligent and can play scrabble"! Badcock jeered as he cleaned his hands with his white handkerchief.

"You obviously are not inclined nor suited to the study of science and as a consequence your ignorance precedes you Mr Badcock or should I call you Bad Ass"? Dennis Sauvage rudely remarked quite irritated by Badcock's constant heckling.

"Have you never heard of antibiotic resistant bacteria"? Sauvage glared at Badcock as he asked him directly in a threatening tone of voice.

"Yes I have "! He replied defiantly.

"Good, how do you think they came about"? Unable to answer Badcock forced a downward smile and crossed his arms.

"By the process that is clearly described on the diagram before you, the one that your boss has just spelt out to you"!!!

"Okay, so what of it"? Badcock snapped back.

"We have trained microbes to interfere with the dissolution of tablets and capsules in the gastrointestinal tracts of humans after they have been ingested. Therefore all of the medications in these infected dosage forms will be rendered totally ineffective! This technological breakthrough has been achieved by programming selected bacteria and virus to use all available disintegrants as energy sources and in so doing the microbes alter the disintegrants physio-chemical properties so that they become hydrophobic in nature, meaning they repel water instead of attracting or accepting it. Hence no more swelling of the dosage form, no sudden generation of internal stress forces and no resultant disintegration of the tablet or capsule and; we have taken further steps to ensure absolute success, we have also programmed the same microbes to render gelatine hydrophobic"! Dr Dennis Sauvage simply detailed without making any slightest reference to the genius behind the discoveries.

"It still sounds fu... "! Badcock was about to swear when the Harshman abruptly stopped him by saying

"What he says makes sense Louis."

"Since when have you become educated you dumb bastard"?

"After I came into possession of the pins" The Harshman's statement caused Louis Badcock to think awhile and abandon his aggressive scepticism.

"Thank you Sir." Dennis Sauvage politely said as he took charge and projected the next series of slides that dealt with the logistics of the operation.

"We have to be very careful how we introduce the microbial contaminants which have been stock piled in readiness."

"You've been working on this for some time"? Louis asked of the Small Dark Figure.

"Correct." It replied and with that Badcock sensed his inadequacy and began to sulk.

"Okay to proceed Louis? Yes? Thank you. We thought it best to inoculate all disintegrants whether they be corn or potato starch, tartaric acid, sodium bicarbonate or methyl cellulose at the supplier level. We will do this under the disguise of performing a government audit. Once the contamination reaches the manufacturing facility it will imbed itself in the machinery and be extremely difficult to eradicate. Our friends the PhD clan will help in this respect and in the distribution of our 'antidepressant, anxiolytic." The Small Dark Figure explained as it pointed to the members of the clan after which it continued to say.

"I was expecting you to make some smart remark about PhD

Louis, let me enlighten you before you do, it stands for Phamhung Distribution, its illustrious founder being Mr Nghi Phamhung, a Chinese born Afghanistan national who has revolutionised heroin transportation worldwide.

"We have never ever been involved with heroin." Badcock aggressively remarked as he took an instant dislike to the Chinese businessman.

"And we never will. Phamhung will assist us with the marketing of our new age antidepressant which is not based upon heroin nor any other opiate or anything that the pharmaceutical companies presently manufacture, it is a by product of our microbial friends." Badcock was tempted to say "More nonsense" but refrained from doing so.

"Dennis will explain the concept." The Small Dark Figure then said. "mRNA is too small a molecule to have any pharmacological effect, therefore it needs to hold hands and develop a strong structure that can act as a Neuro-transmitter within the brain. The best microbial factory for this task is a fungus and the best fungus is.........Louis.... hum"?

"Candida"

"Very funny Louis, try again, nice girl's name though."

"Mushrooms" Louis stabbed in the dark.

"Excellent, now there's a clever chap! So as not to disappoint you we do not use the magical variety but the common garden kind, with one exception, instead of producing black spores it gives white dust full of mRNA, the very kind that we're after"! Dennis proudly stated as he produced a small 15ml amber dropper bottle from the left inside breast pocket of his Harris Tweed jacket complete with customary elbow patches standard code of attire for gifted academics. He then described the bottles contents.

"In here Ladies and Gentlemen we have the elixir of happiness. Two drops under the tongue twice a day completely absorbed sublingually, straight into the blood stream, no first pass hepatic metabolism, pure unadulterated mRNA, our mRNA coursing its way to the receptive target organs."

"What do you call it"? Badcock sneered.

"Hapgen, short for happy genes, Mr Badcock, perhaps you should try some"!

"No thank you! If I want that sort of thing I'd rather sleep with one of my ladies of the night. A different woman each time brings me much…. "

"Heartache I would suggest! You seem the possessive type Louis. I think you're in need of a little stability in you life"! Dennis Sauvage summed up.

"Never! If anyone has caused me to feel unstable it's you"! Badcock uncontrollably shouted as he pointed to the Small Dark Figure.

"It all makes sense now! You syphoned off a considerable percentage of the fortune from my operations in Newburn to fund this project of yours and yes I know why you're doing it; to get into the inner circle of Dot.org." Badcock continued to shout.

"Calm down Louis, I was going to take you with me." The Small Dark Figure unconvincingly said.

"Rubbish! I don't believe you! There's only one available place and you want it for yourself! What do you expect me to do? Sit on your lap"?

Badcock screamed as he jumped to his feet and shook his fist at the Small Dark Figure who remained outwardly calm under the circumstances.

"I'm going back to the real world, I'll make it work, you'll see"! Were Badcock's last words before he charged out of the cellar complex and run up the chimney's internal fire stairs. It was then that one of the PhD clan members spoke, none other than its founder Mr Nghi Phamhung.

"I detect a tension between you two"!

"It has persisted for some time." The Small Dark Figure explained.

"Why is that"?

"We come from rival families."

"One of which sits in the inner circle"

"Your deduction is accurate Nghi Phamhung."

"Hummmm, your problem not mine, tell me more about RNA gay one." Phamhung said in a clipped Chinese accent as he turned towards Dennis Sauvage.

"Glad to Sir; Ribose Nucleic acid is already available in a number of over the counter medications in Europe and the USA. It has been extracted from beer and bread yeasts and used in the treatment of mental retardation and to improve memory in senile dementia. A Splenic source is indicated for the treatment of hepatitis and cancer. As such it is not specific enough and that is why I centred on its messenger variant, the bringer of good news."

Phamhung then signalled for Dr Sauvage to pass the amber dropper bottle across, he studied its precious contents for a few moments as his henchmen looked on knowing full well that he had already worked out the complete marketing strategy.

"This will be no underground or backyard operation. The present name of the product will become the manufacturer. The product will be renamed as a natural dietary nutritional supplement based on brewers yeast and mushroom; it will be sold as a concentrated extract, full of health giving benefits. The promotional pamphlet will give the consumer the impression that it will restore full vitality and happiness.

Some mention of an ancient re-balancing formula will be made. It will be distributed using the multi-level marketing system so that many will benefit. The colours of the label and leaflets will suggest honesty, reliability, the truth. Are you coming with me on this" Phamhung then asked.

"Yes." The Small Dark Figure answered for all.

"Good! Can you supply on demand"? To which the Small Dark Figure looked to Dr Dennis Sauvage for guidance.

"That is not a problem. We have already converted much of Dot.org's farm main building into a Hapgen facility. Inside we have assembled a number of large polymerase chain reactors which can multiply the mRNA exponentially given the necessary ingredients required for the precise biochemical process." Dr Sauvage outlined.

"And the mushrooms"

"These have been fooled into believing that they are in a constant state of sporing. No problems there"! Dennis Sauvage confidently replied

"Providing they continue to believe"!

"They won't revert." Dennis confidently asserted.

"That's not what I have read." Phamhung countered.

"Your source Sir"

"Private researchers like yourself"

"I shall remain diligent"! Dennis Sauvage assured Phamhung as he began to speculate about the illicit and unethical research that the shady Asian might have been involved in.

"No more time for cool behaviour"! Phamhung rasped.

"I can manage to be in two places at once." Dennis Sauvage firmly replied in a tone of voice that indicated his passionate love of the ice.

"Hum, I don't know whether I like that! We will see"! Phamhung philosophised as he stared at the Small Dark Figure. "When do we begin"? He then asked. The greed of the Small Dark Figure wanted it to be yesterday, its patience said day after tomorrow and its intelligence was still calculating.

"May I suggest November 2nd." The Harshman put forward.

"You have the floor, developing one, tell us more." Nghi Phamhung commanded assertively.

"On that date there will occur a major economic disturbance in Australia and England as a result of terrorist activity upon the pharmaceutical industry. It will continue to grow and we may see the downfall of both governmental systems"!

"Where did you get this startling information from"? Phamhung barked impatiently with raised eyebrows as he thought that his spy network had failed him.

"I'd rather not say." The Harshman reluctantly replied.

"Why"!

"Because you may not believe"!

"Then it is not based upon earthly facts. Am I right'?

"You are." The Harshman answered completely unafraid of the self opinionated Asian.

'Do not take me for a narrow-minded cold-blooded businessman, my Chinese ancestry has taught me much about the metaphysical world"!

Sensing that Phamhung was receptive, the Harshman cleared his throat, gathered his astral experiences and gave a short description of the future event.

"There is a place where the soul goes during the time the body sleeps, it is known as the Field of Dreams. There the souls determine the future of the physical world in the days or months and years to come. On one occasion I encountered the soul of one who has brought peace to his part of the world and I understood that he wishes to cause grief to all those who brought much harm and sorrow to his people. He seeks revenge, by what means I could not fathom, all that I could gleam was the date, symbolic in itself and associated with an international horse race. In Australia one such event occurs. If we coincide with that, then the local authorities may conclude that all three are related. They will not suspect us at all, especially as we have changed the nature of our goods from pharmaceutical to purely natural."

"A very clever military manoeuvre, we will prepare November 2nd as the launch date, my deputies here will instruct you in due course as to how much Hapgen we will require and how much of the mRNA needed to sabotage the pharmaceutical companies manufacturing facilities. The price of Hapgen is not an issue, however I caution you not to become over zealous in your ambition to succeed as greed destroys everything." Phamhung concluded, he then spoke in Chinese to his deputies giving explicit orders that he wished for them to follow accurately.

14

PLAN OF ATTACK OPTION 2 SPIRITUAL REVENGE

There was no doubt in Franck Max Climax's mind that whoever was guiding him from above intended him to strike at the pharmaceutical industry. The past days had certainly indicated that and his exclusive copy of the Koran suggested it as well; for it was written that the Entity who had created the world did so in such a fashion so as to ensure that for every animated being there was a natural cure available for everyone of their ailments.

Lumina was probably involved with his spiritual guides. She came to seek his assistance, she wanted him to teach about plants, but Franck knew that the lessons would fall upon deaf ears, for those who ran the established traditional medical industries instilled and spread deafness through their arrogant means, by the fear of change and just by plain greed. Necessity the mother of invention, the driving force behind invention and discovery had to be employed. To shut down the entire drug industry globally was an over whelming task but not impossible. The question was how rather than why, for the latter had already been answered. Franck realised that no matter which avenue he took it would be labelled as an act of terrorism, for all those who come to reform are perceived as such by those in power. Even revolutionism attracted that description to itself.

Franck wished to avoid violence and loss of life however in this instance that ideal would be impossible to satisfy, for the task at hand when implemented would cause immense widespread suffering. He wept at the prospect.

Expedita had provided him with the mechanism of action but not the firepower. There were too many targets; even the alternate medicines were guilty of misleading consumers as to their effectives. To attack or sabotage individual factories was to stir up a multitude of hornet nests.

Extremists had tried in the past by tampering with goods, introducing poisons or issuing threats, to no avail; temporary, fleeting results; long-term incarceration was always the most likely endings for those found out. There had to be a different way, a dramatic theatrical sweep is what Franck sought, something that could and would cause permanent change.

"Necessity, Necessity, Necessity, where do you hide"? Every day he would repeatedly question until his weary thoughts caused him to fall asleep.

The passing days did not provide any solutions, all of his 'friends' it seemed deliberately avoided him respecting his need for privacy. Even his beloved Squirrel's paid him no heed. Franck Max Climax became a lonely solitary man, an outcast of society, a recluse imprisoned by the problem at hand. He did not understand why help was not forthcoming. Instant Karmic Response did not react when he invoked it and he felt as though the answer was behind him and in him all the time. It was not until he saw his own reflection in the full length bathroom mirror one early morning after he had showered that he uncovered the first clue; the markings on his back. In Roman numerals the number 1915 was present.

"What does 1915 mean? What's so significant about that year? What must I learn from its contents? He questioned himself as he felt the raised keloid tissue.

"A whole year to examine, what is it that I must research? Is it a world, industrial, political or science event? Perhaps a brief summary, an overview will give me some idea or the answer? No Time for breakfast, just me and my computer, together we will search for the answers."

"But not so my enlightened electronic friend" Was his conclusion mid afternoon after nine hours of intense dedication. "I wish I knew what 1915 points to." Franck sighed. "I wish I knew where to look." He sighed again and then he slapped himself on his forehead and exclaimed "How stupid, what a fool I've been, my Koran always tells me" Franck thought out aloud as he freed himself from his computer workstation and reached out for the precious book that he always kept close at hand. Franck kissed its black leather cover and solemnly performed his own manual ritual. He then slowly flicked through its pages until he deeply believed it would stop him at the correct page, which it did. However there was an anomaly.

There was no doubt in his mind that the pages had been previously correctly reassembled in proper numerical order, yet the page was numbered 1314, not 348 as it was meant to be. Franck examined the previous page which bore the number 347, the page after 348 was numbered 9, the page after bore 2113, followed by 3113, 1621 and finally 19, then the correct sequence continued.

"Do all of these years have something in common with each other? How the hell am I supposed to find that out? It will take me an eternity! This is impossible! What do I have to work with, let me see; 1915, 1314, 9, 2113, 3113, 1621 and 19. A digital sequence, something left behind for me to decode. What am I looking for? Is it a mathematical problem? Do I use quadratic equations, calculus or do the numbers stand for something else? Sometimes it is better to stop analysing and walk away, perhaps food, that's it food, my brain needs nourishment. A bowl of fresh fruit with ice cream, that sounds good, awfully good as Lord Tingle might say, right then, off to the larder." Minutes later with a kaleidoscope of sustenance before him; which he eagerly devoured, to say the least Franck Max Climax was heard to say.

"Lovely vanilla ice cream; delicious health giving purifying berries, yum, blueberries, strawberries, raspberries, loganberries, absolutely wonderful, the A B C of good health. Wait a minute what did I just say, the A B C, the alphabet, twenty six letters in total from one to twenty six, a digital sequence representing letters of the alphabet, that's it! Mathematical words, let's try it"! Franck continued to talk out aloud as he wrote down the letters of the English alphabet and assigned a number to each.

"What do I have here"? He whispered as he played with numbers.

'Let me see. I'm 1915; perhaps I'm the leader, then 1314, 9, 2113, 3113, that's strange? 1621and 19 I am limited by 1 to 26, so can't have 91 as a number for a letter, I'll have to keep within those parameters, Okay"? He asked himself. "Okay, then we'll probably get the following letters; s , o , m , n , I , b , a , a , c , c , a , a , c , a , f , b , a , s. Scrabble nightmare! This is too much for me! Let's try again, I think I'm comfortable with s o m n, lets try more double digits, then we get I , u , m , good, that spells somnium. Strange word or do I toy around with the letters? No! See what the next numerical sequence translates into; 3113, 1621, 19, it can't be 31 so let's try 3, 11, 3 this gives me c, k, c and 1621, 19 gives me p, u, s, m, puss in boots? Hey!

C, k, c, pus not good to form a word out of, the first three must be wrong, what if it were c, a, m, puscam, not quite. Rearranging we can have, pamcus, sucamp, campsu, campus. Somnium campus; looks good, sounds good, probably an ancient language, now my clever electronic friend translate it into English for." Franck said as he reacted intimately with the computer terminal.

"Dream plain, plain of dreams, esoterical, whimsical…mystical …. tangible; I wonder? How do I access it? I ask you! Natural or enchanted sleep, which one will it be? If it be the latter what spell do I cast? Allah forgive me I should have said prayer"! Franck Max Climax apologetically exclaimed as he mentally grasped for salvation.

"Another hurdle to leap, I know the name of the place but not where it is. How do I get there? What is it about dreams that I do not understand? Do I have to be asleep to access it? What's wrong with day dreaming"? Franck attempted to access the Field of Dreams by activating his 'epileptic fits' but to no avail. His mind wandered aimlessly, uncertain of what it was looking for and then he tried to daydream and failed, as he was not very good at it. Imagination was not one of his fortes.

The afternoon dragged on, the air in his apartment became stuffy, overloaded with his expended energy it began to assume a cloud like appearance, warm, comforting, soporific, it enticed its inhabitant to cat nap. Franck's eyes grew weary, his body similarly so, his head wobbled rhythmically to the words that he repeatedly chanted.

"Somnium campus, Somnium campus, Somnium, campus……….."

The Field reacted and pulled his soul towards it. As Franck's soul 'walked' through the spiritual ether it encountered three separate visions. At first he could detect the smell of gas amongst the forest of trees that he was in. A Stranger ahead of him held a can, sprayed the substance within and attempted to ignite it.

"Why does he seek to hurt me"? Franck anguished as he saw the gas explode and its flames rush towards him with a ferocity that threatened to incinerate him, then he was safe transported by hands unseen. He stood perched on a high brick fence that separated two houses. To his right the neighbours had just returned in their car from doing the weekly household shopping, they exchanged pleas-antries with Franck when suddenly he was repeatedly 'stung' by minute particles of 'flying fire' that fell in countless numbers from the dark cloudy sky overhead.

"Meteorites"! He shouted, "We're being bombarded, the end is at hand"! He panicked but he shouldn't have for the fiery storm abruptly ended as it had commenced and was replaced by a flood of water. From where he was standing in the distance he could see the city's central business district submerged under a torrent of water, which rapidly spread into the surrounding suburban districts and towards him. Then there was peace.

"Father, Father, where are you hiding"? He sung out as he played the game of Hide and Seek as a young child in the grounds of his deceased father's estate, except his father in real life never achieved such success. There was no answer to his constant pleas and Franck relived the pain of his early childhood when his father went away.

"Please Father, I need you, I do, I want to touch you, hold you, please! Where are you? Come to me please"! He sobbed as he fell to his knees and watched his teardrops fall upon the lush grass. Cold and alone he found the strength to straighten up and face the cruel world that awaited him. His father's mansion was a large disused hotel in a sad state of disrepair. Franck stood up and gingerly walked towards it as he whimpered to himself.

"I am strong, I can survive."

Windows were smashed, doors hung off their hinges, paint, plaster and wallpaper had peeled off the walls and ceilings, cobwebs, dust and bird droppings adorned everything else. Not exactly inviting to those who sought perfection; but heaven to those who had nothing below nothing. As He stepped inside the floorboards creaked and he swore that he heard the words,

"You have entered the House of Puzzles." spoken in a low hush.

Franck the child stopped and innocently gazed at his eerie surroundings and became somewhat afraid. He mustered the courage of his convictions and took another step forward again the floorboards reacted and he heard.

"The treasures you seek..." Franck halted and the words halted. He took another step and the words recommenced.

"....are located in the place of dangerous liaisons"! He instantly thought that every suite in the hotel could easily fulfil that definition, more input was required Franck took another step forward.

"Fleeting they might be, everlasting they will always be. Beware"!

Not satisfied, he took another step forward and was met with silence. Franck agitated the floorboards again and silence was the reply. Obviously the cryptic statement implied short-lived relationships, the question was how short? A day, an hour a brief moment or two and yet it also suggested permanency which did not make sense.

'Father, my father, how I wish you were there when I grew up. If this be your house help me once for my life has been a miserable empty void without you. Father"!!!! He shouted at the top of his voice. The sound reverberated and echoed throughout the rooms. The chandeliers clinkered and swayed in defiant amusement as wind chimes do during nature's fury.

Franck stood still, listened and realised that this was the clue to solving the enigmatic statement. He walked about the hotel's foyer and searched for the building's directory, which had fallen from its place on the wall next to the elevators and lay hidden from view beneath a pile of disused furniture. Disappointed that he could not locate it Franck decided to ascend the emergency stairs and see if there was another on the first floor. Gladly there it was on the wall facing the top of the stairs.

"Golden Ballroom West Wing Level three" Is what he wanted to read and with a song in his heart he skipped towards the room of dangers. The West Wing's corridor leading up to the main entrance of the Ballroom was extremely dark and gloomy.

"Not a safe place to be in"! Franck thought as he scampered towards the doors and burst them open with his youthful energy.

The interior of the Ballroom was in total contrast to the rest of the building, pristine, bright, airy and welcoming.

"There's no one here, what is this nonsense? The treasures I seek are located here. This can't be the place. Damn it I got it wrong"! Franck cursed to himself as he lowered his head in defeat.

"Don't be so sad, let's play"!

"Uh! Who said that"? Franck somewhat startled asked as he expected the floorboards were at it again.

"Hello my name is Marshall." A boy replied identical in size and appearance to Franck.

"That was my father's name"!

"Then I must be him"!

"You can't be, you're not old enough"! Franck argued as he studied the young lad.

"Hum, I was hoping you had learnt by now, obviously you haven't"!

"What do you mean, haven't? I've seen and learnt so much more in comparison to my fellow humans."

"That is true." Marshall agreed and then asked "But have you leant about the mansions of the soul and the way of the spirits"?

"No." Franck reluctantly answered.

"Then it is time my son, it is time"!

"Are you really my dad"?

"I am and I see that you are having difficulty with the concept it's really very simple and easy to understand. We spirits do not age, we remain the same, we're all children, full of imagination that feeds and runs the universe. Have you ever played Mothers and Fathers when your body was small"?

"No, but I watched others, I thought it was such a silly game largely because I had no Dad therefore I couldn't relate to the role." Franck regretfully replied.

"Sorry about that. My earthly life was meant to be short in preparation for your earthly existence." Marshall stated as a matter of fact.

"What about the pain"? Franck angrily asked

'It goes away, come on lets play, after all you came for a purpose, which is to alleviate suffering. Is that right"?

"Yes." Franck agreed

"The suffering of children"! Marshall emphasized as he took

Franck's hand and led him through a doorway into the unknown. They had gone from one pristine area into one that was even more so.

"Is this the Field of Dreams"? Franck cautiously asked.

"That it is, careful where you step, better if we keep to the edges, because once you step onto the board without purpose you are likely to change the course of history without knowing it."

"Is this where the future is worked out"?

"Some would like to think that, but there is more to it" Marshall explained as he guided Franck.

"It looks like a huge chess board."

"Not everyone plays" Marshall explained. The statement threw Franck's mind into a state of mild confusion.

"Look around you and see what you can see." Franck obeyed and studied his surroundings. He saw the vast expanse of the chessboard, its players so he thought its observers and then an endless stream of what appeared to be bundles of 'optic fibres' flowing past. The observers floated in and around the chessboard but never touched it, behind them it appeared was a window though which another group of highly intelligent beings watched.

"Is that an electricity or telephone cable"? Franck asked as he pointed to the bundles of 'optic fibres'.

'Neither; these are the silver cords of life that attach your soul to your physical body."

"Where do they go"?

"Home"! Marshall replied.

"But Earth is home"! Franck boldly and ignorantly asserted.

"Earth is nothing more than a spherical laboratory; where life experiments with Transpermia; meaning it is seeded by life forms outside of it. Many souls come from other celestial bodies throughout the universe. When their bodies' sleep, they escape home to be confronted or reassured that what they are doing is good, otherwise they come here to cause future events or observe the process of their creation. Have you ever thought that you were in two places at once or that you were somewhere else and that was the reason why you couldn't find something that you were looking for'?

"On reflection it has often happened to me." Franck agreed and it made him think even further which made him say. "That would suggest to me that heaven is something else."

"Quite right; but we are straying away from the true purpose of your visit, my son. Why have you come here? What is your wish?"

"To shut down all drug manufacture in Australia and England"! The requests intention clearly caused the intelligent beings behind the window to become rather agitated, something that Marshall keenly observed.

"Do you know what you are asking for and the dire consequences it will have on both of the respective populations"?

"I do." Franck solemnly answered as though he was making a marital vow.

"Are you willing to suffer pain beyond your wildest imagination as compensatory payment"?

"I am" Franck once again solemnly replied as the eager groom.

"Then you have one of two choices; enter the Field of Dreams, assume the identity of one of the power figures, plead you case and be prepared to die for your cause or approach those behind the window who cannot interfere with the workings of the world."

"I don't believe that"! Franck answered back. "It has come time for them to act! The world has reached such a level of immoral decay that something must be done to reverse it! I do not think I can achieve anything in that seething mass on the board before me irrespective of how powerful a figure I assume. Those on the other side of the window I conclude must be in heaven, they have achieved; otherwise they would not be there. Correct? They have the power to help correct? But they have not done so for almost two thousand years. Why allow it"? Franck stammered with rage.

"Because, otherwise they would not achieve"! Marshall answered defiantly.

"Then heaven needs to change its rules"!

"You will do that"? Marshall teased

"I am prepared to"!

"To the board, Mr Franck Max Climax, prepare to become a pawn." Marshall commanded.

Franck courageously obeyed and followed closely behind his father. Celestial chess was unlike anything he had experienced before, but then he had no prior recollection of his previous encounters on the Field of Dreams.

Pawns came in a multitude of configurations that suited the intention of the soul. Franck found one that mirrored his needs and stepped onto the board.

His chosen attire instantly came alive and interacted with thousands of other players, he quickly realised that each of his moves was translated into the reality of the physical world. As he strongly put forward his proposition and the reasons behind it the resistance he met was devastating. His pawn was immediately surrounded by sword wielding bishops and hacked to pieces. Someone on earth died and Franck found himself behind the window amongst the intelligent beings.

"Am I dead"? Franck asked as he examined himself, his surroundings and those around him, who remained silent, still and smiled warmly at him.

"This is frustrating! I know that I'm the intruder but I wasn't expecting to be eliminated so quickly. What happens next"? Franck asked in a restrained manner. Again silence and warm smiles were all that he received. Understanding that it was expected of him to remain still Franck did so and took a better look at his confines he then heard the following.

"You are not behind a window as it appears from the other side, you are in fact inside of it and furthermore a window it is not, to the floor it belongs. You are in limbo as we're until you lost and became our salvation and in doing so we shall assist you in fulfilling your desires." The intelligent beings said collectively without moving their lips.

"How can my defeat be your salvation"? Franck queried.

"Because no one ever losses on the Field of Dreams. Irrespective of your personal outcome, by doing battle you have left behind an imprint, one that is never forgotten, given time it will be recognised and taken up by someone else. The geniuses of the world are never usually recognised during their lifetime; however the imprints that they leave behind set the stage for future events. They remain the quiet achievers. Those that accomplish great things in their own time are usually thieves and vagabonds in the political sense and it is these that allow the dead to have their final say on the Field of Dreams." This last point enthralled Franck and he patiently waited for them to explain.

"The dead have thirty calendar days to walk the earth and go through the process of self examination before either coming here and returning to their true homes or advancing to the next level of spiritual existence. Many choose to enter the Field of Dreams and based on their earthly experiences fight to make the earth a better place in which to live."

"Where do I find these people"? Franck eagerly asked concluding that this was the avenue of his future success.

"They are easily identified by their dimness, meaning that they are not as bright as we"!

Franck took a proper moment to analyse those who conversed and found them to be children as his father Marshall was, except they in contrast possessed an extraordinary clarity of depth, something that his father did not. He also deduced that they were a collection of geniuses whose life's work had gone unnoticed and that they had decided to accept imprisonment as a means of obtaining a second chance to change the world. The question was how would they achieve this?

"We understand your quest; you will need to attract sufficient numbers of them to yourself to achieve your goal." The group said.

197

"Not possible! I am imprisoned like you"!

"Remember what we said, your loss is our salvation"! Franck nodded in agreement as though he understood.

"Then prepare to do battle! Come join hands with us and make our circle complete. You are one of us now." Franck obeyed and felt the surge of an incredible love course through his entire being. The window lifted, tilted this way and that before it shuddered and broke free from its moorings and fell like an inconspicuous dust particle from the sky. It danced and tiptoed on the political wavefronts above the Field of Dreams and searched for the imprint that was left behind by a clairvoyant who predicted one hundred years previously of the adverse effects that future chemical treatments for the human race would have. Included in his message was the remedy, the reversal of the greed driven affliction. Every trick had been used by the Masters of Affliction to distort the identity and location of this imprint in the hope that its importance would be lost forever.

"This is impossible, we will never find it"! Franck sighed.

"Little faith delays things! This ship is programmed to find it, let it perform its duty"! The intelligent ones directed.

"Very well" Franck hesitantly replied as he strengthened his grip with those that he held hands with. Then there was silence followed by a blinding flash of light that reduced everything into a sea of tranquillity. Nothing moved everyone was still in complete abeyance of the event.

The intelligent ones smiled and whispered. "Divine intervention at last."!

"Was that God"? Franck exclaimed as he gazed upon the sea of tranquillity.

"No just one of His rebalancing mechanisms, Le Chatelier's Principle. Listen to the music." The intelligent ones thoughtfully explained.

Franck pricked up his ears and listened as the imprints of the eons orchestrated their messages of destruction and rebirth throughout the Field of Dreams. The window that Franck and his companions were in reacted to the various notes and its glass emitted a sound of its own like a child answering its parent's call. Franck and the intelligent ones happily hummed along as they felt that success was only a heartbeat away. Like a mother welcoming its lost child home, the imprint embraced the window's occupants, the intelligent ones were free once again, Franck had his information and the clairvoyants prophesy came true.

Franck once again found himself in the ballroom of his father's mansion. This time it was not empty, this time people and merriment filled it completely, Marshall stood unnoticed by Franck's side.

"Exciting journey" He asked as he mentally applauded the scene before them.

"It was fantastic"! Franck enthusiastically replied as he relived the extraordinary experience.

"Made good use of it and what it provides"

"I shall." Franck Max Climax sincerely replied as he continued to dwell on the subject matter.

"All those before you, will make certain that your dream is realized. The event will not happen globally, that is not its intention, it will be restricted to England and Australia, its timing will coincide with the revenge of those dearly departed who have become increasingly outraged at those who favour horse racing in preference to their spiritual obligations in remembering the Feast Days of All Saints and All Souls. Man must no longer prey on himself or his own kind; he needs to relearn the lesson of love in the physical realm for if he does not then it may be too late once he reaches the spiritual" Franck nodded his head, to signify his understanding and then he asked.

"How will my quest be satisfied"?

"There will occur a genetic paradigm shift that will render all synthetic medications inactive in both man and beast"!

"I thought spirits were not allowed to interfere with the workings of the world"? Franck stated quite confused.

"Sometimes it is necessary to correct"! That was all that Franck Max Climax was allowed to hear; next he heard; drip…drip… thump…thump… restriction….drip….drip….thump….thump… restriction, A vivid memory from the past except this time it was very different. This time Franck embraced it wholeheartedly because he knew it represented his lifeline to the physical world, embellished with the quiet on goings of various physiological monitors.

The bedroom was warm, inviting, peaceful, joyful a tribute to those who had looked after him. Flowers of many varieties adorned every table, silver bowls of fruit sat proudly next to them, almost as offerings to the Gods, all that was missing were burning sticks of incense and the squirrels who came to pillage and plunder and make a mockery of people belief's.

Franck gave a sigh of relief and accepted all of the intravenous tubes that were attached to him, for they delivered the necessary par-enteral nutrition that had kept him alive for the past thirteen days, a time confirmed by the date on the bedside clock radio. Franck caught his reflection in the dressing tables mirror and barely recognised himself. He had lost almost 30% of his body mass. Even though he appeared drawn and gaunt he still maintained a healthy glow.

This time he did not wonder who had ministered to him, neither did he fear who his intruders might have been, instead he gave sincere thanks and then a most peculiar thing happened all those whom he had met in his father's mansion appeared before him.

Franck thought that this was the end of his life and that his life was flashing before him. However it was not, for it was the reverse; it was the pre-life exposure which many privileged souls remember.

You may question this as it suggests that for some; life is pre-determined, fatalistic, but it is not; however having said that; it is important to realise that in order to achieve life's tests it is important to meet the right people.

Those who remember pass with distinction, those who do not flounder.

15

SELF EXAMINATION

They say that abstinence makes the heart grow fonder, but what if it is confronted by familiarity that breeds contempt; surely there exists an avenue, a balance that allows the relationship to survive indefinitely.

In Yvette's mind there was no doubt that Mr Jack Stern was the first proper gentleman that she had ever met who was not a priest and whilst she was attracted to him deep down in her heart she felt that her ultimate destiny in life was to be married to a man of the cloth. It was not an immoral obsession but rather an intuitive feeling, a clairvoyant prediction that demanded satisfaction.

It was not Yvette's intention to hunt down a priest and seduce him into marrying her; this was not her disposition. She was resigned to wait patiently until he, that is the one, arrived and recognised her as being his true eternal soul mate, things would then follow their course naturally.It was a great pity that the admirable Jack Stern was not suitably qualified.

Both he and Brendan O'Reilly were on equal footing, each had rescued Yvette from extreme danger and serious harm and each was extremely handsome, this is where the similarities ended.

Brendan was a quiet man of extraordinary compassion and love, a tad nervous about his newfound abilities, in her eyes he stood as a highly educated gentleman passionate about his vocation. Whereas Mr Jack Stern whilst sharing the same qualities, outwardly brimmed with supreme confidence, sarcastic at times and possessed an unusual humorous theatrical ability that made it impossible for the observer to separate the actor from the individual. Jack definitely made Yvette feel good, in a comforting fashion, like a father or bodyguard; whereas Brendan instilled safety and completeness.

Yvette felt uncertain about Mr Stern, there was so much about him that she didn't understand or know. Their moments together were always pleasantly memorable, however there was something missing.

Yvette felt that she was better for him then vice-versa and in some respects he appeared to be toying with her. There was also another aspect that she dwelled on and that was the way in which each held her in their arms. Jack's embrace was more like that of a close friend or a family member whereas Brendan's was an encounter to lust after. It was on the dance floor that Yvette first experienced the magic of being held by the handsome Father Brendan O'Reilly, it approximated the ecstasy that she often experienced when in deep prayer before the Blessed Virgin's statue.

In the Church of the Coloured Sands Yvette sat as an obedient schoolgirl before the meticulously carved white marble statue of the Virgin which was gowned in ornate blue and gold cloth and she listened to the whisperings of the divine creature. Yvette cast her mind back to her happy childhood and gave thanks for the foster parents who raised her lovingly and never let on that she was adopted, something that she had worked out for herself over the years but remained silent on the matter. She was also profoundly grateful that her foster father never took sexual advantage of her. He was a fine upstanding man who respected the rights of others and would often go to extreme lengths to safeguard them. Deeply religious he taught

Yvette how to pray and in the process introduced her to the mystical ways that stimulated and fed her supernatural abilities, which she understood to be universally normal.

Yvette learnt from a young age to see and hear differently and only discussed her experiences with her foster father who fully comprehended and further encouraged her sensory adventures without feeling jealous at the thought that he could not partake of such glories. He constantly reminded Yvette to keep these mysteries to herself for the world was and is not a safe place for such gifted people. This resulted in Yvette becoming rather reserved and shy but not afraid. She grew into a beautiful woman, blessed with fine features, porcelain like skin, light chestnut coloured hair and hypnotic aqua-green eyes. Yvette did moderately well at school but shunned much of the education thrown at her for she rightly concluded it was all based on man made theories and did not coincide with what she had learnt during her periods of meaningful prayer.

On one such occasion she was allowed to see her biological mother and father, both of whom had been tragically killed during a mindless terrorist bomb attack in central France when Yvette was barely twelve months of age.

She concluded that she was always protected from above and below as well.

The fundamental reason for Yvette being drawn to men of the cloth was that she wanted to share her life with one who had experienced similar events to herself. Sadly she remembered the statistics that a seventy-year-old priest once related to her about his graduating class of 1977. Of the twenty five newly ordained hopefuls, one died within twelve months from terminal pancreatic cancer, fourteen left the priesthood over the next twenty years and walked the face of the earth aimlessly leaving ten to carry on the good work.

The fourteen who had decided to leave did so of their own free will and volition. Each subsequently married and each marriage lasted without incident. Although the sample size was small it nevertheless suggested that the training each received in the Seminary prepared them in all aspects of love. The only arena that it faltered was within the Church itself, being unable to satisfy all of its priests' wishes and desires. Not one of the fourteen married their housekeepers or anyone in the parish, each reinvented themselves and found someone new.

Both Brendan and Jack were new; the latter was the impostor or was he, for without a doubt he possessed a genuine knowledge of love, however Mr Jack Stern did frustrate Yvette sexually after all this time he had not made any sexual advances and this troubled her. Did he consider her sexually unattractive? Was he gay or was he merely being patient? It was true that she herself did not offer any encouragement and perhaps this is where the dilemma lay. Yvette needed time to think, the experience at Mauritius had been beyond belief and she was both moved and touched by being the catalyst that accelerated the conversion of the Catholic Church's Decay.

"Is it my purpose to show others the way? Do I have to sacrifice my happiness in the process? Will my gifts cause me to become an outcast, a hermit, a freak"? Yvette lowered her head into her warm soft hands and felt her tears of emotional distress fall from her sorrowful eyes.

"Oh my father, my dear father, how I miss our intimate talks, our walks through the National park, the touch of your hand, your cute wrinkled smile. I need to come home. I need your guidance to enable me to see for myself. I am so good at doing it for others, now it is time for me to do it for myself. I need to know and with that Yvette made the sign of the cross, kissed the silver Rosary beads that she held in her hands and slowly made her way out of the church.

Brendan was seated in one of the pews close by, he watched as Yvette left the church and wished that he was no longer a priest. Brendan had also been tussling with his emotions, for the women of Mauritius had started to engage him. It was the same as before, the telephone calls at all hours of the day, any silly excuse to talk with him, discrete and indiscrete notes left frequently in the collection baskets at Mass, under the presbytery door, in the letter box and confession times became a real chore. Thankfully he was able to contend with it all and contain it by the use of his newly discovered powers.

Voluntary invisibility, the gift of travelling by thought and bi-location helped to maintain stability, take the pressure off and avoid the stalkers. They were much worse here than back at home.

"Ah home! I wonder if there exists a fragment there that needs to be discovered. How many fragments are there before the Catholic Church is whole again? Certainly the one that was buried here is the encyclopaedia of love." H thought as he reflected on his seminary days and his mentor Father Liam Mackeral. "Curious name for a priest" he often thought "But he epitomized love, he knew how to distil, concentrate and infuse it into the human vessel, Father Mackeral was the ultimate spiritual alchemist! We need more people like him in the church who know how to pick the essences of love and blend them into the universal Parfum that welds people together.

I think I understand why woman are after me; all they seek is the Parfum; unfortunately they don't know it because they do not know or comprehend their own makeup and its subtleties. In order to obtain the rare and elusive human fragrance they offer sex as bait, payment and reward in return."

Brendan convinced himself that his hypothesis allowed him to understand woman once and for all and the nature of their overwhelming attraction towards him, however one question remained, was the perfume of love that he possessed universale? For the first time in his life Brendan felt at ease with his own sexuality and the opposite sex; this relaxation would enable him to explore future and present relationships with a sense of freedom and greater intensity. He never perceived the prostitutes that he had helped to rescue from The Infirmary at Newburn as being a treat to him, on the contrary he felt perfectly at ease with them and it was probably this that helped him all along to develop this side of his personality. As long as they were at his side, the stalkers would he naively concluded exasperate themselves, lose interest and give up the case.

The idea that other fragments existed throughout the world fascinated him and it made him wonder if his earthly purpose was to breathe new life into his beloved Catholic Church by resurrecting that which had been buried.

If this were true he would have to find a worthy successor to take over the reigns of the Church of the Coloured Sands, out of the corner of his eye Brendan saw that this was unexpectedly taking place.

"Come on, drink man, it won't kill you"! Jack sternly commanded as he took hold of Father Bogliani's hand and dipped it into the Holy Font's waters.

"I can't I'm not good enough; I'm not worthy"! Bogliani the drama queen shouted back.

"Utter nonsense! What are you afraid of, socks is it; think you're going to be attacked by a multitude of sock's intent on slapping you to death? Perhaps machete wielding socks, otherwise known as the horrible hackers or maybe it's the vicious Piranha socks you fear"?

"Nnnnnooo…"!

"Drink then"! Jack growled as he patiently waited for his student to take the plunge.

Reluctantly and with much effort Bogliani made the sign of the cross, mumbled "God forgive me" and immersed his entire head into the sparkling waters and took his fill of its health giving properties. He stayed under for so long that Jack wasn't sure whether Bogliani was being repentant or trying to drown himself.

"Oh for God's sake what are you doing now"! Jack bellowed as he grabbed hold of Bogliani by the scruff of his neck and yanked him out of the Baptismal Font. Bogliani gasped for air and Jack asked. "Feeling better"?

"Too early to tell" Bogliani half said and half gargled as water gushed out of his mouth.

"Don't think so, acts instantly especially at the emotional- spiritual level. Feel it working? No? Let's see okay"? Bogliani looked shyly at

Jack as he wiped his face with his tattered handkerchief that was in essence an undone and heavily ironed sock.

"Ready to start Yes? Good! Tell me a story"! Jack commanded.

"About"? Bogliani replied blankly.

"Socks, glorious socks, the foundation of all life, its meaning, socks, socks and more socks"! Jack Stern jeered.

"Are you mad Mr Stern? Have you completely lost your senses"?

"Well then, I do believe we've made progress. Make me a promise; now that you've elevated yourself, no more sermons about socks, scarves, hats or mats"! Jack strongly demanded. Bogliani shook his head in response, however it was not in agreement with Jack's request but more in keeping with his own conclusion; he thought Jack Stern to be quite mad!

"Another thing, now that you're in the Church of the Coloured Sands and you will probably assist in its operation you'll need to properly attire yourself."

"How rude of you Sir"! Bogliani snapped back indignantly as he grew 9cm in height.

"If that's the way you feel, so be it, but do me a favour allow your humility to express itself and take a good look at yourself in a mirror, then come back to me when you have finished and we can talk further."

Brendan like many others who were seated around the church watched the entire event without uttering a single word, the odd muffled chuckle did erupt now and then; otherwise they respected the silence expected within a church. He stood up just as Jack Stern confidently sauntered past.

"Jack, may I have a word"?

"But of course my friend, been a while since we last spoke, easy to see you have maintained the momentum of the initial public reaction." Jack Stern replied in a warm and complimentary manner.

"And you haven't'! Brendan replied as he brushed aside the well-intended flattery.

"Hum, that's disappointing, mind telling me what you're talking about"?

"Yvette of course"!

Jack tilted his head to one side, looked upwards, chewed on his lower lip and replied. "Guess you're right, been too busy with other more important matters"!

"Can't you see she's hurting"?

"Never felt it, thought she was satisfied with her find." Jack accurately surmised.

"Is everything a business to you? Why are you so damn cold and calculating"?

"So others may enjoy the warmth"! Jack answered with a depth of philosophy that befuddled the priest and then he asked. "By the way where is Yvette"?

"She left some time ago quite distressed"!

"I didn't notice."

"You never do"!

"You're being quite aggressive and rather protective as well, if I didn't know any better I'd say you were in love with the creature."

"And you're not"? Brendan fired back in a questioning manner. Jack scratched his dead and replied. "Still trying to discover what love is."

"I thought you knew! I heard your sermons at St Pious. You spoke with such authority or was it bluff Mr Stern"?

Jack did not answer the question; instead he changed the topic of conversation.

"I suppose I'd better find her and make amends." He suggested with downcast eyes.

"If it's not too late"! Brendan cuttingly replied.

Jack avoided the comment and its associated confrontation by looking Brendan in the eye with an analytical innocence rather than belligerence.

"Well Fool! I see you are still here! Hoped you had left for good"!

"Sister Ambrosia, a pleasure as always." Jack courteously replied as he turned to face the pugnacious nun.

"The girl needs her father"!

"Too young I'm afraid." Jack flippantly answered making reference to himself.

"Idiot! She wants and needs to go home"! Sister Ambrosia angrily retorted as she flared her nostrils and flashed her eyes.

"Thank you! You've both been very helpful"! Jack gushed as he hurriedly kissed Ambrosia on the cheek and half walked and half run out of the church.

"And what about you boy, when will you be truthful to yourself about your own feelings? Solitary, solitude, alone and abandoned is not you! Everyone needs someone." Ambrosia's words tore at the fabric of Brendan's inner world and laid bare his soul before him.

Yvette meanwhile from a distance felt Brendan's coldness, she stood alone and forlorn at Mauritius International Airport and patiently awaited her fate. Even though she was endowed with super-natural abilities she did not have the confidence at that time to 'fly' home solo using 'Spiritus Ruah'.

A solid airline flight is what she needed. Yvette had money, her own personal credit card a generous birthday gift courtesy of her father.

The airport's main hall was largely deserted Yvette shivered even though the ambient temperature was a comfortable 29 degrees Celsius and the humidity a pleasant 52%. The ticketing clerk for Air Mauritius was busily considering Yvette's request for a seat on a direct flight to New York City. He made numerous phone calls to his superiors and immigration officials to resolve the problem of Yvette's supposedly lost passport. The afternoon dragged on, the departure time drew closer a vacancy was available, the much needed green light was still red even though the clerk besotted by Yvette's counte-nance ran down every avenue to make things happen. Yvette wanted to do it herself, she did not want to ask either Brendan or Jack for assistance, she needed time to think, to self analyse, to hold her dad and feel the warmth of his paternal love.

"Mom you are a very, very lucky woman! I wonder if you realise that" She thought to herself as she sat in the waiting area and pondered her chances.

The Boeing 747 airliner had landed and was in the process of being unloaded, serviced, refuelled and reloaded before departure. The clerk grimfaced with head hung low approached her. Yvette feared the worst as she saw him flanked on either side by two ugly looking immigration officials.

"Mademoiselle Bell." The one on the left inquired.

"Yes."

"We have a problem with your request for an airline ticket and your present status in Mauritius."

"I don't understand! My passport has gone missing and I need to leave urgently for family reasons"! Yvette gravely explained that made the ticketing clerk feel even more for her.

"We understand, we are not uncompassionate as other countries, we wish to help. My colleague here recognised you from the church, so we conclude that you are not an evil person. Over sea's it is a different matter and even though you are returning home you may run into difficulties." The man on the right solemnly explained.

"What do you suggest I do"?

"That is a simple matter; return to the parish and try to find the missing documents or alternatively go to the American Embassy on the mainland if ours at Port Louis is unattended. One further anomaly, we do not appear to have a record of your arrival in Mauritius" Stated the man on the right.

"That's because computers leak! Sorry I'm late darling just received your urgent message"! Jack profusely apologised as he appeared from nowhere and startled everyone.

"The documents gentleman, up to date passport, entry visa, arrival documents etcetera." Jack brashly said as he handed them over to the officials for their perusal. "And for you Sir, my credit card make certain the young lady boards on time, and business class please." He instructed the ticketing clerk.

The officials took their time in carefully examining the material; finding no fault they gave the nod and allowed the Air Mauritius clerk to finalise Yvette's travel arrangements. She remained silent throughout the whole ordeal and spoke only when she was alone with Jack.

"Thank you." She softly said as she nuzzled her head into his manly chest.

"Have a safe journey." Was his succinct reply, one that Yvette was disappointed with and wished it had been somewhat more romantic. Irrespective of that she pressed herself more firmly into his body and waited in anticipation.

Jack Stern was not one for words, he considered them useless and primitive in all respects even though six thousand nine hundred and twelve languages existed in the world not one of them was adequate. His way of demonstrating his affection was to respond physically, Jack held Yvette around the waist, kissed her gently on the forehead and said.

"Remember I shall always love you, no matter what, go now, travel safe, I shall be with you always."

These words although welcomed and embraced by Yvette's heart, cut deeply into it, for they came at an awkward time. Yvette did not return Jack's affection for she was not ready to do so. Instead uncertain about her feelings, she broke free, brushed away the hair from her face and walked away, not once did she look back. In the aircraft Yvette cursed herself for her stupid actions and felt that she had betrayed Jack. This was not the time to make rash decisions; marriage if it came was a lifetime commitment. Both husband and wife had to be equally happy with the arrangement, neither was meant to suffer, nor become the other's slave. Today was the first day that she felt closer to Jack in a long time she prayed that the closeness would narrow.

Unbeknownst to Yvette Jack had secretly followed her. He watched until she disappeared from view, which was after she had passed through the last check point prior to boarding the flight. He then waited some more and departed to the Genius Loci once the aircraft had safely become airborne.

In two heart beats Jack Stern was back in the USA, Yvette's journey home would take infinitely longer giving her the much needed time to compose herself. She was grateful for Jack's generosity in paying for the first class accommodation. Although she felt a little spoilt it did not tarnish her simple attitude nor cause her to wish for the rich life and then she realised the material dissimilarities between Mr Jack Stern and Father Brendan O'Reilly. One was very rich it seemed and the other had taken the vow of poverty. Although Yvette's entire flight home was uneventful she felt uneasiness in her heart which was caused not so much by the dilemma that she faced but more external in nature as if a foe was watching her ready to pounce at the opportune time.

"Hello Papa, is that you"? She cried like a young child who bravely tried to hold back the tears.

"Yes……..Yvette? Where are you"?

"At…at…. the bus station. Can you come and pick me up please"? She said with a cold tremor in her voice.

"Be there in a flash! Wait a moment I thought you were in Mauritius having the time of your life"? Mr Bell put forward.

"I needed to come home"! Yvette replied in a manner that accurately described her anguish.

"How did you, my child"?

"By plane and bus"

"You sound distressed, stay where you are I'll be there in a flash"!

"Thank you Papa." And with that Yvette cradled the public pay phone's hand piece, dabbed the tears from her eyes and blew her nose.

"Who was that darling"? Mrs Bell asked of her long-standing

husband as she emerged from the laundry carrying a basket of freshly washed clothes.

"That was our Yvette."

"How is our precious darling, sublimely happy as usual"?

"Not really, she's home and sounds very fragile."

"Off you go then, don't dilly-dally; make haste; pick her up as swiftly as you can"! Mrs Bell curtly commanded as she sensed her husband's anxiety.

"I'm going I'm going"! Were the words he shouted back as he raced out of the house and towards his well-kept vintage car.

Mr Alexandre Bell a most appropriate name; considering the meaning of his christian name, which is defender of mankind, drove his second love true and straight to be reunited with the apple of his eye.

Strange how couples marry only to discover later that one of their children becomes or was the object of their seeking affections. Is it because they see a little of themselves in the child and therefore they like their own reflection or is it that the child choose the parent in order to fertilize their love and make it blossom?

In Alexandre's circumstances Yvette was a foster child, an orphan, an innocent victim of mindless violence, a gift for a man who genuinely wanted children but was deprived of them through an unfortunate quirk of nature.

Although his wife Abrielle was open, warm and welcoming, her cervix and womb were not, both of them remained very hostile to Alexandre's sperm. A tragedy because she also, through her intense devotion to him, wanted to provide Alexandre with a child of his own. Yvette was the gift from God, a result of endless prayer and unwavering faith.

Alexandre drove into the bus depot and guided his automobile slowly along the passenger set down area as he kept an eye out for his precious daughter.

It was 8.05pm in the evening, light drizzle fell from the skies with the ambient temperature falling as well. The car's windows began to mist inside making it difficult for Alexandre to easily identify his child. As he rounded the curve in the road there was no mistake about it; there in the public seating looking very forlorn and physically tired stood Yvette.

Mr Bell could see that she was very troubled and needed him. Alexandre brought the car to a halt, switched off the ignition, and sneaked up behind her. He hugged and kissed his daughter and made her feel good once again and then he took her by the hand and bundled Yvette into the warm and cosy interior of his second love.

"No Luggage"?

"I travelled very light." Yvette meekly replied as she shivered with cold..

"Clothes and all"

"I was in a hurry."

"I know you better than that, you were burdened with the weight of emotions and unsaid things. I can tell." Alexandre expertly concluded.

"I could never keep anything secret from you"!

"Except for the things you can see." Alexandre replied making reference to Yvette's supernatural eyesight.

"I'm glad to be home."

"We all feel the same; a good night's sleep for you, we'll talk tomorrow" Alexandre suggested as he safely transported them home.

Yvette readily accepted his idea, extended her left hand, gently rested it on her father's right thigh and sunk her body into the comfortable leather faced passenger seat.

The next day completely refreshed after a good night's sleep, Yvette partook of her favourite breakfast; freshly ground Jamaican coffee and two candied orange peel brioches made by Andre's French Patisserie. Her mother Abrielle did not fuss as much as her dad for she knew her place in the family. The weather outside was bleak in contrast to that of Mauritius. The skies were overcast, winter threatened to arrive early this year; the rain continuously drizzled and yet it was a joy for Yvette to behold.

"Home, wonderful home, with all of its peculiar familiar smells and noises"

She whispered to her father.

"Holidays can be a chore at times." He remarked.

"Mine wasn't at the outset"

"When did it change"? Alexandre asked out of curiosity.

Yvette didn't answer; instead she cupped the hot mug of coffee in her hands and inhaled its aromatic vapours. Alexandre realised it wasn't the right time to labour the point.

"Would you like to go for a long walk this morning"? He asked changing the subject.

"Love to, especially the quaint and colourful places you took me to as a child." Yvette smilingly replied after she finished her coffee and wiped her mouth with a pure cotton table napkin.

"I'll get my coat."

"And mine too please Papa."

"With the utmost of pleasures"

"Thank you Papa." Yvette sweetly said with a smile that melted Alexandre's heart.

Nicely rugged up against the early morning cold Yvette and her Papa gracefully descended the front stairs of their home and slowly walked along the garden path towards the white picket fence. Yvette stopped at its gate and gasped at the inescapable scene to her right.

The front of the adjoining house together with the full length of its perimeter fence was covered with a multitude of crudely hand written placards protesting about one subject or another.

DANGER BEWARE OF THE SPIDER
BATHROOM SEATING CAPACITY FOR ONE FEDERICK!
DANGER THE HOUSE IS HAUNTS!

JOHN GOTS EYES ON YOU WATCHING
DANGER BEWARE THE CAT
KING FEDERICK
DANGER BEWARE THE RATWELOR

BEENAWARE OF THE SNAKE HEINTHEHOUSE

BAR MY WINDOWS LOCK MY DOORS COME INSIDE!

She stared at the bizarre accumulation of words but did not venture closer as she felt the uneasiness that she encountered on the flight home.

"When did this happen"? She nervously questioned as she felt fear slowly creep into her body.

"While you were away"

"Mr Clydesdale died"?

"Yes his immediate family sold the house to an investor who promptly rented it out"!

"Very sad, he was such a cantankerous man."

"To everyone but you my darling" Alexandre solemnly replied as he remembered the joy that Yvette brought to the old man.

"Where's his grave? I 'd like to pay my last respects"

"He was cremated; his ashes were spread across his vegetable garden"! Alexandre glumly explained as he thought it quite bizarre.

"He was the neighbourhood eccentric but nothing like these inhabitants."

"You are very perceptive Yvette. They're a strange lot that rent the property; if you wait long enough you'll spy one of them shortly."

Yvette did as her father said and not wishing to draw attention to themselves she strolled about her parents finely manicured front garden. Within fifteen minutes the clairvoyant soothe-sayer complete with the pertinent regalia and dark brown leather top hat bounced out into the open with another placard under his armpit. The funny little man scurried about the yard like a possessed squirrel looking for a place topbury its precious load. He darted to and fro with hammer in hand and nails in his mouth until he found that special place in which to secure the rotten floorboard and its profound message. Satisfied with its integrated position he jumped into the air, loudly clicked his heels together and rushed back into the house. His performance was more suited to the theatre than to normal members of the public and Yvette questioned the man's sanity.

"He's harmless." Alexandre countered.

"You're not frightened living next door to him"? Yvette nervously asked.

"Not at all, his sorts are harmless."

"I hope you're right." Yvette replied as she looked over her shoulder to make certain the funny little man had stayed indoors. Alexandre wrapped his arm around Yvette's waist as reassurance of his protection and the pair strolled down the tree-lined street outside of their home they turned left and walked towards Newburn.

In the distance Yvette unlike her father saw an eerie figure in the heavy mist ahead, it appeared to be an excessively tall man on a bicycle, he moved towards them without any sign of peddling which was strange in itself as the road's gradient was uphill. Yvette gripped her father's arm in fear.

As the apparition came closer the illusion was shattered and the reality clearly apparent. A tall middle- aged redheaded man dressed entirely in a load brown plaid suit complete with a matching top hat sat motionless upon a small red bike with a blonde male midget dressed in exactly the same attire seated on the bike's cross bar. There was no apparent physical exertion on the part of the riders, the little red bike moved of its own accord, with no motor attached.

Neither Alexandre nor Yvette knew what to make of it and they both stood quite still until the strange duo passed them by.

However this did not happen. The odd looking cyclists stopped at exactly the same spot where Yvette and her father stood. They altered their rigid stone like statue appearance and became fluid. Now life like they turned in unison nodded their heads and with wide eyes, flared nostrils and raised eyebrows they stared at Alexandre and Yvette.

The uneasiness magnified in Yvette's being, excessively frightened she wished Jack was nearby.

"Fear not, we do you no harm. Listen to the big man." The blonde midget croaked in a gravelly voice. The redheaded middle-aged man bowed forward from the waist careful not to dislodge his passenger and removed his brown leather hat, as a gentleman would do.

"Beware fair maiden; beware of the scarred man and the keeper of women, they desire your freedom." He profoundly stated and with no further indication or comment the pair resumed their original positions, became granite faced and drifted up the hill without any exertion on their part.

Yvette dug her nails into her fathers arm; she shook with fear and pleaded.

"Father don't ever leave me, please"

16

WHO'S WINNING NOW?

Australia is without a doubt a nation of people obsessed with gambling and sport. On the first Tuesday in the month of November each and every year the Australian horseracing calendar reaches its climax with the running of The Melbourne Cup at Fleming Race Course, in the state of Victoria. This one solitary sporting event literally halts the nation in its tracks and as a consequence the entire day is wasted. Millions if not billions of dollars are spent on fashion, food, alcohol and gambling, on course and off course at the various state run totaliser agency outlets and private bookmakers. Restaurants, hotels, cafes, racecourses and private venues are booked out for the great one hundred and forty four year singular social event. The hype leading up to, during and after the event is awesome.

In the eyes of the clever terrorist it is a perfect time to strike; unfortunately terrorists are usually a dumb lot and most of their attacks happen by pure luck more than anything else. However on this day of this year when the Cup coincided with the festival of All Souls Day something different occurred.

Harvey Jarwood the manly in disguise Prime Minister gaily sauntered about the extensive grounds of Flemington Race Course.

He had arrived early. 7.30am to be precise, right on opening time, to Harvey Melbourne Cup day was the perfect occasion on which to grease the political wagon. Prime Minister Jarwood was dressed in a grey pinstriped flannel suit, pale blue banker's shirt, imported rose pink silk tie and genuine Texan cowboy boots, the spurs of which were at home reserved for dark erotic occasions.

Champagne breakfast, continental buffets were served at the Hillstands, Corporate Sails, Skyline, Panorama, Gallery and Terrace Restaurant as well as at the various marquees and private enclosures.

By 10.30am in the morning the distinguished Harvey Jarwood was starting to look the worse for wear and on many an occasion he almost made his slip of the tongue into a political disaster had it not been for his ever watchful intervening attaché who was dutifully present to correct the Prime Minister's indiscretions.

"I say, Prime Minister, are you free" Cyril Pinewood asked as he approached his superior.

"For you always darling"! He replied in a high voice that raised the eyebrows of many observers.

"Prime Minister I think it would be appropriate if we visited the fashion arena's" His attaché whispered in his ear and then he gestured to the crowd and said "A little too much Mount Gay rum has brought out his feminine side." His off the cuff remark produced a positive giggle that rippled through the crowd.

"Come on Prime Minister the ladies await."

"Oh yes those things." He mumbled under his breath as he walked three steps behind Cyril Pinewood and admired the rhythmic contractions of his buttock's muscles. Mr Pinewood felt his superior's admiration and smiled to himself.

The fashion house enclosures and adjoining open spaces were filled with a multitude of young bevies dressed in all styles of seductive clothing; a heterosexual's paradise. Harvey Jarwood dismissed his attaché and circulated of his own accord much to the delight of those who flattered themselves in being in the company of powerful individuals. The Only advantage in being homosexual was that both Harvey Jarwood and Cyril Pinewood knew and understood the workings of the female mind and this enabled them to win the majority of the adult female primary vote at election time.

As the morning wore on, Harvey quickly regained his mental and physical balance by avoiding alcohol and consuming large quantities of tomato juice spiked with Tabasco sauce. Lunchtime signalled a change of venue, the Hillstands beckoned; its highbrow wealthy occupants demanded the duo's presence. In that environment Harvey and Cyril were the puppets of the real rulers of the land, the prominent and faceless corporate giants. These were the people who made the rules.

"Worked out who's going to win today Prime Minister"? A senior corporate executive asked as he approached from a dim corner.

"Yes I have been reliably informed that Awesome Twosome stands a very good chance." Harvey Jarwood arrogantly answered.

"Five point one million dollars is a lot of money; enough to tempt many into doing something devious. Are you certain Awesome Twosome is your choice"? The executive asked.

"What are you insinuating Sir"? Harvey retorted whilst he maintained his diplomatic composure.

"Many will lose their money and a privileged few, those in the know will gain immensely, not exactly cricket, by the way, your wager, does it make reference to the horse or yourselves"?

"Utter nonsense, good day to you Sir"! Harvey snapped back, the executive said nothing in return and retired to his corner.

Harvey Jarwood turned his back and accepted a glass of local 'champagne' from the serving tray of a waiter who was circulating around the tables and promoting the excellence of its vintage. Harvey took one sip and signalled by way of a nod of the head to Cyril who immediately came running over.

"What's the matter"? Cyril asked.

"I've just had an encounter"!

"Yummy….you beast"!

"Not like that you fool"!

"What then"?

"That elderly man over there in the corner; in the black suit and polka dot tie."

"Yes what of him"? Cyril asked as he cast his eyes discretely over the location.

"I think he's some sort of investigative officer; probably looking at anything irregular with the Melbourne Cup."

"Are you suggesting, doping, race fixing; paid off stewards and that sort of thing"?

"Keep you voice down"!

"Yes Prime Minister." Cyril instantly obeyed.

"Did you place the bet"?

"I did on the horse you instructed."

"And that was"?

"Woodchips"!

"Excellent I feel very uncomfortable here, let's go somewhere else"!

"I thought you'd never ask"!

"Stop it Cyril! Keep it real"!

"I am Prime Minister I am. The Terrace has a nice mix of people." Pinewood said with authority

"Good, andiamo, it's a little close"!

"To race time Prime Minister"?

"No you fool, to the truth"! Jarwood roughly replied as he gestured to be followed to the restaurant and then he checked his wristwatch.

The announcer's voice blared over the internal sound system advising that the all important race was just minutes away and that the horses would shortly be moved from the public viewing arena to the starting gates.

"I'm now going to hand you over to Mike Charlton who will be your official race caller for this great international event."

"Thank you Tom. Ladies and gentleman welcome to this years grand horse event; the race that stops a nation! Might even stop your heart if you've backed a one hundred to one outsider! We're just minutes away from the Starter shooting his gun; ladies and gentleman place your bets, last minute call to place your bets once and for all." He jovially repeated like a smooth seasoned bingo caller.

"From where I am standing number seven Flashy Underwear has settled in nicely; Devil's Pleasure is proving a little resistant; Happy Maiden is offering no resistance; Pope's Choice has made sure of that! Forequarter; Hindquarter and Royal Quarters have snuggled in nicely; Pheasants Tail and Peasants Pockets seem to be having a quarrel; might have to put the blinkers on; yes' the jockey's signalling; stewards attending; Pheasants Tail is being taken out! Shoestring; Dumb Money; Loose Hands and Titillation are being manoeuvred in; followed by Sir David, Witches Curse and Express Delivery. The last horses are being lead in by the stable hands; no more bets ladies and gentleman; no more bets please"! Awesome Twosome, Woodchips, Pill Popper, Native Boy and Here I Come are in; Pheasants Tail attended to. All gates closed, horses locked in, stewards away, starter's waiting for them to settle; Pheasants Tail still a bit wobbly; Flashy Underwear looks nervous; Titillation fidgety; Express Delivery toey. Starter is looking down the line; steady; steady."

"Bang" Went the starters pistol and with it copious amounts of adrenaline were dumped into the bloodstreams of both horse and humans.

"They're away in this year's Melbourne Cup! Sir David, Woodchips, Pill Popper, Native Boy got away nicely, Devils Pleasure, Loose Hands, Witches Curse and Dumb Money stalled in the starting blocks! Forequarter, Express Delivery, Awesome Twosome, Pheasants Tail stretched out ahead close to the barrier with Royal Quarters leading the way! They're followed three deep by Happy Maiden, Titillation, Shoestring and Pope's Choice; further back it's Hindquarter, Flashy Underwear, Here I Come; then it's Devil's Pleasure, Loose Hands,

Witches Curse and Dumb Money; bringing up the rear is Peasants Pockets.

First time past the winning post it's Royal Quarters leading the way by six lengths followed by Express Delivery, Pheasants Tail, Awesome Twosome and Forequarter side by side; five lengths further back Hindquarter has moved up from the rear of the pack and is just behind Happy Maiden on the rail followed closely behind by Pope's Choice, Titillation, Shoestring, Sir David, Pill Popper, Native Boy and Woodchips; four lengths away it's, Devil's Pleasure, Witches Curse, Loose Hands, Dumb Money, Flashy Underwear, Here I Come and last of all Peasant's Pockets!

Around the turn into the first straight Royal Quarters leads the way; Pheasants Tail starting to find his rhythm, Express Delivery checking his progress, Awesome Twosome 's pumping himself up, Forequarter looks scared, Happy Maiden's smiling as Titillation rubs along side! Pope's Choice, Shoestring, Pill Popper and Sir David keeping pace, Native Boy's keeping Hindquarter and Woodchips at bay! Starting their first sprint Witches Curse, Loose Hands, Flashy Underwear, Devil's Pleasure and Dumb Money are making a move leaving Peasants Pockets and Here I Come at the back of the pack!

Down the straight they go into the back curve; they're starting to bunch up; not good for Happy Maiden one of the favourites boxed in on the rails as are Dumb Money and Sir David.

Royal Quarters is still out front, king of the castle, no contenders in sight, Express Delivery being whipped by Pheasants Tail, Awesome Twosome ain't awesome anymore! Making ground is Pill Popper and right behind him is Flashy Underwear!

Heading towards the two thousand metres mark; it's still Royal Quarters in front, Peasants Pockets and Here I Come have started to make their move; the favourites Happy Maiden, Dumb Money and Sir David still locked in; Pope's Choice and Titillation have pulled out wide making their run; Loose Hands, Shoestring, Witches Curse and Devil's Pleasure seem to be running out of puff, Hindquarters appears to be falling asleep!

Around the turn they come into the final nine hundred meter straight!

Royal Quarters' blue blood has turned blue! Peasants Pockets, Here I Come are gaining rapidly! Pope's Choice and Titillation are in the way; Flashy Underwear, Pill Popper are just Behind Royal Quarters, the whips are out!

Four hundred metres to go! Here I Come has pulled out and passed Titillation and Pope's Choice; Flashy Underwear and Pill Popper are neck and neck with Royal Quarters!

Forget the rest of the pack it's between Flashy Underwear and Pill Popper. The blue blood's dead! Down the outside Peasants Pockets and Here I Come are flying home!

Flashy Underwear has her head in front!! Here I Come is gaining ground!!

Pill Popper's run out of speed, Peasants Pocket's are empty! It's Here I Come and Flashy Underwear!

Flashy Underwear...Here I Come.... Here I Come ... Flashy Underwear

What a race! It's going to be close, very close! Fifty metres and its neck and neck! The jockeys are pulling out all stops!

Flashy Underwear...Here I Come... !

What a race! What an unbelievable race! Never seen anything like it in all of my years! No official results, ladies and gentleman, no official results"!

Pandemonium broke out throughout the entire racecourse, nationally and abroad. Not one of the favourites featured in the top three places, bookmakers became devastated and distraught at the results; many feared financial ruin. A wave of shock and despair swept through the crowds and all those who were involved with the orchestration of the event. Only a few were jubilant at the outcome a first in Melbourne Cup history.

"The race officials are calling for a photo, a photo finish ladies and gentleman, please stay calm, official results in a few minutes." Mike Charlton smoothly announced un-phased by the commotion that surrounded him.

"What bloody nonsense is this Cyril"? Jarwood screamed at his second in command.

"It was on good authority! It was reliable information straight from the horse's mouth."

"There goes a big chunk of our campaign money"!

"How much did you bet Prime Minister"? Cyril Pinewood asked.

"Enough to be worried about"!

"Oh dear"!

"Not to worry Cyril my friend in treasury will attend to it"!

"That's awfully immoral Prime Minister"!

"No Cyril, its par for the course"!

"Yes Sir." Pinewood answered admirably.

"Might as well leave now; no more to be done or said! See you tomorrow."

"Yes Prime Minister." Pinewood obediently obeyed and prepared to make his exit as well. A similar situation was occurring behind closed doors in the jockey's assembly area.

"What the bloody hell do you think you were doing"?

"Nothing boss"!

"That's right nothing! You bloody well lost the race! We'll be ruined! All of us, you, you ass"!!

"But boss, nothing worked! The horse, the dope, nothing! No one could do anything! Ask them"! The jockey defiantly and angrily shouted back as he truthfully explained the circumstances.

"What are you telling me"?

"Something went wrong"!

"Look you pimple faced miserable excuse for a jockey, I don't care how many races we've let you win, I don't care what reputation you've got, you're finished! Understand? Finished"!!! The boss man uncontrollably shouted.

The jockey hung his head low and dropped his helmet to the ground. He was after all telling the truth, this was a horse race unlike anything he had experienced before. The pre-arranged game plan had gone horribly wrong. He couldn't understand why. Nothing made sense it was as if for once the horse with genuine natural ability had won. He feared for his life, millions of dollars had been lost, reputations destroyed, lies, rumours, suspicions would fuel the pay backs, feuds and the inevitable horse wars. Australia's biggest Horse race had become an earthquake that was set to shake its entire crime ridden business to its foundations.

The jockey's boss man was fuming and afraid at the same time for he also was in the firing line from the faceless that ruled the land.

"Well ladies and gentleman the official race results for this years Melbourne Cup are as follows. 'Dead' heat for first place, sharing the line honours are Fancy Underwear and Here I Come, third place was won by Pheasants Tail.

Congratulations to all the connections involved the apprentice jockeys who rode the winners and the trainers. This years Cup has an additional first. It is a shock to see a stud horse winning; normally they are geldings, says a lot for testosterone power. Well horse trainers you might have to consider a new avenue in the future; T-Power! The good news for the punters; Pheasants Tail paid $41.95 for the place; Here I Come paid $37.50 and Fancy Underwear $43.50. The trifecta if you had it paid a staggering $111,650.45.

None of the race favourites featured in the top five placing's. Stewards are happy, no protests, drug swabs are clean. Thank you ladies and gentleman, that was this years Melbourne Cup hope to have the pleasure of your company next year, this is Mike Charlton signing off."

"Prime Minister, Prime Minister, wait, don't go, I've got an urgent telephone call for you"!

"Oh what now, you stupid fool, what do you want"? Jarwood barked.

"We have a national crisis"!

"Yes I know the Melbourne Cup result"!

"No Sir much worse"!

"What could be worse than that"?

"A terrorist attack Sir"! His attaché calmly said. The words stopped Jarwood dead in his tracks, sarcasm gone his rationality destroyed, he did not comprehend, he could not think, his body went into psychological shock and he paled into insignificance.

"Did you hear me Prime Minister"?

"I did." He stuttered as he felt a certain dizziness overwhelm him.

"You'll need to come with me Sir we have set up an emergency briefing in your hotel suite."

"Does any one else know"?

"No Sir all media has been suppressed. We have implemented the somewhat draconian provisions of the Terrorist Act of 1999."

"Good errrr….. I think."

"My sentiments as well, this way Sir we have the maximum security vehicle at your disposal. Pinewood is already on board ready to brief you Sir."

"Unheard of in Australia"! Jarwood muttered as he strove to keep up with his attaches' silent urgency.

Inside the white Ford LTD stretch limousine sat Cyril Pinewood, the head of ASIO and a senior federal police officer.

"Well what's happened, how many injured, who, what, when." Jarwood nervously blurted out as he took his seat. Not one person said anything until the limousine's doors were securely shut.

"It's not what you or anyone of us ever expected and we don't know at this stage what the cause is." The attaché glumly stated as an introduction to the national emergency.

"So it's not a bomb"?

"Far from it"

'Well don't keep me in suspense, what the bloody hell happened"? Jarwood demanded to know feeling increasingly frustrated.

228

"We don't know; all that we can tell you is that people are keeling over left, right and centre, all over Australia. The emergency services can't cope, the hospitals can't cope; the funeral director's can't cope"!

"Mass Poisoning"

"We don't know"!

"Look I'm becoming increasingly annoyed with your ignorance! Tell me something concrete"! Jarwood almost shouted as he felt his temperature rising.

"If you would allow me Prime Minister" The head of ASIO said after he had cleared his throat.

"Yes."

"The primary targets appeared at first to be hospitals. We ascertained from the information gathered that from midnight onwards all narcotics and anaesthetics routinely used ceased to be effective."

"Well give them more a bigger dose, what's the problem"? Harvey Jarwood suggested as an uneducated politician bent on solving a problem by simply throwing money at it.

'Not quite that easy, when I mentioned ineffective I should have said totally. No pain relief, no anaesthesia, nothing. The end result as you can imagine were people waking up during their surgical procedures, patients not being able to be put under, those with intractable pain screaming out for relief. It wouldn't have been so bad if one or two hospitals were affected we could have resolved that; but this isn't the case. Every hospital in the country is involved, public, private, major, minor, nursing homes, doctor's surgeries, paramedics"!

"That's impossible"! A disbelieving Harvey Jarwood harshly concluded

"I agree Sir, it doesn't make any sense that all batches irrespective of their age or substance or manufacturer or country of origin are under attack. What is also rather bizarre is that the illegal drug trade has also been affected, cancelled in effect. Every accident victim, terminal cancer patients, women in labour, people with chronic pain and disabilities cannot be helped and I'm sorry to say that we can't even say 'take two aspirin and go to bed'"!

"I don't believe one word of what you're dealing me"! Jarwood hissed cynically. "Except if what you are saying is true then the drug addicts deserve it! They've been sucking the life out of the social security system far too long."

"There's more Prime Minister." Cyril Pinewood interrupted. "Narcotics and anaesthetics are not the only targets, insulin has also been implicated"!

"All forms"

"You guessed correctly Sir." Pinewood confirmed.

"Tell me this is not happening Cyril." Jarwood almost begged like a small boy as he buried his head in his hands and wished the world away.

"It is. As consolation we are using all avenues of disinformation and assurance to pacify everyone. The situation is very serious, but we are not alone"!

"What do you mean"? Just then the Limousine's ultra-secure mobile telephone rang. Pinewood picked up the phone and received the call

"Good morning, we were expecting your call. Yes, identical situation, yes, same approaches, yes he is, pleasure talking to you." Pinewood politely answered before he handed the handset over to Jarwood. "Prime Minister of England Sir" He politely said.

"Good morning." But before Harvey Jarwood could say anymore the British head of state attacked him with a barrage of gruesome statistics. Jarwood paled progressively until he appeared deathly grey at which point his caller terminated the one sided conversation.

"It's the same in England." Jarwood croaked and then asked. "How could any one orchestrate this? What about the States"?

"You mean America"? The ASIO head asked.

"Yes."

"No word, it appears they are immune."

"Bloody yanks! Always have to be better than anyone else"!

"I don't think that is the case. It probably has something to do with political ideology." The ASIO chief suggested.

"What are you insinuating"?

"That we that is us and England have done something together to upset someone."

"That's impossible"! Jarwood fired back.

"But not if you view our nations' histories or present positions on sensitive issues." The ASIO head hit back. Prime Minister Harvey Jarwood remained silent and secretly postulated to himself the cause of the Melbourne Cup horse race's result and then he asked.

"Have there been reports of similar occurrences within the veterinary industry "?

"Not as yet Sir"! Pinewood said with authority.

"Keep an eye on it and maintain and reinforce present strategies! I don't want any leaks to or by the media! If they attempt to publish the news, block it and if you have to.......... eliminate the journalists"! Harvey Jarwood firmly ordered.

"Are you suggesting…."? His attaché bitterly asked, as he was an advocate of freedom of speech.

"We have the power; why not use it"! Jarwood replied arrogantly as he applied his authority and expected every one to obey his commands without objection. Across the waters in the USA a similar scene was unfolding.

"We have harnessed the power of science to our advantage. Today the foundation day of our humble beginning will revolutionize the way we do business forever. We have silenced our competitors and given those who thwart us something else to do. Our pathway is uninhibited, from today onwards Dot.org through our efforts will achieve greatness and we gentleman will be richly rewarded"! The Small Dark Figure shouted with its arms out wide and eyes directed to the heavens.

There was a general atmosphere of controlled excitement amongst its listeners apart from Nghi Phamhung who always remained stoically indifferent.

"Tell us Mr Phamhung how goes it"?

"All Joy."

"Wonderful just what I wanted to hear. Tell us more." The Small Dark Figure excitedly beckoned.

"Is the name of the product" Phamhung dryly answered.

"Bit corny"!

"Not at all; we had considered many titles such as brewer's joy, all good, mushroom's delight, not one captured the essence of the product and our belief systems. Here take the product and see what I mean." Phamhung said as he magically produced several samples from thin air and handed them out.

The long slim diamond cut royal blue glass bottles were embossed with the products name in gold metallic paint and capped with a solid gold screw top. It held ten millilitres of the specially 'brewed' mRNA enough for thirty days supply based on a two drops three times a day dosage regime irrespective of age, weight or sex.

"This is simply beautiful Mr Phamhung. I apologize for my indiscretion." The Small Dark Figure gushed as it played with the key that would potentially allow it access to the inner sanctum of the organization Dot.org.

"I take it that today is its official launch date."

"It is."

"And our competitors"

"Their produce has been tampered with some weeks ago."

"Excellent"! The Small Dark Figure gushed once again as it eagerly ribbed its hands and jiggled about on its stool. "How about distribution"?

"Only the major cities have been targeted, those with the highest prescribing rates, networks are operating as we speak. It is anticipated that medically unattended people will benefit first of all and that this will create a foundation of convincing anecdotal evidence that will forcibly encourage the sale of the product to those who have became compromised as a result of drug failure." Phamhung expertly explained as one who had done his homework well.

"Excellent how cleverly you have thought this out"! The Small Dark Figure said in a congratulatory fashion. "What are your sales predictions"?

"Based on our own research how does the term exponential sound to you? We trust that you will be able to meet demand"! Phamhung coldly asked in a nonsensical manner.

"No problem"! The Small Dark Figure confidently assured Nghi Phamhung as it spoke for all those involved in the process of manufacturing vast quantities of mRNA.

"Very well now we play the waiting game."

17

AS IT HAPPENED

If anything makes a man into a man it is usually something drastic in nature like an overwhelming national disaster. The gay closet homosexual Prime Minister of Australia Mr Harvey Jarwood sweatied profusely as there were no answers to the immediate drug crisis that had engulfed his country.

Experts were speechless, idealess and for once in their lives much closer to their true intellectual level than ever before. The theories, postulations, hypotheses that the entire scientific world had been built upon vaporized; all that remained was the bare truth, one that demanded recognition; namely, how intertwined all living entities are upon this world, this earth, a veritable sea of genetic material seeking its own perfection through the process of its own self experimentation. No eminent person was willing to accept it never mind whisper its name.

"Pinewood"!! Come in here immediately"!! Jarwood violently commanded via the parliamentary office intercom.

"Straight away Sir"! Pinewood sharply replied and reluctantly dragged himself away from his self adulation that he had been conducting in his hand held mirror in the privacy of his own office.

"It's been two weeks since the Melbourne Cup, what do you have to report"? Jarwood said as he tried to control his temper.

"What would you like to hear Prime Minister, that everything is peachy fine? Well it isn't! This is how it goes. First there were anaesthetics, insulin and narcotics that abandoned us followed by the analgesics, antihypertensives, antipsychotics, anti-anxiolytics, anti-clotting agents, antihistamines, anti-arthritics, anti-arrhythmias, anti-ADHD, anti-nauseants, anti-depressants, antibiotics; anti-flu in fact anything ANTI that you might think of! One even wonders if our anti-aircraft defence system works at all"

Pinewood theatrically recited in true Gilbert and O'Sullivan fashion.

"Makes for quite a catchy satirical tune"! He comically added before he sat down, became silent and twiddled his thumbs.

"For God sake's, man, can't you offer me any salvation"!

"Depends how you're dressed or undressed! Contraception is one that I missed Prime Minister"! Pinewood teased.

"Stop it! Give me some hard facts"!!

"Well if it's hard you want, hard you'll get"! Cyril Pinewood authoritatively replied as he depressed the intercom switch and asked the PM's secretary to allow his first discovery to enter his superior's office. The door opened gently and an elderly man of short stature with heavyset eyes, dark rimmed reading glasses and a mop of white curly hair entered the room.

"Prime minister may I introduce you to Professor Ori Vale, a foremost expert in pharmaco- genetics." Pinewood said as he escorted the professor towards Harvey Jarwood.

"Never heard of him or his field"! Jarwood rudely snapped.

"Rather specialised"! Pinewood hinted hoping that the PM would recognise the Professors eminence.

"More like expensive to the government with no return" Jarwood abruptly retorted.

"Oh my God"! Pinewood exclaimed with his eyes raised to the heavens.

"What now you bumbling Gaylord"?

"Contraception, we're in for a population explosion! Unwanted pregnancies, forced marriages, more strain on the social security system! How Marvellous! Not looking good is it Prime Minister"? Jarwoods penetrating look of murderous intent in response quickly subdued the effervescent Cyril Pinewood who retreated into a neutral corner.

"Professor Vale, sorry about the antics, we're very stressed at the moment as you may appreciate. May I offer you some refreshment"? The PM then politely said as he took charge of the situation.

"Nothing at all thank you"

"Very well, what can you tell us about the present medical dilemma"?

"Before I give you my conclusions I need to talk to your TAG people. Can you arrange that"? The professor asked the PM as he peered over his glasses and analysed his body language.

"But of course. Pinewood get Manoff on the line ASAP"

Pinewood obliged and within moments Manoff was conversing with the Professor and making available the information he sought. Jarwood and Pinewood meanwhile left the Professor and shared a cup of coffee together in the PM's exclusive retreat that was attached to his office but sealed away from it by two sets of double insulated doors.

"Do you think he can help us Cyril"? Jarwood asked sincerely.

"If he can't he can certainly put us onto the right people. He is eccentric, well read, very broad minded; I believe he leaves no stone unturned."

A rap on the inner signalled that Ori Vale was free.

"Well Professor, can you help us" Jarwood asked somewhat sheepishly.

"Only in one respect namely the cause of your problem. It's not the drugs. They check out nicely. All of the tests prove they have been manufactured correctly and will perform ideally according to the tests conducted by the manufacturers and your own TAG department."

Pinewood and Jarwood were dumbfounded by the Professor's statement.

"The problem lies with the patients. There has occurred a genetic paradigm shift; one which has caused people not to recognise synthetic drugs. In effect the human body has thought of these as being rubbish. But since we all vary from individual to individual the reaction varies; so that some synthetic drugs are still having an effect although it appears to be minimal. The cause of it, well, that might be difficult to ascertain, especially if it is shown with time that this phenomenon is restricted to Australia and England. One of the ways it can certainly occur is by the introduction of foreign genetic material into the human body."

"Are you suggesting a viral plague"? Pinewood put forward.

"Unlikely; because it would be a global event, although that is not always necessarily so I think it is more likely to be via mass immunization. Some one has very cleverly tampered with the process and created an attenuated virus, which has managed to activate certain latent genetic defence systems. In effect what I am saying is that the human body has evolved or devolved if such a word exists, into accepting natural therapies only! No synthetics allowed! Your artificial drugs gentleman, are being excreted intact, un-metabolised. I fear you have many hurdles to overcome. If you do not find the culprit then you will need a scapegoat, some one you can set up, that should not be difficult given your resources. If you decide not to go down that pathway and it is suggested and proven that a preventative influenza vaccine was the cause, then you might as well resign in the wake of the economic chaos that will result. To change this shift will require immense scientific effort. It is an enormous challenge. We would need to find the exact locations of the genes and the procedure necessary to deactivate them. It would means going public and even then, considering the way scientists argue amongst each other it will take decades to stumble across the solution.

Gentleman my advice to you is, find the culprit, he holds the answers. I have no further comment, good day." Professor Ori Vale succinctly advised and without any further warning abruptly stood up and left.

"Did I say something to upset him"? Jarwood questioned himself and Cyril Pinewood.

"Or was it me"? Pinewood then embarrassingly asked also thinking the same.

"No matter, we'll sort this mess out. Economic chaos what utter poppy's cock"! Jarwood confidently said as he reassumed his arrogance.

"We're looking for a culprit, an idealist, some one with a quest! Perhaps one we've harshly dealt with before, humm, you don't suppose we've become involved in a battle between natural and unnatural therapies do you"? Cyril Pinewood asked the Prime Minister as his mind raced to find the answers.

"Get Manoff on the line! I want to know if those alternate therapy companies are experiencing the same problems"!

"Yes sir. But before I do, I have someone else that you should meet."

"Another useless money wasting expert, I suppose"!

"Alice would you please admit Mr Eric Moeson, thank you." Pinewood merrily chirped.

The door to the privileged sanctum opened sharply and a lean and learned middle-aged man stepped into the sombre room. His air of authority commanded respect; it came not from his physical attributes but from his advanced intelligence.

"Prime Minister may I introduce you to Dr E Moeson, distinguished microbiologist who researchers for the Commonwealth Health Dept and is presently stationed in Tasmania."

"A pleasure" Jarwood genuinely said as he stood up and offered his handshake, which was politely and promptly swept aside.

"Mr Jarwood, Mr Pinewood, good day to you both." Moeson

answered totally unperturbed by his political company.

"Thank you for answering the call. The task we have for you today is to assist us in formulating a simple, plausible explanation for the Australian public as to why their medication in some cases is largely ineffective." Pinewood explained and then allowed Moeson to dwell on the matter, which he didn't need to.

"I have read you brief and discussed the data with Professor Vale, a close friend of mine. Have you met him"?

"Can't say I have" Jarwood untruthfully replied as he feigned the opposite.

"Pity, he'd steer you in the right direction. There's something that's bothering me. This explanation of yours, it's not intended for a minority of people is it"? Pinewood and Jarwood remained silent and looked at each other.

"Enough said." Moeson quickly deduced.

"Well can you help us" Jarwood impatiently asked.

"I can, however I advise you, keep details vague, any attempt at specifics will land you in boiling oil"!

"We shall take that into consideration." Jarwood and Pinewood answered simultaneously.

"How many idiotic proposals have been put forward with respect to the population's ailment besides the infectious theory? I don't suppose you've considered beer? It's a perfect vehicle for distribution after all we are a nation of prolific drinkers"!

"Surely you jest"? Jarwood taunted

"It is an ideal candidate. Genetically modify the hops and who knows what might happen? Unfortunately nothing will be done about it, for it generates money, tax dollars, unlike the pharmaceuticals that drain treasury's coffers"!

Moeson cynically retorted.

"Did you come to talk politics or assist us in our campaign"? Jarwood taunted once again except this time a little more forcibly.

"I don't like helping your kind. My interests at heart are to prevent public panic, therefore listen carefully, write it down and do with it what you please! You will report that a variant of an enteric gut virus has hit the population. It is asymptomatic meaning it produces no discernable symptoms. People feel well; the only parameter that has been affected is hepatic function; in that regard only a select number of enzymic processes are at risk. Call it a benign hepatitis of short-lived duration. As to its origin you can argue that India was it source. Here is a fact sheet that your health department officials can work from once they stop squabbling amongst themselves." Dr Eric Moeson said as he handed over the document that he retrieved from his leather case, which he had earlier brought in with him. Jarwood and Pinewood vigorously studied its contents like two teenage schoolboys pretending as they did to understand its technical jargon.

"Yes this will be most helpful, thank you Dr Moeson, thank you very much." Jarwood sarcastically uttered as he signalled for Moeson to depart.

The Eminent doctor read their body languages clearly, narrowed his eyes at the political misfits, stood up and left unattended, vowing never to return.

"Harvey I think he has given us a safe way out of the dilemma. It helps us to ameliorate the situation and assists us in not further implementing the provisions of the 1999 Terrorist Act."

"Yes I agree Cyril. We couldn't have kept the media quiet. Sooner or later the truth would have emerged. This way we are guaranteed of pacifying the population at large; now any feedback on the alternate medicines"?

"I haven't had a chance to do as you requested Prime Minister. Remember I called in the other…"

"Oh yes, yes I remember, enough of the excuses, get Manoff on the line" Jarwood barked like a grumpy old dog who demanded attention, just then his phone rang and he reluctantly attended to the call.

"Yes, really, well then that deepens the mystery yes I agree we'll need to convene an emergency meeting."

"Who was that"? Pinewood asked rather curious as to the identity of Jarwood's caller.

"Minister for Health"

"Good news"?

"Seems the majority of alternatives are having problems except for Napp and a handful of others, dry herbs are also exempt."

"Looks as though we've found our culprit"!

"Obviously" Jarwood unconvincingly replied.

At 9pm that night in the closed off, no media or any other personal allowed main committee chamber, an armada of shady characters assembled. Present were Harvey Jarwood, Cyril Pinewood, Annette Manoff, the head of ASIO, the chief of the AFP, a representative of the pharmaceutical manufacturing association, a spokesman for the national doctors association plus the president of the political party in power and the minister for health. Once the doors were shut and Jarwood was satisfied with security he cleared his throat and in a deliberate tone of voice declared the meeting open.

"Gentleman we have a very grave matter to discuss. I take it you all understand that you are sworn to secrecy nothing that is said here today will be remembered or mentioned to anyone outside; agreed"?

Everyone present nodded.

"Good it appears…

"That you have no idea of what you're doing"! The pharmaceutical Manufacturers Association representative loudly exclaimed.

"That's not true"! Jarwood angrily answered back clearly upset that anyone should suggest that he was incompetent.

"We believe otherwise, we stand to lose tens of millions of dollars, we run the risk of having to close down and without us who will fund your next election campaign"?

"We also agree with him"! The medical spokesman shouted.

"Gentlemen keep your voices down! There is a limit to the room's sound proofing"! Pinewood cautioned as he tried to diffuse the situation at which point he opened a file containing several bundles of papers and handed them out to everyone including the Prime Minister who had no prior knowledge of their existence.

"Read carefully this is the proposed strategy." He then proudly added.

Both law enforcement officers thought about the previous damning verbal evidence relating to electoral corruption, both thought it best to ignore the facts and ensure their own survival.

"As you may read we have elected to support the viral explanation for the current medical misfortune. This is our best avenue; it allows everyone apart from the surgeons to keep trading. All surgery needs to be cancelled." Cyril carefully put forward.

"It doesn't need to be, we have alternatives." The medical representative argued.

"I understand, however in the present climate, they that is, the drugs need to be recognised by the body. I believe nitrous oxide might be the only systemic anaesthetic available to you. Anything man made is not tolerated." Pinewood explained to the interjector before continuing on." The medico-pharmaceutical industry can survive if we act cleverly. We will never publicly suggest that complete drug failure has occurred; partial impairment is the go, a condition that can easily be overcome by educating patients to adopt additional health giving measures. Trust me gentlemen this will work. The public at large is stupid. We have kept them that way for decades they will believe us before they believe anyone else it's all a matter of wording" Pinewood cleverly explained.

"In other words you want us to keep them in the dark"? The medical representative asked.

"Precisely"! Jarwood answered in the affirmative for Pinewood.

"If it goes completely wrong then we have plan B; which involves publicly stating that as a result of continued investigations by various governmental agencies the true cause of the problem was tampering by Napp Pharmaceuticals." Pinewood then further explained.

"I hope you have proof" The president of the political party bluntly said.

"We will have! Napp's products are presently unencumbered, meaning, that not one of them has suffered."

"That's not proof, it might be good formulations at play on their part otherwise its purely circumstantial evidence." The APF chief cautioned.

"I'll let Manoff be the judge of that, take the floor Annette"! Jarwood directed.

"I er.... that is the department acknowledges Napp formulations are different. We've had difficulty in accepting their submissions, however since the substances involved are largely innocuous and they, that is Napp satisfied the Code of Good Manufacturing Practice, we could not deny product registration."

"Why haven't their products failed"? The general question was then poised.

"Under the provisions of the TAG Act, Napp manufacturers therapeutic goods, even though all that they do is micronize, blend and pack herbals into capsules and flow through infusion tea bags for specified purposes without the inclusion of any excipients. It was their argument that the blend ensured complete intestinal absorption and gave better results than any herbal given neat. The formulations were a collection of innocuous mixtures without any outlandish claims. We certainly tried to frustrate them by asking for locally conducted clinical trials and papers but at the end of the day we had to relinquish our position and list their products once they engaged the services of an eminent Queen's council. This caused bad blood between the two of us." Manoff slowly explained.

"I believe you recently shut them down and then you retreated." The political president stated.

"That is correct"! Manoff reluctantly agreed her face reddened with the memory of it all.

"Don't you think taking further action against them might be perceived as a personal vendetta"? The political president then asked.

"I think I might be able to shed light on the situation." The ASIO chief said easing the tension in the room. "It may not be known to Ms Manoff that the Catholic Church is involved with Napp. One Archbishop Steven Moulds in the USA has invested heavily in the company. We received information from free lance FBI agents about a telephone call that the Archbishop had with a Mr Star I think they said in which Moulds sought his help to resolve the Napp impasse."

Manoff reacted visibly to this revelation.

"What's a freelance FBI agent"? Jarwood asked intrigued with its definition.

"It is well known that law enforcement officers throughout the world sell information. There is a market for everything; our own also engage in this activity. Freelance agents work predominately for one agency outside of that, their time is their own."

"Doesn't anyone monitor them"? Jarwood asked.

"No one blows the whistle"!

"Hum, not impressed"!

"Welcome to the real world"! The ASIO chief responded. A hush spread throughout the room as each wondered if their lives had been sold to a foreign body.

"Is the Catholic Church in Australia involved with Napp"? The party president asked concerned about the political ramifications at the ballot box.

"It appears not. Archbishop Moulds is a rogue agent who follows the American dream, he is money driven; it's all business to him"!

"No other motives"?

"Not at this stage, what I have told you is based upon the sketchy information that we obtained."

"I don't think we can involve Napp any further. The electoral cost will destroy us we can't become immersed in any sort of religious war." The party president warned.

"I agree but what if the Church seeks to interfere in the nation's politics. What do we do then"? Jarwood asked mindful of the Church's importance.

"Prove the assertion and on this score there is something quite disturbing that I need to relate to you." The ASIO head replied.

"Very well, proceed." Jarwood responded somewhat aloofly.

"In order to obtain as much evidence as possible, we often turn to clairvoyants to assist us in our investigations. Each that we approached gave us the same answer." The ASIO chief paused and looked around the room to gauge the potential reaction.

"Yes go on'! Jarwood impatiently growled.

"It appears that the current crisis is an act of God"!

"Don't give me that religious dribble, what utter nonsense! This is the twenty-first century! Science rules not unproven religious superstition! Give us proper facts man"! Jarwood demanded as he hit his fist on the boardroom's conference table in front of him. The ASIO chief remained silent and shook his head.

'Harvey irrespective of your beliefs we have to ensure our political survival, leave Napp alone, leave the Catholic Church alone, it's hardly a terrorist. Even though only twenty percent of its flock practice their faith regularly it doesn't mean that the rest are immoral. We need to navigate our course carefully. Let's take on board what Pinewood has put together for the time being until more emerges. How say you"? The party president strongly argued.

"Very well" The Prime Minister grumbled.

"And the rest of you, are we in agreement"?

"We're not happy, but I suppose we have to cope the best we can" The Pharmaceutical Manufacturing Association representative admitted.

"Then gentlemen I think we should call it a day"! The party president declared as he rose to his feet. Manoff remained seated her abandoned religious beliefs resurfaced and were destined to haunt her for weeks to come.

"Good work Cyril, keep you finger on the pulse, fine tune the operation, you'll be richly rewarded"! Jarwood falsely but convincingly said as he accompanied Pinewood out of the meeting room. They walked down the corridor and through the member's hall where four sets of paired columns rose over an 'altar' of black granite to support a glazed pyramid canopy. Every time the distinguished Harvey Jarwood walked through the hall he gave thanks to all of his extended family and friends who were instrumental in designing the new parliament house. His family was born to rule and did so according to the desires of the crowned goat. The basic plan of the new parliament was laid out the same as Stonehenge with the missing 'Stone of Scone' taken from Westminster Abbey and placed in its foundation.

The architectural plan revealed the image of the crowned goat, the eyes formed by the two chambers of parliament, the outside forecourt depicted a crown with an all seeing eye in its centre and the giant curved walls formed the basic structure of the goat's face and horns thus completing the occult significance of Canberra.

Harvey rounded the corner that would take him in the direction of his office and as he did so he was rewarded with a wall of Bogong moths!

18

SELECTIVITY

"Woggle, boggle, Bogong; God how I'm sick of these nuisances; can't one just get on with the job of governing as one sees fit? Bleeding invaders! How can we be expected to function? To be seen to be responsible? I ask you. How can we"? Harvey Jarwood muttered to himself as he walked and swept away the moths that plagued the parliamentary corridors of corrupted power.

"Swat to the right, swat to the left, twirl, step forward, twirl, swat to the left, swat to the right twirl, jump"!

"What the hell are you doing Cyril"! Jarwood barked clearly irritated by everything around him.

"Having a little fun"!

"Well I glad some one is; any word on the air conditioning"?

"Yes Sir, completely stuffed Sir! Filters, ducting, fan, outlets, completely stuffed with moths! Time to get the fans out! Only way to cool this place down"! Pinewood smirked.

"Damn it"!

"There's more good news Sir"!

"What's that"?

The moth plague has two variants. Not just the Bogong of 87 but the webbing worm of 89 eating away all the soft furnishings. What an excuse to redecorate, never did like that soothing green décor. Need something more like fiery red, hot, passionate red! Which reminds me, seen the gardens lately"?

"Can't say I've noticed, why do you ask"? Jarwood inquired.

"The second plagues arrived"!

"What second plague"?

"The 97 Argentinean stem weevil; the lawns are completely destroyed. Isn't it strange how history is repeating itself? There is a solution, we could replace them with synthetic grass like they use on tennis courts except some one might think we're fair game and decide to call us plastic like the grass."

Jarwood sighed and rolled his eyes to the heavens it was becoming all too much for him.

"I say Prime Minister you wouldn't by any chance know anyone around here who dabbles in the occult, would you"?

Jarwoods body hair spiked all over, he adjusted his tie and without looking at Pinewood responded." Not at all! I don't mix in those circles"!

"I'm not suggesting that you do; it just seems strange that the morning newspapers have reprinted the news items of a few days ago and have hypothesized that the aboriginal people who placed the original curse on the new parliament house are active again. Perhaps you should say sorry"?

"For what"?

Pinewood bit his tongue and kept pace with the Prime Minister until he looked back and said. "Footprints in the sand"!

"Have you gone completely mad Cyril? What are you talking about now? The bleeding beach is hundreds of miles from here"!

"It was a metaphor sir of the impression that you have left upon this finely sculptured corridor, your footprints sir"! Pinewood explained as he invited his superior to about face and gaze upon the carpet. Each step that Jarwood had taken had ripped up the pile and left behind the outline of his shoe and an imprint of its soles pattern.

"Oh my God what next"?

"Laughter I suppose sir."

"Don't be funny"!

"It's not my intention, listen." Pinewood quietly whispered as he grabbed hold of the Prime Ministers forearm and steadied him.

"It's all around us." Jarwood observed as he spun slowly around and allowed his ears to pick up the faintest sound.

"And it's not via the intercom." Pinewood further observed as he also continued to search for its source. All those in the building awoke from their jobs and curiously walked about.

"More mind games, damn woggle"! Jarwood cursed.

"So you do believe."

"Not really! Just remembering what the ASIO man said about clairvoyants and an act of God. Call house security, they'll sort it out"!

"Yes Sir." Pinewood answered full of admiration for his boss. Meanwhile Jarwood went through an open door to his right and into a large sitting room which had a window to the outdoors it struck the Prime Minister that there were no people outside of parliament house, the area was deserted.

"Strange; very strange"! He thought to himself as he scratched the side of his thigh.

"No one seems to be answering sir." Pinewood said making reference to house security as he bounced into the room; somewhat relieved that he had found his superior.

"Cyril."

"Yes sir."

"I thought you said the grass was dead"?

"Yes I did sir."

"It appears green to me"!

"Let me see sir." Pinewood excused himself as he manoeuvred himself around the P.M. and approached the window. "It is sir; however, it also appears to be moving"!

Once again the hair spiked all over Jarwood's body as he felt something was not quite right. An eerie feeling swept through his entire anatomy and he feared for his safety. He immediately thought of his wife and children and for once in his life lost his homosexual tendencies. Transfixed by the lawn's hypnotic movements the pair was unaware of the security guards who had just entered the room.

"Prime Minister your attention please we are evacuating the building, this way please"! The elderly guard gruffly commanded in true military fashion.

"Evacuation.... what evacuation? I that is we haven't heard" The startled Jarwood rightfully questioned quite annoyed at the guards obvious disrespect.

"The building is under siege. It's not safe to be in here, all personnel are being directed to the nuclear fallout shelter below." The other security guard explained. Jarwood carefully examined him with his eyes and deduced that he was part aboriginal and proud of it. His name badge said it all for it was in the shape of an ancient Waugal, which caused Jarwood to shiver. Doubt crept into the P.M.'s mind. Were these people telling the truth, were they genuine guards or was this an assassination attempt? He looked towards Pinewood for reassurance but nothing came for he had divided his attention between what was happening outside and what was being said inside.

"What exactly is the danger"? Pinewood asked.

Viscous Kookaburra's, poisonous frogs and snakes; no one can leave, we need to take you downstairs for your safety." The part aboriginal rudely and abruptly replied.

"How long for"?

"Until everything settles down." The part aboriginal guard answered clearly insulted by Jarwoods lack of knowledge of the land.

"You make it sound biblical." Jarwood dryly said with the inference that the part aboriginal was ignorant of such teachings.

"It has those proportions; it's a natural phenomenon, a huge population explosion that happens every twelve to fifteen years if the conditions are right. This year the seasons have been good, productive, there's an abundance of food, moths proliferate; beetles multiply and multiply. They attract predators and unfortunately this time Canberra is in the middle of it."

"No curse then"? Jarwood remarked feeling a little more at ease but still remaining a tad nervous.

"The elders would disagree; after all you white men are responsible for their present predicaments"!

Jarwood disregarded the inflammatory statement and avoided making any further comment.

"Do we have to go into the bunker? I'm claustrophobic; can't we stay inside until it blows over"? Pinewood whinged; at which point the elderly security guard violently pushed him aside and Pinewood fell to the floor.

"There's your answer deputy." The elderly security guard replied as he pointed to the wall's air conditioning outlets from which the head of a poisonous snake protruded and hissed aggressively.

"Okay no more encouragements I'm out of here"!

They exited the room and joined the small throng of people that was hurriedly making its way to the underground hiding place. The eeriness that Jarwood felt earlier filled the building everywhere that they went, a mixture of hisses, laughter and thumping filled the voids and escaped through the crevices to culminate in distorted sounds of impending doom. The entrance to the underground facility offered salvation, the sanctuary was vast, well equipped, self sufficient and decorated in soothing green.

"Oh, not more green! What is it with you people can't you think of any other colour besides green" Pinewood whinged as he made his way into the great subterranean palace.

Television screens hung like chandeliers from the ceilings throughout the complex there was no lack of information or entertainment there.

"Did we build this"? He questioned.

"The building yes, the technical stuff no. Like most things in this country it was imported from overseas."

"Good quality stuff I hope"?

"Absolutely, we are obliged to guarantee the safety of your kind"! The part aboriginal acidly replied.

"How secure is it"? Jarwood stepped in and firmly asked.

"It is completely impervious to wind, rain, snow, rats, insects and mice." The part aboriginal mockingly replied Jarwood forced a stiff upper lip, dismissed the guard and went in search of someone who appeared more accommodating and acceptably polite. The entrance to the facility slammed shut; the sound echoed throughout its entirety and was followed by a whoosh of air signalling that it was hermetically sealed, intact and that the recycling process had begun.

"Oh isn't this marvellous"! Pinewood chirped as he danced about and examined all of the nook and crannies before proceeding up a flight of stairs that allowed him to discover the command centre. Inside sat a highly trained army officer expert in the workings of the facility. Pinewood could see that he was absorbed in cranking up the various life support systems.

"Well what do we have here"? Pinewood merrily asked as his eyes darted all over the impressive array of dials; switches and meters.

"This is a restricted area sir, would you please leave"! The army captain sternly ordered.

"Listen mate, I'm the deputy Prime Minister, if you want to keep your job I suggest you change your attitude! In any case if this is so restricted why did you leave the door unlocked"? Cyril Pinewood hit back. The officer ignored the irritating statement and continued with the tasks at hand.

"Look at all the pretty dials, what do we have here"? Cyril sparkled as he pointed to a speckled toggle switch.

"Please don't touch that sir, it activates the solar panels"!

"Tell me more, I need to know more"! Cyril playfully begged.

"In a moment I'm still shutting down the building"!

"Turning it into a ghost town? How spooky"! Cyril gleefully said with a sense of macabre in his voice.

"No sir! I'm tying to make the building less attractive to invaders."

Cyril remained silent and watched attentively. When the officer had finished and was satisfied with the result he turned to Pinewood and gave him a brief description of the various controls.

"This is a state of the art self sufficient facility. All power is off the grid, not from it, solar power capable of generating 110.5kw hours per day from as little as six peak sun hours. We have Atrace Engineering version 6.01 inverters, Ducal C60 charge controllers and a master power supply control panel that produces sine wave quality power. Located in a safe part of the building are housed airtight battery boxes that contain two hundred and forty lead acid batteries, the inverters convert the available electricity into a 240 volt supply. Outside stand eighty solar collector modules mounted on stands capable of three-way tracking these follow the sun as it traverse the sky. An Orion propane generator starts and stops to recharge the solar batteries whenever necessary, these are monitored by a sophisticated computer system that ensures………"

"Everything runs smoothly, very impressive, the taxpayers money has been put to good use. What about the air, water and food"? Pinewood asked interrupting the army officer.

"Swiss manufactured Lowa air filtering system was used in the design of this building; it safeguards against any undesirable agents such as viruses eg smallpox, bacteriologicals such as anthrax, radioactive fall out and even smoke from a forest fire."

"Impressive but who cleans the filters once they're clogged"? Pinewood smartly asked. The army officer evaded the comment and continued on with his memorised description.

"We have an endless supply of fresh water from a tamperproof eight hundred and fifty feet deep well found beneath us."

"Thank you very much, I see I'm wanted." Pinewood excused himself as he viewed a monitor. "I'll come back and talk to you soon.

I'm sure we'll be down here for a few days." He then suggested as he departed to return downstairs.

"Yes sir what did you need me for"? He asked expectantly as he approached his superior who was viewing a large plasma screen.

"Look at this Cyril, Canberra is in a state of chaos"! Jarwood sombrely answered which quickly dampened Pinewoods secret desires. Cyril Pinewood shifted his focus; watched and listened very carefully to the televised news report.

"The Governor General of Australia has declared a state of emergency in Canberra. People are being evacuated. Already many casualties have occurred as a result of unprovoked snake attacks. As many of you are aware from previous media reports, moths and beetles have plagued new parliament house and its surrounding areas. These it seems have attracted countless numbers of frogs and kookaburra's hell bent on a feeding frenzy, which in turn attracted thousands of venomous snakes. Various religious groups are calling it an act of God in retribution for the sins committed by our government. They are saying that this natural phenomenon is in fact five separate plagues and more will follow. The major Christian churches are remaining silent on the cause of the events. Irrespective of this we presently have a nation without an operating government. All parliamentary business has come to a halt." The news presenter paused to allow the cameraman on board the television stations helicopter to transmit the all important on the scene images. When sufficient graphic detail had been shown she continued.

"I believe the Minister for Health and the Minister for Defence have both been air lifted out of Canberra and are both in a critical condition following multiple snake bites. There have also been civilian casualties but at this stage we are unable to give you any reliably accurate numbers.

No word from the Prime Minister or his staff. It is highly likely that they have taken shelter in the emergency nuclear bunker situated beneath parliament house."

Does that mean we could be down here for weeks"? Cyril asked out of concern for his long-term mental and physical wellbeing. Jarwood did not answer instead he sat grim faced and threw his hands up in the air and screamed." The XXX industry will be ruined, what will people do without their latest porn flick"?

"Was that you that I saw in 'Bite Hard' opposite Dawn Under" Pinewood asked cross-eyed just as the all-important red phone rang.

"Is that you Harvey"?

"Yes it is George. I suppose you've heard about our natural disaster"?

"The plagues, yeah, some of our evangelists are making good hay from it." Brian George president of the United States of America replied. "That wasn't the purpose of my call. I understand England and yourselves are experiencing some difficulty with the efficacy of your pharmaceutical products."

"What of it'? Jarwood snapped back clearly offended by the Presidents lack of sympathy and offer of help.

"We appear to have incurred the same problem."

"Really"! Jarwood gloated happy that the yanks were not immune as previously thought. "When did it happen"?

"We believe based on our reliable sources that all batches manufactured from the first Tuesday of November of this year have been affected."

"Across the board"

"Strangely enough no; only antidepressants, anxiolytics and anti psychotic drugs have been selectively targeted. Which makes us think that the epidemiology is different to yours; by the way your country's making the news over here. Used to be we only heard about your bush fires and gay parades. You've really got it going on this time. The evangelist's especially our black brothers are having a field day with your plagues and that small part you had in 'Bite Hard"!

"Really"! Jarwood answered aloofly hoping that no one else was listening to the telephone conversation apart from the army officer who monitored everything in the emergency underground complex.

"I think you may have to revise your racial policies."

"Out multi-cultural approach is working just fine! Thank you very much"!

"By the way what's a Wag…gal"?

"That's pronounced Waugal, Wau…..gul…."! Jarwood sarcastically explained.

"Those black ministers I spoke about are calling it an Angel of God." The President drawled. Then there was silence. "Harvey, Harvey? Dumb Aussie bastard hung up on me. Brian George the president of the United States of America cursed. "Get me the Head of the CIA, time to cancel our protection of Mr H Jarwood! Let the Aussies look after their own"!

Harvey Jarwood's dramatic ending of the telephone conversation further inspired his potential lover Cyril Pinewood.

"What a man"! Cyril thought to himself as he returned his gaze to the television monitor that he was previously watching. The elders of the aboriginal clan the Pickett-Farmers were being interviewed as to the likely cause of Canberra's afflictions.

"I think you should watch this Prime Minister." He said in a low voice as he approached his idol.

"What now"!!

"It's about the Waugal, you know the aboriginal creator, spirit, soul, the one who looks after its…."

"I don't want to know. Go away! I have enough to contend with"! Jarwood shouted as he stormed off in search of a quiet corner in which to retreat and that was exactly what the demure Miss Ivy Humblebug had as well; an overwhelming dilemma; for the incriminating evidence that she once saw in the company of Mr Jack Stern Alias Geoff Stricker, negotiating agent for Napp Pharmaceuticals was now in the top drawer of her bedside table and begged to become publicly known.

Ivy was not in Canberra; she had taken two weeks of her annual leave and returned to the rural town of Hilltop New South Wales some 200km north east of Canberra. Miss Humblebug lived in an old family cottage that was built by her great grandfather at the turn of the century. It was a simple weatherboard dwelling, two bedrooms, a living room, a combination bath/laundry wet area, no formal dining; all meals were eaten at the simple wooden table located in the middle of the kitchen. There was a rear sleep out and the toilet was located in a cluster of overgrown bushes thirty meters from the rear of the house in the garden. Ivy trained herself not to go to the toilet in the middle of the night for that was more than often a harrowing experience.

Every night Ivy would follow the same ritual. At 9pm after watching her favourite television shows for the night she would make herself a mug of hot chocolate made from full cream fresh country milk, imported Swiss chocolate and topped with six creamy marshmallows. Ivy would then consume it slowly whilst seated on the backstairs of the house as she listened to the country noise and admired the uninhibited galaxy of stars above. She would then venture forth to the outhouse, void her urinary bladder and dash back inside into the comfort of her grandmothers bed which held precious memories of all those who had slept in it. Ivy would take her Dear Diary out of the top drawer of the bedside table, write in meaningful notes on her day's activities, flick to its back pages and solemnly recite her nightly prayers as her grandmother had taught her. Then with arms folded in the shape of the cross across her ample bosom she would escape to her imaginary inner sanctum and fall asleep to awake the next day fully refreshed and rejuvenated.

On the fourth night of her official leave Ivy realised that her Dear Diary was not alone for it had company, male company in the form of hundreds of pages of carefully referenced data that detailed the nefarious workings of the TAG team with their various industrial and political affiliations. Ivy remembered the words of Jack Stern.

"If you decide to do something with it your life will probably be in danger! No point in going to the federal police they're in on it! No point going to the political opposition parties they wrote the legislation! That leaves us with two avenues; the senate and the media."

"Which one do you suggest I try? Which one do I try? Which one do I try"? She repeatedly asked herself and her subconscious each night before she fell asleep.

"I feel really tired Father but I need to talk to you some more." Precious Dhaarling said to Max as she sat opposite him in their little hiding place so carefully disguised in the attic amongst the rubbish of their well appointed house.

"Don't you think it's time for you to go to bed? You have had such an exhausting day, first your oral examination early this morning at the university, then working in the pharmacy, coming home and studying some more. You need to stop burning the candle at both ends and in the middle as well." Max Dhaarling said in a caring manner.

"I know but mother expects it, high achievers usually do, she always wanted me to do something meaty, I have no choice and that's why I need to tell you of my discovery."

"Very well child, explain if you're up to it." Max warmly replied.

"Over the past few weeks I've told you about how much this mystery virus, you know the one reported in the media has affected the patients our pharmacy services and I think that you have deduced that the official story as propagated by the Australian Government is very different to what is occurring."

"I thought it might have been and I suppose no individual can or is prepared to do anything about it." Max rightfully commented.

"You guessed it. The upside in our retail outlet is that Mr gosling has become the golden boy. His penchant for alternatives is working extremely well Ramon Abdullah has put his greedy arrogance on hold and allowed Mr Gossling to ensure their survival. Sadly we are the exception to the rule, pharmacies in general are suffering badly, people are no fools, they know when something doesn't work and in this situation Mr Gossling is a rare man better than all of the alternative therapists put together. He has the rare gift of accurately identifying the cause of a patient's ailment and treating it correctly. Strange how the tables have turned; previously the medico-pharmaceutical industry had the upper hand, now that things have changed people are realising the benefits of natural therapies and are even turning inward to find their own solutions all except for one group." Precious paused and Max Dhaarling did not interrupt. "The drug addicts have become a serious menace worse than before. Ramon Abdullah has fifty six methadone and subutex patients in his pharmacy of these only two or three are coping with the ineffectiveness of their drug, the others have gone crazy"! Again Max Dhaarling remained silent and reflected on the problems that they were also causing in his baby stores.

"Theft, robbery, breaking and entering, muggings that's what they are resorting to in order to obtain any illegal drug that might remotely benefit them. Pharmacies, doctor's surgery and chemist wholesalers are being continuously robbed of narcotics, benzodiazepines and pseudoephedrine compounds. None of this is being reported as the authorities cannot diffuse the situation. A media ban is in place."

"Can't Mr Gossling help"? Max asked ambiguously, Precious looked at him sideways and gathered the true nature of his question.

"If given the chance however the problem is deep seated; its origins are thousands of years old"! The statement caused Max Dhaarling to frown and wonder what his daughter had found.

"I am no genetic or anthropological expert yet I have reached the conclusion through historical reading that Opium did not come about by chance. The plant that we harvest Opium from today is known as Papaver Somniferum it is believed to have evolved from a wild strain Papaver Setigerum which grows in coastal regions of the Mediterranean Sea through centuries of cultivation and selective breeding in effect genetic engineering of one sort of another. The Sumerians knew 4000BC about opium."

"Do you think it was them"?

"It doesn't matter for the Opium poppy then reached China about the fourth century AD through Arab traders who advocated its 'medicinal use."

"It sounds innocent to me." Max Dhaarling genuinely expressed.

"I suppose one could conclude that, especially if one refers to the works of Homer's Iliad and Odyssey and Hippocrates prescriptions. It sounds all quite proper until one research's its neuro-pharmaco-logical effects. Heroin derived from Opium is similar in its effects on brain biochemistry to endorphins, the natural opioid's of the body and may I add less potent. It competes with the endorphins for specialised endorphin/ opioid receptors found on the surfaces of some body cells. Our bodies respond by reducing or even stopping production of endorphins when heroin is consumed. Endorphins are regularly released in the brain and nerves and function to attenuate pain; their other functions if any are still obscure, however I don't quite agree with that proposition."

Max Dhaarling sat mesmerised by his daughters learned authority and he realised that he was well and truly in her academic shadow.

"The reduced endorphin production in Heroin users makes them dependent on the Heroin since a lack of either endorphins or Heroin results in extreme symptoms including pain that occurs in the absence of physical trauma, that is what causes the withdrawal symptoms in Heroin addicts as the body take's some time to restore endorphin production."

"Hum, tell me child; what you have just told me, do you think it is applicable to other drugs"? Max asked as he mentally analysed Precious verbal data.

"Most certainly Father, I would venture to say that we could safely include all of the benzodiazepines, anxiolytics; pain relievers, in fact it is my observation that the people taking these chemicals were miserable before and remained miserable after ingesting them." Precious bitterly expressed.

"What are you suggesting"?

"People in western society generally speaking have forgotten how to be happy, however that is getting away from the crux of my argument."

"Which is"?

"That some one began to tamper with the human race more than six thousand years ago"!

"In what respect"? Max asked

"Genetic and environmental"! Max looked Precious in the eye and chewed on his bottom lip signifying that he was mulling the unproven hypothesis over in his mind.

"Supposing this world is one giant experimental laboratory" Precious put forward as an opening chess move.

"Okay"

"Imagine an observer constantly collects data as the experiment proceeds."

"Yes."

"Supposing the observer decided to become the experimenter because it tired of the results; it wanted something new, something more dramatic perhaps even violent."

"Okay"

"The observer decides to interfere, to plant the seeds of destruction in its own time which coincides with the development of the human races."

"Are you suggesting that it foresaw the dependence of humans upon mind altering chemical substances"?

"Possibly and deliberately genetically engineered Papaver Setigerum"!

19

FREEZING HOT

"How much longer must I have to endure these conditions? After all I am the exulted Prime Minister of Australia! What nonsense to have to sleep out in the open in the auditorium of this nuclear shelter! Where are my private quarters? I'm not one of them! I was born to rule! What idiot designed this place? December the third and I am still here locked up with these imbeciles"! Harvey Jarwood thought as he looked around and struggled to adjust to the artificiality of his surroundings.

"No natural light, no breeze, no fresh air, just recycled stuff, what a technological disaster! A death trap for uninformed individuals! I can't survive down here put me back into the real world! Where are the troops? Where's the rescue party? What are the armed forces doing? Just wait until I get out of here, heads will roll, body bags will fill and Generals will be stripped naked"! Prime Minister Harvey Jarwood bitterly whispered.

"No change in Canberra's status this morning viewers; as usual all attempts to remedy the situation have been thwarted by the astronomically huge numbers of atypically aggressive and venomous snakes that inhabit the city"

Was the message that was repeated almost without variation day in and day out by the majority of Australia's national broadcasting television networks.

"All the more reason heads will roll when I escape this hell hole"! Jarwood angrily muttered to himself as he viewed the numerous television monitors spread around the facility.

"Fifteen days of suffering"!!! He then audibly said.

"It's not that bad old chum, at least we're alive and not in the belly of some giant anaconda"! Cyril Pinewood optimistically chirped after he overheard his superior's severe glumness." But then I must agree with you to some extent." He reflected. "All of my prayers have gone unanswered puts one's faith to the test."

"What are you blabbering on about Cyril"?

"My Catholic faith and my devotion to prayer"

"What of it"?

"Well, I've prayed to St Jude the patron saint of hopeless cases, to St Catherine Labourie whose feast day it was on the 28th November she gave us the Miraculous medal, look I have one here in the palm of my hand. We're lead to believe that anyone who has one in their possession will be granted special graces. Today its St Francis Xavier's feast day, I've tried praying to him as well. Guess I'll just have to keep trying until someone listens and does something about our predicament."

"So you don't think this is an act of God"?

"No Sir highly unlikely, more satanic than anything else"! Pinewoods last phrase struck a chord in the evil heart of Harvey Jarwood.

"How many plagues do you think we've had Cyril"?

"It depends how you interpret the situation Sir."

"Meaning"

"Well do we consider the Melbourne Cup as a plague? If so then we could say that it was number one followed closely by the failure of the pharmaceutical drug system, then we had the moths, worms, weevils, frogs, birds and finally the snakes, in all about eight."

"Not seven"?

"No Sir, not seven unless you were to delete some of them and think of them as being coincidental with one of the others then perhaps the sixth and seventh are yet to come." Cyril confidently replied. Harvey thought awhile and then asked.

"You're certain this is no act of God."

"Yes Sir, firmly"!

"Can I have a look at your Miraculous medal"?

"But of course Sir."

"Do you still have the Somalian Army knife"?

"You mean the one you bought for me from that bright red bearded black man in Mogadishu? What was his name again? Me bipin, me beeping, makes me think he was named after a car or some such thing at birth! Wasn't he the one who produced all of those false passports and wanted you to become the Ambassador or was it Minister for Foreign Affairs for Somalia"? Pinewood asked.

"Yes, one of those, the knife"! Jarwood responded quite annoyed.

"The knife, yes of course I do, it's here in my trouser pocket. Must say its very peculiar, gives off the smell of rotting flesh now and then, probably the wood it's carved from. Don't like it much, people think I've farted or I've got some dreadful form of atrocious body odour"!

"I'm certain they don't"! Jarwood wryly answered.

"You haven't seen the looks. By the way do you still have all of those forged passports the red bearded black man gave you"?

"Yes they're a great party joke"!

"As long as that's all they're being used for" Pinewood seriously cautioned.

"I assure you Cyril all is above board."

"Good Prime Minister, here you are Sir, one Miraculous medal, slightly worn and one stinky Somalian Army knife."

"Thank you Cyril, now will you excuse me, my bowels are making themselves known"!

"The old early morning pre-breakfast evacuation, the pressing predictable, pre-parliamentary runner, ol' habits die hard me hearties." Cyril rattled off like an old sea dog who had an intimate knowledge of the P.M's intestinal tract.

"Thank you Cyril"! Harvey Jarwood grunted, rolled his eyes in obvious disgust and turned to make his way to a remote part of the complex leaving Cyril Pinewood to contemplate facing the horrors of consuming another freshly opened tinned breakfast.

Two levels down in the freezing basement hidden amongst the hundreds of piled up cartons of canned food; Harvey Jarwood swept his hair back, drew in his stomach and carefully unfastened the money belt from around his waist. 'For emergency use only' were the words he remembered being uttered by the bright red bearded Somalian as he handed over the "Official Ambassador for Somalia' passport; except that was not its true purpose, for on each page invisibly written were the satanic verses necessary to awake the desires of his evil intentions.

Harvey fashioned a make shift altar out of the cardboard boxes, knelt uncomfortably in front of it and with the utmost contempt dumped the Miraculous medal on top. He then retrieved the Somalian Army knife from his trouser pocket, smelt the handle's wood and revelled in its pungent odour.

"Death death and more death how marvellous"! Harvey whispered as he kissed the evil object; the wood of which came from a tree that boarded one of the many mass graves that dotted the arid Somalian landscape. The tree's roots penetrated deep into the soil and greedily soaked up and devoured the decaying remnants of those who dared to oppose. The wood obtained from the tree's branches was used as inlays for knifes, a handful of which found themselves in the wrong hands.

Each handle had embossed upon it 'Job before joy' as a general philosophy in life, however cleverly written beneath it was 'JOMZ-JEZJJJY' the handle was in effect the Magick Wand, or rod of authority, cut and trimmed on the day and in the hour of the Sun with its characters inscribed on the day and in the hour of Mercury. There was no need to aspergate, fumigate or stain the wand with sacrificial blood as its fibres were made of petrified human remains. These wands were always presented wrapped in silken cloth in all colours apart from black or brown.

Harvey Jarwood's breathing became laboured as he forcibly whispered.

"The power is mine to dissect, to arrest, to cut, to end"!

He carefully extended the hinged knife, no ordinary implement it resembled a mini sword. Upon its blasé was lasered 'Adonay' on one side and 'Athane' on the other. In the relative darkness of his environment the knife's handle began to emit a phosphorescent light the tool necessary to read the passport's satanic verses. Thousands of miles away the bright red bearded Somalian became aware through the psychic network that emergency procedures had been implemented by one of his disciples and he set about preparing himself for his disciple's success. Mr Bipin Greatrex was obsessed with introducing a new breed of man into the political world, the unidentifiable sadistic satanic homosexual. Harvey Jarwood was the first of many groomed to find themselves in positions of immense power; curious that it should start down under and work its way to the top.

Bipin Greatrex marched with great urgency to the mass grave on the outskirts of Mogadishu; it was there that the tree stood from which Cyril Pinewood's army knife was fashioned. The same tree would act as a beacon and attract the necessary forces needed to achieve Harvey Jarwoods freedom. No intelligent individual ever went there; the area had a gruesome reputation for past and present bad events; ones that literally petrified people into staying away. Stories of grieving relatives being found at the gravesite withered, mummified and completely drained of blood and all body fluids scared the locals beyond belief. Bipin Greatrex was unafraid, it was his territory, the tree and he were one; each respected the other, each powerful in its own rite, both realised that together they complimented and completed the darkest of trilogies that beckoned global domination.

Greatrex knelt by the tree's side and waited patiently for its surface roots to tantalisingly invade his body like an insidious cancer. The sky darkened in the immediate vicinity, the wind blew with an intense hot ferocity and the Greatrex chanted continuously making reference to the Seven Hills of Rome and Capital Hill in Washington D.C. The tree stirred into visible life and whipped itself into a frenzy; rigid branches became fluid, twigs rope like, leaves extensions of them, the trunk fashioned itself into a handle and awaited the station owners hand. Greatrex cracked the eager whip the surrounding elements obeyed, vortexes of energy formed, broke apart and reformed repetitively until they reached a common goal and channelled themselves into the three points of the satanic triangle.

"Abracadabra." Harvey Jarwood solemnly said with wide opened arms, paused and then assigned an evil spirit to each letter of the Magickal word.

"A for Adonai."

"B for Buseeognation."

"R for Radisha."

"A for Agnon."

"C for Cados."

"A for Alpha."

"D for Destatur."

"A for Abac."

"B for Beroth."

"R for Ruach."

"A for Agios."

"The demon spirits of power descend I beseech thee, come to my aid, rid me of all of my afflictions, free us of God's plagues, let our Master rule as he was meant to, how dare He (God) makes a mockery of our cherished symbols. I conjure thee the most glorious, efficacious incomparable Lord, the true 'God of Hosts', come quickly without delay, front whatsoever part of the world thou art in, create the answers, satisfy my demands and those of my kind, make thy power known, manifest yourself within the triangle and destroy this circle of false lies"! Harvey Jarwood deliberately and passionately said in a low demonic voice. He took the miniature satanic sword and drove it into the hearts of the miraculous medal. Blood poured forth copiously something he had not expected. Initially he thought that the blade had slipped and cut his hand, not so, the miraculous medal bled unabated. Horrified by the result Jarwood stopped what he was doing; wiped away the dripping perfumed Precious blood from his hand and fingers and threw the sacred medal against the wall. Thousands of miles away Bipin Greatrex observed the vision of what had happened to Harvey Jarwood and momentarily lost faith in his power. Both lay exhausted, their work was accomplished; it was worth it for freedom had been confirmed.

The underground facilities lights flickered once, twice and desperately tried to hold on to no avail, modern technology no matter how well conceived is no match for Nature's fury. The outside solar panels designed as well as they were failed the unexpected meteoric decline in ambient temperature and its associated blitzkrieg. From the clear blue skies overhead tonnes of golf ball sized hailstones bombarded and pounded everything in their path into submission.

They plummeted towards earth as though they had been deliberately sling shotted from above by an army of invisible warriors. The hailstones' velocity was incredible; each broke the sound barrier as it sped towards its designated target, the combination of sound shock waves and direct physical impact reduced every hit to its original components. The barrage continued until all targets were obliterated and the countryside was covered with a sheet of ice metres thick. New Parliament house creaked and groaned under the weight imposed upon it. Its voice could be heard everywhere especially in its bowels where things were made worse by the intolerable freezing conditions.

Darkness filled the underground facility; panic spread like a wild bush fire, only the operations officer remained cool. In his memorized surroundings he activated the necessary switches to bring forth temporary low light, he tapped the ambient temperature gauges repeatedly to check their accurateness, outside minus 65 degrees Celsius, inside minus 10 degrees Celsius.

"What the hell"? The officer grunted as he tried to activate the outdoor surveillance cameras. No result. The buildings groans intensified. "It wasn't built for this! Material fatigue setting in, time to evacuate"! And with that decisive conclusion he activated the appropriate protocol.

As the sirens blared Harvey Jarwood's senses strained to keep control of themselves and him in the pitch-blackness of his secret lair. He fought the disorienting effects of that fright, flight and fight biological defence system an quickly brought it under control to find his way back into the main auditorium.

"What bloody high tech nonsense do we have now"? He cursed to himself before he shouted it out aloud as he stumbled about to discover that the large room was empty.

"Sush no need to shout! There's no one here but me." Cyril Pinewood explained as he approached the wayward Prime Minister. "It's all good news I think." He then added.

"Are you sure? It sounds as if the buildings about to collapse and we'll be both crushed to death." Jarwood anxiously determined.

"Not if we're quick." Cyril confidently replied.

"God it's cold in here"!

"Wait a moment look at the news." Cyril suggested.

"Oh great, here we are in almost complete darkness not knowing what will happen next, signs all around are flashing evacuate and all you want to do is watch television"! Jarwood hysterically shouted.

"Stop it Sir! We are truly saved see for yourself"!

Jarwood momentarily peered at the faint images on the monitor and strained his ears to listen to the commentator's whispers.

"From our permanent on the scene reporter Mike Carlson comes this extraordinary exclusive report, Mike."

"Yes Joslyn as you can see we are standing on a vast sheet of frozen ice, not unlike that of Antarctica. The heavens 'opened up' so to speak a few hours ago at around 9am and dumped enormous amounts of huge hailstones that pummelled the area. Nothing escaped; houses, cars and all of those nasty snakes, all gone, devastated, reduced to rubble. The only ones to survive were the birds they flew the coup hours before the ice storm."

"It looks as if Australia's Prime Minister can finally be rescued." Joslyn suggested.

"Not so Joslyn, the ice is meters thick any rescue party will have to wait until the ice melts."

"Damn it," Jarwood mumbled, as he feared the worse.

"How long will that take"? Jaslyn then asked.

"Even though it is summer perhaps one or two weeks I just hope that the Prime Minister is somewhere dry or at least water tight."

"Could you enlarge on that Mike"?

"When all of this ice melts there's going to be an awful lot of water about"!

"Thank you Mike"

"Pleasure Joslyn" He cheerfully said as he waved goodbye and shivered to indicate how cold his surrounding were.

"Now to our foreign correspondents in Rome and Washington D.C. Jacob are you there, Jacob"?

"Yes Joslyn." Jacob replied as he wiped the perspiration off his face.

"Can you explain to our viewers what you are experiencing in the Holy City"? Before he answered he again wiped the perspiration from his face and took a large mouthful of water from the litre bottle that he carried with him.

"We are experiencing sudden extreme heat, almost like being dropped into a hot air oven. It started at 3am this morning and hasn't let up. We are in winter, the present outside air temperature reads a staggering 47degrees Celsius. Rome's residents are going berserk they think that the city has been hit by some sort of military thermal heat ray"!

"I believe a similar situation exists in Washington D.C."

"Really"

"Yes Jacob, thank you, stay on the line as we talk to Marcus." Joslyn politely but firmly said as the television screen spilt vertically into two images revealing the Washington correspondent on the right.

"Hello Joslyn it's quite late in the night over here around 10pm."

"That's early for some folk." Joslyn quipped Marcus avoided the sharp response.

"As you can see people are walking about quite scantily dressed with nothing left to the imagination and in defiance of our strict dress codes. It is an unbelievable 118 degrees Fahrenheit which translates to about 48 degrees Celsius I believe it is meant to be winter."

"Any speculation on the cause"

"This is America every conceivable reason is already up for grabs, from alien invasions, conspiracies galore, religious rigor-mortis and terrorist tea parties. Some are even suggesting that your events in Australia are the true cause, highly unlikely, but then one never knows"!

"Well we're done for"! Harvey Jarwood sighed. "Stuck in here for another two weeks, let's hope this place is watertight! By the way where is every one"? He asked.

"Through the emergency exit Sir, this way Sir." Cyril Pinewood optimistically said as he directed the PM who appeared very confused and distraught.

Bipin Greatrex felt his disciple's anxiety for it paralleled his own. Bipin did not know what to make of the hidden symbolism behind the Miraculous medal's shedding of Precious blood, but those who had died a cruel death in their pursuit of Somalia's freedom knew and rejoiced in its meaning. The bones of their corpses rattled and banged incessantly causing the ground to shake and tremble, the dust to rise and the vultures to flee. The bones' percussive movements emitted a sound reminiscent of Verdi's Prisoner Chorus and Tchaikovsky's 1812 Overture. The soil moved rhythmically to the beat, the dust formed images of fallen soldiers and fuelled Bipin's determination to succeed at all costs; after all he was the secret organizer of the Somalian war lords, peace would come to the land only when the world reached a critical stage of oil supply, then and only then would he announce the untapped wealth that lay beneath Somalia's deserts.

Thousands of miles away Jack Stern wandered the national park where the Genius Loci was hidden and reflected on the birth of Christ and the importance of the gifts of myrrh, frankincense and gold that his parents received. The wind brought news of the various global events that were presently televised world wide, the trees reacted visibly and started to secrete resin in defence, whilst Jack became aware that a future foe, a Master of Affliction awaited him.

20

HUMAN RIGHTS

Ivy Humblebug kept abreast with the news as it was reported with respect to poor plagued Canberra, political capital of Australia and she wondered if she would ever be called back into active duty. Not so everything was in disarray a testament to centralised bureaucratic power and how it can go terribly wrong. The ice storm guaranteed that it would be months if not years before the TAG building was operational again, providing something could be salvaged that is. The responsibility of that federal department's business was temporarily shifted to the state health departments and it invariably resulted in more chaos due to the individual variations with respect to the interpretation of the complex laws and their regulations.

Ivy continuously dwelled on the importance of the information she possessed and speculated on what might happen once it was leaked and what impact it would likely have upon her personal safety. The pro and contra arguments she had with herself yielded no clear direction for being located in Australia thwarted these. Jack Stern's question 'which one will it be, the senate or the media' she eventually realised was not necessary meant to be in Australia and her analytical mind concluded that the word 'senate' meant much more than the Australian upper house.

'A conclave of educated, intelligent, incorruptible, moral, ethical people' as the great Greek philosophers intended it to be thousands of years ago. An instrumentality that brought forth proper business practices which most importantly guaranteed the respect of human rights.'

Which country should she approach? Would it be one of Australia's political and or miliary allies? Would exposure of the sensitive data in her possession in a foreign land by all means available create sufficient leverage to correct the abominable breaches of human rights as perpetrated by the present long standing Australian Government and its passing into law of all of its proposed parliamentary acts that harboured hidden agendas?

Ms Humblebug's eager mind considered all of the countries that Australia had alliances with and reckoned that irrespective of how accurate and damning the information she had, it would in all probability be conveniently lost therefore the only independent avenue if it had any chance at all might be the United Nations. Ivy mentally checked her available credit card balance and arithmetically deduced she had sufficient funds to travel and stay overseas for about five days.

Then in order to safeguard her future and that of her fellow Australians she would need to copy the privileged information given to her by Jack Stern Alias Geoffrey Stricker in triplicate. Two of which she would forward to the two most influential people within the UN and the last Ivy would stow away in her Grandma's secret hiding place. The original copy would remain in her possession disguised as a complication of burnt music, this she would hand deliver once she reached the USA.

With great care and diligence Ivy set about copying the data by burning the number of copies she required on her laptop computer and once satisfied with the result ventured to the local post office. There she remained low key and calm and went about her 'Official business'; she sent two parcels by International Express Mail, one to the head of the newly formed powerful Human Rights Council and the other to the UN's Secretary General, both contained covering letters supposedly written by A Manoff and J Uzzi c/o TAG's Headquarters Canberra.

With the literary missiles on their way a determined Ivy Humblebug packed her bags, organized her flight on the internet and drove herself at a leisurely pace to Sydney's International airport. After an eighteen-hour wait she boarded Quantas Flight U278 direct to Los Angels California, within twenty-six hours Ivy found herself at New York's J F Kennedy International airport. It was 8am in the morning, quite chilly; a cold Artic wind blew through the metropolis, although alone, Ms Humblebug was not fearful, she was on a mission, a crusade, Ivy hailed down an available bright yellow taxi and had herself ferried to the UN building located on the Plaza bearing its name.

"Is your heating broken"? She asked the taxi driver as she buttoned up her flimsy overcoat.

"No ma'me it's not that cold today"!

"What do you call cold"? Ivy frowned as she visibly shivered and looked outside the windows at the drab surroundings.

"Oh about minus ten degrees, today's warm already three degrees." The Egyptian national replied. "Don't worry lady, you'll be very warm once you're inside the UN, they've got the best of everything"!

"Thank you." Ivy politely answered as she resigned herself to her fate and lost herself in her own thoughts.

Traffic was slow, very slow the Big Apple although grey was welcoming. There was a certain buzz in the air that suggested if you had a dream it could be realised here. Ivy although well-educated and well positioned in life was a little lost like all of us and constantly searched for its elusive meaning.

"We almost there Ma'me, sorry it took so long, I give you special discount, okay"? The Egyptian suggested.

"As you wish"

"By the way what country you from"?

"Australia." Ivy coldly replied.

"First time here"

"No many times before." She cunningly replied knowing full well that he was intent on taking her for a ride. Ivy lent forward and peered at the taximeter. The Egyptian became stone faced as he manoeuvred his taxi towards the taxi rank outside the UN building and stopped the car.

"That'll be…."

"Thirty dollars I think is fair"! Ivy firmly put forward as she flashed her official TAG badge. The Egyptian accepted the offer and said no more.

The wind outside was even colder than at the airport, steam bellowed upwards out of the numerous sidewalk vents.

Ivy was tempted to stand on one of these and thaw herself out before entering the UN building but decided not to as such behaviour might cause suspicion to arise about her true identity. The complex was huge, besides the thirty-one storey main building, there were smaller ones attached to it. Somewhat lost Ivy asked one of the circulating official UN guards for directions and before long Ms Humblebug found herself on the twenty-third floor of the UN building after having passed through three vigorous security checks.

The air was heavy with warmth. The buildings interior décor suggested genuine help was available. Ivy trusted her feeling and knocked on the door of Mr Peter Ima undersecretary to the Human Rights Council.

"Come in, door's unlocked." An elderly cheery voice invited. Ivy swallowed hard, forced the door open and stepped into a large cluttered room in the middle of which sat the middle aged greying Peter Ima and his youthful personal secretary. He stood up, adjusted his attire and greeted Ivy Humblebug.

"Good morning Miss, what time was your appointment"? He warmly asked.

"I don't have one." Ivy answered somewhat embarrassed.

"Oh, then I can't see you I'm afraid. I've confused you with some one else." Ima stated.

"When can I see you sir, its frightfully important"?

"That's what they all say. Let me see now, when's the next available Miss Samuel"? Ima asked his secretary, as he looked Ivy up and down.

"Not until eight weeks from today unless we have a cancellation which is unlikely sir"

"Oh dear, seems you came all this way for nothing miss"!

Tears welled up in Ivy's eyes, the stress of lengthy unbroken air travel, plus lack of sleep started to take its toll. Ivy suppressed any potential sob and pulled out her official TAG identification and handed it over to Mr Ima who studied its significance.

"On official business without an appointment, certain you're in the right office miss"?

"Yes sir."

Peter Ima thought awhile and then asked." Seeking political asylum"?

"No sir, not at this stage."

"Refugee from Canberra, I've seen the chaos."

"Not as yet sir"

"Very well, what do you have for me"? Ima asked as he became increasingly interested in Ivy's unexpected presence.

"This sir" She said as she handed over a disc labelled hits of the 60's, 70's and 80's. "It's not what it seems sir."

"I gather that miss, I'll have a look at it when I get a chance and let you know what I think." Ima said as he toyed with her.

"I can't let you do that sir. I've only got enough money to last me five days then I must leave"!

"Where are you staying"?

"No where sir, I came directly from the airport."

Ima revised his attitude and examined Ms Humblebug more carefully. "The information on the disc"

"Is politically very sensitive sir" Ivy confirmed

"Are you a courier"?

"No sir just a concerned citizen"

"Why not take it to your administration"?

"Because I value my life sir"! Ivy truly replied.

"Then perhaps we should have a look at it." Ima concluded.

"Thank you sir"

"Miss Samuel contact Jonathon will you, have him come up immediately."

"Yes sir right away."

"Miss Humblebug, take a seat won't you? Would you care for some coffee"?

"No sir, a bed would be nice."

"Later miss later." Ima replied cheekily.

Computer expert Jonathon arrived within minutes of being summonsed, he introduced himself and after receiving instructions from Ima took the disc and Ivy Humblebug back to his lair. Once there he made Ivy as comfortable as possible within his messy office and then proceeded to insert the disc into his high powered mainframe computer. He was about to ask Ivy about her mission when the information that he scanned hit him.

"Wow! What do we have here? Interesting, very interesting, Ima's going to be happy with this." He audibly mumbled to himself. Ivy's ears caught note of what he said and asked.

"What can be done about it"?

"Nothing much I'm afraid."

"But you just said Ima would be pleased." Ivy replied quite flabbergasted.

"Yes I know Miss Humblebug but for the United Nations Organization to interfere with a sovereign democratic country, well, that is something beyond its power. I'm afraid all of this needs to be referred to our legal department." Jonathon replied politely as he pointed to the large LCD display screen.

"I've wasted my time" Ivy replied quite despondent and downtrodden.

"Its early days, wait here, I need to talk with Peter."

"Very well" Ivy replied as she half sighed, half yawned and closed her eyes to shut out the anxiety of uncertainty. Two hours of blissful sleep passed by which allowed Ivy Humblebug's troubled mind to rest.

"Miss Humblebug, Miss Humblebug." A young afro-American woman said as she attempted to stir Ivy out of her deep and much needed slumber.

"Yes I need to go to the United Nations. Australia's in deep trouble, its people have lost their freedom, there's no democracy." She feebly replied as her head rolled from side to side.

"Poor dear, you're really exhausted, I think I'll let you sleep a little more." And with that she left and locked the door behind her. As the morning dragged on Ivy's sleep regained her strength and she awoke refreshed to find Jonathon busy at his computer terminal.

"You're finally awake. Good, you must be hungry. Need to freshen up before lunch"? He thoughtfully asked with a smile on his face. Ivy returned the smile, stretched and nodded 'yes'.

"Come with me then." He instructed and led the way to a well-equipped staff bathroom and left Ivy to attend to her toiletries. He patiently waited and then took her to an upstairs staff restaurant and allowed Ivy to help herself to the wide selection of food available. Peter Ima and his secretary Miss Samuel joined them.

"You look much better than earlier this morning." Ima genuinely complimented Ivy as he appreciated her figure.

"Thank you sir, it was all so rushed to get here."

"I can imagine. It must have taken a tremendous amount of courage to do what you did." He verbally applauded.

"Not really sir, I simply delivered a disc."

"Have you read what's on it"?

"Sort of"

"Meaning"

"There was other printed data with it." Ivy responded making reference to that which Jack Stern left behind in her possession.

"Where's that now"?

"I assumed it was all on the disc sir." Ivy said innocently.

"It probably is, however the printed material did you dispose of it"?

"No sir, I hid it." Ivy replied certain that her hiding place was secure,

"In a safe place"

"Very sir"!

"Good." Ima replied satisfied with her response.

"Why do you ask"? Ivy asked.

"The information you gave us is not as black and white as the untrained observer sees. Jonathon here ran a number of ciphers through the data it revealed certain things about Pine Gap, Nurrangee and the Club of Rome."

"What's that"?

"A secret organization, a finance consortium, rumoured to be pledged to infiltrating various political, religious groups with the intention of a world dictatorship. It helped fund the building of your new parliament house in Canberra as the future seat of political world power thus eliminating all forms of true democracy. Unfortunately we cannot do anything about it openly. To take the evidence to the Human Rights Council will achieve very little as we know that certain member nations have been infiltrated and will in all probability vote against any disciplinary action levied against Australia."

"The risk I took was in vain"? Ivy asked conclusively.

"Not so. Eat your food and I shall explain." Ivy obeyed and forced herself to eat in order to bolster her spirits.

"Our legal department has looked at the data and suggested we call in the Virginia Farmboys. They're on their way as we speak." Ima explained.

"Are they a rival gang"? Ivy naively asked.

"You could say that. They are what we need to remedy the situation." Peter Ima replied with a smirk on his face.

"What's the significance of Pine Gap"? Ivy Humblebug asked. "I thought it was only a military installation"? She added.

"Without going into detail suffice it to say that Pine Gap like many other similar installations around the world is necessary for world peace."

"How"?

"Through the process of data collection"!

"If that's the case how come it didn't collect the sort that I presented to you"? Ivy asked distressed. Peter Ima couldn't instantly answer the question and simply said.

"I don't know, I don't think any body does. We rely on people like yourself to provide us with evidence and that is why you cannot return to Australia"!

"Pardon" Ivy questioned visibly shocked.

"We need to change your identity."

"But my family"! Ivy protested.

"Will need to learn to live without you" Ima grimly replied.

"That's not fair" Ivy loudly said as she suppressed her emotional tears.

"It's the price." Peter Ima philosophically stated.

"For what"?

"World peace, the rights of others freedom" Ima stone faced correctly said

"But I didn't collect the data, it was given to me"! Ivy bravely countered.

"You're still involved, you decided to act upon it, therefore you need protection; we value people like you."

"For how long" Ivy ambiguously asked as she tried to come to grips with her situation.

"As long as it takes and then if we think it is safe we might send you back. Now Miss Humblebug finish you meal the Farmboys have arrived." Ima slowly and clearly said as he finished checking his mobile phone's message bank.

The cold wind continued to blow, now colder than before as the land became accustomed to the ice.

"What have I done? What have the tree, Bipin and I done? Oh my God"!!!

Jarwood miserably exclaimed as he emerged through the unimpeded emergency exit to face a white wasteland before him.

"Our celestial competitor the supposed true God of Hosts played our arrogance against us. How dare he make a mockery of our snake symbols the cunning bastard!!! Canberra's destroyed, the future seat of world power is about to collapse, all that building for nothing. The elders at the Club are not going to be impressed. Where to now? Where will we reseat government, bureaucracy? What a mess"!!!! Jarwood cursed himself as he stared in complete disbelief.

"Quickly sir, she's going to collapse"! Cyril Pinewood shouted at the dazed Jarwood who reluctantly turned in the direction to which his deputy pointed.

In front of him the new parliament house built with the funds of the Club of Rome stood completely covered in nine meters of heavily compacted ice. Its central icy spire stretched artificially into the heavens for a full one hundred meters, it resembled a spear ready to strike the wounded animal's final deathblow. Jarwood could hear the goat's head groan with pain as it awaited its inevitable demise.

Harvey closed his eyes and expressed sorrow as the symbolic creature died.

He desperately hoped that like the mythical phoenix new life would rise from the 'ashes' even though the goat's death was of its own doing.

Harvey Jarwood was not alone in feeling the goat's agony, Bipin Greatrex also saw and felt with immeasurable bitterness as he came to realise that the true God of Hosts had assisted the evil forces in the final and unnatural plague. A little ice was what was wanted not the copious amounts that fell. It was sickening to accept that He loved everyone. Bipin cursed profoundly and promised revenge.

The emergence of those held captive in parliament's house underground nuclear fallout bunker was captured by chance by a lonely television stations helicopter as its crew ventured out to record the extent of the ice storm that struck unexpectedly. The news of survivors quickly mobilized the army's rescue helicopters that were on twenty- four hour standby in the designated safe areas surrounding Canberra. As Jarwood, Pinewood and several others were airlifted out and flew across the devastated city, Jarwood continuously and repetitively whispered to himself. "It's my entire fault why couldn't I see? It's my entire fault why couldn't I see?" as he cast his eyes upon the endless rubble, nothing had been spared. Pinewood overhead his comments in the helicopters noisy interior and said.

"It's not your fault sir."

"Oh yes it is! My Family was responsible for Canberra"!!!

"And you are unaccountable for your ancestor's actions"! Pinewood boldly countered but his words fell on deaf ears as an apparently psychotic Jarwood repeatedly chanted in an increasing loud voice.

"It's my entire fault why couldn't I see"?!!!

Pinewood didn't know what to make of it as he observed Jarwood violently shaking his head. In an attempt to cover up he explained.

"Poor soul probably suffering the ill effects of light deprivation claustrophobia and exposure"

The army paramedic on board examined Jarwoods vital signs, measured his pupillary response and then radioed ahead for an ambulance and doctor to be waiting on touchdown.

As the CIA unmarked helicopter landed at Langley in the Mclean CDP of Fairfax County Virginia, Ivy Humblebug feminine emotions descended into turmoil. She was thankful for the thermal underwear that the UN officials had provided for her, it kept the external cold out but she alone would have to deal with the internal variety generated by her anxieties. It would not be easy coming to grips with a new identity and forcibly shutting out thoughts of her family who would undoubtedly be worried sick about her sudden disappearance. Ivy's preoccupation with her thoughts was abruptly interrupted by one of the Farmboys.

"Miss Humblebug we've landed step this way please." CIA agent Leighton Hill coldly and efficiently said as he extended his hand to help Ivy out of her seat. The agents partner Miss April Hako stood by his side in readiness to help with Ivy's luggage.

They escorted her to what appeared to be a CIA holding prison and this made Ivy's body panic.

"What have I done? What's on that damned disc"? She silently thought to herself as she was led into a cold and mouldy cell.

"Wait here Miss Humblebug." April Hako directed. "One of our senior officers will attend to you shortly." Ivy meekly obeyed and sat down on the blanket covered single army camp bed. Both agents left her and attended to their other duties. Time dragged on, the cell's room became colder, darker and more confined. Ivy sat in silence burdened by her worries, her stomach gurgled, her small bowel squirmed and she started to experience hot and cold flushes.

"What do you think sir"? Leighton Hill asked his superior who sat before him and calmly observed Ivy Humblebug's behaviour.

"Double agent? Courier? Informant? Idealist"? Leighton persisted with his questioning.

"Neither one; I think she's innocent."

"What gives you that impression sir"? Leighton asked.

"Her bio-readouts, nothing refers to guilt, exposure or escape." Leighton's superior replied as he pointed to the various monitors that were linked to highly advanced infra-red probes that invisibly dotted the holding cell's walls and ceiling.

"Time to call her in sir"

"I would think so."

"Very well Sir April could you do the honours"?

"Of course Leighton" Hako sweetly replied as she took her leave.

"Thank you." Leighton replied with a wink of his eye.

"Miss Humblebug sorry to have kept you waiting could you accompany me please" April Hako politely asked Ivy who still uncertain sighed with relief for being taken out her harsh environment. She followed closely behind and was led into a plush office some ten minutes later after having negotiated a maze of corridors and stairs.

"Miss Humblebug may I introduce myself. CIA Executive Agent Raymond Halliday, I am responsible for your well being, please take a seat and make yourself comfortable. Need any fluid refreshment"?

"Warm glass of fresh milk would be nice sir."

"Haven't heard that one in a long time obviously you're from the country" Halliday replied as he nodded for one of the agents to fetch Ivy's request.

"Sort of sir."

'Tell me Miss Humblebug, how did you acquire the information that you personally brought in with you and that which you sent by mail"?

"I can't rightly say sir, it was all so bizarre." She replied aware that the CIA was intimate with the UN and they obviously held a file on her identity.

"Do your best we're very broad-minded in here." Halliday openly expressed.

"Very well sir." Ivy cautiously replied as she mentally prepared herself to describe the day that Jack Stern Alias J Stricker infiltrated the TAG headquarters and threatened to expose the nefarious dealings of its chief staff. How the evidence he materially produced was there one minute and gone the next and how she came to discover it in the bedside table at her Grandmothers house.

"Did you at any stage examine the information"?

"Briefly sir and only in relation to the breach of human rights it is a dreadful shame that the people of Australia have had their freedom of choice, their democratic rights restricted to such an extent"!

"Is that the only reason"? Halliday asked unemotionally.

"Yes sir why do you ask"? Ivy asked opened eyed.

"I'm in two minds whether to tell you or not." Halliday indecisively answered.

"I think I already intuitively know." Ivy replied as she took a sip of the full-bodied vitamin enriched milk that agent Hako had brought for her.

"Before the plagues hit Canberra we became aware of certain anomalies that were happening with privileged information out of Pine Gap. A situation that our country's administration was not very happy about especially after we had gone to great lengths to pacify different differing political parties by sharing our acquired information in order to ensure Pine Gap's strategic position"

"To whom did you allow access"? Ivy boldly asked even though she realised that she may have overstepped her authority to question.

"Australian Secret Intelligence Service, Australian Security Intelligence org, Defence Signal Directorate, Defence intelligence Org and their respective affiliations all of which are no doubt answerable to your PM and cabinet.

Our agent network intercepted highly sensitive secret information vital to our country's wellbeing being sold in Africa, specifically Sudan and Somalia by a newly formed black organization determined to imprint and implement their political ideology worldwide, abolishing all forms of human rights in the process and replacing them with a sadistic satanic homosexual totalitarian system that creates in the minds of the citizens the illusion that choice is still theirs." Peter Ima said without batting an eyelid or having any regard for political correctness, which he considered to be an underhanded way of defeating people in any form of confrontation. Ivy remained silent and reflected on the conditions of her employment which included a thorough knowledge and understanding of the TAG Act. Memory of its contents supported CIA Agent Halliday's hypothesis.

"What might surprise you is that this activity was conducted by Australian double agents." Halliday then said after a brief pause.

"Why"? Ivy asked rather stunned at the revelation.

"The world is a funny place. Nations, people constantly jostle for position your present government under the leadership of Harvey Jarwood has progressively drifted away from their allegiance to the USA and has become heavily involved in the Asia-Pacific rim, under the disguise of trade. Your government it has been made known to us has made secret pacts with China and other hostile Asian nations. Given time you will see that the cultural makeup of your nation will shift to predominately Asian-Islamic, Christianity will disappear and the world as we know it will be spilt in half into the north and the south. Our only ally will be the European Union and perhaps Russia once it stabilizes." Halliday postulated.

"Is everything that I've read about the CIA true"?

"That depends."

"Upon"

"What you have read." Halliday calmly replied without revealing his knowledge.

"Assassination attempts, destabilisation, arms/drug dealings, Syrian torture and if you really want a person to disappear you send them to Egypt. Ivy quickly rattled off.

"Speculation at its best"! Halliday fired back. "We are fundamentally an organisation that seeks to protect people's human rights."

Ivy Humblebug considered everything that Halliday had to offer and believed nothing.

"The present Pharmaceutical crisis in Australia is that your doing"? She then asked.

"Hardly, similar events have occurred in England and on our own turf although not to the same degree. We suspect they are independent events."

"Not a form of destabilisation by fanatical elements within the CIA"? Ivy cheekily suggested.

"Not at all, we are very good friends with the British, we enjoy a good understanding with each other"! Halliday defensively responded as he avoided all inferences associated with the word destabilisation.

"Do you suspect an African origin"? Ivy persisted.

"Actually yes and we are very keen to help resolve the situation in England. In our own backyard we feel it is a domestic issue created by person or persons who have a vendetta against the Pharmaceutical industry for what ever given reasons and with respect to Australia we will use their present chaotic circumstances to our advantage." Halliday confidently explained.

"In other words you want Harvey Jarwood removed"!

"It goes deeper than that"! Halliday stoically remarked. Ivy nodded her head to indicate that she understood.

At the Immaculate Conception's altar in St Pious' Church Newburn where Yvette Bell first met Jack Stern alias Fr. Brendan O'Reilly, Yvette knelt in front of the Blessed Virgin's statue and prayed as the hundreds of votive candles in front of her flickered and cast a sea of intermingling shadows on the adjacent walls. The fragrance of freshly cut roses filled the sanctuary and the morning light created an atmosphere of happiness as it entered through the upper stained glass windows and spread itself across the broad expanse of the church. Many people were present, the television broadcast of the miraculous happenings in the previous year guaranteed forever St Pious place in the pilgrims itinerary of holy places to visit. The early morning worshippers recognised Yvette and they admired her extraordinary beauty, many thought that she was a physical incarnation of a heavenly angel.

One however sought to destroy her image permanently, Louis Badcock, Director of The Infirmary, wanted Yvette as his prize, to strip away her freedom, to destroy her virginity, to hold her captive and teach Brendan O'Reilly and that interfering Jack Stern that they were no match for his daring. Mr Badcock had a new weapon comparable if not better than the powers that his opponents possessed.

The Harshman in Louis eyes was bigger, badder and better equipped. Today at St Pious Church he and the Harshman would abduct the lovely Miss Yvette Bell and use her to repossess what rightly belonged to them, namely his original ladies of the night.

"Come my friend, work quickly, silently; make her disappear without a fuss." Badcock whispered as he nervously looked about.

"No problem! I have learnt much; it will be easy for me."

"Good, the Indian Master has taught you well." Badcock surmised as his excitement increased.

"No I found a new one the great red bearded king. He has taught me much about the pleasures of a man's hidden dark places and his passage to joyful pain"! The Harshman replied with a sly smirk, as he looked sideways at Badcocok. Louis avoided the implied sexual innuendo and waved him away, hoping at the same time that his prized hit man had not turned gay.

The Harshman's appearance transformed itself into that of a well attired and groomed young priest not unlike Brendan O'Reilly. He blessed Badcock with the sign of the cross and then drifted down the aisle towards the unsuspecting Yvette who remained deep in prayer. Badcock meanwhile pressed himself into a dark corner and excitedly awaited the much-anticipated outcome.

The Harshman glided to a stop and stood by Yvette's side. He cleared his throat and said. "Good morning Miss Bell, a pleasure to see you back here"!

Yvette did not answer, she was in ecstasy and oblivious to the world outside of her.

"I said good morning Miss, did you not hear me." The Harshman repeated himself except this time a little more forcibly. Again Yvette did not verbally respond, instead her entire body increased its radiant beauty and emitted a heavenly fragrance. Irritated by her unresponsiveness the Harshman tapped her sharply on the shoulder but to no avail.

"Having fun Louis"? Badcock heard a voice say to the left of him.

"Who said that"? He asked quite shaken as he looked around to find no one.

"I'm going mad"! He thought to himself as he attempted to recompose himself.

"Not quite"! The invisible voice to the left of him explained. Louis a little more frantic looked around and saw nothing once again.

"You really should leave her alone, she doesn't belong to you"! The words cautioned.

"What the hell, where are you"? Badcock angrily and loudly blurted out causing the worshippers to look up in his direction as he jumped from his dark surroundings. The Harshman put his finger to his lips and hissed. "Sush this is a holy place of worship, be silent"! His priestly manner infuriated Badcock who stormed towards him.

"What the hell are you doing? Just wake up the girl and let's get out of here!

I don't have time for this nonsense"! Louis abruptly commanded.

"She's in ecstasy, it will be impossible to move her I can't do it even with my new powers." The Harshman correctly explained.

"What utter, utter nonsense"! Babcock spluttered.

"It's true what she say's." A voice to the right of Babcock said making a mockery of the Harshman's enhanced femininity.

Louis looked around madly and asked. "Did you hear that"?

"No sir."

"You must of it was loud enough, what's the matter with you? Must I do everything myself? Here get out of the way you buffoon, I'll take her out myself"! Badcock screamed much to the dismay of those at earnest prayer as he was about to lunge towards Yvette.

"There's only one way Louis let me show you how it's done. Are you ready? Now you see her, now you don't." The invisible person's words teasingly said as Yvette disappeared from view.

"Fine; just fine! What a bloody waste of time and money you've become! Get out of my sight"! Badcock hysterically screamed at the Harshman and then he bolted out of the church.

The Harshman remained calm and retained his priestly appearance. He briefly smiled, shook his head, made a crazy face and addressed his onlookers.

"Prematurely discharged from the mental asylum"!

21

SILENT EXPECTATIONS

When Yvette finally opened her eyes she found herself in her own private heavenly garden amongst the bushes of the rare blue rose that grew in the National Park where the Genius Loci was secretly located. Jack Stern was by her side immersed in his own ecstasy. Yvette instinctively knew that there had to be an important reason for her unexpected relocation and she kissed Jack tenderly on the cheek so as to say 'thank you', he immediately responded by smiling lovingly at her.

'Was I not safe"?

"Afraid not, Badcock and his genetically altered Harshman wanted their ways with you."

"You came to my rescue." Yvette said as she remembered the prophecy.

"Always" Jack softly replied as he reached out and touched Yvette's hand and then added." I constantly keep an eye on you, Brendan and all those I love no matter where I am."

"Is one as important as the other"?

"I have no favourites when it comes to protection."

"I see." Yvette replied somewhat disappointed and she looked away to hide her temporary anguish.

"Please don't say it that way." Jack simultaneously pleaded and cautioned as he raised Yvette's hand to his lips. "You do know that I love you." He genuinely said in a low whisper and he kissed her hand.

"And I you"

"I thought as much." Jack softly whispered.

"But you haven't made any advances apart from embracing, holding and kissing me passionately I would have expected that you would have………"

"There is a reason." Jack replied interrupting her mid sentence.

"And that is"?

"Deep inside I am a rather shy man plus the fact that I don't want to spoil you."

"I find that rather hard to believe." Yvette said visibly quite confused.

"It's true I've always let the woman make the first move and take charge."

"In other words you like being dominated."

"I wouldn't say that, I would rather describe it as being polite and non- invasive. In your case it is even more critical, largely because of your innocence."

"Since when is that a barrier"? Yvette asked trying to understand herself.

"Two reasons. Firstly I detect you are attracted to a man of the cloth and as a consequence you probably feel guilty for having such emotions, secondly you possess the gift of Innocence, a gift that causes you to largely reside in the mansion of your soul, therefore you can see, unlike the millions if not billions of people past, present and in the future, who have spent their entire lives studying so that they might see, but you my precious Yvette have been born with the gift and I do not personally wish to taint or destroy it any way."

"How could you do that"? Yvette asked making reference to Jack's impeccable way of conducting himself as a gentleman.

"By dragging you away from your mansion and immersing you excessively in the physical world which might cast a permanent veil over your ability it was no mistake it was not by chance that we holidayed in Mauritius"!

"You were using me"? Yvette asked as she lowered her head in submission.

"Never it was not like that I simply created the opportunity for you and Brendan to employ your talents, Brendan needs you, I felt and saw the love between the two of you when you danced together."

"You were jealous"! Yvette accurately deduced.

"Momentarily" Jack confessed before moving onto the important issue at hand "It is no coincidence that you are attracted to priests. You were meant since birth to seek one out, it is your vocation, your duty, your destiny."

"But why"?

"So the Church can be saved"!

"Are you suggesting that Brendan and I will marry"?

"Perhaps in minds only, I feel the two of you compliment each other."

"How do you know"? Yvette asked eager to learn the truth.

"Remember what I said a few moments ago about keeping an eye on you"?

"Yes."

"It's not be taken literally; let me explain what is meant by the eye, it is in reality one's subconscious, it sees all, you merely have to command it what to do. Ever since I realised that I was different I have been fascinated with the life of the Christ; through the process of remote viewing I have studied the actual events pertaining to his life as recorded in the ether as opposed to the written word."

'That is why you brought us to Mauritius"! Yvette gladly concluded.

"Precisely however I did not know where to start, I had a general idea but not the exact location and thanks to you we found it."

"You are a very complex man Mr Stern"!

"And you are exceptionally beautiful, a beauty that must be preserved at all costs, Miss Bell."

"Do you think there is hope for us"? Yvette asked as her eyes pleaded for the affirmative.

"What do you mean"? Jack asked anticipating the answer.

"That we might become lovers"

"Still early days, you need to learn more about me and yourself before you make the final decision. Come with me I need to show you something." Jack tenderly said as he helped Yvette to her feet and walked hand in hand towards the ultra-secret northern entrance to the Genius Loci. The keeper of the rose looked on and smiled thankful that Jack had begun to reveal himself to Yvette.

On the top level of the Genius Loci Jack and Yvette stood looking out onto the great expanse of the grasslands before them. Jack was behind her with his hands around her waist, he held Yvette close, this for him was heaven, her warm soft inviting body caused him to remember and appreciate all of the beautiful things in life both spiritual and physical. Yvette held his hands and wished he could stay forever however she knew it was not possible, for life beckoned and both of them had to obediently respond.

"I almost forgot how magical this place is." She said interrupting the mood.

"It never ceases to both inspire and impress me." Jack agreed.

"What was it you wanted to show me"? Yvette asked as she melted her body into his.

"My global balancing act" He replied pointing to his computer terminal, which by now had reacted, to his thought commands.

"Ever wondered what happened to the great geniuses of our world? Jack asked as he prompted the computer to display his invisible website. "Let me say that through the process of institutionalised education and competitive marketing society has managed to kill them off.

In my own way I counter that by finding budding geniuses and bringing their inventions to the fore. I support, I nurture the creative principle, I spend hours seeking them out and then I hand over the information to one of my paid colleagues and they do the rest."

"Which is"?

"They contact the person evaluate what they have discovered and make certain it is brought into the market place." Yvette expected Jack to say that this process created his wealth but was surprised to hear." My colleague and his charge enjoy the 'full' proceeds of the sale even though I receive a small percentage. This circumvents multinational companies buying the discoveries and shelving them for posterity. The masses are entitled to enjoy the best that man can conceive and should not be burdened with substandard goods that rely on image rather than performance."

"Does this mean you support the arts as well"?

"It does."

"A caring philanthropist" Yvette applauded.

"Not quite, I'm just one who wants to make a difference; everyone is entitled to their place in the sun. I suppose I could in some respects be considered to be a champion of freedom for I hate oppression"! Jack stated in a powerful philosophical manner as a list of some of his successful ventures displayed themselves on the computers large LCD screen.

"The results are very impressive"! The head of Dot.org happily exclaimed as he looked directly at the Small Dark Figure and Nghi Phamhung owner of PhD Distribution. "If it continues in this way I think we can offer you that permanent place for you in the inner sanctum." He added.

Badcock squirmed at the thought of it. To him it was all wrong, not the way that the Mafia traditionally conducted business. This was new uncharted territory anything could go wrong.

"Thank you." Phamhung replied. "We couldn't have done it without the brilliance of Dr Dennis Sauvage." "Again Badcock squirmed this time physically and visibly.

"Something troubling you Louis reliving the memory of your recent failed attempt to abduct Miss Bell" The Small Dark Figure jeered.

"Who told you"?!

"Our mutual friend" The Small Dark Figure mocked as he pointed to the stone faced Harshman.

"You traitor"!! Badcock screamed.

"Please Louis, calm down and conduct yourself in a proper manner." Nghi Phamhung sternly commanded to which Badcock took offence and glared back at him menacingly.

"Who the hell does he think he is"? Louis Badcock silently thought to himself. "My day will come." He resolutely promised himself.

"He's right, please; it's not that we're displeased with your past or present efforts, on the contrary, we ear marked you for promotion some time ago, this venture however has grabbed our full attention, it promises to make us billions. Mr Phamhung you may continue." One of the Mafia bosses indicated in a low-pitched gruff voice that clearly had its fair share of expensive cigars.

"Thank you, I am very pleased to report that as of the second of November this year, sales of Alljoy have exceeded our wildest expectations. We anticipate complete national distribution by March of next year"!

"Um that's very interesting. What do you attribute this remarkable success to"?

"Numerous factors; brilliant networking packaging formulation and word of mouth; it seems we did not need to wait for people to exhaust their medical drug supply." Phamhung happily responded as he flashed up a series of power point displays projected onto a large screen by the latest digital technology. "There occurred an exponential explosion in sales within fourteen days of introducing Alljoy using the multi-level marketing approach. The reaction to the preparation was overwhelming; production had to be increased three fold in order to cope with demand."

"Is that within our capabilities"? One of the Mafia bosses asked as he rubbed his hands together.

"It is; the manufacturing process is simple; we can presently cope quite easily." Dennis Sauvage confidently answered.

The Small Dark Figure glowed and gloated at this revelation for it had not previously seen the official sales records although it guessed things were going extremely well. The last projection slide said it all. If one wanted to win Lotto by selecting the six correct numbers out of forty-five, it represented a one in thirty six million chance of winning at the best anywhere between four and twenty-two million dollars, Alljoy posted a probable return of one thousand times these amounts, there was only one downside if it ever happened and that was a counter attack by your competitors. Nghi Phamhung was well aware of this and made certain that nothing was done to attract attention to their operation or its priceless product. He considered himself to be the ultimate intelligent deviant a trait acquired by being a Chinese born Afghan national, one who worked with the CIA in bringing in loads of heroin into the USA, protection by it was always assured. Nothing in any one of his operations was left to chance. Everyone involved with the project was thoroughly screened; everyone was informed without a shadow of doubt as to the consequences should they step out of line, to Nghi Phamhung the Achilles heel did not exist.

"Well is everything under control" Were the first words that Harvey Jarwood forcibly uttered as he stirred out of his coma; certain that it was not a delirious statement Cyril Pinewood answered.

"Yes Sir."

"Good are we in a state of silence"?

"You're in a private intensive care unit, can't get much more silent than that sir." Pinewood answered thinking that was what the PM wanted top know.

"No you idiot! The media! The media"! Harvey Jarwood screamed as he rolled his eyes.

"I don't get your drift."

"You never do! Has anyone leaked the truth"? Jarwood very agitated demanded to know as he nervously examined his surroundings.

Confused Pinewood simply answered "No" and hoped it would pacify his superior.

"Good let's keep it that way"!

"Very well sir."

The nurse in charge of looking after Prime Minister Harvey Jarwood became aware of his awakening and entered the intensive care room.

"How long has he been awake"? She asked in a monotone clinical voice.

"About two or three minutes" Pinewood nervously answered clearly intimated by her no nonsense authority.

"Good." She sharply replied as she expertly studied the various monitors that were attached to the PM's body, Cyril Pinewood allowed her a few moments before asking the obvious question.

"Is he okay"?

"Yes, he seems to be making a steady recovery, the various physiological parameters that we are measuring appear to be normalising."

"What precisely was wrong with him"? Pinewood gingerly asked.

"I'm not the clinician, but if you must know, the chart suggests it was a complex set of symptoms precipitated by light deprivation, sudden onset diabetes and a long standing previously undiagnosed psychosis." The last condition seriously alarmed Pinewood who did not want his PM to be mentally unbalanced, where would that leave him, would he Cyril Pinewood be thrust into the PM's office? Was he ready for such an outcome? Questions, questions so many question to be answered. The nurse left the room and summonsed the doctor in charge of Harvey Jarwood,minutes later he arrived and looked quite relieved that the PM had regained consciousness. He allowed Pinewood to remain whist he conducted a thorough medical examination. He then carefully studied all of the monitors, reviewed

Jarwood's med chart and gave the following orders.

"Cease the haloperidol, diazepam and glucose drip. Start him on oral fluids and light solids, ops every thirty minutes. Intermittent light therapy and he's probably not used his bowels for a while, better give him a good flushing out; never know what nasties have been in his rectum."

"Excuse me doctor." Cyril politely interrupted

"In a moment deputy, I haven't quite finished." The doctor firmly asserted himself as he examined Jarwood's pupillary response and proceeded to listen to his heart function. During the entire procedure Jarwood remained calm and silent although his facial expression was one of distorted madness. It was enough to instil some sense of normality into Cyril Pinewood who for an instant dismissed his affection for the PM and thought of his family and wife.

"You are incredibly beautiful! I wonder if you really look the way we have captured you in plaster." Brendan whispered as he knelt in front of the Virgin Mary's life sized statue housed in one of the side altars in the Church of the Coloured Sands Mauritius.

"Actually she is even more beautiful than you can imagine, there is one who will help you see." A voice whispered to him.

"Is that you Jack playing games again"?

"Not at all, it is I to whom you gave life, except this time you may not recognise me."

"Decay"

"Correct."

"Where are you"? Brendan asked as he shifted his focus away from his dedicated prayer.

"Come follow my voice." Brendan obediently stood up, pricked up his ears radar style and awaited instructions. Decay's voice lead him to the Sacred Heart altar, beckoned him to approach and be one with the Holy Flame which signified the presence of Christ in the Holy Sacrament of the Eucharist. Brendan hesitated; fire was not one of the four elements that he was comfortable with even though he was meant to have mastered it.

"Do not be afraid it is not as it seems." Decay reassured him. Reluctantly with faith Brendan intoned the mystical words that would allow him to reside within the flame. All around him merriment abounded, there was no heat, it was comfortable yet blinding as the laughter of children filled the air with sparkle.

"See what you have caused."

"I suppose." Brendan humbly answered over awed by his achievement.

"We need more; do you think you can deliver"?

"I Suppose." He once again humbly answered.

"Good." Decay slowly said colouring the word with a kaleidoscope of ideology. Brendan recognised its value and asked.

"You have a task for me"?

"Correct; one that you and you alone started."

"Meaning"

"My discovery through the eyes of a loved one" Brendan knew that Decay referred to Yvette.

"What do you wish me to do"?

"Make me complete." Brendan looked perplexed. To him everything was just fine; the Church, the congregation, devotions, pilgrimage etcetera. He thought awhile before poising the next question, before he could do so he was presented with a riddle.

"Frankincense, gold and myrrh"

"The gifts of the three wise men" Brendan mumbled as he shielded his eyes from the ambient lights increasing intensity.

"To the uniformed" Decay deliberately answered as the lights intensity increased once again but this time with altered frequency so that Brendan swore he could hear music.

"Light causes sound"? He questioned.

"Do not be distracted, they are simply reacting to what I an about to tell you for they live a life of silent expectations." Brendan obeyed and awaited further instruction. "The three wise men came with knowledge, a map of destiny for Christ to follow. The Virgin wept when she saw it. How unfortunate for a mother to know the sorrows that her child must endure and yet she accepted them. The man who brought you here has correctly deduced the map through his seeking."

"Tell me more." Brendan thirsted.

"The gold was from India, similarly the frankincense; the myrrh was not from the Hell district of the Red Sea district known as Tehama but from Somalia in the region of Somaliland from there through the Fairs of Berbera the Banians took it to Bombay."

"Are you suggesting that I journey to India"?

"I am."

"And for what purpose"

"To discover the other fragments"! Brendan looked at Decay and realised that he no longer recognised him and he remembered Decay's words. How many pieces were there, where were they located, what would happen once they were all discovered?

"First you need to find, then you will meet resistance; the Masters of Affliction do not wish for peace on Earth, they feed on war. Be prepared, be fore warned"! Decay cautioned as his countenance began to resemble those around them, Brendan closed his eyes and put up his hand to shield his eyes from the light's blinding intensity.

22

BUILD ME UP

Louis Badcock left the Dot.org meeting earlier than anticipated. He could not stand the success of the Small Dark Figure's Alljoy project, nor could he stomach Dennis Sauvage's gayness. Louis was bitterly disappointed with the Harshman, obviously his allegiance's lay with the Small Dark Figure. The Harshman would never replace the D-man he was one of a kind, how he wished for him to return and with that thought Louis Badcock drifted back into the murky world that the Infirmary offered.

"Do you take me for a fool"? The Keeper of the seventy-first level of the celestial staircase bellowed, as he looked the D-man squarely in the eye.

"Of course not"! The D-man faked.

"Really well let me tell you otherwise! Granted you have completed your self-analysis, your judgement, your recommendations, the conditions necessary to advance to the next level, but here everything is transparent, therefore you are rejected! Heaven is wise to your intentions! Very clever of you feigning the want to join our side it was not out of desire or love was it? No! It was a plot, a cleverly disguised move to infiltrate us, learn our strategies and report to your Masters.

How foolish, how naïve do you think we are? Well"!

The D-man remained silent, his face reddened with rage in response to the Keepers verbal onslaught.

"I hold the keys to the seventy-first level of Ascension, there are one hundred and forty-four in all before the final journey comes to an end, for you that is now! You have one of two choices. Co-inhabit the body of that homosexual being Bipin Greatrex and magnify his powers greatly or return to your incorrupt buried body and have your powers reduced by half in which case it will take you approximately one thousand earthly years to regain them," The Keeper offered with a smirk on his face.

The D-man knew his was powerless, he had no show; he had given up his earthly powers which could have been transferred into the spiritual realm had he remained on the destructive side, however once he committed to cross over to those who espoused love he voluntary lost all. An awful decision to make, however he was committed to the Masters of Affliction and wanted at all costs to please them; the D-man calculated his position before making his celestial move. The keeper was in no hurry, patience abounded within him, he watched with amusement as the D-man made his decision. He thought it through and then quite defiantly said.

"If I return to the forest, for Bipin means forest, it will amount to a bipolar existence, a schizophrenic disaster, I loathe homosexuals, give me my body back anytime, no matter its state"!

"Granted"! And with that before the D-man could utter another syllable he was once again one with his two thousand year old body which rested inside a stainless steel sarcophagus seven feet underground in one of the plots located at Newburn's public cemetery, the black granite tombstone above carried the name Ivan Gallows.

The D-man's body resembled an obedient perfectly sealed mechanical device, one prime by the reunion between body and soul and it was humming. Its heart sprung instantly into action, the rich blood coursed through the kilometres of vascular tubing restoring energy and life to all those dormant tissues. The brain responded, it spat out a deluge of hormones to reactivate, rebalance and re-energize all glands and organs. The D-man took in a deep breath of the coffins mouldy air, allowed the available oxygen to do its work and then exerted his full power. The ground above exploded upwards into a one hundred meter column of black dust, the coffin's lid followed quickly behind like a silver UFO emerging from a subterranean base. Those who were at the cemetery for one reason or another and had witnessed the event fled in terror, those who worked there walked towards the gravesite with the expectation that it was just another gas explosion caused by a large decaying corpse who had eaten too much. By the time the workers reached the site the D-man had fled.

"This is the way to make money! Pleasures of the flesh, the world's oldest, most reliable, time tested game, honest, repetitive, enjoyable, addictive" Badcock assured himself as he entered the newly rebuilt and refurbished Infirmary.

Everything and everybody looked good, grand, Louis was pleased, he winked at several of his staff and went upstairs to his penthouse suite. As he approached the door to his den of inequity a strange obnoxious odour filled his nostrils.

"What the hell? Smells like rotting meat, is someone playing a practical joke on me"? Louis fumed as he cautiously pushed open the door.

"Good Lord or should I say Holy Satin"! Badcock said unemotionally even though it was him who had 'killed' the D-man at St Pious some time ago.

"Good to see you too Louis"! The D-man coldly answered.

"I thought you………"

"Betrayed you, hardly, a move on my part to learn more about our enemies."

"Did it work"? Louis asked still in a state of disbelief.

"I'm afraid not, I've lost half of my powers." The D-man regrettably stated.

"At least you're alive." Louis sympathised.

"If you can call it that; tell me where the pins are." The D-man impatiently asked.

"The Harsh man has them, he's learning from them."

"Won't get him far, he's too stupid, get them for me"! The D-man sarcastically said.

'I don't know if I can, the Small Dark Figure's involved"!

"I see, never mind, there is another way, but I need you help."

"Of course"!

"Give me my money." The D-man roughly barked.

"Your money" Louis asked blankly

"Yes my money"! The D-man growled, this time Badcock was not intiminated by his aggression.

"It, it found its way into the coffers of Dot.org." Badcock explained.

"At whose insistence"?

"The Small Dark Figure's, it needed to finance its Alljoy project." Badcock replied knowing full well it was far from the truth.

"Never mind Louis, supply me with cash to get to Canberra Australia."

"Better still let me make all the arrangements." Badcock offered in the knowledge that the D-man would show his gratitude when called on. "How about you shower off, I'll attend to your clothes, let's get them dry cleaned or something, you probably need food, what has it been, six, seven, eight months since you last ate"?

"Longer." Was his reply

"Very well, hand them over, the bathroom's that way." Badcock pointed as he waited for the D-man to shed his stinky clothes.

"I haven't forgotten"!

"My apologies"! Louis excused himself as he rubbed his hands together in anticipation of causing the Small Dark Figure's downfall.

Thirty-six hours later the D-man landed at Canberra's domestic airport. It had been miraculously spared by the ice storm. As he walked out of the terminal's arrival lounge a bitterly cold wind caught his breath.

"Bloody hell what is this, Antarctica"?

"Haven't you heard mate? We're snowed in! Canberra's under fifteen feet of ice and snow." An Aussie Ocker rudely remarked uninvited the D-man ignored the imbecile and proceeded to locate an available taxi.

"To parliament House please" He loudly said as he approached a taxi driver who lent against his cab and idly passed the time of day.

"Can't help you mate! All roads are blocked! Iced over! No access! Only military vehicles allowed"!

"How far"?

"What did ya say mate"?

"Which way"? The D-man angrily asked becoming rapidly intolerant of the yobbo.

"Just follow the signs mate"! The taxi driver stupidly replied oblivious to the D-mans' fury.

"You don't know just how lucky you are.... mate"!

"You taking me on mate" The taxi driver violently retorted as he reached into his cab and retrieved his makeshift metallic club.

"Later mate, later, go play with your male doll friends."

Outraged by the verbal insult the taxi driver lunged at the D-man and struck him heavily on the crown of his head. Un-phased by the cowardly attack, the D-man smiled, opened his mouth and breathed on his unsuspecting attacker. The putrid essence of a thousand openly rotting bodies hit the taxi driver with such a punch that he instantly went down and discharged the contents of his bladder and bowels.

"Have a nice day.... mate"! The D-man farewelled and made his way towards new parliament house. Ivan Gallows alias the D-man walked confidently across the icy expanse. He remained focused on finding the Stone of Scone and accessing its hidden powers. The closer he got the more determined he became, with each forceful footstep the ice beneath him cracked and the slumbering snakes stirred into life, broke free and followed him obediently hissing all the way. The D-man's trek was picked up by the military's radar and a team was immediately dispatched to intercept the intruder who had entered the no-go zone.

No individual irrespective of his or her standing was allowed in or out until the entire area was declared safe. New parliament house came into view; it lay prostrate upon the landscape like a deceased animal that had been fatally wounded through the heart by a long spear. A voice to the right of the D-man rang out.

"Hey you there, stop! You are in a restricted zone! Stay where you are"! The specially trained SAS soldier commanded. Paying no heed the D-man continued his brisk pace and ordered the sea of snakes behind him to deal with the annoyance. The multitude of slithering creatures stopped as one; raised itself on its tail and hissed defiantly at the soldiers who halted their multi-terrain vehicle and battered down its hatches in readiness for battle.

"One enormous ice cube, no visible way in or out, not here, not there, not anywhere. Where are you located? Hum to me sweet Sacred Stone of Wisdom hum to me." The D-man beseeched as he approached a corridor of tall white gum trees that flanked the underground nuclear shelters emergency exit.

A feeble note made its way out of the door and drifted on the air currents lulling the D-man towards it. Acknowledging its authenticity the D-man ran towards it, found the exit door, ripped it open and plunged uncontrollably down the steep stairwell into the cavernous basement below. He landed on his back with a crash but felt no pain, everything was black, the ice storm had completely obliterated all systems. To Ivan Gallows it was home, black was his colour, his ally, his favourite medium, he felt at ease and had no difficulty navigating around once he got to his feet.

"Hum my little lady hum. Call me, I will find you." He seductively whispered as his ears located the source.

The D-man expected the Stone of Scone to be embedded in the foundations of parliament house, but not so. Some one had very cleverly placed it in a black box and cemented it into one of the southern supporting walls. It was not for public view; it was remote, isolated, in a highly restricted area where seldom anyone ventured if at all. A forgotten place except to those who desired access to its secret treasure; it was not easy, codes, codes and more codes.

Auditory, digital, literary, physical, each designed to impede the entry of any impostor, only Harvey Jarwood and his witch knew, something that the D-man had no knowledge of, he would rely on his own talents.

"I am here, come and get me." The Stone continuously hummed.

The D-man strained to find its exact source. Those who hid the Stone went to great lengths to complicate its location. The Stone's pleadings reverberated around the room making its origin impossible to detect. The D-man then realised that half of his powers had been selectively stripped away, his ability to ask inanimate matter the way was missing. He cursed Heaven and shouted profanities as he proceeded to the centre of the auditorium. Once there he listened differentially to the Stones pleadings.

"Stand still, silent breathing, listen, listen very carefully to every note, close your eyes, see with your ears, mind, feel it, see it, locate it, there"! The D-man mentally said to himself as he very slowly completed a three hundred and sixty degree turn on the spot. He repeated the manoeuvre seven times until he was convinced that each trial yielded the same result, then and only then did he walk towards the source of the signal.

A blank wall awaited him. The D-man looked at it in frustration, it was seamless. He studied its features meticulously, 'nothing except for those stupid spelling mistakes'.

'Authoriz'd Personell Only'

"E, L, L." He said out aloud and this time he unexpectedly plummeted into an even darker abyss. The darker it became the brighter it was to him.

"No problem." He muttered as he got up to his feet, dusted himself off and slowly searched his surroundings. This time the hum was more distinct, more easily locatable. The Stone sensed the D-man's presence and increased the intensity of its vibration. He easily found the next portal of entry, the payment complex, a numerical quiz; a correct number sequence was the key. Eleven spaces followed by one space followed by five, above this the words 'numero uno' an impossible number combination for the most gifted analytical mind to crack.

"If I get it wrong what will happen to me? Electrocution, squashing, decapitation, do I have only one chance or is it strike one, two, three you're out"? He thought as he looked at the chequer board layout of the wall that contained the puzzle.

The D-man studied the significance of the eleven- one- five spaces, thought about the owners of the Stone and the Stone itself. Hours passed by, darkness filled his mind, he grew tired, despondent; lethargic, his eyes grew weary, eyelids heavy, muscles became flaccid and Ivan Gallows the D-man collapsed into a heap of supernatural exhaustion. All he could do was dream of numbers and endless lotto machines, picking coloured balls, every number combination a winner, no losers, how stupid, surely a dream of contrary, Danger! Do not believe danger! Wake up! You need a cup of tea; scones would be nice with strawberry jam and freshly whipped cream! Um, nice, delicious, wipe that cream off your face, oh you want another, there you are, can't stop eating, here eat, until you explode! Warning, terrorist attack warning!

The D-man woke with such a fright that the room's darkness offered no comfort. He bumped into objects, stumbled about, tripped and fell until his eyes welcomed the darkness and he could see again. Then he approached 'numero uno' with a fresh mind and reflected on his nightmare.

"Strawberries and cream, doesn't fit, Stone of Scone, scone a fruity bread, afternoon tea delight served with jam and cream, also served with different jams most popular being raspberry, which fits, cream fits, but it is also spelt crème, and can be 'n', but its 'numero uno' does it mean every space is the number one or do I assign numbers to the letters of the alphabet and substitute them for the letters? What do I do"? The D-man asked nervously of himself aware that just above him in the ceiling numerous lenses were focused on him, once again those abilities, which could have told him about their exact nature, were missing.

"Damn it, 'numero uno' I am the one! It applies to me! Not anyone else"! He arrogantly thought.

"Stone of Destiny, Stone of Scone, Jacob's Pillow, Coronation Stone; Jacob's Pillar, Liath Fail, the speaking stone, none of these fit; I helped complete the final triangle and that fool Jarwood and his clan want it for themselves! How dare he, Origin of war, Stone of discord, despair, disruption, destruction, fail me not! Talk to me for heaven has stripped me of my most valuable powers! Ivan Gallows the D-man screamed in frustration.

"Sweet to me, tinged with tartness, what else can I say? But 'Raspberries One Crème'" He added with authority as he glided his fingers across the eleven-one-five empty spaces and awaited his fate. The hostile lenses above, the electronic vultures, glowed, growled and then suddenly and unexpectedly rapidly discharged a flurry of intense light beams of varying vibrancy upon him. Without any warning the chequered wall allowed two of its panels to glide apart revealing a dusty black box. The D-man nervously approached it and lovingly touched it. He sighed relief, briefly remembered what it was like to be human, the memory of which repulsed him and then Ivan Gallows exercised his immense physical strength and yanked the one hundred and fifty two kilo stone from its hiding place. He placed the unlocked black box on the floor, opened its lid and knelt before it to signify his respect.

Ivan gallows the D-man ran his hands over the red sandstone

and breathed in the glorious vapours of myrrh and frankincense that escaped from the stone's infused oils placed there by its original keeper, the biblical Jacob.

The Stone of Destiny changed its tone in response to Ivan Gallow's caresses, it tingled as its lovers fingers traced over the Latin cross chiselled into its surface a remnant of a famous catholic saint's attempt to pacify its evil content for the saint realised that this ancient artefact was the origin of earthly discord created through the misconception that those who kept it in their possession were the true rulers of the world. Beside the Latin cross a rectangular piece of metal was attached to the Stone, upon which was inscribed:

UNLESS THE FATES BE FALSELY GROWN AND THE PROPHETS VOICE BE VAIN WHERE'RE IS FOUND THIS SACRED STONE THAT RACE SHALL REIGN.

This confirmed the Stone's authenticity its true origin not divine.

The D-man chuckled to himself as he reflected on the present day tension that existed in the United Kingdom between the Irish, Scots and English as a result of the Stone's interaction between the races and their use of it to coronate their kings and queens.

As the Stone transmitted all of the evil powers that the D-man desired, he relived its violent history starting with Jacob, the draconian onslaught of king Nebuchadnezzar in 602BC, its stormy passage through Syria, Egypt and Spain, the troubles it caused before it came to rest in the hills of Tara in Ireland.

The download of information came to an abrupt end, connection terminated, only seventy-five percent transmitted.

"What! Give me what I need! Return me to my former self! Why do you torment me! I have work to do" Ivan Gallows questioned, demanded and pleaded with the Stone over and over again until for one brief moment it spoke to explain.

"I cannot for I am precluded by the one who through the eyes of another has discovered the fragment of true peace." Then it said no more and lay lifeless.

23

PINS AND NEEDLES

Ivan Gallows the D-man was back in Badcock's quarters forty-eight hours after being partially reconstituted by the Stone of Scone. Since his reincarnation he continually cursed the keeper of level seventy-one of the celestial staircase and those who had robbed him of his powerful abilities, one of which unfortunately was memory. The D-man now suffered with a form of meta-physical Alzheimer's disease, which caused him much distress.

"Good morning Louis, time to get up"! He firmly said as he physically stirred Louis Badcock out of his deep slumber.

"Oh what do you want now, can't you just leave me alone; can't you see I'm doing my best"? Badcock annoyingly murmured as he comically struggled with his bed coverings.

"It's me Louis."

"Yes I know the marvellous one, the Alljoy King, the future head." Badcock mumbled not recognising the D-man's voice.

Undaunted Ivan persisted with the following threat. "If you don't get up immediately I shall reduce you and your miserable bed to ashes"!

The statement catapulted Louis into sitting up and in the process his bed coverings flew off into all directions revealing his nakedness, unembarrassed a bleary eyed Louis answered. "Back to your normal self"?

"Hardly where's the Harshman"? The D-man demanded to know.

"I…can't rightly say; perhaps you should try the Small Dark Figure's place, he hovers around there most of his spare time."

"Very well"! Ivan Gallows answered as he turned on his heel.

"Remember where it is"? Louis innocently asked.

"You making fun of me" The D-man abruptly growled as he glared at Badcock who openly displayed his family jewels.

"Me never, just being caring as usual"

The D-man left without any further comment leaving Louis Badcock with the impression that he was about to discipline both of his adversaries. Ivan Gallows had no difficulty in locating the Small Dark Figure's palatial residence, which was situated in a semi-rural setting some thirty minutes drive from Newburn's town centre, a perfect location for nefarious under world operations and meditative pursuits. Convinced that his stealth mode was once again operational Ivan Gallows alias the D-man entered the complex and started a thorough search of all buildings, nooks and crannies and would not stop until he found the precious metal alloy pins that were used in the crucifixion of Christ. No one noticed or heard him with the exception of one person namely the Harshman, the Small Dark Figure's newly acquired ally. The Harshman closely shadowed Ivan Gallows as he went about his business; it was not until the D-man was upon the secret hiding place of the pins that he interrupted the potential theft and called him to halt.

"Stop right there"! He bellowed to which the D-man obeyed and slowly turned to face his adversary.

"Who might you be warrior, soldier, pawn, puppet or ignorant victim awaiting sacrifice"?

"Neither"! The Harshman rudely replied as he carefully analysed the D-man's makeup and dimly remembered him from before.

"Very well, where are the pins"? The D-man crudely asked with a tinge of admiration for the Harshman's stupid courage.

"What need have you of them"?

"They belong to me"! Ivan Gallows stated with supreme authority.

"Then you are my biological father." The Harshman mellowed.

"Don't be stupid! I've fathered no child! I am above that sort of thing"! The D-man arrogantly and quite correctly said.

"I came from you." The Harshman meekly said as his eyes screamed "Hello Dad"!

"By what process"? The D-man asked shunning the Harshman's obvious affection.

"Your blood runs in my veins"! The Harshman lovingly said as he battered his eyelids.

"Genetically altered does not make you my offspring! But then again: perhaps it does my son." The D-man coldly replied as he deviously thought of a plan to reconstitute himself as he temporarily abandoned the idea of recapturing the pins. "My God you even look like me! What a handsome brute you've turned out to be! Lost some of your harshness and replaced it with smooth evil power; what a transformation! Full credit to those who performed the experimental procedure"!

"Thank you….dad." The Harshman answered with a hint of gayness in his voice; something that Ivan Gallows found disturbing.

"Tell me do you remember what they did to you"?

"Nothing complicated. I believe they liquefied your congealed blood and transfused it into me and then patiently awaited the outcome."

"Pleased with your newly acquired powers"

"Not really, I'm not the man I used to be, I no longer think for myself, I constantly relive all of your memories, it's quite bizarre." The Harshman said as he shook his head.

"In relation to what I could do or have done"? Ivan Gallows asked fishing for an unusual answer.

"Exactly"!

"Interesting, very interesting"! The D-man calmly replied not wishing to display his excitement, he paused and then said. "As you know Louis Badcock shot me dead."

"That's what we all saw and thought. How come you're alive"?

"I have friends who rescued me however I won't elaborate on that out of respect for their identity."

"Very well….dad." The Harshman gaily gushed as he took hold of the D-mans hand, drew him towards him and embraced him tightly. Ivan Gallows allowed The Harshman a moment of loving and then broke free pretending to be weak.

"The reason I was looking for the pins was in the hope that they might revive me. I am still unwell, my convalescence goes slow now that I accept that you are my offspring perhaps you could spare a pint or two of blood"?

"For you, dad anything I'm just glad to have family again"!

"Very good my son very good now take me to the place where we can perform the transfusion, but before we do please give me those pins, after all a son only learns from his father and you do want to learn"? The D-man asked as he almost choked on his make-believe pleasant nature.

"I do, I certainly do"!

"Good. There is one thing that still bothers me and I hope you can shed some light on it. You seem to be a little on the feminine side."

"Quite right a character trait that I've observed myself, something that I'm not very happy with. I've talked it over with the technicians who orchestrated my genetic transformation and they assure me that once the process is complete I won't need to have any more hormonal injections."

"What sort of injections"? The D-man asked somewhat anxiously.

"Oestrogens and follicle stimulating hormone"

"For what purpose"?

"The explanation given is that these hormones stimulate the

reproductive process beyond the sexual aspect. All replicating systems which involve high cellular turnover are affected, blood, gastro-intestinal tract, liver, skin, nails, hair etcetera. The theory is sound but does it play havoc with my emotions and dress sense?" The Harshman explained as he adjusted his underwear. This was something the D-man did not want to see nor hear, however it did confirm one thing, Ivan Gallows was unique, one of a kind, neither reproducible nor replicable in any sense of the word. The Harshman was doomed to failure, his blood was worthless to Ivan Gallows; he needed another way to reconstitute himself.

"At least it's given you smooth skin and an excellent head of hair." The D-man sarcastically said in a disapproving fashion.

"Does that mean we're not exchanging blood anymore"?

"I'm afraid so, the pins hold the key. Take me to them and be prepared to experience a whole new world."

"Yes dad." The Harshman childishly answered in an almost girlish manner as he wiggled his way towards a pile of junk that lay in the corner of the room. From it he retrieved a heavy box of tools and placed it before the feet of Ivan Gallows. He fell to his knees and opened the three-tiered metal container. Each level was full of odds and ends, nuts, bolts, washers, self-tapping screws, plugs, masonry and wood drill bits, dyna-bolts, a small screw driver set and a collection of different sized spanners. Buried in the bottom of the box was a collection of self sealing plastic bags one of which held the precious pins the Harshman fossicked about until he found the fifteen to twenty centimetre long spikes and with a sly grin on his face handed then over to the D-man, Ivan Gallows carefully unwrapped them and laid them down upon a green felt covered table that stretched across the eastern wall of the room, which the D-man then understood was a large craft room of sorts. The Harshman watched him carefully as he methodically arranged the pins into a tight geometrical pattern and when he had finished the D-man without looking at the Harshman asked the following question.

317

"I suppose you tried to make sense of their markings"?

"Yes I did to no avail."

"I'm not surprised it's not a language of this world." The D-man casually remarked.

"That's why I had trouble."

"Did you try to learn by holding them"?

"Yes I did and that also failed"!

"So you decided to cast them into a handyman's box." The D-man growled visibly disgusted by the thoughtless action.

"Yes." The Harshman sheepishly answered.

"It wouldn't have been the first time"! Ivan Gallows growled in a low voice.

"You've lost them before"? The D-man avoided the question and initiated the sequence that would activate the pin's true nature.

"Apologia Baralamensis, Apologia Baralamensis; Apologia Baralamensis" He softly said three times as he stroked one of the larger pins with his left hand. It immediately sprung into life and projected a beam of light from its tip into the base of the adjoining smaller pin which glowed mercury violet in colour before discharging a series of rays into the remaining pins that reacted by taking in the light transferring their information into photons and reflecting them back into the ether. In the centre of the pin's geometrical pattern a pulsating image of intense digital data formed, the D-man immersed both his hands into its pool of light and washed himself all over before scooping a handful and drinking its contents. Once he had done this the image disappeared and the geometrical pattern was broken. Ivan Gallows nails and hair adopted a metallic appearance, his terrifying glance returned and his breath smelt more horrendous than ever. Ivan extended his hands outwards in anticipation of generating an unstable thermodynamic entropic energy ball, but nothing happened; the space between his hands remained empty. Ivan tried again and again; but nothing happened.

"Damn you Heaven"! He cried

"What's the matter father"?

"Don't call me that you genetic misfit"! Ivan Gallows shouted with rage as he scooped up the pins and ran away under the cloak of stealth leaving the Harshman abandoned and rejected. It was all too much; the Harshman collapsed in a heap from a combination of emotional and oestrogenic overload and he sobbed miserably. The Small Dark Figure happened to be passing by and heard his lament; it peered through an open window and saw the pathetic figure lying on the floor.

"Harshman is that you"?

"Go away"! He responded as he with a limp wrist waved the small Dark Figure away. Perplexed by what might have happened the Small Dark Figure approached his charge and cradled him in its arms and tried in its own way to console him.

"He was so mean to me! After all that I've been through you'd think he would understand! But No! What a cold hearted beast." The Harshman sobbed.

"Whom are you talking about"? The Small Dark Figure asked completely bewildered.

"My Father"! He miserably replied, The Small dark figure searched its mind and then said.

"I thought he died twenty years ago."

"Not him, the other one"!

"Which one"?

"You know, that, that beast Ivan Gallows"! The Harshman howled.

"The D-man was here"? The Small Dark Figure asked concerned at the prospect of his existence and his likely state of mind.

"Yeeeesss….! My genetic father"!

"Oh dear I think I better call in the medico's" And with that the Small Dark Figure telephoned those responsible for the Harshman's physical alterations.

"Well Ivan how did it go, get what you wanted"? Louis Badcock asked the D-man as he sat in one of his apartments comfortable chairs and sipped on a cup of freshly and expertly brewed imported Earl Grey tea.

"Yes and No" The D-man grumbled visibly annoyed.

"Not fully reconstructed"? Badcock asked as he held back his laughter.

"No"!

"What seems to be the problem"? Louis asked as he pondered the proposition that the D-man was potentially useless to his personal ambitions.

"There is something blocking me."

"Explain." Louis asked feigning genuine interest.

Ivan Gallows the D-man pulled out of his coat pocket the collection of fifteen and twenty centimetre metal alloy pins and placed them on the teak coffee table before Badcock, who remained silent like an interested university student awaiting instruction.

"These are more than a device to inflict pain and death"! Ivan Gallows sadistically said as he carefully picked one out and manually demonstrated its needle like sharp point and the flat end that received the hammers blow.

"These collect data." He proudly said as though they were his invention.

"Oh yes and how is that possible." Badcock asked septically with a borderline sneer.

"Whenever I've used these to extinguish a person's earthly existence, the pins took a sample of the individual's blood together with its spiritual essence which were later filtered and condensed into that which would generate an increase in my power to the satisfaction of my Lords."

Badcock was never one for religious hocus pocus or that spiritual metaphysical stuff as he regarded it; however once in his life his mind became interested and he asked a most interesting and pertinent philosophical question.

"If you killed the good guys then what you are saying is that the qualities they possessed could be used for evil purposes"?

"The essence, the power is neutral; its use by its owner is what determines its inclination." The D-man correctly answered.

"Have you ever used your powers for good"?

"All the time, for the good of our cause"! Ivan Gallows smiled.

'I take it our cause does not restrict itself to Dot.org is that correct"? The D-man nodded in the affirmative and Louis Badcock remained silent, sipped his cup of tea and meditated on their brief conversation before asking. "What do you think might be constipa… I mean blocking you"?

"I don't know. It might be that Brendan O'Reilly and whatever he has done or it might be another elsewhere, the world is a big place. Something doesn't feel right, something on earth has changed; there has been a shift in the balance between war and peace, regrettably towards the latter, if it continues we will all be without a job." The D-man grimly explained.

'Let's change the subject, you've had a hectic and frustrating few days, come share a cup of tea with me and watch the international news on satellite television." Badcock suggested with an almost clairvoyant sense of prediction. Ivan Gallows the D-man sunk his six-foot plus athletic frame into one of the chairs especially designed for viewing pleasure as Badcock prepared the beverage.

"There you are my man, enjoy, un-frazzle your nerves, better days ahead." Badcock positively said as he sat down next to the D-man and activated the large sixty-inch plasma screen.

The first item was relatively boring; a documentary dealing with the beneficial properties of rice bran oil and Neem oil, the next raised the eyebrows of all its viewers.

"Bon Soir Mesdames and Monsieur's, welcome to France 2 national television. The biggest news story to break today has come to us from France's former colony, the Island of Mauritius, where it is rumoured that a huge church has appeared from no where in the Chamarel region of the Island. The locals have dubbed it the Church of the Coloured Sands. Furthermore it is reported that the church's baptismal font produces an endless supply of miraculous holy water. Many who have blessed themselves with it, drunk or washed with it have experienced profound spiritual and physical cures. Besides that the church itself seems to be able to instil an inner peace into anyone who enters its interior. Many believe that whilst it may be the waters that are responsible for these phenomena they largely attribute these supernatural events to the unknown priest Fr Brendan O'Reilly who appeared from nowhere. It is further speculated that Fr Brendan O'Reilly and his seven sisters are responsible for the happening. Those who have returned to France after holidaying in Mauritius have spread the word wildly to friends, relatives, church officials and the media. As a consequence we have managed to collect a mass of photographs and video footage that confirms the rumours. The local Catholic priest Fr Bruno Bogliani is part of the event that many are calling an act of God. The Island's government are remaining silent on the matter for good reason. Mauritius's economy is largely dependent on tourism, sugar cane rum and textiles. This act of God is a bonus for the Island. Strangely enough it has not caused any tension amongst the Island's various religions for the Church of the Coloured Sands does not appear to teach any specific ideology. Its main focus appears to be centring upon the abolition of sin as a concept and replacing it with help in discovering one's inner abilities. This refreshing point of view has given a new lease of life to all those who have attended mass leaving them with a sense of appreciation and a vision for the future that they can realize. Those who run the church do not ask for any donations; worshippers, pilgrims and the curious give freely, the money finds it way towards helping the poor of the Island without any loss in amount. The growth of the church is not restricted to the increasing numbers of people flocking to it, the church and its sur-roundings appear to be growing as well without encroaching on any ones territory. A presbytery to house the priest and sisters, a parish hall and a school followed the church, all of these it is claimed just materialised; local tradesman built nothing. The effect needless to say has caused many Christian groups around the world to organise pilgrimages to the Island. What is also most peculiar is the way in which mass is conducted. Even though Fr Brendan O'Reilly says mass in English, everyone present hears it in their own language.

This in itself is a miracle for there does not exist any audio equipment at all, no visible loudspeakers, headphones etcetera. Fr Brendan O'Reilly and his sisters are very shy and prefer to go about their work rather than entertain the media, however having said that it does appear that part of the church's attraction is the priest himself and a young female assistant Yvette Bell. The priest's handsomeness is a real drawcard to the women; they swoon at his sight, whereas Yvette Bell's countenance is incredibly innocent and beautiful. The story about them reads something like this; the group arrived in Mauritius some weeks ago on holiday and spent their time at Club Med with a Mr Jack Stern. After a brief stay they left when the Church of the Coloured Sands suddenly appeared. There is nothing sinister about the circumstances; our research team has identified Fr Brendan O'Reilly as being the same as that seen at the miraculous events that were broadcast live from St Pious Church in Newburn USA, it may well be that we are seeing an extension of that but in another category which might be a modern day transformation of either the Catholic Church or religions in general that is in keeping with the intellectual advancement of mankind." The glamorous young female newspresenter detailed with a passionate warmth and vigour.

"There lies our problem, my difficulty, the roadblock to my destiny. He has discovered one of the fragments"! The D-man cursed in a despicable tone of voice as his available powers surged to the fore. Badcock immediately put a handkerchief over his mouth and nose to filter out the D-man's highly obnoxious mouth odour worsened by his state of visible frustration and anger.

"Blocked powers and diluted, I think your position is compromised." Louis said through his handkerchief.

"You're right, I need help; it won't be easy. This man must be stopped before he brings peace to the world"!

"How many fragments are there"? Louis asked not knowing their importance or their origins.

"Many."

"Then one wouldn't make much of a difference." Badcock naively suggested.

"Do not underestimate it." The D-man warned as he pondered its likely powers and then he continued by saying. "I need help, I may have to visit Bipin the Greatrex in Somalia."

"But not before you help me with Dot.org." Badcock said as though the D-man departure was conditional upon fulfilling his desires.

"Very well" The D-man reluctantly agreed and then he took a sip of his less than lukewarm tea and contemplated his future.

24

AWARENESS

Knowledge is a powerful tool, a precursor to awareness in the workings of the universe. It is often said seek and ye shall find, knock and the door will be opened, ask and it shall be answered. Ivan Gallows alias the D-man was no stranger to this for he was well versed in the darker application of all that he had accumulated. Although his powers were limited he nevertheless would use stealth to gather the help that Louis Badcock required before venturing forth to reconstitute himself and save the world from that abhorrent idea of peace.

Louis had briefed the D-man on all of Dot.org's gossip and the play that the Small Dark Figure was making for the last available chair in its inner sanctum using Dr Denis Sauvage Alljoy as its leverage. The D-man was frustrated with his inability to travel by the thought process and although Louis Badcock was very helpful in providing him with an automobile and an abundance of cash to pay for travel expenses, the D-man decided to pocket the money and hitch a ride unseen on whatever transport was available.

Hollywood on Ice the ice skating show that Dennis Sauvage was part of was presently performing in Denver Colorado It would be the

D-man's first port of call for he wanted to learn more about Alljoy before he acted on Louis Badcock's behalf, after all, ultimately the D-man was answerable to the Masters of Affliction. He would only act if it suited the purpose of their grand plan.

Hollywood on Ice performers were housed in transportable homes in a cordoned off area behind Denver's main sporting arena. Nothing was spared to ensure their comfort, lavish quarters, excellent food and competent trainers. The show was a spectacular mix of different acts with no central theme running through the performance. Dennis Sauvage excelled as the Woki from Star Wars; being tall he fitted the part admirably and thrilled the audiences with his daring jumps and acrobatics all performed with a fully functioning light sabre.

The promoters of the show ensured that security was tight all around, however it did not present a problem for the D-man who walked in unperturbed just like the assassin from the Star Wars movie prequel, The Phantom Menace. It did not matter to him whether Dennis would be present in his trailer or not. As it happened Ivan Gallows arrived during morning rehearsal, the team was being grilled by the choreographers as to position, attitude, speed, carriage and completion whereas the trainers were weighing those not practicing to ensure their physical statistics stayed within the acceptable limits. There were penalties in place for any breaches such as weight gain, excessive alcohol in the urine or presence of any illegal drug although certain substances were 'allowed' in order to improve and sustain performance. The promoters had a very good understanding of film making and the marketing of all of its associated merchandise, the various Hollywood on Ice shows were freely available on DVD, their original music scores on CD plus the associated garments and toys.

The D-man moved about freely and quickly found the location of Dennis Sauvage trailer. Its door was locked, no problem for Ivan Gallows who simply exerted differential pressure to the lock mechanism with the thumb and forefinger of his right hand and walked straight in. The Interior was spotlessly clean, everything in its place, no dust or dirt anywhere, something that you might expect from a microbiologist. The cabin was clearly divided into two sections, Dennis's love of ice-skating and his passion for science.

Behind locked glass doors that stretched to the ceiling on both sides of the trailer were dozens of technical books, some ancient, some new on a variety of topics, biology, biochemistry, genetics, microbiology, neurology and a collection of articles on the way that both astro and quantum physicists viewed the human life process. This immediately gave the D-man the impression that Dr Sauvage was a very clever man although "was he too clever for himself"?

The D-man searched various shelves and drawers expecting not to find anything even though he had a nagging suspicion that such brilliant minds usually harbour some sort of revolutionary desire. As he merrily worked away he became aware that he had in fact stumbled across a transportable mini laboratory, Dr Dennis Sauvage had indeed learnt the art of talking to the micro-organisms and had developed a highly sophisticated yet simple language, one that allowed him to do away with expensive research equipment.

As he flipped through various notebooks, the door opened and Dr Sauvage entered, his eye immediately caught the open floating book that the invisible Ivan Gallows held in his hand and Dr Sauvage watched aghast as the pages flipped over as if of their own accord. Fearing it to be a poltergeist Dennis shouted some gibberish, looked nervously about and bolted outside. The D-man smiled sadistically to himself and wondered why Dr Sauvage was so nervous apart from the obvious supernatural incident.

"What are you hiding Dennis and where"? Ivan Gallows asked himself as he intensified his search.

"Where would you hide the information, private files, computer disc, CD, book, what is important to you? So far all that I've found is your current experimental results. When do you find the time? Perhaps you're not so gay after all"?

Dennis Sauvage returned with a burly black American security guard who brandished a twenty thousand volt stun gun in his right hand and a five foot extendable baton in his left.

"It's in there, go do your stuff"! Dennis nervously urged as he kept away from the trailer's door.

"What a minute, what did you say you saw again"?

"I told you, a terrible smell and one of my books floating in the air with its pages turning over"!

"Alright, alright, just settle down, you crazy woki"! The security guard snapped back as he stepped up into the mobile home. He gingerly peered inside and after a brief moment said. "Everything appears okay apart from that terrible smell. You been experimenting again with your expired food? You know the rules, no pigging out and no snacks after meal times! Where you hiding them stinky scraps'? The black guard authoritatively and rudely asked as he bravely stepped inside and proceeded to examine Dr Sauvage's waste paper bins, bar fridge and the underneath going ons of his extra long bed.

"Forget about that, look for the demon"! Dennis Sauvage shouted from where he was standing.

"Nope, nothing nobody here woki-man lots of mouldy bread woki-man, what you got brewing here woki-man, sure you ain't growing some sort of high, got something new for the cheese industry"?

"Oh never mind, just pretend I didn't call you"! Dennis visibly annoyed retorted as he ushered the black guard out of his private domain and locked the door behind them.

The altercation caused the D-man to shift his focus of thought and he looked at the collection of DVD's that Sauvage had acquired over the years." Mars the Messenger of War' was the title that immediately caught his attention. The D-man loaded the disc into the trailer's inbuilt DVD-television combo as it was called and pressed play. The message 'cannot read disc' flashed on the screen, he tried again, same result and then he decided to try another avenue and inserted it into Sauvages's computer CD-Rom. "access code' flashed up. "Not necessary." The D-man growled as he quickly over-rode the request by punching in a number sequence designed to shock the system into obedience. The opening page consisted of a series of photographs that paid tribute to Dennis Sauvage's dearly beloved uncle who as one read the story died of AIDS, a condition that Dennis would explain was thoroughly treatable by the human bodies own defence mechanisms. The theory he espoused was that as individuals were conceived and born, they inherited all of the survival skills necessary to live a disease free life, from both sides of their parental bloodline, which extended back to the beginnings of the human race. Dennis believed that someone had along the way tampered with this process and introduced the disease factor, which was either switched on or fed by negative emotions. It was Dr Sauvage's intention to isolate the automatic autonomic immune system by introducing a genetic bridge, a messenger RNA that would make the system immune to emotional influence and allow full expression of all knowledge stored within its genetic material.

AIDS to Dennis was not a modern day disease, it was ancient, people had been exposed to it before and survived, that information had been passed on, no one needed to die of that disease.

This enlightenment shocked the D-man the world did not need such interfering fools it was obvious to Ivan Gallows the executioner that Dr Dennis Sauvage's objective all along was to create the world's first universal panacea using the instrumentality of greed for power and money.

"If this project is allowed to continue unabated my Masters will not be pleased, it is my duty; I must put an end to it before it reaches epidemic proportions." The D-man thought to himself as he reflected on what Badcock had told him, namely that Alljoy sales had enjoyed exponential growth and that national coverage was only months away.

'When annihilation occurs people wander about aimlessly even though a few who know how to govern are present amongst them." Cyril Pinewood postulated as he was being whisked away to the state of New South Wales and its capital city Sydney under the protection of the Australian Federal Police Special Ministerial Protection Unit. Pinewood's chief Harvey Jarwood had not been given the all clear and remained in the country hospital on the outskirts of Canberra. The flight by army helicopter was pleasant enough if one could tolerate the excessive noise generated by the overhead rotors beating the air. The journey would end at New South Wales State Parliament House where it was decided Australia's Federal Government would co-exist until Canberra's 'national disaster' subsided and the extent of the damage fully assessed.

"Cyril Pinewood you old fox, we'd thought we'd lost you, good to see you alive! Bet your wife and children will be over the moon with excitement to lay eyes on you once again'! The newly elected acting prime minister of Australia blurted as he extended his hand towards Cyril Pinewood.

"Yes thank you. What a mess where do we start"? Pinewood answered demonstrating his inability to cope with the situation at hand.

"Good question. Did you know we lost the minister for health and the minister for defence"?

"Really"

"Yes both dead. We've replaced them of course, but what a shambles"!

"How bad is it? Are we able to operate"? Pinewood openly questioned the acting PM.

"By bluff alone; people are sheep you know"!

"That's all very well but I need to know the full extent"! Pinewood persisted as he grew quite anxious about the acting PM's answer.

"Taxation's gone, shouldn't have, but thanks to that main frame computer in Canberra being extinguished, the satellite computers aren't coping at all"!

"Which means"?

"Treasury's running on empty, unless we seek and obtain overseas funds. The American's aren't forthcoming, behaving very cagey at the moment, don't know why, World Bank's the same."

"Anything else" Pinewood continued to probe.

"We have no co-ordinated defence, once again problems associated with centralising all of our data in Canberra and that applies I'm afraid to Centrelink, our social security system, foreign affairs and health. Things are chaotic. I'm glad the population's attention is easily diverted away from it, seems beer and sport are keeping the masses happy."

"Solution"

"None I'm afraid"!

"Curious the Americans are not coming to our aid," Pinewood observed as he added, "Wonder what we've done to upset them I suppose we could exist on a state by state system until we rebuild ourselves." Cyril suggested as he grasped for straws.

"Our conclusions precisely; they appear to be self sufficient in terms of raising taxes and whatever federal tax is generated we have suggested they keep and send only a small proportion for us to use in the interim period."

"Well thought out." Pinewood congratulated the acting PM.

"We had no other choice"!

"Explain." Pinewood asked as he stopped walking.

"Rats jumping ship."

"I see, thought as much, many left"? Pinewood inquired as he reflected on the calibre of those who claimed to be capable of governing. "Fair weather politicians" He thought to himself.

"Less than fifty per cent and of those not many with operational grey cells between their ears"

"Always been the case; takes a war or disaster to weed out the riff-raff." Pinewood concluded.

"Elitist." The acting PM taunted.

"Where does that leave me" Pinewood adversely reacted.

"You're more than welcome to your old job! You are now the new acting prime minister and if our beloved Harvey Jarwood does not recover, you're it! No one in his or her right mind will think of challenging you for the onerous position! It's all too hard! Nose to the grindstone for you old chum"!

"Flattered I'm sure. Lead on, I need to know where to start." Pinewood grimly replied as he reluctantly accepted the proposition.

"With the Americans I suggest." The acting PM happily replied as he counted his lucky stars.

Excuse me Mr Halliday, sir." CIA agent Hako said as she stood in Halliday's office doorway.

"Yes April, what is it"? Executive CIA agent Raymond Halliday asked.

"I've received an urgent communication from the White House."

"In relation to"

"The present pharmaceutical crisis sir"

"What does it say"? Halliday asked barely shifting his gaze from his work at hand.

"Do you mind if I come in sir, I feel somewhat awkward standing out here"?

"By all means, close the door behind you, sit down, would you like a coffee"? Halliday quietly asked as he made Hako feel at ease.

"That would be nice sir."

"White, two sugars"?

"You have a good memory sir."

"Comes with the position" He replied as he slid his executive leather chair towards a side table and punched in the codes necessary for the sophisticated upmarket café series coffee machine to dispense its aromatic liquid refreshment. Both remained silent as they watched the technical wonder create a wonderful cup of coffee from humble roasted Kenyan coffee beans.

The aroma wafted around and seduced them into thoughts of

chance encounters and hot steamy lovemaking. Both were single, unattached, it was no secret that they possessed secret desires for each other. The pressure of work, those annoying or unexpected assignments constantly kept them apart, making them increasingly nervous about taking that first step and saying 'hello'.

"There you are April." Halliday said as he smiled and handed the cup of hot beverage to her which was tinged with an invitation of 'I want to know you better'. April accepted it warmly. They sat for a few minutes and said nothing as they sipped their coffees; April broke the silence by handing across the White House fax that she spoke of earlier, Halliday took it from her, smiled and read it carefully.

"No longer a local event as the President initially thought" He commented, read on and then concluded "Very interesting indeed, I'd never have guessed, I always thought they were our friends, how wrong one can be"!

"Me too" April agreed.

"How accurate is this information"? Halliday asked.

"Quite sir, our resources confirm most things"

"Very well convince me." April Hako scanned her duplicate copy that bore substantial notes and very carefully explained.

"When the reports of drug failure occurred within our own pharmaceutical industry, specifically the anti-psychotic and anxiolytic drugs we thought it was the work of a home grown terrorist intent on disrupting the industry holding it to ransom out of revenge for something that might have happened to them or one of their family members. We even thought it was an attempt to discipline the psychiatric industry, the doctors themselves as the failure of the medications to disintegrate was specific to those used in that arena. We even suspected that the perpetrators might have been rival companies who marketed natural therapies, as tension has existed for some time between them and the medico-pharmaceutical companies who have gone to increasing lengths to poo-poo natural therapies due to their lack of acceptable scientific data. When we looked at how well they were doing in the market place, although there was a significant rise in sales of products it was across the board, consequently we could not point a finger at any one specific. Our attention however was directed by the pharmaceutical police...."

"The what" Halliday asked stopping Hako mid sentence.

"The pharmaceutical police sir"

"Please explain."

"This is a private surveillance group funded by a conglomerate of powerful pharmaceutical companies that constantly monitors the activities of rival companies and natural therapy sellers with a view to informing the authorities as to anomalies."

"Which I take it results in unnecessary suspensions in trading, investigations etcetera, etcetera" Halliday concluded being no stranger to the world of shady commerce.

"Precisely sir"

"Whom are they pointing the finger at"?

"Before I divulge that information there is something you should know." Halliday remained silent as he glanced over Hako's sexy physique.

"The tampering of drug manufacture has become widespread; it now involves all classes of drugs, day by day, the FDA is becoming aware of batches failing to meet standards, code of good manufacturing practice, in effect these cannot be released as opposed to what the Australians are trying to get away with. The companies are screaming for our help, saying it is an external act of terrorism designed to bring our nation to its knees. We have a very serious national security issue at hand, one that threatens to undermine our economy by destabilising the medico-pharmaceutical industry and the ultimate effects it will have on the stock market, the value of our American dollar, it will cause immense international embarrassment we may no longer be seen as being the super power. We need to act quickly and properly, not the shoot now and ask questions or provide shaky explanations later." April Hako explained.

Halliday admired Hako's stance and asked. "Very well, what do you propose"?

"Our intelligence sources have compiled the following." Halliday nodded his head to signify 'please continue' and then sipped his coffee some more.

"Several diligent workers within the industry have identified substandard disintegrating agents as the culprits, however it was not as simple as that, the ingredients appeared to have passed quality control procedures until one and only one very astute scientist decided to test several batches for microbial contamination and found that they all harboured a specific virus, presumably found only in Australia."

"Okay that is by the way, it isn't telling us who the pharmaceutical police suspects"!

"I'm sorry I became a little carried away." Hako apologised as she realised that Agent Halliday was making her sexually nervous. "When it became apparent that someone had deliberately sabotaged the drug industry two things happened. Firstly an increase in illegal drug use was noted and then a surprise product called Alljoy entered the market using the multilevel marketing system."

"Its owners"

"No one known to us, however, there exists a vague suspicious link to a one Nghi Phamhung"!

"Say no more April." Halliday hastily responded, as he looked somewhat whitened by the discovery. "Tell me more about the virus."

"Before I do so may I explain the significance of Alljoy"?

"If you must" Halliday abruptly agreed.

"It is a unique product, although cleverly marketed as a herbal it contains a significant concentration of messenger RNA."

"So what of it"?

"The pharmaceutical police as saying it might represent a universal pancea."

"That is a preposterous supposition"!

"I agree sir, however...." Halliday waved away the topic and insisted they discuss the Australian connection in the light of what he had learnt from Ivy Humblebug a few days earlier. "Very well sir." Hako capitulated as she regained her sense of direction and went onto explain the significance of the Australian virus. "The virus is only found among certain species of eucalyptus trees. The Koala bears deliberately avoid them as the leaves cause them great gastric distress and even death."

"Smart bears."

"Promiscuous bears sir."

"Pardon"

"They suffer with Chlamydia."

"Is that how members of the Australian population contracted the disease" Halliday flippantly asked tongue in cheek.

"Australian sexual perversity is not part of our agenda sir." April Hako coldly replied.

"I'm afraid it is considering the dilemma we face with their man at the top"!

"Point taken sir" Hako apologetically answered.

"How did the virus find its way into the States" Halliday asked concentrating on the subject at hand.

"We think it was deliberately imported by some one who knew what they were doing."

"An expert, any leads"?

"No sir, none at all, at least not in the public sector and it is highly unlikely that anyone is involved from our military."

"Very well, where does that leave us"?

"On the hunt" Hako vaguely replied.

"Keep it up."

"Yes sir."

"Another coffee" Halliday warmly asked changing his aggressive mood as he raised his eyebrows and subconsciously dilated his pupils to indicate his level of sexual excitement.

"Perhaps later sir when things settle down."

"We must make time." Halliday suggested as his way of making a date with Hako.

"Yes sir we must." April Hako replied accepting the implied invitation.

As soon as CIA agent April Hako left Raymond Halliday tidied away what he had been working on, assembled the pile of documents that he wanted his secretary to correct, collected his highly secure mobile phone and left the office for parts unknown.

It took him ninety minutes to reach his destination and once satisfied that the area was 'clean' he left his car; entered a noisy atmosphere and dialled Nghi Phamhung's silent telephone number after passing the three-step access sequence.

"Hello Tanner, are you clear? Good, time to talk? Good"! Halliday said in a disjointed fashion as Nghi Phamhung answered each short question. "They're onto your Alljoy; I've made nothing of their discovery, left it inconspicuous, watch your back, you have nothing to fear from us, keep an eye on the multi-nationals. Any news on terrorist cells, need new info to strengthen my position. Not so fast, let me write that down, okay keep in touch." Halliday once again said in a staccato fashion and then abruptly terminated the call. He glanced at his wristwatch, thirty-one and a half seconds, nice and tight. Then he walked slowly back to his car and took very careful note of everyone around him both close and distant without rasing suspicion to himself. Once clear he thought about the relationship between the CIA and Nghi Phamhung, how necessary it was for the CIA to preserve it in order to guarantee its own survival, how instru-mental Phamhung had been in supplying information on emerging terrorist cells whilst leaving sufficient numbers intact to keep the CIA busy. Raymond Halliday would use his position of power with its as-sociated rhetoric as a means of protecting Phamhungs Alljoy venture but he secretly knew that the market place would in its own time determine whether it should survive or die for there was not only the pharmaceutical police to contend with but assassins as well who were expert in the ways of making accidents look natural.

The information that Phamhung had just given Halliday once washed and sanitized would add weight to the idea that the present drug crisis in the USA was orchestrated by the Australian adminis-tration which sought to distance itself from that fact by creating a similar situation in Australia and the United Kingdom. The truth did not matter to Halliday for if it were true that Harvey Jarwood and his clan were creating international political mayhem with information obtained out of Pinegap then and only then would CIA covert opera-tions be put into place once the President was alerted to the situation. However a better option for Raymond Halliday was to be in the arms of his potential lover and wife to be Mrs April Halliday nee Hako.

"I've managed to bring your favourite this time." Vivienne excitedly gushed as she passed the grilled vegetable and brie baguette to Max Franck Climax who was presently known as Robbie the vagabond to the sweet and innocent girl.

"I really appreciate your efforts." He thankfully responded. "I'm sure you will be richly rewarded one day."

"It's already happened"! Vivienne gleefully answered as she took a bite of her lunch.

"How's that"? Max Climax asked.

"Me mum's cured" She proudly stated as tears of joy started to gather in her clear blue eyes before freely cascading down her fine porcelain skin.

"I thought she was seriously sick."

"So did I until the drug crisis hit"? Vivienne replied as she dabbed away her tears.

"And then"?

"She stopped taking her medications and she got better. One of her friends then promised to get some alternate herbal treatments from Germany and now me Mum's just fine. All those years of suffering for nothing! I knew it was those damn tablets that were making her sick! She's not alone, look what today's paper writes"! Vivienne happily said as she took a crumpled copy of the days' London Herald national newspaper out of her shopping bag and found the exact page and article. The story's headline read ' Brits invade continental Europe in droves seeking cures'. Max Climax was already aware but pretended not to know and read the article vigorously, once satisfied with its content, he raised his eyes to the heavens and silently gave thanks for a number of reasons. Firstly that he had caused the multi-nationals great pain, secondly that the people of Britain were given the chance to heal themselves naturally even though a percentage remained resistant to these ideas and persisted in taking ineffective medications in the hope that the placebo effect would see them through and thirdly that illegal drug addicts were being naturally detoxified and consumed marjoram as a way of seeing their day through. The rich attempted to circumvent drug failure by importing drugs from the continent but failed so the article concluded and it gave support to the viral based cause of the national pandemic. The article then continued to discuss the merits of the cancellation of all needless elective and cosmetic surgery.

"Well-balanced article don't you think"? Vivienne asked after observing Max Climax's reading behaviour.

"With respect to pro's and con's of natural therapies." Franck replied

"What about how well us Brits behave in our hour of need"?

"Yes you certainly....I....mean we certainly go about things quietly, methodically and with a dogged determination to succeed even though it might mean seeking outside help." Franck agreed.

"Must be a worrying time for parliament and all those health bureaucrats" Vivienne joked.

"I suppose but at least help is not far away." Franck ambiguously replied.

"As for the article, if it is correctly reported, even customs have dropped their guard and are allowing treatments into the country for personal use only. What do you make of the virus theory as being the cause of the mess"?

"I'm not exactly medically qualified to say, however having said that I suppose I have enough personal experience with the down and outs to accept the fact. Isn't Hepatitis caused by a variety of viruses, A, B, C, D and E? If one of these changed like the flu virus that the experts tell us about every year then it could spread like that and blanket the entire population with long lasting effects." Max shakily put forward.

"Hum good theory for a beggar, you been reading discarded science mags from the bins"? Vivienne jokingly asked as she took another bite of her baguette.

"You guessed right"! Franck Max Climax replied as he smiled gingerly and threw breadcrumbs to the pigeons that patiently paced up and down the pavement seeking their daily bread.

Brendan O'Reilly irrespective of where he found himself would always obey his daily Catholic rituals starting with early Morning Prayer, reflection and when the occasion arose, instruction by Jack Stern.

Today was no exception Brendan quietly finished saying the Our Father as he prepared to sit himself down in the company of the delectable Yvette Bell, the master soul collector Mr Jack Stern and partake of an enjoyable afternoon tea as the Genius Loci was always able to serve compliments of Grandpa.

"The food here is always delicious"! Yvette approvingly said as she took her first mouthful.

"Thank you." She could hear Grandpa seductively saying in her head, he blushed at the verbal innuendo smiled and tried to keep the food in the confines of her mouth. Jack said nothing as he mentally prepared himself for Brendan's instruction.

"I agree especially that circumstances are now different. Then we were on the run now we are more relaxed." Brendan replied remembering the days when they that is he, Jack and the nine girls were on the run from all and sundry, a time of excitement and self-discovery.

"And the food has not lost its intensity"! Yvette said finishing off his statement.

"Perhaps it's the environment"? He quizzically suggested.

"Or its maker" He could hear Grandpa saying in his head. Brendan scanned the room to see where Grandpa was hiding but no luck.

"I also play hide and seek." Brendan heard Grandpa playing with his mind.

Jack allowed Yvette and Brendan to fool around like little children with Grandpa as they enjoyed their food, which consisted of Gravlax, served with a sweet dill mustard sauce, light rye bread, thinly sliced boiled egg, caviar, capers, pickled asparagus and tomato followed by a French style light and fluffy baked lemon ricotta cheese cake and freshly brewed coffee made from Costa Rica beans. Jack remained silent throughout and it caused Yvette to think that he was being threatened by Brendan for her affections. When the time was right Jack interrupted their jovial mood by asking.

"How did religions come about"?

Brendan and Yvette looked at each other and knew that Jack was expecting an answer out of the ordinary, neither one volunteered an opinion until they were certain that it possessed originality. Yvette was first to respond.

"They came about as a result of circumstance and language." She bravely said.

Jack got up from his chair and walked about the table like an eminent professor. "Well said." He applauded her and then looking directly at Brendan he asked. "And their failings are"?

"That there remains a need for understanding which the religions do not supply for they create law without explanation." Brendan cleverly proposed.

"Excellent! So in effect all of them lack a sense of......"? Jack asked as he paced about and watched Grandpa invisibly clear the dishes away. Yvette giggled as the crockery flew past her and when Grandpa stroked the back of her neck once he had finished. Jack came to a halt and watched the visible play with the invisible; he waited patiently for Brendan to elicit a reply.

"Direction"

"Again an excellent deduction tell me qualified priest, supposed learned one, what did your founder leave behind"? Jack asked intensely.

Brendan interpreted this as being a trick question. Who indeed was the founder? Was it Saint Peter one of Christ's apostles, the hundred odd religions professing to be the true Christian faith before they were finally welded into the Catholic Church, or some one else?

"I do not know the man." Brendan truthfully replied.

"First denial"! Jack said coldly as though Brendan was re-enacting the biblical record of Peter's denial of the Christ.

"Surely you have some experience of him"?

"Never" Brendan bluntly retorted.

"Second denial; want to try for strike three"?

"Try the mass." Yvette whispered into Brendan's ear as she came to his rescue. Jack overheard her suggestion and shook his head to signify 'not quite right'.

"I thought it was after all the host and wine were changed into the body and blood of Christ during consecration." Yvette defiantly said.

"Symbolically perhaps but that is not what I am looking for."

"You're not suggesting the keeper of the Church of the Coloured Sands"? Brendan confusedly asked.

"Perhaps"

"Never......... he doesn't remotely look anything like Christ"

"Are you certain"? Jack probed and allowed Brendan time to re-consider his answer.

"I don't think this line of questioning is getting us anywhere"! Yvette argued. Jack remained calm and smiled in response to her determined stance.

"Very well I'll change the question. What did the Christ leave behind"?

"Knowledge" Brendan guessed as he stabbed in the dark. Jack clapped his hands as one would in standing ovation and then he asked.

"Bravo! What was the nature of his knowledge"?

"How the hell am I supposed to know"? Brendan thought to himself as his mind raced and grabbed for proper academic straws to hurl back at Jack. Then he realised that he was nothing more than a pale shadow of Jack Stern.

"He left behind true knowledge." Yvette softly answered on behalf of Brendan as she drew in a deep breath of air and continued "Knowledge of one's true self, one's abilities and how to use them without pollution. Knowledge of the world and how to access it and use it without pollution and knowledge of the universe and how to learn from it and add to it without pollution"

"Very well said, little too much emphasis on pollution, nevertheless I catch your drift." Jack warmly congratulated Yvette.

"Thank you." And with that she reached across and took hold of Brendan's hand so as to offer reassurance and compassion.

Jack studied his charges intensely and then described their relationship in an almost clinical manner. "Yvette, Brendan you were made for each other, you belong together. Brendan you need Yvette's eyes and you Yvette Brendan supplies the love you need to bring forth all of your secret wishes. This is an undisputable fact for in Mauritius both of you started the process with the discovery of one of the hidden fragments of the knowledge that the Christ left behind. This ancient knowledge has been protected over the centuries by a secret society known as Circulus Palari."

"You said process and fragments." Yvette observed.

"Yes."

"Are you therefore suggesting that other fragments exist, how do they fit together, what is the process"? Brendan paled at Yvette's question for he realised the consequences.

"I am still researching all of those areas, suffice to say that it represents a long awaited global event providing we find and put all of the pieces together; assemble the puzzle so to speak."

"Roaming Club doesn't make sense"! Brendan interrupted as he commented on his understanding of the translation into English of the Latin phrase Circulus Palari.

"It does if you consider its origins and its present intentions, however that can wait, we have gathered today to discuss knowledge as Yvette correctly deduced. So far we have discovered a fragment that has allowed you Brendan to expand your knowledge of your true self. Open your shirt and let us see." Jack gently and respectfully asked.

Brendan frowned and wondered what Jack was up to and then he remembered what he had been taught before about the effect that his evolution would have upon the appearance of his crucifix. Brendan removed his priestly white collar from his shirt, unbuttoned the top three buttons of his shirt and pulled out his gold crucifix, which had grown in size and had become further encrusted with precious stones that represented the stages of his development and the acquisition of supernatural powers. Yvette compared it with that of Jack's heavily encrusted one and realised how much further Jack had progressed.

"You've come along nicely, however you still have a long way to go, infant." Jack remarked, a description, which Brendan did not take offence to.

"We need to find more fragments but there will be dangers I warn you." Jack Stern cautioned.

"From whom"? Yvette inquired.

"The Roaming Club and our own people"! He quickly answered without any hesitation, just then Jack's highly sophisticated phone rang, it was His Grace the Archbishop Steven Moulds. Jack waved his hand and the phone was instantly connected to the room's sound system allowing his friends to listen in on the conversation.

"Ah Your Grace, you've found me again." Jack cheerfully greeted.

"Yes Mr Stern my people will always track you down"!

"Such clever chaps, I'll have to try harder to escape your clutches"!

"Very funny Mr Stern" Steven Moulds acidly replied.

"What spot of bother are you in now"?

"None......... the person in hot water is Fr Brendan O'Reilly"!

"Why is that"? Jack asked innocently

"We have decided that his party time is over, back to regular duties for him"! Moulds sternly barked.

"Not pleased with his work in Mauritius"?

"Too sensational"!

"I wouldn't say that, the locals seem exceptionally happy"!

"So I gather from CNN's international news. O'Reilly's caused quite a stir in France unfortunately it's made no impact on our local attendances."

"Perhaps they need Brendan over there that could make a difference; by the way pleased with Napp"?

"Very, was that your work"?

"What's that"? Jack asked in a naïve child's voice.

"Australia's drug crisis"!

"Their what"

"Drug crisis"!! The archbishop screamed.

"That's beyond me your grace." Jack replied playing the ham.

"I'm not so sure Mr Stern." His Grace dryly replied.

"Rid yourself of organised crime"? Jack then asked completely throwing His Grace off his guard by changing the subject.

"None of your business Mr Stern"!

"Apologies I forgot the Church needs to make money, pity it isn't by legitimate means anymore."

"That's quite enough Mr Stern"! Steven Moulds said raising his voice.

"What are you going to do, cast a spell on me, burn me to crisp, turn me into a pillar of stone"?

"Enough Mr Stern"! The Archbishop roughly commanded.

"Exactly why did you ring me your Grace"? Jack asked completely unaffected by Moulds ranting.

"To find Brendan O'Reilly"

"Very well, if I see him I'll tell him you called, God bless you your Grace."

"Just wait a minute Mr Stern. I need a word with you"!

"Exactly which one was it, thank you, apologies, good work, congratulations"? Jack asked cheekily.

"Trouble, Mr Stern, don't go looking for trouble! Now is not the time to change the face of world religion"!

"That's debatable the Islamic's appear to be having a go"! Jack fired back without any regard for political correctness. "By the way Your Grace since when has the Church of the Coloured Sands been considered to be trouble"?

"My advice to you Mr Stern, is, don't go looking for any more trouble and send back Father Brendan O'Reilly once you see him"!! His Grace loudly warned in his standard authoritative, aloof and dictatorial manner.

"Otherwise"?

"He may find himself in excommunicado"! His grace Steven Moulds very slowly and very deliberately replied. Sensing that the Archbishop wanted to have the last say and was about to terminate the call, Jack clicked off and pressed reset on his phone which activated its random telephone number generator to give it a new numerical sequence.

"Only calls when he's in trouble"! Jack remarked as he put away his sophisticated mobile phone and gazed upon Brendan who looked rather despondent. "Don't worry my friend it's always like this when you're onto something new that threatens to destabilize the status quo. Think about it then you'll understand why big bureaucracies irrespective whether they are public or private are so slow to act, change represents threat."

Brendan remained silent almost sulking Yvette put an arm around him and whispered. "We'll make it together."

"I think the Archbishop's call confirmed my suspicions, all the more reason to instruct you on your next port of call." Jack said breaking Brendan's mood, which caused him to perk up and listen attentively after he removed Yvette's arm from his shoulder. Once again Jack adopted the countenance of a learned eminent history professor and said.

"They brought frankincense, myrrh and gold."

"Correct"! Brendan energetically uttered as he remembered the biblical account of Christs birth.

"However" Jack paused dramatically and gestured. "They were not gifts."

Both Yvette and Brendan frowned at the revelation. "They were collectively a map of destiny for the infant, a map that he would have to follow from the age of twelve until the beginning of his ministry which represented the fulfilment of his teachings."

Brendan audibly recounted the words of Decay. "The gold was from India, similarly the frankincense, the myrrh was not from the Hell district of the Red Sea district known as Tehama but from Somalia in the region of Somaliland from there through the fairs of Berbera the Banians took it to Bombay. You will need to journey to India, you will meet resistance from the Masters of Affliction who do not wish for peace on Earth they feed on war." He finished saying.

"You have come well prepared"! Jack complimented the handsome priest.

"Thanks to the keeper." Brendan happily replied with a boyish grin on his face.

"Tonight we reflect on our futures, tomorrow we return to Mauritius and await the pilgrims, nothing like a little controversy to wake up Rome"! Jack smartly said with a mischievous smile.

25

MUTATIONS

When one works for the CIA there is no rest. Amongst its workers the standing joke was that the Central Intelligence Agencies abbreviation CIA really meant 'constantly irritating annoyance' for there was no life outside of it, even when one retired, its memory lingered on and coloured everything that the ex-employee did.

Raymond Halliday sought a restful night's sleep in the comfort of his bed after an agonising day at the office. His female pet Shitzu of three years lay at the foot of his mattress happy that her master was home at last and when the moment was right she crept up the bed, licked Raymond on the cheek so as to say 'sleep well my master' and cuddled up next to him.

Raymond Halliday lived in a spacious three-bedroom apartment courtesy of the CIA, one of the perks of his job. The others included free transport and an abundance of travel overseas. The downside, it was usually attached to company business. Raymond however always saw the positive side and enjoyed the sight seeing and made certain that his passion for chocolate was always satisfied; for no matter where he found himself he would always purchase the finest chocolates available from that locality.

It was four thirty in the morning according to his bedside clock, its companion the black and gold antique French phone starting chiming, its ring tone indicative that the office was calling. Raymond Halliday reached across and picked up the receiver.

"Hello." He feebly answered.

"Good morning Raymond, code P, repeat code P." The duty officer advised which meant that Raymond's presence was immediately required.

"Thank you, be there directly." Raymond's Shitzu sensed that her master was wanted and whimpered so as to say. "Can't you stay longer"?

"Don't worry lady, I'll be back soon." Halliday assured the pedigree dog as he quickly dressed and skipped the customary toiletries by drenching himself with a copious amount of manly body cologne. He was out the door before the Shitzu could make any further fuss.

Code P meant the President of the USA was on his way to attend a briefing of major importance. Raymond pondered its likely content for he had encountered nor detected anything new over the past seventy-two hours. As he drove into the complex at Langley Raymond noticed security had trebled inside and outside, after all one of the world's most powerful men was attending, the symbol of true freedom; an ideal that needed to be protected at all costs.

Executive agent Raymond Halliday was one of the last to take his seat in the assembly headed by the Presidents Secretary of State the forthright Ms Rachel Crank.

"Good of you all to come at such short notice I congratulate you on your dedication. This morning we need to discuss a potential national state of emergency. As you are aware several months ago our nations pharmaceutical industry, was hit by what we then believed to be a domestic terrorist attack, which the FBI and other authorities are presently investigating. This has now been raised to category D1." A ripple of troubled rumours spread through the room, Crank paused for it to subside.

"There appears to be a similarity between what our friends the English and our allies the Australians have experienced. The official story that they have propagated namely a widespread viral epidemic affecting the entire population is not applicable to the US. I sense some of you are about to question category D1. There has occurred an exponential increase in drug failure in the USA caused by a specific virus that has rendered all disintegrants used in tablet and capsule manufacture inert. This virus is foreign to our shores, its only known source, the great continent of Australia." Once again murmurs spread amongst Crank's listeners only this time louder. "Our greatest fear is that this virus in its present or mutated form may spread to other grains and consequently cause a devastating effect on our food supply. The President has ordered the Centre for Infectious Diseases as well as the Federal Agricultural Department to decontaminate all suspect manufacturing sites and stores as quickly as possible. There is a total media blackout on the operation code named 'Clean Sweep'.

In addition we have instructed all of our intelligence agencies worldwide to prepare a short list of persons capable of originating such a brilliant attack. Once we have determined who it is, it should confirm our feeling based on current available evidence that Australia's present long standing Prime Minister Harvey Jarwood is the brain child behind the operation." Rachael Crank coolly said as she turned her head to the right. Brian George the President of the USA recognised the cue and took his place next to her at the podium.

"Good morning ladies and gentlemen. The world as we know it is divided by the equator into the northern and southern hemispheres, which are further polarised into the haves and have-nots by socio-economic developments and trends. There is no doubt in my mind that wealth is more abundant in the north in all aspects of the word. The south suffers and whilst we consider ourselves to be one of the great superpowers, none exist in the southern hemisphere; it is virgin so to speak. It has become apparent to us that Mr Jarwood wants Australia to be the superpower of the south as part of his ideology. He also desires to alienate himself and his country from the USA, an agenda that is imminent. Under the disguise of alleviating the world's refugee crisis Mr Jarwood has been instrumental in influencing Australia's immigration policy to allow predominately rich non Christians into his country thus furthering his cause and distancing Australia from our Christian Union. CIA agents April Hako and Raymond Halliday will confirm that sensitive data collected by our bases at Pinegap and Nurranger has been sold on the African black market by Australian double agents working on their government's behalf, thereby causing Pinegap's military and political strategic position as well as our global network defence system to be put at grave risk. Make no mistake people, these bases are located on prime real estate, we cannot afford to lose them"! A grimfaced President George warned without taking his eyes off his audience.

"Mr President." CIA agent Leighton Hill interrupted as he raised his hand to attract the commander in chief's attention.

"Yes young man."

"CIA special agent Leighton Hill.... Sir; I understand your concerns however I do not comprehend Australia's importance in world's events. It is a small nation by our standards barely twenty million people, primarily used over the years as a pawn in our global foreign policies.

I see no urgency in your presentation this morning. Any information emanating out of our Australian bases can easily be doctored before it reaches the Aussie authorities. Today Canberra lies bare, Mr Jarwood is hospitalised his prognosis suggests he will make a full recovery in time, the federal governments infra-structure is in disarray, why may I ask Sir did you call this Code P meeting? I personally see no danger whatsoever." Leighton Hill both asked and concluded as he openly displayed his confusion by frowning profusely. President Brian George remained unperturbed throughout Leighton Hill's analytical questioning.

"Why indeed Leighton, why indeed, unless it was to put a

wounded animal down, out of its misery"? Brian George snarled.

"At best sir, I perceive it to be a lamb"! Hill aggressively retorted with a tone of voice that clearly showed that he did not want the US to initiate another unnecessary and controversial invasion.

"Supposing sir, the animal was more dangerous, a lion perhaps, what then"? The President proposed.

"Show me I say"! Leighton demanded resolute in his convictions.

"Very well Rachael you heard the man do your stuff"! Brian George confidently directed as a man who held a winning poker hand.

"Straight away sir"! She obediently responded as she instructed the nearby technical attendants to bring down the projection screen from its housing located in the ceiling above the podium.

"Lights please, thank you, projection please, thank you." She politely asked as she readied herself with a powerful laser pointer.

"Here we have a series of pictures taken of Australia's Kakadu National park located in its northern territory. The area is abundantly rich in uranium ore, the subject of much hot political debate over whether to mine it or not for peaceful purposes only. The Federal Government vehemently argues that the area is untouched. These aerial photographs confirm that until one looks more closely using different techniques as the next series of slides demonstrate.

Satellite differential infrared scanning paints a picture of intense activity beneath the surface, a labyrinth of underground mines, tunnels and shafts. Modified nuclear-magnetic resonance of the same and surrounding areas depict transport of mined ore to a close proximity underground refinery producing one hundred per cent uranium rods. From there these are conveyed in radiation proof containers by civilian trucks to the outskirts of the Simpson desert where in the middle of nowhere and only known to the wildlife the vehicles disappear from view into a repository designed to stockpile the uranium. Here are digital photos taken by one of our own double agents working in the area. As you may see a large depository of military hardware exists and behind those closed doors clearly marked with the radioactive symbol, dozens of nuclear warheads.

The technical expertise and equipment necessary to produce these weapons exist behind the same doors. They have been imported from overseas, from mainly the Koreans and I'm afraid to say from some of our own companies, but I must add done or should I say sold in good faith. The Simpson Desert's underground water supply provides the heavy water needed for the manufacturing process.

These findings have caused us great heartache and uncertainty for not one of us ever considered that one of our friends or allies would ever betray us. This has led us to re-evaluate all of our political relationships; it might well become a situation of the U.S.A not trusting any nation that it has entered into a pact with. We need to become even more vigilant for it appears that terrorism does not only originate from those who despise our achievements but from our friends as well! Luckily Australia's geographical isolation can be used to our advantage.

A military strike is out of the question unless; it was disguised as an attack by the Indonesians, the question becomes, when and where and the consequences of its actions. Diplomacy is also not an option

The Australians are very clever; we believe they created their own drug failures as a smoke screen and then attacked our sovereign soil with their form of biological warfare. In some ways we need to do the same, the President and I seek your advice, because fundamentally your department will be responsible for bringing the Aussies back into line.

I'll stop here and adjourn for say forty-five minutes, which should allow you sufficient time to brainstorm the current crisis." Rachael Crank said as she ended the introduction to the morning's hectic proceedings and left to accompany the President who along with his Whitehouse aides had already gone into the adjoining room to enjoy freshly brewed coffee and stacks of flapjacks heavily drenched in genuine Canadian maple syrup.

As a chief Executive officer, Raymond Halliday knew that he would be expected to deliver an iron clad operational proposition, which invariably would be off his own bat and not in association with anyone else. In the department he was the loner, especially when it came to original ideas, accordingly he left for parts unknown within the CIA's complex to mull things over.

Some people sit on the toilet and read the newspaper as a stimulus to evacuate their bowels, Raymond Halliday on the other hand had a curious liking of public toilets; he simply sat on a vacant pedestal, closed and locked the cubicle door and listened to the abdominal performances of strangers on either side of him as they entered and exited, it was his way of obtaining inspiration for his ideas derived from the bowel habits of others. The human body's anal symphony of ridding itself of wastes much like the workings of the CIA.

"Times up back to the conference room"! Raymond told himself as he looked at his wristwatch and prepared to leave the confines of his meditative chamber located in the staff male toilet situated on the same level as the assembly room. With his head fully loaded he took his place and waited for Rachael Crank to reconvene the meeting.

"Thank you ladies and gentlemen, I trust you are ready to provide us with an avalanche of ideas."

One after another voiced their opinions and put forward their strategies in a true competitive spirit,unfortunately for them the President and his Secretary of State had already heard these before and from their top advisors. When all were said and done Halliday as the last remaining survivor raised his hand.

"Mr Halliday, you have the floor, proceed when you will" Were the words that Rachael Crank greeted Raymond with

"Thank you very much; Mr President, Ma'am, fellow agents, there is no doubt in my mind that we have to be very diligent and careful in our approach which will need to cover all bases if it has any chance of striking the menace out. Harvey Jarwood's clan it appears has been very active in Australia's political arena for many decades.

The Ice storm that dealt Canberra its final deathblow has fractionated the present ruling party; luckily for Jarwood the largest proportion of it remains under his family's influence. We cannot assume that all members are aware of what Mr Jarwood is up to but then again perhaps they may well be and it would explain the direction that Australian politics is taking. The dilemma is, if we eliminate Harvey Jarwood, how many more will we need to attend to, or will it be the case of once the king falls his troops will be easily routed?

Will the king's death be natural or unnatural, physical or political? Do we want the operation at Kakadu patent, destroyed, exposed or kept under wraps? The question is what is in the best interests of our nation and with respect to that issue how can we maximize our buddy-buddy relationship with Australia?

Our operation needs to be invisible with a tinge of transparency that allows the Aussies to realise; we are aware, we are watching and we will act"!

"What is your proposal Mr Halliday"? The President asked suitably impressed with Hallidays opening comments.

"Mr Harvey Jarwood's health will deteriorate, Kakadu National Park will experience a natural disaster, the Simpson Desert's underground depository will vanish and Australia's political landscape will change forever under the leadership of Cyril Pinewood." Raymond Halliday confidently put forward.

"I'll leave you to make the necessary arrangements, keep me informed, thank you ladies and gentlemen, that's all for today." Brian George the President of the United States signed off and stepped off the podium and walked towards Raymond Halliday, he extended his hand which Halliday grasped firmly and placed his other hand on Halliday's left shoulder. The President then bent forward and whispered into Hallidays right ear.

"Good work, we're aware of Nghi Phamhung, no slip-ups otherwise he's toast"!

"Yes Sir." Halliday nervously replied as his face whitened.

"You look rather pale, not feeling well"? Louis Badcock said with sublime pleasure as he looked at the Small Dark Figure's sunken features.

"How caring of you Louis"! It sarcastically replied and then waved Badcock away by harshly saying. "Go take your place"!

"Very well my lord." Louis cynically replied as he walked to the end of the conference table and sat next to one of Nghi Phamhung's henchmen.

"I wonder why we're all here, counting the millions are we? Going international are we, well"? Badcock asked in an absurd tone of voice not unlike that of a television cartoon character.

"Silence you fool! I don't know why we have to tolerate your presence"! Nghi Phamhung shouted in a high voice.

"Because I run a successful solid business; you Asian misfit" Badcock retorted; his cutting statement struck a nerve in Phamhung who narrowed his eyes and stared at Louis with murderous intent.

"I wouldn't intimidate him." The Harshman cautioned. "He's come prepared"! He warned.

"My body guards can deal with anyone"! Phamhung defiantly said as he thirsted for blood.

"Oh dear I think you had better rethink your position." The Harshman continued to caution fearful of a sudden bloodbath.

"Why what's he going to do, slap me around like a prostitute"?

"Louis I think you better show him"! The Harshman softly suggested.

"May I introduce Ivan Gallows my personal assistant, a little worse for wear considering he is about two thousand years old and has recently escaped the clutches of heaven"! Badcock proudly announced as the D-man entered the room and stood behind his seat.

"So you are the one." Phamhung concluded remembering what his Chinese ancestors wrote about an invincible warrior; one who had helped their armies win battles hundreds of years ago.

"Perhaps" The D-man growled.

"Well Badcock I may have to change my opinion, obviously you're interested in our venture and you have brought help." Phamhung swallowed hard as he back peddled.

"Not really his presence is coincidental, why don't you carry on and tell us about the Alljoy disaster, I'm sure the leaders of Dot.org would like to hear about it"! Badcock smirked as he sensed the Small Dark Figure's failure.

"Actually it's not as bad as Louis here makes out." Phamhung countered.

"Oh yes it is! I told you... not.... to ....get.... mixed up with gays"! Badcock taunted. The Dot.org mafia bosses looked on stone faced and sat silent.

"Alljoy the product is a very successful product, too successful"! The statement made the mafia bosses smile. "However" Phamhung cautioned. "Its success lies not in its sales but in its effect and therein lies the difficulty." Phamhung explained.

"How can that be considered to be a failure." One of the mafia bosses asked out of curiosity.

"It's embarrassing for me to say." Phamhung faultered

"Let me help Nghi"! Badcock rudely interrupted. "Unlike prostitution or drug addiction where people come back for more, this Alljoy, what a name, Alljoy the latest marketing joke, cures people! One dose and all of your ailments are gone forever! What a brilliant product! Should sell tens of millions make you a very rich dead man"! Badcock dryly said. "In fact it should make every one associated with the venture dead! Question is does it bring people back from the dead I ask you? You think I'm joking, then think again, the world of commerce is not interested in cures, perpetual motion machines, endless supplies of free energy or anything that robs it of repeat sales!

Therein lies your problem, the biggest threat to your survival, the money making machine that wants it all"! Badcock dramatically argued as he forced the issue and looked Nghi Phamhung squarely in the eye who shivered in response.

"How did he know, or is he just guessing? Where did he get the info from"? These were some of the muddled thoughts that ran recklessly through the Chinese born Afghanistan's mind Phamhung put on a brave face and said.

"We have nothing to fear from the authorities, my contact who is very highly placed with the CIA and has the president's ear assured me during a recent telephone conversation. He did warn me to keep an eye on the multi-nationals. I think we should continue Alljoy." Phamhung reluctantly and very shakily put forward knowing full well that his argument was shallow.

"Of course you should Nghi, every common person wants a cure, problem is how many accept a cure exists at all, scepticism, cynicism will become your worst enemies." Badcock sharply countered as he increased his verbal onslaught.

"We shall remain silent and offer no comment on anecdotal evidence." Phamhung defiantly replied.

"I give you fifteen to eighteen months before the magic runs out! Just another flash in the pan"! Badcock loudly predicted.

"We will still make a fortune." Phamhung angrily attacked like a wounded animal.

"At what cost? Have you considered your Alljoy effect on the illegal narcotic market? What if it cures drug addiction, you will effectively destroy forty percent of our business perhaps even more! Clever boy! Congratulations to you both"! Badcock bluffed in the hope that the insinuations would cause sufficient doubt in the mobster's minds to end the project. Silence filled the room everyone pondered the violent exchange of words between Badcocok and Nghi Phamhung.

"How confident are you of immunity from Government forces"? One of the Mafia bosses asked breaking the tension.

"Absolutely"! Phamhung resolutely replied as he took in a deep breath of air.

"Good! We did not get where we are today by being afraid! Continue as normal. We will provide you with extra protection on one condition." The same mafia boss arrogantly stated.

"What will it be"? Phamhung asked expecting the worst.

"We see the solution to the problem as being very simple; make Alljoy weaker, water it down, reduce the content of the gay one's discovery by fifty percent! Then you shall have no further problem, it's all a matter of dosage"! The mafia boss instructed like a stupid bootlegger who was ignorant and completely unaware of the power of Dr Dennis Sauvage's messenger RNA.

"Of course" Phamhung thankfully replied.

"Damn it"! Badcock cursed under his breath and without further comment abruptly took his leave. The Small Dark Figure's countinance regained itself and it shone once again having been given a new lease of life by its superiors.

"You were going so well, I thought you had all of them won over" The D-Man said to Louis Badcock as they walked side-by-side back to where Louis car was parked in the sprawling gardens of the Ricci'c estate.

"So did I" Badcock bitterly replied as he calculated his next move.

"That wouldn't be necessary Louis. Don't even consider it! It will dirty your hands and your chances of entering the inner circle! Others will do the work for you"! Ivan Gallows the D-man strictly instructed as he responded to reading Badcock's mind. Louis stopped still and studied the D-man in detail.

"Your powers grow stronger; you read my mind, your breath as destructive as ever, hair and nails slightly metallic, anything else"?

"Afraid not, no destructive energy on tap, I cannot fly by thought, hence the need for more money"! Gallows reluctantly indirectly asked.

"Where to now"? Badcock questioned.

"Somalia."

"That's a strange destination. What's there besides civil war, poverty and destitution"?

"One who can help me I guess."

"How do you know"? Badcock asked.

"He was one of two choices; I didn't fancy becoming a schizo-phrenic homosexual so I declined the offer"! Ivan Gallows replied with a thankful sigh. Badcock looked at him closely and was pleased that they both shared a dislike of gays.

"Here you are, I've linked your name to my credit card, use it freely." Louis proudly and magnanimously said as he handed over a gleaming gold plated credit card from his leather wallet made from crocodile skin.

"I prefer cash"! Ivan Gallows aloofly said.

"Very well"! Badcock replied as he withdrew the credit card and replaced it with a bundle of one hundred dollar notes. Gallows flicked them through his fingers, listened to the crispness of the currency paper and then brought them up to his nose to smell the colour of the money.

"Uncle Sam's"

"Of course"! Badcock lied, as he knew they belonged to an enter-prising cousin. "When will you leave"?

"Today, drive me to the airport"! Ivan Gallows abruptly demanded as he slipped the money into his black trouser pocket where it would stay until he needed it for casino pleasures. They sat in relative silence as Badcock swiftly taxied the D-man to the local domestic airport, from there Ivan Gallows hitchhiked unseen on numerous domestic and international air flights until he found himself wandering the streets of Mogadisu Somalia unnoticed in search of the faint image of the man, the keeper of the seventy first celestial ladder had imbedded in his memory.

Dirty, dusty, dry and arid, hot, hurried, hassled and lost were the best words to describe the otherwise confident assassin, after hours of aimless trekking.

"Why so glum? You should be happy here, this is your land, the one you created, enjoy the fruits of your labour"! A raspy voice rang out which caused the D-man to come to a halt and reflect on the content of its statement.

"Looking for a way out of you present dilemma? There is a simple way, all ports of call require a passport." The voice then offered in solution.

"Damn this hybrid existence! I hate being human even though it is partially so"! Ivan Gallows cursed and he continued to analyse the words he had just heard." He's here, but where? Ports of call? This is a land locked city! What's next"? He asked himself as he continued to shuffle on.

'Past the P-ought' Ivan read on numerous roadside signs as he passed a profusely red bearded Blackman dressed in vibrant clothes seated behind a much used collapsible card table upon which rested a sign that bore the words 'official Somalian passports available here'.

"Go no further show yourself you are amongst friends." Bipin Greatrex warmly greeted Ivan Gallows in a loud voice, which caused the dust to rise off his 'diplomatic' table. Ivan halted his tedious struggle and materialised into full view.

"Step this way sir, please take a seat, rest your weary soul; let me attend to your needs." Greatrex openly invited as he stood up to greet Gallows. The D-man mentally superimposed Bipin's image over that which he remembered from his encounter with the keeper of the seventy first celestial floor.They fitted perfectly but he needed further confirmation.

"What is your name"? Gallows growled.

"Forest"

"As in" The D-man roughly questioned.

"Trees, lots of them crowed into a vast expanse of land." Bipin answered as he allowed his hands to describe the scene.

"And your other name"? Gallows asked quite disappointed.

"Large and royal" was Bipin's gesticulated reply.

"Waste of time, effort and space.' Gallows snapped back quite irritated.

"Watch your tongue insolent one"!

"Why should I? You're nothing more than a pompous overweight

Somalian who peddles false passports! You're a tourist's joke"!

"That may be but I have direct contact with the Masters of Affliction"!

"Name one"! Gallows angrily taunted.

"Tetra Grammatou..... Good enough weakling" Greatrex insultingly replied.

"Yes! Damn you"!

"Then we will get on famously, you self impoverished runt and if you haven't already deduced it, Bipin Greatrex Gaylord at your service"!

"Why all of this homosexual behaviour"?

"To bring further discord into the human race and please our lords. I just love the one where the guy after fifteen years of marriage and fathering three children decides he is gay and leaves, it's a good one, lots of emotional hell for everyone concerned"! Bipin merrily chuckled.

"You mean there are two cupids"? Ivan asked quite confused as he frowned.

"There is now, one for the heteros and one for those hiding in the closet"! Bipin continued to chuckle unabated.

Ivan Gallows settled himself, homosexuality was abhorrent to him, it was vile, crude and wrong. This was a dirty way of causing pain; Ivan's methods on the contrary were clean, dirt free, surgically perfect. He attempted to gauge how powerful Greatrex was and even though his estimate might prove correct he could not chance disposing of Bipin in his present state.

"What sort of passport would you like"? Greatrex asked continuing the banter.

"One that grant's immunity

"From" Greatrex probed.

"All that prevents me from regaining my powers"!

"What source have you tried"? Bipin seriously asked.

"The Stone of Scone and the Pins of Crucifixion" Ivan Gallows replied somewhat disappointed with their outcomes.

"Two of the greatest sources of power available to demons and you were I believe the keeper of the Pins." Greatrex answered matter of fact.

"Correct"!

"I cannot help you directly I can offer no spell, chant or ceremony that will restore your powers. Heaven has thwarted us as well; your salvation lies in influencing those Roman's sympathetic to our cause. Bring down the miracle in Mauritius and you will be set free"!

"How"? Ivan Gallows the D-man excitedly asked.

"By removing the source; Brendan O'Reilly, remember your past"! Bipin's directive caused the D-man to recollect the crucifixion and the events that led to the formation of the 'rock' and how its coming into being nullified the violence inflicted upon the earth by the Stone of Scone. He then vaguely recollected becoming engaged in the rock's separation and how the four fragments were distributed throughout the world never to be seen nor assembled again.

"Brendan O'Reilly is naïve, unaware of himself or his true powers, He remains confused and muddled, remove him and the church will die, only then will your powers return and our Masters will rejoice. This will assist you with your endeavours"! Bipin Greatrex smiled as he handed over a genuine Vatican City passport, other ID papers and said.

"Be sure to contact the Romans in the Club, they will help you immensely! Your task will become less difficult"!

26

PILGRIMAGE

Although Yvette felt safe in the knowledge that Jack was always close by she still held firm her childhood belief that her dad Alexandre was the real source of her protection, after all he was the one who was always there in her thoughts. Jack Stern represented the physical form whenever she was away from home. At Yvette's insistence Jack arranged for her parents Mr Alexandre and Abrielle Bell to be flown to Mauritius and experience first hand the miracle that Yvette and Brendan's collaborative efforts had brought about. Jack, Yvette and Brendan followed thirty-six hours later using their own specialised form of ethereal transport.

Yvette's parents never had the opportunity of travelling overseas due to monetory constraints they were deeply indebted to Jack's generosity and viewed him as a very suitable candidate for Yvette's hand. Jack sensed this but could not take advantage of it; he remained a true gentleman one who provided and expected nothing in return. It was his pleasure to house Yvette's parents at Club Med where they would enjoy their first overseas honeymoon.

Abrielle had often wished for a tropical island holiday and the Island of Mauritius did not disappoint. It was the time of the year when the vegetation everywhere was green and in blossom, the farmer's fields were overflowing with lush sugarcane and the banana and pineapples crops were overflowing. The sun's light made the scenery a tropical paradise for the avid photographer negating the use of filters to capture the brilliant colours of the island whilst the ocean waters emitted the most unbelievable enticing aqua colour that one could imagine. Brilliant untouched and un-enhanced imagery captured on film. The Island dressed itself in merriment accentuated by the discovery of the Church of the Coloured Sands.

Abrielle Bell was completely besotted by the Island and the facilities that Club Med had on offer. All thoughts that Alexandre no longer loved her vaporised by the first morning of their stay; love was in the air, love for her husband, daughter and life. Mauritius rekindled all of that and it burnt brightly through her eyes. Yvette's accomplishments as important as they were to her mother the rediscovery of the love that bonded Abrielle to her husband overshadowed her desire to visit the Church of The Coloured Sands. Mornings spent walking on the tranquil beach hand in hand and watching the storm clouds gather for the afternoons customary 3pm heavenly wash down were more important, it inspired her to make hot passionate love to her husband and makeup for the years of abstinence caused by her misinterpretation of the circumstances surrounding their marriage. If only she had felt like this before, perhaps she could have conceived naturally, love above all was the strongest force it was capable in her eyes of achieving the impossible. Alas, perhaps it was not too late or was it? Was there still a chance? Her cervix and womb had lost their hostility for once they retained Alexandre's deposits instead of rejecting them Abrielle lived in hope.

"Come darling eat your breakfast quickly. Abrielle eagerly beseeched her husband as he sat opposite her looking quite exhausted after his pre-breakfast bedroom encounter.

"You're in the mood already"? He gulped as he struggled to take a bit of his freshly baked chocolate croissant.

"Perhaps, but I think you deserve a rest for the day my darling, tonight is a different story"! Abrielle with a tilt of her head seductively replied in a low voice as she admired her husband and the numerous finches that flew in and out of the open restaurant.

"Thank you." Alexandre nervously said as he sipped on his freshly squeezed orange juice.

"Good boy! Plenty of Vitamin C makes for healthy sperm and lots of secretions don't forget to eat your scrambled eggs, French toast and fruit platter. You need your strength"!

"Yes Mon Cherie." Alexandre weakly replied as he reflected on his marital life and thought to himself. "When I first met her she was shy eager to please, adoring, then when she discovered she could not bear children everything changed. It was as if lovemaking became a burden, something dirty, I was lucky if it happened once or twice every six months. Even when Yvette arrived it did not change. Still I was not attracted to other women she was the one for me irrespective of how poorly she satisfied me in the bedroom and how she further changed through her job and became the cold condescending dom-ineering prim and proper French woman. Childless women often go like this, it's a pity; childless men like me can either sulk in a corner and drink their worries away or put all of their energies into another love such as an automobile. What's happened to her in Mauritius? All of her has changed; she behaves like a young uninhibited woman! Is it the air, the sun, the resort or the abundance of topless women, what can it be? Can I keep up with her demands? I do not know whether to thank Mr Jack Stern or curse him"!

"Alexandre my darling, your mind seems so far away, what are you thinking about my love"? Abrielle asked recognising her husband's distance.

Alexandre could not lie to his wife and answered. "Mauritius has transformed you into an insatiable sex machine, something I'm not used to"!

"Are you complaining"?

"Not at all, it has taken me by surprise I was conditioned to once or twice a year when you felt like it." Alexandre shakily and secretly confided

"I understand my darling, it must be a strain for you, one minute nothing, the next you have to exercise vigorously on demand, the machine has a mind of its own. Oui" Abrielle paused and changed her mood. "I do not think I will ever be able to undo the hurt I've imposed upon you. I was wrong in my view of our relationship and my body. I saw no sense in making love if I could not conceive a child that is how I was brought up. You thought differently and you sacrificed your right to sexual pleasure by staying loyal and married to me. I completely missed the point, I am sorry; can you find it in you to forgive me"? Abrielle apologised with much pain in her heart and tears in her eyes.

Alexandre reached across and took hold of both of Abrielle's hands and gently smiled. "People marry out of love for love to love; not in order to take advantage of the other person, it did not matter how you treated me I always loved you and still do"!

"I'm sorry Alexandre, I'm so sorry"! Abrielle sobbed as she tried to control her emotional state.

A young well-groomed and tanned GO walked past and inquired in French. "Are you all right Madame, can we be of assistance"?

"No thank you I'm quite........."

"Happy! She's just accepted my proposal of marriage." Alexandre interrupted clarifying the situation.

"Congratulations! I am so pleased for you, it happens here all the time, you know." The GO said in French.

"I thought as much." Alexandre replied.

"Yes Monsieur we locals call Mauritius the Island of Love. Let us congratulate you further, please, yes, one moment." The young GO politely asked as he took his leave and disappeared through a set of doors into the main kitchen. The thoughtful GO's intervention calmed Abrielle and transformed her tears into those of a virgin rather than that belonging to middle aged woman in her mid forties. Alexandre saw the change and commented on her renewed beauty.

"You are as beautiful as the first day I laid eyes upon you"! He genuinely expressed in French as he stretched his body across the table and kissed his wife tenderly on both cheeks.

"I promise never to disappoint you again." Abrielle bravely resolved.

"Just be yourself, my angel." Alexandre softly replied as he smiled at the sight of the chef who obviously loved his food carrying a medium St Honore gateau complete with the traditional bride and groom figurines on top.

"A gift for the love birds, Mademoiselle, Monsieur" The jolly French chef beamed.

"Thank you." Abrielle blushed and she lowered her eyes to feign her modesty.

"I have a further surprise for you both"! The GO teased and then generously said." We have decided to upgrade your facility to that of the bridal suite for the duration of your stay."

"That won't be necessary, we're humble folk, and we'd prefer to stay where we are, everything is so perfect here, and changing rooms might spoil the mood. I like the intimacy of the one that we are staying in." Abrielle explained in fluent French as she looked to her husband for reassurance.

"Yes I agree with my fiancé. But thank you once again." Alexandre said in confirmation.

"Very well Monsieur, perhaps you would be our guest's of honour at dinner tonight and afterwards at the show, yes"? The Go hoped as a trade off.

"We will."

"And how will you spend the rest of the day"? The GO further inquired subtly not wishing to know all of the details.

"I'm taking my wife to be into Grand Balle and let her choose her engagement ring. After that we shall visit the local Catholic priest and arrange our wedding." Alexandre explained in French much to Abrielle surprise.

"Will it be at the newly found Church of the Coloured Sands"? The GO excitedly asked as he reflected on his mental image of Yvette.

"But of course."

At the church the pilgrims from various European countries had already started to arrive in increasing numbers after the France 2 television report, which had been broadcast on other networks.

The multitudes made Brendan quite nervous, stardom was something he hadn't lusted after, Fr Bogliani on the other hand welcomed the attention with open arms and sought to take as much of the limelight as possible. Daily Mass times had to be altered to accommodate the sea of souls who thirsted for salvation. Bogliani proudly ascended the pulpit to deliver his sermon of the day.

"This magnificent building, sniff, sniff, neh, once used to be a dirty old sock abandoned by its owner and left to rot in the fields neh, sniff, sniff! But! It was found and its fabric wove itself into the warm and fluffy atmosphere that you sit in today neh, that you enjoy neh, sniff. The Holy Church is a sock it provides us with comfort, sniff, protects us from the cold, sniff, stimulates our feet into walking in Jesus' steps neh, and causes us to wish that we could wear them on our heads neh, sniff, snort! Our Church is like a universal sock, it can be used anywhere on our anatomy, to care for it, nurture it, sniff, sniff snort neh, so my fellow believers, take your sock and stick, sniff, sniff, snort, and place it where you will"! Bogliani ended leaving his audience completely bewildered.

"What happened to him"? Candy whispered in Jack's ear as they stood side by side in the wings of the main altar.

"Water's worn off"! He dryly replied off the cuff.

"Huh"?

"Never mind I'll explain later." He mischievously whispered as he turned to Brendan who was standing closeby and indicated that he should rescue the congregation from the evil clutches of the distorted

Fr. Bogliani. Brendan stepped forward and ushered Bogliani off the pulpit much to the people's joy.

"Thank you Fr Bogliani for your...er...somewhat 'enlightened and symbolic' homily. May I welcome you ladies, gentlemen and children to our church built especially for all of us irrespective of race, colour, sex or creed, to enjoy and learn from" Brendan's warmly greeted before he went onto expound his knowledge acquired through Jack's ghostly grandpa as to the workings and applications of the universe's catholic, all of which filled in but remained contrary to worldly religions largely through the limitations of language. When mass had finished and they had disrobed in the sacristy Yvette approached Brendan with a warning.

"Excuse me Father, there are many in the church waiting to trick you. They will cause you great harm, be careful what you say today for they are wired for sound."

"Do you know who they are and where they're from"? Brendan asked in reply.

"No I can't, all I see is hidden microphones and recording devices." Yvette truthfully responded.

"Endless possibilities, the media, church investigators, rival religions, fanatical groups, Interpol, government agents' etcetera, etcetera"! Jack glibly interrupted not intending to strike fear into his audience. "But don't worry we'll sort it out. One word of warning only answer questions inside the church, not outside, there you'll be naked, exposed, stay inside and enjoy the result"!

No one really knew what Jack Stern referred to nevertheless they blindly followed his instruction and obediently followed out of the sacristy through the main altar down its stairs and into the church where the pilgrims milled about.

"What's next"? Felicity one of Brendan's charges asked.

"We wait." was the reply.

"For what"? She whispered.

"For them" Jack nonchalantly replied as he looked around.

"Sounds scary, don't you mean interview? By the way I think we look silly just standing here and doing nothing"! Felicity complained as she felt awkward where she stood.

"Let's mingle, you go over there to the font, you to the votive candles, you and you collect the offerings at the main doors and I Brendan and Yvette will stand here and look ridiculous." Jack flippantly declared as he directed various members of his troupe to their duties and then in a very loud voice he addressed all those who remained in the church. "At the beginning of Mass we never ask anyone who possess a mobile phone to switch them off or in fact any other electronic device such as video recorders, portable cassette-recorders or even camera's of any sort. Would you like to know why? Yes? Very well I shall tell you. There occurs a strange electro-magnetic anomaly within these walls that interferes with and prevents all electronic devices no matter what their origin or makeup from working. Many have come away from here quite disappointed for they have no electronic recording of their experience and for good reason, it is intended as a human experience only, nothing artificial can capture that, sorry to disappoint you, have a nice day"! Jack signed off and faced Brendan and Yvette. "Have they left"?

"No but a number are looking very curiously at each other, almost confused and…..somewhat desperate"! Yvette sweetly replied relieved that some of the pressure had been taken off them.

"Good, then remember them well, meanwhile, have they arrived"?

"Who"?

"You know"!

"No I don't"! Yvette replied in an exasperated tone of voice.

"The bride and groom" Jack teased

"Do you know anything about this Brendan"? Yvette asked thinking that Jack had invited a crazy comical couple from Club Med. Fr Brendan O'Reilly ignorantly scratched his head, put his hand to his jaw and forced a downward smile.

"None the wiser Yvette I won't tease you any longer. Your parents will be the first couple to marry in this church. In fact here they come now"! Jack explained as Alexandre and Abrielle entered through the church's main doors. Even though she was far away Yvette spied the large diamond cluster on her mother's left hand.

"Beautiful isn't it"? Jack seductively whispered into Yvette's ear. "It's not the diamond nor its cut or clarity that makes it sparkle, nothing but carbon, an excellent conduit for energy and emotion." Yvette understood and saw that her mother had finally found true love.

"Ah Alexandre, Abrielle, so nice of you to grace us with your presence, Alexandre you look much fitter and leaner than when I last saw you, been working out at the Club? And Abrielle what a beautiful young woman you've turned into, positively radiant, obviously you and Alexandre work out together." Jack flattered the youthful couple in his risqué way.

Yvette's mother positively beamed at Jack's compliments whereas Alexandre blushed and remained somewhat confused about his new lease of sexual life and stood nervously next to his wife reluctantly holding her hand.

"It's a real gem, don't you think"? Jack said with a sense of ambiguity as he referred to the church, raised his hands and spun a full three hundred and sixty degrees on the spot.

"Come momma let me show you around." Yvette seized the moment and broke her mothers grip on Alexandre and playfully led her around the church to explain all of its various features. When they were out of earshot Jack turned to Alexandre and said.

"I see you found the gypsy."

"Just as you said, at Port Louis central markets, quite an experience"! Alexandre replied as he mentally recounted the event.

"She give you a good rubbing" Jack asked tongue in cheek. Alexandre blushed. "You obviously enjoyed it! Where did she do it"? Jack continued to interrogate intimately.

"A gentleman does not tell"!

"Judging by your exhausted state, she rubbed you in more places than one"! Jack smirked.

"I think I'd better join my wife"! Alexandre responded feeling the heat of Jack's questioning.

"Jack need I remind you that is a house of God"? Brendan quietly cautioned.

"Does he want to meet the gypsy as well"?

"What"?

"You never know perhaps his luck will change"!

"Stop being blasphemous,iIn any event who is this woman"? Brendan asked as he tried to reprimand Mr Jack Stern for his insolence.

"Eloise Esmeralda Gonzalez, Spanish gypsy, striking facial features, luscious full lips, piercing brown eyes, long dark wavy hair with a mixture of gold and auburn tips. Dresses flamboyantly, very confident, very happy surely you couldn't have missed her, unless you wanted to. Must be the way she eats bananas! I've often seen her outside church on a Sunday, anyway got to chat with her one day and learnt about her family and how extraordinarily lucky they were and how they were able to transfer this luck momentarily to an outsider by rubbing it across. Obviously Alexandre's encounter enabled him to have a win on the local lottery and vau-la, le diamond ring"!

"You knew all this would happen"? Brendan guessed.

"But of course, it's a matter of observation, otherwise life's very boring and you never escape societies brainwashing! Come on let's have some fun and meet the spies." Jack mischievously urged as he took Brendan by the arm and went onto to say. "Outside we will encounter three groups of investigators, the media's, Vatican City's secret service and......."

"The local authorities" Brendan suggested.

"Goodness no, they're only too pleased we're here. Done wonders for the economy, you've got to be congratulated! Haven't you noticed there's no more poor in Mauritius, the tin shanties have disappeared, everyone's working, everyone's found a purpose in life, you're a modern day hero, a sa....."

"Saviour" Brendan concluded.

"Only if you want to be crucified; entrepreneur is a better choice of words." Jack smartly replied as they walked through the doors and pretended to make their way to the presbytery avoiding admirers as they went.

"Excuse me Fathers." A pretty petite woman in her mid thirties said halting the pair.

"Yes Miss how may we help you"? Jack politely inquired.

"I'm rather confused about the origins of this building."

"Yes." Jack replied offering a semblance of assistance.

"The locals say it never existed and there's no evidence of recent construction work." She stated quite emphatically.

"We didn't have any trouble locating it! Are you certain the locals informed you correctly? Perhaps a little too much rum on their part good day young lady" Jack glibly answered as he authoritatively waved her away and continued onward with Brendan in tow.

"One down two to go." He whispered to Brendan.

"Father O'Reilly a moment please" A very aggressive and brash male rudely shouted as he pushed the petite woman aside.

"Still hot in Rome or should I say hot from Rome" Jack accurately suggested as he interrupted the Roman mid-sentence who although exposed immediately and angrily retorted by saying.

"We cope"!

"The Holy See well not suffering from heat exhaustion" Jack flippantly asked as he made eye contact with the Roman.

"That was some time ago"!

"So it was, almost seems like yesterday." Jack replied as he looked skywards and pretended to shield his eyes from the blazing sun.

"Father O'Reilly........"

"End of conversation Enrico! No time for discourteous buffoons who show disrespect for the opposite sex"! Jack forcibly said as he correctly identified the Roman's Christian name.

"Testa di Cazzo"! The Roman violently blasphemed with his entire body.

"Finocchio, cazzo, porca miseria eh"! Jack coolly replied without batting an eyelid as he expertly returned the compliment leaving the Roman flabbergasted at Jacks repertoire of Italian swearwords. "Come on Brendan let's move on, two down, one to go"! He calmly said as he attempted to usher his friend along which was abruptly halted by the appearance of a stunningly beautiful woman.

"Good morning Fathers, God bless you both. May I introduce myself, I am Sister Expedita Shocker." She said erotically as she extended her open hand, which Brendan eagerly grabbed.

"Good morning Sister, a pleasure to meet you. What order do you belong to"? Brendan stuttered, as he didn't know what to say after analysing her dress.

"An obscure French one, Sisters of Wayward Travellers" Expedita replied with a mischievous smile.

"Come to look after the French pilgrims"? Jack butted in sensing that underneath the habit was the body and mind of a very voluptuous and sensuous woman.

"Actually I'm in charge of a group." Expedita replied with a seductive sway of her shapely hips, which caused Brendan to stare like a little boy.

"Been here before"?

"First time for me"

"Well then allow me to show you around." Jack chivalrously offered as he took charge of the situation. "Brendan will you be alright if I leave you, promise not to talk to any strangers" Jack asked as he treated Brendan like an obedient schoolboy.

"I suppose." Brendan reluctantly answered quite dejected as though his lollipop had been taken away from him.

"Excellent, this way Sister" Jack politely directed as he attempted to lead Expedita towards the church.

"Not so fast! I intentionally came to meet and talk with Father O'Reilly no one else Mister….."?

"Stern, Jack Stern."

"If you could kindly step aside it would be helpful to my cause." Expedita warmly but firmly requested.

"Very well, only too pleased to assist a beautiful woman" Jack obliged with a nod of his head as he stepped aside and allowed the nun full access to Fr Brendan O'Reilly.

"We understand each other Mr Stern that is rare in a man."

"It happens, pity you're a nun." Jack teased in response.

"Nothing's permanent Mr Stern"! Expedita provocatively responded, which simultaneously shocked Brendan and pleased Jack at the same time. "Now Father O'Reilly, take me on a guided tour and tell me everything." Expedita purred causing him to go weak at the knees. Jack flashed a warning look at Brendan which read "careful what you say"! Brendan nodded he understood and left with the voluptuous creature.

27
ROMAN HOLIDAY

As Brendan guided Sister Expedita Shocker around the Church of the Coloured Sands his boyish antics raised many an eyebrow amongst his ocean of established and newly acquired female admirers.

"Is she a nun or whore? What makes her so attractive? Why not me? Trollop! Hooker! Putana" Were just some of the self-examining questions and obscenities that swept the atmosphere surrounding the engaging couple.

"So far Father O'Reilly you haven't told me very much"! Expedita sadly expressed.

"I'm so sorry but that's the way it was." Brendan replied holding back.

"Hum." Expedita said with a little wiggle of her nose as she realised that she would have to change tact if not rely more heavily on her sexual charm.

"Never send a man to do a man's job, substitute a woman instead, she's more likely to get results, multiply that ten times if she's dressed as an innocent sex laden nun." Jack convinced himself as he kept an eye on the highly interactive couple. "I think she's getting a little too hot." Jack concluded as he approached Brendan and Expedita with a view to cooling their lopsided relationship.

"Sister Expedita, my darling, since you're new to the Island and conceivably want to learn as much as you can for your own benefit and those that you are looking after, I suggest I introduce you to Eloise Esmeralda Gonzalez, a Spaniard, she's a local guide who can inform you expertly on everything you wish to know, if she can't then she can transfer this extraordinary hidden talent that she possess called luck! Seems it runs in her family and she just loves rubbing herself onto you"!

"Sounds quite erotic"! Expedita concluded as she licked her bottom lip.

"You didn't even flinch! Let me demonstrate as Esmeralda would"! Jack gestured as he took hold of Expedita's hand and drew her closer.

"Rub your hand and the winning Lotto ticket comes your way! Rub your leg and help comes in all of your travels"! Jack seductively said as he genuflected and caressed Expedita's left upper leg. "Rub your private parts and the perfect man or woman comes into your life." Jack slowly and teasingly said as his hand deliberately drifted past her kneecap and made its way towards Expedita's groin.

"That's quite enough Sir! Have respect for the Habit"! She playfully snapped at him as she slapped his hand.

"Always do Sister, always do." Jack obediently groaned. Brendan meanwhile stood aghast.

"Where do I find this woman"? Expedita seriously inquired as she changed her tone of voice and subject material.

"At Port Louis central markets, you can't miss her, look for the brightly dressed woman with auburn and gold tips in her hair, eating a banana. She'll be surrounded by a throng of eager men."

"All tourists I suppose"! Expedita cheekily asked.

"What else? Good day Sister, a pleasure to have met you, I'm certain we'll be seeing more of each other. Come Brendan we must attend to the Bishop's desires"! Jack flippantly said.

"Excuse me Sister." Brendan reluctantly said not wishing to break up the group. He stepped around Expedita and saw how she visibly reacted to Jack's use of the word 'desires'; her eyes followed Brendan and Jack as they left. Hers were not the only to observe the priestly duo's departure, Yvette and her parents stood nearby.

"I don't like what I see." Ivan Gallows said incognito as he landed at Rome's International Airport aboard an Air America jumbo jet. Moments later he was heard to say. "Damn it looks and feels hot as well."

The D-man's observations were correct; the reciprocal meteorological relationship that Rome and Washington had with Canberra continued to hold true. In spite of Australia's heat Canberra's frozen state refused to melt away in accordance with the natural laws of physics and accordingly the twin cities of Rome and Washington persistently stayed unbearably and un-seasonally hot; two 'saunas' surrounded by winter landscapes. It was later discovered that Canberra's ice had an unusually high latent heat of fusion due to the complexity of the ice crystals formation. Ivan Gallows chuckled to himself as he exited the plane and walked through the various gangplanks towards the Airports arrival lounge. Staff and visitors were scantily dressed, some almost indecently much to the voyeurs delight. Incoming travellers were clearly overdressed; distressed once the wall of heat struck them and they opted to strip down to the essentials. The Airports air conditioning systems had long since failed making conditions beyond intolerable. As Ivan Gallows the D-man meandered about the complex, for the first time in his two thousand year life he felt the stirrings of the human reproductive instinct in his loins caused by the failure of his supernatural abilities to reach their one hundred percent status and block out all of the human response.

Hot glistening bodies slithering to and fro, ample heaving bosoms rhythmically rising and falling, long legs promising valleys of delight, moist sensual lips offering oral sensations were all about him, teasing, provoking, asking "when will you be mine"? Ivan Gallows's brain responded; hormones flooded out, prostaglandins went on a rampage and filled his penis with rage and envy. Lust was in the air, being supernatural had its advantages but it also robbed its bearer of the pleasures of the flesh and Ivan Gallows in his present state desired the latter before he finally recommitted himself to his ultimate destiny.

Ivan Gallows had been denied of all aspects of sexual pleasure from the outset when the Masters of Affliction infused him into a human body it was look but do not touch. Today for once in his life he wanted to know what all the issue was about such a small piece of tissue. One fear lingered in his mind; would the Masters terminate him or would they allow him his moment of discovery as they positioned themselves on the celestial chessboard.

Nervous perspiration dripped from the D-mans face and hissed as it struck the floor beneath him. It tracked his movements as he walked out of the terminal and only attracted the eye of the observant viewer. Ivan Gallows was no stranger to Rome; he was well versed with the city's layout and its peculiarities. As always his arrival would be unexpected, out of the cold, disturbing yet welcoming, it would occur at a time when everyone that he needed to see was in; however he had not taken into consideration Heaven's legacy and he suddenly realised that he was suffering with selective memory loss and the identities of all those that he intended assembling escaped him.

Dazed and confused by his own inabilities Ivan Gallows walked aimlessly about until he found himself in Rome's red light district and in bed with the 'flying mattress' as she was known Isabella Von Zecca; a once famous international catwalk and photography model whose preference for cocaine and rich men whether married or otherwise caused the death of her career. The only difference between what she was doing presently and before was that she was no longer on the catwalk all other aspects of her life remained unchanged with one exception; Isabella knew how and when to keep her mouth shut and give total abeyance to secret information. Isabella became the favourite of Rome's powerful and elite, the concubine of many.

Ivan Gallows had no childhood memories, no suckling at the

breast, nor being born from a woman, he was an adult when he was summonsed to do his work upon the world. He lay along side the motherly body of Isabella Von Zecca and slowly felt his way about her naked body with his fingertips.

Isabella considered him to be an experienced lover although he was doing nothing more than exploring her body with a child like simplicity. His and her climax had come and gone and he wanted more. Ivan Gallows re-entered Isabella body and used his instrument of love to fathom the depths of her emotion. He thrust slowly and mentally gauged the intensity of each stroke, the effect it had upon him and the result it had upon her, pleasure was a matter of stiffness, speed, closeness and angle.

Isabella was right to allow this man into her chamber, it was more than fate, he was a gifted lover, a rare encounter never to be forgotten, his movements made all of her past experiences meaningless.

"Ivan my love do you not tire of what you are doing"? She softly asked in her romantic Italian accent.

"No it is my first time, something new, I'm enjoying it and want it to last forever." He replied in the manner of a young and sexually inexperienced boy who showed no respect for his parents or his lover's comfort.

"Most men only last three or four minutes naturally, longer if they inject their members or take erectile drugs, even then they suffer discomfort after their first climax, but you…….."!

"Want to last forever"! Ivan said with an insatiable look in his eyes.

"I'm getting a little dry." Isabella complained making reference to her lack of vaginal moisture.

"I can fix that"! He eagerly answered as he flooded her with another copious ejaculation.

"I guess you can." She moaned as she felt her body respond to his. Time dragged on and Isabella grew weary of her new lover, the novelty had worn off, the excitement dissipated and the stimulation instead of being pleasurable became painful. She briefly considered her life in danger as she recognised the assassin in Ivan Gallows.

"Have I made a slip of the tongue, have I learnt too much, am I a walking liability, is this to be my fate, endless pleasure before dying? My extinction performed by a man who is superhuman"? She questioned herself as she deliberately tried to break free.

"I want more"! Ivan Gallows whinged as he roughly fondled her generous breasts.

"You're hurting me! Please respect my feelings"! Isabella softly pleaded.

"But I want more"!

"Perhaps I could another woman." She suggested as she altered her position.

"You're my first I want you and no one else"! Ivan Gallows whimpered.

'Why did you come to Rome"? Isabella asked changing the subject.

"To meet someone who can help me." The D-man vaguely replied as he continued with his pelvic thrusts.

"An appointment"

"Nooooo.....something else, that's right, the red bearded Somalian told me to find a......Roman club." Ivan Gallows stuttered with nervous energy.

"A club or the Club" Isabella next asked thoughtfully.

"Perhaps"

"Which one"? Isabella persisted.

"I don't know! I just want more this is sooo beautiful"! Ivan moaned as the next orgasmic wave swept through his body and caused him to fill her once again with his reproductive juices. Unfortunately for Isabella this was one of her days off in the week, no other lovers to attend to. On working days she restricted them to two a day, one before lunch and one for later in the afternoon free for relaxation and shopping. Isabella's wardrobe desired nothing; it was up to date with the latest designer creations both local and imported, an outfit to please everyman and every occasion. What would her salvation be? How would she escape the grovelling and groaning of this sexual fiend? She needed to shower, to clean, to mop up, remove all of the secretions from her exclusive linen and mattress. As Isabella agonized on her escape the front door to her posh apartment unlocked and swung open.

"Good afternoon Senorita." A voice from the doorway politely said. "Luisa cumma to clean, is okay"?

"She's early! What a God send"! Isabella mentally applauded to herself.

"Come on mister time to get off, my cleaning lady's here"! She said with a dramatic sense of urgency as she did not want them to be caught in the act.

"But I want more"!

"Later, first tidy, wash, go out for a meal, meet your friends, then we can….." Isabella said in staccato fashion as Ivan pumped madly away.

"Oh, alright, if I must, not happy, Ivan sad now" The D-man grumbled as he withdrew and rolled out of her bed.

"Go into my ensuite, wash yourself, clean"! Isabella shooed him away like little bird and then stopped to admire his still erect penis and wondered how it hadn't suffered any ill effects after being erect for over three hours.

"Senorita everything okay? You have gentleman client? I leave now." Luisa tactfully called out in broken English.

"A friend, Luisa, distant cousin, please come in"! Isabella almost begged in Italian as she threw on a flimsy negligee.

"Yes Senorita, whatever you a tella me, is okay, I ask no more, the usual"?

"Yes thank you Luisa, the usual." Isabella said with her back to Luisa as she hurriedly spruced herself.

Ivan Gallows found the shower invigorating, he enjoyed the pulsating jet of hot water hammer away at his anatomy and likened it to his manhood which he looked at and concluded. "This is what makes the world go around, nothing else, nothing more; I could easily become a slave to sex"! He fantasized as he washed his reproductive member over and over again.

Luisa the broad minded mother of eight had by now entered Isabella's boudoir and patiently cleaned until Ivan Gallows had completed his ablutions. When it became apparent that he wanted to stay in there for an eternity she entered the bathroom and rapped on the water closet's sliding door.

"Excusa mister, you gonna be much longa, I needa to finish okay, I hava other how you say, jobs to go to."

"Apologies, I'm finished, one moment'! The D-man growled after he snapped out of his day dream and stepped out fully naked to the admiring eyes of the middle-aged woman.

"Very nice-a, very nice-a" Luisa loudly complimented Ivan Gallows as she eyed his splendid phallus. The D-man said nothing in return; he grabbed one of the bathrooms large hanging towels wrapped it around his waist and walked out to find his clothes freshly pressed to perfection and neatly laid out on Isabella's bed.

Isabella stood in the middle of the room dressed in a figure hugging floral print complete with sweetheart bodice, ideal for hot sweaty conditions; she wore a pair of comfortable open suede shoes and a very pretty gold and red hair clip in her expertly styled hair.

"Come we eat now." She said in her Italian accent. The D-man obediently obeyed and dressed quickly so as not to keep his lady waiting. Isabella sensed that the power struggle had shifted within their brief relationship and she no longer feared him. All of the painful pleasure that she had endured with him had it appeared ended and she thought that she had complete mastery over him.

Ivan Gallows and Isabella Von Zecca emerged hand in hand from the main entrance of the building in which she had her luxurious apartment and walked in the direction of their final eating place that shouted 'great food here' as her nostrils determined, the restaurant would reveal itself to be quaint, rustic if not dirty, the service below average, the food simply sensational and the ambience eccentric. The love struck superman with his dominatrix sat at a corner wooden table that was in much need of repair, it creaked, was uneven and possessed endless carvings on its top left behind by lovers who wished to leave behind a memory of themselves. Isabella ordered for both of them choose the drinks and signalled a male admirer to join them.

"Ivan this is Buddha the harmonica man." She said as the cheery round faced gentleman joined them.

"Pleased to meet you Mr Ivan and you my princess a pleasure as always"! Would you like for me to play a tune for you"? He asked as he produced a well worn German harmonica out of his shirt's breast pocket. "Always carry it with me, practice every spare moment." He happily related as he awaited further instructions.

"Something romantic, would be nice Buddha." Isabella sweetly requested, the word romantic was foreign to Ivan Gallows. Buddha played an old standard the evergreen 'three coins in the fountain' with a passionate rendition that fitted the restaurant's atmosphere perfectly. At its conclusion he returned the musical instrument to its home and asked.

"What did you think"?

"Bravo maestro, I have much to learn." Ivan genuinely praised Buddha with much gusto.

"Well said, you're new to Rome"?

"No I've been here countless times except on this occasion I seem to have lost my itinerary."

"Meaning" Buddha inquired thinking that the D-man had been adversely affected by the extreme heat and was probably suffering with some sort of dehydration which led to his disorientation.

"Whom I was meant to converse with" Ivan Gallows ashamedly replied.

"Perhaps I can fix that for you."

"How's that"? Gallows asked as he looked around to see if he could recognise anyone.

"They don't call me Buddha for nothing. I am the man of wisdom and answers."

"Ivan seems to think that he has to attend a club of Rome." Isabella put forward in a low voice.

"An ancient organisation started almost two thousand years ago, very secret, very strong and very dedicated to its goals and objectives, has tentacles everywhere." Buddha whispered and then he asked. "What business might you have with it"?

"I need to regain my strength and…." Were the opening remarks that Ivan Gallows used before he detailed his predicament, when he had finished Buddha thought a while and cautiously advised.

"I think we can help you, Isabella bring him to this address tomorrow at two fifteen in the afternoon, we will assemble a conclave to remedy his situation."

"Very well Buddha, will you stay and join us for dinner"? She asked hoping that he would say yes.

"I would be a fool to resist such glamorous company"! Buddha graciously accepted the invitation.

Dinner was a pleasant passage of time, a much needed learning experience for Ivan Gallows emotionally, mentally and physically. Not quite superhuman his body cried out for sustenance and introduced Ivan to taste, smell and flatulence. Isabella's choice of food contained all those ingredients that fully satisfied the tastebuds, nose and stomach and in Ivan's case his libido.

"Eat your asparagus, that's a good boy"! Isabella seductively said in the mood for love again.

They Finished their meal with cappuccino coffee's a selection of dark chocolates that had been kept in the refrigerator to protect them form the excessive heat and a small glass of fine Italian brandy, after which Buddha excused himself and left the love birds to bill and coo.

Naked, eager and aroused Isabella Von Zecca lay on her back in her semi darkened bedroom and made herself comfortable in her luxurious bed. She softy caressed the inside of her velvety smooth thighs before touching her erect clitoris; she then ran her hands over her abdomen and across the nipples of her ample breasts.

"Let me do that." The D-man softly growled as he unexpectedly removed her hands from her fountains of life and knelt next to her, stroking the areas that she had just touched.

Isabella offered no resistance; she stared with dilated pupils at her lover and noticed for the first time that the tips of his hair crackled with energy as did his fingertips. The electricity that he transferred to her body caused Isabella to react in pseudo climatic fashion. The excitement in Ivan Gallows grew as he conducted his foreplay, it approximated the joy he felt when he was about to terminate a designated victim, Ivan shifted his position and lay on top of her, he stretched towards Isabella's throat and eagerly sucked on it as his right hand grasped it and started to squeeze, she readily opened her legs in response and adjusted her hips to accommodate his blood engorged penis which began to behave like one of his fingers discharging electricity along its full length. Isabella's vagina squirmed as Ivan's love member prodded and probed, his pubic hair crackled and its proximity to her clitoris sent it into raptures of ecstasy. Her mind struggled to cope with the experience of overwhelming simultaneous vaginal and clitoral orgasms. Ivan on the other hand carried on regardless and was tempted to extinguish her life had it not been for that shred of humanity within him which spoke to him saying.

"She's a creature of life, a giver of life, harm her not"! The words caused Ivan to loose his destructive tendencies and he looked upon the woman with caring eyes.

"What's the matter, why did you stop"? Isabella asked sensing his anxiety.

"I'm sorry I almost hurt you"!

"When"? She replied feigning ignorance.

"Now"!

"I thought you were just trying to be macho." She made it sound as though she was guessing.

"I never had a mother, father, brother or sister to show me the way. Perhaps I did choose to find out after all"? Ivan vaguely replied as he remembered Yvette Bell's image at St Pious Church on the day he sacrificed his superhuman status, crossed sides, protected the innocent and lost his physical life for the first time.

Perhaps his choice was about discovering what Heaven had to offer instead of infiltrating it in order to unveil its next move on the celestial chess board where the game it played against the Masters of Affliction was to change the diverse thinking of the masses by using the least number of players. Pure love physical love took hold of him as had Isabella Von Zecca in a way he thought not possible.

"Are you an orphan"? She caringly asked.

"I can't explain, you might not understand"! Ivan answered not expecting her reply to be.

"Many of my encounters are placed very high up within the Church; they have shared information with me not for public ears"!

28

PRIEST HOLE

Two fifteen in the afternoon; 22 Piazza di Santa Cecilia was the time and place Buddha wished Ivan Gallows and Isabella to meet him. Rome's unwavering ambient temperature of 33.3 degrees Celsius irrespective of time of day caused all manner of plants to blossom profusely well before time. Ivan Gallows enjoyed the scenery as he walked arm in arm with the highly desirable aristocrat Miss Isabella Von Zecca. It was a brisk four kilometre walk to St Cecilia's church in trastevere, one of the tituli, the first parish churches of Rome, known as the titulus Ceciliae.

The first church built on the site was in the 3rd century or 5th as some might argue. When the church was rebuilt by pope Paschal the first (817-824AD) as the result of a clairvoyant prediction a priest hole was incorporated into the building and enlarged and improved upon by subsequent constructions especially in 1822 and 1889. The priest hole was usually an artfully contrived hiding place not only for the officiating church staff to slip into in case of emergencies but also where the vestments, sacred vessels and altar furniture could be put away at a moments notice. To escape the priest hunters those persecuted ran along subterranean passages to hide between walls and bury themselves in impenetrable recesses and entangle themselves in labyrinths and a thousand windings. The entrance to these places was most cleverly disguised to the human eye but not to Ivan Gallows who had no difficulty in hunting down his prey.

Buddha the harmonica player waited at the large water vessel, a cantharus, in the centre of the beautiful courtyard in front of the church. Flowers bloomed everywhere in a dazzling array of colour.

"I'm pleased you made it." Buddha exclaimed as the couple neared him. "Come the others are waiting." He added as he guided them past the church's wall that contained several medieval tombs, inscriptions and fragments of sculpture, before he opened a side door into the main church.

Buddha then lead then through the church took a turning to access the corridor off the right hand nave towards the chapel of the Bath or Balneum Cecilae. In front of the sanctuary stood Saint Cecilia's beautiful effigy sculptured by Stefano Maderno; when Ivan Gallows and Isabella passed by it stirred into life and screamed; "Murderer"! as it remembered the beheading that the saint had suffered.

"It wasn't me." Gallows tried to convince his stunned audience.

"Wrong turn my apologies." Buddha excused himself happy that he had brought them there. "Genuine article" He thought making reference to the D-man. "We were meant to go upstairs; how silly of me to forget! Let's turn back"! He directed as he took the correct path that would allow entry to the church's upper gallery, which is presently used as the nun's choir.

The gallery is closed to the public most of the time with the exception of Sundays at 11am, Tuesday and Thursday between 10am and 11.30am. Buddha had no difficulty in entering the sanctuary, which housed a fresco by Pietro Cavallini, entitled The Last Judgement painted around 1293AD. Many thought it to be a turning point in the history of art, an important inspiration for the emergence of the renaissance style. The painting startled Ivan Gallows as he took its intended meaning personally.

"Come let's study this magnificent work more closely"! Buddha enthusiastically urged as he took Ivan and Isabella by the hand and caused both of them to disappear from view. Unbeknownst to them, a concealed entrance to the priest hole existed in the right column that flanked Cavallini's fresco. Isabella squealed with fright, Ivan remained calm; Buddha smiled as they squeezed their bodies through a winding, mouldy tight corridor that smelt of persecution and death. Isabella felt like a modern day treasure hunter in search of pirates buried treasure.

"Mind your step we're almost there." Buddha whispered as he led the way. "Left, right, left, almost like a dance hey? One two three in you go"! He joyfully said as he stepped sideways and pushed his guests forwards into a dimly lit oval chamber.

"Stand there, stay quite still, don't move, your helpers will be here directly." He cautioned as he positioned the pair in the centre of the room.

Ivan Gallows looked around unafraid and adjusted his eyes to brighten the image in his mind in contrast to Isabella who feared for her safety. The walls were littered with ancient symbols and hieroglyphics, which the D-man readily recognised and these as one scanned along became modernized in their text amongst which was included a record of the D-man achievements.

The floor was a parquetry of precisely arranged large and highly polished slate slabs. Buddha the harmonica player took his position on what appeared to be a numbered tile, tapped it rhythmically and with hands joined together ironically assumed an upright praying position. Four individuals seated in cane chairs suspended on ropes descended from the ceiling, each member alighted and took his respective position on the floor to complete the five points of a precise pentagon. Three were quite clearly distinguished members of the Vatican's elite whereas the forth appeared to be a grotesque reincarnation of a seventeenth century seafaring thief; Pigtail the Peg leg Pirate as he was known stepped forward. Isabella looked him up and down and found him to be completely abhorrent! She couldn't imagine anyone making love to him let alone her!

Five foot two, eyes not blue, shaven head, black braided pigtail five feet two, right leg entirely missing, replaced by a titanium rod, his sadistic specialty intestinal drainage accomplished by cutting the rectal sphincter free and dragging out the entire length of the digestive system through the incision site whilst the victim was still alive! Isabella sensed his perverted pleasure and it made the D-man saintly by comparison. Pigtail licked his lips and wiped away the excess saliva with the dirty sleeve of his black shirt.

"You have served Rome well over the centuries D-man, what brings you here"? Pigtail asked knowing full well what his response would be.

"I need restoration"! Ivan Gallows hesitantly said as he glanced at Isabella.

"We are well aware there stands an impasse to your progress." Pigtail replied offering neither assistance nor sympathy.

Deeply disappointed by the pentagon's disinterest Ivan Gallows angrily shouted. "You're not giving me any help"!

Immune to such behaviour Pigtail simply replied. "Strange as it may seem the answer lies within the Church itself, indirectly so, kill it and you will be whole once again"!

Confused by his statement Ivan Gallows stared at the menacing figure and said. "Shall I start with each one of you"?

"Obviously the heat has dulled your mind! Must I explain"? Pigtail violently replied which caused Ivan Gallows to search his memory for the answer but it eluded him. Pigtail then continued his verbal assault.

"You failed to recognise it! You incapacitated it and then you let it free! Now it threatens to destroy our decades of rule! We speak D-man of Father Brendan O'Reilly! He is the church you were to destroy! Instead you failed through your grandiose idea of dying! Now look at you a threat to no-one, useless to us! Pathetic! …Go!!!

"But…….." Ivan Gallows sobbed.

"But nothing we will take care of the mess you created."

Isabella tugged at Ivan Gallows sleeve as a faithful wife woul do, signalling. "Come darling we are wasting your time let's go"!

Disillusioned and embittered by the encounter the D-man sub-missively lowered his head and forced his way out of the Priest's hole as he would think of it in the future with Isabella in tow. Buddha felt Ivan Gallows's grief and once the pair were out of earshot he glared at the other members of the almighty Pentagon and firmly criticized them by saying." You could have helped him:"!

"He has exhausted all avenues it is out of our hands. My derogatory statements are enough to inspire him." Pigtail arrogantly retorted. Buddha knew this to be untrue and he engaged in a heated and torrid exchange of words with the peg leg whilst the others meekly looked on.

Ivan Gallows meanwhile had descended to the church's ground floor and stood before St. Cecilia's finely crafted effigy. Once again it stirred into life but on this occasion said nothing.

"Tell her I wasn't the one"! Ivan begged of it. The statue smiled and nodded to signify 'yes'.

"Does that mean you're innocent"? Isabella asked the D-man as she held him arm in arm.

"Only of her death" Ivan replied "Only of her death." He repeated regretfully as he reflected on the countless numbers he had dis-patched to the satisfaction of the Masters of Affliction. Perhaps it was time to make amends, the question of what side to belong to demanded resolution. Why do people argue? Is it because they do not understand the other person's point of view, their perspective? Would arguments cease if people became fully informed or would they continue unabated as a result of cultural upbringing? Peace offered no excitement. War, conflict, competition gave everyone a sense of purpose, desire, achievement, satisfaction. Isabella Von Zecca introduced Ivan to physical love; even there peace did not exist!

Ivan Gallows the D-man concluded that peace like orgasm was short lived, elusive, unpredictable and hard fought for, destruction on the other hand was continuously on tap eager to satisfy the demon inside of us; accordingly he wanted it all, ready access to sexual orgasm as well as his lost powers. Ivan Gallows was unwilling to compromise; two thousand years of celibacy was enough, he wanted in, whenever and wherever he saw fit!

Isabella examined Ivan Gallows far away gaze and identified the fiendish promiscuity in his face and realised she was the first notch on his gun's handle. Nevertheless she resolved to remain true to him until cast aside by his vagrant tendencies.

"I have other contacts." Isabella offered breaking the mood.

"What do you mean"? Ivan growled in a low voice as sparks of electricity crackled from his morning glory.

"There are others that I know of who dabble in the occult."

"What here in Rome in this supposed Holy City"?

"Yes there are the mystics, the alchemists and the ancient gypsy's who know of the underworlds little creatures." Isabella mysteriously explained.

"Where do I find these people"? The D-man growled.

"First you must tell me what you seek, the information you gave Buddha is too confusing for me and we must be careful for if those that I know become frightened by your actions or desires they will flee never to be seen again." Isabella very carefully cautioned. Ivan Gallows the D-man looked at her sideways and grunted in response.

"How could you do that to me? She was positively….."

"Embracing"? Jack answered stopping Brendan mid sentence.

"Yes for the first time in my life I've become physically attracted to a woman"!

"Instead of running away from them what a pity; well that's what physical lust does to you. Must be all of that testosterone talking, now where's the real Brendan O'Reilly I ask you"? Jack authoritatively teased as he raised his eyebrows in a questioning manner.

"Right in front of you"! Brendan quickly fired back.

"What did you want me to do, leave you alone with her? She's not interested in you; she's a spy for God's sake, actually no"! Jack corrected himself.

"What do you mean spy"? Brendan asked somewhat scared.

"When you're in the spotlight people investigate, that's the way of the world; fuels the gossip columns, want to know more"?

"But I'm only doing my job, what I'm supposed to do, how can they possibly complain'? Brendan grumbled somewhat confused.

"The problem is you're operating on foreign soil without a missionary's licence. The local government wouldn't complain, you're doing marvels for tourism, Rome on the other hand if you grow too big for their boots will see you as a threat rather than an asset, especially if none of the donations reach Rome's coffers. Offer them a portion of the wealth and see what happens." Jack suggested.

"Really"

"Really, money talks my man"! Jack philosophically said.

"Wait a minute, you're speculating about everything and everyone"! Brendan argued as he snapped out of his love struck daze.

"You're probably right however the fundamental problem of being outside of your parish, dioceses, country of origin and on unofficial holidays you must admit needs addressing. Father Bogliani is the official Catholic Church's representative answerable to some black African bishop I imagine, you on the other hand, the handsome charismatic stranger has come riding into town with a bevy of beauties and overnight builds an empire. By the way when you constructed this place did you include a priest hole'? Jack inquired.

"A what" Brendan frowned misinterpreting the question.

"Didn't they teach you anything in Seminary School"? Jack scoffed

"Obviously not"! Brendan dryly answered.

"Well let me explain courtesy of my priestly uncle's tuition. A priest hole is a cunning hiding place built in many a Catholic Church or home especially in England during the reign of Elizabeth the first when an Act of parliament was passed prohibiting the Church of Rome from celebrating its religious rites on pain of forfeiture for the first offence, a years imprisonment for the second and life for the third. Not much fun for its priest and made worse should one of them convert a protestant to Catholicism. A separate law provided for the death penalty as it was considered to be an act of high treason." Jack dramatically explained as he emphasised the words, law, death and high treason. Brendan gulped hard at the newly acquired knowledge.

"Afraid of the boogey man" Jack further teased.

"No." Brendan courageously replied.

"Good, two things, get to know this building better and let's keep your powers even more secret as we develop then further"! Jack suggested as he thought about possible future events.

29

REVEALED

Another Code P summons had been issued except this time it was for a restricted number of people, not everyone was to know it was for the ears of the privileged few. Present as before was the President of the United States of America Brian George, the Secretary of Sate Rachael Crank, a handful of their top advisers and members of the CIA; Raymond Halliday was the first speaker.

"Good morning Mr President, Secretary of State, ladies and gentlemen. I have given the matter of Australia's hidden aggression much thought and have come up with the following plan which ideally should cover all bases." He slowly and confidently put forward. "In keeping with Australia's recent natural disasters, I speak of Canberra's plagues which culminated in its freezing over, I thought it best if that trend be continued with a meteor storm in the area's that have attracted our interest. Our military has perfected a powerful portable Tesla plasma ray that can easily be transported on one of our stealth bombers and adapted into its armoury allowing the pilot or gunner to accurately focus the beam and inflict maximum damage upon any target. Flight tests have revealed that air to ground strikes produce an impact zone that very closely resembles that of a meteor impact.

The Tesla Plasma ray weapon can produce variable beams allowing us to vary the size of the 'meteor' that will strike the targets at Kaka du National Park and the Simpson Desert. There is a need to inflict other strikes so as to create the illusion of a localized meteor shower. It is our intention to flood the illegal Uranium mine in Kakadu and to completely seal off the Simpson Desert depository. Mr Jarwood will be disposed of medicinally; we have a CIA operative within the ranks of Australia's Army Corps, a specialist so to speak. I will arrange for him to visit Jarwood and administer a cocktail of legal drugs that will in effect 'fry' Mr Jarwood's brain. It will not be the first time that we have had to interfere in Australia's politics." The President ignored this last comment and allowed Halliday to proceed.

"The timing of the 'meteor' strikes needs to coincide with specific weather conditions for added dramatic effect! I've listed all of that in this brief, which I hold in my hand." Halliday concluded as he readied himself to deliver the multiple copies in his possession.

"Thank you Raymond. I am certain we will act upon your recommendations." Brian George openly and warmly commented before he responded to April Hako's raised hand. "Miss Hako you have something to add"?

"Yes I do Mr President some of which does not include good news I'm afraid"! She vaguely said.

The President remained unmoved. "You have my permission to continue." He cautiously replied.

"Recent documentary and photographic evidence has revealed the full extent of Australia's ambitions. The depository in the Simpson Desert is not what we initially thought it to be. Whilst there is no doubt that Australia wants to achieve superpower status in the Southern Hemisphere it is presently conjectured that it wishes to destabilize the balance of power in the Northern Hemisphere through the sale of unsanctioned purified Uranium not intended for peaceful use. Days after we showed the pictures taken inside the storage bunker all of the Uranium rods were shipped to overseas destinations. The world has become hungry for Uranium ever since the Russian stocks post communism has been exhausted. North Korea, China, the Middle East Arabic countries and Russia itself are competing with each other and paying exorbitant high prices for black market supplies. Shipments to the Middle East are conveyed via the military under the disguise of provisions sent to peace- keeping forces in the region. North Korea and China deliveries are cleverly disguised as raw materials in transit whereas the Russians are via the two-way Opium trade routes. Australia is no longer an ally Sir, it is a country hostile to American interests, as a result we need to look very carefully and closely at all of our international friends on a national and individual basis without exception." Hako deliberately and convincingly stated before she went on the say. "Therefore in the latter context it is imperative that we look at ourselves and find those apples that are prepared or already have made the barrel rotten"! She firmly concluded as she slowly turned to look at everyone in the room in an attempt to gauge their emotional reaction.

Raymond Halliday thought of his pet Shitzu as she scanned his face.

"Do you have anything to offer Miss Hako"? The President politely asked.

"I do Mr President." Hako replied as she aggressively flipped through her report. "The CIA grants favours to those who help us and sometimes these are rather unpalatable as they fuel certain immoral and illegal practices on our sovereign soil it is a compromise that we are not proud of Sir"!

"Specifically what are you referring to Miss Hako"? The President coldly interrupted.

"The protection of Opium trafficking into the USA from Afghanistan in exchange for ongoing information relating to the exposure and identification of terrorist groups new and old, especially those that are intent on harming the Union Sir"!

"Names Miss Hako names"!

"Yes Sir, Nghi Phamhung is our prime suspect Sir"! Hako unemotionally replied.

"What of him? I guess he's the good guy providing he hasn't abused our generosity by flooding the market with Heroin." The President grinned and expected everyone around him to do the same.

"Phamhung has repeatedly bitten the hand that feeds him; Sir"! The statement caused the President to loose his smile and he crossed his arms across his chest in defiance.

"Mr Nghi Phamhung is involved in two very sinister operations; the sale of Australian Uranium to the Middle East and to China and the distribution of a substance known as Alljoy here in the USA. The second activity is considered to be an act of terrorism as the success of the product was dependent upon the selective collapse of the pharmaceutical industry which was also orchestrated it appears by Nghi Phamhung." Hako caught her breath, took a sip of water to moisten her dry mouth and vocal cords. She then adjusted her well-cut designer jacket before proceeding.

"Before you continue, if what you have just told us is true, it creates enormous diplomatic problems for our administration. We are virtually guilty of protecting a major terrorist who it seems is hell bent on destroying the fragile Middle East situation." The President bitterly surmised.

"Yes Sir that would appear so and not wishing to be disrespectful I gather it would annihilate your chances of re-election by eliminating the Jewish vote entirely if it became public knowledge, Sir"!

Brian George forces a downward smile as did many in the room not out of any sense of loyalty or sympathy but rather out of concern for their personal survival, as each new incoming administration caused the mighty winds of change to blow. The CIA staff liked President George for he was a fair man who thought things through.

"Tell me more about Phamhung."

"Yes Sir. Nghi Phamhung freely travels the world on his Chinese passport as a well to do businessman, openly conducting his many legitimate business ventures, which we view as a smoke screen that camouflages his shady deals. Phamhung has been the focus of a deep ultra-secret undercover surveillance operation over the past ten months that has provided us with concrete evidence as to his nefarious conduct. I must say that it was not easy as his system of doing business relied upon a sophisticated oral cipher. It took us endless hours of diligent work to break the code." Hako slowly explained as she gave herself a pat on the back and was expecting the President to do the same. Unfortunately his mind was elsewhere. Hako then signalled for one of the attendants to summon the outside guards and block off all entrances to the meeting room. 'Tragically Sir that information quite clearly identified and incriminated Agent Halliday as over stepping the CIA's policy on reciprocal aid"!

Executive CIA agent Raymond Halliday on hearing this accusation quickly calculated his next move as two heavily armed security guards approached him from behind. The President looked directly at Halliday and awaited his defence. Raymond Halliday didn't bother standing up instead he remained seated in a passive undisturbed manner.

"It's all true Sir, I bent and broke the rules and received generous rewards in return. I'm not ashamed of what I did or what I received, it was for the American good." He calmly stated in a well-controlled voice that inspired trust.

"Miss Hako." The President asked looking for further clarification, meanwhile Halliday cursed himself inwardly. "I fell for her charms it completely threw me off guard! Damn sexual misadventure, no more, never again, I'm staying away from ambitious corporate females."

"Mr President we have in our possession sufficient audio-visual evidence to show that Agent Halliday received substantial monetary payments which never found themselves in the CIA's slush fund. We assume that Halliday has cleverly stashed these away as he appears to live a relatively austere lifestyle apart from his love of chocolates and dogs Sir." Suppressed laughter rippled through the audience. Halliday immediately stood up and addressed his peers.

"Everyman has his idiosyncrasies and peculiarities, mine as you have just heard are clearly defined. As to the monies, the manner in which I operate is on a "I don't trust anyone basis"; therefore whatever I received from Nghi Phamhung was used to pay my secret informants, those who exist in the subcultures of the criminal-terrorist under-world, these are my checks and balances, my confirmations and if a surplus exists that money is donated to honourable Christian charties something that Agent Hako would surely have come across when she or any one of her operatives checked my office and home on many occasions." He calmly said as he thought. "Well April I think you failed to get into my pants in more ways than one, no promotion this year"!

"Plausible, quite plausible, makes sense to me Agent Halliday I don't think we should labour this topic any longer, Agent Hako do you have anything else to add"? President George asked as he demon-strated his annoyance with her and pleasure with him.

"Yes Sir I do with respect to the Uranium and the Middle East."

"I'm all ears Miss Hako, proceed." The President abruptly commanded.

"The Uranium is in pelletised form, easily disseminated, making it extremely versatile and allowing the manufacture of multiple nuclear explosive devices of varying capabilities.

"About time the Arabs had the upper hand"! The President said openly much to the surprise of his listeners, which he readily observed and therefore realised that he needed to clarify his statement. "No one in a true democracy has the right to hold the upper hand. No one singular group is allowed to dominate others by any means possible. I think it is time for the Middle East to look after itself and if the Arabs have nuclear weapons well and good! I'm sick of seeing and hearing; a young Arab boy was shot dead by an Israeli soldier because he threw a rock at him then the Arabs learn to shoot guns only to be confronted by tanks, so it escalates, tanks bombarded by airplanes, missiles counteracted by invasion and so it goes. Once the

Israeli's know the other side have proper weapons that can potentially destroy masses of people perhaps at long last peace will come into the region and the Israeli sprawl will stop. Damn the Jewish vote! There are many more people to think about in the Union we cannot pander to the privileged few! I do not believe in the concept that any certain group of people are born to rule"! The President strongly asserted. This facet of his behaviour endeared him to the masses, for President Brian George thought out aloud, analytically, bravely, ethically, morally; he was a President of the people. "Gentlemen the plan is as follows, leave the current shipment of Uranium in the Middle East, try to retrieve stocks from North Korea and China, observe the Russians but do not interfere they will be our allies one day in case the Chinese become rogues. Not a word about our knowledge, no leaks, keep Nghi Phamhing on side, Halliday follow through on your Aussie plan. Now to domestic matters; Hako you're the bringer of good news what have you to say"? Brian George cheerfully asked.

"My team has as a result of investigating Nghi Phamhung listed a number of scientists capable of causing such pharmaceutical grief." Hako answered somewhat jaded.

"And your investigations have lead you to conclude"?

"The most likely candidate is this man Dennis Sauvage PhD un-employed microbiologist, brilliant, eccentric, gay ice skater."

"Happy in his sport in other words" The President flippantly suggested "A little more than that Sir"!

"I see, are there any promiscuous gays in the CIA willing to help"? The President asked.

"In this age of equality, I'm certain we could rustle up a few."

"Very well put your spurs on and get that whip cracking"

"Yes sir." Hako obeyed as she hurriedly shuffled her papers together not knowing whether the President was making a personal reference to her bedroom antics.

"I wish you had never told me about the priest's hole" Brendan whinged.

"Priest hole get it right, otherwise people will think you're some sort of pervert"! Jack cautioned.

"Fine, but I can't stop thinking about that nun Expedita Shocker"!

"Wish you would, not the time nor place for it"! Jack continued to caution as he walked about the Church of the Coloured Sands in an attempt to discover the illusive priest hole.

"She's so beautiful"! Brendan sighed as a young boy struck down with a bad case of puppy love.

"So is Yvette." Jack advanced.

"Not the same"! Brendan sharply replied.

"I agree."

"You do"? Brendan asked quite surprised.

"Yes I do, nothing against the girl, she's supernaturally gifted, a virgin, exceptionally beautiful but she lacks a certain attractiveness that makes men lust for a woman. I'm fond of her, I love her but I couldn't, wouldn't and don't desire to make love to her. You on the other hand…" Jack explained as he scanned the churches numerous walls.

"She does nothing for me." Brendan surprisingly answered.

"Are you certain"? Jack asked as he stopped what he was doing.

"What do you mean"?

"I saw the two of you intimately dancing, enjoying body contact, rumba wasn't it? She was putty in your hands and you my young handsome devil responded amorously to her body language." Jack clearly remembered.

"You were there"? Brendan asked quite surprised that he hadn't detected Jack's presence.

"I certainly was"!

"Why didn't you come over and join us, it was a marvellous gathering." Brendan recalled.

"Jealousy, mild form of, never experienced it before, thought it best to depart undetected." Jack replied with a mild degree of embarrassment.

"I see." Brendan said as he closely examined Jack's eyes for the truth and then he asked. "What if Yvette discovered Expedita Shockers sexiness within herself"?

"Still wouldn't"!

"Why"?

"I don't want to destroy her innocence." Jack genuinely replied with moral intent.

"Does that mean she is cursed to remain a virgin"?

"Only until her work is done." Jack intuitively concluded and then he asked the question. "Supposing you were given permission by Rome which one would you choose"?

"I don't know."

"Good answer. Marriage is difficult, I know because I have observed and listened to others. First it is fired by lust then love follows bringing with it discovery and joy. A lifetime is insufficient to learn the entire world of the other and tragically it is interfered with by the arrival of children and the mundane things of life. Lovers turn into parents who fight and bicker over trivial matters, absurd things, money, desires, haves and haves not. Lovers become opponents, gladiators; guerrilla's not realising throughout their warfare that love binds them together. Lust gives way to diplomacy until old age robs them of youth and its reckless ways leaving them spent and wondering what it was all about. Learn this lesson well before you venture onto the path of mental madness." Jack warned philosophically.

"Is that why you are single"? Brendan asked as he detected Jack's marital fear.

"I am still looking and enjoying it, by the way had some fantastic encounters"! He proudly responded with a glint in his eye.

"All virginal" Brendan cheekily replied remembering the conversation they once had on the beach outside of Club Med.

"For the first time, it's all about the first time, the excitement, magic, ecstasy and speaking of which, it lies before us"! Jack joyfully exclaimed as the priest hole reluctantly revealed itself.

"Why should such an ancient structure need one"? Brendan seriously questioned.

"We will always be persecuted my friend, irrespective of time and place! Come let us see what treasures await us"! Jack happily expounded as he stepped inside the entrance that was brilliantly incorporated into the wall beneath the church's huge northern arched stain glass window. Inside darkness greeted them followed by the hush of silence, the moistness of freshly formed dew and the scent of roses. "Waiting for your eyes to adjust to the Dark? Don't bother, turn the lights on instead"! Jack commented as he felt Brendan aimlessly groping about.

"There is no switch"! Brendan anxiously and nervously stuttered.

"Imagine you're at the Genius Loci, clap your hands rhythmically until you work out the sequence. You know how good us Catholics are at the rhythm method"! Jack instantly joked.

"Does everything have to be sexual"? Brendan asked in desperation as he tried different combinations of sounds.

"Only occasionally, you're not doing a very good job of turning the lights on; perhaps I'll use my torch instead"!

"You brought a torch"? Brendan sounded quite exasperated.

"What did you think I would do, project light from my fingertips"? Jack sarcastically replied as he flashed the torch light about. "Small rectangular closet big enough for maybe twelve people, no more, strange considering its ancient symbols, there must be more." Jack muttered as he inspected their surroundings. "We can either go up, down, through or out." He surmised. "Which do you prefer my friend"? Jack asked Brendan who looked non-plus-ed.

"Out would be good this looks like a dead end." Brendan suggested.

"A decoy perhaps; causes them to move to another priest hole, a clever move to frustrate your pursuers. I bet they're all identical with one exception; this one's different for it possesses the body and soul of a woman." Jack seductively deduced as he ran his hands over the chambers walls. "Long legs, a well of succulent nectar, a button of desire, fountains of life, embracing arms, fingers of delight" He chanted as he searched for the feminine outline that would open according to the strength of his emotions. "Let me make you laugh, giggle and swoon as I tenderly touch your inner moon"! He romantically said as he magically pressed both of his hands upon two large interlocking stones that surrendered to his loving commands.

Brendan thought Jack to be quite mad even more so when Jack repeatedly said. "Sexercise....... it's all about sexercise"!

"What are you going on about now"? Brendan sighed as he observed Jack's pelvic thrusts.

"Games that adults' play"

"What about them? Can't you stop being blasphemous? Can't you have respect for the Church, just for one minute"? Brendan demanded to know out of frustration.

"We're not in the Church we're outside of it, in any case stop changing the subject. What I was about to say is they're sexual blueprints"! Jack explained.

"What are"?

"Games, football games"!

"How"? Brendan asked fearing the worst.

"Well let me explain. In your seminal fluid there exists as a result of evolution, blocker sperm, killer sperm and fertilising sperm, all as a result of making certain that your genes are successful in contrast to your opponents."

"What opponent"? Brendan shuddered to think.

"The guy who left his deposit in the woman before or after you, in the good old cave man days when promiscuity ensured the survival of the fittest"!

"It's different now." Brendan sharply stated.

"True, now we have sport to satisfy the sexual appetites of the masses"!

"Are you crazy"? Brendan loudly asked totally bewildered by Jacks obscure thinking.

"The football represents the fertilising sperm, the goals its target is the egg, your team members are made up of blockers, killers and strikers, all sperm striving to make themselves fertile, in other words win the match, win the competition by scoring goals, fertilising the egg. You get to watch that's what is so fascinating also explains why so much pornography exists"! Jack explained cryptically with his head cocked to one side.

"And I suppose practice time is......"

"Masturbation"! Jack said finishing Brendan's sentence.

"Can we please change the subject"? Brendan pleaded as he felt his sexuality starting to respond.

"Afraid not, she only responds to 'dirty' talk"! Jack replied mercilessly as he continued to caress the two stones that glowed with increasing intensity to his touch. "Come show me your points." Jack teased. "Hot and hard your turn Father Brendan" Jack said rather pleased with his efforts as he stepped aside. Brendan reluctantly stepped forward and placed a hand on each exposed nipple he blushed as he allowed his senses to experience the moment.

"Not what you expected"? Jacked asked knowing full well that he had misled his friend all along.

"They're so soft, so enchanting, so.... almost as if they wished for me to explore them further." He analytically deduced as he eagerly experimented with the artificial foreplay.

"A lesson to be learnt my friend. All those who appear hard, rigid, impenetrable are in reality easily converted to display their softness. Let go and allow your hands to drift downward and through the hollow of her desires." Jack seductively directed as he pointed to the red pulsating light that approximated the belly button. Brendan without any hesitation obeyed, closed his eyes and slowly drew his fingers in a serpentine fashion towards the spot as he fantasized about the owner of the outline.

"You can stop now." A gentle voice commanded. Brendan froze and nervously opened his eyes to gaze upon the naked body of a young and exceptionally beautiful woman. The only part of her svelte anatomy that was shielded from view was her mons pubis, which was covered by a ruby red loincloth. The woman's breasts, half covered by her wavy golden chestnut crowning glory were equally perfect in size, shape and attitude. Her body was curvaceous, limbs delicate but strong, neck like a swan; face radiant with love and devotion.

"Oh my God you're real! I thought I was playing with a piece of stone."

Brendan profusely apologised as he felt his embarrassment overwhelm him.

"You weren't to know." The young maiden excused him.

"I think you should make Fr O'Reilly here aware of whom you are." Jack interrupted in a gentlemanly fashion.

"I shall." She serenely replied as she smiled at him in a way that suggested she approved of his awkward caresses. "I am she who ensures the survival of the true church. I am the source of its fertility I am Luvera welcome to my world." She royally decreed as she invited the pair in.

What Jack had detected before suddenly struck Brendan. "The freshness of morning dew and the smell of roses" he reminded himself as he closely examined Luvera who walked before them. It was not overly warm where they were and yet Luvera's skin showed no signs of goose bumps, it appeared different to normal as though it possessed an outer transparent simmering film that protected it from extremes of temperature and perhaps as Brendan thought enhanced her curvaceous body, which he much admired. "The female body is such a beautiful work of divine art I congratulate you my Lord" He secretly prayed as a sense of deja vu descended upon him. The area that the Goddess of Fertility led them to was equivalent to an underground hothouse accommodating one thousand white Iceberg roses in full bloom. The air was heavy with their dew soaked scent. In the middle stood a beautiful naturally formed white granite altar perfect for symbolic sacrificial ceremonies marred only by one thing; from its centre an endless supply of Holy water bubbled up and cascaded over the altars edges and defied gravity by spiralling upwards into the Church of the Coloured Sands Baptismal font. To the right of the altar where the dry ground started stood an oak table covered with a lace table cloth upon which sat a Stuart crystal vase with twelve long stemmed white Iceberg roses perfectly arranged. Brendan boldly walked up to the reality of the vision that he held at the Genius Loci when Jack demonstrated the unbreakable union between the future and the present. Brendan remembered what Jack had said at the time. Jack who was close by whispered into Brendan's ear. "Remember the scene because before you know it you will be there"!

"We have been waiting a long time for you Father Brendan O'Reilly." Luvera regally confirmed as she stood by his other side. Brendan stood open mouthed, motionless and closed his eyes. The trio stood together and waited for Brendan to make the first move.

"If Jack was right as this instance shows, will everything given time that I have dreamt and desired come true"? Brendan thought to himself before he asked the following question. "How...er.... long have these been here"?

"Since you were born and before when the prophesy was made"! Luvera sweetly answered as she stroked his back with her right hand. "Each rose represents an individual, the vase the person who assembled you and the table the foundation of your beliefs." She further explained.

"I firmly believe that I am addicted to sex"!!! Ivan Gallows hungrily admitted as he thrust his love member into Isabella Von Zecca warm and willing body.

"I'm glad you have." She moaned wishing that he were materially rich as well.

"I want all my powers back, my wealth and a freedom to do anything I wish without compromise. After serving two thousand years of imprisonment without quarrel upon this lonely planet I deserve a reprieve, a pardon." Ivan Gallows the D-man convinced himself as he increased the frequency if his thrusts.

"You'll never get it if you spend all day in bed"! Isabella warned halting his actions temporarily.

"Are you tiring of me"? The D-man roughly growled as he forcibly grabbed Isabella's hips and pulled her violently onto his massive member causing her much pain and discomfort as the head of his penis hammered the mouth of her cervix. Her pain intensified his pleasure.

"No....."! She screamed. "I was merely making a suggestion." She sobbed.

"What is that"?

"Remember what I said"?

"No I don't." Ivan Gallows rudely snapped back annoyed that his insatiable lust had been interrupted he was on a mission, a sexathon, wear out this woman and go onto the next until his penis had no more to give.

Isabella sensed his madness and resigned herself to an uncomfortable fate fearing for her life. After half an hour of intense activity and numerous ejaculations Ivan was partially satisfied. He disengaged himself leaving Isabella physically and mentally traumatised. Demonstrating no mercy he looked upon his dishevelled prey and sarcastically said.

"Whore now that you're satisfied, take me to your ancient friends otherwise I shall terminate your miserable existence here and now"!

Isabella slid her ravaged body out of her luxurious bed no more and wearily walked towards her finely crafted Italian wardrobe. In it she found her thread bare, worn and torn outfit, the one that attracted the underworlds gypsy's, she struggled to put it on; fearful exhaustion had stripped her of her energies. The D-man watched impatiently as she lethargically readied herself. Completely unkempt and elderly in appearance she with head hung low struggled to whisper. "We can go."

The sophisticated, glamorous head turning high-class woman

was gone. Isabella Von Zecca momentarily returned to her origins as the impoverished roman street kid fending for herself as best as she knew how. Pick pocket, thief, liar cheat were her past ways until one day she chanced to help what she thought was a fellow member of her class. A young girl brutally and senselessly bashed and left to die by a group of drunken British backpackers.

The victim turned out to be an ancient fairy-leprechaun who possessed the ability to take on human form. Isabella tended to her wounds and nursed her until she was well again. Isabella's unselfish actions permanently endeared her to the creature and she was introduced to its world of ancient mystics, alchemists and the gypsy's of the unseen underworld, the one that exists beneath the surface of the earth.

Isabella Von Zecca painfully led the way, her pelvic floor agonised with each step, she could feel the blood ooze from her pummelled cervix onto her underwear and steadily drip onto the hot pavement below. Her appearance caused the underworld's spies to take note and soon the air was full of their whisperings. The D-man was immune to them and followed closely growing impatient at her tardiness.

"Make a move on whore"! He roughly commanded. Isabella remained deaf to his urgings and shuffled her way towards an intersection that would bring her salvation. She passed row after row of Bambino cars of varying ages, states of repair and colours until she appeared to stumble on something discarded on the sidewalk and she fell sideways into the open door of a speckled automobile and disappeared from view.

Fearing that she had been abducted the D-man ran towards the vehicle and grimly looked inside. It was empty, no Isabella. The D-man frantically searched the car to no avail, she was gone and with her all chance of recapturing his former supernatural strength so he thought as he withdrew his large muscular frame and peered down the empty street.

Click, open, shut! Click, open, shut! Were the repetitive noises he heard behind him as he stood still Ivan Gallows turned sharply on the heel of his foot and squinted hard at their origins.

'Car doors, who's playing games with me'? He thought as the noises recommenced behind him once more. Again he swivelled on the heel of his foot, this time his increased frustration caused his hair and fingernails to crackle with all manner of aggressive electrical discharges; had he been at full strength he would have most certainly annihilated the annoyance with an unstable entropic energy ball.

"Oooo..oh I'm over here, come and get me you brute" Isabella Von Zecca's voice seemingly rung out from parts unknown.

"Huh"? Ivan Gallows grunted as he scanned the street.

"Doors to the front, doors to the back, left one, right one, which one will it be"? Her voice continued to tease as the Bambino's car doors opened and closed chaotically.

"A glimpse here, there and everywhere. Now you see me now you don't"! The voice of Isabella Von Zecca heckled as a fleeting image of her pathetic body appeared here and there thoroughly confusing the D-man.

"Pay back time you bad, bad brute"! The voice of a young unspoilt child squeaked behind Ivan Gallows as the sound of a heavy Irish club whooshed through the air and struck him heavily on the back of his neck.

It disconnected his consciousness from the physical world and he descended into a pit of darkness.

"Comfortable? You bad, bad, beast"! The same young voice asked some time later as Ivan Gallows resurfaced onto a sea of murky reality. "Yes it's gloomy but nice. We call this our ancestral suite. Perhaps you recognise some of our mummies? What's the matter cat got your tongue afraid to say anything"? The fairy-leprechaun said in answer to Ivan Gallows silence as he examined as best as he could his subterranean surroundings, which he realised, were rather constricting.

Ivan Gallows lay entombed in the open sarcophagus of a deceased Catholic saint whose skeleton lay beneath him and caused him much discomfort, physically and spiritually. The two foot two white skinned fairy-leprechaun with pink hair, hands and feet who had spoken to him sat on an elevated shelf above, looked down upon Ivan Gallows and sensed his immeasurable pain. "No freedom I'm afraid, this is your incarceration, before the trial." He said with glowing purple pastel eyes.

"What trial"? Ivan Gallows growled.

"You stand accused of causing grievous bodily harm to one of our friends"!

"She enjoyed it"! Ivan arrogantly retorted.

"Typical male"! The fairy-leprechaun angrily responded as she watched Ivan Gallows struggle to break free. "Supernatural you might be, strong enough to be free I cannot see, stay with us you will until we see fit to take your fill."

"What gibberish are you taking, set me free this minute"! Ivan Gallows demanded furiously as he thrashed about. The fairy-leprechaun simply tolerated his tantrum; half smiled, jumped down from the shelf and walked away taking with it the light that had illuminated the secret undiscovered catacomb.

In a larger void a long corridor away Isabella Von Zecca lay naked on a polished black marble slab, she was surrounded by a choir of eight fairy-leprechauns all two foot two, white skinned, pink hair, hands and feet, who chanted in esoteric tongues never encountered by human ears.

By her side ministering to her mortal wounds was an ancient creature taller than the rest who stood three feet two, a giant amongst the others, with another difference; he was pink skinned, with white hair hands and feet. He arrested the bleeding, rebuilt all of her ruptured tissues and then he erased all traces of the D-man from her memory, all of which he achieved through the mystical realignment of her bodies energy patterns, those that were generated by and fed the tissues that the process of life gave birth to. Pleased with his efforts the ancient creature in true fairy tale fashion sealed his work by kissing her tenderly on the lips. The choir of eight fairy-lepre-chauns applauded the outcome.

"Another triumph Master"! They cheered in harmony.

"It was nothing! She was very co-operative, she wanted to get well"! He replied. "Where is the one that inflicted the pain"? He then asked intent on revenge.

"This way Master" The female fairy-leprechaun happily replied that had kept him in check.

"Why can't I get of this forsaken box? Is it you? You worthless bag of bones that holds me back"! Ivan Gallows cursed and anguished as he fought against the confines of his coffin and the cosmic glue that held him rigidly in place. "It should not be difficult to escape and yet I am powerless. Who are these creatures? Why haven't I ever encountered them? Why wasn't I ever warned of their existence"? He continued to pry as the deceased saints skeletal bones dug deeper into his flesh.

"Curse you I wish I was free"!

"Clockwise is this the brute that abused our precious Isabella"? The ancient fairy-leprechaun asked.

"Yes Master"! The small female fairy-leprechaun who had kept the D-man under observation answered.

"Ancient you are, wise you are not; fetcher of the stick thrown by the Masters of Affliction is all you may claim. Much debt you have incurred, much destruction you have wrought on the world above, nothing below and here is where it ends for the Karmic debt you have incurred must be repaid.

No one is immune, no one is exempt, it is neither right nor wrong, always present, always demanding, exceed your quota and you will find yourself here"! The ancient fairy-leprechaun solemnly stated in a monotone voice that was neither threatening nor humorous.

"What hideous creature are you to attempt frightening me"? Ivan growled as he felt a surge of his power.

"I am Underone, he who has walked the corridors in the bowels of the earth, teaching those who discovered our world the secrets of life, love and peace. See how we light the path before us." Underone the ancient fairy-leprechaun authoritatively answered as the whole anterior surface of his boy emitted a bright light whereas his posterior remained dormant.

"You are nothing more than an overgrown Irish folktale"! Ivan Gallows countered in a raised voice as his strength continued to grow.

"Leprechaun's we are not, fairy-leprechauns are we the original hybrid that once split into two allowing leprechauns and fairies to inhabit the world above. Those who choose this path lost most of their powers whereas we retained and elevated our knowledge." Underone meticulously explained in the hope that the D-man would understand.

"Look here underling you are wasting my time, I'm leaving"! Ivan Gallows bellowed visibly irritated intent on breaking out of his incarcerated state.

"Yes I suppose you are now that you sense your powers returning. However let me show you why you will remain where you are"! Underone quietly answered as he magically swept the air with his hands and redirected Ivan Gallows energy fields.

"I can't move, breathe, my heart my............."

"Yes Mr Gallows sudden health crisis? Perhaps the air down here has caused you to experience asthma, angina......well......answer me." Underone suggestively asked as he teased and closely observed Ivan Gallows facial grimaces and bodily contortions as he struggled to stay alive. Underone stared at the D-mans erratic eyes and reached deep into his soul.

"There is always one below superior to the likes of you. I am that one and will remain so until I foolishly discard my innocence. Your punishment will be to live the life of a saint and you will start by attaching yourself to his goodness." Underone said as he released Ivan Gallows from his anxieties and caused the deceased saint's skeleton to weld itself permanently back to back with that of the D-man.

"Arise Ivan and enjoy the granting of your desire"! Underone commanded much to the enjoyment of the nine fairy-leprechauns who sat and watched from the shelves above.

"Are you mad? This is not my wish"! Ivan Gallows hysterically shouted as he felt the weight of goodness upon his shoulders.

"Perhaps not but stay like this, you will, imprisoned for twenty eight days as payment for hurting our friend. The choice is yours, remain below and walk the bowels of the earth alone or escape to the surface and hide your hideous appearance from humanity, for believe me if you will, you cannot caste off your saintly attachment." Underone's words further infuriated Ivan Gallows hysteria and he violently extracted his muscular frame from the saint's coffin. All of the fairy-leprechauns dissolved into their surroundings and watched as he hopelessly tried to disengage the saint's skeleton that was deeply imbedded in his anatomy and had fused itself into his own skeletal structure, bone to bone.

Frustrated beyond his own comprehension, he dismissed any idea of adopting the creatures of light philosophy and he searched for a way out. His environment suddenly became pitch black as fairy-leprechauns switched off, not a flicker of light anywhere. Ivan Gallows stood perfectly still, adjusted to his saintly burden as best he could and strained his body's tactile receptors to detect the faintest suggestion of a breeze, a current of air that pointed the way out. It came from his left side, less than a whisper but enough to be considered a friend, something the Greeks wrote about. Ivan Gallows very slowly and ever so carefully turned so as not to disturb the delicacy of his situation and then step-by-step walked with his newly acquired 'friend' until the outside world greeted him with amusement.

The exit to the external world came in the form of a disused aqua duct built by the Romans centuries ago. The mouth of it adjoined a fashionable shopping complex and was used as an undercover eating area. A naked Ivan Gallows walked towards the daylight and assumed invisibility and hoped that his external skeleton would follow suit. The sight of a motley coloured and ancient skeleton walking backwards caused the near naked shoppers to stop, stare and gasp at the 'apparition'. Many fled, others remained where they were and stood aghast. Security was called and many arrived to investigate the bizarre sight. Ivan Gallows remained focused and continued to walk undisturbed, fiercely determined to flee this hideous city; as he did so he caught his reflection in a store window out of the corner of his eye and uttered an audible obscenity which was enough for the security guards to draw their weapons.

"Halt stay where you are"! One of the burly guards commanded as he pointed his high voltage Tazer.

Ivan Gallows immediately obeyed and the saintly skeleton became lifeless. Four others joined the burly guard and with lumps in their throats they surrounded the unlikely looking skeleton. Ivan Gallows knew he was not exempt to physical harm and waited patiently like a cobra to strike. The skeleton by itself would not be enough therefore he decided to materialize into full view.

"Madonna! Jesus! Santa Maria"! The guards exclaimed as two of them dropped their loaded revolvers and fled leaving three to confront the monster. Sensing their inabilities Ivan Gallows without the slightest warning hit them with his hideously vile breath and followed through with a flurry of fists that rendered them all unconscious. He then disappeared into an extra large gentleman outfitter and furiously rummaged through its clothes on sale until he found a pair of pants, overcoat and hat large enough to accommodate him and his Siamese twin.

30

DIPLOMATC CHANGE

After the last Code P meeting Malcolm Halliday busied himself and others in readiness for the 'meteoric' strikes on Australia's outback. Everything was in place including the medical removal of Prime Minister Harvey Jarwood all it required was the Presidents nod of approval, no signature, no documentary evidence nothing!

Throughout his entire effort Malcolm Halliday could not arrest, stop nor slow his mind from worrying about the CIA's relationship with Nghi Phamhung. The biggest concern he had was keeping quiet the Chinese- Afghanistan's trafficking of Australian processed Uranium to the Middle East. If the information were ever leaked to the Israeli's it would become hell for Malcolm Halliday and President Brain George. How ambitious was April Hako ambitious enough to blab her way into his position? Where did her political allegiances lie? Had the President ordered all of the gathered information destroyed? Would ignorance be his only defence? That was the problem of having free time on your hands it causes the mind to panic unnecessarily. Malcolm Halliday sat grimfaced at his work desk the past few days of intense dedicated work had caused him to age and he decided that once the President gave the green light he that is Malcolm would journey to parts unknown together with his beloved Shitzu and leave his problems behind. CIA Executive Agent Malcolm Halliday closed his eyes and retreated into a world of meditative escapism and waited patiently for the Presidential okay.

"Agent Halliday a word please"! April Hako voice thundered after she gave his office doorframe a sound rapping.

"I'm sorry I was miles away." Halliday apologised making no eye contact with his once secret love.

'We have a situation Sir"!

"Very well come in and explain it to me." Halliday politely said as he stood up to invite Hako in and offered her a chair in which to sit in.

"Thank you sir but I'd rather stand. I've come to summons you to a meeting with the President." She abruptly replied.

"Very well I'll gather my papers and we can leave straight away." Hako said nothing as she observed Halliday calmly fill his attaché case with numerous manila folders. "Quite a performance you put on the other day, if I didn't know better I'd guessed you were after my job"! Halliday joked.

"I'm hard working, not ambitious nor scheming, I expect to be promoted on merit alone"! Hako replied with a hard edge to her monotone voice. Halliday took her no nonsense answer as a sign to remain silent and he accordingly did so.

President Brian George together with Rachel Crank and an assortment of top advisers waited in the ultra-secure conference room within the CIA's Langley complex. It was a room intended for one's ear's only, no records apart from that. Good in some respects, bad in others, you had to keep a sharp mind, photographic memory and no misinterpretations. This meeting room was the graveyard of many an agent summonsed previously. Halliday thought himself too young to die. Entry into the conference room was via three sets of double insulated doors, after passing through a rigorous security check.

Halliday entered the room and recognised everyone apart from two individuals.

"Agent Halliday, Agent Hako, please take your places over there, thank you. May I introduce you to the British Ambassador to the USA Paris August and to Mr Alfred Woodside from the British Secret Service, their presence today heralds a change to our....er your plans." President George haphazardly explained before addressing his British guests. "Paris, Alfred, these competent CIA agents before you have come up with a well thought out scheme to discipline and reign in Australia's long standing government which has behaved much like a naughty schoolboy."

Hako and Halliday both nodded so as to acknowledge their guests, Hako remained indifferent whereas Halliday reserved his openness out of displeasure for British Diplomacy, which to him meant 'smile at your opponents while you knife them in the back' diplomacy to Halliday was the epitome of hypocrisy and accordingly he thought of his Shitzu to disguise his disgust.

"The plan and its sequence as you have learnt is brilliant and I was about to authorise its execution had it not been for your urgent diplomatic intervention. Agent's Hako and Halliday your ears please it appears Australia's activities in the Southern Hemisphere have attracted the British interest. Using International Cricket as a smokescreen Harvey Jarwood has forged strong links with South Africa to capitalise on the nations enormous wealth both natural and intellectual, with the intended end result being, Australia's unilateral Declaration of Independence from England. Paris August here has received special instruction from the British Prime Minister Bernard Townsend to directly and personally instruct us that they will assume responsibility for Mr Jarwoods political assassination and therefore we have been politely asked to leave that aspect of our plan to them."

"Will it be along the same lines as when Australia's Governor General dismissed their federal parliament some decades ago"? Hako asked having been fully briefed on Australia's political history.

"I'm not at liberty to say, that is a matter for our PM and the Home Office to determine." Paris August coldly answered in her highly polished plum voice.

"Will your Queen have a say"? Hako persisted.

"Again my hands are tired." August arrogantly and aloofly reiterated which cemented Halliday's philosophical convictions regarding diplomacy.

"I think we can safely rely on our British friends to deal with their own, after all they do have a Commonwealth of Nations to administrate. I think it is a good move for it takes away the responsibility of that aspect from us and given the British excellence for dealing with sensitive matters will provide a cleaner result. Furthermore I am more than certain they will be able to infiltrate the minds of the powerful select in Australia into supporting the monarchy instead of a republic especially when money and power are at stake." President George half heartedly said.

Agent Halliday was not happy with the concept, it didn't sound right. To him it was more about Britain grabbing the international limelight, fooling itself by not letting go of its glorious superpower past. How much of his plan had the President divulged to the Brits? Malcolm crossed his arms and gritted his teeth Brian George sensed his disapproval.

"Any qualms" The president asked Hako and Halliday.

"If you're happy with their proposal so are we." Halliday replied with the sharp edge of his tongue.

"Hako"

"No reservations Sir, the only question I have is with respect to timing." April thoughtfully answered.

"Paris"? The president inquired of August

"As I said before, that will be a matter for our PM and the Home Office."

"Much like cricket I suppose'! Halliday acidly put forward before he went on his verbal rampage mocking the great British institution.

"Short legged maidens out for a duck as mad dogs and Englishmen go out in the midday sun to watch the spinners, tossers, knock three sticks over and cheer 'Rule Britannia' bleeding ridiculous"!

'Halliday mind you tongue we have important guests"! President George quickly rebuked the insolent CIA agent.

'No apologies Sir! I take my leave you may discipline me later Sir"! He sharply retorted as he stood up abruptly clearly dissatisfied and stormed out of the meeting.

"My colleague is very sensitive about his work, you'll have to excuse him, I think he feels that his plans have been undermined and sabotaged." April Hako apologised once Halliday was out of earshot.

"Point taken Miss Hako; please reassure him we meant no harm, it is our way. Mr President perhaps we could adjourn on that note"? Paris suggested as she signalled Arthur Woodside it was time for them to depart.

"Bleeding Brits how dare they! Imperial imbeciles! You watch they'll mess it up"! Halliday thought to himself as he strutted to his office with the unwavering intention of finishing work for the day.

"President George you have my permission to do the work yourself now that you've let the bleeding Brits in"! Halliday continued to mentally seethe as he neared his office door. The three red phones on his desk blinked furiously demanding immediate attention. "I'm not in find someone else! You can all go and............yourselves"! He openly cursed as he gathered his pile of top-secret documents and threw them into his private safe to remain locked away until he had sufficiently simmered down and was agreeable to work for the office once again. Malcolm Halliday punched in his security code into the safe's keypad and closed its door. Satisfied he turned his office lights off and left for the day uncertain that he would return the next. The emotional fury that stormed inside of him drove the CIA's personnel out of his way as he whirl winded in a straight line to his parked car.

The subterranean fully enclosed car lot was empty and strangely cold. Halliday approached his company car and activated its remote.

The car failed to respond. He pressed 'unlock' again with the same result. "Strange I just replaced the batteries; no matter I'll open the door and disengage the alarm with its key" was his mental solution. Two minutes later thinking he was free to depart Malcolm seated behind the steering wheel inserted the key into the dashboards ignition switch and turned it to stir his 'beast' into life. Nothing, the mechanical horse refused to stir, its heart lifeless.

"What now? Another setback! What a day! Bet it was those bleeding Brits"! He thought in frustration as he calculated his next move. "Check all electrics." He muttered to himself as he reached under the dashboard to pull the bonnet release lever.

"Battery terminals dry, secure, no corrosion, water levels okay, fuses all fine, electrical connections intact, no loose wires, no cut wires, no cracks in coil, starter motor ready, fuel lines full. Why won't you start"? He pleaded with the car for an answer.

"Because Agent Halliday we have the final say"! A voice came as the beast's engine burst into life startling Malcolm into hitting his head on the raised bonnet. Recognising the voice Halliday peered around the corner of the vehicle and saw President Brain George standing next to the driver's side with a small electronic device in his hand.

"Company property, we decide when it goes when it stays"! The President of the United Sates warmly explained.

"Very well Sir looks as though I'm stationary"! Halliday angrily concluded.

"You're behaving like a jilted lover Malcolm, drop the act"! The President strongly advised.

Halliday bit his upper lip and feigned lack of aggression, a lowering of defences, but in reality he was ready to attack his commander in chief for betrayal and treason. Halliday lowered the car's bonnet and gently closed it in contrast to his violent mood. President George stood alone, no body guards, he was well aware of Malcolm Halliday's self defence capabilities but he was also keenly intimate with his agent and with that confidence in mind he clicked the device which he held in his left hand and the CIA's 'beast' went to sleep.

"You're alone"? Halliday allowed his astute nature to observe.

"Naturally our professional intimacy needs to be preserved at all costs."

"Then why did you involve the Brits"? Halliday verbally scalded the President.

"I had no choice. They've been very active; their spy network detected and uncovered some of Jarwood's plots and when the hits on the pharmaceutical industry occurred on three continents they suspected a common thread. Rather than working alone they decided to share their information with us and proposed we collaborate on the final solution." The President truthfully related.

"I see and you saw it fit to hand over my brilliant strategies." Halliday harshly criticised his superior.

"This is what they received." Brian George in defence said as he handed over a blue print copy of the intended operation. Malcolm Halliday took the highly secretive papers and thoroughly speed-read their contents to his total surprise.

"You're no Judas Ischariot"! He surmised.

"Never will be my friend. The Brits are okay but they still live in the 18th century, this is the new world for people like you and me, before they know what is happening it will be over and done with, all that will be left for them to do is sort out Australia's political mess providing Her Majesty is bothered"!

Hoping that the President had not deceived him Halliday persisted with his line of questioning. "What of my proposals"? He asked.

"Operational as of today with some additions, I have commissioned another high altitude stealth bomber to simulate meteor trails in the stratosphere or ionosphere by the use of Tesla plasma rays, can't have hits on earth without shooting star's can we"? The President joked. Halliday laughed at the implied dark humour and extended his hand out of friendship.

"I'm sorry I doubted you Sir."

"You're excused but don't do it again." The President cautioned as he embraced Halliday and patted him several times on the back.

"Yes Ambassador what news have you for me" Bernard Townsend United Kingdom's Prime Minister asked.

"All good Prime Minister, Woodside and I were privileged to view the American's solution to the present pharmaceutical crisis in the light of their accumulated secret service data. We met with the President, the secretary of State, their top advisers and high-ranking CIA officers. I am pleased to say that they have albeit reluctantly allowed us to deal with Harvey Jarwood in our own way." UK's ambassador to the US Paris August slowly detailed.

"Excellent when do we act"? Bernard Townsend excitedly asked as he did not exactly have fond memories of Harvey Jarwood on the contrary he found the man to be quite obnoxious.

"All in good time Prime Minister. Harvey Jarwood is still hospitalised, not good cricket to hit a man when he's down."

"Agreed keep me informed." Townsend ordered.

"Shall do Prime Minister, Woodside's on his way back home as we speak, he'll fill in the details once he arrives home, one of our top men, excellent field operative knows how to sniff things out, I'm more than certain you'll be pleased with the outcome." August confidently said in true British cryptic fashion.

"Good work Paris, keep an eye on the Yanks, still don't trust them." Townsend ended the conversation and cradled the secure direct line to the States.

"Agent Hako"

"Yes Mr President." April obediently answered as she stood up to meet Brian George as he entered her office unannounced.

"Have you found the agents we need to accommodate Dr Dennis Sauvage"? The President asked.

"Not within our department Sir, that activity is frowned upon, our policy is strictly the employment of heterosexuals Sir."

"Solutions, Hako, solutions"? Brian George demanded to know.

"The military Sir" Hako unashamedly answered.

"Which branch"?

"The infantry…. I…. mean the Army Sir." Hako's comment made the President laugh. "What's so funny Sir"?

"It's visual Hako, a visual joke; the use of gays improves fitness, running ability." George cryptically answered.

"I don't understand." Hako frowned

"Let me explain. This guy goes into a gym and asks for a programme to help him loose weight. The assistant takes him to a window and shows him the one she had in mind. Behind the glass is a big room with a buxom blonde in a skimpy bikini being chased by an overweight man. She yells "You can have me if you catch me".

The customer goes "wow" and asks, "What's this called"? The assistant answers "This is our standard silver treatment; there is a gold version available." Thinking gold means two blondes the guy signs up, pays his money, is stripped down to his jocks and is taken to the golden room. He waits nervously. Then this big burly Scandinavian male blonde walks in holding a short whip. The guy looks surprised and says, "What's this"? The Gay Swede answers in a squeaky voice. "Gold standard ducky, start running"

"Very funny Sir, hope it didn't happen on your election trail." April falsely relied pretending to suppress her laughter.

"I thought you'd like that, so you see Miss Hako perhaps the Army's enlistment of gays carries with it a secret ulterior motive, the improvement of our troops stamina."

"A somewhat bizarre conclusion Sir; Dr Sauvage does very well when the Army is in town. It appears he scores after the show with many of his male admirers especially if he sneaks out and ventures into the same nightclubs that they frequent." Agent Hako tastefully described.

"Can we orchestrate such rendezvous'"?

"Very easily Sir, we have a base close to where Sauvage's Ice Show is presently performing. I've arranged for a number of uniformed men to attend one of the weekend mattinee's."

"Under what pretext"?

"Extraordinary selective R & R Sir"

"Sounds good and then"? The President asked.

"They will be invited back stage to meet the artists and hopefully sparks will fly."

"Let's hope he's in the mood."

"I should imagine he is Sir, he's had no steady relationship for over a year. His last sexual partner died tragically, a victim of equipment failure, trapeze artist, buckle broke, snapped his neck"!

"Was the show cancelled"? The President respectfully asked.

"Only Sauvage's commitment to long term relationships; he now prefers one night stands." Hako disapprovingly replied.

"He's not worried about sexually transmitted diseases or AIDS"?

"I think he's got that covered Sir."

"How do you mean Hako"?

"It's in his Alljoy Sir."

"I don't understand." The President sounded perplexed.

"I've had several expert people look closely at it Sir, very closely, it appears to have disease limiting capabilities"!

"What are you saying"? Brian George asked as both his interest and enthusiasm intensified.

"Our researchers detected large amounts of Messenger RNA; no sense was made of it until we decided to interview those who sung Alljoy's merits. Without exception everyone who consumed the substance had their health status reversed." Hako explained and expected the President to react cynically to her statements. Brian George thought awhile before engaging in further conversation, which made Hako temporarily nervous.

"This discovery by Sauvage was no accident; it was deliberate. Question is why? Perhaps one of his past lovers or gay friend or even family member died of AIDS or some other incurable disease; as a consequence it caused him to seek out a universal panacea. I want this man! Do you know what it means, a genius in our midst a god send for our military programme." US President George exuberantly exclaimed.

"I'm afraid I've lost you Sir." Hako vacantly replied deep science was never one of her strong points.

"We produce defensive biological weapons, we like the rest of our competition have no real antidotes, Dennis Sauvage could possibly work them out for us, it will give us the edge we are looking for, I want this man, I want to meet this genius, bring him to me once you've captured his attention." The President ordered as he rubbed his hands in anticipation.

"Very well Sir." Hako obediently answered.

"And Hako"

"Yes Sir."

"Make certain he is treated gently, this man is very gifted, we must see to it that he is satisfied and remains happy and gay at all times."

"Yes Sir you have my word on it." Hako assured the President as she swallowed hard.

31

MISCHIEVOUS INTENTIONS

Louis Badcock felt at peace with himself, it no longer mattered whether he ever made it into Dot.org's inner circle. What was important was the continued success of his revamped Infirmary and its franchise. Ever since he had changed the mix and nature of its clientele the venture's success grew exponentially, the only limiting factor would always be the acquisition of girls who knew how to perform to the satisfaction of the customer and themselves as well.

Louis lay on the lush green grass beneath a spreading Elm tree heavy with summer foliage; it grew in the middle of the sprawling gardens at the rear of the Infirmary. Numerous hedges dotted the landscape each pruned and fashioned into an erotic work of horticultural art that depicted a highly suggestive sexual position. In the centre of the garden a large white porcelain fountain sculptured in the form of two intertwined lovers bubbled cheerfully away as its waters up sprayed in all directions bringing life and joy to the numerous multi coloured choi which inhabited the circular pool that formed its base.

It was peaceful there and for a brief moment the warm sunshine embraced Badcock's body as a young woman would do and with it came memories of Felicity, Naomi, Brandy, Candy, Samantha, Brittany, Jamie and Holly; those that he had lost to Fr Brendan O'Reilly.

"The girl's I wish I'd loved before"! Louis whispered to himself as he fantasized being naked in their presence and satisfying each one as she desired.

Louis knew he was deluding himself, Mr Badcock was driven to power, to succeed and he wanted it his way, so much so that Louis Badcock's mind started to misbehave much like that of a mischievous child who calculated ways of causing mayhem in an effort to satisfy his compulsive tantrums. Louis found the Small Dark Figure always demeaning and irritating, the Harshman a biological experiment gone horribly wrong, Brendan O'Reilly a permanent thorn in his side and Jack Stern the devil himself.

"I am the man! I have always been the Man! Sophisticated daring! I am where I am because of who I am! My past circumstances were unfortunate, accidental! I am on the path again Dot.org needs me! It is incomplete without me"! Louis Badcock used these self-generated affirmations to convince himself of his own importance. Badcock's mouth tightened and became a narrow slit in his face, his eyes filled with ambitious hatred as he raised his body off his comfortable grass bed. Firmly focused on his next series of moves Louis tapped the water fountain twice before setting off back to the Infirmary.

Out of the corner of his eye he saw the black eerie shadows of a human skeleton slowly stretch before him as though it was sent to strike him down and withdraw his soul into the underworld. Louis heart shivered, his respiration paused, his facial blood drained and his legs refused to move. The shadows moved closer until the skeleton's bony arms and legs encaged him.

"Did you miss me Louis"? It asked in a low and seductive voice that threatened to extinguish him. Badcock wanted to scream but his vocal cords and lungs refused to co-operate.

"Grim reaper Angel of Death? Is it my time? Have I entered into a pact in the past that I forgot about? I don't remember"!!! Louis in a state of extreme agitation questioned himself as the skeleton repeated its question.

"Did you miss me Louis"? Afraid to answer Badcocok tried to break free.

"It's no use we're destined to be together forever"!

"Go away you smelly bag of bones"!! Badcock finally shouted after he regained his lost strength.

"But Louis I love you come with me"!

"Damn you let go"!! Badcock screamed as he squirmed to discharge his bony leper.

"Very well" The skeleton replied as it released its haunting grip. Badcock was about to make a run for it but his courage caused him to turn instead and face his adversary.

"D-man.......what the hell happened to you"? Badcock exclaimed with a shocked look on his face as Ivan Gallows materialised into view.

"Misfortune with fairies"

"Gays did this to you"?

"Leprechaun-fairies" Ivan Gallows detailed.

"Small gays" Badcock comically asked as he raised his perfectly manicured eyebrows to demonstrate his sheer disbelief.

"It's not all bad, couldn't fly home but sure scared the pants off those who tried to stop me coming back"! Ivan Gallows dryly joked.

"I know the Somalian's have pigmies but leprechauns"?

"It wasn't there; the Greatrex couldn't help me so I ventured to Rome and met with some dark cleverly disguised Vatican heavies. They were nasties. A woman who earlier befriended me promised to introduce me to ancient mystical alchemists." Gallows grimly explained.

"They did this to you"?

"No I never met them, along the way I was bushwhacked by these little pink haired white people. It was so bizarre. They inflicted this curse on me." Ivan reluctantly and ashamedly replied.

"To stop you from defeating O'Reilly"

"No ....out of punishment"!

"For"

"Hurting their friend" Ivan Gallows proudly said as he perked up.

"Who was"?

"Isabella Von Zecca high class whore"!

"She probably deserved it"! Badcock arrogantly and disrespectfully suggested at which Ivan Gallows the D-man looked away in shame.

"What are you hiding"? Badcock sternly asked, as he looked intensely at Gallows who avoided his stare. Sensing he held the upper hand Louis repeated the question and Gallows answered in a hushed whisper.

"I lost my virginity; I partook of the pleasures of the flesh and got carried away. It started out fine but then I tasted the violence in sex and exerted myself"!

"You almost killed her"! Badcock correctly deduced.

"Yes."

"I see. Is your punishment permanent"?

"No"!

"For how long"? Badcock inquired as he stepped forward to examine the ancient skeleton.

"Twenty eight days."

"That's not long. Is it your own"?

"It belongs to a deceased saint"! Ivan Gallows glumly answered quite disturbed with its description.

"Oh dear I suppose you're of no use to me then." Badcock concluded in a raspy voice.

"I wouldn't say that! Every cloud has its silver lining. I can still disappear and animate this skeleton to scare people. It took a little while to work out the mechanics, now all is fine, a world class act." The D-man proudly replied as he recounted his Italian adventures.

"Very well Mr Contortionist take your bony puppet into town and steal a bundle of mobile phones, sim cards and extra credit. Meet me in my apartment, come through the secret entrance and buzz me when you arrive." Badcock commanded with a sly smile.

"Yes Louis, be back directly." Ivan Gallows half growled and half grovelled as he disappeared from view with his 'Siamese twin' firmly attached and walking backwards.

"I've been at this eighteen hours a day, seven days a week and seem to be getting nowhere! It's late; I'm tired, exhausted, all I want to do is go home"!! Cyril Pinewood bitterly complained to himself as he scratched his head and searched for answers to the avalanche of administrative problems that lay before him.

"What is it with this system? No matter which department I approach it is always the same! Yes sir we will look into it, but first we will have to devise a policy to suit your requests. Committee's need to be put in place, firstly to identify the parameters of your wishes and then to clearly define what you are intending to accomplish. Once we are satisfied and everyone is clear we will set up the next committee to come up with workable suggestions. Once everyone is happy we will tender out the work and employ the most satisfactory candidates providing they are happy with the contract that we offer. If not then we start all over again. This is bureaucratic madness! There is no government here! We are a two-tiered governmental system, the elected buffoons who know not what law they are passing and the idiots who administer the law that they know nothing about! Can we please start again! I am tired of dealing with people who have no respect for their departmental minister. They listen not! They act not! They do not! The system is so deeply ingrained with dead wood it needs a massive fire to reduce everything to ashes and start again. How to avoid the behind the door corruption and graft from happening again? This nation borders on anarchy the only thing stopping it is multi-culturism and the social security system that feeds it"! An exasperated Cyril Pinewood analytical mind rambled on as Cyril held his heavy head in his hands.

"Acting PM Pinewood"!! Harvey Jarwood's secretary loudly and disrespectfully uttered as she barged into his sanctuary. "You are a wanted man"! She threatened as she pointed a finger at him.

Her words snapped Pinewood out of his gloomy mood and he stood to attention as a well trained and obedient private in the army would do.

"Is there a bounty on my head"? Pinewood submissively whimpered.

"By all and sundry; I have the Americans, the English, Koreans, Indonesians and a dog parlour operator on the lines seeking your immediate attention"!

"One at a time I can only take so much more today." He bitterly complained.

"I suggest you start with the Korean, he's awfully mad"! Jarwoods secretary stated in a firm manner as in her mind she almost ran the nation prior to the unexpected plague of troubles.

"Tell him I'll call back, perhaps he could invade South Korea or detonate a few nuclear weapons while he's waiting."

"Very smug of you Sir; head's or tail's" Jarwoods Secretary flippantly asked as she flipped a fifty-cent piece into the air.

"Always preferred a bit of tail"

"Male or female"

"Always female" Pinewood defiantly replied too tired to blush for having been found out.

"Are you sure? I've heard contrary rumours, unofficial gossip plus that look in your eye when you're............" Jarwoods secretary taunted.

"Exaggerations and preposterous nonsense fuelled by political dissidents"! Pinewood madly asserted in his defence.

"Friends then"

"Nothing more"! Pinewood aloofly replied.

"Heads it is, which means Brian George followed by Bernand Townsend. I'll make the necessary arrangements, keep your conversations brief"! Jarwood's secretary curtly said as she rushed out of the room.

"Bloody woman thinks she rules the country"! Cyril Pinewood mumbled to himself as he casually swept his full head of hair back into place and adjusted his crumpled attire. The desk tops Commander telephone system's Number 5 line flashed rhythmically almost it seemed to the 'Stars and Stripes' melody and demanded to be heard. Pinewoods right cautiously approached it and hesitantly picked up its handpiece and automatically placed it against the side of his head; guessing the time of day in the USA he greeted the American leader.

"Good morning Mr President how are you doing"? He cheerfully asked in complete contrast to his tired and gloomy self.

"Not bad for a second timer"! Brian George energetically answered indicating that it was his second term as the Commander in Chief.

"What do I owe the pleasure of your phone call to"?

"Just checking on Jarwood"

"Still in a coma, gone to pieces I'm afraid. I've heard they're thinking of transferring him to a mental institution that specialises in the latest treatments." Pinewood reluctantly informed his caller, as he did not wish to become Australia's permanent PM.

"My spies tell me your administrations not holding up too well."

"We're managing." Pinewood bravely replied in an attempt to save face but he knew full well that the situation was chaotic.

"I haven't contacted you to offer charity."

"Or the American way of doing things" Cyril unexpectedly interrupted which precipitated a deadly silence from the President; Cyril meanwhile remained un-phased and calm and awaited further discussions.

The American people are very concerned about the integrity of the Australian government and the impact it is likely to have upon our global network of military bases." Brian George then after a brief moment very slowly explained.

"What are you hinting at"? Cyril asked with pricked up ears, his mind having zoomed in on the ambiguity of the word 'integrity'.

"Whispers, damning whispers"

"In relation to"

"The stability of our relationship" The President replied in a low tone of voice.

"Meaning"

"Rumour has it your administration wants to go it alone"!

"Where to"? Pinewood sincerely asked becoming somewhat confused, as all of this was new to him. Jarwood had kept great masses of political activity secret to himself. "I know nothing of it"! He then added.

"Your tone of voice sounds convincing acting Prime Minister Pinewood. Perhaps we should give you the benefit of doubt. Just remember our Australian bases remain American soil and we will do everything to protect their sovereign nature"! Brian George firmly warned and then without further notice he terminated the call disallowing Cyril Pinewood any opportunity of confirming his understanding of the nebulous situation.

"Line 3 Mr Pinewood" The office intercom blared.

"Thank you." Cyril replied a little shaky and rattled by his previous caller.

"Cyril Pinewood is that you? You old fox! Bearing up under the pressure of it all"? Bernard Townsend warmly inquired in a fatherly fashion.

"As best as I can.....considering" A preoccupied Pinewood vaguely answered as his mind continued to dwell on his previous caller's conversation.

"How's your Health Department coping with the drug crisis? Found the culprits? Not by any chance South Africans? Heard you've had a great influx lately, we aren't entirely pleased with their past efforts, hope they won't adversely influence you." Townsend rattled off.

Cyril Pinewood tried to get his head around what the British PM was insinuating and once again he focused on the ocean of political secrecy that Jarwood floated on.

"I have no comment." Cyril truthfully answered.

"Not been made privy then"?

"Afraid not"

"Good then there's hope for all of us. Need to look after British interests, our investments in Australia." Townsend cryptically said.

"News to me" Pinewood thought to himself as his mind raced into overdrive.

"Need any help restructuring"? The British genuinely offered.

"No I think we're managing."

"What about the cricket team"?

"Why would he want to discuss cricket at a time like this unless it's to seduce me into novel ways of subtle yet deadly interrogation." Cyril thought to himself before he committed himself.

"No South Africans on the playing team nor in reserve and no matches planned with the South Africans until our house is in order." Pinewood answered in good sporting fashion.

"Well said I'll leave you to carry on, keep up the good work and by the way glad to see that you've finally lost your fondness of men. Good night." Bernard Townsend tongue in cheek clicked off.

"Just don't sit there doing nothing! Acting PM line 4 if you please! Get on with it"! Jarwoods secretary sharply ordered as she cracked her oral whip.

Feeling almost completely drained and confused Pinewood mustered his remaining available energy's and attended to the next caller.

"Ah haarow, that you Jalwood" The unidentified Korean asked. Cyril strained to understand the man never mind putting a face to the voice.

"Pardon"

Whele is lest of oul shipment"?

"I'm afraid I don't know what you are talking about." Pinewood slowly articulated as he looked out of his office window to confirm that it was indeed full moon weather. "Three lunatics in a row" He mumbled

"Look could you please speak up I am having trouble understanding you"! He then slowly and firmly asked the Korean.

"Lacist Forleigner" was the reply.

"What is it you seek"? Pinewood then asked dismissing the caller's inflammatory remarks.

"Lest of oul shipment, wheat, wheat! You know floul beads, calgo not all there"!

'That's not the only thing that's not there"! Pinewood mentally concluded.

"Give me your details I'll attend to it first thing in the morning." Cyril politely promised as he changed his attitude and waited patiently for the Korean to supply the necessary information, nothing but a blank line. "Hello, hello…..strange fellow"!

"Line number five, hop to it"!

"Bloody hell what do you think this is some sort of emergency hot line"? Pinewood almost verbally rammed the words down the secretary's throat.

"Good evening Acting Prime Minister, this is Acacium Rackmanagym Indonesian Minister for foreign affairs, we've spoken before."

"Agreed"

"Our government has been observing your countries state of affairs for some time and we must regretfully inform you that we are severing diplomatic ties with Australia. Our embassies plus all staff will be recalled back to Indonesia immediately. Effective today you will no longer need to worry about Bali belly; Australian Citizens are no longer welcome"! Acacium grimly and cold-heartedly proclaimed after he cleared his heavily smoked throat.

"Oh what's his problem? Shortage of shark fins? Why don't they just stick to making pineapple soup"? Pinewood sighed in response to his aggressive caller whom he thought to be a bit of a crackpot.

"Very well I shall inform our officers to publicly redirect our Australian holidaymakers to Thailand, and then we will hold numerous press conferences to explain why"! Pinewood acidly replied in response to Rackmanagym's official announcement and then he had the sublime pleasure of being the first to hang up.

"Line number six, lucky line six, bingo! Best call of the night left to the last, just like a fine wine"! Jarwoods secretary jeered.

"Bet you're lying"! Cyril miserably muttered as he fought off his aversion not to perform his duty.

"Hello this is Cyril Pinewood how can I help you'?

"By taking this blasted FiFi, FuFu, FaFa or whatever it's called off my hands! I've had enough of it! This is not a boarding house for wayward animals"! A highly pitched and highly-strung unidentified voice demanded.

"I'm sorry the only thing I recognise in your description is FuFu, some sort of delicacy from Ghana or is it part of their stable diet." Pinewood questioned both himself and his caller.

"Very funny Mr Pinebark just get someone to come over and collect this menace before he turns all of my dogs gay"!

"To whom am I speaking"?

"Triple A dog-groomers Mr Pinechip"!

"Tell me more."

"Some weeks ago this government paid private courier deposits the white mongrel complete with written instructions and photograph, to be exotically clipped, shampooed and toe nails painted in a variety of psychedelic colours." The owner of Triple A angrily stuttered.

"What does it have to do with me"?

"I don't believe this! Because mate Mr Splinteredwood you're the blasted owner"!

"I am"? Cyril answered quite bewildered.

"Look mate the documents cite you as the registered buyer"!

Not wishing to antagonise his caller and further inflame the situation Cyril Pinewood politely offered an apology.

"I am very sorry with all that has happened. The dog slipped my mind; personal survival was and is presently paramount. I will make arrangements to have the randy animal collected tomorrow; your bill will be fully paid with a little extra for all of the inconvenience that AAA parlour has had to put up with." Without anyfurther ado the dog groomer shouted an unmentionable obscenity and rudely terminated the call.

"Well Mr Pinewood, Mr Cyril Pinewood you're finally aware"! Harvey Jarwood's secretary firmly stated in no uncertain manner as she crept into his office and absurdly towered over him supported by the fact that she was only 1.60metre tall. "About time you became a man, never thought of you as being gay! He took advantage of you and your silly naivity"!

"What are you insinuating"? Cyril defiantly answered as he blushed momentarily.

"Jarwood's betrayal he very cleverly seduced you into falling in love with his femininity. Examine yourself; the squeakiness in your voice has disappeared, your wrists are strong and your regularly speak to your wife on the phone. Things you never did before or probably did before Jarwood appeared on the scene. Am I right"?

Pinewood grim faced stood up closed his eyes tightly so as to shut out the image of Jarwood, released the tension in his jaw muscles and quietly said. "Thank you I think I've had enough for one day. I need to go home."

"Before you do sir a little present for you" Jarwood's secretary said as she thrust a computer disc into his hand.

"What's this"?

"Evidence of betrayal on it you will find documents, which you will have no recollection of ever signing. Good night sir"!

As the chauffer drove the white limousine through the streets of Sydney, Pinewood nervously activated his lap top computer and inserted the re-write able compact disc that Jarwood's secretary had provided him. Every document contained on it that he viewed confirmed her conclusions. Harvey Jarwood had used and abused Pinewood's infatuation and it was made worse much to his escalating horror by the realisation that every piece was designed to cement Jarwood's vision of Australia becoming the first Western Communistic Society of its kind brutally fed by a storehouse of legislation, protected by the social security system's army of bureaucrats. The government chauffer continually observed Pinewood's reaction in the rear vision mirror as he fiddled with the automobile's stereo system and other controls.

"You look a little troubled tonight Prime Minister, more than usual I venture to say"! He boldly said breaking the internal silence.

"Not really, the day was a grind with a flurry of overseas calls at the end, nothing I could not handle. Know anything about a dog and AAA grooming"?

The Chauffer pondered the question as he played with the cars dashboard computer. 'Can't say I do, is it important to national security"?

"Never mind" Cyril sighed as he slowly scrolled through the secret and highly confidential parliamentary documents. The chauffer continued to silently observe Pinewood until he saw Cyril's eyes widen with disbelief then he quickly looked away.

The final page read. "A present for you, a gift, to access it type in your wife's Christian name followed by her nickname, otherwise known as a term of endearment."

Pinewood dismissed the written insult and obeyed the directions. The sum of $15,000,000 US dollars in Pinewoods name flashed up on the screen followed by the prompt. "What to know more"? Cyril typed in "yes". The computer responded by providing depository details. A highly secretive Swiss bank account located in Hong Kong accessed only after a series of identifications had been satisfied. Not one of the documents that Cyril had previously viewed made any reference to this 'reward' and consequently he became suspicious as to its intention.

"All gay infatuations cease to exist I am a man and a man I shall stay"! He confidently said to himself as his subconsciousness dwelled on the enigma.

"Is it a trap or is it a test? To prove I wish I knew. Is it only me that can physically access the money or is it someone else's in my name only? Does it matter? Probably not! What I fool I've been to fall in love with a man. Shameful! Senseless! Why was I attracted to his femininity rather than my wife's? What was missing? Femininity a sexless attribute seemingly equally distributed amongst males and females the cause of so much chaotic confusion." Cyril regretfully told himself as he furrowed his brow and looked away in disgust.

"Having difficulty making your decision sir"? The chauffer warmly asked as he made eye contact with a rather disturbed Pinewood in the rear view mirror. "I gather by your body language that you are rather reluctant to take the bait."

"This is ridiculous"! Pinewood snapped back.

"Par for the course sir, not unlike a Hollywood movie where it's either the butler, gardener, maid or chauffer that is the culprit. I've watched every move you've made in the back seat." Pinewood nervously scanned his immediate surroundings not knowing what to expect or what to look for.

"Too micro for you to detect" The chauffer commented as he took a deviation and drove the limousine into a deserted industrial area.

"This is not the way home! Stop this car immediately and let me out"! Pinewood violently shouted as he attempted to open the rear door.

"Afraid not sir; you are not my master I am answerable to others"! The chauffers words struck a shaft of terror deep into Pinewood's soul bypassing his heart. "It will do you no good to struggle sir, the doors are doubly locked, the windows bullet proof and me completely isolated and detached. Stay quiet and all will be well. Agitate yourself unnecessarily and a gloomy fate awaits you." The chauffer calmly explained as he drifted the car into a dark parking spot next to a collection of uninviting warehouses. He put the automobile into park exited the vehicle opened the boot retrieved several items of clothing plus a high voltage stun gun.

"Mr Pinewood if you please." The chauffer beckoned as he, with stun gun in hand ready to shoot at a moments notice, opened the rear door. Cyril by now the epitome of desperation slowly slid out of his seat ready to take advantage of any opportunity to escape.

"Think otherwise Mr Pinewood"! The chauffer cautioned as he stepped back to allow the acting PM to emerge. "Put these on"! He then roughly commanded as he handed over a black leather mask complete with cut outs for the eyes and mouth each fully zipped so as to allow selective sight and speech. At the back a long zip ran down the full length to allow easy pull on and keep the mask securely in place. The other item of clothing was a disposable pair of bright yellow plastic overalls with a button up trap door located in the seat of the pants.

"This is absolutely degrading! I feel like a freak out of a television advertisement for roadside assistance! God it's hot in here, can't breathe, can't hear, my skin's crawling or is something crawling on me"? A panic stricken Pinewood thought as he finished putting his vestments on.

"This way Sir" The chauffer gestured with the stun gun as he directed Cyril down a spooky laneway and followed closely behind. "Stop right here. Now listen very carefully your name is Crassus, say very little, you're here to observe, it will explain all of the difficulties you've been experiencing.

Do not, I repeat do not engage in any games, cite polyps, fissures, haemorrhoids. Overuse as an excuse, otherwise your life will never be the same again, do you understand"? To which a meek and subdued

Pinewood nodded in the affirmative. "You are entering via a member only side entrance, it will grant you immunity from suspicion. I have the key, no I'm not one of them; I'm simply the keeper of the key intended for the PM's pleasure." The chauffer bluntly stated. "Now go in, become wise, exit when you wish, no-one will take any notice, today is race day, welcome to Gerbalis"! He added as he shoved the mentally unprepared and frightened acting PM through the door.

A rather fragile Cyril Pinewood found himself in a small dimly lit cubicle. The door opposite to him appeared to be locked the door behind him similarly so, not knowing what to expect he tried to force both but to no avail and then a metallic electronic voice rang out.

"Stay still scanning in progress." Cyril immediately became motionless and watched as a series of red laser beams traversed his body. "You may enter Crassus." The electronic voice announced as the door before him opened of its own accord.

"Obviously the markings on the mask or an electronic implant allowed me entry." Pinewood concluded as he stepped forward to view the horrendously bizarre scene before him.

There was no doubt in his mind that this warehouse had been especially sound proofed for the noise levels inside were deafening. A frightful blend of pleasurable screams groans of disbelief and hysterical laughter fuelled by chemical addiction battered his eardrums. A circus of frenzied activity, a sideshow of sexual freaks totally immersed in their anal delights, all dressed as he was in varying colours and styles.

Gerbalis was not a society devoted to flower arranging or anything remotely to do with Gerbera's on the contrary, its intention was the worship of the trained Gerbil and its ability to explore, burrow and ravage the delicate and highly innervated rectal mucosa.

Tonight was treadmill night and as the same suggests Gerbils of different genus were put through their paces before speeding off into awaiting and dilated rectal orifices enlarged through the insertion of cardboard tubes. Two types of recipients were present; normal and gaseous, the latter would either participate in the cannonball event or remain silent.

The explosive propellant was naturally developed methane gas generated by gastrointestinal bacteria fed on a pureed mixture of beans, onions, prunes and Brussels sprouts, at the distal end of the cardboard tube a small remote controlled piezo-electric ignition device was fitted that when activated caused the methane gas to ignite and expel the Gerbil in a ball of flame much to the on lookers aberrant delight and the projectors love of pain. The participants invariably loudly shouted "Armageddon" as the cue that they were about to ignite the available intestinal gasses. Prizes were presented for the longest trajectory, largest flaming ball, survival or death of the unfortunate rodent. Cyril Pinewood was aghast with abhorrent disdain that wanted him to flee his surroundings; however his eagerness to learn the truth caused him to circulate freely.

"Cheesmani" A solid rectangular man announced as he thrust his hand forward.

"Crassus." Pinewood replied as he accepted the formal handshake.

"Good evening"?

"Yes."

"Enjoying yourself"

"Yes, looking forward to seeing records broken." Pinewood falsely yet convincingly answered.

"Me too Hurrianae and Hoogstraag stand a good chance; don't know about Dunni I think he's ruined his chances after experimenting with petroleum lubricants and liquids.

"Heard about that, believe he needed plastic intervention." Cyril feigned and then he said. "Thought his walk was a little strange."

"How do think the women will go"?

"Er….can't say I've ever seen them performing here." Pinewood replied guessing.

"Actually you're quite correct it's the first time we've let them in. Keep an eye on Famulus, Vivax, Pussilus and Nigerius, I think they may well surprise us with their pelvic floor abilities. The rectangular man jokingly said in a loud voice.

"Keep that in mind, got to circulate.' Pinewood somewhat agreed as he excused himself.

"Who was that? Must try to identify people, hard to do considering the circumstances, perhaps when it gets a little quieter" Pinewood thought as he net worked his way about the crowded warehouse and met a confusion of names such as, Diminitus, Simoni, Zakaria, Pyramidium, Floweri, Watersi, Nanus, Agag, Rex, Afra, Robusta and Emini. His ears quickly learnt to adapt and they filtered out the annoying background noise enabling him to identify the voices of high-ranking officers from various law enforcement agencies as well as several federal cabinet ministers. As he was about to leave the master of ceremonies proudly made the following announcement.

"Attention fellow Anal-ists. I have extremely good news for all of us! Principilis is being transferred to a mental hospital run by none other than our beloved Bonhotei, it is hoped that under the care of Sacramenti he will make a full recovery and continue his grand work in promoting the ideals of Gerbalis"!

The crowd cheered and clapped thunderously in response before breaking out into joyous chorus and chants.

"Gerbalis, Gerbalis, Gerbalis, desert rats for ever."

Pinewood saw the crowd's eyes becoming glazed over with a psychotic obsession and he hurriedly departed fearful of the fact that he would have to join them in order to defeat them.

32

IRON'S HOT

Cyril Pinewood arrived at work looking extremely haggard and unkempt. He had not had a wink of sleep all night. The Gerbalis experience had over stimulated his subconscious and his moral attitude into a state of acute insomnia. Any word that commenced with the three-letter combination GER acerbated his sleep-deprived anger.

"What sort of twisted society am I raising my children in"? Cyril questioned himself as he glanced at a photograph on the wall that depicted geraniums in full blossom. "Poor blighters, subjected to such degrading filth"! Pinewood silently cursed as his mind raced forward to the up and coming Gay Mardi Gras that was held annually in Sydney New South Wales, one of the biggest in the world. An event which originated in 1978 as a protest march and in commemoration of the Stonewall riots, all those who participated in that era faced police arrest and unemployment as homosexuality was a crime until 1982. Many 'died' for their socially unacceptable behaviour; as a result the wider community embraced their 'martyrdom' and its cause.

The police and armed forces entered macho style floats in subsequent parades however the gay element amongst their ranks was never publicly made apparent nor condoned. The Mardi gras was a political quagmire, a wetland of murky waters where many a desperate politician went to resurrect their ailing careers before they went down for the third time.

The big event lasted four weeks and featured many cultural, artistic, activist and social events that included the launch party, fair day, parade and its after party. In this entire world event contributed in excess of one hundred million Australian dollars into the New South Wales state economy.

Cyril Pinewood's office was full of documents and books beginning with GER, geriatric, German,

"A geriatric German with a giant gherkin strapped to his waist acting as a green studded dildo standing on a bed of floating sauerkraut! Stop it! Focus! Stop this endless preoccupation with gays and gerbera's. What did I just say, gerbera's. Gerbalis, I wonder"? Cyril Pinewood suddenly thought as he switched on the office computer and did an Internet search for Gerbalis. Within 4.58 seconds one hundred and twenty five matches were found one of which included The Rainbow Syndicate. Cyril Pinewood's eyes locked onto it and pounded on his minds door to allow the information in. Reluctantly Cyril admitted to himself he had to learn and he slowly and diligently read the following paragraph about Rainbows purpose.

"We are here to provide a chat channel for gay, lesbian and bisexual world players. By making 'use' of the 'secret' feature in the club system we are able to keep the privacy of our members and the purpose of our worldwide club intact. The following are active recruiters to our cause and have agreed to have their names appear on this site. Womb, Pansy, Lickbanger, Wushichou, Gaelan and Gerbalis; members identities will never be revealed except with their permission."

"Gerbalis, Gerbalis, Gerbalis"! Pinewood repeatedly said to himself as he postulated the society's potential impact upon civilization. "A worldwide recruiting agency for a homosexual revolution in response to their suppression by heterosexuals in a pattern similar to the male domination of females; first demonstrations, protest marches, then unabated publicly supported gay parades followed by homosexual infiltration into fashion and music, both powerful pseudo-political arenas. Religion and true politics were left to those who kept their true natures ultra-secret."

The recruiter 'Womb" played on Pinewoods mind and he decided to review the information on the disc that Jarwood's secretary had given him on the previous night. Thirty minutes on he found that which he sought. A private members bill dated October 2001 appropriating five million dollars from Medicare for it was written funding research into the effects of excessive alcohol consumption on the endometrium before and after sexual intercourse.

"I don't think so! Pure bunk ham"! Pinewood reacted as he cross-referenced this finding with others on the computer disc, which revealed written authorities for payment of varying amounts to various insurance companies situated in New South Wales under the disguise of helping the state government out with some 'natural disaster' that occurred co-incidentally at the same time with the financial difficulties that the Gay Mardi Gras faced which threatened its demise. The amounts totalled five million dollars. Cyril Pinewood concluded it was a scam designed to keep the event afloat and allow the public assembly of Rainbow's members from all corners of the globe in Sydney.

"Wonderful use of taxpayer's money" Pinewood cynically remarked as he examined his present political position.

"Absolutely perfect, no resistance! Got them eating out of my hand"! Louis Badcock proudly congratulated himself as he terminated his call to the pharmaceutical police, an organisation responsible for putting real threats and quack's out of the market place usually by the most violent means available much to the populace's delight.

"If they don't do the job I've alerted the FBI and CIA in the interests of National Security as a back up"! He sadistically added as he threw away the misappropriated mobile phone that Ivan Gallows had brought him.

"You really don't like it" The D-man observed making reference to Badcock's competitor the Small Dark Figure.

"My compulsion is beyond obsession, it fuels my desire to annihilate it once and for all"! Louis sternly stated as he placed his hands on his hips, boldly spread his legs wide apart to demonstrate his courage and then said making reference to Gallows appearance. "I'm sure you know how constricted and caged I feel"!

Ivan remained silent, pensive and juggled the remainder of the phones that he had stolen.

"One last person to contact, mobile please" Badcock roughly demanded as he snapped his fingers. The D-man displeased with Badcock's attitude resentfully obliged.

"Useless! Sim card"! Badcock crudely barked as he pointed to the fact that the phone was inactive.

Once again Gallows obliged this time a little more resentful.

'Well hello is that the fun guy"?

"Pardon" Archbishop Steven Moulds asked audibly irritated by his caller.

"Aren't you the mushroom with the ten inch stalk"?

"Very funny Mr Badcock"! Archbishop Moulds replied as he accentuated bad and cock.

"Um fancy a drive down Hooker's Parade or Vain Street"?

"Not today thank you Louis"!

"Are you sure? I'm surprised you haven't made arrangements to sample our new stable of eager girls. What's the matter lost your interest"? Badcock irreverently teased.

"What's the purpose of your crank call, Louis"?

"I thought that you like I miss the original bevy of beauties." Badcock said knowing full well how frequently his Grace had dipped his stalk. "Let me persuade your highness." Again the archbishop said nothing as he contemplated hanging up on Badcock. "It would kill two birds or should I say two ugly situations with one stone."

"And what might they be"? The Archbishop finally asked.

"I that is we get our girls back and you reign in that trouble maker O'Reilly before he causes any more damage."

"It's not that simple. Matters have become complicated. I'll need time to think about your proposal. I'm not one to be blackmailed into doing anything rash"! Steven Moulds truthfully answered as he anticipated Badcock's threat of exposure. Meanwhile Louis conjured up all of his memory's images relating to the Archbishop, past, present and imaginary.

"Let me see, kissing under Holly, sipping on Brandy, sucking on Candy, fondling Felicity, nudging Naomi and your favourite the athletic Brittany, those long legs, well developed thighs, defined calves…………"

"Aaaaahhhhhh…" The D-man suddenly groaned. Badcock quickly put his hand over the telephone's mouthpiece and said.

"Sush…. It's not meant to turn you on, control yourself you sick bastard! Stop reliving your sexual experiences with that Italian floozie…"

"It's not what you think"! Ivan Gallows grimaced as he bent over in pain.

"Go and relieve yourself, the bathrooms over there you'll find plenty of lotion"! Badcock acidly replied before he returned to the Archbishop. "Lovely long slender arms, firm double D cup breasts, perky nipples…" Louis seductively said as Ivan Gallows continued to wince with excruciating pain.

"I think you should listen to him." Jack Stern cautioned as he materialised into view. Outraged by his intrusion Badcock threw the phone he was holding at Jack who casually stood his ground and watched the projectile travel towards him in slow motion before it disintegrated into a hundred small pieces.

"What were you saying about long muscular legs and ample bosoms Louis"? Jack asked as he directed Badcock's attention to the D-man who lay convulsing on the floor in a fashion similar to a woman giving birth.

"I bet you're wondering what's going on is that right Louis? Well let me enlighten you. It's like this. You see my crucifix, lovely don't you think with all of those jewels encrusted on it"? Louis looked on dumbfounded as his mind searched for another weapon to hurl at the annoying Jack Stern. "More than costume jewellery; insert it here and watch the magic begin"! Jack instructed as he removed the precious item from around his neck and plunged it into the sternum of the saint's skeleton that was fused to Ivan Gallows.

"Observe carefully, watch what happens next." Jack continued to instruct as he slowly turned the crucifix a full three hundred and sixty degrees until a discernable click was heard and with that all of the Infirmary's penthouse suite's lights died, all of its window curtains darkened, stretched themselves tightly across the window frames and barred any light from entering, everything was cast into darkness, Louis Badcock's eyes struggled to adjust and he stumbled as he searched the apartment for one of his many hidden loaded revolvers.

Jack meanwhile assumed invisibility after he removed his crucifix and moved into a neutral corner. He smiled in readiness at the comedy that was about to begin.

"In life following conception many of us start off as twins in the womb before one is absorbed by the other. Today Mr Gallows you have been given the unique opportunity of reliving the event and you Mr Badcock had been blessed by observing it ringside." Jack said in a velvety voice that lay halfway between a medical consultant and a wrestling announcer. "Did you by any chance remember to bring the ultrasound device Louis"? Jack joked as Badcock desperately tried to find his cache of weapons.

"You should really watch this Louis, you might learn something. By the way what sex do you prefer, boy or girl"? He asked tongue in cheek. "Blonde, brunette, redhead, what say you"? Jack asked as he watched Badcock intensify his awkward search in the pitch darkness.

"To your left Louis, that's right, a bit further on, you're getting hotter, stop, careful where you step, on all fours now, that's a good chap." Jack with his perfect night vision guided Badcock 'the lamb' to reach his useless endpoint. Badcock didn't know whether to trust or thank Jack Stern as he opened a cupboard that he hoped contained the assortment of assault weapons.

"I think you want the one loaded with Teflon coated armour piercing bullets; you might stand a chance"! Jack suggested before he asked. "Did you bring sunglasses"?

"What"? Badcock screamed hysterically as he cocked the silver plated Browning 9mm automatic and scanned the apartment with gun in hand, his senses strained to pick up the faintest evidence whether it was sight, sound or the smell of Jack Sterns whereabouts.

Jack Stern the patient one stood invisibly still, unafraid and completely in control, whilst Ivan Gallows continued to experience the agony of being reunited with his twin. Badcock dismissed the D-man's groaning and thought he had located Jack Stern and squeezed off several rounds. Annoyed with his aggressive attitude Jack Stern redirected the flight of one of the bullets and caused it to ricochet off a metallic object and hit the gun out of Badcock's hand, without further warning the penthouse's walls and ceilings it seems were saturated with and discharged a light of such intensity that everything in its patch was rendered transparent to the point of not being there with one exception, the saint's skeleton that was attached to Ivan Gallows. Badcock raised his arms to shield his eyes to no avail, as he could see straight through them, he closed his eyes with the same result, nothing could be shut out, excluded; the bizarre circumstances caused his head to spin uncontrollably until he could stomach it no more, he violently vomited nothing it seemed until he could no longer heave.

Jack Stern remained in his neutral corner and patiently observed the abundance of creative light assemble and channel itself into the saint's skeletal structure where after taking advice from its dormant DNA built its body anew.

"Arise Saint Ignatius" He solemnly commanded once he saw the saint's eyes open and he was satisfied that it was sufficiently protected against all future insults to its physical and spiritual well-being. The naked saint glowed with light and enthusiasm as it rose to greet Jack Stern.

"Born before your time, destiny finally realised"! Jack remarked.

"What is your bidding master"? The saint asked as he bowed from the waist and stretched the hapless D-man in the process.

"To keep this beast at bay for as long as you can. What do you think Louis, a good suggestion? Like your Siamese twins? Pity they're back to back doesn't make for a good long-term relationship unless they invite another couple over"! Jack spoke to a somewhat dazed Badcock who was busily stepping in and out of his own vomit.

"Wouldn't be much good in maternity"! Jack dryly commented just before Badcock lost balance, fell forward and slid face first on the penthouse's expensive floor covering giving himself a bad carpet burn in the process. Jack walked over to where he was laying and issued the following stern warning into the ear of the semi conscious brothel owner.

Mr Badcock, Mr Louis Badcock, hear me well. Please be advised on the pain of death to leave the honourable Brendan O'Reilly, his eight charges and the incomparable Yvette Bell alone! By the way I think your apartment is in bad need of refurbishment"! Jack concluded as he gazed upon the devastated and whitewashed interior in which nothing escaped the brutal bleaching inflicted by the incoming light. Jack Stern then solemnly blessed St Ignatius with the sign of the cross and disappeared from view.

33

SHOCKING NEWS

Once acting PM Cyril Pinewood had become familiar with the extent of the selective homosexual invasion of Austra-lia's political and administrative system he could no longer look at rainbows, small rodents or flowers in the same way again, gone was the magic associated with anyone of these.

There was a way out one that people with little backbone invari-ably take; to jump ship, to abandon, to depart or simply put ran away at breakneck speed And yet he felt that Harvey Jarwood's secretary wanted him to stay for she saw him as being the right man in the right place at the right time. There was a reason for this. Ms Penelope as she preferred to be addressed possessed a rather harsh attitude to life hardened by the fact that after fifteen years of marriage and having given birth to two children, her husband Ronald decided he was gay and left her for another man. Penelope consequently developed a pathological hatred of homosexuals and bisexuals and it was rumoured that she had been responsible for several mishaps at various gay carnivals especially those frequented by Harvey Jarwood incognito. The then Prime Minister never knew how close the enemy was at hand. It was Ms Penelope who had instructed her colleague the chauffer to take Cyril to the warehouse and educate him in the' parliamentary ways' as an incentive to ridding Australia of the vermin that sought to destroy the fabric of its society and those of others. She had in her own way waged war for over a decade against the Rainbow Syndicate's secret cause and could not believe her luck when Canberra was hit by the series of plagues. There was no time to waste; Cyril Pinewood was the man, granted he had been initially confused by Jarwood's charismatic femininity but now with that monster hospitalised and a state of national emergency in existence she was convinced to the absolute that the traits of honesty, fair play, resourcefulness, intelligence and determination would enable Pinewood to turn Australia's fortunes around and return it to its former 'lucky country' status.

It was 1:45AM in the morning; Cyril Pinewood lay next to his loyal wife and embraced her from behind with a mixture of love, lust and the seeking of reassurance. True restful fulfilling sleep had eluded him ever since he stepped into the shoes of acting PM and tonight was no different. The faint noise of the hallway's telephone ringing reached his ears and it increased in loudness the longer he refused to obey its call. Neither half asleep nor half awake a grumpy Cyril Pinewood trudged his weary body towards the incessant racket.

"Hello." He feebly answered as he positioned the cordless handset against his stubbled face.

"Top of the morning to you"! Brian George brightly and cheerfully greeted.

"How did you get my telephone number"? Pinewood asked annoyed that his supposedly silent number was public knowledge.

"We've got you under twenty-four hours surveillance! Can't have anything happening to you as well"!

"What do you mean by "you as well"? Cyril asked somewhat confused.

"You haven't heard then? That's not unusual for you Aussies! Always slow at your game"! Brian George brashly stated with authority then he continued to say. "You really should spend less time sanitising the news and just allow your media to do its job and report like it is"!

"I'm a little muddled; it's almost 2AM in the morning what could possibly be so urgent for you to telephone me at this ungodly hour"? Pinewood naked and hostile aggressively questioned the American President.

"Well boy probably two minor bleeps on Australia's history! The death of your PM Harvey Jarwood and the freak meteor hits on your Kakadu National Park and Simpson Desert.

"I've heard nothing"! Pinewood weakly replied, as his mind became increasingly muddled.

"That might be the case boy, but here its hot news, big news, released within thirty minutes of the events happening. Go to your computer and I'll patch you in." Brian George abruptly said and then patiently waited for Pinewood to obey. Pinewood with cordless phone in hand tried to remember which room harboured the family's endless source of Internet joy. After opening several doors including the linen closet and cleaning cupboard he finally struck gold and entered the right room. Tired, gloomy and anxious Cyril cranked up the out of date electronic box and parked his naked bottom on the cold vinyl covered chair.

"Who's your mother"? He gasped when his delicate testicles hit the icy seat.

"What was that boy"? The president asked pretending not to have heard Pinewoods exclamation.

"Nothing just talking to the dog"

"Lap.... floor...or guard"?

"Neither, toy actually." Pinewood honestly answered as he moved the fluffy stuffed Dalmatian away from the computer's keyboard.

"Are you ready"?

"Yes I think so." Pinewood answered after the computer had fully booted up.

"Very well type in the following website address, it will take you directly to the television station that is broadcasting the stories right now. You will find it quite comprehensive. We'll send our official condolences to the Australian people later today."

"Very kind of you.... I think"? Pinewood stuttered somewhat confused but glad that his sexual apparatus had slowly started to warm up.

KBW-49 the Information Television Station aggressively filled the computer monitors screen, Frank the cleverly dressed jovial presenter was at his entertaining best, rattling off one wise crack after another.

"Well Janice it makes you wonder what those Aussies have done wrong to incur the wrath of God"? He blurted all smiles.

Janice sat next to him and felt rather uncomfortable. She was not used to being in the studio as she was undoubtedly the ace in the field reporter who filed astonishing stories and received the coveted National Television Award for journalistic excellence following her remarkable coverage of the events at Newburn's St Pious church.

'I don't think we can assume that Frank." She replied with an artificial smile barely showing her teeth.

"Oh I don't know! Let's look at it on face value. Canberra's hit by those plagues and now this; Kakadu National Park semi devastated and an unexplained nuclear explosion in the Simpson Desert and to top it off their Prime Minister has been wasted! I mean assassinated! All in one night of feverish frenzied activity! You can't tell me there isn't any divine aspect to this"! Frank theatrically argued as he overused his arms by gesticulating them madly about.

"For once Frank you may be wrong! We have obtained amateur videotape evidence before and after the meteor storm. I'm certain our viewers will find it fascinating." Janice said in a no nonsense and calm manner in contrast to Frank.

"Once again viewers our illustrious award winning Janice has provided us with a scoop and whatever you are about to see is exclusive to us! Janice."

"Thank you Frank. As you and our many valued viewers can see on this footage the sky to the west of Kakadu has many shooting stars flying through it prior to the singular brilliant flash which represents the big one that struck the National Park. The amateur cameraman who shot this film is a fellow American back packer."

"I didn't know you loved roughing it Janice"! Frank interrupted.

"Depends what it is Frank"!

"Huuummmnn…say no more Janice!! Have you had the video examined by experts to ascertain the nature of the projectiles? Perhaps it was spare space junk re-entering the atmosphere or Superman on one of his off days"?

"Frank do you ever stop it"?

"Only trying to be helpful, you know adding a little colour"! Frank shyly replied as he adjusted his jacket and loud tie. "Why is there no sound"? He then observed.

"Thank you Frank. I wish there was no sound coming out of you"! Janice mumbled under her breath. "Retired Astro-physicist Doctor Neil Beckett who previously worked for NASA confirmed that the trail pattern is consistent with meteors and further considers that the number coupled with the strike is most likely the result of a medium sized asteroid fragmenting before it reached the earth's atmosphere. The explanation for the absence of sound is rather complicated; suffice that the radio-magnetic radiation emitted by the large object was sufficient to interfere with the video cameras sound recording system."

"Lucky we have sight"! Frank once again interrupted.

"Yes! We are blessed in that department"!

"Unlike the Aussie's hey"? Frank jeered. "So tell me, what about the nuclear explosion in the Simpson Desert, it wasn't one of ours was it"? He then cheekily asked with a mischievous glint in his eye.

"Its pure speculation based upon eye witness reports and their interpretation of the mushroom shaped cloud."

"Who were they"? Frank asked on behalf of the viewers.

"Indigenous people, Frank, indigenous people"!

"You mean the Waugal fearing Aborigines"? Frank disrespectfully surmised.

"No comment." Janice replied as she rolled her eyes in minor disgust.

"I say you don't suppose they were high on something like methylated spirits, aftershave lotion, no that's not quite right, petrol, paint thinner, glue, photocopy toner, spray deodorants, hair spray, that's seriously wrong, have you ever heard of a sweet smelling aboriginal? Under the influence they'd be seeing mushrooms everywhere, in the sky, over the water, on the land, little ones, big ones, pink ones, blue ones, real and magic"! He said with a straight face and total disregard for political correctness. Janice waited for the dust to settle before she intervened.

"We've heard rumours that experts from Pinegap are journeying as we speak to the explosion site."

"Good old Yankee's to the rescue." Frank patriotically sung as he whipped out a miniature American flag and shook it madly about as he asked. "Do we have close up shots of the damage at Kakadoooooo on my Didgeridoooooo"?

"We do." Janice replied trying to keep a straight face. "The same cameraman fearlessly went in search of the crash site and supplied us with this." Janice then allowed the videotape to run before further commenting. "As you see a huge explosion has occurred in the National Park, fuelled by what seems to be superheated steam."

"Can you explain that to our viewers Janice"? Frank asked as he stroked his chin and attempted to look serious.

"The asteroid was white hot if not in a semi molten state, it caused massive surface destruction when it impacted by virtue of its immeasurable inertia and then it continued to penetrate the earth's crust until it hit an underground river and vaporised its waters which you can plainly see knocked the cameraman off his feet"!

"Two explosions Hollywood eat your hear out"! Frank yahooooed

"Luckily we have secured our fellow American's cell phone number."

"He's injured"? Frank asked as he changed his tone of voice and caused concern amongst the stations viewers.

"Our expert Dr Neil Beckett suspects that the resulting vapour cloud looks suspiciously radioactive"!

"Conclusions Janice…. conclusions"

"Either a secret military installation or an illegal underground uranium mining and processing operation." Janice coldly replied. Her statement sent an icy shiver down Cyril's spine, which caused his mind to snap to attention. "I can't tell you any more until Dr Beckett examines the videotape in detail."

"This puts a whole new slant onto the story. I can see speculation galore, endless conspiracy theories and mindless chitter chatter. Changing the subject, tell us about the late Harveeeeey Jarwood." Frank grimly said as he pretended to be shattered by the incident; but just as Janice was about to present the news item he abruptly interrupted by saying. "Did we have another convenient American on the scene"?

"This time the story comes via the police scanners."

"I always knew KBW-49 was resourceful." Frank jovially commented.

"We understand that a blanket has been put on the murder which occurred as the PM was being transported by armoured guard to a mental hospital that specialises in difficult cases. There are no survivors."

"What do you mean; no survivors"? Frank dramatically uttered so as to startle KBW-49's viewers and sensationalise the finding.

"Just that"! Janice bluntly replied.

"This blanket you spoke of, was it designed to allow them, the authorities that is, to concoct some fabricated story about his demise, I ask you"? Janice remained silent and gazed at Frank in sheer disbelief.

"Well then looks as though we let the cat out of the bag and poked a few holes in their plan"! Frank smirked as he congratulated himself on his accurate insight.

34

CLEVER DECEPTION

The shocking news that U.S. President Brian George had relayed to Cyril Pinewood kept him up for the remainder of the night. Cyril could find no solace in his bed or from the welcoming warmth of his wife's body. He knew he had to come to grips with the ongoing bizarre events otherwise he would succumb to sleep deprivation and be of no use to anyone.

"Damn the astronomical mishap, damn Harvey Jarwood, damn everyone and everything! It's all so absurd; nothing matters! I no longer care whether it goes or goes not! Today I start caring about my family and myself. No good being the martyr, who the hell cares about me? Everyone is looking for someone else to be the Mr Fix-it, well it's not me"! A determined Cyril Pinewood convincingly told himself as he clumsily made breakfast for himself and his still slumbering wife.

He prepared the meal as quietly as he could, keeping the decibels low and was about to assemble everything on the breakfast tray when he heard a faint knocking on the front door. Cyril stopped what he was doing and cautiously approached the house's main entrance. The outline of a small petite woman cast its shadow on the doors glass insert. Cyril Pinewood analysed whom it might belong to and coura-geously unlocked the door.

"Good morning sir, I am the bearer of good news and bad news"! Ms Penelope whispered in a low husky voice as she tried to contain her sublime pleasure. "Harvey Jarwood is dead and as for the good news."

"I am the new PM"! Pinewood completed her sentence.

"How did you possibly know? All of that was kept hush-hush, not a leak anywhere"!

"Except in the USA where it's presently national news. They're calling it 'Terrorism Hits Australia." A dejected Cyril Pinewood answered and then he violently added. "I'm tired, grumpy and ready to punch anyone who causes me any further grievance"!

"Well we had better perk you up Prime Minister....breakfast"?

"I've already prepared it."

"Let me have a look, stand back"! Ms Penelope happily chirped as she forced her way into his kitchen, but before doing so she signalled the chauffer to join them. "Oh Prime Minister you call this breakfast"? She exclaimed as she poked the burnt pieces of toast and overdone scrambled eggs that resembled bits of coagulated leather.

"Not exactly befitting a man of your status or your ever faithful wife God knows how she put up with you I admire her virtuous patience. Yes I know you grumpy old bastard you didn't want any irritations this morning! Aren't you glad I'm here to protect you? Now sit down not another word and watch how breakfast should be made." Ms Penelope authoritatively said as she eagerly dived into her task.

Pinewood meekly obeyed and sat on one of the bar stools next to the chauffer who had already made himself comfortable.

"At least the budgie's sounding happy this morning." Ms Penelope observed out of the corner of her eye as she expertly went about fash-ioning the meal. Pinewood silently nodded in response as he cast his vacant gaze upon the caged yellow bird.

"Think he's happy caged up like that"? Ms Penelope asked.

"We let him out occasionally." Cyril sadly replied.

"Not exactly back to nature is it"?

"Suppose not."

"Glad we understand ourselves. Call your wife and the children will you. I'm about to serve up."

"Yes ma'am." Cyril quietly obeyed as he left the kitchen dinette area quite subdued and returned moments later with his family in toe.

"Good morning Mrs Pinewood, children, please be seated, I've just rescued your breakfasts from your.... adventurous and somewhat cavalier husband."

"In other words Ms Penelope he made a right botch-up of it."

"At least his intentions were admirable." Cyril smiled at the positive comment and waited for everyone to be seated including the chauffer and Ms Penelope once they had ministered to everyone's needs including their own.

"It's rather pleasant having your company this morning Ms Penelope." Mrs Pinewood genuinely said as she took a mouthful of her freshly prepared food

"I agree I would have preferred less dramatic circumstances however." Cyril candidly said as he appreciated his food. Mrs Pinewood reacted visibly and looked directly at him for an answer. Cyril felt the heat of her gaze and obliged.

"Early this morning our time the American Media machine reported multiple meteoric hits in the Northern Territory and the death of our PM. I can't say any more until I investigate both incidents and make an official statement." Pinewood unemotionally stated knowing that his wife fully understood the protocols involved.

"Well then that changes things completely! I suppose I'll be seeing even less of you, thought it wouldn't last forever, excuse me will you." She tearfully exclaimed as she stopped eating and left to confine herself in secure warmth of her bedroom.

"Poor dear comfort her Mr Pinewood. When you have done a good and proper job of it joins us and we will help you with your investigations." Ms Penelope suggested as she continued to enjoy the fruits of her labour.

If it wasn't stressful enough before it was certainly unbearable now. Sooner or later Cyril Pinewood realised he would have to make a decision pertaining to life's pathways the road that he was presently on read martyr on every passing signpost, a description that did not fit him comfortably. Every now and then an exit presented itself but the uncertainty of it thwarted Cyril and caused him to remain indecisive.

This morning was a slow motion blur, all sights and sounds appeared distorted, muffled, nothing was real anymore, a continuous slow motion event like one experiences during a motor car crash, the body's inbuilt neuronal mechanisms designed to protect its owner. Everything was suspended just like the private jet that Cyril Pinewood found himself on from Sydney to Melbourne. Ms Penelope and the chauffer were in charge.

"Approaching the corner of Swanston and Bourke St's central shopping precinct" The Chauffer calmly advised as he drove the Victorian state government fleet vehicle slowly down Swanton St. Pinewood sat in the rear seat next to Ms Penelope and reminisced on his past days as a carefree Melbournian University student studying the arts and law. He remembered his first brush with homosexuality.

"The cricket loving transvestites of Melbourne, what a bunch of weirdo's this place hasn't changed much"! He whimpered as he recollected the daily abuse he received from the local lunatics as he would come to call them.

"Your man is over there, across the road see"? Ms Penelope instructed the PM as she pointed her finger discretely whilst the chauffer negotiated the car into an available loading zone and then displayed the official government dashboard notice that would confer immunity against parking fines.

"Who am I looking for? There are thousands of people out there." Pinewood mentally exhausted asked in need of further direction.

"Stop being a pansy, for God's sake look! Over there, on top of the mountain! The Hoola hoop man." Ms Penelope forcibly said.

"He's a circus act."

"Doesn't stop him from being smart"?

"Hope you know what you're doing"! Pinewood grumbled as he alighted out of the car and followed instructions. He carefully navigated his way around the endless throng of tourists who stopped and stared aimlessly, when the moment was right Cyril crossed the street to be confronted by an unkempt Australian yobbo coming at him in the opposite direction.

The social security liability was dressed in a bright but dirty blue and orange heavily ripped tracksuit and was wearing nothing more than a pair of worn out black rubber thongs. The yobbo stopped Pinewood in the middle of the road's tramway tracks.

"You have forty-eight hours to change your clothes you faecal excuse for a human"! He violently shouted at Cyril and then kicked an empty soft drink can that lay before him. Stunned by the unprovoked attack Cyril stood still and watched as the yobbo ran off down the street and played 'chicken' with the Bridge Rd grey tram that rumbled along which would have reduced Pinewood to pieces if he hadn't responded to its horn blast and stepped out of its way only to be closely missed by another travelling in the opposite direction.

"Nothing changes." He convinced himself as he settled his frayed emotions and approached the Hoola hop man who was obviously pleasing the crowd no end with his pelvic antics at the corner of Swanston and Bourke St.

The elderly busker was clothed in a full flowing flowery dress, wore bright red lipstick, dangling earrings and had a headpiece made of plastic tropical fruit on his head. He stood on a pedestal that was covered by a cloth that bore vibrant tropical motifs and smiled endlessly.

Cyril Pinewood found a spot in the tightly knitted crowd and waited a full thirty minutes to no avail and thought to himself. "This is stupid! What possessed Ms Penelope to bring me here? All this basket of fruit does is gyrates his pelvis and keeps that plastic ring moving! Big deal"!

"Well my man pleased to see me"? The Hoola hoop man happily greeted as he looked directly at Cyril who stood close by. "You come to see Gee Pee that's right Gee Pee not tee pee, see pee, wee pee or dee pee no, no me Gee Pee! I'm the curer of all your ills." He said in an awkward blend of Jamaican and Malaysian accents.

"Who are you"? Pinewood asked.

"I told you my man, I Gee Pee, Ja-malay, my mother Jamaican, hot woman, my father Malay, worn out. I gyrate all day long, look see, people love me, hoop to the left yes, hoop to the right no, in the middle who know"? Gee Pee the seventy three year old Ja-malay with a perfect set of white teeth gleefully said as he sung the merits of his magic circle.

"You're not a doctor yet you seem to know things." Pinewood slowly remarked as he nervously frowned.

"Correct! Some call me the gyrating prophet. Your happy friend see me all the time"!

"What happy friend"?

"Gaylord Jarwood." Gee Pee laughed out aloud. "He come to me, not in me, all the time! You understand"? Gee Pee asked with a twinkle in his eye.

"Not really"!

"Then me explain. When happy one wanted to know what others were doing he come and see me first. Then he do funny business with papers. You know accounts of members who were private."

"Afraid not"

"Sad very sad you work on words. It become clear to you! Now what you want to know"?

"Oh yes, the meteors and Jarwood's demise." Pinewood tactfully asked.

"Very serious stuff; I ask hoop. Please no touchy it belong to Gee Pee, only let Gee Pee see, no one else very serious..........with happy one not hurry curry, funny curry, groovy curry more like nasty goreng that your culprits...and.... and.... space rocks not hit earth... hot dogs your sauce!

Pinewood frowned.

I see Gee Pee not successful...you want see yes"?

"Of course"

"Okay but no touchy otherwise Gee Pee no more...first you give Gee Pee money" Pinewood located his wallet and extracted two one hundred notes.

"I no likey.... money...plastic, slimy like your government Gee Pee want metal"! Pinewood extracted a hand full of mixed coins and proceeded to select the one and two dollar denominations

"Gee Pee not happy lookie over there.... Proper metal shop... he sell you good coin.... go"! Cyril Pinewood saw what the ancient Ja-malay hinted at and made his way to the coin seller, hurriedly purchased a legal tender two hundred dollar twenty four carat gold coin and returned with it post haste.

"That better, now here your present." Gee Pee said as he dropped a plastic bubble into Cyril Pinewood's hands.

"What the hell? This is a child's token, something you buy out of a vending machine"! Pinewood angrily said quite agitated.

"Not so, Gee Pee give you Table of Truth, you put it together and hold tight. Gee Pee not lie you see soon. You not be angry. Gee Pee good man always good man." The Ja-malay truthfully replied as he continued to gyrate.

"Table of what" Jarwood still somewhat annoyed questioned.

"Table full of treasure, he who takes fill pass into next life, he who do not come back again and again"!

"Very philosophical is that it, any more"? Pinewood asked feeling somewhat jaded by the whole experience.

"You come back anytime when you want to know more. Gee Pee

always here…rain sun wind."

"Always"

"Not Saturdays, Sundays Gee Pee go elsewhere."

Pinewood's mind boggled as to what 'elsewhere' meant. Cyril stern faced did an about turn and walked west into Bourke St Mall in search of a free singular metal seat one of many that bordered the tramlines that ran down the centre of the street. Luckily a few were available the acting PM choose one outside of David Jones Department store and was about to open the plastic vial that was given to him when the obnoxious unkempt yobbo the one dressed in the orange and blue ripped track suit appeared once again.

"Forty six hours and thirty minutes and counting remove your faecal self from these streets"! The yobbo coarsely screamed. This time he was armed with a Hessian sack full of empty aluminium cans and he violently threw one after another at the unsuspecting Pinewood who avoided them as best as he could albeit comically. Shoppers, locals and tourists looked on with a mixture of surprise and mirth. Embarrassed by it all Cyril sprung to his feet ducked and weaved as his audience pointed fingers and thought his misfortune was a free street act, part of Melbourne's Art Festival.

The now official PM pocketed the plastic vial containing the supposed Table of Truth and bolted across the street into the Myer's Department store, he ran at break neck speed and erratically weaved in and out of display counters sending stock crashing all about him. Store security was called and numerous guards were quickly mobilised. Convinced that the yobbo was a hair's breadth behind him Cyril found the escalators and sprinted up on after another until he reached the forth floor; there he made a dash out of the building across the enclosed interconnecting walkway towards the other Myers Store that housed electrical, bedding and household goods. No sooner had he rushed into the building he was then seized upon by three burley guards.

"You can stop running sir! Calm down! We're here to protect you!

It's all right, there's no one after you." The three combined to utter in a manner designed to pacify the PM. Cyril still extremely edgy breathed hard, his heart racing, his legs ready to make a break for it looked around nervously.

"I'll pay for any damage. I'm very sorry." He shakily and apologetically said as he became a little more settled.

"We quite understand. Yakov the yobbo doesn't normally behave like this, he's usually subdued, you must have done something bad to spook him"!

"Bad I haven't been here for a decade"! Cyril replied fuming at the baseless suggestion.

"Too busy saving Australia acting PM Pinewood, is that right mate"? One of the burley guards cynically taunted. "Brave of you to venture out alone, left your undercover cops at home? Give them the slip"?

"Typical just typical, let me guess, de-facto wife, three kids, large social security cheque, works for undeclared cash, milks the system because it wants to be milked, thinks all politicians are gay. Mate"!! Pinewood bravely threw these inflammatory words into the face of the cocky and disrespectful security guard and awaited his brutal response as he coldly stared him in the eye. Tense moments passed, each not giving any ground until one of the gentler guards intervened.

"Perhaps you could come with us, we'll need you to fill in an incident and damage report."

"Glad to."

"That won't be necessary PM." Ms Penelope sharply indicated. "We'll send some people down to clean up this mess, this way sir."

All three guards stepped back and made way for the Pm's determined secretary, she was not in a mood to be tampered with.

"Thank you, this way PM the car is down stairs." Ms Penelope led a relieved Cyril Pinewood out of the store and into Little Bourke St where the chauffer was waiting.

"Take me somewhere quiet, these people are nuts." Pinewood still a little ruffled bitterly complained.

"Shall do sir" The chauffer acknowledged as his mind raced through numerous possibilities.

"Feeling drained Prime Minister"? Ms Penelope genuinely asked as Pinewood settled into his seat.

"More than that, quite shattered actually, I feel a little more secure now." Cyril Pinewood prematurely answered as the deafening sound of an enormous crash filled the vehicles cabin.

"Get out of the car now"!!! The chauffer shouted as he just managed to escape from his driver's seat seconds before a heavy industrial dumpster descended from nowhere and flattened the vehicle. The force of the impact threw all three occupants onto the sidewalk and street followed by shower of shattered glass and other debris. . Each shakily clambered to his or her feet and panicked. Yakov the yobbo was behind the wheel of an industrial rubbish collection truck that he had rammed into the rear of Pinewoods vehicle in an attempt to seriously maim if not murder the new PM. He reversed the heavy-duty vehicle, swerved around the squashed government car and fearlessly sped down the street with forklifts in the down position. The sudden shock and consequent fright was too much for Cyril Pinewood and he discharged the contents of his stomach on the sidewalk. The smell of his own vomit acerbated his falling blood pressure and he fell heavily to the ground temporarily losing consciousness. Ms Penelope and the chauffer with guns drawn rushed to his side and stood vigilant until the paramedics arrived. They mutually agreed that Melbourne was not a safe place for the new PM. Once he had regained consciousness with the help of a little smelling salts, oxygen and a glucose intravenous drip, they bundled him into an available police car and under armed escort ferried him back to the airport. They breathed a little easier once they had boarded their private jet and were in the air on route to Sydney.

Cyril Pinewood looked extremely pale; a good measure of Jager-meister in Ms Penelope's mind would soon overcome that hiccup and restore the PM to his normal colourful self. He thankfully accepted the herbal infusion, threw it straight down his throat in one manly swig and stretched out on his extended seat to fully relax his body. Once the various herbs had done their job Cyril retrieved from his trouser pocket the plastic vial that Gee Pee had given him. He examined its contents very carefully and realised that there were more than four legs and a table top inside.

Cyril Pinewood repositioned himself and placed an empty breakfast tray that was nearby on his lap. He pulled the vial apart and poured its contents onto the tray's hard surface.

"Bloody hell what's this; an exercise in microsurgery Lego for ants"? He mentally sighed as he surveyed the veritable mini three-dimensional jigsaw puzzle. His anxiety did not go unnoticed.

"Would you like some help Prime Minister? A woman's fingers are more delicate, here let me help you." Ms Penelope kindly offered to alleviate his frustration. Cyril Pinewood gladly accepted and watched as she expertly assembled the pieces.

"You've done this before." He guessed.

"Perhaps" She enigmatically replied as she handed over the finished article and added. "For you sir, enlighten yourself."

35

HOT DOGS AND CURRY

Cyril Pinewood thanked Ms Penelope for taking the time to assemble the Table of Truth and was surprised how rigid the completed item was.

"Are you certain you didn't fuse this thing together"?

"I am."

"Very well, thank you for your timely efforts." Cyril gratefully said as he took another sip of his recharged Jagermeister and juggled the table with the fingers of his left hand. He studied it carefully and thought to himself.

"What am I supposed to do with it now? No instructions, bloody marvellous. Do I squeeze it, tap it; poke it, maybe I should sing to it? One bleeding mess after another! Gee Pee the cure-all I think not! My legs feel heavy; it's so nice in here floating above the clouds, on the clouds, rest at last…" Cyril calmly told himself as his body glided into the sleep mode.

"We have wigs, all sorts of wigs, all colours, styles, lengths, wigs for bald people, celebrity people, healthy people; sad people, no matter your state we have one for you"! The spruiker sang out aloud at the entrance to a by invitation only fashion parade. Cyril Pinewood stopped to admire his wares but was soon whisked away by his partner for the night. Cyril was present in spirit alone, partaking of an event that took place eleven days earlier in the hot and humid suburbs of Jakarta. Before he realised what had happened Cyril had eluded all checkpoints and stood amongst high-ranking government officials and top ranking military personnel. The elite group of individuals flanked both sides of a long catwalk and eagerly awaited the much anticipated fashion parade.

"We have wigs all sorts of wigs, we have uniforms all sorts of uniforms, army, parade dress and genuine combat! Korean, Chinese, Taiwanese, all match perfectly; all come with pretty blonde boy Port Arthur Style…you like"? The master of ceremonies asked in a clipped fashion as he strutted about the crowd with his radio microphone close to his lips.

"Okay five minutes…you people which style you like…. then we show you available elite…five minutes ladies, gentleman" Cyril Pinewood's body twitched as his subconscious reacted to the profound out flowing from the Table of Truth. "Well which one you decide…. Korean…excellent choice…time for killer's selection…. observe cat…. walk and screen behind it. Look… see…read… then you select…. Mr Training…if you please… music…lights…. action"!

Drums, loud drums, percussion, deafening percussion, pulses of light, dark skinned assassins in jungle greens, cartwheels, double somersaults, hop skip jump, slide, crouch, shoot, retrieve, bullets flying, walls shattering, people ducking, panicking, fleeing what next? Lights, blinding lights, no remorse, exhibition over, choice or no choice, officials too frightened to speak, military stand proud, job well done, the elite demonstrate their prowess, no choice simply send in the troops." Pinewood's body twitched again this time a little more vigorously.

"Darkness once again, fast forward time, it's now, lonely country road, I Cyril am on it, not walking, in a transport vehicle, heavily camouflaged ambulance, next to the driver, two cars in front, army truck complete with eight SAS at the rear, all four in radio contact with each other, everything running smoothly, five hours to go before they deliver the package, the happy one, Gaylord Jarwood. Routine delivery, everyone relaxed but vigilant, not expecting trouble, then four explosions, bang, bang, bang and bang. Four wheels blown, four front tyres almost like winning Lotto, left, right, left, right symmetry not possible, unbelievable, confusion. How did this happen? Red alert! Ambulance shuts down! Personnel stay inside…. lock down! Torches flash everywhere, fifteen people on the ground, perimeter established, guns at the ready, others examine the damage. Four further explosions, left, right; left, right, someone's marking you down, no longer random; we're the targets! All lights out, night goggles on! We've been trained for this, no problem, routine. What's this, blonde wig running across the terrain, a distraction, do not engage, repeat do not engage! Funny I thought I was next to Dave, he's dead, no sound. Mr Saville Row alias Jarwood also dead no sound! Everyone's dead but me! Heavily protected, armed and dead! Useless equipment! Our opponent's superior in all respects! Pay back time for interfering with their fishing rights! Australia's part of Indonesia's archipelago one giant landmass, Australia the biggest island, we belong to them, our waters their waters, it all makes sense.

Endless Australian tourists rotting in their jails for nothing, why didn't we learn, the blonde wig is back, its cruel wearer walks around unemotional, shades of Port Arthur massacre, same accuracy, same expert, not copy cat, but repeated! Why did we disarm? PM lays dead, extra precautions useless! Matter of time, before we become them! Once again dark, not so silent, this time I'm gliding, floating; extraordinary sky ship. I'm no tourist, Navy-Air force, Uncle Sam, hot dogs with mustard, New York side walk, heavily badged elite, highly trained, covert operatives, only selected missions, never reported, answerable only to the President himself! Warnings on internal fuselage "Tesla

Plasma Ray version SPWRX9" access code complicated, restricted to five people I'm one of them. Stealth bomber flies on Tesla technology, stationary, it hovers, silently, position assumed, sister above ready to complete fireworks, here they come, streaks of light through the stratosphere, target locked on, Kakadu National Park, underground goings on, identified, isolated, confirmed! Fire one! Fire two! All over decimated, natural looking, man with video on ground, one of us, transmitting data soon, US TV stations receptive, great news! Blink of an eye second target, Simpson Desert, sky show already in progress, magic mushroom time! One strike, chain reaction, everything's vaporised, everything's hot! Fungus is born; we're out of here!

Why is the truth so abstract? Something he didn't tell me! Don't think I like this table! There must be other tables to partake from, supposing there aren't, explains why romance was born, that's better, I can take it now, but not forever, don't think I want to come back, can't I just live in my fantasy world? Much nicer this make believe"! Cyril Pinewoods eye lids began to flutter upwards as sleep hormone retreated back into its neuronal caves shut their doors and allowed alertness to exert its influence.

"You're back in the real world enjoy your cat nap Prime Minister"? Ms Penelope jovially asked as she sipped on her half cup of freshly brewed coffee. Pinewood feebly answered in the affirmative as the experience left him feeling rather drained and euphoric.

"Learnt about the in's and out's of various things"?

"Disturbingly so, I'm afraid."

"For your own safety"

"And that of my fellow Australians; however I may need to qualify that statement considering the events of today."

"Thought about your next course of action"? Ms Penelope asked as she searched his eyes for a clue.

"Not really, fleeing Australia is presently very attractive given the eleven to one ratio." Pinewood suggested as he scratched his head.

"I don't understand."

"The answer lies in the disparity between our and the Indonesian's population." Pinewood replied as he reflected on the Indonesians assassination of Harvey Jarwood and the American's discipline of Kakadu National Park.

36

WHITE OUT

"Lot's and lot's of uniformed men in the audience tonight, I do love a man in uniform, brings the beast out in me"! Dennis Sauvage whispered to another gay ice skating performer as they both peered through a rip in the stages heavy crepe curtain.

"I'm getting hot just looking at those handsome devils don't think the ice is going to keep me cool tonight"! He predicted as he scanned the slab of oval ice and its perimeter. "Look at the Captain over there he's just gorgeous,and in just the right position for me to fall tonight and land in his lap! Lucky boy, lucky me"!

"Stop it Dennis! You know what the boss thinks about fraternising with the audience"!

"Haven't been caught yet few close shave's though." Sauvage remarked unashamedly.

"Come on let's get costumed up, curtain call in less than fifteen minutes." The fellow performer urged as he took his tall well-defined muscular frame to the dressing room.

The well-cut music form the Star War's film The Empire Strikes Back blasted its way into the auditorium and accosted the ears of everyone present, it dramatically heralded the ice shows tribute to the sci-fi adventure movie as the professional skaters dressed as Imperial guards, aliens of all sorts and the main characters of the movie stroked around the rink in readiness to demonstrating their individual gymnastic skills. Then the auditorium's lights dimmed and went out, the skaters disappeared and the show started in earnest.

The crowd thrilled to the exhibition of jumps; double and triple axels, double loop combinations, flips, lutzs and the seemingly endless spins performed in all manner of bodily contortions, upright, sitting, laybacks and more.

The troupe also used a mini-trampoline and Russian swing to catapult skater's five to ten meters into the air before they landed into a bed of powdered snow. The feats were daring and dangerous and required an expertise of the highest calibre. Dennis Sauvage as the Wookie dazzled the audience with his back flips and reverse double somersaults.

"One Imperial guard down, two to follow, outside edge, that was cutting it fine, power through, right edge, three turn, backward crossovers, flip back, over I go, oh that feels right! Big air, loved that one, caught the ice nicely, blades gripping perfectly, turn to forward crossovers again. Light sabre out, activated, throw it into the air, on target on cue, explosion, down it comes glitter and all fantastic! Power away, brief rest, coast, deep breaths, bit hot in here, legs fine, thumbs up from Mr Overseer, right next sequence. Hans Solo here I come, comedy, kids, adults love it, clown around that's it, something's not right, definitely not right, left blade doesn't feel secure, movement, probably me, the excitement of those handsome boys in the audience, the captain, God hope some of them think like me, here's wishing! Forward crossovers, six in total, left inside three turn, turn on the heel, Mohawk, whoops… one Wookie's in the air, armed forces here I come"! Dennis Sauvage the highly disciplined skater calmly thought to himself as he lost control, flew into the air, twisted mid flight and fell headlong into the audience.

Cheers of thunderous laughter accompanied Dennis Sauvage's

mishap, a natural conclusion considering the madcap comedy that preceded it. The slapstick continued as a sideshow as six army officers shot up from their seats, magically produced a full length American flag and draped it over Sauvage's limp body indicating that the Wooklie was dead. The spotlight fell on their performance as they ceremoniously carried Dennis Sauvage out of the auditorium. The overseer was furious.

"Who re-wrote the script? I didn't give permission for any improvisations, some one find Dennis...I want answers"! He furiously erupted even though the crowd delighted in the show's humorous accident. Moments later the news was not good.

"Can't find him boss"

"Understudy you're on, well go on then, don't stand there like a stunned Wookie, three two, one you're on"! The overseer impatiently commanded as he took hold of the understudy's arm and flung him onto the ice much to the audience's surprise, which initially gasped and then applauded rapturously. Dennis Sauvage was also on ice, one of a different kind.

"Are you comfortable sir"? Air Marshall O'Ryan politely asked in a deep manly voice as he adjusted Dennis Sauvages thermal gear.

"Oh yes, are you my hot date for tonight"? He asked as he surveyed the Air Marshall's finely chiselled facial features.

"Afraid not sir, I'm the transporter the entertainment officer will appear later."

"Awfully cold in here" Dennis observed as the surrounding air stung his face.

"No insulation military aircraft deliberately built lightweight for maximum speed and carrying capacity."

"Aircraft"

"Yes sir you're on board an Army-Navy turbo prop plane."

"Where to"?

"In you're in the Army now, soldier" Air Marshall O'Ryan proudly stated.

"I would prefer the Navy."

"Don't worry sir the incidence of your kind is equal in both."

"You're teasing." Dennis replied delighted at the prospect.

"Genuine classified statistics sir"!

"Hum what will I do, boot camp, hard on training, full body contact, um? Sounds so deliciously exciting"! Dennis gushed as he fantasized about possible and future sexual adventures.

"None of that sir, you're officer material, I believe you have been personally conscripted by the President for R&D purposes; I am lead to believe you're somewhat of a bug expert." Air Marshall O'Ryan dryly replied.

"At your service boy, however boy, since you're my inferior, tell me exactly where you are taking me, that's a direct order boy"! Dennis Sauvage grinned and bluffed as he relished his new position of authority. Annoyed at his statements inference Air Marshall O'Ryan sharply tightened Dennis Sauvages buckle that held him securely in place and in his seat.

"Firstly sir, you haven't been processed and secondly that information is highly classified, have a nice trip"!

"Ground crew in position" The commander in chief of the tactical unit asked as he donned his night goggles.

"Yes sir." His second in commanded positively answered.

"Markings correct"?

"Yes sir check"!

"Photographer, cameraman"

"Yes sir check."

"Uniforms uniform"

"Check sir."

'Excellent! Time to commencement"

"Three minutes and counting"

"Invasion sequence"

"Snipers in place will take out guard dogs and guards on duty using tranquilliser darts. On command power supply cut all systems shut down, team One from the north, team Two from the east, casualties will be minimal however all life threatening resistance will be countered by shoot to kill sir."

"Excellent…phase one …snipers on standby." The commander in chief said as he examined his wristwatch in readiness to give the order. "On my mark, steady…extinguish all perimeter guards."

"Yes sir"!! The commander in chief waited patiently for his second in command to report.

'Area black and secure sir"

"Send in the raiding party's, helicopters alpha, beta search lights on, wipe the area clean."

"Yes sir."

Satisfied the commander in chief took his leave from the highly sophisticated electronic command centre on board the heavily disguised emergency aircraft and returned to its cockpit. As the aerial control centre descended in the pitch-blackness to commence its visual sweep of Dot.org's farm the activity on the ground was frenzied.

Debilitating gas grenades exploded left, right and centre, outside, inside, high-powered pencil thin light beams sought out their prey, facsimile DEA (Drug Enforcement Agency) agents stormed the facility and nullified everyone and everything. Only one random employee was able to get to his mobile phone, ring The Small Dark Figure and leave the shortest of short messages before being knocked unconscious.

In the midst of the pandemonium the false DEA agents worked professionally and expertly, nothing was overlooked; all details were attended to, fast, invasive and destructive, just as it was predetermined. Dot.org's Alljoy manufacturing plant lay decimated, no memories, no process, no recollections, no records, only vague fleeting flashbacks amongst those who dared to remember. Dennis Sauvage's Messenger RNA Hapgen ceased to exist, the life taken out of it, the polymerase vats stripped of their reactive DNA.

"You have done well comrade! We have not seen such high

quality for a long time"! The grubby Russian arms dealer declared as he finished examining the sample of radio active Uranium in his peculiarly crude way. "What did you say its source was"?

"Kakadu" The American double agent replied.

"How did you manage to obtain such a fine sample"?

"No comment comrade"!

"Well it is good to see that the East and West share a common goal." The Russian replied thoughtfully.

"The world needs the Eagle and Bear if it is to survive, otherwise the Dragons will have their ways."

"Wisely said my friend when can you deliver the shipment"? The Russian asked as he poured two generous portions of Finnish vodka to stave off the winter cold. "Here you are my American friend Budem"!

"Spasibo"! The American answered as he savoured the delights of the wheat grain alcohol and considered answering the Russians questions as he gazed upon the icy landscape that represented the lonely Finnish- Russian border.

"Let me start out by saying that allies are not always friends, it is sometimes better to become friends with your enemies, at least you know where you stand and what to expect." The Russian nodded his head in agreement and took another swig of his vodka. "Our people the Americans have learnt a bitter lesson from those living in the great Southern continent."

"You mean South America"? The Russian eagerly asked as the alcohol stirred his loins to think of hot Brazilian beauties doing the samba on his naked lap.

"No"

"Africa"?

"Not exactly"

"What then I know of no other land apart from Antar…i…ca."

'Try Australia" The American answered without being patronising.

"What of it"? The grubby Russian asked as he wiped his mouth on the sleeve of his well-worn overcoat and then pretended to look rather perplexed as he could only vaguely recall images of galahs and kangaroo's.

"We have military bases there."

"Like us Russians comrade"!

"You jest"?

"Like my friend Yannick! That is a character I tell you! Poor peasant! A deluded scoundrel but entertaining none the less" The Russian laughed as he emptied his glass of vodka down his eager throat. The American double agent meanwhile wondered where this line of conversation was taking them.

"Ah yes the stories I could tell you of Yannick! Travelled the world in his mind and brought back souvenirs from wherever he went. I see you do not understand. Here let me pour you another glass. Zum Wohl"!

"Pohjanmaan Kautta"! The American countered in Finnish.

"I see you know your languages, perhaps you and Yannick were travel buddies"? The dirty Russian laughed loudly to which the American simply shook his head and sipped on his ice-cold vodka.

"Yannick the rabbit lived poorly often he would go away from the village in which he lived and return with souvenirs for the country that he had "romantically" visited. With these he would seduce the lonely and single women and have his ways with them by filling their heads with fantasy and the promise of helping them to escape their dreary existence. Yannick would bring back toy kaola's from Australia, Swiss watches; designer sunglasses from Italy, parfums from Paris; you name it, Yannick would journey there and bring it back for you providing you shared your bed with him. Yannick was a con man with an insatiable appetite for women. He preyed on their ignorance of worldly affairs and in essence brought them nothing but cheap hope and copies of the things they desired the most. Yannicks expedidi-tions were disguised journeys to average paid seasonal work in out of the way places. Once over he would find his favourite importer of Chinese made goods and lustfully arm himself for his next conquest."

He colourfully described in his rich Georgian accent after which he drained his glass.

"Almost sounds like the American dream."

"With one exception" The Russian growled. "He became a little too adventurous and double crossed his friend."

The American remained quiet and unmoved as the Russian poured yet another generous portion of vodka and continued with his story.

"Yannick took me for a blind fool and made a play for my beautiful girlfriend of many years while I was away on serious business."

"Yannick's no more"! The American coldly concluded as he grasped the significance of the Russians colourful anecdote.

"Dispatched to parts unknown so my American friend in this age of plagiarism where nothing is sacred this sample of yours will it stand the test of time or will it like Yannick's treasures fall apart? Genuine Kakadu or cheap copy from Chinatown" The American remained poker faced and examined his negotiator while he calmly played with the lead lined bullet shaped container that housed the uranium sample.

"The artificial hot stuff is Uranium 233 derived from neutron bombarded Thorium 232, this is high quality Uranium 238 with traces of Uranium 235 about 0.99% add a little green salt and smatterings of Randon and you have Kakadu Creole style." The American playfully answered as he threw the 'hot' item at the Russian.

"Still doesn't prove anything"! The Grubby Russian slurred after a chilly pause. "All it suggests is that you are a good salesman"!

"Fair assumption, supposing I told you that the shipment is free"!

"Then my friend it is time to part company"! The Russian roughly said as he stood up and grabbed his bottle of Finnish vodka and screwed its lid tight.

The American sat dumbfounded at the Russians abrupt reaction; he was about to speak when the Russian explained.

"Our glorious country, our Mother Russia is no longer run by political idealists they have been replaced by shady accountants. Everything runs on figures Mafia style. For me to accept your gift would cause havoc with their mentality, everything is business, no favours, these are seen as future blackmailing. Three things I want you; source, cost, delivery"!

The American double agent sighed heavily as though he had been checkmated; he bit his lip and looked downwards to give the impression that he was down trodden.

"Does Nghi Phamhung mean anything to you"?

"Sounds like a bizarre torture ritual where you would hang you enemy up side down from the knees." The Russian replied as he face assumed a simpletons' appearance.

"Phamhung is the ultimate wheeler dealer who has misled the US on numerous occasions. He pretends to sell us vital information relating to active terrorists groups whilst orchestrating the sale of illegally mined Australian Uranium. Luckily we managed to intercept a large shipment destined for either Korea or China."

"Great detective work on your part"! The American avoided the compliment.

"As to the cost, black market figures are always substantially higher than commercial when it comes to items of war, one thousand US dollars per kilogram would not be unrealistic for what we have on offer." The Russian remained serious for a moment and then burst out laughing his mirth echoed throughout the frozen landscape. The American held his ground and sipped confidently on his remaining vodka.

"Well comrade it seems we have a deal however do not expect any hard currency in exchange for your wares. Instead let us offer you gems from paradise." The Russian jovially said as he extracted a dirty brown leather pouch from an inside pocket of his fur lined overcoat. He gently untied the top and carefully poured out pure white and coloured diamonds into the palm of his gloved hand.

"Genuine Argyle diamonds cut to perfection." He proudly said as he allowed the artic light to fire up the collection of exquisite gems. "I told you comrade we have bases in Australia! Now when can you deliver"?

The American double agent smiled and reached for his mobile phone. He selected the appropriate number and when it answered he cryptically said, "Seal hunter satisfied" and disconnected the call.

Moments later the Russians mobile phone rung with extreme urgency, he retrieved the annoying device, as he did not have much respect for modern technology and activated its screen. "Not possible...."! He roughly grunted as he glared menacingly at the message.

"What's the matter comrade, eagle's become too intimate with the bear"? The American flippantly asked as he looked over the Russians shoulder and read the drop off co-ordinates for the Uranium shipment.

37

LOVE NEVER FORGETS

"Good morning viewers! Good morning to those who have stayed up late and a very good morning to those who have got up really early! One o'clock in the morning is pretty early for the likes of me! I usually do the day shift"!

Frank the boisterous news presenter at KBW49 sung out in his normal theatrical manner complete with comic facial expressions.

"Today we bring you a special presentation via our European friends France 2 Television. We thank them very much as we thank all those who make KBW49 the great information station that it is. Mauritius is the focus of our attention and hasn't it been an unusual week so far Janice"?

"Yes thank you and good morning to you Frank. Australia's long standing Prime Minister was assassinated, Kakadu National Park was hit by freak meteor strikes and the as yet unexplained nuclear explosion in Australia's remote outback not to mention our own domestic stories."

"Those Aussies are having a real tough time I almost feel like sending in the troops to help them out"! Frank said blowing his trumpet.

"Very charitable of you Frank, perhaps we could inform our viewers about our involvement with France 2."

"My pleasure Janice, my pleasure" Frank howled.

Janice hated being in the studio with and being seated next to Frank the buffoon. His aftershave was overpowering, his deodorant repulsive and whatever he sprinkled into his underpants made her want to heave her heart out. Janice secretly wished she were on location with those lucky, blessed French journalists.

"As some of you already know a certain Father Brendan O'Reilly rose to national prominence after the televised events at St Pious church almost one year ago.

We will now show you an edited version, what you are about to witness is genuinely real. This is not a computer-generated stimulation I mean simulation, it may be offensive to some and cause distress in others, it is intended for mature open-minded viewers, KBW49 does not endorse its content." Frank read almost correctly according to the political protocol before him. After the filmed and edited sequence had been televised Frank went on to describe the next set of circumstances.

"Father Brendan O'Reilly and his seven sisters it appears are very good at uncovering things or put another way he is very good at taking things off. In Newburn it was the sea of corruption separate to the miraculous healing statue of the Blessed Virgin Mary located in St Pious Church. Now on the Island of Mauritius in the region of Chamarel they have unveiled an ancient church of unknown origin and have given it the apt title of Church of the Coloured Sands. One of its central feature's is the baptismal font, which continuously overflows with life giving water. There is more! Watching can only explain what is really happening. Any comments Janice"?

"Leave it to France 2, I'm feeling a little nauseous, if you would excuse me, please." Janice politely asked as a wiff of Frank's underpants caught and held her breath.

"Poor lady; nevertheless folk's the show must roll on! Are you there Josephine mon amour, lovely name Josephine, exotic oui"! Frank blared as he raised one eyebrow, winked and adjusted his earpiece.

"Good morning Frank, a pleasure to speak with you and your many viewers. It must be early for you." The attractive journalist greeted in her highly polished French accent.

"Never too early to make sparks, I mean speak with you Josephine." Frank replied amorously.

Josephine accepted the compliment graciously before proceeding with her description.

"Through our mutual efforts a broad section of Europe and North America will watch a live coverage of Mass said by Father Brendan O'Reilly within this remarkable Church of the Coloured Sands.

Father O'Reilly it was rumoured not only discovered its invisible structure but also advertised it. He has through his sermons and I must say handsome looks caused quite an international stir. Further the rate of miracles that have occurred here is extraordinarily high. The women of the Island and those who have journeyed here are without a doubt besotted by the man. Brendan O'Reilly is rapidly achieving religious mega- stardom and yet he remains shy and elusive. We plus many others have tried on many an occasion to interview him without success, either we have been thwarted by jealous women eager to lunge at him or his seven highly protective sisters intervene."

"Lucky man, wish some of his charisma would rub off onto me, God do I need a good rubbing"! Frank exclaimed raising both of his eyebrows.

"Contrary to popular belief it is purely platonic."

"What is? Oh that I'm sure we all believe it." Frank replied tongue in cheek.

"Believe what you may Monsieur. May we return to the church? Today you will witness extraordinary if not supernatural happenings"

Praise the Lord, tell me more Josephine, more importantly tell me when"!

'We are aware that recording devices repeatedly fail inside this magnificent building. We do not therefore guarantee that we will be able to film the actual Mass and this becomes a contradiction in terms."

"Precisely just what I was thinking"1 Frank agreed trying to look intelligent.

"Having said that, take a look at this. The church measures approximately eighty meters in length by sixty meters in width; one would expect that it could house say two to two and a half thousand people, my assistant Mr Benoit has countered the worshippers as they have gone in. How many so far Benoit"? Josephine asked her twenty four year old cameraman from Lyons.

"Twelve thousand seven hundred and fifty six and still counting"!

"That's amazing, tighter than sardines, God do I like it tight'! Frank said loudly in amazement.

"You are wrong Monsieur, everyone is seated in comfort."

"Impossible"!

"It is happening as we speak. Benoit see if you can film inside using the telephoto lens." The young man obeyed and the image filled the screens of countless television sets around the world.

"Is this some kind of optical illusion"?

"No Monsieur I give you my word."

"Are you shrinking them witch of the North"?

"No." Josephine sweetly replied and avoided the insult.

"What if anything is a likely explanation"? Frank asked appearing non plus-ed for the benefit of his viewers.

"Like I said before it is just happening."

"Anything else" Frank persisted.

"We need to go inside and see" Josephine warmly concluded as she signalled for Benoit to accompany her, both visibly hoped for the best, both made the sign of the cross across their bodies. Frank mirrored their actions and attempted to stir up his viewing audience.

"It has been rumoured ladies and gentlemen that no electronic devices however sophisticated work within the wall of the church. So everyone cross your fingers, toes, eyes and more and pray like never before"! He profoundly urged as he and his viewing public 'walked' in time with Benoit's camera.

"So far so good" Frank whispered as Josephine and Benoit crept reverently into the church's foyer. "All I can say is that it appears to be truly universale in accommodating anyone who chooses to enter."

Josephine the seasoned investigative journalist examined everything as thoroughly as she could and then using the video camera's advanced lens system searched for finer details. The first anomaly that she detected was the absence of an amplified sound system and yet everyone it appeared could hear perfectly well once Mass had begun. Next she wondered why Brendan spoke in French, was it out of courtesy for the large contingent of French pilgrims?

"Benoit what language do you hear"?

"French"

"Thank you." Not satisfied she asked other worshippers randomly.

"English, Swiss, my native tongue, Mauritian, Afrikaans, German, Austrian, Russian, Belgian, the results floored Josephine who was about to contact the KBW49 programme manager on her mobile phone and ask him to conduct a similar phone survey when she was startled into realising that Brendan stood a few meters away from her. Josephine's heart raced, excitement spread like wild fire through her body and she could feel her skin tingle as she reacted visibly to his wonderful magnetism. Josephine swooned, as did the others around her and then from the corner of her eye she saw that Brendan was also upon the altar and other places as well. She reached out and touched him and was not disappointed.

Brendan spoke with a tonal quality that melted your heart, a voice reminiscent of all the great crooners who possessed the common ability to swoon the masses.

"Today my fellow human beings I wish to talk about love. I have read and studied hundreds of articles upon the subject and I must admit that I have not even begun to understand it myself. However what deeply disturbs me is how affluence within a society destroys relationships. I fear that we have personally lost the ability to discover and form new relationships. Everything it appears is electronic, Internet driven, people hide behind a computer screen, a code name and are afraid to be unmasked, exposed. Chat sites…impersonal, dating services…impersonal, gone are the days of hand written letters, messages that overflowed with romance, feeling and emotion. Men have lost the ability to communicate with women.

The Internet satisfies the adventurers in lustful love. The chase, the infatuation, erotic text messages, SMS's, all devoid of romance, empty meaningless words all dispatched to score, hit the target. Has the developed world gone completely mad? It's all about me, no longer the other person! How sickening that, men consider love as being an accounting forum!

Lava Dates…. meet your hot number here; let her erupt all over you!

Call Me Quick…. girls at your doorstep in a flash

Hot for U Asian…. Phillipino, South American, Russian, women from poor countries made ready for you

Is this how we should treat women? Men keep spread sheets, dossiers, whiteboard tables, scoring cards on their encounters; love to them is a hunt, a military exercise, devoid of romance, honesty and morals; they plot and engineer meetings for impersonal sex. Once the 'kill' has been executed, once they drain their equipment they forget and move onto the next target.

Women on the other hand in underdeveloped countries use 'affluent' foreign men to escape their oppressions and poverty, whereas those in developed countries use men to satisfy their fantasies.

Then the so called educated with have us believe that love is totally chemical in nature. It is driven by the hormones oxytocin and vasopressin, heighten these and she will love you forever, just keep supplying her with chemicals and you will have a sex robot until you tire of it!

I am ashamed of my own sex; it mistreats the beautiful creatures of our human race, namely women! They are not pieces of meat! They are warm, loving, loyal, passionate beings capable of achieving anything they set their minds to and what do we do.... we destroy them!

A man came amongst us two thousand years ago to teach about love and how we should care for each other. He dared to challenge the organised crime within the synagogues, he dared to cherish women and rescue them from the slavery imposed upon them and he dared to be an individual. The result is documented in religious history."

It was then that Brendan paused and realised what he said and hoped that no one would uncover the origins of his seven 'sisters'.

"One normally associates people's appearance with a particular place, my charges look completely different to when I first found them, no one will recognise them here." He confidently thought to himself before he bravely said.

"Women should be allowed to enter into any field of endeavour according to their talents and wishes, it is their right; there should be no impediments"!

Those in Rome who wielded the Church's immense power were not taken by Father Brendan O'Reilly's sentiments. The Pentagon namely the three high-powered elite, Buddha and Pigtail the Peg-leg Pirate sat and calculated their move. "This man is trouble he needs to be silenced"! They collectively thought.

"Women are entitled to equality befitting their gentle natures, yet this is not the purpose of my homily although the subject matter is related. What I am about to narrate is a true story which will confirm that Love Never Forgets. I could have suggested Love Alway's Remembers but somehow it does not ring true." Brendan held his audience captive; his listeners sat like little four-year-old children at the knee of their favourite grandparent who eagerly awaited their bedtime story.

"Many, many years ago in a large Austrian city there lived a pretty young maiden by the name of Leannie who worked at the local hospital as a nurse. Leannie worked happily at her job for it was her vocation and she was deeply dedicated to it and as a result she was the most wonderful nurse you could ever meet. Leannie was engaged to a fine young man called Peppy; he was extremely handsome and attracted admiring looks from women wherever he went. Peppy was a professional handyman and a very good dancer. He was expert at his job and never without work. This bothered Leannie for the overtime that he was expected to do cut into their precious time together. Patient and loving for that was her nature; Leannie tolerated his circumstances for she understood that all of the extra money that he earned would help establish them for the future. The highlight of the week for both was going to Saturday night dances and cabarets.

Leannie longed to be in Peppy's arms, held close and tight, swept away by the magic of the music and his brilliant dancing moves, a desire that rarely came true. Once they entered the dance hall, women of all ages and marital status threw themselves at him until he reluctantly gave in to their endless begging. Two or three dances with Peppy were the most that Leannie would experience on any given occasion; Peppy would always apologise afterwards at the end of the evening. "These women mean nothing to me you're the one I love and will always love" Leannie would simply smile and accept his affirmations but as time flowed on she became despondent and felt that she could no longer compete with all of his admirers; sooner or later Peppy would falter; consequently and with much pain in her heart she broke off their engagement and set sail for Australia to be with her elder sister. Peppy was devastated.

Two years later Leannie married a Lithuanian man by the name of Vidas, a dental technician by trade. Together they lived an intense life and dreamed of having a large family, a wish that was shattered by an unfortunate car accident; Leannie was a victim of being in the wrong place at the wrong time. She was driving home along the freeway when a young male hothead in a high powered four wheel drive rammed into the back of her modest car, mounted it and threw it across three lanes of traffic before it disintegrated in the crash barrier. The extent of Leannie's injuries made the doctor's declare her infertile. Vidas was happy to have his wife alive at least they had each other. He resigned himself to becoming a childless couple that would happily pour all of their affections upon Leannie's niece and nephew. When Leannie's father passed away Vidas suggested that her mother should move in with them and he made arrangements for their house in the hills to be altered in such a way so as to allow everyone their own privacy including the pet dog.

The years dragged, everyone was relatively happy considering until Vidas complained of a persistent lump underneath his jaw, one that did not respond to herbal, homeopathic nor pharmaceutical preparations.

"It's probably nothing." He would stubbornly say when questioned about it for it did not go unnoticed. Finally after much persistent nagging he finally gave in and visited their general medical practitioner who initially thought it to be a sebaceous cyst or an infected lymph node. The abnormality did not respond to oral antibiotics or any form of topical therapy.

The doctor decided to surgically remove the annoyance and he sent it to pathology for histological analysis. The news was not good.

"I always thought the Spanish Dancer would get me." Vidas nervously said on hearing the pathologist's report.

"At least it is treatable, but not by chemotherapy. Radiation is the best choice. I suggest we start treatment as soon as possible." The doctor grimly suggested as he literally pointed the bone at Vidas.

"Why the urgency"? Vidas asked as he felt a coldness penetrate every joint of his body.

"It is always better to destroy any cancer in its early stages." The doctor candidly remarked before he described the therapy. The oncologist has instructed the radiologist to use a narrow radioactive Radium beam to ensure minimal damage to surrounding tissues, but

I am sorry to say you will probably loose most of your teeth"!

Vidas laughed loudly at the therapy's probable side effects.

"What's so funny"? The doctor asked as he furrowed his brow.

"Oncologist's die from cancer, cardiologist's suffer cardiovascular disease, psychiatrists have nervous breakdowns, anaesthetists gas themselves to death and we gifted dental technicians loose our teeth! Ironical isn't it? Just as my dad always predicted"!

The Spanish Dancer was not a nice woman she was down right nasty. She started slow and steady by ripping his teeth out and removing half his jaw; then she stopped and stared as the doctors rebuilt his ravaged body, briefly allowed Vidas a rest and the illusion that all was well before she with supreme arrogance tossed her long raven hair back and rapped her castanets to summon her army of death. The soldiers listened to every beat of her heel striking the ground and marched onward and outward dumping an ocean of cortisol into his veins. Vidas lost appetite, grew weak and weary, slept day in and day out and became unbearably aggressive as his will to live plummet with his weight. Leannie his devoted wife and nurse cared for him with a loving tenderness.

She forgave him for all of his mindless indiscretions until the day he died. All was still and emptiness entered her life once again as it did when she left Peppy. It was during this time that she had a reoccurring nightly dream that featured two very sad children who repetitively cried "Moma where are you"? It lasted all of four weeks. At first Leannie dismissed it as the workings of her subconscious mind pinning for Vida's memory but this was not so. She would later discover through a clairvoyant that it was the souls of children that had chosen her as their earthly mother. The haunting dreams ceased when they could wait no longer and decided reluctantly to move on."

Brendan paused briefly to gauge his audience's level of participation. The people in his congregation sat mesmerised, his words had caressed their ears and stirred their hearts; they thirsted for more, even the men surprisingly.

"Thousands of miles away to the East, Peppy has suffered a similar fate. The woman he took as his wife had died suddenly from an aortic aneurism. Lila was her name and she was not dissimilar in appearance and temperament to Leannie. Peppy loved her but not in the some passionate way as he had loved Leannie. He felt guilty at her death because he thought he had deceived himself and her in not loving her as much as he had loved Leannie. His guilt was further magnified when he remembered how often he thought of Leannie when he was with Lila and he wondered if she ever knew.

Peppy had settled in a part of New Zealand's South Island that resembled and reminded him of Austria. He established a very successful and profitable 'Rent A Handyman' business and was not short of dollars nor womens' attentions. Of these Lila was the closest in some respects to Leannie and these virtues he cherished the most. Peppy and Lila did not end up having any children either for reason's unknown to the medical profession.

In the months following Lila's sudden unexpected and tragic death Peppy felt very alone although he was never without the pleasure of a woman's company. A well to do widower was the target of many women's affections, luckily Peppy was wise to this. Every night just before he fell asleep Peppy would whisper with a mixture of guilt and love "Leannie where are you I miss you so"! His patience was rewarded only because Peppy exerted his faith and never stopped believing that some one would answer which came in the form of a repetitive dream.

Lila dressed in a pale chiffon flowing dress came to him with two children in tow. They would laugh, play and sing songs of London and its courts. Lila would then show Peppy a sheep's head and say, "You must go there." The reoccurring dream drove Peppy almost insane; it made no sense, deprived him of sleep and continuously tormented his emotions until one of his worker's wife who was heavily into the occult lent him a book on the proper interpretation of dreams. Still it made no sense; it was a lot of mish-mash, koodle-moodle as the Germans would say. Even so the dream would not go away; it persisted with a dogged determination until Peppy opened his mind. The significance of the sheep's head did not dawn on him until one of his fellow Austrian workers joked out of the blue "There are no kangaroo's in Austria" this allowed Peppy to put two and two together and realise that Leannie was possibly in Australia. But where; what did London and courts have in common? Was it legal, regal or seagull and what about that blasted sheep's head?

"Ach du liebe Schnapps und Sauerkraut"! Peppy would often curse when he was stressed or needed a break.

There was not much point in telephoning home as his family members had turned their backs on Leannie after she broke off the engagement. She was nothing more than a distant unpleasant memory. Lila was showing him the way, a test of his love, he felt that she had in a round about way forgiven him otherwise there was no purpose to the dream.

"Why must I go to a sheep's head? What does that mean"? Peppy would often ask himself as his mind searched for answer obvious or otherwise. He decided to try the world's library namely the Internet for clues on his workplace computer late one night. The three words; London courts and sheep threw up fifty five thousand nine hundred matches none of which were very promising, next he tried London courts Australia, this time five million two hundred and thirty thousand matches presented themselves. The first reference was London Court Perth Western Australia it had its possibilities. Peppy then followed the link to Western Australia.com and allowed his eyes to wander about the site aimlessly until they detected an abstract impressionistic representation of a sheep's head, Western Australia's state map was the best example, Peppy's heart leapt and shouted "She's there" but his intellect demanded stronger proof. Faced with this dilemma he asked the woman who lent him the dream interpretation book for guidance.

"Your heart never lies to you, follow it and you will not be disappointed"! She told him with the utmost authority.

RESURRECTION IN MAURITIUS

"How long must I go for"? He asked.

"As long as it takes, one can never rush true love, the signposts will guide you." Peppy accepted the woman's wisdom, packed his bags and journeyed by air to Perth Western Australia. There he found suitable three star accommodations within walking distance of London Court, a combination of residential and commercial premises built in 1937 for the wealthy gold miner and financier Mr Claude de Bernales. The designers intended to create a structure reminiscent of Tudor England but as one walks through the Court a sense of France and Southern Spain makes itself apparent. Peppy found this to be true on his first day out and he understood why Leannie would frequent the tourist attraction. The Court's collection of quaint shops and café's provided visitors with a perfect blend of old fashioned surroundings and service. All that was missing were people dressed in period costume. If Peppy remembered Leannie's habits correctly, the chocolate, shoe and international food stores would be the ones that she was most likely to frequent. Would she be alone or with a friend, had she changed much, was she still working as a nurse, had she remarried questions that Peppy hadn't even considered before leaving home, questions of intellect not of the heart.

How many of you seated today identify with Peppy's pain? Cherish the moments you spend with your loved one, moments that you otherwise take for granted. Learn without losing your individuality what pleases and displeases them.

Peppy became acutely aware of Perth City's tight security cameras were everywhere spying for the viewer's pleasure. It was the middle of winter, an unseasonably wet and windy one according to the locals who knew no better, statistically it was average. Would such 'wild' weather keep Leannie away?

The dreams had stopped and no further help was forthcoming. Peppy was left to his own devices. He spent every day between 8am and 6pm aimlessly walking the streets, up and down London Court until it became a frustrating abhorrent ordeal, much like an outdoor

502

prisoner. Days became weeks, weeks, which weakened his desire. "She's not coming, I got it wrong, fourteen more days and I'm leaving, but I can't I need a friend."

Peppy consulted Perth's Business and Government White Pages telephone directory and located a local chapter of the Austrian Club. He rang the number and spoke with a very friendly middle-aged lady who upon hearing his plight invited him to the Saturday night's dinner and dance. There were a few tickets left for sale and she would reserve one for him. The day of the dance was truly miserable. One cold front after another swept through Perth and its metropolitan area, hailstorms, torrential rain, wind gusts up to 110km/hour with the consequent energy blackouts threatened to cancel the Old Austrian Club's social event for the night. Peppy remained optimistic dressed himself suitably for the night's occasion and the gloomy weather outside.

He admired himself in his apartment's full-length mirror and smiled to himself in remembrance of all those young females half his age that had tried to pick him up for a hot date. There was trouble getting a taxi, not uncommon for Perth even at the best of times. He waited patiently for a full hour and then some more before he obtained the services of one driven by an illegal immigrant. Peppy gave the appropriate instructions of where he wanted to go and hoped the Club had not sold his ticket as the taxi driver deliberately took the extra long route to Maddington where the Club was situated.

"Not a good night for party. I think lights out soon. Many repair crews on road." The taxi driver commented in broken English just as they finally reached his destination.

"Perhaps they have candles, adds to the romance" Peppy replied.

"You want woman? I fix you up with good one! Come with me, I show you good place, plenty women, hot, cheap, clean, I take you"?

"No thank you, this is my place, my kind of people, thank you anyway."

"All right mister that $59.50."

"Here's $30.00 next time take the direct route"! Peppy firmly reprimanded the driver as he left the money on the passenger's seat.

"You cheat me mister, I call the police"!

"Don't bother I'll do it for you"! Peppy forcibly replied as he produced his mobile phone and faked punching in the emergency number triple zero. The taxi driver sped away and nothing more was said or heard about it.

The Austrian Club was alive and well. Tyrolean music played by a live band filled the surrounding air and challenged the winter's storm to change its mood. The car park was full; Peppy saw that the Austrians remained as always resilient under the extremist of conditions, a tremor of excitement run down his spine and urged his feet to step forward and enjoy days gone by. Peppy quickened his pace to keep up with his pounding heart and was soon inside immersed in the European hospitality that he had so long missed. There was no need for him to previously fear, the middle-aged woman who promised to reserve a ticket for him was present and true to her word.

"There you are sir, a pleasure to welcome you to our club" She kindly greeted him as she handed over the reserved ticket.

"I thank you from the bottom of my heart Fraulein." Peppy chivorously said flattering her in the process.

"I'm afraid I'm a little too old for that." She remarked obviously taken by his sweeping compliment.

"You will always be a Fraulein to me"! He replied as he removed his overcoat and handed it to the young female cloakroom attendant who admired his handsome features.

"The ticket includes your evening meal here is the menu for tonight. You will find our kitchen prepares excellent cuisine."

"Thank you, I'm certain I shall enjoy myself thoroughly." Peppy predicted as he excused himself and made his way towards his allocated table. He left the foyer and walked towards the joyous sounds of happy music and the smell of stomach satisfying food.

The auditorium was massive by club standards it easily seated four hundred people, had a more than accommodating polished wood dance floor and a stage for the performing musicians.

A state of the art kitchen was located to the right, next to it the main bar, where beer and schnapps flowed freely, around the corner a separate bar existed for the cultured wine drinkers who only consumed the finest Austrian wines and spirits.

The evening's activities had already commenced some forty- five minutes earlier. Couples whirled and twirled around the dance floor in sync to energetic polkas and gallops; others sat in silence devouring their delicious food which never failed to satisfy their high expectations whilst the remainder made up of lonely and single individuals scanned the room looking for fun and romance.

Before Peppy had reached his table or even taken his seat a young lady from an adjoining table rushed over and asked him for a dance.

"Perhaps later I would like to eat first." Peppy warmly replied with a smile that made the girl even weaker at the knees.

"Promise"

"Yes promise." He happily replied leaving the girl happy beyond measure.

Peppy quickly worked out he had to order from the kitchen and the meal would be conveyed to him once the chef was satisfied with its appearance. Peppy choose Geselchtes which is smoked bacon thickly cut and served with crusty bread as an entree, Tafelspitz as the main, prime rump steak boiled and garnished with horse-radish, apple sauce, chives and served with roast potatoes or knodels, light fluffy dumplings made from flour, potatoes, semolina, bread rolls, ricotta cheese and yeast. It was a toss up between Apfelstrudel and Sacher Torte for sweets. Judging by the amount of Apfelstrudel going out it had to be extremely good. Coffee could wait until he needed reviving. Alcoholic beverages were not included in the price of admission; Peppy avoided these, for the atmosphere was intoxicating enough.

Peppy could feel numerous eyes upon him as he enjoyed the

memories of Austria which were infused into the food that he ate and he engaged in meaningless conversation in his mother tongue with the people assembled at the same table. The young lady whom had asked him for a dance before was by his side again by the time he had taken his last bite and she eagerly asked.

"Are you ready"?

"Very well let's dance." He answered with a suppressed sigh not wishing to disappoint her any further.

The polkas had finished replaced by slow waltzes and erotic tangos. She clung onto him with such desire that it made it difficult for him to manoeuvre her around the room. Two dances later they parted company much to her disappointment as the tempo changed and the orchestra announced for couples to take position for the social barn dance. Around and around they went, in and out, swapping, changing, increased body contacts, more impressions, abundant awakenings, peppy a rare specimen amongst men, gentle, talented, fun, a joy for all women; history repeating itself until as an act of God would have it the lights went out.

"Schnapps und Sauerkraut"! He cursed as he fumbled his way in the crowd of dancers, people laughed, giggled, kissed and more, men pinched, squeezed and tickled their whores who resisted not until the lights came on for a brief moment before the wind, the tree and the outside power line resumed their battle.

The storm threw the wind against the tree and forced it to bend to its will, the mighty eucalypt took root and refused to budge shedding a few minor branches in the furore that ensued. The wind obedient to its master whipped the tree with the electrical power line causing it to 'bleed' but the resilient tree would not yield. The wind continued its lashings until sparks flew into and lit the night sky with an enormous discharge of electricity. The power line lay spent, ripped away from its moorings, useless to the storm. Inside the Austrian club everyone remained safe, unfazed, with no emergency lighting, dozens of candles of all sizes, shapes and colours were hastily lit.

The orchestra's musicians switched on their music stands battery powered lights and continued playing to soothe the savage beast outside. The melody's sweet notes enraged the winter storm and it retaliated by shaking the whole area with an awesome barrage of thunder and lightening.

Instead of becoming frightened or submissive, the defiant orchestra shivered once only and then took advantage of the storm's energy by delivering a perpetual, strident and boisterous rendition of Johann Strauss II Thunder and Lightening polka.

In the midst of the mayhem Peppy was shunted to and fro by the seemingly endless line of women eager to be with him for a brief moment or two. They sped past tables, chairs, the kitchen; other couples and then something familiar, a scent halted everything, like a dog who has never forgotten his family; Peppy's olfactory senses reacted to a fragrance from a time long ago, distinctive, individual, lingering and unforgettable.

"She's here, no doubt about it"! He convinced himself as he allowed his nose to lead the way until he was centimetres away from the woman of his dreams. Leannie stood with her back to him and was chatting with one of the kitchen hands. Peppy bravely reached out and nervously touched her on the shoulder. "Fraulein… bitte zum tanz" He gently asked in Austrian as he for once stood alone.

Leannie unaware slowly turned around to face the stranger uncertain who he was. The years had been kinder to Peppy, he had hardly aged, Leannie gasped with surprise. "What are you doing here"?

"I came to find you."

"How did you know"? She asked feeling somewhat embarrassed.

"Love has a way." Peppy quietly answered as he took hold of her hand drew it towards his lips and kissed it tenderly. Leannie avoided eye contact withdrew her hand and coldly replied.

"I'm still in mourning, this is bad timing."

It was not the answer Peppy expected; he had travelled thousands of miles, waited and searched patiently for weeks. " I understand"

Is all that he could reply as his heart remembered the first time Leannie had torn it apart, then with a remaining glimmer of hope he produced a business card with his contact details. "Call me when you are ready." He politely offered, turned on the heel of his shoe and disappeared into the darkness of the winter's stormy night.

"Aaaahhhh" The congregation sadly groaned as it felt Peppy's painful frustration. Brendan stood poker faced not wishing to reveal the stories ending, he waited for the worshippers to settle down and end their speculations before he continued.

Weeks after he returned home Peppy had one final dream of his deceased wife. This time the children had gone; London, its courts and the sheep head no longer featured instead Lila floated by his bedside in a full-length white flowing dress that gave off a bluish tinge of light; tied around her waist was a thick gold braided cord. Lila radiated an angelic aura that filled the room with heavenly light; she smiled serenely and softly whispered into his ear.

"Thank you Peppy for loving me in the way you did, it meant so much to me. Perhaps we will meet again this was my gift to you, goodbye." She ended making reference to the previous repetitive dream.

Lila's words haunted Peppy's moral and ethical side for months to come. He dammed himself daily for not loving his wife one hundred percent of the time. He dammed himself for remembering Leannie and then he blamed himself for his wife's death thinking that somehow through unseen forces he had caused it. Peppy sought help from as many people as possible in order to solve his dilemma, not one remotely provided him with a satisfactory solution, poor, poor Peppy; unhappy distraught Peppy; alone once again and afraid that he had wronged and destroyed a fine woman.

When his spirits had reached an all time low and he seriously considered abandoning everything in his life and starting afresh in a third world country the telephone rang unexpectedly one day at three o'clock in the morning.

"Hello Peppy here, what mach's du"? He drowsily answered.

"Peppy it's me Leannie."

"Yes." He answered still immersed in his dream world.

"Have you time to talk." She asked completely oblivious to the time difference between Western Australia and New Zealand.

"Yes." Peppy replied becoming increasingly alert.

"I thought about what you said."

"Yes."

"Do you still want to find me"?

"Yes." He guessed rather than answer with some reservation.

"Then can I come and see you"?

"Of course" He shakily replied.

"It might be a while." Leannie explained

"Why is that"?

"Vidas invested our money badly, it's very messy; mother is trying to sort out our finances."

"Give me your details, I'll arrange everything." Peppy boldly suggested as he threw caution and all of his worries to the wind.

Brendan paused once again and took a sip of water to lubricate his throat and re-hydrate his vocal cords.

When Leannie arrived two weeks later it was initially strange and awkward for both of them, no longer in their early twenties life's experiences and the passage of time had changed them both. They had married different people and were single once again in altered states, a fragment of their previous love for each other tentatively lingered; however it was weakened by Leannie's fear that Peppy would abandon her once he learnt that she was declared by the doctors to be infertile.

At Peppy's insistence Leannie stayed at his well-appointed house in the guest room. They started out as two separate people sharing the same house until they felt comfortable with each other's feelings, it was then and only then that they confided their deepest fears to each other. Things changed, Peppy lost his personal blame and felt that his deceased wife Lila had helped him to find Leannie, obviously

509

she still cared for his earthly happiness and made the road open for him to freely journey wherever he wanted.

Leannie never suspected that Peppy was relatively well to do; it was not her intention to take advantage of a wealthy man. She postulated that either divine providence or love as Peppy had put forward at the Austrian club had brought them together once again.

Leannie helped Peppy in his business, she was a very efficient bookkeeper and an excellent first aid officer; her presence brought a new freshness to his Rent a Handyman business venture which was much appreciated by staff and customers alike.

Strangely enough their relationship throughout remained platonic, meaning they had not entered into sexual intercourse with each other. Leannie was shy and Peppy would only commit to the act when he had convinced himself that he truly loved her, it was one of Peppy's ultimatums to himself.

"You must love a woman truly before you make love to her otherwise you are nothing more than an animal which acts out of reproductive instinct."

It was then that Yvette looked at Jack Stern and wondered how many woman he had bedded and under what circumstances. She thought for a while and reflected on the days when they shared lazy afternoons in bed at their Club Med chalet, topless Yvette would lie on Jack's naked muscular chest, he would warp his arms around her and gently caress her virginal breasts without proceeding any further, it both delighted and frustrated Yvette in that she did not understand where she stood with him until the day Jack explained that he did not want to ravage her innocence.

As chivalrous as his rule may sound Leannie found Peppy's reserved behaviour frustrating. She thought that he did not find her sexually attractive and was seeing other women on the side for there was no shortage of female admirers. Peppy on the other hand was simply nervous, he wanted to make a move but didn't know what brought Leannie pleasure. After all she had been with another man, could Peppy compete with the memory of another expert lover? Did it matter? Would love find a way?

It so happened that Leannie's birthday fell during her stay with Peppy, a date that she did not mention but one that Peppy had never forgotten. On the morning Peppy arose earlier than usual and went to great lengths to prepare an expert breakfast for the occasion. On a large hand carved serving tray Peppy had arranged a selection of Austrian style pastries that he had fetched from the local French Patisserie, scrambled eggs with gravlax and lettuce, Greek style yoghurt with fresh blueberries and a jug of percolated Viennese style coffee. He also brought a large gift wrapped heavy package and a vase of red roses.

"Good morning my sweetness happy birthday"! He gently whispered into Leannie's ear after he had placed the breakfast tray on the bedside table.

"Pardon… what time is it"? She drowsily asked as she stirred out of her deep slumber.

"Time to celebrate the occasion of your glorious birth"!

"Mein himmel; you remembered, what an unexpected surprise, thank you my darling, but you shouldn't have." Leannie exclaimed as she spied the smorgasbord of food and the vase of red roses. "How beautiful, how thoughtful of you"!

"It was my pleasure."

"You went to a great effort, there's enough food here to feed five people, please join me."

"If you insist"! Peppy replied and waited patiently for Leannie to make herself comfortable before he placed the tray on her lap and then drew up a chair next to her. Halfway through their meal Peppy picked up the package off the floor and nervously presented it to her. "For you"!

"Oh thank you, you shouldn't have, the roses were more than sufficient"!

"Please open it." Peppy said nervously as he left to insert a compact disc into the bedrooms modest hi-fi system.

Leannie fumbled with the gift wrapping and opened the cardboard box to discover a leather bound telephone book.

"A very practical present; what made you think of this." She asked clearly demonstrating her confusion by frowning.

"I thought if you were intending to stay longer you should have your own personal copy, perhaps you should flick through the pages to familiarise yourself with its contents." Peppy nervously suggested as he pressed play on the hi-fi system.

"It's a telephone book how complicated can it be"? Leannie asked clearly perplexed.

"Try it."

Leannie picked up the book by its spine and rapidly thumbed her way through its pages, as she did so, a little gift wrapped box fell out , it had been cleverly concealed in a void cut out in the centre of the telephone directory. Peppy watched anxiously and hoped.

"What's this Peppy"?

"Open it I hope you like it." He replied as the music started to play on the bedrooms modest audio system. Leannie closed her eyes and hoped as much as Peppy that it was what she had wished for. The red and gold wrapping came away easily to reveal a small blue velvet covered box, Leannie held her breath as her fingers trembled with excitement as they struggled to open its lid. Inside sat a yellow gold engagement ring that held a 2.5 carat brilliant cut white diamond that shimmered and sparkled with an intense fire that was fuelled by true love.

"Oh Peppy what does this mean." She asked after she had wiped away her tears of surprise and joy.

"That I want you….no…I mean …would you consider spending the rest of your life with me"? He nervously stuttered as the melody Quando Quando played on the stereo. Needless to say Leannie had no hesitation in saying yes.

Well I suppose ladies and gentlemen, you expect me to tell you that this story ended like a fairy tale and they lived happily ever after? I would like to but as you all know life has its ups and downs, they quarrelled and loved as any genuine couple in love but they never became angry with each other. Leannie sold her house in Australia and together with her mother settled in with Peppy and surprise, surprise; twins were born to her within two years of their marriage!

A medical miracle, perhaps, Peppy has his own beliefs on this score; he is firmly convinced that his first wife Lila had something to do with it for he constantly remembers her parting words " This is my gift to you" Peppy now has the opposite dilemma, does he stop remembering his first wife?

38

EVERLASTING VIRGIN

Max Dhaarling locked himself away in the 'dungeon' as it as called by the staff of the Babystore. He had had enough of retailing. Max like many of Australia's disillusioned population decided to watch SBS's delayed telecast of France 2's coverage of the mass at the Church of the Coloured Sands. He had seen the promo on the previous day and perceived the event to be an answer to his prayer.

Max Dhaarling never got over Expedita Shocker she remained a haunting memory one that reminded him of a childhood sweetheart. The Babystore provided its staff with a middle of the road 70cm colour television complete with an inbuilt DVD player; it was securely bolted to the floor and wall. The entertainment unit was purchased for the purpose of assisting staff to 'chill out' whenever the need arose thereby reducing absenteeism and improving productivity. Max Dhaarling listened intently to Brendan O'Reilly's sermon word for word and when he saw a glimpse of Expedita Shocker in one of the front pews near the main altar his heart faltered as he reflected on his life and his relationship with his wife. Max Dhaarling ultimately realised that he was tired of his wife's constant lecturing it infected everything she did and touched. She was obsessed with achievement; there was no family life, no intimacy, only work, work and more work. Investigate every angle to maximize the dollar, worship the dollar, please the dollar, kiss the dollar, live and die for the dollar.

Merry Dhaarling's unwavering preoccupation with wealth slowly and surely drove Max and his daughter Precious away from her. She was completely and utterly consumed by Western style materialism, something that Max Dhaarling found hard to come to grips with. He often thought about the life he left behind and concluded that irrespective of the glamour that Western society projected he was not suited to its way of existence. Max Dhaarling longed for the simple Sudanese ways, his soul thirsted to relive and experience the sweet idyllic village life that he had enjoyed before the soldiers came and almost destroyed everything.

Perhaps there was no need to have been enlisted by the unseen Franck Max Climax or arranged to be married to the older Merry Dhaarling and exported to Australia, speculation and doubt originating out of the mind of a successful businessman.

Father Brendan O'Reilly's homily teased, tormented and tore at the heartstrings of Max Dhaarling. What ever His name was that lived two thousand years ago perhaps He had the right idea for peace irrespective whether it was on an individual, national or global basis. Max Dhaarling identified with Peppy's dilemma; Titi was her name of Nigerian parents, born in the Sudan, she was Max's first and only love. She came with a certificate of virginity, a document contrived and issued by the village only after a thorough examination of the girl's intimate and private 'oasis'. Max and Titi would often joke about it, they loved each other intensely and deliberately saved themselves for their wedding day a measure of their mutual love. Max was devastated when the soldiers came and took Titi as a prize.

Although Australia was good to Max, its disintegrating society had an adverse effect upon his brother Acku. Unable to find one of his own kind that he could relate to either male or female, Acku invested in a blue-eyed mannequin, not the living variety, the ones that various stores use to display their merchandise. Acku's was soft, with fully flexible limbs, hour glass figure, a head of genuine human hair, porcelain like skin, natural feeling large breasts, perfect in every detail, ageless, complete with fully functional genitalis, only Acku and Max knew of her existence. Acku ate with her, talked to her, slept with her and more, she was always receptive and never suffered with a headache, He even offered her to Max when he felt that his brother needed a release from his sexual tensions. Max always declined saying it was not right as she was Acku's woman and he needed to respect that. Max saw much mistreatment of the opposite sex in Australia and as a result he detected an undercurrent of aggression towards males. Merry he felt had been influenced by it; she was now the perfectly structured woman in all respects, appearance, behaviour and dress. Everything about her was automatic, no spontaneity, no frivolity, no gaiety, everything was regimented by her desire to achieve, and stay focused, no distractions and above all no tomfoolery.

Brendan O'Reilly had become unwittingly a champion for women, did this priest realise what he had embarked upon? Max felt sorry for him and secretively wished him well, thanked him for his enlightenment and the strength and courage to find Titi if she was still alive, perhaps like the story that Brendan had just told 'Love finds a way'. With courage and strength came faith, Max Dhaarling returned to his executive office and pretended to work normally for the rest of the day. As he did he recovered all of the essentials needed to journey back home from their secret hiding places, his stash of credit cards, American dollars, and his Australian and Sudanese passports both of which were kept up to date. Max then organised a plane flight via Air Mauritius to Mauritius and a connecting flight from there to the African continent where he would travel by bus and train until he reached home. In fox like fashion Max covered his trail, he left a message on his residence's answering machine advising that he would be home no earlier than midnight if not after, on the pretext that he had been invited to a children's warehouse fashion showing which would be followed by a sumptuous a la carte dinner at a nearby Italian restaurant. Max knew that Merry could not attend as she was in the hectic time of the academic year with many assignments to mark and lectures to prepare. It all fitted so well together, escape was his. Max decided to stay the night at a motel under his Sudanese name and then go by taxi to Perth's international airport. He left the Babystore at 7.30pm, locked it securely, took one last lingering look at the building and his achievements, breathed deeply and took his first step for home.

Max unlocked his car and threw his battered valise case onto the passenger seat. Once behind the steering wheel he inserted the key into the ignition switch and was about to turn the engine on when a low voice from the rear said.

"Did you think you could leave without me"?

Max literally froze, his breathing stopped, his face reddened, perspiration beaded on his furrowed forehead and all the hairs on his body became erect. He gazed into the rear vision mirror to see who was there; nothing. He mentally searched for a weapon of self-defence after recalling that there had been a spate of car hijackings recently. He sat still and thought it best to say nothing and let the voice speak again.

"Well answer me"! The voice firmly demanded, Max could not and in his frightful state had difficulty recognising the intruder.

"I said did you think you could leave without me"? The voice asked a little more insistent but still no image of its owner. In a split second decision Max decided to make a bolt for it, he reached for the door handle and forced it down, nothing, it was locked.

"How the....."?

"What's the matter can't escape"?

The ordeal became frightening beyond all respects, Max hadn't felt such fear since the day when the soldiers came and ravaged his village. He reached forward and activated the car's remote to electronically deactivate the car's central locking system and he forcibly attempted to escape once again. Every move he made was countered he was trapped.

"Would you like an explanation"? The voice teased with a sublime pleasure that resembled a snake about to partake of its kill.

"Yes" Max feebly answered.

"I've got the other remote"!!!

"Who would want to play such a sadistic trick on me? Why hasn't he already attacked me, why the agony'? Max rapidly thought as he mustered up the courage to turn around and face his tormentor.

"Surprised to see me"?

"Precious! How could you do this to me"?

"Because you were leaving without me, that's why"! She replied as she removed the voice modulator from her throat.

"How did you know"? Max asked as shame crept into his body.

"Us women have a way of knowing"!

"Does that mean you mother knows" Max asked visibly shaken at the prospect of it being true.

"Don't be silly she's all wrapped up in herself! So Pap where are we going"?

"Home"

"You mean the Sudan…yippee." Precious shouted with a gleam in her eyes.

"Yes."

"For joy"!!! She happily exclaimed.

"What about your studies"?

"I'll finish them in England or maybe not, perhaps I'll satisfy my genetic memory first." Precious theorised.

"What are you talking about"? Max asked rather perplexed.

"It's the new buzz, the hot topic of discussion, they now believe that each one of us is born with memories inherited from our ancestors all conveniently stored in our genes. I should have no trouble settling in, so come on let's go"! Precious explained as she mentally set sail for the future.

"Go where"?

"To the airport silly two tickets on Air Mauritius"

"Two" Max said as he plainly demonstrated his confusion.

"Yep two; I hacked into your computer at work, I've known for weeks that you were up to something, so I kept close tabs on you, aren't you glad"?

Max had to agree he reached over and kissed his daughter on both cheeks and then after a moment he said. "Can you help me find Titi"?

Alexandre lay quite still on the soft double bed mattress in the Club Med chalet; he was naked, partially covered with a white cotton sheet to keep the chill off him caused by the overhead oscillating fan. Abrielle he thought was busily preparing breakfast in the aftermath of their early morning lovemaking. He could hear her footsteps but not the clutter of dishes and then he remembered the Club provided all meals including late breakfasts and lunches.

"What are you doing darling." He gently asked as he turned his head in her general direction.

"Just testing the waters my sweet" She responded.

"Is there something wrong with the tap water"?

"No my precious, my own water"

Curious as to what she was on about Alexandre rolled out of bed and walked naked to where his wife was standing. Abrielle stood by the bathroom sink and was dipping what appeared to be a mini-spatula into a container of yellowish fluid.

"What did you say you were doing"?

"Testing my waters"

"Why would you do that"? He asked having little medical knowledge and totally none when it came to women's physiology.

"Because my body's changing" Abrielle explained with a smile

"It comes with age." Alexandre vacantly and dryly commented.

"Unlike your precious car, which never dates" Abrielle fired back wounding her husband in the process. Alexandre gritted his teeth and admitted to himself that his lifelong love affair with his car had approximated pseudo-sex. Abrielle ignored her husband momentarily as she continued to stir the mini spatula in the golden liquid.

"Times up" She then said as she extracted the device and examined its surface. "Oh my God that explains it"! She gasped with delight.

Still uniformed Alexandre looked blankly on and cautiously asked. "Explains"?

"Why my breasts tingle and I've been passing lots of water."

"Probably too much wine and you reaction to my fondling" Alexandre bravely put forward.

Abrielle's facial demeanour changed as she proudly said. "I'm pregnant"!

"Not possible"!

"What do you mean"?

"The doctors they… and your age… "! Alexandre stuttered out of sheer disbelief.

"They were wrong and I am young enough to carry." His wife defiantly answered proud of her achievement.

"Did you read the test correctly"? Alexandre asked not wishing to be disappointed by a false result.

"I'll do it again, I bought a two test pack in any case the test is 99.9% accurate. It only looks for human gonadotrophic hormone, which is only present during pregnancy. Alexandre looked on nervously and quietly observed as Abrielle repeated the test, which yielded the same positive result. Alexandre's eyes became moist with emotion; a teardrop escaped and ran down his left cheek followed by another. Abrielle sensed his elation and tenderly embraced him. "All going well; we shall become a natural family." She whispered.

"What about Yvette"?

"I'm no fool Alexandre I've seen the gleam in her eye, she's in love, it won't be long before she leaves us, then what will you do"?

"How do you think she will react to the news"?

"Joyously especially if it's a boy, I know she loves the person you are and the way you were a father to her. I don't think that she could have wished for a better person."

"And you"?

"I think I failed Yvette in some respects probably because she was not my own, With the birth of our baby everything will change, she and I might become closer, but then again if she marries her husband may fulfil everything that is missing in her life. We'll worry about that when the time comes, come my handsome man make love to me"!

"But you're pregnant"!

"Orgasm's are good for the uterus and a healthy uterus means a healthy foetus"!

All through Father Brendan O'Reilly's moving homily Yvette and the girl's like the others in the congregation thought about their lives in depth. Each dwelt on their first love and the lasting effects it had upon them. The question repeatedly arose, were they meant to be with that person for the rest of their lives? Yvette had been kissed before, she was no stranger to light foreplay but not the heavy sexual stuff; no one however had quite the impact upon her like Mr Jack Stern and although she thought of him as being more of a father or brother she had to admit that it was this quality that made her feel comfortable. Yvette remembered the day when Jack watched her cleaning the bathroom floor at St Pious Presbytery; it was then that she fell in love with him and although she denied it love had a way of knocking at her heart's door to clearly display the one she was meant to be with. The same love dispelled all of the fears and misgivings she might entertain about his past.

Brendan O'Reilly received a standing ovation at the end of the mass's concluding prayer. The applause mainly came from the women and it was obvious that it humbled him further. He remained on the altar to offer his thanks and answer any questions. Yvette meanwhile ushered Jack into the sacristy once there she completely out of character looked him straight in he eye and quite forcibly said.

"I want to make love to you and I won't take no for an answer"!

"Very well but what about your innocence" Jack asked as he played along.

"It will remain intact after all we live in a constant state of virginity"! Yvette cheekily replied.

"You've been taking to Brendan."

"One could say that, well what about it"?

"Very well is now a good time"? Jack replied catching Yvette off guard by calling her bluff.

"I suppose but not here…" Yvette hesitantly replied and before she could add anything more Jack took her hand and whisked her away through the process of Spiritus Ruah to the foyer of the Grand Hotel Europe located on Nevsky Prospekt, the main avenue in the most romantic city outside of Paris France, namely St Petersburg USSR.

With no identification whatsoever upon him Jack Stern approached the somewhat stand offish manager on duty and spoke to him in fluent Russian. Within a matter of moments after the pleasantries had been dispensed with Jack had the previously stiff and starchy man grovelling at his side. The manager attended to Jack's every whim and fancy, nothing was too much trouble, the Russian thrust a golden key into Jack's hand as he kissed him robustly on both cheeks in true pheasant style. Jack thanked and rewarded him with a handful of American dollars, which were eagerly accepted.

"What did you tell him"? Yvette asked somewhat dazed by Jack's impromptu performance.

"You wouldn't want to know."

"Please don't leave me in suspense, I need to understand you."

"Very well, as it happened, this famous hotel has attracted many eminent people, the likes of Sir Elton John. P Tchaikovsky, President Bill Clinton etcetera, etcetera.

I merely told the manager that I was part of Bill Clinton's entourage and that I was here on official business preparing for yet another stay. My recollection of his visit convinced him that I was authentic."

"How did you do that and how is it that you can speak Russian"? Jack smiled and looked at Yvette sideways as he drew her near and whispered.

"Firstly I remote viewed the past events and secondly I can't speak Russian I let the ether do that for me." Yvette pretended to understand as she admired her lavish surroundings. "What would you like to do first? Take in the sights, be wined and dined or explore the incredible world of reproductive endorphins"?

"Two, one and three sounds good to me"

"Thank you it will be my honour to escort you mademoiselle." Jack said in a truly chivalrous manner. He led the way and showed her the varied restaurants that Grand Hotel Europe had much pleasure in publicising.

L'Europe Restaurant specialise in French and European cuisine impeccably served in its lovingly restored Art Noveau interior, live music accompanies the unrivalled culinary experience in an elegant and intimate atmosphere…is how the brochure read. The restaurant also boasts the finest new and old world wines and to top it all off a selection of excellent international hand made cigars.

"I hope you don't smoke." Yvette said reservedly

"Or drink to excess or do drugs or fool around or gamble." Jack solidly replied in a tone of voice similar to that of an innocent choirboy. "Next the Caviar Bar and as you can see it is the perfect place to go if you're looking for the true taste of fine Russian Cuisine.

The restaurant's setting was stunning just like the previous; Art Noveau was also adopted for the interior complete with marble décor, mirrors and a water fountain.

"This, mademoiselle, represents an adventure for your taste buds, a fine selection of Caviar and a superb assortment of domestic and imported Vodka's served crisp and cold.

"Whom have you brought here before"? Yvette timidly asked expecting to be disappointed.

"Only my father; it appears my family has a Russian heritage. I believe my ancestors were cooks in the Tsars kitchen, everything they prepared was ni-yuk"! Yvette giggled and realised that Jack did not take himself seriously and enjoyed laughing at himself.

"'Now we're between the Mezzanine Café and L'Europe Restaurant so let's find the former." A short walk and they were there; Jack opened the French style doors and allowed Yvette to enter first. "The Mezzanine Café is a relaxed and utterly delightful café in the heart of the hotel. As you may see it has a soaring glass canopy that spans the original structure to allow soft natural light to filter through during the day and 'the white night' of summer in the evenings. This is the place for fresh breakfast pastries, afternoon tea is traditional according to Russian customs; it is the most appropriate time to enjoy the hotel's famous homemade almond cake."

"You say that so well, almost as if you were a highly qualified and cultured tourist guide."

"I am certain mademoiselle intended that as a compliment, please look around and feel the ambience before I escort you to Rossi's the Italian restaurant located between the Lobby bar and Chopsticks Restaurant on the main level."

"Now you're joking Chopstick's Restaurant"?

"It's true here look at the hotel's brochure." Jack explained as he politely pointed to the information on the open page of his pamphlet.

"My darling this is all too much for a simple girl like me, show me where the poor people eat, perhaps I will feel more at ease there."

"Very well however I feel I will have failed you if I didn't offer you dinner at one of these world class restaurants."

"Let me think about it."

"Very well" Jack replied as he took hold of her precious warm hand and lead her downstairs through the hotel to the outside. Sensing that she was cold, Jack walked briskly and took Yvette to the Bolshoi Gostiny Dvor Department store a few blocks away on Nevsky Prospekt.

"You certainly know your way around."

"Like a homing pigeon."

"Are you certain you're not related to Russian Royalty"?

"Not at all as I said before cooks in the Tsar's kitchen, probably spent their entire lives peeling potatoes or beetroots."

"What are we doing here"? Yvette asked as he guided her through the department store's main doors.

"Finding you some warm clothes"

"I'm okay." Yvette protested.

"Not from where I'm standing, I see goose bumps on goose bumps, which suggests to me you at chill factor 9 otherwise known as shivering uncontrollably."

"It's excitement"! Yvette proudly said.

"Yeah, let's not dilly dally; what style would you like, Western or Eastern"?

"How about Russian peasant"

"I see you're already setting the mood, next you'll be telling me you want me to find you a barn complete with a haystack." Yvette flashed her eyes as to say yes. "Come on Miss Country girl lets find your peasant clothes."

Expecting that he would be bored and impatient with helping a woman to shop for clothes Yvette was pleasantly surprised to discover how helpful Jack was. "You know Mr Stern you're quite the accomplished gentleman, I would almost say that you could become a very good butler or gentleman's batman."

"I never realised you thought of me as being a superhero." Jack countered tongue in cheek as he admired Yvette's final choice of elegant and inexpensive clothing. Black velvet skirt, white cotton peasant style blouse with colourful trim, soft leather Spanish made knee- high boots and a fawn camel hair overcoat complete with fur trim.

"I'm ready please show me the sights, my handsome batman."

"Sush, someone might hear you, I'm supposed to be incognito, undercover, remember? In any case I'm famished, it's after 2pm, let me take you somewhere rustic." Jack insisted as he took Yvette down the Nevsky Prospekt to where it intersected the historic Moika Canal. There they found a genuine Russian style Izba or peasants hut that was better known as the Sverchok Restaurant, inside it provided a warm and authentic atmosphere complete with hearty Russian fare according to old traditions. Jack and Yvette seated themselves in an enclosed cubicle that was furnished with hard wooden chairs and table. The wall behind them depicted a romantic night landscape lit by the light of the full moon. They both ordered tasty Georgian Shahliks. The meal was not without incident.

A troupe of traditional Russian skomorokhi- kukolniki (clowns) suddenly appeared from nowhere and ran amuck ensuring that the patron's visits were both entertaining and enjoyable. They performed slapstick comedy, magic tricks and acrobatic juggling until they were dazzled by Yvette's beauty and then they fell at her feet, each attempted to outdo the other in order to win her affections. Jack attempted to reward them handsomely by offering a handful of American dollars but they refused saying that to behold such beauty was reward in itself. As they departed one of them hurriedly said in Russian.

"Go to the church of the Resurrection of Jesus Christ it is almost as beautiful as you."

"Jack what did he say"? Yvette asked out of curiosity.

"He said you should visit a nearby church, its beauty almost matches yours."

"How sweet; can we"?

"As soon as we finish our meals, which by the way are coming towards courtesy of more clowns" Jack replied as he drew Yvette's attention to the parade of colourfully clad donkeys that trotted out of the kitchen. Each had a dwarf perched on its back that balanced two trays of freshly prepared food. The dwarves performed a little balancing act before fanning out and distributing the dishes to their respective tables.

"Looks and smells absolutely delicious; what a generous portion"

Yvette exclaimed as she blossomed in the restaurant's atmosphere.

"Mine too, probably intended to fuel our internal fires." Jack deduced as he heard his stomach screaming. "Yippee food at last"!

The Georgian Sashlik dish was just heaven it had Jack purring like a large fat cat. Yvette ate half of her meal, as she was intent on remaining dainty. They both consumed non-sweetened black tea with their meal. Jack left behind a generous tip for all concerned.

"The church of the Resurrection of Jesus Christ is better known to Petersburgers as the church of the Saviour on the Spilled Blood or even some argue, the Church on the Blood, as it marks the spot on which Alexander II was fatally wounded on March 1 in 1881. The church was looted after the revolution and turned into a warehouse for the Small Opera theatre after World War II, as it was almost destroyed. In 1970 after it became a branch of the St Isaac's Cathedral museum, steps were taken to restore it to its former glory. In 1997 it was re-opened. It contains more than 7500 sq meters of mosaics that link Alexander's II murder with the crucifixion." Jack slowly described in a highly polished voice as he pointed to the mosaics that dealt with the subject and then he realised he was taking to himself. Yvette had wandered off to admire the Konostasis Mother of God with Child. Jack walked up behind her, put his arms around her waist and tenderly whispered.

"I think you're in your element. Perhaps you would like to visit more Russian orthodox churches"?

"I didn't realise that the Russian people were so religious"!

"That's what has kept the Russian nation and its people so strong and united."

"Please show me more, as much as you can." Yvette pleaded as her soul thirsted for an abundance of knowledge.

"Very well my sweet, you do realise that there are hundred's of churches here."

"Yes but I only want to see the orthodox one's."

"Very well, when you finished here, we'll see as many as we can in the time remaining and then the rest tomorrow." Jack calmly suggested as he mentally sighed and waited patiently for Yvette to complete her admirations.

They then went by taxi to their next destination, which was the Alexander Nevsky Monastery complex. At one stage the complex was home to an impressive sixteen churches, which unfortunately suffered at the hands of the revolution, it wasn't until 1989 that steps were taken to stop the destruction of the buildings and the trading in graves. Only five churches survive; the Holy Trinity Cathedral, the Church of the Annunciation, the Church of St Lazarus, the Church of St Nicholas and the Church of the Holy Mother of God. Jack Allowed Yvette to freely explore the complex and examine whatever she wished. They talked little until they reached the Monastery's graveyard, home to the final resting places of many of the great names in Russian culture. The Tikhvin Cemetery contained Tschaikovsky, Rubinstein, Muggorgsky, Rimsky-Korsakov, Glinka and Dostoevsky. Yvette recognised several of these names from her love of classical music.

"Birds of a feather flock together." Jack commented as he strolled around the grave plots.

"Deliberate or accidental" Yvette asked as she considered the mathematics of such an occurrence.

"Probably neither"

"So much culture, so much emotion, these people are deceased and yet this place is rich with their achievements, one could acquire so much inspiration by just sitting here." Yvette philosophised as she reached out with her sensesand glided towards Dostoevsky's tomb where she sat down and became transfixed. Jack the perfect gentleman as always joined her and waited patiently. His mind did not remain idle and it quickly remote viewed the events at Mauritius.

"Enough culture for one day, wine and dine me senior, I am yours'! Yvette suddenly said without any warning.

"You've become inspired." Jack replied as he shifted his concentration back to the present world.

They walked hand in hand as lovers do back to the main gates of the Monastery's complex and as they did the evening's chill followed them closely behind and whispered into their ears tales of ghosts and beings that do unmentionable things when no one is around. Yvette was frightened to look behind whereas Jack dismissed it as spiritual folly and kept her close.

The Caviar Bar was Yvette's choice of venue for dinner that night. She ordered a selection of fine caviars with condiments for entrée.

"I've never tried the real stuff before. I thought I would, it will help prepare me to become a good lover. An acquired taste especially if I am expected to swallow"!

Jack simply smiled at her inexperience and erotically said. "To be eaten in small portions otherwise the taste can be overwhelming." He then demonstrated the elegant way of consuming the delicacy after which he added. "One then either washes it down with ice cold vodka straight from the freezer or champagne."

"I like this stuff, cold, smooth and warming at the same time." Yvette confidently said as she threw the second shot of Russian vodka down her throat. "Oh that feels good." She added as the liquor fired up her oesophagus.

By the time she had finished her plate of food Yvette had downed six shots of three different vodkas. They did not appear to have made any impression upon her. A nearby waiter commented in a low voice to his colleague on Yvette's drinking ability.

"That French woman really knows how to hold her liquor."

"Lucky man" His friend replied as he turned to gaze at Yvette who sensed his inquiry and returned the look, which frightened the waiter, no end.

"That girl is creepy"!

"What do you mean"?

"I feel as though she sees me completely naked."

"Don't be stupid! Attend to your duties! Remember everyone here is welcome! Snap to it"!

In reality what he had sensed was true. Yvette's ability to see had been altered by the alcohol she had consumed.

"You have a mischievous smile on your face, what are you thinking"? Jack inquired as he detected Yvette's childish pleasure.

"That man over there has a tattoo on his abdomen just above his penis, it reads, "people slayer" The woman he is with also has one, it reads "slay me" They are ex government agents, both out of shape, shaggy, podgy, overweight, too much of the good life courtesy of the Russian mafia, bad people, racketeers, fingers everywhere, here, there, Pakistan...that's odd...perhaps we need to go there one day." Yvette explained in a low whisper.

"And me what do you see"?

"A very nice gentleman, somewhat complex and mysterious"

"Nothing more, no nakedness"

"A lady does not tell. In any case that would spoil the surprise for me. By the way I suggest we order the potato pancakes with wild mushroom sauce as our main meal. Everything else on the menu is how do you say...spoiled"! Yvette said after peering into the kitchen.

"Very well you have the eyes."

Yvette reached over and took Jacks glass of vodka and downed it in true Russian style, it was obvious to him that she wanted to drink from the same cup that he did. The pancakes came and went, the vodka flowed freely and all the while Jack wondered what Yvette's intentions were.

"I feel floaty oh so floaty, oh so floaty, I feel high, take me with you and let me feel you all night." Yvette sang as she stood up and enticed Jack with her body language to embrace her from behind. "Come take, come take me and let me feel you inside, for I love you and never want to forget that ride"! She sang melodically. Jack by far the more sober of the two swept Yvette off her feet and carried her in his arms. One under the back of her knees the other under her shoulders. Yvette held onto Jack tightly, her hands wrapped around his neck, which she kissed passionately. "You're so strong, you're so strong, carry me away, my knight." Yvette lyrically said as she pointed the way to the elevators.

Jack bowed to the dining room staff and patrons as a gesture of thanks and took his 'bride' for the night to their hotel suite. The room was lavishly appointed.

"This is fit for a king." Yvette giggled as Jack opened the door.

"Makes you feel special"?

"Overwhelmingly so you may let me down now, I need to attend to ladies matters."

"Very well mademoiselle, the bathroom is......"

"I can find it I'm not drunk you know....just a little happy." Yvette replied assertively as she left his embrace.

The luxurious suite was equipped with His and Hers bathrooms. They were identical apart from the colour scheme and the Russian symbols that depicted boy and girl. Yvette choose the wrong bathroom. Jack meanwhile made certain that the "Private do not disturb" sign was hanging on the outside door handle which he made certain was locked. He then dimmed the suites lighting, located the master bedroom, hung up his clothes, showered quickly, towelled dry and perfumed his body with the complimentary toiletries that the hotel had provided. Naked and refreshed Jack took his athletic muscular physique to bed and awaited his 'mistress' for the night. He passed the time by remote viewing the current events at Mauritius and whatever held his interest. Jack felt his body soften and relax as the bed moulded itself to suit his mood.

His heavily encrusted crucifix lay on his manly chest, its jewels merrily sparkled as his mind drifted off and explored newly discovered metaphysical worlds. Jack was oblivious to Yvette's presence until he felt her delicate soft hand touching his flaccid penis.

"You slipped in very quietly." He softly commented as he turned his head to face his beauty.

"You were miles away, for a moment I thought you did not want to know me."

"Hardly, are you certain about this"?

"I'm a little nervous."

"Is that why your hand's shaking"?

"Sorry." Yvette apologised somewhat embarrassed as she withdrew her hand.

"That's okay don't let it worry you, its fun to be clumsy." Jack said with warmth and tenderness as he touched her nose with the finger of one hand as his other ran down the lateral length of her body.

"You certainly know where to touch a woman"!

"Comes from years of experience"

"Had a good teacher"? Yvette asked as she explored the depths of Jack's blue eyes.

"One of the best"

"Care to share your experiences with me"?

"Not really it might offend you." Jack mindfully responded and before she could object he kissed her tenderly on the lips. It was a long lingering kiss, different from the rest, an invitation to explore.

"Kissing is meant to be good for you." Yvette purred after their lips parted.

"How's that'?

"It lowers the blood pressure."

"And orgasms are rewards for partaking in creation." Jack correctly added.

"I don't know whether that last kiss elevated or reduced my blood pressure."

"A kiss that imparts a sense of protection by its giver causes tension to vaporise in its beholder; but a kiss that inflames the passions causes more." Jack slowly explained. Yvette's lips moist and warm slowly opened allowing Jacks tongue to enter, which was greeted by hers and like its owner was shy and submissive. The tips of their tongues touched each other, tenderly, lightly; exquisitely, their taste buds mustered their numbers and savoured the sweetness of their lover's oral secretions, a complex mixture of tastes left behind by the food they had eaten and the chemicals that their bodies had produced during their gentle foreplay. Jack was the observant one, Yvette the explorer driven by emotional desire.

Jack continually caressed Yvette's body as they kissed, he knew all of the correct acupuncture points relating to sexual performance and he let his knowledge guide his fingers and hands. Jack listened carefully to Yvette's breathing, heard the increased loudness of her heartbeat and saw the changes in her nakedness. When Yvette opened her eyes they sparkled like her smile, Jack returned the gesture and observed the pupils of her eyes pulsate intensely with true love. Unlike Jack Yvette was not completely naked she had retained her briefs, something that he guessed would have happened.

"I'm so hot, what are you doing to me." Yvette moaned as she threw back the ornate bed covers.

"My honourable duty" Was all that Jack said in response as he admired her glowing countenance.

"You're very good at what you do Mr Stern, she must have been one fantastic teacher."

"What makes you think it was a she"?

"Only girls know how to please themselves." Yvette cheekily replied. Jack smiled at her forthright answer.

"So Mr Stern this ductus-longus-shortus thing of yours, how good is it"?

"What did you call it"?

"Ductus-longus-shortus"

"Sounds like Latin."

"Latin…ish the girls coined its name after all the priests they serviced." Yvette explained.

"The girls"

"Yes our girls, you know, Brandy, Candy, Felicity…. "

"Okay what else did they tell you." Jack teased as he sensed that Yvette had done homework on the subject.

"Well they had me practice on……"

"Fruit"! Jack interrupted. "First you started on a banana and then you worked your way up to a Lebanese cucumber or was it a zucchini, is that right"?

"Sort of, quite a curious little thing isn't it"? Yvette asked making reference to Jack's still flaccid penis.

"Yet it grows on you with time"! Jack was about to say, "No pun intended" when Yvette started to expertly caress his elevated testicles and the base of his penis.

"Hum the girls were right it does swell up"!

"As you can see…it's…based…on a remarkable bio…logical… hydraulic system." Jack groaned

'You must have lots of little men in there pumping their hearts out, careful now don't want to over do it, otherwise it might explode"!

Jack closed his eyes and let the waves of sexual ecstasy flow over and through his body. Yvette shifted her body's position and moved her head towards his erect manhood, which swelled even further with anticipation she held it with reverence and whispered to herself.

"It looks clean, smells clean, do I or don't I? I've had plenty of 'practice' but this is the real thing, oh my God what do I do next? Can there be harm in this? Let me think about this…suddenly my body feels heavy, my arms, my legs, my head…I'm so tired….so terribly tired….too much ….too soon….I'm exhausted…..I want to do it….I need this man….I….I can't keep my….eyes….open….Mother of God help me….give me….str…gth."

What was meant to be an unforgettable night of passionate love making in St Petersburg didn't eventuate. The waves of sexual pleasure subsided they flowed back to their origins all was calm again. Jack lay quietly frustrated; he resigned himself to falling asleep as he was. The room was warm but not warm enough, without disturbing the slumbering virgin he reached down and drew the bed covers over them and then took a few moments to relax himself mindful of the fact that Yvette still held his penis. The melodic sounds of Russian music being expertly played by an orchestra located in one of the hotel's nearby restaurants entered the room and filled Jack's ears, it caused him to reflect on the day's events and focus on, of all places Pakistan, until his mind had enough and the Angel of Sleep seduced him into the Field of Dreams.

39

DARK HORIZONS

Jack Stern was no stranger to the Angel of Sleep she would summons him when something important needed seeing to. It began when Jack was a young lad, a vetting time to determine his candidacy for positions vacant, nothing glamorous, well paid, nor prestigious, they were to the contrary. The young Jack Stern loved his dreamtime adventures he eagerly looked forward to them every night, besides the challenges he became smitten by the angel.

As the years progressed the angelic visits became infrequent, irregular and although Jack would never admit to it he was secretly looking for someone on earth as beautiful as that heavenly being, a wish impossible to translate the spiritual into physical reality.

The Angel of Sleep was always kind, tender and forgiving no matter the circumstances. She rescued Jack from many a mutilation on the Field of Dreams and he often wondered if she had ever incarnated on earth. Once he was brave enough to directly poise the question but to this day he has never received a reply.

The Field of Dreams that represented the earth and all of its living creatures was extensive to say the least. One had to know one's way about it, tonight was no different tonight Jack Stern needed a guide for the Masters of Affliction had been very busy and although Jack intuitively sensed the growing opposition to Brendan O'Reilly by those in power he needed to thwart them now and not later. The Angel brought Jack to a place he had not been before.

"Do you see it'? She gently asked

"What am I looking for"?

"Christ's imprint aided and embellished by all those who followed him."

"Nothing glimmers here it is lifeless." Jack concluded after his eyes scoured the inhospitable dark and gloomy landscape.

"Yet there is life, there is movement."

"By dark and hideous creatures so revolting that one fears for the lives of millions." Jack said in response as he began to see with his heart. "They enlarge before me, their souls tainted by their evil intentions magnify the actions they wish to perpetrate upon the earth. I feel powerless to stop them." Jack despondently said as he watched the grotesque creatures wield their mighty swords.

"Why attract such feelings"? The Angel sympathetically asked as she stood next to him and reached out to touch his hand. "If one has an Achilles heel do you not think that all of them as a group share the same failing? Let me explain further. A crowd of people with a common purpose acts as a singular body, it possess a heart and soul, it will fight in a co-ordinated fashion until it is challenged or its goal is satisfied and then it dissipates into its collective individual members as quickly as it was formed. The speed of its dissolution is dependent upon how soon some one discovers its weak spot or has the power to cut off its head. The former is always easier."

"I accept your philosophy however I am hampered by not knowing which bodies on earth these incredibly disfigured and ugly spirits inhabit."

"Then my good student, watch them carefully in this timeless void for as long as you need to catch a glimpse of that which will help you to identify them on earth then and now."

Jack reached for his crucifix and squeezed it tightly with his right hand, as he did so it caused a light to pulsate weakly in the midst of the darkness, the light a glimmer of hope for the millions sent the hideous creatures into such a heightened state of frenzy that they unwittingly attacked each other. Pleased with his efforts the Angel bade Jack farewell leaving him to re-enter his sleeping body.

Jack Stern slowly opened his eyes, in St Petersburg it was close to 9am in the morning. Neither he nor Yvette had shifted their bodies during the night, Jack's eyes moistened with tears as he gazed upon Yvette's innocent radiance.

"You really are meant for me, such a rare rose, I hope I can always protect you from the evils of this world." He mentally whispered to himself just before he slid out of the bed.

"Come now continue to sleep my child, you are so fair, so innocent, so chaste, I wish I can keep you like this forever" This time he audibly whispered these words as he continued to admire and appreciate Yvette's extraordinary beauty. Jack collected all of Yvette's belongings, neatly folded and placed them into a laundry bag, which he attached to his wrist once he had clothed himself. He then approached the bed in which Yvette slept, leaned over and wrapped her snugly with the luxurious coverings.

"Too much alcohol and excitement let me take you to papa." He softly said as he lifted her slumbering body and through the process of Spiritus Ruah whisked both of them to where Yvette's foster parents were staying.

"6.10 am a good time for people in love to wake up. Better not disturb the lovebirds you never know what they might be doing? Something obscene perhaps; creak, creak, creak, certainly movement over there, don't think I can put her in bed with mama and papa, they seem a little athletically preoccupied! Let's try the spare room, hope mom doesn't holler too loudly when she……….. You need your sleep." Jack quietly commented as he discreetly made his way invisibly about the Club Med chalet.

"A double bed, most appropriate, there you are my angel, sleep well until I see you again." Jack sweetly said as he gently lowered Yvette onto the bed and covered her with a sheet. He stood for a moment to admire her radiant innocence before he kissed her passionately on the side of her neck and flew into the eye of a raging hurricane located in the Pacific Ocean in readiness for his next battle.

Abrielle, Alexandre and Yvette were oblivious to each other's presence; luckily the amount of vodka that Yvette had consumed rendered her senses comatose, inert, and relatively unable to detect the canoodlings of her foster parents.

"Are you certain it is safe"? Alexandre asked very concerned and feeling guilty at the same time.

"Of course my darling, it is completely sealed off, my cervix is plugged; our baby is safe." His ecstatic wife answered feeling more complete after a glorious early morning love making session.

"I don't know if I can do it again, can we stop for a little while please"? Alexandre begged his wife once he managed to catch his breath and his racing heart had slowly settled down.

"Of course my darling, after a nutritious breakfast and lots of vitamin packed fruit juice we'll have you revving and roaring to go before you know it."

Alexandre swallowed hard and forced a smile. After all a miracle had occurred in Mauritius, his wife had become an insatiable fertile nymphomaniac. Abrielle was pregnant, he would be a father and God willing the yet unborn child would decide to be a boy. Alexandre reached out and lightly touched Abrielle's abdomen in the region of her uterus just past her mons pubis.

"No longer maybe baby, no further disappointments, baby makes three"!

"Have you forgotten about Yvette already"? Abrielle asked curious with respect to her husbands vague muttering.

"Never, on a spiritual, emotional and mental level she will always be my child, however this one is different." Alexandre replied making reference to their developing foetus. "Solely because it is of our flesh and blood, we had a say in how it was formed and in how it will look. The child will have our genes, it will not be a biological stranger; this does not mean that I will love Yvette any less. She came at a good time,she filled a gap and created a new one by her departure."

"You make it sound so mechanical." Abrielle concluded.

"I do not mean to, I am sorry and I am sorry to say I am hungry.... Breakfast time"!

"Alexandre wait a moment we're not alone, some one's in the apartment! Listen the other toilet has just been flushed."

"Probably the cleaner" Alexandre answered unafraid.

"Even so I'm sacred"!

"Very well I'll ask them to leave." He replied as he rolled out of bed, found his black elasticised underwear on the floor just underneath their bed and slipped them on. Alexandre silently made his way out of the master bedroom into the passage way and as he rounded its corner he caught a glimpse of the naked back of a young girl re-entering the spare bedroom. His animal instincts aroused he could feel his entire body not excluding his groin, stirring into action. Alexandre felt like a young stud, a champion; a warrior ready to pounce onto anything that was likely to cause trouble or give him pleasure. Alexandre advanced towards the door and forced it open to find a young maiden lying in bed and moaning.

"How did you come in here? What is your name? Out with it"! He roughly bellowed as he towered over the fragile and prostrate girl who assumed the foetal position upon hearing his threatening words.

"My name is Yvette Bell, I do not know where I am and I do not feel very well."

"Yvette? My Yvette"

"Is that you papa"? She replied barely recognising his voice.

"Are you all right"?

"Too much C and V too much"!

Thinking the worst and not knowing what the letters stood for,

Alexandre's mind panicked and thought of endless pessimistic possibilities. Cocaine, crack, cock, violations, vagina, after all she was naked apart from her briefs and apparently in pain. Both she and Jack Stern had disappeared the previous day to parts unknown, what was Alexandre meant to think?

"Tell me Yvette, what happened."

"Like I said too much C and V"

"Which stands for"? Alexander timidly asked fearing the worst.

"Caviar and vodka"

"Where"?

"In St Petersburg" Yvette painfully answered. "Jack took me there, I wanted him to make love to me."

"And did he"?

"No papa! It's all my fault I've failed him! I'll probably never see him again! I'm such a failure"! Yvette sobbed.

"Did he take advantage of you"? Alexandre asked as he felt his protective nature came into play.

"He's too much of a gentleman; I wanted so much for it to be perfect! I even asked the girls to teach me how to really please a man in bed and what did I do? I feel asleep on him" Yvette continued to sob with her hand over her mouth as her tears fell on the bed sheets. Not knowing what to say Alexandre excused himself.

"I better get your mother she knows better than I what to do in matters like this."

"Thank you papa, thank you." Yvette answered as she felt the painful anguish of her failure well up inside of her.

Alexandre returned moments later with Abrielle who glowed all over in stark contrast to her foster daughter who looked very pale and distraught. Yvette's relationship with her foster mother had never been as close or intimate as that with Alexandre, yet Yvette felt a need to feel and hear a mother's soothing words and touch.

"Oh mama I feel so bad! I've done a terrible thing! I'm so ashamed! Please hold me tell me it's going to be all right, please"! Yvette begged as she reached out with her arms.

Abrielle outwardly touched by Yvette's sorrowful state climbed into bed with her and allowed Yvette to lay her heavy head upon her bosom. Abrille cradled Yvette in her arms and held her tight. Alexandre sat silently at the edge of the bed and watched as the poignant scene unfolded before him. Abrielle continuously stroked Yvette's head whilst she whispered unbridled assurances into her ear. Even though the early morning air was heavy with heat and humidity, Yvette felt cold and needed a mother's bodily heat to keep her warm. It was not long before she fell asleep. Abrielle signalled to her husband that he should depart for the main restaurant and enjoy breakfast alone.

"We're a family, I'm staying." He firmly said in a low voice as he made himself comfortable. The hours passed Yvette's body worked overtime to rid itself of the ingested alcohol and its depressant effects whilst Yvette drew extra energy from Abrielle to help facilitate its actions.

"Never again" Were the first words that Yvette uttered as she stirred out of her unnatural sleep.

"Feeling better"? Her foster mother asked appearing to be caring.

"Yes thank you, at least I can think a little more clearly once again. What possessed me to drink so much"?

"Fear of the unknown and the acquisition of Dutch courage." Alexandre answered on his wife's behalf as he stood up to leave mother and daughter alone.

"It's rare for us to share a moment like this. I thought you cared for nobody but your father and those Catholic icons." Abrielle coldly expressed without even looking at Yvette once Alexandre was out of earshot.

"I'm very sorry if my actions gave you that impression." Yvette apologetically replied.

"We are talking decades you do realise that."

Yvette refused to answer on account of her foster mothers change of mood. Instead she raised herself up and looked inquiringly into Abrielle's eyes.

"You've changed, there's something different about you." Yvette surmised as she scanned her foster mother's body. Abrielle somewhat aloof and arrogant simply smiled back at Yvette. "You're pregnant"!

"I certainly am." Her foster mother triumphantly announced.

"Alexandre and I are going to be a real family at long last. You of course will be of no relation to the child. Your foster father is overjoyed at the prospect of becoming a father. It will probably change his relationship with you, so I suggest you hurry along and find yourself a husband instead of spending useless hours praying to those lifeless statues of yours"!

The words cut deeply into Yvette's soul and wounded her terribly. Abrielle had no conception of Yvette's supernatural gifts; she was only interested in destroying the bonds that existed between Yvette and Alexandre. Yvette without saying anything further bravely left her bed leaving Abrielle to gloat over her victory.

Yvette had no difficulty in finding the clothes that Jack had neatly packed. She dressed lightly and once she had finished left on foot to walk the distance to Chamarel and the Church of the Coloured Sands. Alexandre did not see her go as he was busily watching the television's Sky network.

As Yvette walked through the main gates of the holiday resort the ever-attentive taxi drivers offered her transport, most at an agreed bargained price with the exception of one who having recognised her pitiful state offered it for free. Yvette refused all.

"The walk will do me good, I have much to think about." She genuinely replied with half a smile.

In true Christian spirit Yvette hung her head low as a sign of complete humility and obedience and slowly trudged her way home. The rapidly soaring ambient temperatures made the journey laboriously difficult, the sun beat down fiercely and without mercy upon her anxious body, a body dangerously dehydrated by the previous day's excessive alcoholic intake. Yvette's body struggled to keep cool and obey its master's commands, her physiological compensatory systems cried out "Stop we cannot take any more! Abort! Rest or die"!

In her stressful state Yvette made an error in judgement and strayed off the main sealed road onto an old abandoned lonely stretch of gravel road that ran through lush sugar cane fields. The densely packed vegetation barred all breezes from entering their domain and as a result the atmosphere within was confined, breathless, restrictive and stifling, Yvette's body could no longer cope with the increased burden of environmental insult and without any further warning it let go and she collapsed face down into a road side ditch.

40

TOUCH AND GO

In the eye of the tiger all is calm, skies are blue but outside of this the storm rages and causes death and destruction to human life and property alike.

Jack Stern was there as part of his ongoing education to master each of the four elements and in so doing learnt that everything in life is political. The Pacific hurricane given the ridiculous name of Percy was the epitome of this behavioural concept. Percy drew his strength from the latent heat released from the hot, humid air that rose from the agitated waters of the ocean, its vibrational anger derived by the endless streams that washed away human emotions and carried them into the seas. Day by day the violence built up until it caused the oceans to reach boiling point. Disorganised clusters of showers and thunderstorms became organised, a creature was born out of the coalescence that was destined to vent the full fury of its negative energy and force on anything that stood in its path. Some where within this mighty beast of whirling air lay an Achilles' heel. With arms and legs drawn tightly into its body the animal of the air spun with an awesome ferocity and sought to destroy the origins of its emotion, fed by the ocean its only adversary was the land, for it smothered its source of life and quelled its existence.

Jack stood upon the calm ocean waters and surveyed his sur-roundings a fine example of a political storm in Nature. The ocean was the ally of the air and the land was the enemy of both deter-mined to protect its inhabitants. Well aware of Percy's strength Jack wondered what measures he should take and to what depths or heights he would need to go in order to placate the beast.

Did one go about it head on or did one circumnavigate the problem and seek peripheral assistance?

The hurricane's thunderstorms were bonded irreversibly, there was no wind shear; it blew strongly and without any deviation or variation in the same direction, only one factor was not homoge-neous and that was the water itself, the very source of its life. Ocean water can only sustain a hurricane when it is approximately 27 degrees Celsius in temperature. Such warmth causes large amounts of water to evaporate and make the air very humid.

However to what depth was the water at 27 degree's Celsius Jack questioned himself as he sought a solution.

"Hurricanes come and go quickly, therefore the depth can only be relatively shallow otherwise the entire world would repetitively breed an endless supply of monsters." He concluded as he sought the friends from the deep.

"Fish's big and strong heed me please, gather together, fan the cold waters from the deep towards the sun to help me please." He beseeched them as he moved about Percy's open eye.

"Fish's of the deep heed me please, find it in your hearts to spare those who hunt you from harm, they will in return spare you in numbers. Cool the tempestuous waters with your knowledge of currents and time. I promise I will make you mine." Jack poetically asked as he marched around the margins of Percy's open eye close to the wall of death. He stretched out his arms to signify his welcoming embrace and continued to preach his message until the giants of the ocean floor answered his call.

Percy's eye grew calmer, bigger with Jack's determination to alter the hurricane's appearance until the eye fully opened engulfed the face of the storm, one blink it was gone; all was quiet once again. Jack thanked and blessed all those who had helped him, the creatures of the sea, the cold ocean currents and his mentor the Angel of Sleep whom he loved dearly. Satisfied with his achievement Jack by the speed of thought returned to the Church of the Coloured Sands, the grounds of which and its surrounding roads were a hive of activity, pilgrims and opportunistic locals everywhere. It hadn't taken very long for the traders to set up stalls and traffic in all sorts of religious souvenirs, postcards, samples of holy water, T-shirts, rosary beads and more.

"Where would they be without the church"? He cynically mumbled to himself as he materialised in the crowd. The interior of the church was abuzz with all sorts of people seeking their own personal salvation. Brendan's seven sisters were busily helping them as best as they could each according to their individual merits and talents.

Jack approached the ever-vivacious Candy "I say Candy my sweet, have you or anyone of the others seen Yvette"?

"Not since the both of you disappeared early yesterday afternoon. Where did you go"?

"St Petersburg."

"Where's that"?

"Russia." Jack politely answered as he returned Candy's smile.

"That's different"!

"The Venice of the North"

"Sounds romantic" Candy enviously purred.

"It's meant to be."

"Did anything happen? I saw that look in Yvette's eye." Candy cheekily remarked.

"Afraid not" Jack disappointedly replied.

"Let me guess, she fell asleep on you."

'An inevitable outcome"

"I hope she didn't leave you high and dry"?

"I coped"! Jack answered truthfully.

"A thorough gentleman, I wish I could meet a man like you."

"You have" Jack replied ambiguously leaving Candy wondering as to what he meant. "I'm a little worried about the girl I may need to excuse myself, thank you for your help." He went onto to say just before he kissed Candy on the cheek and disappeared from view.

Instead of 'landing' in Yvette's foster parent's Club Med's love nest he 'arrived' on their front doorstep and knocked on its door frame. Within moments Abrielle half dressed answered the call.

"Who's there, please"? She asked somewhat agitated at being un-expectedly disturbed.

"It's me Jack Stern. Is Yvette with you"?

"No she isn't"! Abrielle rudely and abruptly answered not bothering to open the door. Impervious to such obnoxious behaviour Jack stepped closer to he door and asked.

"Do you know where she's gone"?

"Not at all, she left without warning this morning. Didn't bother telling us where she was going"!

"I see; did you by any chance have an argument"? Jack asked becoming somewhat alarmed.

"That's none of your business! Alexandre, Alexandre come here at once and get rid of this annoying man"!

Abrielle's husband came running like an obedient attack dog frothing at the mouth, he ripped open the door expecting to find an intruder or worse instead he was confronted by the saintly image of Jack Stern.

"Er... ah... Jacque... Abrielle what nonsense is this? Mr Stern is not..."!

"Yes he is! He was becoming aggressive, demanding and threaten to knock down the door just because I told him off for what he did to Yvette"!

"I don't remember Yvette saying anything like that"! Alexandre said coming to Jack Stern's defence.

"She told me differently, you weren't there"!

"We'll discuss it later, go back to bed, I'll attend to this"! Alexandre firmly said absolving her of any further involvement. Abrielle threw her head back in defiance and stormed off.

"I'm terribly sorry Jacque, I had no idea, please come in."

"I'd rather not just tell me where I can find Yvette." Jack asked sharply

"I cannot I left her with her mother, next thing I knew she had slipped away."

"Happy or sad"

"I do not know, but I have some wonderful news … Abrielle's pregnant"! Alexandre happily replied changing the subject.

"That explains everything, thank you and good day." Jack abruptly said visibly annoyed at their lack of parental concern. He spun around on the heel of his foot and departed briskly towards the resort's main gates. Along the way he questioned every GO he encountered as to Yvette's where abouts, each regrettably gave the same 'I don't know' answer. Undeterred Jack interrogated every taxi driver present at the main entrance whether they were seated in their car, standing about or taking shelter in the large security kiosk. Only one remembered Yvette coming through that morning and the general direction she took. Jack thanked the driver profusely and then started to track Yvette's 'scent' like a well-trained bloodhound using his highly developed remote viewing ability.

Jack Stern cleared his mind, closed his eyes and intoned the necessary mystical words to help him see the history of the road's early morning travellers. There were many however what helped Jack to distinguish Yvette from the others were her tears of anguish amongst the many raindrops that marked her passage. He dutifully followed them taking special care not to miss one marker until he reached the point where Yvette had strayed from the road, from then it was easy, for only her image came into view. He stood quite still, watched as he remote viewed and became both shocked and grief stricken at her pitiful sad state to the point where her exhausted body could take no more and she collapsed face down into the roadside ditch.

Knowing where she lay, Jack ran with all of his might towards her crumpled body and came to a skidding halt at her side. Yvette was unconscious; her clothes were wet and muddied by the afternoon's deluge of rain. Luckily the drench had not filled up with water otherwise she would have surely drowned. She lay still, very still, hardly breathing; it was obvious to Jack that several creatures from within the sugar cane fields had examined her. Snakes had slithered across her body, foxes had nibbled on her exposed ear lobes and her naked legs bore numerous large insect bites.

"What happened to you? How could anyone let this happen to you? I thought you were safe with your foster parents! How wrong was I? Oh my precious darling, I've failed you miserably"! Jack tearfully whispered as he fell on his knees, turned her over and cradled her in his arms. "Come on lets make you better." And with that Jack Stern transported both of them to the Genius Loci.

"It's about time you got here"! Grandpa loudly exclaimed in his ghostly manner.

"I just found her"! Jack snapped back defiantly.

"It took you long enough! All my life I've looked after this one and you come along and almost spoil everything"!

"What are you taking about? Are you suggesting you already knew Yvette had met with an accident"?

"Maybe"

"For god's sake why didn't you do something about it"? Jack angrily asked visibly annoyed at his grandfather's lack of action.

"Not allowed to"

"Fine" Jack grumbled as he stood before his Grandpa with Yvette in his arms. He stared briefly and then asked. "What now"?

"To the pool" Grandpa proudly commanded.

"I don't think hypothermia is a particularly good idea, I've just rescued her from one episode already"!

"I'm not taking outside silly! The new pool, the one I've just finished building, this is the Genius Loci remember sonny"? Jack reluctantly accepted the reprimand and followed Grandpa closely behind.

"Here we are laddie"

"It was meant to be an indoor swimming pool not an ocean, she'll drown in there"! Jack loudly remarked as he gazed upon the extent of Grandpa's efforts.

"Sorry…. Forgot…. Now let me see…. Aqua ductus longus-shortus…. there that's better"! He joyfully said quite satisfied with his magical ability.

"Is that okay sonny, she won't drown now, put her in that's a good lad, gently does it, she'll be well in no time, completely healed, mind, body and soul, I guarantee it"! He added as the ocean sized enclosure contracted into a full sized therapeutic bath. "Water temperature's right, isotonicity just perfect, nutrient content spot on, living entity fully active, all we have to do is wait and observe; how's your nursing skills"? Grandpa jokingly teased.

"Fine just fine… what's this ductus longus-shortus"? Jack asked remembering the previous night when he and Yvette engaged in pre-liminary foreplay.

"Seemed an appropriate description"

"You were there? You sick twisted spirit"!

"I'm allowed to watch"! Grandpa proudly confirmed.

"You perverted voyeur"!

"Doesn't that mean I'm normal? Two negatives make a positive"! Grandpa cheekily deduced. Jack rolled his eyes in disgust.

"I suppose you've watched all of my encounters"!

"Maybe yes maybe no! In any case what's more important is that you stop being such a gentleman with the ladies. Start making the first move, take control be a little more aggressive, dominant otherwise the girls will think you are either gay or disinterested"!

"Since when have you been the relationship expert"?

"I've had my experiences"

Jack shook his head in disbelief and muttered to himself before he changed his line of questioning. "What did you mean; you've looked after her all of her life"?

"She's special"

"Yes I know that! I have ambitions of making her my…."

"It was no accident that her biological parents were murdered"! Grandpa stopped jack mid sentence. "She was meant to be killed as well, luckily we intercepted. Jack instinctively knew what his Grandpa was hinting at.

"I'll need to double my efforts."

"More than that sonny, she's part of the puzzle; she must stay alive at all costs! She possesses the purity of heart and those extraordinary eyes."

"It was in her best interests that she fell asleep on me and we didn't make love." Jack surmised.

"Doesn't affect the heart, she will remain pure irrespective of that. There is only one way to protect her, keep the limelight away, focus it on some one else, let her do her job but never give her credit otherwise they will try again to extinguish her flame. She is a rare rose amongst all of us, guard her well love her with all of your heart."

Jack heeded Grandpa's words well, bowed his head and accepted the responsibility.

The purified oceanic waters that grandpa had engineered coursed their way around and into Yvette's body; they cleared away all manner of debris, her tissues responded and in a time normally ascribed to the miraculous rebuilt themselves anew. Yvette de-aged began to stir; she shed the day's traumatic events and let them slip away never to be thought of again. The beautiful maiden opened her sparkling blue eyes and welcomed her surroundings.

"I'm alive." She thankfully whispered as she gazed at Jack and his ghostly Grandpa who both smiled. "Thank you and sorry about last night" She apologised as she wondered why Grandpa had blushed.

"It was fun must do it again." Jack playfully said as he squeezed her hand.

"Except this time I promise not to fall asleep."

"It was heaven just being with you and feeling the softness of your body next to mine."

"Enough said my darling, enough said"

Grandpa approved and faded from view.

41

IMMORTAL TRAITOR

Days after Brendan had delivered his breath taking homily the Island of Mauritius erupted into carnival atmosphere as did the solidarity of women worldwide, for once there was a man who believed in and fought for women's rights and causes.

Money flowed into the Island from the pilgrims' pockets and from all over the world via mail as donations for the Church of the Coloured Sands. Everyone on the Island was happy, everyone prospered in his or her own way even the homeless received some share of the wealth.

The President of the government was especially pleased and decided as a gesture of his appreciation to approve the expenditure of government monies for a week of national celebration that would mark Father O'Reilly's discovery. The festivities would take the form of numerous street parties, bonfires, fireworks and a parade through the streets of Port Louis.

President Casseem Ringagain a practising Hindu was taken by Brendan's first homily and from that point onwards he predicted great things for the priest's future and that of the Island. Casseem came from a family of wonderful party throwers and it was no effort for him to quickly orchestrate an unforgettable event. At the insistence of his seven 'sisters' Brendan accepted the presidents invitation to breakfast at Government House unaware of what lay in store for him, as he had been totally consumed, immersed and preoccupied with his vocational responsibility of proper pastoral care at the newly discovered church.

Brendan and the girls left the church to care for itself in the early hours of the morning of the day's presidential meeting and journeyed to the three storey colonial styled house at Port Louis. Jack Stern and Yvette were still away although Jack once he was satisfied that Yvette's physical wounds had healed returned briefly to inform the others that they would be absent for another day or two. Candy made great mileage out of the news and teased Jack mercilessly.

"What's the game you're gonna play? Let's see who fall's asleep first? Hey Jack the lad"! Jack returned the flirtatious compliment with a nod and a wink of the eye.

The healing of physical trauma requires complete nutrition, a robust constitutional and rest whereas the emotional and spiritual require an abundance of genuine loving energy. Following her rejection by her foster parents Yvette had been on the verge of dying from an irreparable broken heart had it not been for Jack Stern's timely intervention.

They sat hand in hand on the lush green grass in the National Park's forest that was part of the Genius Loci and admired the heavenly creature as it went about attending to the needs of the invisible rare rosebush that only the pure of heart and gifted could see. Yvette likened the creature's devotion to that of Jack's and felt eternally safe in his company. She knew that when lovemaking would happen between the two of them Jack would not disappoint, all that she needed to do was stay sober and alert. Dutch courage was no longer on the menu, anxiety and fear had to be dispelled, things should be allowed to flow, happen naturally without any sense of anxiety filled urgency.

Yvette and Jack talked about meaningless things before they

ventured onto their childhood and early school yard experiences, something that they should have done ages ago. Yvette's discovery of the first fragment of the true Catholic Church had propelled them into a world of furious activity and driven a small temporary wedge between them. There was a need to take a breather away from it all and yet Jack could not, for his destiny was intimately bonded to Brendan's. Jack did not want to become a super hero even though he realised that he was already at that status, invisibly so and whilst he romantically and intimately interacted with Yvette that portion of his subconscious assigned to remote view continued its honourable duty unabated.

It detected the rumblings at the Church of the Coloured Sands, worshippers had been forcibly expelled under threat of death and all doors bolted shut. Jacks field of view was split in two, one half filled by the Yvette's angelic features the other by the violent events that occurred at the church, even as Jack watched he could not draw himself away from Yvette's side until the keeper of the rose started to fret as many of the bush's blossoms started to shed their petals.

"Jack my darling something's wrong"!

"Yes I know." He replied not wishing to answer the call.

"What is it"?

"We're under attack"! Jack answered solemnly.

"Surely not here" Yvette asked nervously as she looked around for potential assailants.

"Correct"

"Our Church in Mauritius" She guessed.

"Correct" Jack replied as he stood up and lifted Yvette from the grass.

"By whom.... Badcock" Yvette half proposed as she faced Jack and put her delicate but strong arms around his waist.

"Not as yet, perhaps he or another will turn up later. Our present villains are members of the Catholic Church, I think I need to go but not until I'm satisfied that you are safe with Grandpa."

"I'm coming with you." Yvette defiantly said as a faithful spouse and she drew Jack firmly towards her.

"Afraid not, you're not powerful enough. I made a promise to keep you secret."

"Don't you mean safe"? Yvette asked as she pressed her ample breasts against his chest and hoped her sexuality would convince him otherwise.

"Secrecy breeds safety. Please let me go for this is neither the time nor place for us to exchange bodily fluids." He seductively whispered.

"Oh very well" Yvette submissively agreed as Jack tenderly broke her embrace and lead her back to the mountain hideaway.

"Make certain you turn everything upside down! Smash it; smash it open if you have to! I want to find the switch and shut this monstrosity down"! Pigtail the Pegleg Pirate ordered as he stomped about the floor of the Church of the Coloured Sands and made his way up the altar.

"Nothing here" Was the constant and repetitive finding that infuriated him as each ruthless mercenary systemically attacked and demolished suspect hiding places.

"What's the matter with this thing"? He cursed as he drove his peg leg into the altars marble floor. "Why don't you work? Damn it! Come on blast this place into non existence damn you"! Pegleg screamed as he exerted all of his might on the satanic weapon.

"It doesn't work in here and by the way what a horrible rat's tail you've got growing out of the back of your head"! An invisible Jack Stern whispered into the left ear of an already heavily frustrated pirate.

"Who said that"!

"The voice of your conscience"! Jack replied in a low convincing voice.

"I have none"!

"Correct Mr Ischariot, Mr Judas Ischariot"! These words stunned and arrested Pigtail the Pegleg Pirate's animations. He stood as still as a statue, only his eyes moved and his ears strained to catch the location of his tormentor. Hopeless under the circumstances as the mercenaries continued to wage war against the hapless church in an almost deafening fashion.

"You're wondering how I know." Jack further teased.

"I'm known as Pigtail, I am a modern day pirate."

"You're still wondering. The scene is very clear, thirty pieces of silver for betrayal, dobbing someone in, a handsome return for pointing the finger, could be a permanent profitable venture, providing you did it long enough. But then, some one got wind of what you were doing, you had to disappear! Death is the best avenue, permanent; no one to follow you, seek revenge! Very funny the way you went about it!

Your pursuers from a distance saw you jumping out of the tree by the edge of the cliff, rope around your neck, the other end attached to the branch, they saw you drop, swing once, twice, the branch break and your body tumble into the deep ravine. The crowd ran to see you die, they saw a lifeless body, crumpled, bleeding profusely and took you for being dead and left your body to be devoured by the creatures of the world that attend to such matters. They recorded it incorrectly into history. But you Judas Ischariot in your dying state struck a deal with the devil and gained immortality. The devil through his perverted sense of humour did not restore you entirely. The peg leg came as a reminder of your association with Jesus, seemingly a punishment until you discovered its power. But I remind you it doesn't work in here! Want to come outside and play"?

"I'm Pigtail the Pegleg Pirate on a mission to sink this ship and steal its treasures! Guards come up here quickly! I'm being attacked"! Pigtail hoarsely screamed, his face turned blood red with violence. "Search every square metre of this altar swing your bayonets, guns, he's here, hit something; protect me"! Pigtail frantically shouted as he turned full circle.

"Eleven soldiers and you, that makes twelve. What do you call them? Can't be the Swiss guards, they're reserved for Rome, perhaps the swish, that sounds better, let's get the whip cracking shall we"? Jack calmly suggested as he fiercely yanked on Pigtails pigtail and pulled him straight down. Pigtail landed heavily on his back, the fall knocked the wind out of him, whipped and jarred his spine and filled his head with grievous pain.

"You dirty fighter"! He madly cursed as he squirmed in agony on the ground whilst his guards ran amuck searching for the unseen.

"Lads I'm over here." Jack ahoyed as his voice signalled his likely presence.

Each of the swift and swish mercenaries spun around and took aim. Jack briefly came into view, the guards fired their guns at him, one after the other, each swore that they had hit their target, each was dumbfounded as to why Jack Stern remaining standing.

"Forget to load your guns with real bullets? Firing blanks? Put some lead in your pencil, come on, you're real men, beer drinking men, rowdy men, ones that rape and pillage! What's the matter with you? Eleven to one and I'm still standing" Jack seriously taunted.

"Cut him to pieces"! Pigtail hysterically commanded shattering the stunned silence that pervaded the group.

"Careful you might hurt yourselves" Jack cautioned as his image stepped towards them.

The mercenaries descended upon him wildly slashing and stabbing at his anatomy. They felt his pain and saw blood profusely splatter and flow in all directions until they realised it was their own. They had attacked each other, those in the inner circle lay dead; five in total, of the remaining six, three sustained life threatening puncture wounds whilst the other three escaped injury free. Pigtail the Pegleg Pirate stomped his peg leg repeatedly out of sheer frustration.

"How many times must I inform you it doesn't work in here"! Jack flippantly reminded Pegleg as he invisibly circled his adversary. "Swish guards look a little tattered! I enjoyed that game, what shall we play next? Hide and seek? Spank the monkey? I know what about betrayal? There's a fun game. You pretend to be Jesus and I'll be Judas.

Those three soldiers can be your disciples. I'll even pretend to be Pontius Pilate since I'm such a gifted actor. We'll cut to the chase and nail you to that big wooden cross behind the altar. What do you say? Sounds like fun to me."

Pigtail could no longer stand the mockery. "You blaspheming bastard! You have no idea who you're up against! You can't escape! We'll track you down and kill every one of you! No one escapes our wrath"! He threatened as he drove his peg leg into the altars marble floor.

"You really must learn to control yourself; otherwise you might do yourself a mischief! Visited the doctor lately? You seem a little tense, it wouldn't surprise me if you've got some sort of immortal hypertension, could be serious even life threatening! Can't have that, can we"? Jack responded completely un-phased.

Distraught Pigtail blindly rushed off the altar and swept down its stairs, he missed his footing, tumbled and crashed heavily onto the Church's floor.

"Goodness me, are you all right? What a mess! How did you manage to get your peg leg stuck in your ear"? Jack feigning concern said as he invisibly created the illusion that he was by Pegleg's side rendering first aid. The three remaining mercenaries followed quickly and surrounded their boss. Jack remained silent and floated away.

"Who the hell was that"? One of them asked.

"Careful"! Pegleg cautioned, "He's not one of us."

"Okay who was that angel"? The same guard corrected himself as he helped Pigtail to his feet. Pigtail violently dissociated himself from the soldier and issued further orders.

"Never mind him, what you saw was an illusion, an attempt by this haunted place to scare us off. We came to find the switch to shut this miserable place down! Let's get on with it"! Pigtail roughly barked as he dusted himself off.

"You're saying the angel was a ghost."

"Yes! Fan out and continue your search! There's nothing to fear, it can't hurt you"! Pigtail bravely and convincingly screamed.

The three remaining mercenaries swallowed hard and cautiously went about their work much to the annoyance of Pigtail who expected them to be overtly macho. Jack meanwhile remained dangerously mischievous and floated above them inconspicuously. The mindless destruction of the church did not bother him for he knew that once he had rid the building of its vermin it would restore itself completely.

"Look for the priest's hole." Pigtail agitated.

"Pardon"

"I said look for the priest's hole"!

"What sort of perverted bastards do you think we are"? One of the trio answered back.

"Stop your tom foolery, it's a term"!

"Yeah like man-hole, water hole and ass…. "

"Keep it to yourself! You are looking for a cleverly disguised secret entrance"!

Jack watched vigilantly as the mercenaries followed Pigtail's orders and when it seemed that one of them might stumble across the ancient escape route he acted. One of the soldiers stopped what he was doing and stood transfixed facing the altar.

"What are you doing"! Pigtail demanded to know out of frustration. His loud words shocked the soldier briefly out of his trance and he feebly responded.

"There were eight men on the altar a minute ago now there are six."

Thinking he was over come by nerves Pigtail curtly answered. "They probably went off to tend to their wounds"!

"I don't think so." The soldier replied once again transfixed. "Now there are…. five…." He paused and then uttered. "Four…. three…."

Pigtail stopped his search and stood within metres of the priest hole. He watched dumbfounded as each mercenary disappeared from view.

"Is this still an illusion because I am becoming very frightened?

Rockets, tanks, aerial bombardment, snipers, land mines, and grenades I can take but this is something else! This is not real this is outside of my league! What do I do? Who is my unseen enemy? Where do I go"? Was the final question the soldier could ask before he also disappeared from view; one after the other until it was only Jack Stern and Pigtail the Pegleg Pirate that remained.

"Well Mr Judas Ischariot alias Pigtail the Pirate still think it's an illusion"?

"What have you done with my men"?

"Oh you mean those hired thugs? Dispatched then to parts unknown, great test of their survival skills; thought I'd better do that, don't want to soil this sanctuary, enough blood spilt already if you know what I mean"?

"Murderer"!

"Not exactly true, didn't lay a hand on them, try again"!

Pigtail wished his immortality was complete with supernatural powers however that was not part of the deal, his satanic mentor wished to remain the superpower, no one was allowed to challenge his position unlike the God of Hosts.

"Nothing to say; sorry can't chat, have work to do, enjoy your stay"! Jack said as he faded from view, quickly accessed the priest hole and securely locked it behind him. Next he approached the wall of bosoms and devotedly caressed two of them until Luvera the Goddess of Fertility appeared.

"Good morning Mr Stern a pleasure to feel you once again."

"Likewise my lovely lady, are you very busy today"? Jack sincerely asked as he admired Luvera's divine beauty, which reminded him of the Angel of Sleep.

"Always, especially now, two thousand years of unfinished work to catch up on." She replied somewhat reservedly.

"Bother I thought as much! Forgive me I might have to put a hold on that." Jack stated somewhat ashamed, as he knew the ways of these creatures.

"I beg your pardon"!

"There are people upstairs who wish to destroy this sanctuary once and for all! I think it best if we put it into hiding until…. "

"You find the missing pieces, yes I know." Luvera said as she finished his sentence.

"How did you"?

"I was there when the stone was crafted. I had a say in its origins and formation. I remained loyal to it that is why you discovered me here in its bowels." Luvera explained as she fondly remembered conception and then she said. "In any case you can't go making it disappear only the keeper, Decay or Brendan O'Reilly have the power to do that."

'Be that as it may I nevertheless hold the key." Jack proudly said as he displayed his encrusted crucifix and then added. "Better than a Swiss army knife"

"Do you have a secure hiding place"?

"Of course"

"Where may I ask"?

"Genius Loci; where my grandfather lives." Jack correctly answered.

"A splendid choice" Luvera confirmed as she bowed her head and smiled radiantly.

"Let the process begin"! Jack impetuously suggested as he grabbed Luvera's warm hand and attempted to go in search of the church's 'off switch'.

"Before we do Mr 'impatient Stern' whom have you encountered that wishes this part of the stone completely destroyed"?

"One Pigtail the Pegleg Pirate; otherwise known as Judas Ischariot"

"Him"!

"Yes him"! Jack confirmed.

"What do you know of him"? Luvera asked anticipating Jack's in depth revelation.

"I saw him at the crucifixion in a state unrecognisable to the others. He had a hand in the theft, destruction and scattering of the stone given to Saint Peter by the most cunning means.

He influenced Peter to set up shop in Rome thereby guaranteeing the survival of the Roman Empire and with it came money, land, property, debauchery, sex, war, scandals and the death of millions. He banished Saint Andrew to the East and he is probably influencial in preventing the second coming of any Christ, basically he sold his soul to the devil and gained immortality in return."

"You've done you homework well Mr Stern"!

"Thank you, providing my remote viewing is accurate."

"Believe me Mr Stern, it is. Keep up the good work. Having said that there is no need for unnecessary labour; allow me to take you to the place that you seek."

"Will there be fireworks"? Jack excitedly asked as he thought of Pigtail.

"Only, if you want them my little boy."

"Oh thank you that would be marvellous"! He happily replied pretending to be a naïve eight year old.

Luvera carefully meandered about the 'bowels' of the Church as she had previously called it until she reached the source of the Holy Waters that gushed upwards into the overhead Baptismal font. They both stood behind the unique granite altar that channelled the waters upwards.

"Beautiful isn't it." Luvera admirably half stated and half asked. Jack nodded in the affirmative. "To think that three little atoms when joined together produce such a wonderfully precious versatile liquid an absolutely brilliant work of art"!

"One woman and two men wrapped up with each other"! Jack flirtatiously commented as he saw the sexual connotation.

"Men"! Luvera uttered in subliminal disgust as she shook her head slightly.

"At your service, when do you want me to stick it in"?

"There will be none of that Mr Stern. Position yourself for the ride of your life"! The goddess of fertility retaliated as she stepped behind the unprepared Jack Stern, gripped his trouser waistband at the hips and forcibly threw him into the jet of spiralling Holy water.

The molecular Ménage a trois was suddenly shattered by Jack Stern's arrival, the woman in essence was non other than Luvera herself, her two male accompaniments eunuchs by Jack Stern's standards, became instantly jealous by his presence and immediately dissociated themselves from Luvera leaving her free to exert her will and with that the Church of the Coloured Sands transformed itself into a whirlwind of cosmic descent. Upstairs coincidentally Judas Ischariot alias Pigtail the Pegleg Pirate beamed with enthusiastic joy in the belief that he had correctly cracked the main altar's code that would bring the Church of the Coloured Sands to its knees. He gloated with satanic anticipation as the roof of the almighty structure began to disintegrate revealing clear skies above in total contrast to his malevolent mood.

"Dust to dust banished forever, a world full of the goodness of evil"! He madly chuckled as the church continued to vaporise and as it did so streams of cold air came rushing in through the open doors and swirled around him threatening to gather him up and deliver him to the heavens. Pigtail grabbed the main altar's top and held on tight, confident that he had the necessary strength to survive. Everything around him increased exponentially in strength, everything tore at him and everything tested his mettle.

"You promised fireworks"! A disappointed Jack Stern yelled at Luvera as the wild waters churned him over and over.

'Very well come with me.'

"How"?

"Swim to the edge, a salmon can do it."

"Do I look like a fish"? Jack fired back as he tried to find his balance in the turbulent waters.

"In other words you have only mastered hot air and even then you didn't do it by yourself"! Luvera's destructive reasoning made Jack think as he struggled to find a way.

Such words as "think like a fish" would normally not affect the unflappable Jack Stern, however given his present circumstances and the fact that he was dealing with a 'touchable' being as opposed to the untouchables, Jack Stern felt very vulnerable and increasingly weak. Luvera stood silent before him and observed his agony meticulously, when it was apparent to her keen eye that Jack was about to flounder miserably she placed both hands upon the altar and intoned in Latin "Aqua Cessare" A command that ceased the flow of waters and with that one exhausted Jack Stern landed on his back upon the altar like a sacrificial animal and gulped for air like a beached fish.

"Rally yourself Mr Stern! It's time for the fireworks this way please"! Luvera charmingly said as she started for the priest hole's outer chamber. Jack wearily obeyed, rolled himself off the altar and fell limply to the ground. He spent a precious thirty seconds recuperating enough strength and energy to enable him to stand on his feet unassisted and then he slowly followed the Divine creature.

"You did very well Mr Stern."

"I can't imagine how." He truthfully replied as his exhaustion prevented him from feeling any pain.

"Really let me show you the fruits of your labour." Luvera as charming as before said as she opened the priest hole's outer door and ushered Jack into the rampant chaos. The church's transition was literally feeding a small ferocious hurricane with no eye. Jack instinctively grabbed onto anything that he could in order to prevent himself from being blown away. Luvera meanwhile stood serenely nearby, hardly ruffled by it all. Jack stared in total disbelief, which prompted the Goddess to give him the courtesy of an explanation.

"I think and act as a fish." She calmly said as she extended her hand. "Take hold I will protect you." Jack accepted her offer without any hesitation, weaker than before he leant heavily upon his benefactress.

"This Mr Stern is your accomplishment."

"I don't understand how I caused this." He weakly replied.

"Then you have not learnt the intimacy between air and water. It does not matter for now, apart from the occasional lightning strike I cannot offer you any fireworks, however, observe your adversary up there, Mr Stern, a spoilt brat always stamping his feet and causing trouble, perhaps we should heal his affliction." Luvera suggested as she pointed her finger at the grief stricken Pirate who was dealing with more than he had bargained for.

She summonsed the ambient carefree energies and commanded them into action by saying "Resurrectus tibia novus" three times.

By then the floor of the altar upon which Pigtail the Pegleg Pirate was located had started to vaporise and instead of being blown away the actual altar itself remained suspended and hovered above the commotion. Pigtail hung on with all of his might, his legs whipped up behind him, a bizarre and pitiful sight. Then something changed; his legs descended or did they? The storm had not abated! What had caused this strange inexplicable occurrence?

The base of the altar converged into a point and from it emerged a slender multicoloured shimmering snake, which grew in size as the base of the disintegrating altar feed it. The snake hissed and spat reptilian obscenities until it spied Pigtails peg leg and fancied it for its own. Pigtail thought the snake to be a fellow devil in disguise, come to rescue and reward him on his efforts, but instead the snake opened its toothless mouth and started to suck in the tip of Pigtail's peg leg.

Judas Ischariot alias Pigtail the Pegleg Pirate was being forcibly stretched in two opposite directions, upwards by the tornado's fury and downwards by the devouring reptile. The pain was excruciating even for an immortal. Pigtail's peg leg was not entirely artificial its core was his own tibia and fibula; the rest was a conglomerate of materials unknown to man.

Jack watched horrified as the snake stripped the peg leg's outer coverings away until all that remained was Pigtail's own living bone. "What now"? Jack thought to himself, as he instantly doubted Luvera's supposed beauty. Sensing his loss of admiration Luvera remained steadfast and continued to support Jack Stern's weight.

"It's not as bad as it looks"! The Goddess remarked as she lovingly looked into Jack's distant eyes. "Miracles do happen! I've saved the best for last." She cryptically added.

"I don't want to know, my actions have caused me to sacrifice my friend! He stands no chance"! Jack sorrowfully mumbled regrettably making reference to Brendan.

"This is not the time to loose your faith just because everything around you is vanishing. Look how well Judas Ischariot is doing, he is born anew"! Luvera justifiably said as she drew Jack's attention to Pigtail no longer the Pegleg Pirate, nevertheless a pirate he remained. Jack snapped out of his delirious state that had been induced by exhaustion. Pigtail the Immortal Pirate clutched onto the remaining piece of floating altar. The snake, the peg leg were gone in their place a completely new and rebuilt lower limb, the same as the original was present.

"Now he'll have to do things the hard way, instead of stamping his feet and destroying those around him. Goodbye Pigtail, away with you until we meet again." Luvera said as she waved him away.

The hurricane condensed and converged upon Pigtail alias Judas Ischariot. Like a giant vacuum cleaner it picked him up, transported him into the heavens and when it ran out of puff unceremoniously dumped him into the turquoise waters of the Indian Ocean.

"One less supernatural fiend for you to worry about come Mr Stern, take me home I'm yours"! Luvera coyly said as she continued to support him.

Even in his weakened state Jack abandoned all thoughts of Yvette and he cheekily asked. "Are you seeing someone"?

"Quite the upstart Mr Stern, you are obviously the expert in Greek Mythology. The answer to your question is no and the answer to your other question is yes."

"What other question"?

"The one you were dying to ask me all along." Jack replied by appearing innocent of the fact, Luvera took it as a compliment and ended the suspense by saying.

"Do humans marry immortals"? Once again Jack remained shyly innocent with a lust that caused him to blush intensely which he could not hide.

"Take my hand Mr Stern."

"I've never let go."

"Then hold it tighter, are you ready"?

"Yes." Was all that Jack remembered, the word's image imprinted on his mind as they traversed the entire length of the universe and arrived on a world beyond the sum total of all of Jack's life experiences.

Two suns, four unequal orbiting satellites and colours unimaginable yet recognised as though he had been there before.

"Where are we"? Jack asked as his soul thirsted for the knowledge.

"On a world in the Universe known as the one without limitations; everything you see here is my handiwork. This is the cradle of life where everything is truly free, a concept beyond human comprehension. Once an idea is conceived here and embraced by all, the entity leaves to test its abilities elsewhere."

It was then that Jack reached into his pocket and discovered the fragment of the true Catholic Church, the one that bore Luvera's touch and had been activated by Brendan's immense love. The fragment hummed with an excitement almost as great as that of Jack's, it was glad to be partially home even though it yearned for its missing brothers and sisters.

Luvera escorted Jack on a whirlwind tour of the Planet of Fertility, he attempted to take in and remember as much as he could before he felt the urge to return to earth.

"I feel your calling." Luvera calmly said as she stopped navigating. Jack appreciated her sensitivity and briefly flashed a thankyou smile. "We can return another day; I'll race you back, ready…. Steady…. Set…."

"Wait a moment I've never done this before! I don't even know where I am." Jack protested.

The Universe is smaller than you think; it is only your exaggerations that enlarge it"!

"But.... but...." Jack continued to protest as Luvera freed herself from his embrace and faded from view.

42

EXAGGERATIONS

Outrageously weak, disillusioned, confused and completely abandoned are probably some of the words that applied to Jack Stern's pitiful state.

Supposedly alone on a planet in the Universe with no limitations what was he meant to do? Fantasize about his method of departure or wait patiently until his Angel of Sleep or Grandpa would eventually come looking for him. The former was a poor chance the latter also a bad bet, quite erratic lately totally preoccupied with building. No one else apart from Luvera herself except she seemed intent on teaching Jack a lesson, Gods know why , unless it had something to do with exaggeration, a state usually associated with emotion and he had certainly been reduced to such a state.

Jack sat down on what he thought was lush grass and tried to adjust himself to his new world of indescribable colour. Everything was bright, yet not blinding, two suns in the sky but not excessively hot, four satellites and no discernable astronomical tension, every-thing lush but no water, none had he seen anywhere during his tour.

"No water how will I survive? No food what will sustain me? No shelter where will I sleep"? Jack questioned himself hardly moving.

"As beautiful as it may seem it is a desert devoid of animated life. Everything appears to be in balance nothing appears to dominate anything else," He though as he feebly studied his surroundings.

"What did she do to me? I have never in all of my life felt so drained! It's almost as if I am about to die! That stream of holy water what was so miraculous about it? Why did my immersion in it cause the church to undergo such a tortuous and drastic transformation? All I wanted was a simple off switch and blink it was gone instead I've had life drained out of me! Luvera Goddess of Fertility nay I say, she's more likely to be a demon of destruction! Remove me and Brendan's all alone, can or will he cope? There are many enemies plotting his downfall.

There are many.... many.... ways.... The universe is smaller than you think.... It is.... Sm..all we humans magnify our importance's and insignificance's by our exaggerations.... Ex..age..rations. I am being rationed I am the object of the rationing. Rations only occur during shortages, war, disaster, why me, of what indispensable value am I that I should be dealt with in such a manner? In this world of no limitations what will cause me to regain my strength? How is it the air that I breathe supports me, the light that fills the atmo-sphere warms me; the matter that I lay upon envelopes me? It grows steadily up and around, in and out of my body curvatures, nooks and crannies I am so weak that I cannot even resist its advances. I wish I could sleep forever. What spell has she cast upon me? Am I to sleep for a hundred years and await a Goddess to stir me into life? Is this my tomb? My destiny? Is that my failing my previously hidden undeniable wish to marry an immortal Goddess made apparent to me but only through my weakness? What other failings do I have? Why do I doubt myself? What purpose will it serve? This is not me! This is an exaggeration! I am closer to home than I think! Home is next door, I can feel it, touch it, smell it, see it I can.... "!

"He does waffle on, anyone would think that he was delirious! Can't he see we're looking after him! Come on Jack wake up, there's a good lad. Enough of your self pity and your personal brand of psycho-analysis snap out of it"! Grandpa in his own way said as he monitored his grandson's progress and increased the concentration of the swimming pools physiological energisers at the Genius Loci. "Luvera you really have done it this time! Stressed him out to the max! I don't know whether I should report you to your superiors"?

"I'm auto.... "

"Autocratic"! Grandpa shouted visibly disturbed.

"No"!

"Auto-immune"! Grandpa tried again gesticulating wildly.

"No"!

"Automated" Grandpa frustratingly barked.

"No"!

"Let's try audacious, abhorrent, abominable, authoritative, auton-omous, autopsy"!

"I'm not the Angel of Death"! Luvera hit back.

"To my Grandson you are! You almost killed him! Didn't you realise how dangerous it was to use a human to reverse miraculous holy water"? Grandpa aggressively asked.

"Of course I did! Mr Stern appeared to be made from stern stuff"!

"Very funny"

"I don't know what all the fuss is about! He's not dead"!

'Just about" Grandpa fumed.

"Stop exaggerating! Fetch Yvette and have her kiss him."

"It's not that simple"! Grandpa argued to the contrary.

"Human ghost"!

"Are you insulting me"? Grandpa hoarsely screamed.

"Not at all, merely defining your limitations"!

"Did someone call my name"? Yvette sweetly asked in her soft voice as she stepped into the large chamber that housed Grandpa's therapeutic swimming pool.

"It was mentioned." Luvera coolly replied as she folded her arms.

"Was it important"? Yvette inquired, as she innocently looked

Luvera up and down.

"Let me introduce you my precious child, this is Luvera the Goddess of Fertility." Grandpa calmly said after he regained his composure.

"A pleasure to meet you I think. What happened to Jack? He looks very pale almost grey"! Yvette gasped with a shocked look on her face after she saw Jack languishing in the pool.

"He had a rough encounter helping me dismantle the Church of the Coloured Sands it was our way of protecting the fragment." The Goddess of Fertility unemotionally explained.

"He shouldn't be grey, I've only seen that in dead people." Yvette commented as she recollected the numerous funerals that she had attended at St Pious Church.

"Fairytale stuff" Luvera fluently suggested.

"What are you implying"? Yvette asked becoming somewhat hostile as her motherly instincts activated themselves. Luvera remained silent and allowed Grandpa to answer on her behalf.

"You'll need to kiss him truly."

"Role reversal, very well I understand." Yvette answered as she very quickly grasped the situation and accepted its challenge. She walked over to where he lay, bent over while she held her long hair back with one hand and kissed him tenderly for a lengthy while until she felt his heart beat stronger. Jack deliberately kept his eyes closed, relaxed his jaw muscles, allowed his lips to part and with it came an invitation for their tongues to caress each other.

"Bit more erotic than fairytale stuff"! Grandpa cheekily remarked as he spied the couple's oral intensity.

"Who said fairytales are for children"? Luvera asked as she envied Yvette.

A newfound strength coursed its way through Jack Stern's arteries and veins. He felt its origin, which was Yvette's radiant innocence and vowed to protect her at all costs. "I love you." He freely admitted as a tear drop rolled down his left cheek.

"How touching." Luvera dryly said as she interrupted the lover's intimacy. They ignored her verbal intrusion and continued to admire and respect each other whilst Grandpa stood nearby and approved.

"Mr Stern it is only a woman's love that will see you through; help you make a full recovery. I suggest you convalesce for a few days before venturing out. It will mean staying in bed and kissing for hours on end, something you will obviously enjoy"!

"Everyman does"! Grandpa interrupted as he fondly remembered many of his earthy sexual encounters with the opposite sex.

"What about Brendan? He needs my help." Jack wearily asked visibly disappointed with his state of physical exhaustion.

"No he doesn't! If you continue to protect him he will never become fertile, nor realise his full potential, you have done quite enough"! Luvera authoritatively warned. Jack heeded the Goddess's words, reluctantly nodded in the affirmative and resigned himself to the belief that irrespective of his evolutionary status with respect to humans he was midway between them and the angels and much further away from the Gods who used him as a pawn in the games they played on earth. He couldn't decide whether it was a blessing or a curse much like intelligence.

43

CONTROVERSIAL SHUTDOWN PART A

The Mauritian President Casseem Ringagain considered himself to be somewhat of a playboy, one who was eager to acquaint himself with the opposite sex especially if they were good looking and receptive to his reproductive motives. Race was no barrier for Casseem was a colourful mixture in himself, part French, part Chinese, part Indian and part English his genetics reflected both the diversity of the Island's cuisine not to mention its population's racial makeup.

The President hardly slept the previous night out of sheer excitement at meeting not the extremely handsome and charismatic Farther Brendan O'Reilly but rather his seven sensational sisters. The man whose reputation for throwing highly successful and memorable parties made every conceivable effort to ensure that his work would not go unrewarded and that he would at least snare one of the lovelies for the night.

Bright and bushy tailed, groomed and grinning President Ringagain waited with trepidation in the main foyer of parliament house with a handful of his top governmental staff for his guests to arrive. Apart from Casseem who agonised how long it took for every minute to pass, everyone else appeared calm and participated in idle chitchat. The tension in President's Ringagain mind was freed by the chiming of the front door bell. It was not your average ding-dong or ding-a-ling instead it delivered a pleasant Creole tune much to the amusement of the visitor and annoyance of the buildings many staff. President Casseem rushed to the door, pushed aside its normal attendant sending him scurrying to the floor and robustly opened it.

"Good morning Father! I'm so glad you accepted my invitation! Come in please, you and your lovely ladies and…." The President gushed redfaced.

"Thank you Sir, I hope you do not mind but I have brought along Sister Ambrosia. Mr Jack Stern and Yvette Bell could not make it and I thought considering how much good work Sister has done with the poor you would extend your hospitality to embrace her." Brendan openly said.

"Marvellous! Stupendous! I'm… I'm… overjoyed! She… could… er … er attend"! Casseem faked as he extended his hand and secretively thought to himself as he bowed from the waist. "What is that old battleaxe doing here? God I hope she's not the guardian for the day otherwise I'm doomed"!

Sister Ambrosia crinkled her face, squinted forcibly at his lies and restrained herself from yelling "liar" Instead she graciously welcomed his impromptu answer with a wry smile and a nod of her head.

"Come this way please, my house chef's have prepared a sumptuous banquet in recognition of your good work." President Ringagain beckoned as he led the way followed by his attentive and well-trained staff. Brendan allowed the girls to go first, he and Sister Ambrosia brought up the rear.

"Your friend that fool; you know the one I mean." Ambrosia abruptly said.

"Do you mean Jack"? Brendan amusingly asked.

"Yes, yes! Has he made a decent woman of Yvette"?

"Do you mean has he had sex with her or asked her to marry him"?

"Both"! Ambrosia meanly demanded.

"Neither I suspect; outwardly I detect no change in the damsel." Brendan correctly replied.

"You're protecting him! You know otherwise! I'm no fool I know what's going on! How could you possibly associate yourself with such an upstart"? Ambrosia aggressively asked.

"Put it this way, he's a little unusual and it takes a little while to get used to, in fact I think I'll never fully understand him, too...."

"Deviously complicated"! Ambrosia rudely interrupted finishing Brendan's description and then she firmly said. "I have! I put him in the league of a loner, a string puller; a faceless man that lurks in the shadows orchestrates people and reaps the profits. I don't like the man at all. I think you and he should part company"!

Brendan was momentarily taken aback by Ambrosia's caustic deductions; he determined that the nun's bitterness was probably due to a past memory that Jack had conjured up and therefore he suggested. "Hum... Jack's very good at unmasking false people, something they absolutely detest, especially the...."

"What are you saying"? Ambrosia angrily asked ruffled by Brendan's perceptive accuracy.

"Nothing at all Sister just making an observation about a man one I do not know intimately, yet one that I cannot deny." He calmly replied as he stopped walking.

"Pity there are no cocks around here" Ambrosia acidly retorted making a biblical reference that Brendan quickly identified. "In any case what about all of the donated monies"?

"I thought generous sums had been forwarded to your charity."

"Yes they have."

"So"?

"What about the rest"?

"I don't know I'm no book keeper" Brendan freely admitted.

"Just my point, a dark faceless man who wishes to take advantage of people"! Ambrosia hammered her point, this time a gloomy doubt infiltrated Brendan's mind and he remained silent and a little shaken by the insinuation.

"Why so gloomy Father, you are in Mauritius the Isle of merriment, come let nothing disturb you, today is another day in paradise, come a banquet awaits you one of many"! President Ringagain sung as he approached Brendan and ushered him towards the perfectly laid out breakfast table that overflowed with flowers and fresh fruit arrangements. It was located on the spacious rear balcony of Government house overlooking the nearby ocean.

Once Brendan and all of the others were seated President Casseem snapped his fingers and his catering staff sprung into action.

"Ladies, gentleman, as you are of American origin I thought it best not to inflict upon you so early in the morning our Creole ways but rather to tantalise your tastebuds with a fusion of French-American dishes expertly prepared by our own well travelled chefs. Entree... entree... subito... s'il vous plait! First cast your eyes upon our vast yeasty delights located on the sideboard behind you. Country walnut, chocolate, pumpkin and pine nut breads, brioche, hazelnut twist, Danish pastries, almond, chocolate and strawberry croissants"! Casseem expertly described in his rich accent as he slowly pointed to each delightful creation. Satisfied with his delivery the President walked over to where the girls were seated and enjoyed brushing his anatomy 'accidentally' against their exposed limbs. As he walked about he playfully touched their crowning glories and softly rubbed each one on the shoulder as a measure of determining their individual warmth and response, then he brightly announced.

"Now that I have sufficiently distracted your attention it is time for the unveiling of your breakfasts. Unfortunately there is no choice each of us receives the same. Attendants if you please"!

Behind each of the seated stood a waiter with silver service in hand the covered plate was ceremoniously lowered before each invited guest, all apart from Brendan felt like royalty, then on Ringagain's command the silver domes were lifted in unison to reveal artistically arranged eggs benedict with smoked salmon, crepes filled with Cointreau flavoured cream containing fresh mandarin pieces and a selection of fresh local fruits. The waiters then presented each person with a multi-layered mock fruit cocktail.

"Light and highly delicious, a perfect blend of tastes just like the company I enjoy here today." President Casseem jovially expressed with a sense of theatrical exaggeration. He then went around the table and offered each guest tea or coffee to compliment his or her breakfast whilst he continued to gauge, which one would be his for the night. The only one who responded more than amorously to his hot subliminal moves was Sister Ambrosia. Casseem then seated himself next to Brendan and attacked his breakfast.

"You know Father Brendan you are a very clever marketer"! President Ringagain commented as he cut into his eggs benedict.

"I didn't know I was anything of the kind."

"Now, now, Father do not play dumb with me; being Hindu I know the limitations of religion and how hard it is to recruit new members especially if all of its customs are boring. But you Father have breathed new life into your church! What a stroke of genius! A handsome priest to attract the women and seven delectable young sexy women to seduce the men"! Brendan swallowed hard and hid his embarrassment. "You must have spent years developing the concept and that voice of yours, tell me, was it that, that you used to recruit these lovelies"?

"I'd rather not say. Successful marketing has its secrets and I would like to…"

"Keep it to yourself. Yes Father I quite understand, however, there is one other matter; the church, how did you manage to come by it? There are no official records of it ever having been built although some of the locals the one's whose ancestors were slaves brought in from Madagascar by the Dutch tell me that there exists folklore stories about the Island having been once inhabited by strange beings. Perhaps you could shed some light on the subject." President Casseem genuinely inquired as he slowly chewed on his food and looked Brendan in the eye.

"Afraid not, we came to Mauritius for a holiday courtesy of my friend Jack Stern."

"Yes I believe you stayed at Club Med. Some of the GO's that I am familiar with mentioned their frustrations to me." President Ringagain related with a gleam in his eye as he remembered how fertile the grounds of the resort were for him and how many foreign ladies he had managed to bed down.

"It wasn't intentional." Brendan excused himself.

"It never is with handsome men." Casseem dryly replied adding support to Brendan's excuse in a roundabout way before he took a sip of his warm coffee and said. "Then I am told you went into the wilderness and discovered the Church so to speak"!

"Yes." Brendan cautiously answered as he wished Jack were present to diffuse Casseem's abstract line of questioning.

"I see, strange, very strange"! Casseem Ringagain replied as he stroked his chin. Brendan meanwhile pondered his precarious situation. "No matter as long as it continues to bring us prosperity what difference does it make as to how it came about" He then said after a pensive pause. "Ladies, Sister Ambrosia is there anything else we can offer you? No alcohol I'm afraid, you have a busy schedule ahead of you today unlike some of the drunken locals who are inebriated before the sun rises, pity they haven't partaken of the Holy water."

"Even the good Lord does not believe in a universal panacea." Ambrosia boldly put forward philosophically as she choose a strawberry croissant from the sideboard and returned to her place.

"An interesting point of view coming from a Catholic, perhaps I have misjudged you." Casseem said with a wink of his eye as he feigned interest.

"Perhaps you have, let me remind you sir that I am about fifteen years your senior."

"Age is no barrier." Ringagain flirted.

"Next you'll be telling me that Holy Orders are no barrier either"! Ambrosia teased seductively as she bit into her croissant and allowed its creamy contents to erotically spill from its edges and the corners of her mouth. Brendan guessed it was Ambrosia's way of protecting his ladies and he extended this realisation into believing that her suspicions about Jack Stern might well be true, a money hungry string puller, the seed of doubt, the first denial.

The jovial and relaxed atmosphere that President Casseem the self-confessed ladies man had created caused everyone to linger for longer than normal. Once they had appreciatively consumed their fill the girls found favour with the man of a thousand amusing anecdotes and they started to crowd around him on the open balcony. Sister Ambrosia seemingly jealous was not pleased and made several fruitless attempts to water down the President's fiery and charismatic ways. Finally in desperation she wedged herself between Candy and Ringagain and bellowed.

"Mr President judging by your body language I can see that you are a lover of dance. The tango for openers; followed by the waltz, then a brisk quickstep before culminating with the bedroom mazurka as the climatic finale. Don't you think it's a little early in the morning for that sort of thing"?

"Mother Superior has spoken! Perfect timing otherwise we would have missed out on all of the festivities. My apologies, I like you Sister prefer the evening! Now my gorgeous Mademoiselles we will have to continue our little affairs later." The completely unflappable Casseem answered in his affable style.

It was then that the cloud of despair lifted itself from Brendan's mind and he was able to remember President Ringagain from a past time.

"Long sideburns, a moustache, a goatee or two, hair in different styles, cut and coloured to suit the prowl. At Club Med you were there, ready to pounce on the unsuspecting young and middle-aged who sought romance, but that was not you, find, fondle, fornicate and forget was your motto! Thank God for Sister Ambrosia, at least you got him right! Thanks for protecting my girls, hope you're wrong about Jack"! Brendan thought as he angrily scrutinised the lecherous President who remained intent on scoring that day and was oblivious to Brendan's disgust.

"Come my lovely ladies our somewhat outrageous cavalcade awaits us." Casseem proudly announced as he quickly checked the time on his wristwatch and ushered his guests out. Two government attendants in fancy dress suddenly appeared and led the group downstairs.

'What is that fool up to now"? Ambrosia suspiciously asked in a low voice as she kept a sharp eye on the Presidents movements.

"Jack's not here." Brendan commented in answer to her question.

"Not him, the other one! Wake up man! God knows what makes you so special"? Ambrosia caustically replied as she quickened her pace. Brendan accelerated to keep up and remained silent, content to let matters unfold at their own pace.

In the open front courtyard stood eight gaily decorated transport trucks on the tray of the first aptly named Music Maker was a fifteen-piece brass band complete with a bright and breezy percussion section. The talented musicians played a potpourri of jazzed up American songs mainly from well-known Hollywood movies out of respect for the guests of honour heritage. The second to fifth floats were corporate in nature. The first a vivid explosion of the Mauritian National flag in all shapes and sizes followed by dozens of young boys and girls on bicycles proudly sporting their country's standard flag on upright poles attached to the bicycles rear frame a second wave of adult cyclists followed them on touring bikes fitted with portable fibreglass rods bearing the American flag which had been hastily but correctly printed in one of the Island's many textile factories.

The third in line left no doubt as to its intention. The 'Booze Bus' was a cut down, cut out passenger bus, with seats removed, full of good home grown Mauritian rum in glass and plastic 250ml bottles. The latter catering for the down trodden and fallen, every drop is precious to the drunk; plastic breaks less easily than glass. Attached to the bus was another bus without its engine, loaded to the hilt with more rum and in the middle of the pile stood a native colourfully dressed as a pineapple his job was to satisfy as many of the thousands who had decided to attend the festivities out of curiosity than any religious fervour. The Christians could keep their ecstasies to themselves all that these people wanted was good old fashioned flavoured ethanol to fuel their needs and desires. Sadly for them the next float bore a four-metre tall Paper Mache statue of the Blessed Virgin Mary on one side of which stood a sacred cow and on the other an erect dragon in full plumage. Behind these sat an Indian-Chinese ensemble that played a fusion of music from both cultures. Out of the chaos that ensued one could recognise some sort of discernible melody although it was difficult to do so.

The fifth float was a tribute to the dead but not forgotten Dodo bird. The loathsome bird or nauseating fowl as it was called back in 1507 by the Dutch sailors. A wooden plaque depicting the Mauritius coat of arms was securely bolted to the top of the truck's cabin. On its tilt tray was a menagerie of make believe stuffed Dodo's sitting under a replica of the Tambalacoque also known as the Dodo tree, scattered around the birds were an assortment of Malay head dressings made from the feathers of the Dodo's and used in religious ceremonies.

Audio speakers set around and in the Dodo tree continually blared out a two-note pigeon like doo-doo sound in various tones much to the annoyance of a group of irritated crab-eating macaques who sat idly in a cage nearby, contemplating. Banners ran down the full length of the vehicle, one read 'Mauritius never as dead as the Dodo' whilst the other said ' Mauritius Island of Life' Brendan found this particular float a little creepy as the hidden forewarning made the hair on the back of his neck stand up on end.

The next float was empty it was reserved for Father Brendan O'Reilly and his bevy of beauties, who were expected and requested to appear in bathing costumes courtesy of the President himself and designed by a world famous couturier to whom the Island's textile industry was much indebted as the majority of his creations were manufactured there.

"Isn't this a little over the top"? Brendan asked defending his girls' modesty as the President distributed the garments.

"It's a warm day, nice to see girls lightly attired, a little cheeky perhaps, nothing wrong with looking at lovely long legs, a little belly button and mustn't forget the cleavage! Sex sells Father sex sells! Come along my lovelies do this for El Presidente I promise you will be richly rewarded"!

"Where's mine"? Ambrosia sharply asked looking wounded at being forgotten.

"My apologies Sister; as Yvette could not make it perhaps you could try her costume on for size"! The President jokingly said as he passed over the spare garment and then he added. "It will be a good measure of how well your body has stood up to the test of time." Ambrosia snatched the goods from his hand and walked off in disgust. "We have assembled temporary change rooms around the corner." He shouted after her. Satisfied with the manner in which he had handled Ambrosia Ringagain turned to Brendan and smiled broadly.

"Don't tell me you have an outfit for me as well"! Brendan shakily said in an elevated voice.

"Calm yourself Father, no such luck I'm afraid. All you'll have to do is sit in that chair over there and wave like the Queen of England." Casseem politely directed as he pointed to the regal float.

"I'm not a lady nor am I a …. '!

"Yes… yes I know that but then again I have heard rumours." The President dryly said as he raised one eyebrow. Brendan remained un-phased, dismissed the remark and decided to take his position as Casseem intended.

Everything on the royal float was decorated in shades of red and gold. The central ornate 'throne' was raised and surrounded by eight mushroom shaped stools, all very pretty. Brendan saw no point in protesting or complaining about the floats overall appearance, he gingerly took his seat and although uncomfortable waited patiently for the procession to start.

The float behind him was reserved for the Mauritian President Ringagain. Its theme was overwhelmingly sedate; nothing out of the ordinary, plain boring, for it was his wish not to upstage his guest's of honour, apart from one minor detail. The huge 'VOTE FOR ME' placard that lay face down on the truck's tray just waiting to be picked up and waved about. It was in Casseem's character to take advantage of any given situation. The very last float was for the 'troop's as Casseem fondly described them. These were all manner of men highly trained by black African insurgents to take care and resolve any ugly situation that might damage the President's reputation or his persona. They were very capable at their job and apart from them there was no other police presence. On this occasion the 'troops' resembled a bowl of fruit salad. Each officer was dressed in carnival attire that reflected the fruit of his choice; fifty men in all and not one piece of duplicated fruit.

Brendan sat pensively upon his throne and stared at the restless macaques in front of him as he thought. "Clever monkeys, how did anyone manage to capture you? Was it food or sex? Two things important to the animal, how important are they to me? I haven't 'touched' myself since seminary days. Enforced guilt is a powerful restraint but unnatural. Why do so many people wish to control others? Why me? How important is it to be blindly obedient? I'm out of the cage free to move about and yet I feel no freer than you poor macaques! There is no difference between us! Sometimes I wish I were like you! Mr Jack Stern where are you? How is it that on such an important day as today you are missing? It troubles me my friend, it troubles me."

"What a wonderful day! Drivers to your vehicles, ignition on, everyone on board, time to head them out, Port Louis here we come"! President Ringagain sung out as he pretended to be a flamboyant circus ringmaster.

"Come my gorgeous trapeze artists, my seductive pole dancers, on board, you glamour puss's. Hey O'Reilly why so glum? Let's make you a little sexier! Rip that shirt open give us a peek at your pec's come on macho man." The President asserted himself as Brendan's girls sauntered out of the makeshift dressing rooms in true catwalk fashion. President Casseem was right the seven ex prostitutes looked positively radiant in their designer outfits, elegant, chic, naughty and nice.

"Now Mr O'Reilly come here"! Casseem commanded as he approached Brendan and stood between his open legs. "Bend forward that's a good boy there that should do it. Oh my God don't you have a big one, bet you've had plenty of comments"!

"Actually no I keep it hidden" Brendan shyly replied as he blushed deeply.

"Well it's out now for all to see"! President Ringagain smirked as he made reference to Brendan's encrusted crucifix, which sparkled, merrily in the full sun. "Up you come girls. What do you think? Does he look like a rock star or what"? Casseem proudly asked as he displayed his sartorial efforts. Their reaction was mixed which caused Ringagain to carefully study Brendan's hair. "Hum a little too sedate, needs a bit of wildness let's give him that wind swept look"! Casseem coarsely suggested as he expertly ruffled and combed Brenda's receptive hair into a style similar to that of the one and only King…Elvis. 'Okay let's rock and roll"!

The cavalcade sprung into action, the girls giggled with excitement, the macaques jumped about and the President leapt off the Royal Throne onto his own ride. The road from Government House to Port Louis was relatively uninhabited, strict orders had been given to congregate and concentrate the revellers at the harbour town.

The theme of the party was aerial, as Ringagain believed it should symbolically represent the gifts of the Gods in bringing prosperity to the Island. Hundreds of novelty kites filled the air, makeshift hot air balloons as well; piñatas suspended from cables that had been strung across the streets completed the dazzling display. The latter were the hot topic of conversation for both adults and children alike. They floated to and fro in the early morning sea breeze and teased their onlookers. The variety of shapes had one and all guessing as to their contents.

There were, Hula dancers, fairies, bumblebees, ponies, pirates, treasure chests, Dodo's, stars, pineapples, monkeys, the sun, quarter moon, clowns, sea horses, flying fish, footballs, dolphins, coconuts and more, all tantalisingly close yet distant enough to remain untouched. Their descent was timed to coincide with the scheduled 2pm fireworks, each piñata was complete with multiple drawstrings, one correct pull and its contents would be discharged over all and sundry.

As the floats neared the harbour the assembled crowds of people erupted into thunderous applause, welcoming cheers and whistles. The girls were elated, Brendan felt uneasy and Ambrosia's suspicions were confirmed. President Ringagain had hoisted his huge 'VOTE FOR ME' placard and vigorously waved it about, up and down.

"Got to make hay when the sun shines; by the way Sister you look gooood in that outfit"! He glibly remarked as he continued to stir up the crowd with his political antics. Even the macaques reacted vocally to Ringagain's actions.

"Bleeding monkeys disgusting dirty creatures." Ambrosia acidly grumbled as she turned away to greet the awaiting crowds which were clearly divided into two groups, believers and non-believers; givers and takers.

The trucks completed a circuit of the harbour before stopping at their final destination, the open dock area that was surrounded by an abundance of shops. In front of these were several marquees erected by some of the more exclusive hotels on the Island specifically for one purpose only, to display their world famous culinary skills.

The girls were especially taken by the goat cheese with Espelette red pepper and balsamic vinegar, Brendan stayed clear of the panned scallops on a bed of mashed sweet potato with wasabi sauce as he had been wasabied before by Jack Stern back in Newburn, instead he played it safe by partaking of the scallops and camarons duo, palm hearts salsa with chardonnay. Food was everywhere, for all to enjoy, at the docks, on the waterfront, in the markets, all courtesy of the Mauritian Government.

Within half an hour of stopping, the 'Booze Bus' was empty, the pineapple dry and the scheming macaques deliriously happy. The cunning monkeys had been able to snatch two plastic rum bottles from passers-by and cleverly unscrewed them with their teeth, unlike other primates they did not pour out the rum and lap it up from the ground, instead they had through observations of humans learnt to drink straight from the bottle a sip at a time, a technique which prevented the fiery liquid from burning their delicate throats; much better than eating naturally fermented fruits the macaques were drunk in no time, inhibition free, wise as an owl, they plotted their escape.

Not one of Brendan's troupe exhibited any degree of gluttony or alcohol abuse, they remained refined, reserved and thoughtful, they acted with a sense of decorum and truthfully expressed their opinion of all the dishes they tasted in a manner that did not insult the chef's efforts nor their reputations. Sadly this was not true of Bruno Bogliani, the stinky sock man, who believed that everything in the world nay everything in the universe could be explained by socks. Bogliani's highly developed sense of smell, which came about as a result of years of 'starvation', quickly led him to find Brendan and the Girls. He was there for the 'kill' he methodically swept through all of the exclusive marquees as a lowly swine and devoured everything in sight.

"And to think you ran the church before Brendan arrived"! President Ringagain said quite disgusted, without reservation as he stepped into the marquee that Bogliani had decided to plop himself into and make his own.

"My God, man; do you not have any shame? You are meant to be a man of God! What do you think you are doing"? Casseem roughly barked as he observed Bogliani drowning his thirst from wine bottles that he held in each hand. Bruno swallowed hard, caught his breath and belched loudly for his own amusement.

"In this hand I hold a white sock hic... and in that hand I hold a red sock! They're normally known as wine skins however I prefer to refer to them as socks! The red one here is absolutely delightful! Nice fruity sort of mouldy mushroomy flavour, whereas the white, what a joy. Acidy, and repulsive, reminiscent of one hundred day old unwashed well-worn socks! Would you care for some"? Bogliani slurred as he took another swig from the left then the right, left again, right again, until Casseem stopped him by shouting at the top of his voice.

"You are a disgrace! People like you ruin everything! Just make me one promise, stay in here until the party finishes"!

"Can do, as long as the socks don't run out" The thought of it made Bogliani cringe and Casseem storm out of the marquee.

The president took a series of deep breaths and bravely stepped into the full sunshine. Merriment abounded everywhere, in the peoples chatter, amongst the clutter of dishes and on the breeze's shoulders as it carried the sweet notes of happy music throughout the harbour. Bogliani the 'stinky sock in the drawer' could stay where he was indefinitely as far as Ringagain was concerned! The President made certain that the 'socks' from which Bogliani drank would not run dry, with that loose end tied up Ringagain realised it was time to formalise the celebration and he went in search of Brendan and his girls. Although the marquees had been reserved for the exclusive pleasure of his guests it wasn't long before some of the more inebriated locals under the influence of the local rum decided that they also should be allowed to sample what the Island's exclusive resorts had to offer. With little security in place the chefs could do nothing more than oblige the demanding crowds until supplies ran out. Ringagain offered no help apart from the occasional smile, as it was not his intention to host a twenty-four hour eating marathon, with the help of his fifty pieces of 'fruit' he quickly located Brendan with some of his girls.

"There you are my international rock star"! Casseem jovially exclaimed as he approached Brendan from behind and laid both of his hands upon the priest's handsome shoulders.

"Great street party, just love the food, you've outdone yourself Mr President"! Brendan automatically responded without turning around.

"Sorry about the crowds, I suppose everyone wants to get into the act and touch you, especially the women, judging by the fullness of your pockets you seem to have accumulated hundreds of phone numbers."

Brendan blushed and reluctantly turned to face Ringagain.

"Lucky man I wish I were so sexually popular! You must have quite a reputation"!

"Based on fantasy and fiction, nothing more" Brendan truthfully replied as he discarded the contents of his pockets.

"Do you mind if I keep them"? Casseem wickedly asked with a lecherous gleam in his eye as he stooped down to pickup the scraps of paper from the ground.

"Not at all, providing you intentions are honourable! I would hate to think that you would take advantage of any vulnerable woman by suggesting that if she granted you a pleasurable favour you would in return arrange a rendezvous with me"! Brendan replied with a tilt of his head as he studied Casseem's evasive eyes.

"It's time to pronounce you King for the Day my lord." Casseem said evading Brendan's accurate supposition. "This way please the stage awaits you, come Father, ladies this way if you please." The president eagerly directed as he thrust the discarded telephone numbers deep into his trouser pockets. Brendan decided to finish eating his hand made chocolate praline, he then cleaned his hands with an impregnated paper towel and followed.

The president's highly trained pieces of 'fruit' forged a pathway for his guests of honour through the mingling crowd. As they made their way towards the stage the group passed by the Dodo float and Brendan immediately took pity on the languishing macaques. The poor animals had been left out in the full heat of the midday sun, which coupled with their intake of alcohol, and lack of drinking water had left them somewhat bewildered and dangerously dehydrated. Not wishing to make their release obvious Brendan very briefly slowed his pace of walking. In less than two footsteps, he mentally intoned the correct mystical words, intimately reacted with the macaques' steel cage and before anyone realised what had happened, both the cage door's lock and hinges fell apart. Brendan smiled with content and winked at the disbelieving primates.

"There you are my funny furry friends enjoy your freedom, perhaps one day you can teach me to be as free as well." He spoke with his eyes as he managed to look at each individual just before they all escaped into the crowd. Brendan then returned to his normal gait and looked nonchalantly around as if nothing had happened.

In front of the stage lay dozens of abandoned bicycles, their riders having discarded them after positioning their respective flags either American or Mauritian on or about the stage in one of the allotted holders. The nations flags formed a dazzling display of coloured movement that represented an ideal backdrop for the 'King of the Day' namely Father Brendan O'Reilly. President Casseem scampered up the stairs followed by some of his pieces of 'fruit' once everyone was in place and the area secured he invited Brendan and the girls to join him.

The scaffolded platform was a good four metres above ground, sturdily built it could accommodate at least fifty people on stage. In the centre stood a podium complete with four microphones; three of which were assigned to the amplification system that delivered sound centrally, to the right and left with the remaining microphone intended for the local radio station's direct broadcast 'Fanfare for the common man' sparkled from the numerous hi-fidelity speakers positioned around the harbour and city, it was the grand musical signature that the President always used whenever he was present at important public gatherings.

"Good afternoon men, women and children of Mauritius! Are you enjoying yourselves"? He bellowed. The crowd let out a huge roar that resembled a muddled 'yes' in many languages.

"I can't hear you"! Casseem screamed back in true theatrical style. Again the crowd roared except this time even louder.

"Good! Very good! Thank you for turning up today and making this celebration such an enormous success! We will mark this Calender day henceforth as a Mauritian National holiday in honour of Father Brendan O'Reilly and his remarkable discovery. He will live in our hearts for as long as Mauritius exists"! The president proudly exclaimed with a huge grin that displayed his pearly white teeth and said much for his political ambitions. Just then the first aerial bomb went streaking upwards into the sky and exploded overhead as if on cue.

"I see our children are becoming restless, be patient little ones the piñatas will be yours shortly, just ten minutes away on the sound of the second explosion they will drop and you can jump up and rip them open once you pull the right string." The President paused so as to make certain everyone understood the promise.He then looked at Brendan who stood to the left of him with five of his girls.

"Father O'Reilly through your undying efforts you have brought unparalleled prosperity and a new meaning to the Island of Mauritius. We thank you and in return we crown you 'King of Mauritius' for the day and give you a key that will open any door you wish." The president's words of praise were followed by the second aerial bomb exploding in the sky. All of the children present immediately stopped what they were doing; dropped their drinks and food and gazed upwards. Rapturous gibberish spread everywhere like wildfire as the piñatas descended and the children eagerly jumped every which way they could to disembowel the gift laden creatures. The noise of the excitement was deafening a convenient distraction that allowed the unexpected and unannounced appearance of Archbishop Steven Moulds, Brendan's superior. His Grace resplendent in black, not a smile on his face, grim as the reaper, floated up the stairs and stood between President Ringagain and Brendan O'Reilly. The Archbishop was not alone, at the bottom of the stairs stood six sinister figures. Brendan remained calm for he had spotted his Grace in the crowd and had intuitively expected his arrival days earlier. The girls thought the Archbishops presence was auspicious, not one of them suspected otherwise nor did Ringagain's pieces of 'fruit'.

France 2's roving international journalist Josephine and her cameraman Benoit from their vantage point also thought that His Grace's presence was a seal of approval. The pair had spent the morning filming as part of their report. Benoit zoomed in with his camera to record the happenings on stage. President Casseem it appeared was exchanging pleasantries with the Archbishop and was biding his time until the children's commotion died down.

"Ladies and gentlemen of Mauritius, what a surprise for me, His Grace Archbishop Steven Moulds has journeyed from America to personally bless this occasion, please give him a warm welcome." The President sung out. No response, everyone it appeared was preoccupied with the piñatas and their contents. Casseem Ringagain repeated his previous words; again no response from the Island's people, the wind blew his words out to sea.

"Are we on air"? He asked quite annoyed.

One of his security guards immediately responded by saying. "I'll check."

"What's happening Benoit"? Josephine asked as she strained to hear what was being said on stage.

"Technical problems with the sound"

"At the mixing station"

"No that looks intact" Benoit answered.

"Scan the perimeter, use telephoto function as far as it will go."

"Yes Madame." Benoit confidently replied as he adjusted his newly acquired high powered lens.

"Find anything"? Josephine impatiently asked as she squinted to pick up anything unusual.

"Power supply intact, wiring okay....." And then Benoit laughed.

"What's so funny"?

"The monkeys have disconnected the wiring from the backs of the speakers, look they're sitting on them and chewing the cable leads." Benoit explained as he allowed Josephine to see through the camera's eye piece.

"I've never seen anything like this in my life. You might expect one or two but it appears they have attacked all of the speakers, most strange. We can still use it for our story. Film each one then pan back to the stage, I suspect there is something going on up there as well."

"What do you mean you're here to suspend Father O'Reilly? He is our saviour our hero"! President Ringagain shakily asked completely flawed by His Grace's intention. He was quickly surrounded by his pieces of 'fruit' once they sensed that he was potentially in danger.

"Instruct your guards to relax! I am unarmed"!

"What about your men downstairs"?

"They mean you no harm, they are here on my orders to escort Brendan O'Reilly and his undesirables back home."

"Yeah his seven stinky sexy socks"! Bogliani slurred as he stumbled his drunken way towards Ringagain.

"What accusations are you making sir"? The President firmly asked as he rapidly assumed the grandeur of his political office.

"Firstly Father O'Reilly is out of his jurisdiction, he has not been given any permission to conduct Catholic business here on Mauritius. The priest in charge of this diocese is Father Bruno Bogliani a very capable man"!

The President put his hand up to his mouth and attempted to muffle his laughter. It came out more of a splutter than a cough, his face reddened and tears flowed out of his eyes. "Is there more"? Casseem snorted as he reached for a handkerchief to wipe away his moisture.

"Irrespective how sensational the reported events that have occurred in this Island are the Catholic Church remains non committal until it has performed its own thorough investigations, this holds true for Father O'Reilly's involvement with St Pious Church last year. There are many unexplained anomalies that have reached our ears and we feel it necessary to recall Father O'Reilly from his 'holiday' immediately before he does any further damage to his or the Church's reputation." His Grace arrogantly dictated as he stretched to his full height and towered over the seemingly submissive Casseem. It was then that Brendan appreciated how tall the Archbishop really was.

"What sort of anomalies are you hinting at"? Ringagain inquired with the sharp edge of his tongue as he stood his ground and returned the Archbishops piercing look.

"There's quite a number. Perhaps I should allow Father Bogliani here to list them all, after all drunks and little children never lie."

"Thank you Father 'stinky mouldy socks', I am the priest of this Island, everything must go through me and my socks! They must be obeyed at all times! Therefore Father Brendan O'Reilly comes under my jurisdiction, whatever he does, whatever he collects must meet with my approval. At no stage did this, this tourist come and ask for this! I was shoved into a dark corner, stripped of my rights by him and that blackguard Jack Stern! It was all a scam to fleece the locals and pilgrims of their money and socks"!

"Strong words Father Bruno, but who is speaking, you or the alcohol and where is your proof'? President Casseem challenged as he acted as the devil's advocate.

"Firstly all of the donated monies have disappeared! I and Rome have checked! No bank accounts here on Mauritius or anywhere to account for the wealth that these religious crooks have accumulated. Secondly these seven holy sisters that O'Reilly parades, these seven sordid sticky sexy socks are common used socks frequently ridden and worn by many; in other words they are whores! Common whores! How dare he let whores onto the holy sanctuary of the altar and allow them to give out communion! Sacrilege! Blasphemy! Complete and utter contempt for the Holy Eucharist"! Bruno ranted and raved before returning to his devoutly drunken state. His verbal tirade made Brendan wish he had never encountered Jack Stern, the second denial. Father O'Reilly remained speechless, he had no defence; all that had been said dressed him as the sacrificial lamb. President Ringagain looked to Brendan for a rebuttal of the accusations but none was forthcoming.

"You seem to have the upper hand Father Bogliani or shall I call you 'Bog' as the locals do"? Casseem asked in a threatening manner.

"You are more of a fool than I thought! You Mr President like the thousands have been seduced by the mass illusionist, the magician; there is no Church of the Coloured Sands! The land lies bare"! Bogliani triumphantly announced as he delivered the death blow.

"I think you have had a little too much to drink! You suffer with sock induced delirium tremens! Guards take this blithering idiot away"! The President commanded as he distanced himself from the alcoholic madman.

"Just one moment Mr President; what this fine upstanding man has just told you albeit somewhat incoherently is true. There is no church! Bogliani show him"! Archbishop Steven Moulds authoritatively interrupted.

Bogliani obeyed and produced from his left hand trouser pocket a mobile phone.

"Activate it my good man and wait for the call." His Grace instructed as he simultaneously signalled his men below. Within a few moments the phone stirred into life.

"Hello Father Bruno Bogliani, yes, yes I understand, very well." The unsteady priest answered obediently and then he handed the telephone over to President Ringagain who looked in total disbelief at the transmitted images.

"This is a joke, an attempt to discredit Father O'Reilly, a set up by one of your people; I don't believe any of it"! He said quite disgustedly as he shoved the phone back into Bogliani's hand.

"Well Mr President playing hard to get is not exactly your game. Perhaps you will believe one of your own"? The Archbishop smirked.

"What are you saying"?

"That we are not liars, we are here to protect the Grace of God and therefore we alerted your Commissioner of Police as to the disappearance of the Church of the Coloured Sands. I understand he is there now, give him a call, it should clear the air so to speak." Steven Moulds confidently said as he put his arm around Bogliani so as to say 'good job done my son'.

President Casseem Ringagain looked sternly at Brendan O'Reilly who appeared rather distraught and withdrawn, almost afraid to speak. The President dialled the Commissioners number and waited for the comedy to end.

"Hello Commissioner, where are you, at Chamarel? What do you see? Say again, I understand. Prove it to me; activate the camera on your phone, yes, that's what I want, thank you." The President abruptly commanded as he stood still and carefully observed the transmitted images. "Damn it! It's true, no church, well O'Reilly what do you have to say for yourself"? The President screamed visibly infuriated at being taken advantage of.

"I'm innocent." Brendan feebly put forward.

"I can see how. Your friend's not here, he's probably absconded with the money leaving you to take all of the blame."

"By the way if I may once again interrupt"? The Archbishop excused himself in his polished and aloof voice.

"What is it"?

"There was a point that Father Bogliani missed which will more than disprove Father O'Reilly's self proclaimed innocence." The president was all ears. "Observe the crucifix hanging around his neck, rather beautiful don't you think, rather ornate, thick eighteen carat gold, chain, the cross is encrusted with many precious gem stones. Perhaps you should ask him where he purchased it and by what means."

"I can answer that"! Bogliani piped up as he seized the opportunity of driving the sword deeper into Brendan's soul. "He ordered it from the jeweller at Grand Baile, I saw him myself, custom made, paid with cash received from the worshippers"!

The President always believed that a man was innocent until proven guilty as the French did, but today it was difficult considering the evidence at hand and so he suggested to His Grace. "I think this man needs to be suspended until further notice."

"I totally agree we may even have to consider Anathema"! His Grace savagely replied, it was then that one of Brendan's girls namely Brandy, came to his rescue quite unexpectedly.

"Excuse me Archbishop do you remember me" She sweetly asked.

"Can't say I do"

"Are you sure"?

"Yes quite! Why do you ask"? His Grace aloofly responded.

"Because you've tried this sordid, sexy sock on many an occasion, haven't you'? Brandy sourly replied making reference to herself.

"I don't know what you mean"!

"Oh yes you do! It wasn't until you pronounced Anathema that I placed you! You're that horrid lecherous bastard Mr Ductus Longus; you've had every one of us! You're Mr Badcock's lackey! You've come here to destroy everything"!

"Rubbish! Absolute rubbish"! His Grace screamed back.

"I'm not afraid of you mister, I know right from wrong unlike you ceremonious, pompous, self- righteous religious freaks! You don't want Brendan; he's a threat to Rome! That's what this is all about!

The church he found was real! I was there I lived, breathed and loved it. I don't know how you made it disappear, but one thing is certain, Brendan is innocent and you are the bad guy"!

"Have you quite finished? You mad possessed woman! How dare you insult my title"!

Unmoved Brandy automatically fired back by saying. "Artificial man made nonsense, nothing more, which created a self indulgent, self propagating hideous monster"!

These words inflamed the Archbishop's temper and in the heat of the moment he lost control and blurted out." None of you were any good I've had better"!

The statement was meant to represent a violent and degrading personal attack on each one of the girls but it backfired.

"Did I just hear you admit to having sex with these fine women"? President Ringagain curiously asked with raised eyebrows.

"Not at all; I merely suggested that they are not good practicing Catholics"!

"I see, Bogliani what do you say"? The President intensely questioned Bruno who stood nearby.

"Monkeys"

Casseem thought that was an absurd answer and replied. "Pardon"

"One monkey two monkey three monkey four; five monkey six monkey seven monkey more; eight monkey nine monkey ten monkey, eleven; twelve monkey. Thirteen mon…. salami"? Bogliani rhythmically recited in the voice of a young boy as he spied all thirteen monkeys lining up at the rear of the stage. Each held a thirty-centimetre piece of hot Hungarian salami in one of its hands. "Your Grace do you believe in reverse bestiality? I think those monkeys over there want to play hide the salami"!

Brandy grabbed Brendan by his shirtsleeve and physically pulled him away leaving both Bogliani and the Archbishop to defend themselves. The macaques flashed their eyes and bared their teeth. The hair rose on the backs of their necks and they pulled themselves up into threatening balls of fury ready to pounce and insert their hot fermented meats into any available orifice. Ringagain distanced himself from Bogliani by slowly side stepping until he reached the head of the stairs. The Archbishop and Bogliani remained stationary keenly aware of the physical harm that the macaques might inflict if they attacked.

"Don't worry God is with us, he will protect us." His Grace whispered.

"Are you sure because I'm not"! Bogliani shakily responded.

"Of course I am, trust in what I say and observe"! The Archbishop confidently said as he turned and stepped forwards to face the warlike creatures. "Now my good little monkeys I am the Archbishop listen to me and do shoo away, you heard me, shoo away that's right shoo away. You see Bogliani they are already pacified, they have laid down their arms and are removing their putrid bodies from this fine dais, now I can rule in peace. President Ringmaker you may return."

"Again"

"What was that Bogliani oh yes Ringover, come on over"!

"No again"

"What is it with you Bogliani? Must you always be such a constant source of irritation? What exactly are you driving at? What if I've forgotten what's his name does it matter whether I refer to him as Ringback; up, finger, leader, master, worm…well"?

"Monkeys say krra! Krra! Krra"! Bogliani replied.

"Are you mocking me? You stupid transvestite! Guards come up here immediately and take charge of the situation"! The Archbishop rudely commanded, as he grew tired of his surroundings.

"Krra, krra" Continued to sound everywhere.

"Stop that infernal noise Bogliani! Behave yourself"!

"It's not me! They're everywhere"!

"Enough of your madness guards where are you? What's taking you so long"? His Grace Steven Moulds furiously demanded to know.

President Casseem Ringagain stood at the top of the stairs and looked down in horror. He blessed himself by making the sign of the cross on his body with his right hand, unusual for a Hindu; also unusual was the fact that another twelve monkeys had mysteriously appeared from nowhere. With adjustable spanners in hand they behaved like expert riggers and busily went about dismantling the stages scaffolding. The first to go with an almighty crash were the stairs leaving everyone on stage stranded; with the crash came the sound of broken heads and bones, the groans of injured men and the screams of agony. The macaques delighted in calling 'krra, krra' repeatedly as a triumphant war cry. Brendan hadn't expected his freedom to take this path and he felt for the downtrodden.

"Bloody Mauritius no wonder the Island looks like it's either half built or half destroyed! Which is it? Bogliani get a rope or something and lower me down before this infernal structure collapses"!

No answer came.

"Bogliani answer me! Have you lost your senses? Are you mute"? Steven Moulds demanded to know as he stared at the dumbfounded priest.

President Ringagain was also speechless for his past had caught up with him.

Casseem Ringagain originated from a poor Hindu family, something that irked him for Casseem wanted to be as affluent as the rich Parisians that frequented the Island. Intuitively he knew he would not achieve success at home largely because he was not in the academic ways; however Casseem was very resourceful and cunning. He soon found a way to make huge sums of money on the African continent. Jamacacco was his gladiator who fought his battles and won handsomely both in the ring and at the bank. This soldier of war was a twenty-eight kilogram male monkey from the species Simian dominated by the Gibbon. Gentle and harmless with Casseem who treated him exceptionally well, Jamacacco was ruthless in the dog pit where most of his contests were fought. Casseem cleverly travelled the length and breadth of the African continent in many disguises with his monkey. He would act the half-wit, the simpleton, the idiot, the easy target with gold in his pockets to spare and invariably find himself amongst the corrupt warlords, politicians and excitement starved miners. The plot was simple. First engage in random meaningless discussion about the local fauna then make reference to the local guard dogs and insinuate that a monkey could easily defeat them.

Second let disbelief and tempers run wild and allow the challenge to be issued. Ignore it, inflame it until you cannot escape from it and a money wager is made as the proof of the pudding. Always act like the patsy, the sucker, the sitting target and be lead into the fight as the underdog. Cry for your pet and watch as he surprisingly wins, collect your fortune, say he was very lucky and leave.

Jamacacco's mode of attack or rather defence was to tumble about, elude his assailant until he was able to pounce on his arm or chest giving him an opportunity to strike at the canine's windpipe and rip it out. The Gibbon's skin was tough and flexible it rendered him impervious to the dog's teeth. When his opponent proved difficult and it looked as though he might loose, Casseem causally dropped a thirty-centimetre piece of wood into the ring and Jamacacco used it to bludgeon his adversary to death.

As time went on Casseem noticed a change in his companion as though he had developed a moral side and refused to fight anymore under the pretext that animals kill to feed and not for pleasure. Consequently Jamacacco escaped and was never to be seen again by Casseem until today.

Somehow the muscular and highly intelligent Gibbon had managed to stowaway on an ocean going vessel and make his passage undetected to Mauritius where he quickly established his precedence and helped the Islands macaques prosper amongst the humans. President Ringagain had heard rumours from the locals about a highly organised pack of primates performing lightning raids on food stocks, cigarettes and liquor supplies but he dismissed these as ramblings of the collective alcoholic mind. Today Jamacacco stood before him, older, wiser and meaner. The Gibbon was armed with a twenty centimetre dehydrated piece of salami, like the rubber hose it would inflict much pain and leave little evidence of attack. Jamacacco was taller and heavier than Casseem had remembered. The primate stood one metre ninety-five centimetres tall and weighed thirty-five kilograms. Casseemm wanted to say 'hello' but he remembered how he had mistreated his 'friend' Jamacacco in the months before his escape and he wondered if the animal had returned to discipline him on this public occasion.

"What are you all standing around for? This is ridiculous! It's a monkey! A stupid monkey! Just like the others perhaps a little taller! Shoo go on shoo! I'm not afraid of you! Just don't stand there disobediently"! The Archbishop madly raved as he took charge of the situation.

Jamacacco stayed where he was and tilted his head from left to right as he gauged each person on stage, Casseem he thought to be two faced, Bogliani a priest who needed to 'come out', the Archbishop a double crossing dictator, Brendan O'Reilly similar to himself and the five ex-prostitutes, ravaged creatures who needed re-birthing. Jamacacco bared his white teeth to reveal his razor sharp incisors capable of slicing a man open and delivering him to his maker within minutes. Casseem recognised it as a forewarning of impending attack; he crept closer to the platforms edge and looked down for a soft place to land, however all that awaited him were collections of thorny bicycles in every direction he looked.

"Damn you monkey if it's a gift you want here have some shiny stuff"! Steven Moulds impatiently blurted as he threw a handful of coins at the primate.

The Archbishop's actions incensed Jamacacco and he unexpectedly leapt a good four metres into the air and landed heavily on the cleric's back.

Brendan gasped and thought twice about going to his superior's assistance as the Gibbon whipped His Grace with the dehydrated piece of salami about the ears inflicting stinging, ringing pain. The Archbishop in desperation tried in vain to dislodge his attacker Bogliani rushed in to help but was rewarded with a good slap to the face. He fell comically backwards as drunks do, landed heavily on his backside jarring his coccyx and thought twice about helping again as he nursed his aching face and bottom.

Archbishop Steven Moulds became further incensed and outraged but somehow managed to control his temper, he made numerous frantic attempts to grab one of Jamacacco's darting limbs and wrench him off his body but the gibbon was far too quick. The extremely agile primate in a lightning move changed his body position and hung himself upside down on the Archbishops back; he wrapped his powerful legs around the Cleric's chest in a prolonged vice like grip which caused His Grace to stop breathing until he turned blue. Jamacacco then arched his back and savagely whipped the back of the Archbishops oxygen starved legs starting from the lower calves and ending at the upper thighs just short of His Grace's buttocks and family jewels which he thoughtfully spared. Unable to breathe unable to stand the Archbishop lost consciousness and fell forward onto his right side cracking two ribs in the process. As the Archbishop's body descended the Gibbon relaxed his grip, changed his body position and rode Steven Mould's back as if it were a surfboard, he used the priest's inertia to propel himself forward and in mid flight rolled himself into a tight ball and hurled himself at the unsuspecting President who had briefly taken his eyes away from the action.

Jamacacco struck with such ferocity that its force catapulted Ringagain into the air; the gibbon skidded to a halt and watched the President's distorted body streak away before it momentarily hung in space and then plummeted into the harbour's murky waters.

"Two devils with one stone" A satisfied Jamacacco thought to himself as he dusted off his hands and emitted a loud extended 'krra'.

Bogliani panicked and thought he was next; he tore off his shoes and started to suck on his month old socks. Brendan stood open mouthed, sad and glad at the same time, a conflicting mixture of emotions, whereas the five girls could not contain their elation which just happened to coincide with the exploding fireworks overhead and the children's cheers of joy below.

"What a beautiful majestic creature! Look how proud he stands! So muscular... boisterous and yet... so gentle" Brandy commented as she observed how the sea breeze caught and played with the gibbon's blonde and white fur.

The ex-prostitute's accurate description caught Jamacacco's ears and he responded amiably. In an almost human like fashion he preened the fur from his face and sauntered ambiguously towards Brendan. President's Casseem's pieces of 'fruit' remained at ease even though the animal had dispatched their employer to a watery playground. Brandy knelt on both knees and with arms outstretched welcomed her 'hero' the four remaining girls crowded around as Jamacacco approached. He hesitated for a moment before he nuzzled into Brandy's ample bosoms and gently wrapped his long arms around her neck. The interaction brought back fond memories for both of the past loves they like others shared between the animal species. Brendan laid his hands upon them to 'consecrate' their union and whispered "thank you"

The fireworks had reached their crescendo, as had the children's preoccupation with the piñatas; soon everything would be less frenzied, time to relax, with belly's full and minds pacified the afternoon siesta beckoned, a perfect time for Brendan to depart.

"Ladies I think we should go. There is nothing left for use here. Let's go home, join hands please." He softly said in a tone of voice that suggested he was less than a winner.

"We can't." Brandy exclaimed as she clung tightly onto Jamacacco.

"We can't take him with us, he belongs here with the others; they need him." Brendan wrongly assumed.

"I don't mean him although I would love to have him. What about the others"?

"Others"

"Yes the others! Have you forgotten we're a family! What about Jamie and Holly? Wake up father! Stop feeling sorry for yourself! I know what anathema means."

"You do"?

"Yes, shall I mention a few? Louis IV in 1324AD, Henry II of England, Philip I of France in 1094AD and the most famous of all Martin Luther in 1521AD" Brandy confidently rattled off.

Brendan remained silent, he gazed innocently at the fiery ex-prostitute and contemplated his circumstances until he realised that he needed the girls' collective wisdom as much as they needed his protection.

"Does any one of you remember when you last saw them"? Brendan asked as he turned to scan the populated area below and watched as the wind blew the remaining firework debris away.

"I'm fairly sure we became separated in the second or third marquee. Holly took a fancy to one of the visiting pastry chefs from France." Samantha remembered as she joined Brendan's side and searched the ground below for her companions' familiar faces.

"To the marquee then, the sooner we find them, the sooner we depart"! Brendan said with a sense of urgency even though his heart felt heavy at the thought of abandoning the island paradise.

"Don't fret you'll be back, you need me"! A voice whispered in Brendan's ear.

"Nice of you to say that Samantha; thanks for the reassurance."

"Huh"?

"What you just said to me."

"Wasn't me." Samantha explained looking somewhat perplexed.

"Then who did"? Brendan frowned as he looked around him. No one owned up except for Jamacacco who behaved otherwise. The

Gibbon released his hold from Brandy and approached Brendan, he held out his hand as an offering of peace, which Brendan freely accepted. Jamacacco then placed the priest's hand upon his head and spoke to him.

"How long will you stand around and look pretty? If it weren't for your friend Jack Stern none of this would have happened.

You have gifts but you are afraid to use them. Why? You must ask yourself. Is it because you are guilt ridden or is it because of your upbringing and education? I was like you once, obedient, did everything my master instructed, never questioned anything until one day I tired of killing. I began to think freely, I freed myself, no one freed me; I did it on my own and accepted the consequences. I feared the worst but none come. I waited and waited and could wait no more, it was time for action, my action, my thoughts, my words; I am here. Remember my words well for you will need me and I will be here. We are all related, what separates us is our preoccupation with ourselves and our choices."

Then there was silence as Jamacacco removed Brendan's hand.

"He likes you." Brandy affectionately remarked.

"That he does, perhaps it's not a good time to become mushy or sentimental." Brendan sheepishly replied as he heard the Archbishops groans. "He'll be as angry as a bear with a sore head! We better leave ASAP because I'm so scared... Candy"!

"God damn it that hurts! Bogliani where are you? Come here, help me up, you short stocking freak! Come here at once"! His Grace bellowed as much as his pain-ridden ribcage would allow.

"Yes your Grace at once your Grace"! Bogliani indistinctly uttered as he half gagged on a saliva soaked stinky sock.

"Ladies I think we should go, join hands, I'll do the driving Samantha, if you could select the co-ordinates." Brendan asserted as he intoned Spiritus Ruah and transported them back to the marquee where Samantha had remembered last seeing the missing Holly and Jamie.

"They're not here"! Felicity disappointedly said as she frantically scoured the enclosures interior. "In fact no ones here it's deserted. Every ones gone plus over here signs of a struggle." She then added after she had analytically swept though the marquee.

"Don't panic I'm sure they're somewhere safe." Brendan optimistically guessed.

"I don't think so! If Brandy is right about the Archbishop then Mr Ductus Longus up there is here for two reasons, shut you down and do Badcock's dirty work! This is no idle speculation on my part, let's fan out and find our missing sisters"! Felicity quite dramatically suggested with an air of aggressive determination.

"I think we should stay together, safety in numbers. I need to see each one of you close by out of the corner of my eye, you're my children, my charges, I care immensely for you; I really do." Brendan awkwardly and somewhat nervously said as he halted Felicity in her tracks. Apart from his mother Brendan had never really opened up to any member of the opposite sex. It was the same for his seven girls although each one had opened her legs and allowed hundreds of men in, they distanced themselves from any involvement associated with that activity and remained closed hearted. Brendan was the first man ever that each wanted to share her intimate thoughts and secrets with but somehow in the whirlwind of 'success' that they had been vacuumed into that desire had been thwarted. They wanted to tell him how glad they were to be Badcock free, contraceptive free and theatrically free, some even harboured a yearning to have Brendan's baby driven by their unrestricted freedom to ovulate.

Brendan's party of six quickened its pace and swept from one marquee to another without success. Jamie and Holly were no where to be seen. Brendan's nervousness increased and everything around him started to irritate his senses. What if Felicity was right about the Archbishop doing Badcock's dirty work? How many men had His Grace brought with him? Out amongst the crowd Brendan could hear the Archbishop madly shouting orders at the top of his voice as he waved his arms about like a crazy Italian ordering pizza. Father Bogliani with a dirty sock dangling from his mouth ran to and fro not knowing where to go, like a confused and obedient lap dog he blindly followed His Grace's ravings and constantly ran around in circles.

From where they were individually standing Archbishop Steven Moulds and Father Brendan O'Reilly briefly made eye contact. Brendan could feel the hatred in the Archbishop's eyes, it shocked him back into normality and he quickly averted any further conflict by expertly looking about to detect any foreign foes. It was then that Brendan decided to test his newly emerged hearing and he tuned his ear to the babblings of the macaques as they scurried about and talked to each other.

Jamacacco had remained true to his word and instructed his 'flock' to locate Brendan's missing girls which wouldn't be difficult by virtue of their impressive designer bathing costumes. To the untrained observer the macaques appeared to be stalking adults and children in an attempt to steal bags of lollies or bottles of drink, but in reality each carefully combed the area and reported its findings.

"Lollipops, pretzels, butterscotch delights, chewing gums, sugar cubes, pestitudes alight, burning here, there and everywhere, the cleric's army is flaming good, six lay injured, twelve others abound, girls in hiding waiting to be found." Each constantly chanted to itself and others as its eyes burrowed into every nook and cranny seeking the damsels in distress.

"Feel the air, smell its scent, listen for murmurings and muffled cries, watch the thugs where they go report to me when you know." Jamacacco screeched as he joined the hunt.

No one took any notice of the roaming macaques apart from Brendan who decided to follow inconspicuously by assuming invisibility but certain that his girls were close behind. Good for him but bad for them, their shapely figures attracted eager eyes and hungry hands from boys as young as eleven years of age. The blatant assaults in their private parts caused Brendan to extend his invisibility and the group of six stumbled and jostled its way unnoticed through the simmering crowds. When they had reached an open space Brendan halted and listened to the childish simplistic rhymes of two groups of macaques as they poetically chanted to each other.

> Little bits of paper wicky wacky woe,
> Silly bits of paper wicky wacky woe
> Meaningless bits of paper wick wacky woe
> Glorified bits of paper wicky wacky woe
> In a pretty buiding wicky wacky woe
> Greedy little people wicky wacky woe
> Sitting in a blue penny wick wacky woe
> With our lovely ladies wicky wacky woe

A smile spread across Brendan's face as he remembered days gone by when he gave religious instruction to groups of uninhibited school children.

"Do any of you know where to find blue pennies"? He asked "Perhaps at the markets, otherwise the only other place that has that description is the Blue Penny Museum on the Caudan waterfront." Brandy explained.

"The Museum specialises in"?

"Stamps" Brandy curtly replied

"Far from here"? Brendan asked as he looked to the macaques for directions.

"Just around the corner if we backtrack two hundred metres."

"Very well take us there my pretty." Brendan said as he turned about face.

A combination of instinct and observation proved advantageous, it wasn't long before they stood amongst the royal blue lamp posts in front of the heavily guarded building that represented a giant sized doll house. The building housed two of the rarest stamps in the world;

the Mauritian 1847 'post office' penny orange and twopence blue. Mauritius was the fifth country in the world to begin issuing postage stamps back in 1847. The Mauritius Commercial Bank formed a consortium of local companies in 1933 to purchase the stamps at auction in Switzerland in 1933 for posterity.

Brendan could heat the faint voices of Jamie and Holly inside the Museums main entrance, he also detected others belonging to four gruff men and this worried him. Remembering that his gifts were defensive in nature Brendan instructed the five girls to remain outside and to amuse themselves by chatting up the security guards whilst he went inside to summons Holly and Jamie.

Brendan often wondered what would happen if he used his powers in an act of aggression; would they ever consider him unfit as a host or would they turn a blind eye according to circumstance. In the past Brendan had never had to make the first move and he desperately hoped it would be the same on this occasion. He felt the anxiety of the fight, flight and fright response build up inside of him in contrast to the comfort he experienced within the confines of his beloved church especially the Church of the Coloured Sands. Now that it was gone he felt naked, alone, abandoned, vulnerable. Brendan hoped that he would not display any negative emotions or anything that would give anyone the impression that he was weak.

To his advantage the hot and humid weather more than adequately camouflaged his nervous perspiration. Father Brendan O'Reilly discoverer of the first fragment of the true Catholic Church bravely stepped inside the Blue Penny Museum and allowed his eyes to accustom themselves to the buildings interior lighting, out of the corner of his eye Brendan could see Holly and Jamie tucked away in an obscure part of the ground floor. He sensed that they pretended to be at ease but in reality all was not well, they were surrounded by four massive 'watch towers'.

"There you are my pretties, I was wondering where you were and what you got up to. We've just finished with the official formalities so it's time to pack up and go home; I'm rather bushed with being on display." Brendan gushed in an almost effeminate way as he walked towards the group of six.

Afraid to say or do anything both girls half smiled and remained still whilst the four 'watch towers' formed an impenetrable wall between them and Brendan.

"They have made other arrangements Father Brenton"! One of them grunted sarcastically.

"Yeah... they're coming with us to dinner at sex"! Another added.

"At sex you're New Zealanders"!

"You making fun of us"

"Merely making an observation which includes the fact that you are probably heavily tattooed and scarified ex rugby players and Maori's to boot"! Brendan said in a weak voice as he bravely stood his ground thoroughly amazed at his own words.

The four massive 'watch towers' grimly smiled, acknowledged each others intentions and without warning ripped open their floral Hawaiian long sleeved shirts to reveal their 'moko', their individual coat of arms, their identity, their status, all expertly done by a highly esteemed Tohunga-ta-moko. Pentagrams, crosses, magic vampires, dreadlocks and more were etched and permanently painted into their abdominal skins amidst a myriad of spirals in honour of the crooked one, the serpent.

"Impressive! I see that your artist has borrowed symbols from the Picts of ancient Britain. You know those small dark Mediterranean aborigines of Britain who were a major thorn in the side of the Roman Empire" Each of the massive 'watch towers' took offence to Brendan's comments, each started to grunt like a bull, each flared his nostrils and prepared to charge.

"Constantius Chlorus hated these little semi-naked 'Picti' and the Hiberni (The Irish), but mostly the 'Picti'; known as barbarians, pirates, the painted ones, they had connections everywhere much like yourself." Brendan meekly continued without even taking a breath or notice of the 'watch towers' agitated states. "Judging by the extent of your labyrinth of spirals, I dare say you consider yourselves to be half human, half serpent; anti-Gods in the spiritual sense and Gods in the sporting. Am I right"?

"Enough! Cease or decease"! Brendan swallowed hard as did the Museum's Malaysian security guards who looked on from a safe distance. They were very afraid to act as they recognised the significance of the Maori's tattoos "Bad Divine Trouble".

"Leave now"! The massive Maori 'watch towers' bellowed in unison.

"Not without my girls"! Brendan defiantly answered.

"Shesha-Maka dispatch this weakling to the underworld"! The largest Maori known as Uraga- Manu commanded.

"With pleasure" Shesha-Maka replied as he calculated his deathly move.

"Sarpa-Tane, Pannaga-Anewa, blind side, maul, knock on dummy"! Uraga-Maka then cryptically signalled to the other two, his words ignited the fires of war in their eyes.

The glare of their stare caused Brendan to feel uncomfortably hot and he momentarily lost concentration which allowed the 'killers' to pounce at once. They moved with such frightening speed that both Holly and Jamie gasped in horror, the Malaysian guards looked away and everyone expected Brendan to be reduced to a bloody mess. Instead there came the sound of a thunderous collision as two immense bodies sandwiched a third and the trio fell into a heap.

"What's the matter with you off your game bro"? Shesha-Maka dazed and dizzy angrily questioned his mates as he scrambled to his feet.

"Must a misjudged my timing, you got him Sarpa-Tane"? Pannaga-Anewa roughly replied as he looked for traces of Father Brendan O'Reilly.

"No"

"Then where he is"?

"Over there and there"! Uraga-Manu the largest Maori shouted as he pointed to Brendan's image in multiple locations.

"Not possible! This man a devil"!

"No devil, a magician playing tricks with your mind! Look through to find the real man"! Uraga-Manu cleverly directed as he joined the hunt.

"These men are no fools! I need to draw them away from the girls before I can make my move otherwise I stand no chance." An invisible Brendan thought to himself as he keenly observed his adversaries. One by one he turned off of all of his artificial images until one remained which stood next to a priceless collection of stamps.

"Red herring don't bother bro"! Uraga-Manu quite correctly deduced and turned about face with the hideous intention of grabbing either Holly or Jamie and terminating her existence.

Brendan quickly substituted the false image with his own and aggressively yelled. "You are wrong"!

These three little words briefly stopped the massive Maori in his tracks but his subsequent actions were not what Brendan had hoped for. Uraga-Manu violently signalled the three other warriors to once and for all eliminate Father Brendan O'Reilly leaving him free to enjoy the sublime delight of murdering one of the girls. Brendan sensed the evil energy build up inside of the man and he knew that he had to act instantaneously as he was dealing with four mighty seasoned warriors who were afraid of nothing, immune to tricks and false trails, in effect four satanic demi-Gods.

Brendan decided to place his life at risk by physically challenging Uraga-Manu head on, right in front of the girls, however his decision was not made quick enough, before he could do or say anything the massive Maori had moved with such furious intensity that the fingers of both of his hands were about to forcibly clamp themselves around the defenceless throat of Holly. In the spilt second available to him Brendan intoned Spiritus Ruah and imagined he would be able to save his precious girl by wedging himself between her and Uraga-

Manu. In that instant before anyone could finally act the buildings entire lighting system went out, with it came screams of unbridled horror, terror and deathly pain, piercing sirens, abstract sounds that bounced off the walls and caused widespread pandemonium, smells of animal droppings, wet fur and freshly spilt blood.

Brendan hadn't moved at all, nothing had touched him; he shook his head in disbelief, dejected he lowered it and accepted the pain of his failure. In the pitch-blackness the outline of four yellow hissing serpents' gone berserk made themselves apparent. Theirs' was not a pleasant experience nor for those who dared to watch. A complex pattern of sensory, motor, mental and affective symptoms associated with Kundalini Syndrome engulfed their bodies and souls, precipitated by near death and fuelled by accumulated unnecessary meditative practices, in essence a spiritual emergency, one that threatened to engulf everyone around them. A precipitous pranic awakening gone wrong, depersonalisations, altered perceptions, the threat of body-soul dissociations, all of these flew around the room as willowy witches wishing to cast their fatal spells upon the unsuspecting.

Brendan grasped his crucifix and squeezed it with all of his might so much so that it imbedded itself deeply in the flesh of his hand. He had never experienced anything so frightening, neither past exorcism's; ghosts, Badcock or the D-Man remotely approximated his present danger. Brendan's mind panicked, he repeated the Hail Mary, the Lord's Prayer, various intercessions, incantations and powerful mystical words to no avail. He could feel a deathly presence wishing to rip the soul out of his body; he was undoubtedly the designated target of the day. The Archbishop obviously wanted Brendan O'Reilly to vanish completely and mysteriously.

Within the hand that held his crucifix Brendan could feel a hot fluid escape, it seeped between his fingers and trickled down his hand before it dropped onto the Museums floor and formed a pool, from it emerged a white whispery light.

Brendan fearing it was his very own soul stood statue like and nervously awaited his fate. The hot fluid continued to fall drop by drop, it did not splatter when it hit the pool on the ground instead it simply coalesced with it without increasing its size. The pool acted as a reactive crucible transforming each drop into a living white light. The snakes hissed with excitement eager it would seem to partake of the white light's essence. They hungered for its taste and feverously encircled it; their activities frightened Brendan even more which worsened his rigidity. Their hisses of disapproval and derision filled the room as they exhausted themselves by spitting their vile secretions at Brendan in the expectation that they would dissolve Brendan's outer mantle and increase the flow of the white light.

The pool of liquid on the floor reacted favourably to the serpents' demands and channelled upwards forming four fingers of delight, four fingers to fondle, four fingers to suckle, four fingers of satisfaction. Each snake struck at one of the available tentacle like nipples, each gulped down the white light's magical elixir and each expected the life force to drain out of Brendan's non-compliant body. Their feeding frenzy resembled starved Piranha fish and they continued until the light went out and darkness returned.

Brendan was still alive 'God knows how' he strained his eyes to accustom them to the dark but it would not relent. Brendan sensed that death was all around him; he assumed that apart from the serpents he was the last man standing within the Museums complex. Time ticked by like a count down to an inevitable event much like ready, steady, go; except it was more like five, four, three, two, one. Explosion to the left, explosion to the right, in front and behind, pieces of bloody carcass flew everywhere, three hundred and sixty degrees, airborne or not, they descended and vaporised into thin air;

Little bits of ticky tacky
Little bits of woe
Silly bits of paper
Where did they go?

were the next words Brendan heard once the ringing in his ears caused by the explosions had subsided; Jamacacco all smiles stood before the exhausted priest and nodded his head in approval as he dropped his hands.

A bewildered Brendan O'Reilly looked around the brightly lit room. The four Maori 'watch towers' lay dead exterminated by their own ambitions, Holly and Jamie stood behind Brendan both shivered uncontrollably, all of the displays and exhibits were reduced to nothingness. Brendan's ordeal was over, flexibility returned to his body and he opened his hand to inspect the damage that his crucifix had inflicted upon it. Both the palm of his hand and the crucifix were intact, no impression, no scar, no permanent mark.

"What, how"? He asked as his mind tried to work out what had happened.

Jamacacco eased Brendan's burden by answering. "I defeated the demi-Gods physical side; you defeated their spiritual essence by getting blood out of a stone. There is nothing more to say except when you need me I am here, farewell my friend farewell." And with that the primate shook Brendan's hand with both of his, howled 'krra' and departed.

"Come her Holly, Jamie, let me embrace you both. I thank the heavens and others for your safety." He gently said as he wrapped his arms about both of them and felt the softness of their combined warmth; he breathed in the sweet scent of their regained innocence and vowed never to let them go.

44
CONTROVERSIAL SHUTDOWN PART B

Days after he had eaten from the Table of Truth a grievous anxiety spread throughout Cyril Pinewood's body much like an aggressive malignant cancer. His subconscious meanwhile laboured to find answers to all of the perplexities that he had encountered and that lay before him unresolved.

Cyril Pinewood's problem solving mind became so active that day merged into night, daydreams became night dreams and vice versa. There was no delinearisation, no compartmentalisation between AM and PM.

In an desperate attempt to stave off any permanent physiological damage Cyril Pinewood resorted one night to swallowing a handful of his wife's out of date prescription sleeping pills. The hypnotic drugs unlike proper naturally induced sleep hormone did little for his insomnia; they did however suppress his nervous system and relax his tense muscles. In a pseudo comatose almost zombie like state Cyril Pinewood lay next to his seemingly ever faithful wife in the soft king sized bed located in the master bedroom of their own home.

"Answers, I need answers; details, I need details; I need detailed answers, that's what I need"! A frustrated and exhausted Cyril Pinewood at 2am in the morning mumbled incoherently as he tossed, turned and jumbled the bedcovers to uncover the demure, non-complaining Mrs Pinewood who responded by adopting the foetal position to conserve body heat.

"Never again; why did I do it? What possessed me apart from desperation? Why didn't I listen to my wife"? Cyril recriminated himself as his body reacted adversely to the excessive number of tablets labelled benzodiazepine he had consumed.

"Never mix alcohol and drugs! How many times have I heard, read and seen that? Nah! It will never happen to me! Well it has! Here I am a complete blithering mess! Little wonder considering what I have seen!

Secret homosexual political society; the assassination of my political mate Harvey, the bombing of Kakadu and the Simpson Desert, will I be next? What if I don't play their game? What a mess! What a bleeding mess! I wish some one would comfort me! A stranger perhaps! Some one to tell me, it's alright, it's going to be alright"!

"That you calling me brother" A Voice rang out in the mists of Cyril's muddled mind.

In his dream like state Mr Pinewood answered. "It is how did you know"?

"I remain connected to everyone I meet and see for I am Gee Pee the Ja-Malay who heals all, what do you need of me tonight, brother"?

"Answers, details, detailed answers"! Cyril's mind erratically answered as an image of the brightly clad oracle formed before his half opened eyes.

"To what brother"?

"Everything"! Cyril sobbed as tears welled up inside his eyes.

"Gee Pee give you everything, just look-see all you have to do is look-see." The image smiled as it delved into Cyril's openly flustered mind "If you want to see what Gee Pee see you take a look-see underneath me then you see all. Gee Pee very busy! You call me again when you need me, bye from Gee Pee" and with that the image and its associated dream drifted away.

A certain peace descended, Cyril Pinewood felt somewhat comforted even though his body battled the effects of the benzodiazepine overdose.

At 7am on the same morning a groggy and bleary-eyed Cyril Pinewood's mind awoke to the sounds of children playing in the rumpus room below. His body meanwhile had managed during the remaining hours of the night come to terms with the careless and overt chemical assault to itself. Acting PM pinewood 'opened' his eyes and found himself lying on his right hand side with his arms and legs securely wrapped around his wife's warm inviting body from the rear. One of his arms was around her waist whilst the other nestled neatly in her bosoms handsome cleavage.

In that moment he fully appreciated what he really had prior to his infatuation with Harvey Jarwood and how he had almost lost it. Such early morning body contact in the past would have led to a rapid escalation from fondling to rampant lovemaking. Now it was different, the years of disinterest and abstinence on his part caused their marriage to become politically plutonic.

Cyril needed to work overtime in order to rekindle his wife's sexual interest. The death of Harvey Jarwood was certainly a blessing in this respect providing Mrs Pinewood did not believe that Cyril had come out of the closet, a concept that he himself would need to sort out irrespective of what Ms Penelope or others might have suggested.

Today was a step in the right direction. Cyril held his wife's body with love, a deep irrepressible love, an undeniable love; a love not reborn but rather brought back from a foreign place unsuited to its intentions, but it remained ambiguous for part of it still lusted for those parts shunned by the majority of heterosexuals. A diplomatic compromise was needed so cleverly disguised at the best of times that all parties known to him remained exclusive of each other and completely satisfied. Bisexuality, clever, daring, exciting, what a challenge!

"What a stupid idea"!

"Who said that"? Cyril questioned himself.

"I did! Now get out of bed and join me, we're together at last"! Harvey Jarwood's voice roughly commanded.

"But you're dead! In any case why am I hallucinating your presence" Cyril's mind raced to determine.

"Because you are as well; dead that is"!

"Absolute nonsense; I'm in bed snuggled up to my wife and enjoying it! Go away I've had enough of you. I'm turning over a new leaf"!

"Turn then! Move your arm, bet you can't"!

"Of course I can't it's underneath my wife, I'm pinned down"!

"Then move something else"!

"Very well I'll prove it to you, you... you... horrible nightmare." Pinewood stuttered as his body refused to co-operate.

"Convinced"? Harvey Jarwood's ghost asked as it hovered nearby.

"No! It's just a bad dream"!

"Soon to become worse here let me show you." Jarwood's ghost responded as it reached out and took Cyril Pinewood's spiritual essence by the scruff of its neck and yanked it mercilessly out of its tomb.

"Bloody hell that hurt, now look what you've done"! Pinewood screamed as his body and soul detached.

"No silver cord! Do you see a silver cord"? Jarwood asked.

"Can't say that I do" Pinewood glumly replied as he looked down at his lifeless body.

"Then your dead get used to it"!

"But how"? Pinewood asked.

"Watch and learn if you want to otherwise let me take you to paradise, my paradise."

"Is it that good"? Pinewood asked as he started to feel the joy of his new existence.

"Nothing like you ever imagined before unless you remember some of your more bizarre and unearthly dreams in which case you were given a rare glimpse."

"I'm so excited, take me I'm yours"! Cyril squealed in a high-pitched camp voice as he wholeheartedly hugged his soul mate who returned the embrace. The two then floated away with Cyril asking a thousand questions.

"Any heterosexuals"

"Banned"

"Gerbils"

"Lots plus all manner of erotic games with all sorts of extraterrestrial creatures from different dimensions"

"Wow I can hardly wait."

Mrs Cyril Pinewood was also awake. She was more than certain that her husband had died during the night; he had finally taken the bait, not rat poison that was appropriate but too slow, instead, mislabelled tricyclic antidepressants a handful of which would guarantee cardiac arrest. She felt for a pulse, none at the wrist, groin or throat, limbs lacked muscle tone, body felt cold, she was finally free. Her children's laughter downstairs echoed her satisfaction, her pleasure and her liberty. Mrs Pinewood rolled out of bed and kept her back to her deceased husband, she never wanted to set eyes upon him again she was after all a woman betrayed.

She went about the bedroom entered her walk in wardrobe, selected bright sunny clothes, neatly dressed herself, brushed her hair, applied sufficient makeup to compliment her outfit and beauty and then left to greet the day. On her way out she retrieved a mobile phone that she kept in a secret hiding place and activated the programmed overseas private number. Mrs Pinewood glanced at her wristwatch it was 8:10am which corresponded to 10:10pm the previous day for the person she was required to contact, the phone on the other end of the line rang without end until after twenty odd rings a voice answered.

"Good evening" Was all that the recipient said in a low non-descript tone of voice.

"MCP here, good news, the obstacle has been removed." Mrs Pinewood gladly stated.

"Excellent I shall inform AW and PA immediately. Stay where you are a mop up crew will be there shortly. Welcome back and once again good work on forwarding that disc to me, it will further strengthen if not seal my case." And with that the recipient terminated the call.

For the next few hours Mrs Pinewood behaved as if nothing had happened. 'Daddy was asleep' was her explanation for the children. She partook of breakfast, played with them in and outside the house and once they tired of the games did a spot of gardening in the front yard until she was interrupted by the arrival of the cleanup crew all attired in proper Australian uniforms particular to their trade. They went about their business expertly and efficiently by removing all traces of foul play and substituting them with the 'official story'. Once Mr Cyril Pinewood's lifeless body was squared away the tall and stocky commander in chief approached to advise of their progress.

"We've cleaned the house from top to toe as you requested just in time for your 'guests.'"

"Splendid."

"Bearing up Mrs Pinewood"? He asked

"As best as I can." She replied as she feigned a stiff upper lip tinged with grief.

"Excellent! Keep up the performance. Once we leave, give us about twenty minutes and then you may telephone all and sundry."

"Very well" Mrs Pinewood said as she half smiled and prepared to usher the 'cleaners' out.

"No thank you Mrs Pinewood you have been of immeasurable service to her Majesty, until we meet again." The commander in chief genuinely replied as he extended his hand in appreciation.

"Soon I hope." Mrs Pinewood warmly responded with a gleam

in her and a shift in her body position a she accepted his honourable gesture.

If it wasn't bad enough that Mr Harvey Jarwood was assassinated days earlier it was now far worse with the death of Mr Cyril Pinewood Acting PM of Australia especially since through his timely intervention and creative diligent work he was able to create some degree stability within a country devoid of its centralised power.

The news of his death sent shock waves throughout all departments and devastated the likes of Ms Penelope, Harvey Jarwood's secretary and his chauffer both of whom were secret recruiting and training members of Gerbalis. The situation further deteriorated when an emergency convened session of both houses of British Parliament was televised worldwide by BBC News and relayed to major TV corporations around the globe including Australia's own ABC.

"My fellow elected members and lords, we are here today to remedy a grave matter one that threatens to destroy millions of peoples lives unless it is quickly acted upon. We are above all the oldest governmental system in the world, the stability of which owes much to the monarchy; we have over the centuries imparted our knowledge of administration into the countries that we have colonised and I dare say we have done it exceedingly well"! The Prime Minister of England Mr Bernard Townsend impeccably dressed in a Saville Row hand mad suit said with authority as he eyed every member in the House.

"Here, here"! His audience loudly responded everywhere.

"However; sometimes slip ups do occur, it is with deep regret that I report one today. The blunder through an unfortunate set of circumstances has extended itself over a long period of time and therefore there is no one in particular that we can blame. If one was to assign guilt perhaps one should choose the political system itself; a monster bearing many tentacles; however we do not need to be part of it if we from today apply ourselves diligently, morally and ethically! 1900 was when it all started. An Act of British Parliament brought into force the Australian Constitution and over the years as a result of much bickering, various Acts once again passed by ourselves we have streamlined for want of a better word its operation and the running of the Australian Parliamentary system which is best described as a Constitutional Monarchy with our queen as its head. The last pertinent Act passed by us in this regard was the Australia Act of 1986. To the outsider, to the un-informed, to the non thinker all appeared above board, however this was not the case at all for preceding all of this on the 1oth January 1920 the League of Nations which Australia had joined came into force and with that Australia became a sovereign nation under International Law. This was in effect its declaration of independence!

A momentous occasion one would think but not so! It was deliberately and completely ignored by both the Australian politicians and its judiciary for one very important reason and that my learned colleagues was…! All colonial law had been extinguished!

You would think that they the Aussies would have had the gumption to frame a new Constitution. Not so! That weird mob; that vacant lot in the arid land down under did nothing! They and I point the finger squarely at the long line of Australian Governments and their associated judiciary have since 1920 continued to use the Australian Constitution Act of 1900(UK) as a confidence trick of monstrous proportions with one singular intention; to maintain power”! Bernard Townsend visibly angry firmly concluded. He did not hide his disgust instead he paused to allow his powerfully delivered piece of history to sink into the receptive minds of his listeners.

Ripples of concern, waves of disbelief, fleeting conversations with regard to technicalities of law, grunts and groans, reverberated around hallways and doorways of parliament until they simmered down.

“Authority over the Australian Constitution lies not with the Australian Government nor with the Australian people, it rests solely with the United Kingdom. Only we have the authority to repeal it, which remains our absolute prerogative regardless of any past, present or future political promises! This authority is non transferable"! Bernard Townsend shouted as he banged his fist on the lectern before him.

"Australia, its states and territory have no legal basis for its current political or judicial system under International Law. The country sits on two chairs and is destined to fall in the middle! I feel dreadfully sorry for the five and half million migrants who falsely believe that they hold Australian citizenship. Why and how did we allow this precarious situation to happen? At some point somewhere in history we lost the plot through our own diplomatic and political bumbling, by turning a blind eye we became blind, we were obsessed with cricket, we overly fostered Australia so that it became a great sporting nation and nothing else! A cultural wasteland! Sport was its lifeline, its obsession; nothing else mattered to its populus!

A good game of cricket, some fabulous footie, a beer and pie was all that the Aussie bloke wanted, shiela's came and went with contempt, religion, morals and ethics were non existent, we the British people failed them, its cunning politicians and bureaucrats reduced the world's richest nation over time to the level of a third world country!

Ladies and gentlemen, your Majesty whom I trust is watching this broadcast and who will telephone me on the Royal blue phone once I have delivered my speech, I hold in my hand a copy of a disc, a computer disc that I received several weeks ago, it explains where all of Australia's richness has gone." Bernard Townsend held the disc up high above his head and swept it through the air with it came ripples of concern and disbelief which fed the winds of speculation that flew about Parliament house until they finally subsided only then did Bernard Townsend present his findings.

"After I took office I had always been keenly aware that there existed an unresolved political problem with and within Australia. I like the rest of my colleagues and indeed my predecessors did little

627

about it, as the country appeared to be stable in all respects, I like the rest of the others ignored snippets of information that suggested official corruption was rife within its boundaries." Bernard Townsend toyed with the disc of damnation, which happily sparked and radiated light in all directions in stark contrast to its content.

"This disc ladies and gentlemen tells it all, people, places, account numbers, bank balances. The work of a dedicated whistle blower, a genius, most probably a disgruntled taxpayer" He said tongue in cheek and deliberately did not reveal any further details as their list of names included members of the British Empire.

"We the Government of the United Kingdom would have gladly not minded allowing the Aussies to use the constitution we originally wrote for them, it really didn't matter providing they had been honest about it. The dishonest approach is what killed the Golden Goose! Let me explain further. A handful of very clever influential and highly placed people after World War II had finished put up the argument in secret meetings with the relevant government departments that all laws arising out of Australia's Constitution were invalid for reasons mentioned previously, therefore they reasoned that under the circumstances they were not required to pay any form of taxation and accordingly did not!

Two sets of accounting books, one for them, the other to appease any nosey people were kept. The high ranked officials the ones at the very top who ran the various departments including taxation were in on it as were both sides of the political fence. A freely elected dictatorship, one political system with two heads working in unison, manipulating the masses, the divide between the haves and haves not worsened, deepened, broadened, 'keep them poor' was the secret ideology of an ultra secret society." Bernard Townsend paused once again and mindful of his own country's sexual orientation regulations made neither mention of Gerbalis nor any reference to homosexuals.

"Modern day criminals, legal embezzlers, above the law, what law, no law, none for them, many for those who struggle to earn their daily bread. Keep them poor, crumbs from the table, if they whinge change the racial mix, distract them with rhetoric, empty words, keep them guessing, keep them poor! Today Ladies and gentlemen it is incumbent upon this British Parliament to Act! We must uphold the essence of true British Democracy; we must protect and rescue our Anglo-Saxon brothers and sisters who have journeyed thousands of miles to inhabit a foreign land down under, we must free them from the oppression that they endure, they belong to Mother England and She I say will not let them down"!

"Hurrah, bravo, splendid, smashing" were just some of the praises that empted from the frenzied mouths of the normally highly reserved members of parliament. Some broke into song a chorus or two of 'Rule Britannia' filled the air.

"Today ladies and gentlemen we take back Australia"! Bernard Townsend shouted with all of his might over the top of his vociferous colleagues.

In the midst of the commotion there were pockets of quiet discontent especially amongst those whose names unknown to them appeared on the 'list', the very people that Bernard Townsend had strongly criticised, one of them was none other than Franck Max Climax alias Lord Tingle, self made millionaire, a highly polished peer of the realm complete with a voluntary atypical neurological dysfunction. Lord Tingle rose to his feet and with the utmost pretence attempted to stretch to his full height, shuffled about and then comically descended to the level of the English Prime Minister.

"I say, settle down, ladies and gentlemen, we're not going to war, let's assume some measure of civility please"! He very loudly said as he bravely used his arms as a gesture of lowering the noise volume within parliament house. Partially successful he re-iterated the request.

"A little more decorum, a little more sush please, perhaps we could debate exactly how we are going to take Australia back." Lord Tingle openly suggested and then he looked strangely at the PM as he falsely struggled to retain his upright stance.

"Are you alright Lord Tingle"? The PM genuinely inquired.

"MS playing up a little, damn awkward at times, don't mind me, carry on regardless." He graciously replied with a wave of his hand.

Bernard Townsend without any hesitation pounced on the words 'carry on', he made a quick cutthroat sign across the front of his neck and once satisfied that the broadcast team had acted upon his instruction invited the gallery of politicians to debate the matter. To the outside world the televised emergency session of British Parliament had reached the first intermission point, an interval of thirty minutes before transmission would resume, it gave all invited political analysts and viewing public the opportunity of airing their say and wildly speculating on the methods available to effect the 'take back' of Australia. As one can imagine the possibilities ranged from the sedate to the bizarre depending upon the persons age and ethnic background.

"As you have sufficiently calmed this house down perhaps you could enlighten us with your thoughts Lord Tingle"? The PM coldly asked mindful of his lordship's involvement in reducing the world's richest nation to that of a third world country.

"I think fellow members and lords that we should not adopt a gun-ho approach, we are after all British. We do not shoot from the hip instead we carefully evaluate situations and make decisions that satisfy the entire international community of which we are a major part, otherwise we embarrass and ostracise ourselves seriously. In essence what I am suggesting is that International Law takes precedence, it needs to be obeyed first"! Lord Tingle proposed in a less than lukewarm fashion that sort to attract the sympathy vote.

"And what International Laws apply Lord Tingle that could possibly allow those raping Australia to continue? Something out of the United Nations Bill of Human Rights"? Bernard Townsend aggressively asked as he gazed about the auditorium with clenched fists and mouth. The question threw many.

"There's no need for such hostilities, I totally agree with you that such vagabonds need to be brought to task, but I for one do not think that we have the right to invade Australia."

"Who said anything about invasion? I don't remember mentioning the word at all! Perhaps you are worried about the countries multi-national makeup? Hum"? Lord Tingle with his back to the wall remained silent and reluctantly allowed the Prime Minister to continue, while he planned his retort.

"Approximately two hundred and thirty six different nationalities inhabit the arid Australian continent of which fifty might harbour terrorist cells and connections, unless you Lord Tingle possess some shred of overwhelming evidence that these and Australia itself poise a threat to world peace then I think military intervention is inappropriate! The Aussies simply lack good house keeping practices; we Lord Tingle shall assist them in this regard. Do you catch my drift"? The PM firmly asked as he coldly stared at the seemingly defenceless peer.

"Yes I do, however it, meaning your approach does not negate any aspect of International Law"!

"Oh my God you really are harping on with this pathetic aspect! Have your say then! Enlighten us"! The PM said in a manner that threatened to expose Franck Max Climax alias Lord Tingle's nefarious dealings in Australia.

"Be careful Lord Tingle." The voice of a child cautioned as it drifted into Franck Max Climax's head.

"Marshall what are you doing here"?

"Come to protect you."

"Against"

"You've been exposed, they're onto you." Marshall warned as he materialised before Franck's eyes and floated merrily to and fro.

"Nonsense I'm immune, no one remembers me; I've got non-recognition ability."

"And instant karmic response in the days before you got involved in milking Australia's wealth. You entertained greed and it robbed you of some of your powers, the more money you wrongly accumulated the more your abilities diminished." Marshall frowned.

"How was I to know? I did it for the good of my people." Franck protested

"Are you sure Mr Franck Max Climax are you absolutely certain my son, my only beloved son"?

"Yes."

"Then why haven't you distributed the funds"? Marshall curiously asked.

"I was saving it."

"For"

"The right time" Franck alias Lord Tingle correctly answered.

"What did you mumble Lord Tingle? What was it I hear? What time is it"? Bernard Townsend bellowed.

"I'm sorry; I seem to have lost my train of thought." Lord Tingle excused himself.

"Then let me remind you, International Law! Not the International Date Line nor Greenwich Mean Time, International Law! Get on with it time is wasting"! The PM Impatiently ordered.

"Yes of course, International Law and its application to the current situation...

"That incident at the crosswalk outside Kensington Gardens, when the Asian tried to run you down with his car was an assassination attempt"! Marshall glowingly said as he floated before Franck's eyes.

"Never"!

"No instant karmic response that night, it was us protecting you, waiting to see what you would do with your falsely acquired Australia wealth.

"You still look lost Lord Tingle, either say your piece or let us get on with it"! Bernard Townsend roughly insisted.

"I... I... think that..."

"International Law is not applicable! Quite right! The Hague or more correctly The Vague wouldn't have a clue what to do! Now Lord Tingle would you mind stepping aside just over there if you will, thank you" Bernard Townsend commanded as he pointed to the place that he expected Lord Tingle to position himself. The PM then produced a list of names from his breast pocket and with the utmost sublime pleasure read them out in quasi-sensational fashion after which he said. "Would those whose names I have just mentioned please come down and join Lord Tingle, we have a special surprise for you." Every named individual dutifully presented him or herself and eagerly awaited their 'reward'.

"Well, well look at that, sixty seven names in total, missed out by two, damn shame sixty nine would have suited me better, how extraordinary, all Lords not a commoner amongst them"! Bernard Townsend hissed as he watched the assembled lot being surrounded by a platoon of heavily armed household guards.

"Don't look so frightened my lovelies; you've been gathered here today to make a snap decision. Live your lives in exile or turn over your ill-gotten gains! No excuses please, no ignorance, you know what I mean; stories like I didn't know, my grandfather did it; its old money, won't work. The facts speak for themselves, Res Ipse Translator." Bernard Townsend sarcastically said as he surveyed the captured aristocracy.

A simmering arrogant hatred boiled up inside of them and many called upon the Queen to intervene whilst parliament looked on dumbfounded.

"Afraid not chaps! I have Her full authority, settle down and I'll explain the situation to you! It's like this, are you listening Lord Tingle or are you still taking to the little people"?

"All ears thank you PM"

"I'm so glad and so happy you brought up International Law, wonderful stuff you know, creates boundless co-operation between nations, terrific amounts of treaties and endless agreements! So there we have it, this is your choice! Bit restricted I suppose but nonetheless manageable. You lot look confused! Too cryptic? Need clarification? Very well brace yourselves"! The PM slowly and dramatically teased.

"The cunning lot, the ones without shame, no better than the dregs of society except perhaps they are better than you in maintaining their honesty, honour amongst thieves, international thieves you became, raiders of the lost continent. To day you pay your dues, strip you of your title I say not, reduce you to poverty out of the question, let you enjoy your wealth a good idea, but the question is where? The nations we have befriended will say no to your entry, bar your stay, how then will you enjoy your wealth? Any ideas? Any clues? Sadly gentlemen and I use the description loosely, I cannot offer any solutions. A Hercules aircraft awaits you, it will dispatch you parts unknown even to us from there armed with your passports, banking details and your own wits it will be up to you to survive. England bids you farewell"! Having issued those soul-destroying words Bernard Townsend turned his back on the guilty, silently waited for the guards to clear them from the auditorium and then picked up the Royal blue phone.

The remaining politicians meanwhile remained awfully still afraid to utter a single syllable or even breathe loudly. Each was aware of the others presence and consciously made an attempt to keep quiet.

"You never needed the money you know." Marshall whispered in Franck Max Climax's ear as he along with the sixty six peers were being escorted out of parliament house.

"Why not, how do I fund my nation"?

"It's easy"

"How" Franck asked as he kept pace with the pack of peers.

"Work is money, willing hands create wealth; idle hands do nothing"! Marshall confidently said.

"How do I pay them"?

"Print your own currency. A hard working nation creates its own richness. Banks have no money; they lend the money they don't have fifteen to twenty times over. If every depositor decided to withdraw his or her money the banks wouldn't be able to provide it, they would collapse." Marshall accurately said as Franck Max Climax seriously contemplated the proposition.

"My son you have routed the nations that bloodied Sudanese soils with the blood of its own people, you have brought peace back into the land and given its people their freedom but this is not enough for it to survive Sudan must become a self sufficient country dependent upon no-one. Expose yourself as its hero, lead the nation, develop the country but never allow it to lose its identity, leave the western society to itself for its shortcomings and its preoccupation with materialism will destroy your soul, preserve your culture, limit your numbers, life is about the afterlife, I need say no more for I know that you understand." Franck Max Climax heeded his father's words and nodded his head in agreement and smiled in contrast to the glum faces that surrounded him.

The image of Her Majesty the Queen flashed up on a large LCD screen above the speaker's chair, below Bernard Townsend listened intently on the Royal blue phone and followed Her Majesty's orders, he placed the handset into a communications device that acted as an input for the audio-visual system and switched it on, Her Majesty's voice came across loud and clear for all to hear inside and outside of the British Parliament.

"My loyal royal subjects, today will go down as one of the most important and memorable days in our modern history. Over the past three decades we have learnt much about negotiation especially in our dealings with the Chinese and the loss of Hong Kong and its territories. One hundred and twenty years of investment lost to us.

Australia represents another major investment in more ways than one, however we have also been very lax in our duties towards it and this infant nation has turned itself into something of an unruly spoilt brat. A number of weeks ago I was presented with sufficient well-documented and cross-referenced information that carefully showed me the decision that I make today. In front of me sits a document that begs my signature, as I sign with the Grace of God the following Acts of British Parliament namely:

The Colonial Laws Validity Act of 1865 (UK)

The Commonwealth of Australia Constitution Act 1900 (UK)

The Statute of Westminster 1931(UK) and finally the British version of the Australia Act 1986 (UK) effective from today are repealed"!

Her Majesty the Queen then solemnly put pen to paper and signed the all-encompassing document.

"Australia ladies and gentlemen is once again a fully dependent colony of Great Britain. On the question of International Law I have it on good authority by senior officials of the United Nations that our unilateral decision is sound.

45

DIPLOMATIC AFTERMATH

After two and a half weeks, once all the dust real or otherwise had settled US President Brian George convened a top-secret meeting of all staff involved in the 'Kakadu Strike'.

In the 'For one's ears only' assembly room at the CIA's Langley headquarters, Rachael Crank, Leighton Hill, April Hako, Raymond Halliday and an assortment of top ranking political and military advisers gathered in readiness to greet the President. The atmosphere was unusually tense and uneasy given the success of the mission.

"Ladies and gentlemen upstanding if you will, I give you the President of the United States of America"! A burley CIA security guard loudly announced in his Texan drawl as he opened the heavily armed door to the secure chamber. All present immediately stood up and clapped their hands out of respect for the Commander in Chief and his office.

"Thank you and a very good morning to you all. Please be seated." The President warmly greeted. "I see that we have quite an agenda to plough through today; of all the matters before us which one ladies and gentlemen do you consider to be the most important? I'll give you a moment or two to make your decisions." The President then added as he made his way to his reserved place at the elongated oval conference table.

Brian George twiddled his thumbs and forced a downward smile as he looked inquiringly into each person's eyes as she or he tussled with the hidden complexities of the question. When no answers were forthcoming the American President vacated his chair and walked around the circumference of the table with his hands in his pockets.

"I ladies and gentlemen am not looking for specific answers designed to please the Presidency, on the contrary I prefer substantiated, unpalatable and wildly original submissions. Let us consider for example the ramifications associated with the assassination of Australia's Prime Minister Harvey Jarwood.

Was the murderous act an isolated incident restricted to its own locality? What was it meant to represent? An act of terror against Australia or a payback for Australia's involvement in East Timor or ladies and gentlemen was it something more sinister? The President slowly and deliberately asked with a good measure of theatrical ability as he continued to pace about the room.

"I for one do not believe it is isolated." April Hako was the first person to speak up.

"And why is that Miss"?

"Because the bombings at the hot tourist spots in Bali and Indonesia have targeted multi-nationals and not specifically Australians"

"Perhaps it was co-incidental." The President countered.

"No Sir the height of the bombings occurred during the Northern Hemisphere's winter when predominately northern Europeans and Americans went in search of warmer climates." April Hako calmly asserted

"Whereas the Aussies holiday there at all times of the year for shopping, surfing, spirits and fornica......"

"Yes Sir." April Hako quickly replied cutting the President off mid sentence.

Brian George assumed a somewhat pensive stand, stroked his robust jaw and concluded. "In effect predominately affluent Christian cultures."

"Quite right Sir"

"The origin of the terrorists Agent Hako"

"Home grown Sir"

"Under whose influence"?

"Neither Afghanistan, Arabic nor Korean, most probably Chinese if our sources are correct, unfortunately it would seen Mr President that we have been partly responsible for the spread of their Communistic ideology." April Hako proposed.

"How's that." The President asked anticipating the answer.

"By helping with its economic success" Agent Hako replied with a despondent half smile.

"Which ultimately gravitates to a political-economic problem with military overtones caused by the theft or duplication of intellectual property developed by us?"

"Quite right Sir"!

The President thought awhile as his political and military advisers squabbled amongst themselves.

"The Port Arthur Massacre Agent Hako, Chinese influenced"?

"Worse Sir and more serious than that Mr President entirely orchestrated by them with the Indonesians present as observers"

"Enlighten us further Agent Hako." The President politely commanded as the international ramifications associated with the event hit everyone in the room.

"The tragedy demonstrated a number of things. How easily the local police were diverted to another location, how ineffective all three law enforcement agencies namely, state, federal and their own secret service were in identifying the real culprits and furthermore

Sir and this is most probably the crux of the objective, how effort-less it became to manipulate their Prime Minister into disarming Australia. We suspect the Indo-Chinese have a long term plan to invade Australia now thwarted by the British Government's decisive act to take back administrative control of that nation."

"Very impressive Agent Hako, I commend you on your good work, which leads me to conclude that we need to watch the Chinese very carefully." The President stated coldly.

"They are definitely a growing concern Sir, if we are not careful nor diligent in our approach they will ruin our economy by flooding the market with cheap substandard goods. Now is a good time for policy changes Sir." April Hako knowing that she was probably out of place hesitantly put forward.

"I take on board what you say." Brian George agreed.

"There is more Sir, if you will permit me." The President nodded his head and allowed April Hako to move to centre stage.

"Our National Security Systems are being continuously attacked by Chinese computer hackers and by continuously I mean not day by day, hour by hour but rather minute by minute. It's the same for the British. We have upgraded and expanded every conceivable counter measure short of physically locating hackers and sending them into cyberspace." April Hako carefully detailed.

"I take it that is on the agenda"?

"No comment Mr President, however may I say that we have taken steps to silence our own people?"

A hush descended into the room out of a fear that April Hako's comment meant that the CIA had liquefied undesirable Americans.

"Many of our major Universities have for some time effectively pressured congressional politicians to deal with American companies who supposedly breached human rights whilst doing business in war-torn African nations. I believe our agency was instrumental in supplying a list of companies dealing with Sudan. Your prede-cessor Mr President forced and ordered American companies out of Sudan in 1997, foreign corporations less receptive to US University campaigns, US Foreign policy and global calls against human civil rights violations quickly filled the subsequent void. A major offender is Petchin a Chinese owned and operated oil and natural gas Company."

Raymond Halliday and others in the room remained silent and somewhat grim faced as Agent Hako detailed her findings, out of grave concern that they would be found out. The President remained pensive oblivious to their obvious fears.

"In other words we boobed it."

"I'm afraid so Sir." Agent Hako affirmed,

"Ladies and gentlemen, strategies please and by that I mean measures successful to our acquisition of foreign oil at a reasonable price until we develop alternate reliable energy sources." The President swiftly ordered as he returned to pacing around the room. Once again he gave his hand picked personnel sufficient time to come up with some spur of the moment suggestions, Brian George meanwhile recalled many of his Chinese adventures that caused him to distrust the emerging superpower.

First and foremost it was the Asian way of speaking English that continually irritated and bemused the President at the same time. The letter R was L and vice versa for example the classic fried rice invariably pronounced flied lice.

"Harro, preased to meet you Mr Plesident, a preasure to meet you and aahhh have you for this momentoss occassioon. We have aahhh aahhsembred ourer finest musishians to enteltain you! Prease ova hear"! The Chinese Presidential assistant jovially said as he grovelled and guided Brian George along the red carpet to his designated seat in the richly decorated Beijing Concert Hall.

"Tonight we have you something special" He gushed with a face that resembled two slits for eyes, two dots for a nose and one hundred teeth crowded into a tiny space called mouth. The stage curtains opened and revealed a large symphony orchestra. All members were

Chinese nationals, the cream of their elite musicians; they were met with a round of thunderous applause.

"Obviously something to look forward to" Brian George muttered to himself as he settled into his armchair and gave a modest golf clap.

The orchestra tuned its instruments with an obvious animated fervour, music to everyone's ears apart from Brian George who found it particularly jarring. After an agonising seven minutes of fine tuning where every note played was ever so slightly off key thanks to the tonal range of the Asian ear, their illustrious conductor Ai Bong-chew a five foot one inch 'giant' glided onto the stage, swept his jet black hair back and stepped onto his podium.

With his back to the audience he politely bowed from the waist to the orchestra, once to the left, once to the middle and once to the right, then he spun around on the balls of his feet and repeated the act of respect towards the audience. When all was relatively still he spoke into the microphone attached to his coat lapel, first in fluent Chinese and then in erratic English.

"As we aahhh have the USA Plesident hear tonight, we play a seerection of tunes from Bloadway forrowed by Borelo, aahhh thank you, aahhh hope you enjoy thank you"! Ai Bong-chew proudly announced before he threw himself into the musical wok of desire.

The resulting sweet and sour sound scape caused US President Brian George to almost abandon all sense of political correctness and stampede out of the concert hall towards the brink of diplomatic disaster by expressing his true feelings. The 'off' Broadway musical potpourri drove the President's mind into overdrive.

'Anni get your gun' brought forth "I wish I had a gun"! South Pacific's Bali Hai; "More like Bali belly"! Chicago "Give me the mob anytime"! And Grease "Can I please slip on a banana skin and slide out of here, please God please; before you see a grown man cry"!

The orchestra's last piece a powerful rendition of Bolero produced images of Chinese water torture. Completely exhausted by it all and suffering from a massive thumping tension headache the President raised himself up and gave a standing ovation more out of appreciation that the concert was over than anything else.

"Aahhh I see you rikee Mr Plesident, you want Ai to play more"? The conductor asked from where he stood. Brian George shook his head in the negative and pointed to the anatomical location of his bladder.

"Aahhh you have Chinese syndrome."

"Badly" Brian George confirmed as he briskly stoke off in search of the men's room.

The audience laughed as soon as he exited the main auditorium and the President could feel that he was the butt of the conductor's Chinese jokes.

The Chinese Presidential assistant who had earlier attended to Brian George came running in search of the US President in the desperate hope that he did not understand the Chinese nor Mandarin language.

Brian George's recollections of Chinese bathrooms and the customary post concert buffet dinners were also disturbing; the urinals were invariably small and just 18 inches above floor level. One had to point accurately when passing urine plus have the ability to voluntarily control the force of the flow otherwise one suffered urine splattered trouser legs and shoes.

"Everything okay Mr Plesident"?

"Yes thank you."

"Aahhh good you come this way I show you good time" The Chinese presidential assistant assured Brian George once he had found him washing his hands in the men's bathroom. The President looked at him sideways and wondered what he meant by 'come this way'. Undaunted the Chinese presidential assistant took Brian George by the arm and led him to the concert's hall ballroom in which all of the prominent and influential political and business leaders had assembled to greet US President Brian George with one common goal; to milk him of information whilst giving nothing in return apart from false smiles and raised eyebrows.

"Our eight wolrd famous Ilon chefs have ploduced for enjoyment by you, how you say in Amelica, feedbag buffet all you can aahhh eat splead! We havaahhh all main legionat cuisines, Hui, Yue, Nin,X-iang,Su,Lu,Chuan,Zhe come you see." The Chinese Presidential assistant proudly beckoned as he led Brian George to a vast expanse of food.

Before the US President stood eight, horse shaped tables neatly arranged into the shape of one giant horse, behind each table stood the physically drained and nervous chef responsible for that regions culinary efforts.

"You rikee Mr Plesident"

"Overwhelming where do I start"? Brian George replied, as a large plate was trust into his hands by an overzealous kitchen hand.

"I give you best dishes"! The Chinese Presidential assistant confidently said as he escorted Brian George around. "Here we havaahh General Tso's famous chicken, one for me three for you, thenaahh Zongi, Baozi, Congee not on plate, aahhh too messy, instead give you bowl, thenaahhh you need Kung pao chicken, give you good kick in bradda, then aahhh leather eggs with sea urchin for starters, what you think"?

"Can hardly wait to dig in"!

"Okay, prease sit oova there, I keep you company, see everything. Like Horsehoe, we China bling you ruck okay"?

"Okay." The president hesitantly replied as he cast his eyes on the mishmash of food before him.

"He was right, they are Iron Chefs, everything has either been beaten to death, fried alive or steamed into submission! Why did I bother coming over here? Damn politics"! The US President thought to himself just before he made it look as though he was enjoying his meal.

"You wantaaahhh more Mr Plesident" The Chinese Presidential assistant annoyingly asked just as Brian George forced himself to consume a horribly disguised leather egg.

"Not at all, perhaps you could get me a doggy bag for later." He replied.

"No dog on menu, we know you aahhh dog lover, pity we glow vely good table dog."

"Shitzu"

"Aahhh no too small special bleed just for lestalaun." Brian George rolled his eyes in disgust. "Come you try now eulo-asian fusion sweets."

"Very well if I must" Brian George replied as he hid his sigh.

The dessert buffet was impressive. The Chinese contribution was largely sliced fresh fruits, a sweet warm soup, which was mostly sugar water, an assortment of fruit jellies and a Moon cake special American style cake.

The European aspect was predominately French-Viennese prepared by a supposedly highly trained Chinese pastry chef. US President Brian George forced himself to select equal amounts of the opposing cultural cuisines. It was the President's wish to save the best to the last and he therefore commenced with the Chinese desserts.

"This is bleeding awful"! He thought as he half smiled and half chocked on one of the tasteless wonders. Brian George then washed down the offensive sweet with a good measure of Mai-long-slong domestic beer that he hoped was formaldehyde free.

"Bad choice what the hell why would you want to destroy a perfectly good Pilsner recipe by incorporating rice and rye, are these people mad"? The President mentally cursed. "Perhaps there's some salvation in these sweets" He hoped as he attacked one of the French style pastries. "Looks good tastes like cardboard, all body and no soul, another example of the bastardisation of the European race and its abilities by Asian infiltration, God help us and the US, why do they all want to be western"? He thought to himself as he reflected on one of his young female staff members, Ingeborg Chin, a Chinese-Swede. "Mother Swedish, father Chinese, a very confused individual in all respects."

"There is a glimmer of hope Mr President." Agent Hako confidently spoke out breaking the groups silence and the Brian George's train of thought.

"Let's hope it is more than that April." The President responded as he drifted back into the present reality.

"Over the past two weeks a new spiritual leader has emerged in the Sudan."

"What of it Agent"?

"His chosen name is FM 1 a Nubian from the northern Sudan. It is rumoured that he is a descendant of Egypt's twenty fifth ruling dynasty that existed around 730BC thus making him a legitimate ruler of the country whether it be Egypt or the Sudan. Accordingly he has won much favour amongst the Sudanese people so much so that the present regime is feeling very fragile and nervous given the fact Queen Tiye of Egypt was Nubian, the wife of Pharaoh Amenhotep III, mother in law of Nefertiti and the grandmother of King Tutankhamun."

Agent Hako's comments caused the meetings military adviser's ears to prick up with thoughts of an American assisted governmental overthrow.

"Quite an impressive pedigree providing he is related. Pity about the name, do you think FM 1 is sympathetic to American policies"? The President asked.

"Difficult to say, his philosophy of rule is based upon the following ideology. 'Whatever you do, do it as beautifully as you can, but before deciding to do it, first ask yourself, what will it bring to the people, animals, even the vegetables and waters and to the environment' April Hako slowly explained.

"A local or global Messiah Agent Hako"?

"Once again difficult to say Mr President for FM 1's philosophy can be interpreted both ways."

"In which case our track record is much cleaner than that of the Chinese"

"Agreed Mr President may I correct you in saying that FM 1 is not as black as you may imagine."

"Very well Agent Hako point taken; full reconnaissance on him and all Chinese companies operating in the region. Find any dirt on them to our advantage. Keep a watchful eye out and make certain nothing happens to FM 1, if God is on his side the Sudan may well blossom once again." A God fearing Brian George authoritatively said with a nod of his head and then asked. "Any thoughts about China ladies and gentlemen in terms of how we slow down her influence upon the world's economic, military and political landscapes."

In less than a second one of his less than scrupulous wildly imaginative advisers jumped to his feet and rattled off his multi-pronged plan of attack.

"Economic, health system and military is the way to go Sir! First let's get stuck into those rice munching suckers! Hike up import duty on all Asian goods get it made in the USA! We have the technology, we have the people we are self sufficient Sir!

Next let's attack their internal operations, Heard of Project China Sir! It's an extensive epidemiological study being conducted to observe the relationship of disease patterns to diet principally the move from the traditional Chinese diet to one which incorporates rich western style foods and animal proteins. There is a very strong correlation between the emergence of cancer, diabetes, heart and other diseases as a result, let's make them sick by promoting more fast food chains in their country Sir! Lastly thanks to the Kakadu strike we have arrested the flow of Uranium out of Australia to China thereby limiting their nuclear capabilities and let's keep it that way Sir! Finally Sir let's hack the hackers and declare war on those rednecks Sir"!

"Very original good concepts, food for thought I'll consider it."

"Thank you Sir"! The adviser said with a sharp click of his heels.

"At ease soldier"

"Thank you Sir." And with that the overly patriotic adviser sat down and remained intensely focused on the issues at hand.

"Any further suggestions, no? Very well let's advance to the topic of the effectiveness of the Kakadu strike. Agent Hako our bottle of information brief us." The President politely ordered as he sought relief from the previous adviser's intensity,

"Yes Sir I'll need to find the appropriate file, please bear with me." She answered somewhat apologetically as she sorted through her paperwork.

"No need for that Agent, you're a clever intelligent woman, present off the top of your head, if you will."

"Yes Mr President." April Hako shakily replied as she felt the pressure of being put on the spot. "The er precise nature and method of attack by our military left no doubt in the locals mind that it was indeed a meteor strike and nothing else but that. This was further reinforced by the 'natural insertion' of genuine meteoric particles or tektites into the strike zone, in other words we peppered or salted the area."

"Just like in the good old gold rush days."

"Precisely Mr President, luckily no one of any real importance or authority went to investigate. The Park Authority took control of the situation and milked it for what it was worth, I believe the Tektites were scooped up and sold as souvenirs to the gullible tourists."

"So far so good Agent, what about the British"? Brian George asked in congratulatory fashion as a smile spread across his youthful face.

"I think we are on rock solid ground with them and we need not fear about the patency of our defence installations in Australia even though they add little to our global military defence network." April Hako suggested ignorant as to their true importance.

"A situation Agent that might need to be revised and ratified in the light of the recent Indo-Chinese alliance" The President cautioned.

"Agreed Mr President" April nervously replied.

"Proceed"

"Thank you Mr President we are lead to believe by our informants with the British Parliament that the English know very little about the illegal trafficking of radioactive instable Uranium from Australia. Sixty-seven high-ranking Lords have been 'expelled' from the country for the involvement in the 'raping' of Australia's wealth. The present British Prime Minister is intent on cleaning up the corruption that exists in the Houses of Parliament but may not go so far as to impeach the Nation's Aristocracy. I dare say that he is rather preoccupied with matters at home plus the administrative restructuring of Australia and its legal system." April Hako explained and then she sensed it was time to pause.

President Brian George listened very carefully to every word that April had uttered as he paced about the room. The accuracy of her findings made him realise how damn hypocritical and illusionary international political friendships between countries were. The USA spied on England as much as the English spied upon the Americans. Human life on earth was nothing more than territorial in nature amongst all of the races that inhabited mother earth. Once again his political and military advisers squabbled amongst themselves. April Hako waited patiently for the Presidents signal to continue instead he decided to clear the air himself.

"I wish them luck! Diplomacy has never been their forte. They lost us, their attempted prevention of WWII was a disaster, they gave back Hong Kong and as far as the Middle East goes what can I say. The only thing in their favour with respect to Australia is the apathy that pervades the nation, a disease, which allowed minority groups to dictate their wants to the government without question. Question is given the present circumstances will the British abandon their quest and hand back the land to its indigenous people or will they put an end to the Mabo nonsense? Having said this I have come to the conclusion that it has come time for the Presidency of this great nation to declare that we are no longer the world's policeman. No

Minority group within our Union no matter how rich or poor, influential or otherwise has the right to expect or receive any exclusive or preferential treatment. The Constitution shall not be misinterpreted by anyone to satisfy their hidden ideological agenda's. Ladies and gentlemen God does not have favourites and if this be true which I believe it is then it must be the same for the USA. I shall make an official statement within the next forty-eight hours, meanwhile double if not triple your efforts in the Middle-East for we are withdrawing our armed forces, it's time Israel went it alone, we cannot continue to sacrifice innocent young American lives for a vain cause." Brian George passionately and solemnly said with an evangelical tone of voice.

The inspiration for his stunning decision came from remembering Father Brendan O'Reilly's sermon 'Love never forgets' for Brain George had sought the Presidency of the USA out of love, to serve its people out of love and ensure to the best of his abilities that families remained intact, in love, free from all harm and threat, whether domestic or imported.

"But Mr President their oil, we're dependent on it" Many in the room protested.

"I appreciate what you say but understand me please. I do not make this decision lightly, it may even cause me to lose the Presidency however it is more important that we look after own people than become involved in conflicting baseless ideologies for which there are no solutions. Once I make this clear, I think you will find that the Arabs will be more than eager to share their oil reserves with us. We can no longer mix business with religion or politics. I'll wager some of you by now depending upon your networked status in life will either view me as part saint or complete sinner. This does not particularly bother me. I took office for the good of the country not the reverse. Mr Halliday upstanding if you please"!

"Yes Sir Mr President" Raymond Halliday replied as he nervously snapped to attention.

"Nghi Phamhung captured or free"

"Er... Capt... er... free I think" Halliday weakly mumbled.

"Why is that"?

"I thought it would be to our advantage"

"How" The President angrily demanded to know.

"He kept us informed as to potential terrorist attacks"

"You don't seriously believe that do you Agent"?

"I have no reason to doubt it Sir much of his information proved reliable it enabled us to..."

"Little bombs half finished, bits of highly suggestive electronic equipment, pieces of scribbled upon maps, scrapped schedules, never a culprit, lots of arrested innocents, fertilizer packers, air conditioning technicians, but never a terrorist, everything done to make you look pretty and your informant justified." The President boldly interrupted. His cutting remarks shredded Halliday's already tarnished reputation and left him psychologically bleeding.

"Nghi Phamhung played you Mr Halliday, have you at least confiscated their spoils of war"? The President then sharply asked.

Raymond Halliday swallowed hard, made difficult by a parched throat and mustered his scattered thoughts. "I don't know what you mean Mr President."

"Never mind one day you'll understand! I have a new job for you if you're up to it"!

"Yes Sir what might that be"? Halliday timidly asked as his mind licked its wounds.

"I want you to watch over Father Brendan O'Reilly."

"Who"?

"Father Brendan O'Reilly an American Catholic priest of Irish descent, you may have seen something of him in the media."

"Can't say I have Sir"

"Then familiarize yourself with him, you atheistic fool! Until further notice this man is you number one priority! There is something special about him and I want him protected, do you understand

Mr Halliday"? The President roared as he exercised his Office's full authority.

"Yes Sir"

"Good! April Hako"

"Mr President"

"Hand over the priest's dossier to Agent Halliday and assume complete responsibility for Nghi Phamhung I want him reined in"!

"Yes Sir"! Agent Hako confidently replied as she willingly accepted the assignment.

"Not so confident now you pathetic little power hungry megalomaniac? Just desserts to you, a generous portion yes in keeping with your greed! I doubt if Dot.org will want to have anything to do with you"! Louis Badcock mockingly sneered as he dressed down the Small Dark figure outside of Dot.org's boardroom.

Inside behind heavily guarded closed doors the members of the organisations all-powerful inner-sanctum contemplated the fate of those summonsed. They included the Ricci twins, Louis Badcock, The Small Dark Figure, Nghi Phamhung and his PhD clan, Dennis Sauvage, the Harshman and the D-man. The Small Dark figure did not respond it sat motionless, listless as it looked away in disgust at its own failures. Badcock's jeers were nothing compared to its own self-criticism and mental flagellation. Louis Badcock sensed victory and gloated in his own self-glory.

The Ricci twins remained neutral. The Harshman preened himself as a Gaylord would do, whilst the D-Man obsessively contemplated how to rid himself of his smiling Siamese twin who appeared to hold the upper hand.

The doors to the privileged boardroom opened and a burley sinister looking American-Vietcong hybrid stepped forward. "They are ready, go in" He barked in a surly manner.

Everyone timidly responded and shuffled their way through three sets of security doors and three high security passageways before entering the exclusive chamber. Once there a large room differentially lit confronted them, before them in almost complete darkness sat four masked effigies at a bench that smelt of illegitimate authority and deceit. Nervous and unsure as what to do the assembled group awaited instructions.

"Sit over there." The sane American-Vietcong hybrid roughly said as he came up behind the group and shoved each person into their allocated plastic chair.

"Careful"! Badcock hissed as he was forcibly pushed forward.

"Oh you're such a man's man"! The Harshman gaily uttered as he felt the hybrid's biceps and brushed his other hand across the hybrid's trouser front.

"Enough of that; sit and be quiet"!

"Whatever you say big boy"! The Harshman once again gaily replied un-phased.

Meanwhile the D-Man glided past and as he did so Saint Ignatius blessed the hybrid. "In the Name of the Father, Son and Holy Spirit; May the Peace of the Lord descend upon and be with you."

"Huh"? The hybrid exclaimed somewhat disturbed at what he had just seen.

Without any warning the lights suddenly extinguished, complete darkness descended and everyone apart from the four effigies and hybrid felt a sense of dread fill their hearts, minds and souls.

The American-Vietcong hybrid donned a pair of dark polarized sunglasses in anticipation whilst the Small Dark Figure and Badcock simultaneously realised that up to date neither one had met any real member of Dot.org's inner circle. These remained faceless unidentifiable individuals who relied upon emissaries to distribute and retrieve orders and information for the good of Dot.org.

Frightened by their circumstances the Ricci twins allowed their bowels to discharge silent but deadly alterations to the room's atmosphere; the four effigies remained unmoved with one exception their masks glowed in different colours, one pillar box red, the second sky blue, the third sea green and the remaining sun yellow.

"Now you've done it." The Harshman jokingly said under his breath, bad timing on his part for he was the first to be put under the 'spotlight'.

The four effigies masks eyes came alive, they blazed and focused eight highly intensive and penetrating narrow infra-red rays upon the Harshman's unsuspecting anatomy, he winced in pain as each ray hit him and he very quickly broke into a profound sweat caused by the heat of the moment.

"What explanation do you have for your current state"? The four effigies asked as one in a heavily altered metallic voice.

The Harshman put up his hands to shield his eyes, trembled with anxiety and stuttered out an answer plausible to himself "I am a bio-logical experiment, what you see is a result of medical science."

"Absolute nonsense; chemicals do not cause one to become gay! Emotional desire produces chemical abundance not the other way around! Today choose your pathway in life, as you are, is useless to us, as you were, is ideal"!

Realising what they were implying the Harshman instantly reverted back to his original state of mind. The cold-blooded killer mentality firmly re-established itself in his entire body and drove out any shred of feminine sensitivity. The Ricci twins in response continued to emit silent and now far more deadly atmospheric al-terations, Louis Badcock gagged on the pungent odour to the point of vomiting, the Small Dark Figure remained immune to all about it.

"You may go." The four effigies said as the Harshman stretched up and allowed harshness back into his face and hands.

"What abomination do we have hear"? The effigies then coarsely asked as they made reference to the D-Man and St Ignatius and focused their attention on the artificial Siamese twins.

"May the Holy Father bless you all including the robots"! The saint accurately said as he made the sign of the cross."

"Silence"!

"You do not frighten me"! The saint defiantly answered and then retaliated by saying "I have experienced far worse in my many lives"

"Silence or we shall…"

"Kill me? I don't think so"! Saint Ignatius replied as he exerted his full strength, stood up and walked boldly towards the four effigies dragging the hapless D-Man behind him. The hybrid attempted to block his path but the saint swung around and let the D-Man's flying arms knock the hybrid off his feet, one, two, three and land unconscious.

"Stop what you are doing"! The effigies screamed as the saint drew closer.

"Afraid not"!

"We will kill you"!

"What with; toy robotic lights? Try again"! He flippantly taunted as he seized one of the effigy's heads and ripped it from its moorings exposing a lifeless torso and a nest of detached tangled computer wires.

"Meetings over we can all go home now, off you go, don't lolly or loaf about, there's much work to be done, away with you all"! St Ignatius stated quite firmly as he exercised his full power and waved his audience away. Not one offered any resistance, which was not the case in Rome where another secret meeting was underway.

"Now that you've lost your superpower you're no use to us anymore"! Buddha the harmonica player surmised as he made reference to Pigtail the Pegleg Pirate's loss.

"I still have influence"! Pigtail retorted.

"But you're no longer supernatural! No thunder stick, no more stomping of the feet, no more I can move you off this planet! You're back to normal flesh and blood"! Buddha hoarsely screamed intent on eliminating Pigtail.

"What of it? I still have influence"! Pigtail loudly protested to the others present namely the three highly placed Vatican elite who together with Buddha and Pigtail made up Rome's powerful pentagon that steered its religious juggernaut through the ages for its own benefit. As usual their secret meeting occurred in St Cecilia's spacious upstairs priest hole.

"Perhaps he is right" One of the elite put forward.

"In what way"? Buddha acting as the devil's advocate aggressively questioned.

"Strategic policy, investment opportunity, matters of confounding theology, destruction or the discrediting of newly discovered archaeological biblical remnants, in effect anything that threatens our exalted positions." The same elite argued.

"Point taken but thanks to one Brendan O'Reilly Pigtail no longer the Pegleg Pirate is one of us, a mere mortal"! Buddha angrily deduced.

"Perhaps but then perhaps not; losing the limb does not suggest loss of immortality, we can rely on others to extinguish the anointed ones"!

"Like whom"?

"The D-man" The elite proposed.

"Have you seen him lately? He's having a back to back love affair with another man"! Buddha comically stated highlighting its absurd aspect.

"We are aware of the situation and have people working on finding a solution. However given it is St Ignatius who is attached it may prove difficult." One of the other elite although irritated solemnly and calmly answered.

"Another one of Brendan O'Reilly's pranks"

"No there appears to be another anointed one by the name of Jack Stern. He is known to us in a remote sort of way we are lead to believe that he has helped the American Archbishop Steven Moulds with various financial matters. He comes from a religious background." The third elite member answered with a worried look in his face.

"Then it appears he is well versed in our ways." Buddha concluded.

"That is a plausible argument Mr Harmonica player, especially if he had anything to do with the Mauritian discovery, a particularly worrying time for all of us."

"Why"? Buddha asked with raised interest.

"Pigtail, enlighten Buddha." The second elite commanded as the Harmonica player had not been fully indoctrinated into the ways of the Pentagon.

"The rock upon which Christ's Church was built was not St Peter as popularly promoted and believed, it was an actual physical entity that Jesus welded together from the four elements by an advanced understanding of mystical alchemy, in effect a transmutation of ethereal essence. If allowed to persist the wealth of this world would have taken on another form and all of us would have become impoverished. A feverish hunt was made for the 'rock' and once found my master Lucifer was sufficiently powerful to introduce the tinniest flaw into the creation causing it to fragment into four parts which were distributed by four independent invisible agents to parts unknown, thus guaranteeing our power and wealth over the masses forever." Pigtail recalled as he recounted his steps in the historical series of events.

"Your fear is that Brendan O'Reilly discovered one of the fragments in Mauritius." Buddha suggested as he raised one eyebrow.

"Correct." replied all three elites and Pigtail.

"Is there a genuine need to be afraid"?

"Very much so" An outwardly and deeply disturbed Pigtail replied.

"Why."

"The Church of the Coloured Sands as it came to be known had all of the hallmarks of Christ's creation. Every man, woman and child was accommodated according to their beliefs, religion and language. This represented the first real threat to war that controls planet earth." Pigtail painfully explained as he felt for his missing pegleg.

"I see" Buddha hummed as he dwelled on the significance of Brendan O'Reilly's discovery and remained quiet.

Pigtail the Pegleg Pirate then attempted to terminate the heated debate by saying. "Irrespective whether he that is Brendan O'Reilly discovered the fragment by chance or not we cannot take any further risks…"

"In other words you don't have the fragment"! Buddha concluded after it dawned on him that it was the most likely explanation for Pigtail's behaviour.

46

KBW 49

"Hello viewers! What a line up have we for you today! Welcome to KBW 49 your mega information station twenty-four hours a day, always first with the top stories, always first with the real inside information, always here to please, awe and shock you"! Frank bellowed in his own peculiar theatrical style similar to that of a wrestling ringmaster all that was missing was the phrase 'get ready to rumble' but then one never knew when Frank was likely to slip it in. He paused momentarily and then lowered his voice to create an aura of suspenseful mystery. "We've been holding off with some of our stories until our in the field investigative journalists had finished their work and polished it to perfection, Janice"!

"Yes Frank." She softly answered subtly annoyed as being in his presence for two reasons, his loud and brash manner and that overpowering nauseating aftershave that smelt of unmentionable anatomical parts. "God knows who he is trying to attract." She thought to herself.

"Your team I believe have surpassed themselves"! Franck praised adding to the hype.

"It would seem so." Janice proudly answered with reservation, as it was she who was the principle driving force behind all of the inquiries.

"What a choice we have today, it's almost like entrée, main meal, sweets and afters, which one shall we choose? It's so difficult! Do you think it matters? What time of day it is Janice"? Frank asked in a camp sort of way, as his wrist appeared looser than normal so as to confuse his co-host.

"It shouldn't do." Janice replied as she rolled her eyes.

"Very well then, perhaps we should have a domestic first"! Frank gaily proclaimed as he began to roll up his shirtsleeves and loosen his wide secret agent tie designed to eliminate the competition and impress the ladies thereby increasing his chances of hitting the bullseye.

"Domestic it is, let's do it Janice I've been holding back far too long, it's all pent up, time to blow off... some steam and speak my mind"!

This time Janice was visibly afraid, not knowing whether or whom Frank might attack. Had some one whispered in his ear and told him how much she despised him, was this payback time? Janice gritted her teeth and awaited the inevitable onslaught.

"You know Janice I've never liked you, I've found all of your sweetness damn annoying and nauseating. Why can't you loose control once in a while"?

"We're on television Frank"!

"I know, I know, I know, I'm not a fool, that's why I am saying this, it's the perfect introduction to the difficult and hard line decision that our President Brian George made yesterday. Can you begin to imagine how many nasty people he's going to hurt? He's one brave man"!

"Look Frank this is not exactly what I had in mind! Could we please return to our original programme line up"? Janice begged.

"Noo... oh"! Frank screamed back like a spoilt brat with arms folded and rigidly refuse to budge on any point.

Realising she wouldn't get very far with him Janice abdicated and gave him a free rein. "Go on Frank tell us what you've found"!

"Well…. it goes something like this"! He said with an impish lisp. "According to my sources this is the just the beginning of a series of major upheavals in American Government policy. The President thinks we should become more intimate with the Mexicans. Andale! Andale! I say! Personally I'm sick of purchasing high priced designer clothes made in China. Honestly have you seen some of their stuff? Absolutely hopeless! I was in one of those Direct Factory Outlet complexes the other day trying on all sorts of clothing labels! Well I couldn't find one proper size anywhere! I'm a regular sort of guy so you would expect large, a generous portion yes, to fit me. What do you think I ended up with… let me tell you! A three pack of men's briefs, not one the same size as the other plus… all of the package holders were off to the side.

How in God's name am I supposed to get my package into one of those? Stretch it? Not only would I look ridiculously bent over but I would walk funny as well! Then there was the three pack of sports socks. Two lefts', two rights' and one pair marked middle! I bought four T-Shirts and five business shirts, the sizes ranged from XS to XXXL and they all fitted! Okay I can live with that! I bring home the merchandise and remember the wise words of my mom; I decide to wash everything before wearing it. Hijole,Que Onda!! Guacala!!(Holy cow, what's happening, that's horrible, bad move) My laundry ends up a toxic wasteland. The washing machine dies from a lethal dose of formaldehyde and lead poisoning"!

"That's terrible Frank." Janice replied as she like others in the TV studio tried to suppress their laughter.

"Si montas un camello, no te vallan a salir ampollas en las nalgas" A red faced Frank then blurted out.

"Does a bear shi…. In the woods" Janice roughly translated.

"Entirely wrong"! Frank countered with authority as he wiped his beaded forehead. "If you're going to ride a camel you're gonna wind up with blisters on your butt! Is the correct translation, in other words through our greed we made the Chinese a superpower. We missed out on the ten billion dollar arms sale to them because of our anti-communism stand, the Russians on the other hand saw the opportunity, they leapt at it, got the contract and saved their asses from economic disaster. Let's go with the Mexicans I say otherwise we'll all end up No hay de queso no mas de papas"!

"I don't have cheese or potatoes either"? Janice hesitantly guessed.

"Broke Janice broke! Let's get behind Brian George and save our country from this nonsense! Mexico here we come! Gabi es Buena onda, Buena vista, taco's tequila and hot Latin babes! (Good vibes, good view, good food, liquor and Senorita's) Janice mentally translated his statement to be as she pretended to listen to Frank's political philosophy.

Agua con el china perro, hijo de puta puta madre (Beware of Chinese dog, bastards, prostitute mother) I always say"! Frank bravely ended his monologue with no regard for political correctness.

He viewed the concept with complete contempt and disdain; this flamboyant news presenter believed in speaking his mind and damming the consequences, However He would respect the rights of others providing they did the same.

"Anything else Frank" Janice inquired almost afraid to ask the question.

"Yeap! I'm finally proud to be American! I believe in the Presidency! He's bringing our boys home, God bless the man; he has Mucho Huevos (big balls) let the rejoicing begin! Vamonos de revention! (Let's party)"

"Since you're in that frame of mind, let's stay on the political pathway, God bless England? How say you"? Janice asked with a playful smirk on her face and a glint in her eye.

"I'm not as passionate about the English as I am about my own, however having said that I am pleased that they are putting their house in order."

"You mean with respect to Australia" Janice asked intrigued by his comment, which raised suspicions in her mind as to how much Frank really knew.

"Not at all my informants tell me that sixty odd peers of the realm were dispatched to parts unknown for knowingly and illegally syphoning off Australia's unprotected wealth." He boldly stated.

"Big sweeping statement Frank"! Janice cautioned.

"Do you think I'll become James Boggle's next assignment"?

"James who"?

"You know MI5 and all that secret agent stuff."

"Depends what you're spreading or intending to spread."

"Information"

"Do you have it on you"? Janice asked with a sharp tongue and a penetrating stare. Un-phased Frank smiled and returned her look.

"Deep in the palm of my hand it lies, nothing up my sleeves, no slight of hand, just hey presto and peel it away." He said as he magically produced a small retractable scalpel blade from his shirt's breast pocket and proceeded without any delay to perform surgery on his open hand.

Frank's unexpected and swift movements caught his audience unawares and all were aghast as a consequence. One of the studios more astute cameramen quickly dismantled his apparatus and zoomed in at close range to televise Frank's doings. Frank made a deep lateral and bloodless incision across the palm of his left hand, just 3centimetres above his wrist, then he cupped the same hand which allowed a pocket to appear from which he extracted with the aid of a pair of surgical tweezers a 2.5 centimetre square piece of pink paper. Frank then relaxed the hand and glided the handle of the scalpel blade holder across the incision and it instantly fused back together. Spellbound his audience awaited the next chapter in the phenomenon, Frank looked around, ceremoniously laid the pink paper square on the white desk top before him and gently coaxed it into life by snapping his fingers. The four top flaps that held it together unfolded and created a horizontal cross, the creation then apparently flipped over of its own accord and from its centre a thirty centimetre paper 'skyscraper' erupted in a flurry of activity. Each of its 'walls' listed the names of the missing British peers complete with their private home addresses and mobile phone numbers, including Franck Max Climax alias Lord Tingle.

"I call it my 4 T acquisition." Frank proudly said obviously pleased with the delivery of his illusion.

"4 T" A stunned Janice weakly responded

"Yeap stands for titillating terrifying tattletale tower, my powerful phallic monolith"! He smirked, tongue in cheek.

"What can I say"? A breathless Janice stuttered.

"You could try breath taking! Wow! How did you do it? Can I have some? You want to teach me"? Frank cheekily suggested.

"Is there more"?

"Depends upon what you would like to see and hear."

"Surprise us" Janice now somewhat girlishly inclined yelped with excitement.

"Call it what you may, conspiracy theory, hidden agenda, wild speculations, it does not matter, my reliable overseas informants suggest that since the loss of Hong Kong Britain has struggled financially, so much so, that during the 1990's almost fifty-five percent of its population existed below the poverty line, they desperately needed cash otherwise Britain faced becoming an elite third world country."

"Similar to some African states" Janice interrupted.

"With one exception, the African nations are exceedingly rich in natural resources."

"Okay; where are you taking this"? Janice asked raising one eyebrow as she shifted her position on her stool.

"The administrative takeover of Australia is a political confidence trick, a stunt. The sixty odd peers were not individually distributed to parts unknown but taken to a remote secret military debriefing centre where they were persuaded to reveal their 'legal business' methods used in draining Australia's wealth." Frank said with an ambiguous authority as his eyes scanned everyone in the studio to see if they had grasped the reasoning behind the British action.

"It doesn't sound plausible."

"But it is, remember the film 'Catch me if you can'"

"What of it"

"The outcome" Frank teased.

"Was that he was caught"! Janice fired back seemingly annoyed.

"Congratulations! Did you remember the end credits"?

"Sort of" Janice vaguely answered now visibly annoyed.

"Then you would have read that the brilliant confidence trickster was subsequently employed by the government and banking agencies to prevent future fraud."

"Sixty odd experts volunteered by their past ready to take over the departments of finance, taxation, social security, health, reserve bank etc, etc"

"Yeap, you just got a hole in one my Pennsylvanian beauty"! Frank said bursting at the seams with an over production of male pheromones, which in itself was a sufficiently strong olfactory signal to change subjects.

"Brendan O'Reilly"

"What of him" Frank asked feeling rather jaded that the spotlight was off him.

"He was meant to be our feature story"

"Alright if you must" Frank grumbled as he fiddled with his shirt sleeves and readjusted his secret agent tie.

"Our France 2 reporter Josephine filed this report with us earlier this week, Josephine are you there"?

"Bonjour Mon Ami Yes I am here in the beautiful Island of Mauritius enjoying the sun and sand." The vivacious journalist replied as her image formed on the studio's large television monitor, her virtual appearance sent Frank's pheromone factory into hyper drive. He wished, he sighed and trebled at her sight, he fretted, he moaned, and howled like a dog. He went weak at the knees, his mouth watered, saliva escaped from the corners of his mouth as his tongue signalled its eagerness to perform erotic delights on the young maidens sweet curvaceous body. He sat transfixed as rigid as his reproductive member.

"I believe you and Benoit canvassed the entire Island leaving no stone overturned so to speak."

"Yes that is correct Janice." Josephine responded in her rich and velvety French accent, one that drove Frank wild with sexual excitement.

"Tell us more." Janice politely asked as she quietly observed Frank's uncontrollable animal behaviour from the corner of her eye and wondered where and what his hands were doing at that moment in time.

"As we are all aware things were moving along very nicely until the day of the National celebration which marked the discovery of the Church of the Coloured Sands. On that day everything went horribly wrong. The Church disappeared, Father Brendan O'Reilly was confronted by an Archbishop from America and consequently disappeared and President Ringagain flew into the harbour and almost disappeared forever." Josephine smiled with a tilt of her noble head at the end of her humorous description of the bizarre events.

"Sounds rather comical" Janice suggested.

"Yes if it were not so tragic! I suppose you are right, a typical French tragic comedy, full of pathos, slapstick and er how does one say; supernaturale themes."

"Very good Josephine, very good" Janice complimented her colleague and allowed her to continue.

"The whole Island's population is devastated, Father Brendan was much loved by all, he touched the hearts of everyone who met or saw him, whether close up or from a distance such was the charismatic magnetism of the man. Shy and reserved he spoke with a universale authority and never asked for anything in return. The generous offerings and gifts that he received he gave away to Sister Ambrosia who distributed the wealth amongst the Island's poor. She not only feed and sheltered them but more importantly in creating new industrial ventures gave them employment with a good measure of self esteem attached."

"The Island doesn't miss him! They just miss the pilgrim hordes and their pockets stuffed with foreign currencies"! Frank bitterly and rudely interrupted as he preened his hair. Both women ignored his unwarranted ranting.

"My thorough investigations led me to believe that Father Brendan O'Reilly is a genuinely honest man, not a hint of being a shyster and I do not believe in the official story." Josephine emotionally stated as she raised her voice in his defence.

"Which is"?

"The Catholic Church in Rome has finally released an official Vatican statement on Father Brendan O'Reilly it reads:

The Royal Conclave of Cardinals has decided in their wisdom to suspend the American priest Brendan O'Reilly from all of his duties. Detailed examination of videotape footage of the events that occurred at St Pious Parish, the Church of the Coloured Sands and the Mauritian Carnival day in honour of Brendan O'Reilly suggest that the afore mentioned priest possesses mass hypnotic powers. The Church has always held the position that such abilities and their practice are satanic in nature. Furthermore the Church does not condone the priest's behaviour in living with or caring for a considerable number of ex prostitutes and allowing them to defile the sanctity of the Holy Altar whether it is real or illusionary."

Janice put her hand up to her mouth and bit hard so as to distract her disbelief. She was there at St Pious Church, she had witnessed the events first hand, she knew what she had seen, heard, touched, felt, it was no illusion, it was not mass hysteria, it was real, everything was real, as real as the D-Man, Louis Badcock, the seven prostitutes and the Sandrino's whose story helped her to win the coveted National Award for Journalistic Excellence.

"Yes Mon Ami this is how they treat heroes perhaps it is not a French tragedy after all."

"Let's talk about us." Frank blurted out aloud breaking the silence that ensued.

"Which one is us"? Josephine asked somewhat bemused by his proposition.

"Me and you"

"Are you sure you don't mean Janice and yourself? I've seen the way she looks at you Monsieur; I believe she thinks you are quite the conquering devil."

"Really" Frank answered flattered by the comment and equally disappointed by the fact that Josephine remained distant to his advances. He looked in Janice's direction and fluttered his eye lids and eyelashes that bore a hint of mascara. Janice bit harder. Josephine could feel that all was not well and she instinctively introduced the next topic of conversation.

"The letters B and B are synonymous worldwide with the famous sex kitten Brigitte Bardot here in Mauritius they stand for the highly eccentric Bruno Bogliani whose claim to fame is socks. Every sermon he gives is about socks in fact he is so obsessed with the clothing item that he has a sock theory about the origin of the universe. Father Bogliani believes that God is a master sock weaver. Here is the interview that we conducted with him a few days ago at the Church of the Coloured Socks."

The video footage showed Josephine, her cameraman Benoit and Father Boglaini outside his church which resembled a multicoloured sock infested Red Cross or blood transfusion centre.

"Father Bogliani what made you decide to decorate your church in this unique fashion"? Josephine asked as Benoit panned the building with his camera.

"Our heavenly Father is the master weaver of all that exists; neh, sniff, sniff snort, therefore it was right and proper that we represent him in this way. Everyday you put a sock on you are entering the

Father, sniff." He bravely answered as an empty headed individual devoid of all common sense and acquired insight.

"I see; must be quite the experience"! Josephine replied in the affirmative whilst trying to look serious. "Is it the same inside"? She then asked as she pointed to the derelict church.

"Even more wonderful, come and see" Bogliani beckoned as he strutted off in his high heels to open the building's front door. Josephine and Benoit followed closely behind. Benoit took the opportunity to film Bogliani's honky tonk way of walking.

"And the Word was made into a sock and came down and dwelt amongst us, it came to comfort, heal, nurture and warm, such is the power of the Lord"! Bogliani solemnly expressed as he ushered his guest into the hall of divine sockimania.

Washing lines loaded with hundreds of pairs of socks spanned the interior of the church. Everything and anything else that stood, lay or hung was sockified. It was an amazing sight, a labour of passionate love, an eccentric expression of true love and devotion; artistry taken to new heights of three dimensional collage Josephine, Benoit and the viewing audience were overawed by the sheer volume and arrangements of the socks. Bogliani beamed from ear to ear triumphant in his outstanding achievement, not one square inch of the church lay bare.

"Absorbent, acrylic, active, angora, anklets, arthritic, embolic, athletic, basic, bed, blanket, bleached, blended, bobby, booties, cable, cashmere, casual, colourfast, cotton, crew, cuffed, cushioned, cycling, deodorant, diabetic, dress, elastic, executive, fancy, filamentous, fish mouthed, flammable, flat, football, golf, graduated, high twist, hiking, hunting, knee highs, knee warmers, knitted, lace, lambs wool, layered, legwarmers, lisle, lycra, marls, mercerized, merino, metallic, micro-fibre, mid-calf, mock-rib, mono-filament, neat, nylon, paired, patterned, polyester, polypropylene, pom, pouched heel, rack, rayon, reciprocated, reinforced, ribbed, running, Shetland, shrunk, silk, ski, slipper, slouched, soccer, spectator, spilt, stirrup, stocking, stretch, support, surgical, tennis, terry, texture, therapeutic, thermal, tube, wader, walking, welted, woollen, work, worsted, wrapped... is just a few species that I can mention; left alone they cross pollinate and multiply to produce endless variants, look carefully and you can see sonking (socks having sex) going on in the corner over there"! Bogliani quickly said in one breathe as he pointed to where he thought the socks were 'having it off' or to put it more politely pairing with each other.

Neither Josephine nor Benoit wished to venture into the church out of fear of being smothered to death by a sudden avalanche of apparel. Everything looked ticky-tacky, fragile; ready to collapse at any given moment in time.

"How did you manage to acquire such a er collection"? Josephine gulped as she two steps back into the relative safety of the main door frame.

"The Lord works in strange ways." Bogliani explained angelically as he remained where he was.

"So do thieves"! Josephine harshly answered in contrast.

"The Lord is not a thief"! Bogliani sharply rebuked Josephine as he maintained his innocence.

"Only his servant's are." Josephine replied this time sarcastically.

Bogliani did not answer instead he silently immersed himself into this creation and became oblivious to everyone about him. His unresponsive vacant state resembled that of a petite mal epileptic fit. Benoit focused the camera onto Josephine who read out the following accusation.

"Father Bogliani we have it on good authority having widely interviewed many prominent local and overseas citizens that you have misappropriated on more than one occasion donations intended for Father Brendan O'Reilly."

Bogliani did not respond he stood stone faced as a deaf and dumb mute who had been straight jacketed. Josephine waited a good two minutes, sufficient time for him to elicit a defence, before she continued with the findings of her unbiased and impartial survey.

"This miracle of the socks is testament to how crazy the man has become. No one comes here anymore, people are afraid to enter the building as rumour had it that Bogliani by his over zealous and fanatical nature had attempted to cocoon worshippers by wrapping them securely in body stockings." The pre-recorded segment ended there.

"God that sounds alien"! Frank dryly stated making reference to major sci-fi films.

"You're very correct Monsieur. The Mauritian police intervened after several missing person's reports had been received. All of the people were discovered in the building. Each had been bound and gagged with socks, wrapped in what appeared to be Kevlar reinforced material and hung from the church's rafters. Luckily not one person had been permanently injured."

"Religious freak, monster"! Frank viciously lashed out in an attempt to agitate the viewing public." Why hasn't he been put away"? He then demanded to know in a harsh raised voice.

"It seems Bogliani is being protected by the Church in exchange for his knowledge about Brendan O'Reilly and his discoveries." Josephine explained.

"Bastards"! Frank wildly erupted.

'Was it he who made the Vatican aware of other matters such as Father O'Reilly's involvement with the ladies of the night"? Janice asked.

"That and more, we believe Bogliani originated the rumours of mass hysteria and theft even before the American Archbishop arrived. The discovery of the Church of the Coloured Sands had put his 'sock' I mean his nose out of joint, to many he continually behaved as a jilted lover even though members of Brendan O'Reilly's troupe had accepted him into their fold and strove to educate him in their ways. The entire argument in fact his behaviour was driven by one of territorial religious jurisdiction. On the following videotape, which has no audio recording of the conversation between the filmed individuals largely due to the distance, it was taken from and because the public address system had seemingly failed Bogliani accuses O'Reilly of adorning himself with highly expensive jewellery out of the coffers of the Church. This finding came to us from a group of expert lip readers, who meticulously studied the tape provided by us, they also made another startling revelation, in the heated exchange between the American Archbishop Moulds and…. "

"Who"?

"His name is Moulds, Steven Moulds." Josephine cordially explained amused about having been interrupted.

"A most appropriate name" Janice sharply concluded as she reflected on the true purpose behind his Grace's sinister presence.

"The young ladies remembered Moulds as being one of their regular clients"!

"So it wasn't Moulds who informed on O'Reilly." Janice put forward.

"Definitely not, it would have served him no advantage unless it guaranteed him the return of his fleshpots which begs the question, could he have been acting on some one else's behalf"?

"Most astute of you Mon Ami anything else" Janice then asked sensing that the plot was about to thicken even further.

"The monkey knows how to kick butt! I just love that monkey! Did you see what he did to that black devil and how he bowled that Ringagain over! What a ridiculous name! Hello pleased to meet you, what's your name?

Ringagain! Strange I don't think I have your number! Ringagain! Look old chap I just told you I don't have your number! Now if you would excuse me I have other more important and normal people to talk to"! Frank said out aloud in an improvised posh English accent as he played the part of a condescending Lord of the Realm interacting with a frustrated Ringagain.

"You're quite the character Monsieur." Josephine cheerfully remarked as she muffled her giggle.

"I do try to please, especially when it comes to us." Frank replied in a seductive tone of voice as he repeatedly fluttered his eye lids and eyelashes that bore a hint of mascara.

"This next piece of news should please you Mon Amour." Josephine erotically suggested as she returned his advances.

"Tell me what is it"? Frank eagerly asked as his reproductive organ reignited its spark.

"This morning police raided the Church of the Coloured Socks upon the advice of one Sister Ambrosia"

"Don't tell me Bogliani wanted to have sock with the nun"?

"Far worse"! Josephine glumly replied.

"What could be worse than that"? Frank curiously asked.

"Some one had finally socked Bogliani once and for all"!

"Never"! Frank shouted quite astonished.

"It is true, the coroner was called in and forensics is presently at the scene conducting their business."

'Details" Frank asked becoming hot underneath his collar.

"The most I can tell you is as follows. Sister Ambrosia was ordered by the Government to bring Bogliani his daily meals; the priest was virtually under house arrest following his multiple abductions. Sister for her own safety would leave the sealed meals in an air and water tight insulated receptacle capable of holding two days supply near the front door of the church. Very often Bogliani would not collect the meals and they would gradually build up and then empty again. Sister Ambrosia's suspicions were raised today when she made her early morning delivery. Inside the receptacle that had been emptied the previous day sat meals from days prior to that. How did she know? Each meal was colour coded according to the day of the week and time of day, a system that Ambrosia developed herself to prevent accidental food poisoning. Only she knew the code. When Sister delivered today's she found meals from four days previous, it seemed strange and against her better judgement sister took the risk and popped her head inside the church's main doors. The interior had been stripped bare, no socks, no statues, no altar, nothing, except for one lonely human cocoon that swang eerily from the rafters above. Father Bogliani had been well and truly socked. His hands and feet were heavily bound nine times over, he was gagged, a rolled up Italian football sock had been stuffed into his mouth and his head had a small black elastic sport sock stretched over it causing his nose to become horizontal, Bogliani was then encased in a body stocking, hung upside down and consequently died from an unpleasant suffocation." Josephine very slowly and grimly detailed.

"The Angel of the Sock came to collect him"! Franck morbidly said."

"What"

It sounds better than the Angel of Death"! He then said in defence.

"Any clues, motifs, Josephine" Janice then asked the France 2 news correspondent.

"Suspects are many, in fact the Island's entire adult population ranging from those who had been abducted by him to grieving worshippers and members of parliament."

"Retribution in other words"

"Perhaps" Josephine replied without volunteering any further information. This made Frank itch like a curious flea infested feline.

"How long was the holy salami hanging for" He then asked in a manner that suggested days rather than hours.

"At least forty-eight hours if not more" Josephine hesitantly guessed based on her recollection of the interview with Sister Ambrosia.

"Gave him plenty of time" Frank ambiguously commented. Josephine and Janice looked at each other non-plus.

"Honestly Frank what are you on about now" Janice whinged.

"Spooky things; think about it, he could have escaped like the great Houdini or better still come back to haunt us. Imagine the headlines

'Sock covered ghost terrifies locals', 'Men women and children go barefoot afraid to wear socks', 'Exorcist called in to purify sock factory of evil spirits'.

"Frank"!

"It's okay Mon Ami let him have his humour, it helps me introduce the next topic of conversation." Josephine calmly and politely suggested.

"Oh very well" Janice grumbled as she steadied herself; saw the merits of her colleague's proposal and took a long breath to further calm her frayed emotions. Frank on the other hand hyperventilated with excitement; Josephine's encouraging words were music to his mischievous mind.

"It was most appropriate Monsieur that you mentioned ghosts."

"Why is that my French lovely" Frank amorously asked.

"Because Mon Amour at the site where the Church of the Coloured Sands once stood, folk lore has it that a ghost inhabited the area"

"Bogliani's"

"No my friend; think about it, Bogliani was not dead then."

"He might as well have been. I heard his sermons were deathly." Frank acidly replied.

"Respect for the dead, please Frank, respect"! Janice sanctimoniously demanded.

"Respect for him? I think not! Why should I? He was a foot fetish feeling fanatic"!

"Frank behave; please" Janice begged as she reddened in the face and felt her blood pressure rise dangerously high.

"You're blushing"! Frank observed completely misinterpreting her circumstances and then smugly added. "Must be my powerful aftershave, finally weakened your defences"!

"Josephine the story please" Janice nervously pleaded as she mopped the perspiration from her forehead.

"It is always important Mon Ami and my invisible viewers to return to the beginning, the origin, the when's and where it all started, Oui? In the case of Father Brendan's discovery the region of the Coloured Sands and its surrounding districts and peoples is of particular interest. In the days following the disappearance of the Church of the Coloured Sands, Benoit and myself canvassed the area seeking answers to a multitude of questions. We obtained anecdotal reports from the farmers, local residents of the area, onlookers, stallholders and pilgrims who had remained behind; from it we conclude that the holy man is not a master illusionist"!

"I don't agree"! Frank unexpectedly counter attacked in true adversarial fashion. "I have proof to the contrary, just look carefully at this selected piece of footage.

One minute there is the priest with several of his lady friends on stage, lucky bastard! Then in a blink of an eye they gather themselves, hold hands and they're gone, never to return! There is no evidence of camera malfunction, there is no break in continuity, nothing; all is good. Question how did they disappear? Were they really there to start with"? Frank asked with one eye brow raised and his head tilted to the left. Janice was afraid to speak Josephine thought it amusing.

"Frank you are the typical American, brash, bold, perhaps a little loud mouthed, we gave you the Statue of Liberty but we did not give you the freedom to bomb the world. Violets my dear Frank explain it all."

"Brendan O'Reilly was blown off stage like a pansy"? Frank insolently asked.

"I do not think so, just listen for a moment and you may learn something! Historically our Napoleon the one who married Josephine was a devout fan of the flower. On every wedding anniversary he sent her a violet bouquet. 'Our corporal violet' as we so fondly nicknamed him when he died he even had a violet filled locket around his neck."

"How touching"!

"Zeus the powerful Greek God loved a nymph by the name of Lo, to hide her from Hera his jealous wife, Zeus changed Lo into a white cow. When Lo wept over the taste and texture of coarse grass Zeus changed her tears into dainty sweet smelling violets that only she was permitted to eat. Blue violets say 'I'll always be true'." Josephine sweetly concluded with a smile.

"Just like me"! Frank crooned in an attempt to endear himself with her. All that Janice could do meanwhile was to image Frank-making love to a cow.

"You may think that this has nothing to do with the priest Brendan O'Reilly however it is not so. Many people have testified that the Church of the Coloured Sands was born in a plot of land known as the purple quadrangle which was inhabited by a ghost and guarded by several mysterious creatures that resembled red-eyed winged humanoids that stood over nine feet tall. The purple quadrangle was a formidable forbidden place; no one dared to go there out of a fear of being frightened to death.

Needless to say violets grew in the plot all year around without any regards for the seasons. It was like that for centuries until Brendan O'Reilly arrived. Once the church appeared the violets disappeared, as did the ghost, however glimpse's of the red eyed winged humanoids still occurred, when the church disappeared so did the violets and the quadrangle became barren."

"What a wonderful fairy tale Josephine, you have done yourself proud"! Frank whimpered as he pretended to show part of his feminine side. Josephine completely ignored his pretence.

"On the day of the church's disappearance even though it had been declared a national day of celebration, pilgrims still came in numbers to partake of the church's healing baptismal waters and immerse themselves in the atmosphere of the church's extraordinary interior. Along the surrounding roads stall keepers happily did a brisk trade until many 'soldiers' arrived. These hired mercenaries drove the worshippers out of the church and bolted its doors shut disrupting everything in the process. No one could get back in nor dared to go back in. The sounds of loud gunfire coupled with fierce explosions scared them away"!

"What happened next"? Janice gasped, as did the majority of KBW 49's viewing public.

"Eye witness reports suggest that the main roof of the church caved in and a violent mini tornado erupted shortly thereafter. What caused it to occur no one knows or can explain. As the tornado grew in strength the building's entire structure vaporised to reveal one last bizarre scene. At the main altar a distorted man hung on desperately as a large serpent attempted to devour one of his legs before he was sucked away into the heavens. Several astute bystanders videotaped the entire sequence of events commencing from the moment the 'soldiers' arrived. We were very fortunate in obtaining copies of these complete with signed affidavits as to their authenticity." Josephine then broadcast the unedited video footage taken from a number of vantage points and allowed all and sundry to dwell on the televised material.

"The identity of the man at the altar" Frank asked this time seriously.

"Unknown, not a cleric nor local and unlikely to be a pilgrim" Josephine intelligently postulated.

"Why"?

"Our theory is based upon one singular camera angle taken by an intrepid tourist who trusted in his own belief. This fearless man ran towards the disintegrating building and took remarkable close-up shots of the bizarre scene with his semi-professional digital video camera. Look carefully as we slow down the frame rate per second and you will see what we mean." Josephine explained before she went onto surgically describe how Pegleg the Pigtail Pirate lost his supernatural limb. Frank the buffoon was the first to speak.

"There is much hidden symbolism here. I for one interpret the snake as being a guardian of the sacred place, the man a threat to the integrity of the church. The snake has attacked the man and it appears, stripped him of something sinister, a cancerous growth perhaps and it made him whole again before he is whipped away."

"That is plausible as is the opposite, namely that deceit as represented by the serpent lies within the church." Janice offered as an alternate argument. "I take it the Vatican has not seen this footage"? She then wisely concluded.

"Correct." Josephine truthfully answered without making any additional comment.

"That leaves Brendan O'Reilly in a rather precarious and ambiguous situation, one that is further clouded by long columns of lingering doubt as to his true intentions." Janice strongly argued unemotionally as a devil's advocate would do.

"It almost seems to me as though the priest is involved in the occult which would explain his need for prostitutes"! Frank said in a low voice as he stroked his manly jaw thus adding weight to Janice's point of view, which she found comforting.

"An interesting point of view in this age where everything requires a scientific explanation otherwise it is cast into the realm of witchcraft. We have already established that Brendan O'Reilly is not a thief as to satanic practices I need to refer you back to the recordings dealing with the church's vaporisation.

Every recording stops at the same point, once the man at the altar is sucked into the heavens the recordings stop, but my dear friend the eyewitnesses did not. The tornado posed no threat to anyone near its vicinity it appeared self-contained, beyond the boundaries of the church's walls all was still. Once the man at the altar was gone a heavenly being appeared in his place. A young lady by all accounts, she tamed the serpent and it also disappeared. The structure of the church then became transparent, glass like, smaller and smaller until she held it in the palm of her hand. Many people then noticed a young man lying on the ground at her feet, a fallen gladiator; her knight returned from battle in protection of her honour, she appeared pleased with his efforts but he lay still, very still as if he had been mortally wounded. The young maiden dropped to her knees and without any effort on her part scooped the warrior up in her arms and faded from view." Josephine slowly and emotionally described in detail leaving no one in question as to what had transpired. She then closed the book of notes from which she had read.

"Another fabulous modern fairy tale should make a great movie"! Frank flippantly jeered as he itched to get out of the studio into a suit of armour and fly into Josephine's embrace. Janice meanwhile dabbed away a few fallen tears; she had always been old fashioned when it came to matters of the heart.

47

FRAGMENTS

Have you ever been in one of those situations where you knew that you were innocent, when everything you did was for the benefit of your fellow man and yet there were those who deliberately sought to undermine you, to tarnish your reputation, your image, to make mud or any other undesirable smelly substance stick forever just by altering people's perception and understanding of the true facts. Brendan O'Reilly felt like that as he and his only true friends sat together and watched KBW 49's report on the big 70 inch 'plasma' screen on the fourth level of the Genius Loci.

Seven beautiful born again virgins, the enchanting Yvette Bell, the enigmatic Jack Stern, Grandpa his ghostly relative nestled together, tight and cosy with Brendan in the middle, in full knowledge that they were bonded for life and furthermore the Vatican's reaction was confirmation of the fact that Brendan had truly discovered something of significance.

"Um that should produce an interesting cocktail of international opinion amongst the world's people." Jack lightly concluded after he stood up and clapped his hands to shut down the complex's sophisticated television screen. "Question is how much and what will they believe"? He next asked.

"I thought it was a well balanced presentation." Yvette quickly replied coming to Brendan's defence as she reached out and held his hand warmly just as a devoted wife would do.

"Comic and serious" Jack reacted inquisitorially to Yvette's impression.

"Not like that, more… er… along the lines of truthful and … er… fabricated."

"In terms of content it didn't go into any great depth, I for one thought it was based upon opinion intermingled with bystander commentary." Jack accurately replied as he prepared to point his finger at the visibly devastated and disillusioned Father Brendan O'Reilly who languished on the leather couch next to the highly supportive Yvette Bell.

"No need for that Laddie." Grandpa bluntly interrupted as he floated next to Jack and instructed his grandson with a wink of his eye to curl his threatening finger. Jack understood and refrained from making any further comment for he already knew Grandpa had something important to say.

"My children the events at Mauritius confirm a very important behavioural trait." Grandpa said without moving his lips. "Whenever something new is discovered it is either wildly overregulated or destroyed as it invariably poses a threat to someone. Brendan you unfortunately did not discover anything new; however you did rediscover something old, something borrowed and almost new." Grandpa chuckled after making the indirect reference to marital matters. A quick minded Jack and Candy smiled at its humorous intent whilst the others remained engrossed in the mystery that was about to unfold. Seeing that he held his listeners captive Grandpa decided to proceed with his monologue.

"One like you who lived two thousand years ago in the Middle East whom we called the Christ forged a principle that stood to banish poverty and slavery amongst mankind from the face of the earth! Can you imagine the effect this had upon the Masters of Affliction who continuously work hard to control the world of deceit in which we live here on earth? It was horrific! It was hell for them to see peace on earth even if it lasted five minutes! Damnation! Vexations of vexations! Earthly happiness and bliss represented afflictions, agony, anguish; a bottomless pit that lead to Hades otherwise known as heaven to us mere mortals. Once the peacemaker was dispatched from earth the lies started followed by endless aberrations and distortions until hundreds of Christian faiths existed, each claimed to be the true Catholic religion as founded by Christ; a headache for everyone including the Roman Empire. In 324AD British born Flavius Constantinus issued a decree commanding all presbyters and their subordinates to journey to Nicaea and bring with them the testimonials they had orated to the rabble. Emperor Constantine saw the opportunity to create a new and combined state religion protected by law. Two thousand two hundred and thirty one scrolls, legendary tales of gods and saviours plus a record of the doctrine orated by them were presented.

Can you imagine what sort of puerile assembly it was with so many cults represented? Three hundred and eighteen bishops, priests, deacons, subdeacons, acolytes and exorcists gathered to decide upon a unified belief system that encompassed only one God. After eighteen months if not longer of complete and utter satanic gibberish, the useless ballots short-listed five prospects. Caeser, Krishna, Methra, Horus and Zeus. Emperor Constantine made the final choice and Hesus Krishna became the official name. He then instructed Eusebius the historian to compile a uniform collection of new writings developed from the primary aspects of the religious texts submitted at the Council of Nicaea. His words were as follows 'Search ye these books, whatever is good in them retain, but what whatsoever is evil cast it away. What is good in one book, unite ye with that which is good in another. Thus brought together ye shall call it The Book of

Books, make them to astonish!'

When his instructions were fulfilled Constantine then decreed the new testimonies would be thereafter be called 'The word of the Roman Saviour God' he then ordered all earlier manuscripts and council records burnt, further any man concealing original writings would be beheaded.

I see my Laddie remains un-phased by my commentary whereas you Brendan appear a little green around the gills. The next piece of information might cause you to spew!

Today's New Testament contains narratives from the Ancient Indian Epic, the Mahabharata verbatim, passages from the Phenomena of the Greek statesman Aratus of Sicyon similarly so, also included are extracts from the Hymn to Zeus written by Greek Philosopher Cleanthes, two hundred odd words from Thais of Menander, one of the seven wise men of Greece, quotes from the semi-legendary Greek poet Epimenides and seven passages from the curious Ode of Jupiter. Christ's birth is identical to the Fable of Mithra, the Divine Son of God and messiah of the first king of the Persian Empire around 400BC.

Surprise, surprise Mithra's birth was attended by Maji who had followed a star, a star from where I ask you? Guess? The east and they brought gifts of gold, frankincense and myrrh. Shepherds came flocking in excuse the pun, to adore the newborn that came into the world wearing the Mithraic cap. Ouch that must have hurt! Wonder what his mom screamed when he was born. Obviously the popes liked inflicting pain on women because they wore these caps of various designs and attachments well into the fifteenth century. Sexist sadists!

Mithra was one of a trinity and after they drenched, I mean anointed him with honey he stood on a rock, which became the emblem of the foundation of his religion! Sounds familiar? There's more! A last supper; held with Helios, a handsome god crowned with the shining aureole of the sun who drove a chariot across the sky each day and returned to the east at night; also present at the supper were eleven other companions! Guess what happened to Mithra? He was crucified on a cross bound in linen, probably not of his choice; his body placed in a rock tomb and he... that's right rose on the third day or around March the twenty fifth which coincided with the full moon of the spring equinox, a time now called Easter after the Babylonian goddess Ishtar. Mithra promised to return to earth in person! His, the second prophesied coming, hallelujah, praise the Lord for he will banish the gnashing of teeth and the tearing of clothes forever! There will be no more dentists or seamstresses"!

"Grandpa"!

"Yes Laddie"

"Don't get carried away." Jack cautioned.

"There's no wind in here"!

"Carry on."

"Heckler"! Grandpa snapped back before continuing on with his monologue.

"The salvation of deserving souls was to happen during the fiery destruction of the universe, this was the major Mithraic doctrine. Practisers of the faith partook in a sacred communion banquet of bread and wine, encountered this before? Of course you have, it is known to you as the Eucharist, the Christians weren't the first, the Mithraitics beat you to it by four hundred years! All of this comes to you from the learned writings and interpretations of eminent scholastic historians; question is how true is it? Is all of this a red herring, a fox's trail to lead one down the wrong pathway, an attempt to discredit Christ and his achievements? Certainly Constantine was instrumental in destroying all pre-Nicaean documents, yet fragments remain, but not in sufficient numbers to challenge the established authorities. This is what awaits you, what will confront you; face you; afraid? Shaken? Nervous? Anxious? Scared?

It's a long way down before you make contact with the watery depths of knowledge, the Church of the Coloured Sands took you to the diving board, are you prepared to dive in once more"? Grandpa challenged, his words did nothing to inspire Brendan into action, as he was still coming to grips with the ghost's excellent rendition relating to the origins of the modern day Catholic Church and its theology. He knew that Grandpa was not lying for two reasons, firstly it was not in his nature and secondly within the Genius Loci where the finite met the infinite it was impossible to do so. The seven born again virgins were of no help, as it appeared that not on of them had any measure of a proper Christian upbringing, which left Yvette as the source of meaningful comment. However before the beautiful maiden could say anything constructive Jack took centre stage to further compound the problem of the Church's true identity.

"Thank you Grandpa, I take it your accurate information is based on the universe's spiritual archives"?

"But of course."

"Excellent, the topic I wish to dwell on is that of virgin births. Long before the Christian era commenced there were in many pagan places pictures of virgin mothers with their children. Such pictures included scenes of the Annunciation, Incarnation, Birth and Adoration; a common saying among ancient pages was 'The gods have lived on earth in the likeness of men'. Two thousand years before the Christian era, Mut-em-ua virgin queen of Egypt was said to have given birth to Pharaoh Amenkept III who built the Temple of Luxor upon whose walls is represented… "Jack paused mid sentence to clap his hands three times so as to activate the complexes highly advanced 'plasma' screen and depict all of the images he wished to make reference to. "Here we have the 'Annunciated' God That announces to the virgin queen she is about to conceive, next the 'Immaculate conception' the God Kneph mystically impregnates the virgin by holding a cross to her mouth, bet this will be the last time you kiss your crucifix or the Archbishops for that matter! You'll probably think twice about it in future! Yvette, Brendan, ladies! No response; bit of blushing okay! Then we have the 'Birth' of the man-god and finally the 'Adoration' of the newly born infant by Gods and men including three Maji who offer him gifts." Jack slowly described as he pointed to the last of the images that he flashed up on the large television screen.

"Another virgin birth of Egyptian origin is that of Horus who is said to be the parthenogenetic child of the virgin mother Isis. Brendan, ever been to the catacombs of Rome? No? Pity, for in there black statues of this Egyptian divine mother with infant still survive to this day, these were worshipped by early Christians and absorbed into their faith, the Virgin Mary is represented as a Black Regress, her face often veiled in true Isis fashion. The statues of the goddess Isis holding the child Horus in her arms were exported to neighbouring and remote countries where they acquired new identities. Christian in Europe, Buddhist in Turkestan, Taoist in China and Japan, religious plagiarism at its best! Other pre Christian statuettes and engravings of divine mothers and child were found on ancient Athenian coins. Who said there was no money in religion? Amongst the relics of Carthage, Cyprus and Assyria similar figures are often found and are known under a great variety of names according to the sect, for example, the mother was known as Venus, Juno, Mother Earth, Fortune etcetera, whilst her offspring had names such as Hercules, Dionysus, Jove, Wealth etcetera, in India the same figurines popped up under different titles. In many other countries outside of Egypt variants of the story of the virgin birth of gods are told. Attis the Phrygian God was said to be the son of the virgin Nan who conceived him by putting a ripe almond or was it a pomegranate in her bosom, one can only speculate what would have happened if she had played around with a banana, cucumber or zucchini! So there you have it a super short history dealing with the veneration of virginity. Factual, mythical, mystical or romantic which one will it be; which one do we apply to the Christ"?

"I believe it to be factual." Yvette strongly voiced "And I base my argument on the fact that the Blessed Virgin Mary continues to this day to make appearances all over the world."

"Well said my angel, but what sense can we make out of all of this." Jack asked the group in the style of a well-seasoned lecturer. "Brendan, no? Still struggling with the history of the Catholic Church? Anyone play chess? Chess I said Felicity not chest even though I might add you do appear to have a rather good set"! Jack concluded with a borderline indecency in his voice as he smiled with highly suggestive 'come to bed' eyes that made Yvette question his ability to remain faithful in any long-term relationship.

Not one of the group had any initial inkling of the tangent that the highly accomplished gentleman Mr Jack Stern was on, with the exception of Grandpa who stood close by albeit nonchalantly

"Yvette, virgin of virgins, tell us what you know about the Blessed Virgin's apparitions, but before you do so perhaps you could enlighten us as to what you saw on the first day that you 'chanced' to discover the Church of the Coloured Sands." Jack politely asked as he looked down on Yvette who maintained her grip on Brendan's hand.

"Countless numbers of violets"

"Certain there wasn't more, something or somebody that you were afraid of"? Jack intimated in his line of questioning.

"Not that I am aware of." Yvette pretended.

"Very well" Jack replied rather unconvinced as his manner showed as to the truthfulness of her statement.

"What I think Jack is trying to ask is did you see a winged humanoid with piercing red eyes as reported on KBW 49." Felicity explained as she repositioned herself on the couch to face Yvette. The question caused Yvette to blush deeply and lower her head partly in shame and partly in painful embarrassment. A lonely teardrop escaped from her left eye and trickled down her left cheek.

"What's wrong my dove"? Felicity caringly asked as she reached out to touch Yvette who by now had many tears cascading down both cheeks, one after the other.

"You're such a monster"! Brenda shouted at Jack as he stood up to face his foe as warring bucks might do. "Why can't you just leave things alone? Why must you constantly prod and probe until you upset people? Are you happy now? Look at what you've done! Totally unnecessary! It's bad enough that you've shattered my faith in the scriptures there's no need to destroy this maiden's devotion! I wish I'd never met you! Come Yvette let's go"! Brendan shouted uncontrollably as ever fibre of his body shook with rage as it tried to divorce itself of its pent up anger and frustration.

Jack remained calm whilst the girls looked on and gulped with trepid anticipation fearing a violent barroom brawl was about to erupt.

"You got it all wrong Brendan"! Grandpa boldly interrupted as he floated between the two potential belligerents.

"Really, I don't think so! This man is nothing more than a cunning bastard intent on filling his pockets with gold! Not one person means anything to him! Sister Ambrosia was right! He's nothing more than a cold-hearted string puller, a manipulator of the worst kind! Entice you into his web of charm with gifts from the super-natural, before you know it the big black spider alias Steven Moulds comes along and bites your head of! Great, give me more! What am I supposed to do now? I'm a has-been, a flash in the pan! Suspended, without a church or home! I will always be known as the hooker's keeper! Great! Better still why not just call me the religious pimp and get it over and done with! 'Give me a call Father and I'll arrange a hot nun for you tonight!' In house prostitution at its best run courtesy of Father Brendan O'Reilly"!

These final cutting comments struck deeply into the hearts of the girls for it reminded them that irrespective of what they did with their future life they would always be hookers. Candy was the most visibly upset, she cried uncontrollably as she relived the memories of her torrid earlier years, Brendan had allowed his 'defeat' at the hands of the Vatican to virtually tear him apart and this artificial emotional monster threatened to disintegrate the integrity of the group that Jack Stern had so carefully brought together. The atmosphere became thick with contrasting emotions, confusion, despair; a lack of direction momentarily raised their ugly heads until the accomplished Jack Stern snuffed them out by intelligently saying.

"Enough of this; air your personal grievances once and for all, but do not do it in the 'poor me' aspect for it will achieve nothing! Sit yourself down and stop making a fool of yourself! Then listen and learn Brendan"! Jack sternly commanded with a piercing look that grabbed Brendan O'Reilly's whimpering soul by the scruff of its neck lifted it up, shook it about before forcibly sitting it down. He then stepped to the side leaving Brendan to contemplate his fate and approached Candy who continued to shed tears unabated. With the utmost tenderness and compassion Jack lowered himself to his knees and knelt before the grief stricken young lady. The many years spent with his priestly uncle coupled with the long hours in adoration before the Holy Sacrament of the Altar when in exposition cultured within Jack an unusual understanding that made him an almost perfect confessor.

This trait in association with his highly developed intuition and ability to remote view enabled him to easily and accurately ask the following question which was not for his benefit but rather for Candy and those who were prepared to listen.

"If someone had called 911 the chances of reviving her would have been about ninety five per cent, is that correct"?

"I don't know." Candy replied bitterly as she remembered the circumstances surrounding the unexpected news of her half sister's death. "It all happened suddenly! One minute she was there, bubbly, a gentle beauty, extremely happy, everything was going well, she had managed to overcome all obstacles, reunite herself with her four year old daughter after leaving the X rated film industry, she had a new man in her life, handsome, wealthy, educated he helped her to kick her drug habit and then... she was no more...thanks to that so called 'father' of her child"!

Jack and the others remained silent out of respect.

"He called her on the pretext of sorting it out, it was a trap, before Roxanne knew what was happening she was drugged and gang raped by a collection of his druggie mates all of whom had paid for the pleasure. I don't want the same thing happening to me. Once a hooker always a hooker they say no matter how hard we try to absolve ourselves it sticks! In Roxanne's case it was worse! The two hundred odd films that she starred in made her a prime target, I'm the lucky one so far and it's all so strange because religion caused the both of us to end up in the flesh industries.

Our mom was really stupid, a trailer trash girl, pregnant at seventeen to one man and then pregnant at eighteen to another. Alcohol, low self-esteem and insecurity were her downfall. She turned to religion and got mixed up with this religious fruitcake he became our step dad and gave us biblical hell, made us feel worse than worthless, all in the name of God. I prayed day and night to be rescued but no one heard me. All three of us were beaten on a daily basis until we got used to it. If we missed out we feared the next day because that would be the day when the pain returned. He was a sadistic bastard who acted in the name of God. He punished mom, made her work two jobs while he stayed at home and had his ways with Roxanne when she hit puberty and her breasts became as large as melons.

He never touched me because I didn't have that easy look about me. Roxanne and I had to run away and prostitution was the easiest way out for us, especially when Louis Badcock's talent scout appeared on the scene, we both felt guilty for leaving mom the way we did.

Mom was a survivor; we later heard on the grapevine that mom decided to fight back. During one of her daily beatings, which usually occurred in the bedroom of their trailer, mom retaliated by hitting him over the head with the bedside copy of the bible, this made him absolutely ballistic, he jumped onto mom and tried to strangle her with both hands as he repeatedly screamed 'blasphemous bitch, Satan's whore' luckily mom had held onto the bible, in her semi conscious state which was rapidly sliding into oblivion she lashed out to save her life. No one can quite understand or explain what happened next.

It appears that the bible opened up, its hard cover became very rigid and one of its corners acted like a sharp knife that cut into his face and sliced his right eye in two. The searing pain and instant blindness caused him to let go. Mom gasped for air, rolled out of the bed and stumbled her way out of the trailer, she fell down its front door steps and passed out.

Many of the trailer park's residents when they heard the commotion stopped what they were doing and rushed out to see if they could help. Mom lay in a heap, battered, bruised and bleeding, her neck was swollen and her eyes still bulged from the attempted strangulation. Her pulse remained slow and steady but her breathing was laboured. Some of the residents feared her throat had been crushed; they administered first aid as best as they could until the paramedics and police arrived.

Others with weapons in hand gingerly went inside mom's home in search of her assailant. They found him dead in the bedroom his body lay face down on the floor. When they turned him over they saw that the sharp corner of the bible hard cover had sliced through his right eye, cheek and forehead and was deeply imbedded; it had penetrated his brain. Ironic isn't it that the source of terror had become the instrument of death"?

"It's the good and bad that exists in all things." Jack tenderly explained as he raised himself up off his knees, pulled Candy towards him and embraced her fully as a caring and protective father would do.

"Please don't ever let me go." Candy whispered as her body trembled and melted into his.

"I promise." Jack whispered back into her ear mindful of the importance of his commitment.

The other girls crowded around, only Brendan and Yvette remained seated and somewhat distant. Once all of the healing was complete Jack released his embrace and let Candy go and turned his attention to Yvette.

"How about you, sweetness of sweetness, what do you remember about your parent's death"?

"Nothing, I was only month's old at the time"! Yvette defiantly snapped back as she edged closer to Brendan.

"He can't protect you my darling and I won't let him. Once you accept that perhaps you will tell us what you can recollect after all we do remember from the word go, in triplicate, in every cell of our bodies, perhaps you would feel more comfortable describing one of your recurring nightmares"? Jack coldly elicited as he stood tall and aloof a side of him that Yvette instantly took a dislike to.

The slowness of her answer caused Jack to reply on her behalf. "Outside from nowhere two round glowing embers appear at the window, inside the car all is peaceful, attached to mommy's breast everything is secure, daddy happily chats away, all is fine, not long before journey's end, then a flash, a bang; mommy where are you, nothing there but two glowing red embers, is that how it goes my dearest"? Jack coldly asked.

"It does." Yvette weakly replied, as she rested her head on Brendan's shoulder; who responded by cradling it with one hand.

"You saw the glowing embers in Mauritius but you did not flee for you knew they belonged to the one who had protected you."

"Yes, but I also damn him! Why didn't he protect my real parents"? Yvette bitterly sobbed.

"I can't answer that question and I'm not going to speculate for who knows the minds of the gods? I surely don't, but then I'm not here to inflict pain. I feel people's pain, I identify with it and I wish to extinguish it. I find salvation in humour, you my precious seek it in your devotion to the Blessed Virgin Mary; unfortunately we live in the world of deceit which presently is propagating its era of disinformation, one of the mechanisms that it uses to keep humans bewildered, confused and unable to progress peacefully. Moments ago we learnt of its application to the scriptures, the consequence of which has stifled people's spiritual and physical evolution. The Masters of Affliction have tentacles everywhere armed, ready to destroy and disorientate. Your Blessed Virgin Mary is no exception. Many high ranking clergy as well as non believers and sceptics regard claims of Marian apparitions as nothing more than rampant hallucinations. The 'seers' they argue are so overcome by superstition that it causes them to deliberately lie and create the hoax so as to draw attention not only to themselves but to the economically depressed region which they inhabit. Why you may ask, because pilgrims invariably bring in 'big money', nothing is sacred it's almost as if sacredness these days has to prove itself.

One of the most famous and highly venerated if not visited Holy Sites, namely Portugal's Fatima is presently the subject of hot debate. This so called place of 'heavenly lights' is purported by paranormal investigators to be nothing more than a clever Jesuit cover up in which a truly alien phenomenon in the UFO context has been converted into a major religious event.

Fatima's five main apparitions that occurred on the thirteenth day of each month between May and October 1917 established a kind of template for many of the great visionary events which followed and included the essential 'sun dancing in the sky' phenomenon.

Dr Fernando Armenez one of the principal researchers concludes, after studying all of the available recorded statements, that the four 'seer's' had in reality communicated with telepathic little humanoids from a different dimension. It was the local Jesuits Armenez claims who were instrumental if not completely responsible for the application of religious terminology to the extraterrestrial encounters.

Not unlike your situation Yvette, where people stated that you were rescued by an angel during the explosion that engulfed your father's car and instantly killed both of your parents. Yvette my precious without a doubt you have the 'eyes' to see such creatures it must be both comforting and disturbing to posses such a gift which explains your partially timid and withdrawn nature made worse I suspect by your foster parents recent rejection of you. My suggestion if you are willing to embrace it, is do nothing until one of them comes to their senses and attempts to contact you, which I fully appreciate will be especially difficult as you are very close to your foster father, perhaps it is time to spread your wings and embrace another male whom you are comfortable with." Jack proposed more like a counselling health professional than anything else.

Yvette in response looked silently at him, thankfully at Grandpa and quite confusedly at Brendan. Sensing that no one was about to say anything Jack took a deep breath and rattled off the next part of his soliloquy.

"Well then what do we make of all of this mishmash that Grandpa and I have presented to you today? Not very much apart from conjecture, speculation and endless heated argument! There is another way, something that ties it all together and that ladies and gentlemen is poverty!

Three billion people today live on less than two dollars per day; of these one third cannot read a book in their own language or sign their name. Three of the world's richest people's wealth is greater than the combined gross domestic product of the poorest forty-eight nations, one quarter of the world's countries. Fifty one percent of the world's wealthiest bodies are corporations! In the poorest nations it is most likely that debt repayments are extracted directly from people who neither contracted the loans nor received any of the money.

Thirty thousand children die every day due to poverty, they the weak and meek in life die quietly, invisibly in some of the poorest villages in the world far removed from the scrutiny and conscience of the world. Yet this sadness also occurs in the wealthiest nation on earth which has the widest gap between the rich and poor of any industrialised country, this distance between the rich and poor when analysed globally and historically clearly shows that in the year 1820 the ratio between the two was about three to one, by the year 2000 it had stretched itself to eighty to one!

Twenty percent of the earth's human population who do not live in a third world country or below consume eighty six percent of the earth's resources including water. Under the influence of globalisation which started in the 1980's the poorest nations as one might guess have suffered immensely for a variety of reasons, their economic growth, individual life expectancy, education and literacy dramatically fell whilst infant and child mortality rose equally. Disturbing statistics, but not as disturbing as the vast amounts of monies spent on ridiculous items such as; pet foods, seventeen billion dollars, cigarettes in Europe alone fifty billion dollars, narcotics five hundred billion worldwide and wait for it a staggering nine hundred billion on military armaments! Out of all of this the total wealth of the top eight million people around the world rose approximately nine percent to thirty two trillion dollars this year alone giving them control of one quarter of the world's financial assets, in other words 0.13% of the human race controls twenty-five percent of the world's wealth. Every law written is for their benefit one which they are extremely reluctant to relinquish"! Jack slowly and dramatically explained with a bitter edge to his voice and then he audibly mumbled under his breath. "The rich are usually cunning, immoral and unscrupulous bastards"!

"How does one overcome one wealthy person never mind the eight million that you mentioned"? Yvette asked visibly disturbed by the extent of humanity's wretchedness.

"A very good question, my dear, one that constantly makes me ponder as to the origins and diversity of life here on earth. But that is beside the point or is it? Supposing the gods that put this place together do not have ultimate powers? Supposing, they themselves are evolving and are therefore limited in their own abilities."

Brendan was not impressed with Jack's suppositions however the others including Yvette found Jack irrespective of the content of his argument entertaining to say the least largely due to his theatrics. Brendan bit his tongue and remained silent for he wanted to see where Jack's line of thinking was taking them.

"Life upon this fertile heavenly body called earth I deduce is based upon a repetitive and magnifiable blueprint which is accurately and clearly represented by this image." Jack confidently put forward as he commanded the Genius Loci's advanced television screen to display a fully colonised Petri dish, which he could plainly see none of his audience had previously encountered.

"This circular plastic dish is flooded with a nutrient agar solution which supports all manner of micro-biological life. Upon the surface of the agar many circular colonies of bacteria represented by the different coloured dots exist in perfect harmony with each other or do they? Each one of these 'furry creatures' has found its place in the 'sun' and 'farmed' the fertile 'soil' to support itself." Jack explained as he pointed to the various specimens in the Petri dish.

"Each it appears respects the space of others and through a mutual understanding of each others needs they get along quite famously; greed does not appear to be part of their make up. Enlarge this blue print until you reach the complexity of mankind and you will have a different story, which leads me to believe that someone tampered with the blueprint thus causing earth to become a war zone. All is not lost, in the far reaches of the Universe, Love and Peace existed, it heard of earth's turmoils and it decided to send emissaries to cause a change. One by one they were eliminated until Love and Peace decided to play celestial chess and confuse the Masters of Affliction. Multiple virgin births, numerous attendances by the three wise men, countless Marian apparitions occurred to create diversions, smoke screens until the Masters of Affliction tired of the game and allowed the real saviour to slip through. He taught and spoke of peace, question is, was education sufficient, was there another way? Master of Earth, Wind, Water and Fire, he welded the ethereal essence of each to create….Brendan any ideas"?

"Not really Jack."

"What about Peter… 'You are the rock upon which I'… vaguely remember that phrase from the bible"?

"Yes what about it"? Brendan coarsely replied.

"No symbolism, there was an actual physical entity, a fragment of which our lovely Yvette here discovered in Mauritius. Grandpa, will you do the honours please"?

"But of course sonny." He cheerfully replied just before he drifted away.

"What was your involvement in Australia'? Brendan then asked Jack changing the subject completely while Grandpa was away.

"Your Archbishop pleaded with me almost on his hands and knees for me to help sort out one of his financial dilemmas." Jack replied greatly exaggerating his Grace's request.

"Which I take it involved the pharmaceutical industry."

"Perhaps" Jack reservedly answered.

"The subsequent failure of the same industry"

"Yes"?

"Your doing" Brendan asked quite intensely.

"Not at all, beyond my capabilities and not part of my desires." Jack flatly answered.

"I think you know more than you are letting on"! Brendan harshly challenged in an attempt to discredit Jack's persona and force him into telling the truth, as Brendan perceived it to be.

The accomplished Jack Stern remained un-phased even though he anticipated Brendan's next accusation.

"How do I know that you're not one of the Masters of Affliction and that everything to date has been cleverly orchestrated to eliminate me"! An agitated Brendan O'Reilly rather nervously demanded, as he was unsure of how many of the others present shared his suspicions.

"How intelligent do you think I am"? Jack softly but firmly asked in response with a innocent smile on his face.

"What the hell! You're asking me to estimate your IQ? This has noting to do with all of the matters at hand! This is outrageous"!

"Settle down laddie, my question was not meant to be a military diversion, it merely seeks a factual response."

"I don't believe you! Of course you're intelligent, probably very intelligent, a brilliant mastermind in disguise who has cleverly…"

"Done nothing but support his friends, their interests, well being and vocations in life"! Jack interrupted and when Brendan had momentarily settled down he went onto to say. "With intelligence comes morality; the truly rich people of this world are usually financially poor compared with the stupid but street smart financial dinosaurs that roam the world and strip it of its assets. If I were in your shoes I would probably behave the same way and trust nobody until the dust had settled. Take my hand my friend and let me pacify things for you." Jack openly invited as Grandpa and Luvera silently entered their midsts.

"Did we miss anything"? Grandpa happily asked without moving his lips as he held one arm loosely around the waist of the stunningly beautiful goddess.

"Let me introduce you to a member of divinity, ladies and gentlemen I present Luvera, Goddess of Fertility, God you're beautiful"! He cheekily said as he admired her perfectly proportioned hourglass figure and amble bosom.

Apart from Jack Stern everyone else stared in disbelief and remained speechless as they carefully analysed the goddess from top to toe. Yvette although she had encountered Luvera before did not recognise her as on that occasion the Goddess had been dressed differently with an aura of sinister arrogance. But to Jack Stern irrespective of her mood she was always magnificent.

"Now that you've reached immortality perhaps you could make a play for her." Jack flippantly suggested to Grandpa changing the mood.

"Nah she's too young for me"! He replied with a double wink of his left eye.

"In any case I don't think she could keep up with me"! He then remarked as he mischievously squeezed her waist where her 'love handles' should have been and without any inhibition spontaneously kissed her on the neck.

"Oh Grandpa you're such a randy ghost! We won't feel safe at night now that we've seen you in action"! Both Brandy and Candy delightfully squealed.

"No danger of that ladies; nothing physical is possible I'm afraid, it's all purely cerebral"! Grandpa confessed.

"That's the best kind, the one that starts around you belly button, moves around teasingly; rises and falls and then streaks up to explode in your head"! Brandy purred as she licked her lips in remembrance of past great and overwhelming orgasms.

"It's all about fertility and your comment Brandy is the perfect cue on which to allow Luvera to explain events on earth." Grandpa said as he grabbed the essence of her exclamation and reluctantly let go of the beautiful creature. Even before the Goddess spoke Yvette could see that Jack was smitten by her.

"All of creation has always been under the influence of Harmony, but certain Gods became restless, somewhat curious as to what would happen in the absence of Harmony. They wanted more and argued that I should make things even more fertile than what they were. These Gods vigorously campaigned for the elements of Harmony namely Earth, Wind, Water and Fire to be spilt and allowed to do what they wanted to do without restriction. The four elements had always lived happily in Harmony, not at all connected with each other like tongue and groove but rather locked in by a floating key that represented the corrective factor. Planet earth was chosen as a place of experiment for the gods even though they cherished and relished the prospect of seeing what increased fertility could produce feared for their own safety, as they knew that unleased Harmony could possibly destroy them. Earth, Wind, Water and Fire made their home on planet earth but the corrective factor was not allowed, it was banished, cast out to float upon the various solar winds until it found a place to rest. Without corrective factor on earth, greed, chaos and deceit ran rampant."

Luvera described in a voice contrary to that when she carried Jack back to the Genius Loci for reconstitution. Some of her haughtiness had disappeared and had been replaced by a loving nature tinged with regret for having succumbed to the bullying of others.

Grandpa floated next to her and gave her an unexpected 'It's not your fault hug', which Luvera deeply appreciated. "Thank you" she whispered before continuing with her description of the celestial events.

"As mankind evolved and random individuals were blessed with the ability to hear the voices of the four elements a body of collective wisdom formed and was kept secret away from those who ran greed and chaos. This secret society soon realised that Earth, Wind, Water and Fire wished to be reunited in Harmony made seemingly impossible by the absence of corrective factor. However this assumption was proven wrong as the incorruptible materials necessary for its formation existed on planet earth, what was missing was the highly evolved soul who knew how to weld them together.

The anointed one whom you call Jesus was one of the first who was successful in this task. Unfortunate for him there was one who also existed at the same time, he was aware of Jesus' capabilities and shared the same knowledge to the contrary. You know him as Judas; this one was instrumental in destroying the reunited four elements. He is still alive today but thanks to Mr Jack Stern, Judas has momentarily lost his 'divinely' acquired super power of the opposite kind.

The Gods who thirsted for increased fertility have not had their desires extinguished; planet earth serves as the role model for other inhabited planets. They will do everything in their power and by all means possible to certify their stamp of authority, therefore by the most devious means unimaginable they have prevented other god's from rectifying the mess on earth leaving the salvation of the planet in human hands alone.

Jesus was not a god but a highly evolved soul. At birth he was given a map of his destiny in the form of gold, Frankincense and Thyme, all of which represented the incorruptible materials necessary to fashion corrective factor. Harmony once again existed on earth and it caused greed, chaos and deceit to fear for their very lives.

Harmony was referred to in your recorded history as being the 'rock' upon which a church or more precisely peace would be built. Its animating principle was the abolition of all forms of war brought about by people's individual understanding of each other without necessarily sacrificing their own moral and ethical beliefs or their own evolution. Hence it allowed everyone to attain the same level of comprehension irrespective of his or her evolutionary status as you can imagine this outraged the gods who did not support this dichotomy.

Jesus was not the only one to be scourged and humiliated; the 'rock' was also subjected to such atrocities by those who ruled the region at that time. Unlike Jesus it did not 'bleed' nor could any thorn penetrate its outer mantle. It was not until the transformed Judas returned from the dead that circumstances changed. Like the proverbial egotistical spoilt brat who demands everything, Judas angrily stamped his newly acquired leg and the 'rock' split into its four elements. Judas through his blind arrogance assumed that it had come about by the destruction of corrective factor but he was wrong. One of the four elements in the nick of time reached out and hid corrective factor within itself. What I do not know is whether or not it is injured for the forces required to disassociate Earth, Wind, Water and Fire are immense.

Not satisfied with his efforts Judas collected the four fragments of the 'rock' and took them to the highest mountain in the region. There he arranged them as the four points of a perfect square, stood in the middle of it and with an almighty sudden burst of ill humour stamped his leg to dispatch all four into the beyond so that no one including himself would ever know the location of any fragment." Luvera then paused and smiled serenely.

"Can we see 'earth'"? Brandy excitedly asked, as she from a young age was always intensely interested in all sorts of mythology, however she did wonder whether the Church of the Coloured Sands was in fact Earth. Brendan thought Decay might be it, Jack knew otherwise.

"Stop it you mischievous creature"! Grandpa shouted as he tried to restrain a mole like creature that squirmed in his arms. "Oh very well then have your way"! He said as he finally gave in and let Elech scurry about the floor and explore its new environment. "Cute, isn't he"? He asked in a roundabout way uncertain of anyone's response.

Elech was a distorted star nosed mole with small front paws, one of which sported six claws whilst the other had seven. His rear legs were massive, both ended in a club shaped paw that sprouted nine claws. His fur was jet black, each fibre was the same length as all of the others and extremely shiny. A black ball of fluff that ran awkwardly about and managed not to run into anything; one eye was blue, the other green, no apparent ears, mouse like teeth and nose that was bright Mexican red in colour.

"Not exactly what you were expecting"? Luvera deduced judging by each individual's reaction. "Elech does not normally look like this, earth's atmosphere and his separation from the others has caused the distortion, you could say that he looks cute-ugly"!

48

HOW WHY WHEN WHERE

Some would say that the combination of KBW 49's news special, Grandpa's expose on the origins of the Catholic Church, Jack Sterns treatment of virginity and Luvera's explanation of celestial events and their impact on earth was all to much for them to take in within a short space of time, those however in the Genius Loci namely the accomplished Jack Stern, Father Brendan O'Reilly, Yvette Bell, Grandpa and the seven young ladies all found it rather exciting, like a breath of fresh air which heralded the expiration of everything old and stale, a sweeping away of all that which obstructed Peace in its relentless quest to re-establish Harmony on earth.

It was afternoon tea time, the perfect occasion to relax and mull over the events of the day whilst enjoying the richest of coffees with an assortment of the most delicate pastries available in the world. Jack as always was the perfect waiter attending to everyone's needs in terms of their choice of coffee and its preparation thanks largely to Grandpa and his innovative inventive ways with modern technology. Grandpa had found a disused discarded Bar-Charisma coffee machine on a rubbish heap outside a five star hotel's restaurant that was being refitted and he decided to put it into good use once he had finished repairing, modifying and cleaning it to perfection. Result, coffee prepared the spiritual way, heavenly to say the least.

The pastries were no exception. Grandpa enjoyed travelling the world in his ladies outfit and purchasing first hand pastries from the finest French, Austrian, Swiss and Swedish Patisseries and then transporting them back faster than the speed of light leaving nothing behind apart from correct payment for goods purchased. It was almost as if he had gone out of his way to deliberately impress Luvera. Her presence had restored peace causing Brendan to feel quite sorry for his unfounded outbursts.

"I owe you an apology." He humbly and sorrowfully whispered as Jack delivered the priest's cup of freshly made coffee.

"Think nothing of it, done that before." Jack replied as he brushed away the apology and set down the next cup of coffee before Naomi.

"These pastries are divine." Luvera joyfully remarked as she partook of a heavenly raspberry and marzipan multi-layered creation.

"If you think that is good you should try the mixed fruit tartlet complete with orange liqueur infused custard filling and chocolate covered shortbread base." Grandpa seductively offered as he fantasized about the two of them in bed making hot passionate love, Little did he realise that his thoughts were quite transparent to the goddess who took charge of his fantasy and soon had him screaming words of orgasmic delight.

Jack Stern hoped he was next in line but he quickly abandoned the prospect out of respect for Yvette who frowned more out of curiosity than disfavour at Grandpa's sexual outburst.

"You really are…. the Goddess… of Fertility… "! Grandpa stuttered before falling asleep, as spirits are likely to do following post orgasmic exhaustion.

"Excuse me for a moment." Luvera politely asked in her serenely royal way as she faded from view taking Grandpa with her.

"She's giving him seconds"? Candy boldly asked as she stared in disbelief at what had just transpired. "How did she do it? I didn't even see her touch him! She appeared to be enjoying her food with both hands, next thing Grandpa's goo-goo gar-gar"!

"The mind is a powerful instrument." Jack coolly remarked as a matter of fact as he kept himself busy with the coffees.

"Nah, I don't believe it, she had to touch him somehow, somewhere"! Candy persisted.

"Ask her when she returns." Jack suggested as he expertly finished adding the final decorative touches to his own mugga chino.

"Ask me what Mr Stern"? Luvera softly purred as she materialised in her seat.

"The girls, I mean we were wondering how you managed to satisfy Grandpa without touching him." Jack nervously explained completely consumed by her ravishing beauty.

"Very similar to a wet dream, you'll learn more about it in the afterlife. But enough of that, there are more important matters at hand. The three undiscovered fragments; any ideas"

"They could be located on any point on a number of circles close or distant to the impact point." Brendan confidently put forward and once he saw that he had every ones attention went on to say. " All we need do is find the tallest mountain in the region and after making a number of assumptions we can easily predict the precise location of the three remaining elements namely Wind, Water and Fire."

"This sounds rather vague, you've been watching too many American television police shows its not the way to go about it. If Earth has taken the form of a mole what have the other three decided to adopt? Secondly if Corrective Factor is damaged what do we need in order to repair it and how do we repair it? Thirdly is each fragment guarded by a winged humanoid; if so it might make it easier for us providing the humanoid has shown itself and created a local folklore" Jack countered in detail.

"No, you're wrong, my idea is sound and much better than yours and I'll show you why"! Brendan retorted as he rapidly left his group of friends and went in search of a large atlas of the world in order to prove his point of view leaving them to speculate on his suppositions. Luvera was amused, the girls thought him funny, Yvette was sympathetic whilst Jack remained as always highly analytical.

"He's back to being cute." Naomi girlishly commented.

"More importantly he's back on track." Jack observed in between taking bites of food whilst he compared Yvette with Luvera as subtly as he possibly could.

Brendan confidently returned in a flash with a large detailed fold up map of the world that measured 150 centimetres by 100 centimetres and without saying a word neatly positioned it on the table in such a manner so that all could clearly see his theory put into practice. He then produced a clear cellophane transparency that had a protracted set of cross hairs drawn accurately on it complete with a series of concentric circles of various diameters and he placed it over the map.

Brendan then aligned the cross hairs on the highest mountain in Palestine and rotated the cellophane until one of the cross hair arms ran through Mauritius in the region of Chamarel where the Church of the Coloured Sands once stood and measured the distance form it to Palestine, then he reproduced if on each of the remaining arms and proudly proclaimed 'Voila there we have it' and expected a standing ovation for his gallant efforts instead he was met with.

"Hum, you're assuming equal trajectories, equal mass, equal propulsive force, no external force's, no meteorological influences, no other behaviours on the part of each fragment and you've come up with water, water and it looks like either the mountainous region of China or somewhere in Mongolia"! Candy brutally commented as she analysed Brendan's primitive mathematical model. "Surprised, don't be, I was an A grade student before spreading my legs."

Brendan blushed deeply, the others giggled whilst Jack smirked. Devastated by his own naivety and thoroughly embarrassed by

707

Candy's deductions Brendan hurriedly attempted to wrap up his diaster.

"Leave it there my good friend, you meant well, all is not lost." Jack offered in consolation as he studied Brendan's feeble attempt. Luvera's fertile presence meanwhile caused Brendan's distracted mind to wander, all of a sudden the transparency's cross hairs represented two pairs of naked women seated back to back with their legs spread wide open, Brendan then saw himself standing before them hand in hand with Luvera as she taught him that it was both unnatural and unfortunate for any man and woman to go through life and constantly miss out on the ecstatic joys and health giving benefits that the art of proper love making brought forth. The lesson caused all sorts of turmoil in the idealist's mind for it had been programmed by the aberrant ideas of proud men rather than by the wisdom of the humble god's. Brendan looked Luvera straight in the eye and sought guidance.

"I always knew that the fairer sex were stronger and smarter than us! Can you imagine men having babies, there would be no end of complaining, men were never designed to tolerate pain! These weaklings invented the first anti-depressant! It's called beer! They consume it in vast quantities and make themselves look tough by suppressing women. The cretins"! Jack comically rattled off as he studied the response of his female audience who couldn't quite work out whether he was being serious or not.

"Let me guess Mr Stern, you were a stand up comedian before you learnt how to make it stand up"! Candy ambiguously purred in a low voice that accentuated the sexual nature of her provocative statement.

"On demand and no hands"! Jack cheekily responded tit for tat.

"Enough of the innuendo" Yvette intervened.

"I didn't know we had any." Jack sheepishly answered.

"Any what"? Yvette asked with raised eyebrows.

"Innuendo, you know Italian suppositories"!

708

"For God's sake"!

"Is he constipated as well"? Jack Flippantly asked.

"This is getting out of hand." Yvette frowned.

"At least it's fun, oh very well then, let's get back to those boring fragments. Candy if you please, enlighten us with your academic excellence." Jack invited as he pointed to the world map that lay before them.

Candy pushed her chair back, stood up and poured her ample breasts over the table; with a keen eye that resembled an expert jeweller's seeking flaws in a well cut gem, she scanned the entire map and made highly suggestive noises as she went.

"Will you be taking into account gold, frankincense and thyme"? Jack asked as she voluptuously moved about.

"Perhaps"

"Three wise men" Jack proposed

"Never met one, never mind three"

"Star of Bethlehem"

"Rock and roll singer"

"Away in a manger"

"Stoned on something" She outrageously answered without even batting one eye lid. "There that should do it" She then said as she repositioned herself.

"Do what"? Brendan curiously asked as he struggled to identify what she saw.

"Keep my breasts in place of course"! Candy innocently answered as she slumped back into her chair and looked rather pensive.

"Conclusions" Jack asked referring to her findings.

"I need new underwear"!

"It's going to be one of those days"! He thought to himself as he flashed a laughter filled smile. "Could we stay focused"?

"Oh you mean the cross hairs, most unusual. Two pairs of naked women seated back to back with their legs spread wide apart." Candy replied blank faced.

"Where"?

"Right there"! She replied as she rested her right hand's index finger on the spot.

"There's nothing there"! Jack replied after he had examined the spot close up.

"That's because you haven't touched it, try again"! Jack obeyed and did as Candy had instructed.

"Wow, it's almost as if they leap out of the map, nice Brazilians"!

"Precise... ly" Candy agreed as she wildly nodded her head.

"It's your discovery Candy share its description with us, if you please."

"My pleasure Mr Stern" She graciously replied as she lent forward and took command of her audience. "Before I start I need to make an admission. The longer I spend in the company of Mr Stern and Yvette and the more I interact with this complex in the mountains the more clairvoyant I become, there is something magical about this place, its people, there is an overwhelming feeling of belonging. I remember as a child I longed to go to the mountains, my mom would take me whenever she could afford it, which was seldom." Candy paused as to allow any questions. The accomplished Jack Stern listened patiently with interest, he had already remote viewed the scattering of the 'rocks' four elements and awaited confirmation of what he had seen, Brendan meanwhile couldn't decide whether his vision of the four naked women and its associated lesson was a clairvoyant event or simply Luvera tampering with his mind.

"The four elements were not scattered as some of us imagined, Earth, Wind, Water and Fire are highly intelligent entities; may I hold Elech please." Candy asked hoping that someone knew of the creature's whereabouts.

"Here we are." Brandy reluctantly answered as she lifted the mischievous mole from underneath the table and handed it over. Brandy blushed as she did so and madly fanned her face with the closed fingers of one hand to hide her embarrassment.

"Licking in between the toes"? Luvera correctly asked.

"How did you know"? Brandy stuttered.

"It's her favourite pastime, erotically satisfying, isn't it"?

"Quite." Brandy reluctantly confessed as her facial cheeks heated up once again.

"Elech's got a very unusual tongue technique."

"You can say that again"!

"But that's not the entire story." Luvera explained.

"Really"

"It's the saliva that does the magic, salt of the earth, body and soul." She carefully explained as half of the girls shed their foot coverings in anticipation. Candy on the other hand had her ears full.

"Stop that, it really tickles." She begged as the cute and ugly Elech nuzzled its star shaped nose into her neck, licked and nibbled at her ear lobe and firmly dug its claws into her soft skin.

"Settle down Elech, you can't burrow into every woman you see"! Luvera cautioned. She paused to see if her words were headed before she advised Candy. "You have all of twenty seconds"!

Candy understood, she held Elech under its armpits, closed her eyes and felt its memory's vibrations. "Upon a mountain top on a flat piece of ground, a sinister man wishes to strike the earth with his thunder stick. Animals, animals everywhere, appear from nowhere, hot and cold, wet and wild, dirty and squirmy, cocks, dragons, salamanders and rams, foxes, peacocks, ravens and damns, fill the space with annoyance as things go wrong, cats, cats and more cats, kittens, small, fluffy, naked and cuddly, appear once, twice and then no more! Pain in his leg, fire in his blood, lions and tigers seek to strip his limbs, he the dark one strikes the ground, a wave of shock spreads outwards from there, clears the air, all is still, the fragments of their own accord gone to nowhere"! Candy very dramatically and poetically said with eyes closed in cryptic staccato fashion, exhausted she dropped the cute and ugly Elech.

"An intense vision; lets give her a moment, shall we, more coffee anyone"? Jack asked making light of the situation.

Candy's ears enthusiastically welcomed the suggestion, her hands automatically reached out to grab the lukewarm beverage and brought it up to her thirsty mouth and downed the liquid's complex blend of natural ingredients in a matter of seconds, revived and refreshed she energetically exclaimed "I'm ready now" and as she did so she propped up her breasts in readiness for the next line of questioning.

"Is it too early for alcohol"? Yvette innocently asked, as she perceived everyone was in need of a more spirited infusion.

"I second that proposition." Jack gladly agreed as he activated the concealed bar into action. "In honour of our guest Luvera may I suggest a humble mortal version of Nek-tur of the gods, ice cold Scandinavian Vodka, full bodied Jamaican coffee liqueur and the finest Darjeeling tea blended to perfection."

"Is that the best you can do Mr Stern"? Luvera questioned as she tried to catch Jack off guard.

"Under the circumstances I would venture to say yes, any mead will not do you justice. The nectar of the Irish fairies, Goibniu and Diancecht which it is rumoured granted one immortality is presently out of stock and to make matters worse I've just run out of Persian wine bin no: 6000BC" Jack stated quite provocatively which caused Luvera to remember Persian days of old when she drank the wine of the first harvest six thousand years before the birth of Christ.

"You are a man of many facts and figures"!

"The latter is my speciality"! He replied tongue in cheek in the hope that the goddess would appreciate the hidden compliment; Luvera however remained quietly elusive and unpredictable. Jack took her state of mind as the signal to start mixing his original proposition, he had hardly left his spot and turned his back when he heard the magical clinkering of fine lead crystal Aware that he had been upstaged Jack pretended not to have heard the fine subtleties of the noise and continued to walk in the direction of the Genius Loci's extensive bar.

"Mr Stern care to sample the Nectar of the Gods"? Luvera seductively asked as she swept her hands through the air to fill twelve hand crafted lead crystal claret glasses with a fiery fluorescent and phosphorescent liquid.

Jack remained calm even though he could feel the excitement of an eminent chase and he slowly turned around. "You're toying with me"!

"Not at all, try it, you'll find it delicious, isn't that right ladies"?

"Yes Jack please do; it's not a trick" Candy reassured him having sampled the elixir with no ill effects.

"I'm certain it isn't but that is not the problem. For it to be the true Nectar of the Gods Luvera would have to be putting herself in danger of being banished forever; the true Nectar of the Gods grants mortals immortality; at best this is probably a divinely inspired Persian wine." The accomplished Jack Stern confidently argued with a tilt of his head.

"Bravo Mr Stern bravo, now that you have outsmarted me or more correctly outplayed me perhaps you would do me the pleasure of partaking of a eight thousand year old essence." The Goddess coolly responded as she proffered the glorious life filled elixir.

"Its aged well, not a hint of oxidation, nor any interaction with a cork, obviously stored in some kind of celestial container, complex, heady, visions of comets, asteroids, black holes, red dwarfs, gigantic stars, soft on the palate, tingling after taste reminiscent of gamma or x-ray radiation, definitely alien"! Jack expertly commented after he had swirled the viscous nectar around his mouth.

"Alcoholic content Mr Stern"

"None your highness, intoxication probably comes via some sort of inherent energy source that fires off more neurons than we thought ever possible."

"Very astute of you Mr Stern"!

"Thank you, your highness." Jack ceremoniously answered as he bowed from the waist and observed the effect the wine had on his companions. He then asked. "The origins of this exceptional celestial beverage brings us back to frankincense, thyme and gold, could these be the materials necessary to forge Corrective Factor"

"Oh I don't know about you but I for one don't have any thyme for frank's incestuous ways, as for gold, gimme, gimme, more"! A rather tipsy Brandy blurted. "Oh dear did I say something out of space, I mean place"? She apologetically asked as she took another sip of the comforting elixir.

Brendan with some of the others drank in moderation so as to allow the magical brew to expand his inquiring consciousness. "How did Cugly end up in Mauritius"? He asked.

"Whom did you say" Yvette curiously inquired.

"Cugly, Luvera said it herself, Elech over there is cute and ugly."

"So you invented a new word'?

"Yes, quite clever I thought, would you not agree"?

"It has its merits." Yvette warmly answered with a muffled giggle.

"As must my other observation, Candy's clairvoyant description differs greatly from that of Luvera's in relation to the scattering of the four elements. Can we be certain that Cugly is in effect 'Earth' or does it represent another red herring designed to protect the location of Earth at all times. In Mauritius I did not interact with a mole, it was a geological specimen, a type of rock not a furry creature." Brendan said making reference to his discovery at Chamarel.

"What are you suggesting" Yvette asked without exerting any undue pressure.

"Perhaps we are dealing with two separate issues."

"Explain"

"The concept of re-establishing Harmony by the fusion of the four elements and the other; there are in fact four geological artefacts which fit together and serve another purpose. We saw that the first fragment could do."

"Granted" Jack agreed.

"One wonders what roles the other three play and what the entire reassembled structure is capable of."

"What a brilliant inquisitive deduction, I take my hat off to you sir." Jack loudly applauded as he looked around and signalled for the others to do the same. "Now what about the gold frankincense and thyme" He then asked.

"You really are most persistent on this point. I think they are places we are meant to see rather than anything else." Brendan suggested.

"Frankincense is not a locality it's a bleeding herb." Jack comically blurted out in a high voice.

"Yes I know that, I'm thinking more about its origins."

"Which are"?

"Wait a minute, it's not gold, frankincense and thyme, it's gold, frankincense and myrrh, since when has myrrh been substituted with thyme"?

"I thought they were one and the same, in any case I like thyme." Jack replied in the same high-pitched child like voice that he used previously.

"Next you'll be telling me, Constantine was responsible for changing thyme into myrrh"!

"Not as good as water into wine"! Jack flippantly replied as he held his glass of nectar high for Brendan to see.

"You're making a mockery of this"! Brendan angrily concluded.

"Not really, just introducing another variant."

"Which is"?

"Thyme"! Jack cheekily explained.

"I thought we had finished with it"!

"Only after you listen to what I have to say." Jack brightly replied in his boyish fashion.

"Very well" Brendan grumbled like an old discontented man would do.

"Tradition tells us that thyme was the bed straw of the Virgin

Mary and the newly born child. Happy with that, here comes the interesting part!

Thyme due to its matted growing pattern easily hides the small secretly constructed houses of garden fairies who toil all night washing leaves, herding insects, painting flowers and generally cleaning up and tidying the plants ready for the next day." Jack slowly detailed as an expert storyteller spinning a yarn to an audience of receptive ears.

"Oh great next you'll be telling us that Christ was away with the fairies." Brendan shouted.

"Not quite, he went away with the fairies is more exact."

"Oh Buddha"! Brendan swore.

"A little thyme goes a long way."

"What now"? Brendan gasped.

"Jesus, Joseph and Mary in the Middle-east"

"Yes, what of it."

"Thyme came from the Mediterranean or did it." Jack teased.

"Go on, surprise us further." Brendan moaned as he rolled his eyes.

"The Alps, Iceland and Russia are other unusual places of harvest."

"Fine, just fine, more areas for us to visit I suppose."

"On bee's wings we shall travel."

"What do bees have to do with thyme"? Brendan sharply asked as he tried to make sense of Jack's expose.

"Bees are the messengers of the fairy world, how good are you at buzz, buzz"?

"Can we possibly be serious for one minute, please"? Brendan begged quite exasperated as he sought relief from Jack's flippancy.

"Very well, do you remember what they taught you in seminary school about the three wise men"?

"Vaguely"

"Would you like to tell us what you remember"?

"It's very patchy and sketchy." Brendan honestly replied.

"Better than being itchy and scratchy" To which all present burst into belly shaking laughter, Jack joined in and then suggested once he composed himself. "Perhaps I might help."

"Please do"! Brendan almost sarcastically replied.

"According to Herodotus who was around 500BC the trees that grew in Arabia and bore the frankincense were guarded by winged humanoids of various sizes and colours. Diodorus Siculus in the second half of the first century BC wrote ' all of Arabia exuded a most delicate fragrance' even the passing seamen, seamen not semen ladies, if you please could smell the strong fragrance that brought health and vigour. He also mentioned gold mines so pure that no smelting was necessary for the mined precious metal. Frankincense together with coffee and there is where I stop to ask the Goddess for permission."

"Yes Mr Stern you may proceed but before you do, from where do you obtain your knowledge"? The enchanting Luvera serenely asked.

"From that wicked man...... Grandpa"

"Enough said, continue."

"Thank you my lady. In the region bordering Somalia and Ethiopia an archangel came down and taught the natives the importance of frankincense and how to brew coffee properly, something that Grandpa has done today by reconstructing this beautiful Bar-cha-risma machine, so there you have it, if gold frankincense and myrrh represented area's of importance we must journey to their places of origin, no point going to China, they have the most bizarre name for frankincense, they call it 'nipple shaped fragrance'!

All humour aside the Chinese did discover through their fasci-nation with acupuncture and bodily energy flow that frankincense and myrrh open up the meridians and collaterals associated with consciousness. Would any one care for some Qi-li-san"? Jack hu-morously asked as he produced a small vial out of one of his trouser pockets and held it up for everyone to see as he described it contents. "A highly resinous mixture of dried dragons blood, myrrh, frankin-cense, cinnabar, musk and borneol to mention a few"

"Er, no thank you, perhaps another time, I'm a little full, were some of the polite comments that reached Jack's ears.

"Luvera" Jack propositioned the goddess with a wry smile.

"Did nothing for me Mr Stern"!

"Me neither." Jack said in agreement.

"This is all very interesting, but where does it leave us"? A frustrated Brendan asked looking very confused and lost.

"I honestly don't know." Jack truthfully announced as he hung his head sufficiently low to indicate his own struggling inabilities.

"Great just great, what are we supposed to do? Travel the world and look under every thyme bush, find a fairy and ask, do you know the way to San Jose'?

"Steady on, it's not that bad"!

"Yes it is, we dealing with events that happened eight thousand years ago! It's worse than looking for a rusty needle in a hay stack"!

"I agree, but there must still exist sign posts in recorded history that will have us locate the three missing fragments! Luvera could you please show us the first fragment please." Jack sweetly asked.

"I don't have it here on me, your Grandpa put it away for safe keeping."

"Then it could b anywhere, we'll just have to wait until the old fool wakes up"!

"I don't understand how it is going to help us"! Brenda lashed out.

Jack reflected on the priest's accurate remark. " I guess you're right, we might as well refer to the map"

"Map, what map, you had a map all the time"? Brendan angrily snapped.

"Sort of"

"Out with it then"! Brendan demanded.

"It's not that easy."

"Why"?

"Because those who wanted the four elements to disassociate themselves from Harmony want it kept that way. The map is more in the way of a solution, one that can only be carried out by a human being who needs to work out the complex puzzle that keeps disharmony raging here on earth." Jack solemnly explained to which Luvera nodded her head in agreement.

"One of the sign posts I deduced to be music. Many of the great composers through their own humility argued that they did not write the music; they heard it in the ether. Saint-Saens while he vacationing in a small Austrian village in 1886 composed Le Carnaval, a musical suite of fourteen movements, each of which describes particular animals and fossils. I cannot but marvel that Candy's clairvoyant description of the scattering of the four elements parallels and mirrors this musical feast. It is almost as if Saint- Saens's work describes the event. I wonder if Saint-Saens also saw in his mind the scenes that he transcribed into music." Jack explained with some degree of emotion, as music was always dear to his heart.

"Animals; hey; that should provide us with a short list. How many do we have to interview"? Brendan cynically remarked in an attempt to ruffle Jack's feathers.

"Lions, hens and roosters, tortoises, elephants, kangaroos, fishes, long eared animals, cuckoo in the woods, jungle birds and swans." Jack rattled off.

"Apart from Skippy the kangaroo, it looks as though we're off to the jungle to fight the lions and tigers, swing like the monkeys and laugh with the hyenas." Brendan quickly assumed.

"The gold came from India, the frankincense from ancient Nubia in the Sudan and the myrrh from the Red Sea Region and thyme from the Alps. Expect the unexpected! A distorted mole carried, cared for and hid the first fragment that was Earth. Distortion is the key, to India we will fare and search amongst its distortions to discover the second fragment whether it be Wind, Water or Fire"! Jack firmly declared, as he remained mindful of the dangers both natural and supernatural that they would face.

"Good evening Stephen." A very brash Badcock boldly and

without hesitation bellowed down the Archbishop's direct telephone line.

"Yes what is it that you want"? His Grace harshly replied.

Badcock quickly detected the cleric's sombre mood, obviously he didn't like the subsequent media attention levied at him following his exposure at Mauritius, nor it was apparent the religious chastisements he undoubtedly received from his superiors. Rome was not pleased and neither was Louis Badcock. This popular renegade Father Brendan O'Reilly represented a real threat to the Roman Empire, which lived on in the form of the Roman Catholic Church following the Council of Nicea. This colossal business did not want a second coming of a Christ, like any enterprise its survival was dependent upon war without which neither progress nor peace could comfortably exist.

"How good are you at exorcisms"?

"Never done one; why do you ask"? His Grace aggressively barked annoyed at being disrupted by Badcock's telephone call, especially since he the Archbishop was in the middle of watching his favourite adult only DVD.

"We are in need of some assistance."

"Problems with demons, dragons, poltergeists or women" Steven Moulds acidly replied. The reference to women made Louis Badcock's blood boil as it reminded him of his failure to retrieve those rescued by Brendan O'Reilly.

"Do you know of anyone"? Badcock abruptly asked.

"It can be arranged; first you must inform me as to the type of entity we are dealing with" His Grace now a little less aggressive inquired.

"A saint"!

Badcock's startling revelation caused his Archbishop to 'jump'. "Are you serious, all of our saints are dead"!

"Not this one."

"Do not jest with me or the Church, it is bad enough that we are partners"! Steven Moulds rudely remarked as he contemplated slamming down the phone. Badcock sensed the Archbishops imminent intention and pre-empted it by saying.

"I'll ring you on your mobile."

Within a minute Archbishop Steven Moulds' mobile phone's loudspeaker blazed away.

"Moulds here"! He reluctantly answered.

"Turn your phone onto audio-video." Badcock sharply instructed. The archbishop obeyed and watched horrified as the transmitted images displayed themselves.

"What sort of bizarre abomination are you showing me Louis"? He shouted into the phones microphone as his body became wet with nervous perspiration.

"Our mutual weapon Ivan Gallows alias the D-man held captive as the Siamese twin of a diametrically opposed Saint Ignatius, I think he calls himself."

"Impossible"!

"To all and sundry perhaps, but I can positively assure you this is for real"!

To be continued

www.ingramcontent.com/pod-product-compliance
Lightning Source LLC
Chambersburg PA
CBHW020240030726
47499CB00001B/6